LYNN FLEWELLING

author of

BOOK THREE

TRAITOR'S
MOON

"A NEW STAR IS RISING IN THE FANTASY FIRMAMENT."
—Dave Duncan, author of *The Gilded Chain*

DON'T MISS ANY OF LYNN FLEWELLING'S DAZZLING FANTASY NOVELS

The Nightrunner Series

LUCK IN THE SHADOWS
STALKING DARKNESS
TRAITOR'S MOON
SHADOWS RETURN
THE WHITE ROAD

The Tamír Triad

THE BONE DOLL'S TWIN
HIDDEN WARRIOR
THE ORACLE'S QUEEN

BANTAM BOOKS

ISBN 978-0-553-57725-9

U.S.A. $7.99 Canada $10.99

9 780553 577259

50799

EAN

Praise for *Luck in the Shadows,*
the first book in the NIGHTRUNNER series

"Part high fantasy and part political intrigue, *Luck in the Shadows* makes a nice change from the usual ruck of contemporary sword-and-sorcery. I especially enjoyed Lynn Flewelling's obvious affection for her characters. And at unexpected moments she reveals a well-honed gift for the macabre."

—Stephen R. Donaldson, author of *This Day All Gods Die*

"Memorable characters, an enthralling plot, and a truly daunting evil. The magic is refreshingly difficult, mysterious, and unpredictable. Lynn Flewelling has eschewed the easy shortcuts of clichéd minor characters and cookie-cutter backdrops to present a unique world peopled by characters who are truly of that world. I commend this one to your attention."

—Robin Hobb, author of *Ship of Magic*

"A splendid read, filled with magic, mystery, adventure, and taut suspense. Lynn Flewelling, bravo! Nicely done."

—Dennis L. McKiernan, author of *The Dragonstone*

"An engrossing and entertaining debut novel. It opens up a new fantasy world that is ripe for exploration—full of magic, intrigues, and fascinating characters . . . the kind of book you settle down with when you want a long, satisfying read."

—Michael A. Stackpole, author of *Eyes of Silver*

"Flewelling is another new writer bringing vigor back to the traditional fantasy form. . . . highly engaging. The author has a gift for creating characters you genuinely care about."

—Terri Windling, editor of *The Year's Best Fantasy and Horror: Eleventh Annual Collection*

Bantam Books

Published by Lynn Flewelling

Traitor's Moon

LYNN FLEWELLING

Bantam Books
New York Toronto London Sydney Auckland

TRAITOR'S MOON
A Bantam Spectra Book / July 1999

ISBN 0-553-57725-5
Published simultaneously in the United States and Canada

PRINTED IN THE UNITED STATES OF AMERICA
OPM 20 19 18 17 16 15 14

DEDICATION

For our folks, Thelma and Win White and Frances
Flewelling, for their continuing love and support. I prom-
ise I'll write you that serious novel one of these days!
Thanks for liking these so much.

ACKNOWLEDGMENTS

Sincerest thanks to all the folks who continue to keep me sanc, fed, and free of crumbs. Believe me, it's a full-time job.

First and foremost, my husband and best buddy, Dr. Doug, past whom no chapter goes unmaimed. And he cooks! The Dynamic Duo—editor Anne Lesley Groell and agent Lucienne Diver—and to the good folks at Bantam Spectra and the Spectrum Literary Agency, who keep *them* sane, fed, and free of crumbs. The Usual Suspects—Darby Crouss, Laurie Hallman, Julie Friez, and Scott Burgess, and my family. Assorted new readers, Michele De France and NextWavers Devon Monk, James Hartley, Charlene Brusso, and Jason Tanner. Finally, kudos to our local swordsmith (and how many of you can say that?), Adam Williams, for his technical advice and general kibitzing, and to Gary Ruddell, for giving form to my inner visions.

Thank you all for your support, expertise, and in-flight feedback.

Additional gratitude for the Eagles reuniting just long enough to record their *Hell Freezes Over* CD. It got me through some weary days and nights, when "You can check out anytime you like, but you can never leave" pretty much summed things up. But I got over it.

A FEW REMARKS FROM THE AUTHOR

Ever since the first Nightrunner book came out back in '96, people have been asking if I'm writing a trilogy. It's an understandable assumption, given the genre, so I thought I'd seize this opportunity, here in the third book, to lay that question to rest once and for all.

This is not a trilogy.

This is not a trilogy.

This is not a trilogy.

And the first person who asks if it's a pentology gets a sterling silver fountain pen straight through the heart.

Okay, I wouldn't really do that. I love that pen.

I have nothing against trilogies, it just isn't what I've set out to do here. The Nightrunner series is exactly that: a series of interrelated tales about the lives and adventures of some characters I have a lot of fun with. There will be more books, as inspiration strikes.

So, do you need to read the opening duology, *Luck in the Shadows* and *Stalking Darkness,* to understand this book?

Probably not.

Then again, I have two kids to put through college.

Yes, you absolutely need to read the first two books. So do all your friends and relatives.

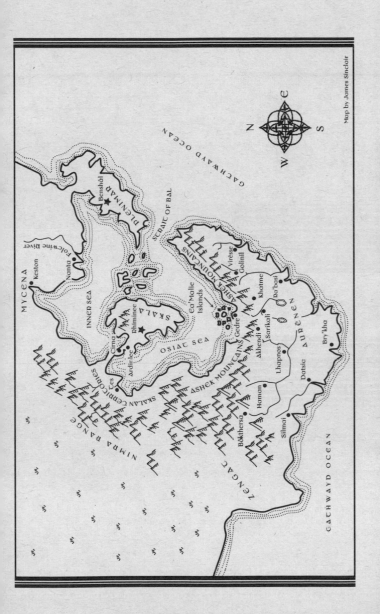

Map by James Sinclair

Traitor's Moon

1
DARK HOPES

The sleet-laden wind buffeted Magyana, whipping wet strands free from the wizard's thick white braid as she trudged across the churned ground of the battlefield. In the distance, the tents of her queen's sprawling encampment billowed and creaked along the riverbank, black specters on a dun plain. In the makeshift corrals, the horses huddled together, their backs to the wind. The unlucky soldiers on sentry duty did the same, their green tabards the only spots of color against this grim palette.

Magyana pulled her sodden cloak more closely around her. Never in all her three hundred and three years had she felt the cold so keenly. Perhaps faith had kept her warm before, she reflected sadly, faith in the comfortable rhythms of her life, and faith in Nysander, the wizard who'd been a part of her soul for two centuries. This damnable war had robbed her of both, and more. Nearly a third of the Orëska House wizards were dead, centuries of life and learning snatched away. Queen Idrilain's second consort and two younger sons had fallen in battle, together with dozens of nobles and countless common soldiers—sent by blade or disease down to Bilairy's gate.

Magyana's grief was mingled with resentment at the disruption of her orderly life. She was a wanderer, a scholar, a gatherer of wonders and tales. Only reluctantly had she taken Nysander's place at the aging queen's side.

My poor Nysander. She wiped a wind-smeared tear from her cheek. *You would have relished all this, seen it as a great game to be won.*

So here she was, winter-locked in the wilds of southern Mycena, a nation once more bathed in the blood of two bellicose neighbors. Plenimar stretched greedy talons westward toward Skala's borders and north to the fertile freeholdings along the Gold Road. This harsh second winter had slowed the fighting, but as the days now slowly lengthened toward spring, the queen's spies brought daily reports of the unthinkable; their Mycenian allies were considering surrender.

And no wonder, Magyana thought, reaching the outskirts of the camp at last. It had been just five days since the last battle. These ravaged fields where farmers had once cut sheaves of grain were sown now with a crueler crop: shredded banners, broken buckles, arrow heads overlooked by scavenging camp followers, and the occasional pitiful scrap of human remains, frozen too hard for even the ravens to peck out. It would yield a bitter spring harvest with the thaw, one she doubted any of them would be here to witness, now that things had gone so horribly wrong.

The Plenimarans had surprised them just before dawn. Throwing on her armor, Idrilain had rushed to rally her troops before Magyana could reach her. One side of the queen's corselet had been left unbuckled, and during the ensuing battle a Plenimaran arrow found the gap, piercing Idrilain's left lung. She survived the extraction, but the wound quickly festered. Plenimaran archers dipped their arrowheads in their own excrement before a battle.

Since then, a host of drysian healers had exerted their combined skills to keep her alive while the wound putrefied and fevers melted the flesh from her bones. It was agony, watching Idrilain fight this silent battle, but she refused to order her own release.

"Not yet. Not as things are," she'd groaned, clutching Magyana's hand as she panted and shook and laid her plans.

Reaching the queen's great pavilion, Magyana sent up a silent prayer. *O Illior, Sakor, Astellus, and Dalna, now is the hour! Give our queen strength enough to see our ruse through.*

A guard lifted the flap for her, and she stepped into the stifling heat beyond.

Huge tapestries suspended from the ridgepoles overhead enclosed the audience chamber, already crowded with officers and wizards gathered by the queen's summons. Magyana took her place to the left of the empty throne, then nodded to Thero, her protégé and coconspirator, who stood nearby. He bowed, his calm, aesthetic face betraying nothing.

The tapestries behind the chair parted, and Idrilain entered leaning on the arm of her eldest son, Prince Korathan, and followed by her three daughters. All but plump Aralain were in uniform.

Idrilain took her seat and her heir, Phoria, placed the ancient Sword of Ghërilain unsheathed across her mother's knees. Bold in war, wise in peace, Idrilain had wielded the ancient blade with honor for more than four decades. Now, unbeknownst to all but her closest advisers, she was too weak to lift it unaided.

Her thick grey hair fell smoothly over her shoulders beneath her golden circlet, hiding her thin neck. Soft leather gauntlets covered withered hands. Her wasted body was muffled in robes to hide the extent of her decline. The drysian's infusions blunted the pain enough not to tax her exhausted heart, but there were limits to even their powers. It took Thero's magic to limn the semblance of flesh and color in the queen's cheeks and lend false power to her voice. Only her pale blue eyes were unchanged, sharply alert as an osprey's.

The effect was flawless. The pity of it was that such deception must be practiced on Idrilain's own children.

The queen's two consorts had given her three children each, the two triads as different as the men who'd fathered them. The elder three—Princess Phoria, her twin Korathan, and their sister Aralain, were tall, fair, and solemn.

Klia, the youngest and sole survivor of the second three, had the same handsome features, chestnut hair, and ready wit as the father and two brothers for whom she still wore a black baldric. Of these six, it had always been the eldest and youngest girls whom the Orëska wizards watched most closely.

Skilled and fearless in battle, Phoria had risen through the ranks of the Queen's Horse Guard to High Commander of the Skalan Cavalry. Nearing fifty now, she was as renowned in military circles for her tactical innovations as she was at court for her blunt speech and ill-starred barrenness. While her merits as a warrior might have been sufficient for the crown in her great-grandmother's day, times had changed and Magyana was not the only one to fear that Phoria lacked the vision to rule a nation touched by the intricacies of the wider world.

Just before his death Nysander had also hinted to Magyana of a breach between heir and queen, but was forestalled by some oath from revealing more.

"We are the oldest of the Orëska wizards now, my love. No one knows better than we how precariously the common good balances on the edge of Ghërilain's Sword," he'd warned. "Keep close to the throne, and to all those who might one day sit upon it."

Magyana turned her attention back to Klia and felt a familiar surge of fondness. At twenty-five, she not only commanded a full squadron of Queen's Horse, but had demonstrated a talent for diplomacy, as well. It was no secret that a good many Skalans wished she was the firstborn.

Idrilain raised her hand and the assembly fell silent. "We will lose this war," she began, her voice a husky wheeze.

Magyana silently guided a stream of her own life force into the woman's ravaged body. The connection brought a backwash of pain, threading her veins with the dull crush of Idrilain's suffering and exhaustion. Magyana forced herself to breathe slowly, letting her mind rise above it and retain its focus. Across the room, Thero was doing the same.

"We will lose this war without Aurënen," Idrilain continued, sounding stronger. "We need the Aurënfaie's strength, and their wizards to turn the tide of Plenimaran necromancy. And if Mycena falls, we will need Aurënfaie trade, as well: horses, weapons, food."

"We've done well enough without the 'faie," Phoria retorted. "Plenimar hasn't managed to push us back from the Folcwine, for all their necromancers and abominations."

"But they will!" Idrilain croaked. An attendant offered her a goblet but she waved it away; no one must see the tremor in her hands. "Even if we manage to defeat them, we shall need the Aurënfaie after the war. We need their blood mingled with our own again."

She gestured imperiously for Magyana to continue.

"The power of wizardry came to our people by the mingling of our two races, human and Aurënfaie," Magyana began, reminding those who needed reminding of their own history. "It was the Aurënfaie who taught our first wizards the ways of Orëska magic." She turned to the Royal Kin. "You yourselves still carry the memory of that blood, the legacy of Idrilain the First and her Aurënfaie consort, Corruth í Glamien. Since his murder and the closing of Aurënen's borders against us three centuries ago, few Aurënfaie have come to Skala and so their legacy dwindles among us. Fewer wizard-born children are presented at the Orëska House each year, and the abilities of the young ones are often limited. Because wizards cannot procreate, there is no remedy save a renewed commerce between our two lands.

"The Plenimaran's attack on the Orëska House cut down some of our best young wizards before the war had truly started. The fighting since has thinned our ranks still further. There are empty beds in the Orëska's apprentice hall now, and for the first time since the founding of the Third Orëska in Rhíminee, two of the House's towers stand empty."

"Wizardry is one of the foundations of Skalan power," Idrilain rasped. "We had no idea, before this war began, how strong necromancy had grown in Plenimar. If wizardry is lost to us when they are so clearly gaining strength, then in a few generations Skala *will* be lost!"

She paused, and Magyana again felt Thero's magic joining her own as she willed more strength into the queen's failing frame.

"Lord Torsin and I have been negotiating with the Aurënfaie for over a year," Idrilain went on. "He is there now, at Virésse, and sends word that the Iia'sidra has at last agreed to admit a small delegation to settle the matter."

Idrilain gestured at Klia. "You will go as my representative, daughter. You must secure their support. We will discuss the details later."

Klia looked grave as she bowed her acceptance, but Magyana detected a flash of joy in her blue eyes. Satisfied, the wizard quickly skimmed the minds of the others. Princess Aralain glowed with relief, anxious only to return to her own safe hearth. The rest were another matter.

Phoria's expression gave nothing away, but the jealousy that gripped her left the bitter taste of bile at the back of Magyana's throat.

Korathan was less subtle. "Klia?" he growled. "You'd send the youngest of us to a people who live four centuries? They'll laugh in her face! I, at least—"

"I do not doubt your abilities, my son," Idrilain assured him, cutting short his protest. "But I need you here to assume Phoria's command." She paused again, turning to her eldest daughter. "As you,

Phoria, must step into mine for a time. My healers are too slow with their cures. You are War Commander until I recover."

She grasped the Sword of Ghërilain in both hands. On cue, Thero levitated the heavy blade, allowing Idrilain to pass it to her daughter.

Though Magyana had orchestrated this moment, she felt a chill of premonition. The sword had passed from mother to daughter since the days of Ghërilain, the first of the long line of warrior queens, but only upon the mother's death.

"And Regent?" asked Korathan, rather too quickly for Magyana's taste.

Or for his mother's, it seemed. Idrilain glared at him. "I need no Regent."

Magyana saw a muscle jump in Korathan's jaw as he gave her a silent bow.

Are you so anxious for your sister's honor, or to see her on the throne? wondered Magyana, brushing the surface of his mind a second time. The Afran Oracle might prevent male heirs from ascending the throne, but it had never prevented one from ruling from behind it.

"I must speak privately with Klia," said Idrilain, dismissing the others.

Night had fallen and Magyana retreated into the shadows between two nearby tents, waiting for the rest of the assembly to disperse. Somewhere above the blanketing clouds, a full moon rode the sky; she could feel its uneasy pull as an ache behind her eyes.

When the way was clear, she slipped into Idrilain's tent again to find Klia bent anxiously over her mother, who lay slumped back in her chair, fighting for breath.

"Help her!" Klia begged.

"Thero, fetch the drysian," Magyana called softly.

The younger wizard emerged from behind an arras at the back of the tent, accompanied by the healer Akaris. The drysian held a steaming cup ready in one hand, his worn staff in the other.

"Get some of this into her," Akaris instructed, giving the cup to Thero, then touched the silver lemniscate symbol of Dalna hanging at his throat. He placed his hand on the queen's drooping head and a pale glow engulfed both of them for a few seconds. She went limp, but her breathing had eased.

Thero and Klia carried her to the cot at the back of the tent and tucked heated stones in among the blankets.

Idrilain opened her eyes and looked wearily up at the others. Thero offered the cup again, but after a few sips she turned her head away. "This must be settled quickly," she whispered.

"You have my word, Mother, but maybe Kor's right," Klia said, kneeling beside her. "I'll look like a child to the Aurënfaie."

"You'll soon teach them otherwise. Korathan was the only other choice, but he'd frighten them to death."

"I understand. I just don't know what I can do that Lord Torsin hasn't tried already. He knows the 'faie better than anyone in Skala."

"Not quite everyone," Idrilain murmured. "But Seregil would never go—not with Korathan—"

"Seregil?" Klia looked up at Magyana, alarmed. "Her mind's wandering! He's still under ban of exile. He can't go back."

"Yes, he can—at least for the duration of your visit," Magyana told her. "The Iia'sidra has agreed to his temporary return as your adviser. If he will go."

"You haven't asked him?"

"It's been nearly a year since he and Alec were last heard from," said Thero.

Magyana laid a hand on Klia's shoulder. "Fortunately, we know someone who can find them. Don't you think that red-haired captain of yours would welcome a journey back to Skala?"

"Beka Cavish?" Klia smiled slightly, understanding. "I believe she would."

Korathan and Aralain had accompanied Phoria back to her tent, where she sat silently over her wine, waiting for word from her spy.

Korathan paced restlessly, chewing on some thought he was not yet ready to share. Aralain huddled in a fur robe beside the brazier, nervously clasping and unclasping her soft, ineffectual hands.

Since childhood Phoria had despised Aralain's timidity and reliance on others. She'd have ignored her completely if Aralain had not been the only one who'd managed to produce an heir to the throne. Her eldest, Elani, was now a tractable girl of thirteen.

"I don't understand why you're so opposed to this plan of Mother's," Aralain said at last, arching her brows in that annoying way she had when she wanted to be taken seriously.

"Because it will fail," Phoria snapped. "The Aurënfaie insulted our honor with their Edict of Separation. Now we're giving them another opportunity, and at the worst possible time. When we most need to appear strong, we're seen running for help from those least likely to give it. Their refusal will almost certainly cost us Mycena."

"But the necromancers—?"

Phoria gave a derisive snort. "I haven't met the necromancer yet that good Skalan steel can't deal with. We've grown too dependent on wizards. These past few years Mother's been ruled more and more by them—first Nysander, and now Magyana. Mark my words, this fool's gamble is her doing!"

Phoria was nearly shouting by the time she'd finished and was pleased to see Aralain properly cowed. Kor had stopped pacing, too, and was watching her warily. Womb mates they might be, but she never let him forget who held the power. Satisfied, she forced a thin smile and went back to her wine. A few minutes later, a soft scratching came at the tent flap.

"Come!" she called.

Captain Traneus stepped inside and saluted. The man was only twenty-four, considerably younger than most of her personal staff, but he'd proven remarkably close-mouthed, loyal, and eager for preferment—a most useful combination—and she'd groomed him as a second set of eyes and ears. In turn, he had amassed a useful cadre of informants.

"I kept watch as you ordered, General," he reported. "Magyana returned to the queen's tent under cover of darkness. I also heard the voices of two men inside: Thero and the drysian."

"Could you hear what was said?"

"Some of it, General. I fear the queen's health is worse than we've been led to believe. And Commander Klia is having doubts as to whether she is equal to the task the queen has set for her." He paused, shifting uncomfortably under Phoria's probing gaze.

"Was there something more?" she demanded curtly.

Traneus fixed his gaze somewhere on the tent wall behind her. "It was difficult to make out the queen's voice, General, yet from what I was able to hear, Idrilain believes the commander is the only one of her children capable of carrying out the mission."

Phoria's fingers clenched momentarily on the arms of her chair, but she schooled herself to patience. Much as the words rankled, she knew they would only strengthen her position with the others. Korathan's face had darkened. Aralain was studying her fingernails.

"The queen plans to send Lord Seregil with Klia," Traneus added. "Apparently Magyana knows where to find him and that young man of his."

"Mother's pet Aurënfaie brought back to heel, eh?" Phoria sneered.

"Don't be hateful," Aralain murmured. "He was always kind to us. If Mother didn't mind that he left when the war began, why should you? It's not as if he'd have been any use as a soldier."

"And good riddance!" Phoria muttered. "The man was a sensualist and a fop. He clung to rich young nobles like a tick to a dog's back. How much of your gold did he help spend, Kor?"

He shrugged. "He was an amusing fellow, in his own peculiar way. I imagine he'll do well enough as an interpreter."

"Keep a close eye on my mother and her visitors, Captain," Phoria ordered.

Saluting, Traneus disappeared back into the night.

"Seregil?" Korathan mused. "I wonder what Lord Torsin thinks of that? He's more of your opinion, as I recall."

"I can't imagine Seregil's people will be in any hurry to welcome him back, either," Phoria agreed, dismissing the matter. "Now, as for this mission of Klia's, we'll want an observer of our own among the company."

"Your man Traneus?" suggested Aralain with her usual lack of imagination.

Phoria spared her a withering glance. "Or perhaps we should begin with someone Klia trusts, someone she'll speak openly around."

"And someone in a position to send dispatches," Korathan added.

"Who, then?" asked Aralain.

Phoria arched a knowing eyebrow. "Oh, I have one or two people in mind."

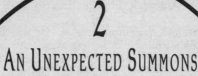

2

AN UNEXPECTED SUMMONS

Beka Cavish paced the ship's foredeck, scanning the western horizon for the first dark line marking Skala's northeast territories. It had been a week since they'd ridden out from Idrilain's camp; it might be another before they rejoined Klia for the voyage south and she didn't take well to inactivity.

She plucked absently at the new gorget hanging at the throat of her green regimental tunic. The captain's brass seemed to sit more heavily against her chest than the plain steel crescent of lieutenant. She'd been perfectly content leading her turma and they'd made a name for themselves as raiders behind the enemy's lines: Urgazhi, "wolf demons"—bestowed on them by the enemy during the early days of the war. They wore the epithet as a badge of honor, but it had been dearly bought. Of the thirty riders under her command today, only half had come through those days and knew the truth behind the silly ballads sung across Skala and Mycena, knew where the fallen bodies of their comrades lay along the Plenimaran frontier.

The turma was at full strength now for the first time in months, thanks to this mission. Never mind that some of the newer recruits had only just lost their milk teeth, as Sergeant Braknil liked to say. Perhaps, Sakor willing, they could be taught a thing or two before they all found themselves back in battle.

Less than a month before, Urgazhi Turma had been slogging through frozen Mycenian swamps, and even that was better than some fighting they'd seen.

Fighting across windswept sea ledges, the waves red with blood about their feet.

Beka leaned on the rail, watching a school of dolphins leaping ahead of the prow. The closer she came to seeing Seregil and Alec again, the more the memories of their last parting after the defeat of Duke Mardus rose to haunt her.

That brief battle had cost her father the use of his leg, Nysander his life, and Seregil his sanity for a time. Months later she'd had a letter from her father, saying that Seregil and Alec had quit Rhíminee for good. Now that she knew the reason, she wasn't so sure arriving with a decuria of riders was the best way to coax them home.

She gripped the rail, willing those thoughts away. She had work to do, work that for at least a little while was sending her back to those she loved best.

Two Gulls was barely large enough to merit the title of village. One poor inn, a ramshackle temple, and a dicer's throw of shacks clustered around a little dent of a harbor. Micum Cavish had spent a lifetime passing through such places, wandering on his own or on Watcher business with Seregil.

These past few years he'd stuck close to home, nursing his bad leg and watching his children grow. He'd enjoyed it, too, much to his wife's delight, but this journey had reminded him just how much he missed the open road. It was good to find out that he still knew instinctively where to show gold and where to guard his purse.

Five days earlier a mud-spattered messenger had ridden into the courtyard at Watermead, bearing news that the queen required his service and that of Seregil and Alec. It fell to him to talk his friends out of their self-imposed exile. The best news, however, had been that his eldest girl, Beka, was alive, whole, and on her way home from the war to act as his escort.

Within the hour, he was on the road with a sword at his side and pack on his back, heading for a village he'd never heard of until that day.

Just like old times.

Sitting here now on a bench in front of the nameless inn, hat brim pulled down over his eyes, he considered the task ahead. Alec would listen to reason, but a whole troop of soldiers wouldn't be enough if Seregil dug his heels in.

"Sir, sir!" a reedy voice called. "Wake up, sir. Your ship's coming in!"

Micum pushed his hat back and watched with amusement as his excitable lookout, a lad of ten, came scampering up the muddy street. It was the third such announcement of the day.

"Are you sure it's the right one this time?" he asked, then winced as he stood. Even after a day's rest, the scarred muscles behind his right thigh ached more than he cared to admit. The wounds left on a man by a *dyrmagnos* went deep, even after the flesh healed.

"Look, sir. You can see the banner," the boy insisted. "Crossed swords under a crown on a green field, just like you said. There's Queen's Horse Guard aboard, all right."

Micum squinted out across the cove. A few years back, he wouldn't have had to.

Damn, I'm getting old!

The boy was right this time, though. Taking up his walking stick, Micum followed him down to the shore.

The ship dropped anchor in deep water and longboats were lowered. A small crowd had gathered already, chatting excitedly as they watched the soldiers row in.

Micum grinned again as he caught sight of a redheaded officer standing in the prow of the lead boat. Old eyes or not, he knew his Beka when he saw her. She spotted him, too, and let out a happy whoop that echoed across the water.

At a distance, it was easy to see the girl she'd been when she'd left home to join the regiment, all long legs and enthusiasm. From here, she looked too slight to bear the weight of chain mail and weapons, but he knew better. Beka had never been frail.

As the longboat drew closer, however, the illusion dissolved. A mix of authority and ease emanated from her as she shared some joke with a tall rider standing just behind her.

She has what she always wanted, he thought with a rush of bittersweet pride. Just shy of twenty-two, she was a battle-scarred officer in one of Skala's finest regiments, and one of the queen's most daring raiders.

It hadn't given her airs, it seemed. She was out of the boat before it ground up on the shingle.

"By the Flame, it's good to see you again!" she cried, throwing her arms around him, and for a moment it seemed that she wasn't going to let go. When she did finally step back, her eyes were bright with unshed tears. "How are Mother and the children? Is Water-mead just the same?"

"We're all just as you left us. I have letters for you. Illia's is four pages long," he said, noting new scars on her hands and arms. Freckles still peppered her face, but two years of hard fighting had sharpened her features, stripping away the last vestiges of child-hood. "Captain is it?" he said, pointing at the new gorget.

"In name, at least. They gave me Wolf Squadron, then sent me and my turma home. You remember Sergeant Rhylin, don't you?"

"I always remember people who save my life," Micum said, shaking hands with the tall man.

"As I recall, it was as much the other way 'round," Rhylin replied. "You took on that dyrmagnos creature after Alec shot her. I don't think any of us would be standing here if you hadn't."

The comments drew curious stares from the bystanders and Micum quickly changed the subject.

"I only count one decuria here. Where are the other two?" he asked, waving a hand at the ten riders who'd come ashore with them. He recognized Corporal Nikides and a few of the other men and women, but most were strangers, and young.

"The rest sailed with Klia. We'll meet up with them later on," Beka told him. "This lot should be enough to get us safely where we need to go."

She glanced up at the afternoon sky, frowning slightly. "It'll take a while to ferry our horses in but I'd like to cover some ground before nightfall. Can we get a hot meal in this place before we go? One that doesn't include salted pork or dried cod?"

"I've had a word with the innkeeper," he replied, giving her a wink. "I think he can come up with dried pork or salted cod."

"So long as it's a change," Beka said, grinning. "How long will it take us to reach them?"

"Four days. Maybe three if this good weather holds."

Another look of impatience creased Beka's brow. "Three would be better." With a last restless glance at the ship, she followed him up to the inn.

"Whatever happened to that young man you wrote us of last year?" Micum asked. "That lieutenant what's-his-name? Your mother's beginning to get notions about him."

"Markis?" Beka shrugged, not looking at him. "He died."

Just like that? Micum thought sadly, sensing there was more to the story. Ah, well, war was a harsh business.

• • •

The weather held fair, but the roads grew worse the further north they went. By the second day, their horses were sinking to the fetlocks as they plodded along what passed for roads in this stretch of wilderness.

Easing his bad leg against the mud-caked stirrup, Micum scanned the jagged peaks in the distance and thought wistfully of home. Little Illia, just turned nine, had been picking daffodils in the pasture below the house the day Micum left. Here, in the shadow of the Nimra mountains, snow still lingered in dirty drifts beneath the pines.

Beka still hadn't explained the exact reason for their journey, and Micum respected her silence. They rode hard, making use of the lengthening days. At night, she and the others recounted battles, raids, and comrades lost. Lieutenant Markis was not mentioned around the campfire, so Micum made it his business to get Sergeant Rhylin aside one morning when they'd halted to water the horses.

"Ah, Markis." Rhylin glanced around, making certain Beka was out of earshot. "They were lovers all right, when they found the time. Cut from the same cloth, too, but his luck ran out last autumn. His turma ran into an ambush. Those who weren't killed in the fight were tortured to death." Rhylin's eyes got a pinched, distant look, as if he were squinting into harsh light. "A lot's made of what they do to our woman soldiers, but I tell you, Sir Micum, the men fare just as badly. We found the remains—Markis hadn't been among the lucky, if you take my meaning. The captain didn't speak for two days after that, didn't eat or sleep. It was Sergeant Mercalle who finally brought her out of it. Mercalle's buried more than her share of kin over the years, so I guess she knew what to say. Beka's been fine since, but she never speaks of him."

Micum sighed. "I don't imagine she likes to be reminded. And there's been no one since?"

"No one to speak of."

Micum had a good idea what that meant. Sometimes the body's needs overrode the heart's pain. Sometimes it was a way to heal.

The road finally grew drier as it wended up into the foothills. By early afternoon of the third day, Beka could see out over the tops of the trees behind them to the lowlands they'd traversed the day before. Somewhere beyond the southern horizon lay the Osiat coastline and the long isthmus that connected the peninsular country of Skala to her mainland territories. The rest of Urgazhi Turma were probably cooling their heels at Ardinlee by now.

"You're sure we'll reach them today?" she asked her father, riding beside her.

"The way you've driven us, we should get there before suppertime." He pointed out a notch in the hills a few miles ahead. "There's a village up there. Their cabin lies up a track just beyond."

"I hope they don't mind a crowd."

The sun was a few hours from the western horizon when they reached the little hamlet nestled in the cup of a valley. Sheep and cattle grazed the hillsides, and she could hear dogs barking in the distance.

"This is the place," said Micum, leading the way into town.

Villagers gawked at them as they rode into the muddy square. There were no temples or inns here, just a little shrine to the Four, festooned with faded offerings.

Just beyond the last cottage an enormous dead oak spread leafless branches against the sky. A trail wound up into the woods behind it. Following it for half a mile or so, they came out in a high meadow. A stream ran through it, and on the far side stood a small log house. A wolfskin was stretched to dry on one wall, and a spiky row of antlers of varying shapes and sizes decorated the roofline. In the kitchen garden near the door, a few speckled hens scratched among the dead leaves. A little way off, a byre sagged next to a corral. Half a dozen horses grazed there, and Beka recognized Alec's favorite mare, Patch, and two Aurënen horses. The chestnut stallion, Windrunner, had been her parents' gift to Alec during his first stay at Watermead. The black mare, Cynril, Seregil had raised from a colt.

"This is it?" she asked, surprised. It was peaceful. Rustic. Not at all the sort of place she associated with Seregil.

Micum grinned. "This is it."

The sound of an ax came from somewhere beyond the byre. Rising in the stirrups, she called out, "Hello at the house!"

The ax fell abruptly silent. An instant later Alec loped out from behind the byre, his fair, unkempt hair flying around his shoulders.

Rough living had left him as shaggy and gaunt as he'd been the first time they'd met. Gone was the citified finery he'd adopted in

Rhíminee; his tunic was as patched and stained as any stable boy's. He'd be nineteen in a few months' time, she realized with surprise. Half 'faie and beardless, he looked younger to those who didn't know him, and would for years. Seregil, who must be sixty now, had looked like a man of twenty for as long as she remembered.

"I believe he's glad to see us," her father noted.

"He better be!" Dismounting, Beka met Alec in a rough hug. He felt as thin as he looked, but there was hard muscle under the homespun.

"Yslanti bëk kir!" he exclaimed happily. *"Kratis nolieus i'mrai?"*

"You speak better Aurënfaie now than I do, Almost-Brother," she laughed. "I didn't understand a word of that after the greeting."

Alec stepped back, grinning at her. "Sorry. We've spoken almost nothing else all winter."

The beaten look he'd had back in Plenimar was gone; looking into those dark blue eyes, she read the signs of something her father had hinted at in his letter. She'd asked Alec once if he was in love with Seregil, and he'd been shocked by such a notion. It seemed the boy had finally figured things out. Somewhere in the back of her mind a tiny twinge of regret stirred, and she squelched it mercilessly.

Releasing her, Alec clasped hands with Micum, then cast a questioning look at the uniformed riders. "What's all this?"

"I have a message for Seregil," she told him.

"Must be quite a message!"

It is, she thought. *One he's been waiting for since before I was born.* "That's going to take some explaining. Where is he?"

"Hunting up on the ridge. He should be back by sunset."

"We'd better go find him. Time's running short."

Alec gave her a thoughtful look but didn't press. "I'll get my horse."

Mounted bareback on Patch, he led them up to the high ground above the meadow.

Beka found herself studying him again as they rode. "Even with your 'faie blood, I thought you'd be more changed," she said at last. "Do I look much different to you?"

"Yes," he replied with a hint of the same sadness she'd sensed in her father when they'd met at Two Gulls.

"What have you two been doing since I saw you last?"

Alec shrugged. "Wandered for a while. I thought we'd head for the war, offer our services to the queen, but for a long time he just wanted to get as far from Skala as possible. We found work along the way, singing, spying—" He tipped her a rakish wink. "Thieving a bit when things got thin. We ran into some trouble last summer and ended up back here."

"Will you ever go back to Rhíminee?" she asked, then wished she hadn't.

"I'd go," he said, and she caught a glimpse of that haunted look as he looked away. "But Seregil won't even talk about it. He still has nightmares about the Cockerel. So do I, but his are worse."

Beka hadn't witnessed the slaughter of the old innkeeper and her family, but she'd heard enough to turn her stomach. Beka had known Thryis since she was a child herself, playing barefoot in the garden with the granddaughter, Cilla. Cilla's father had taught her how to carve whistles from spring hazel branches.

These innocents had been among the first victims the night Duke Mardus and his men attacked the Orëska House. The attack at the Cockerel had been unnecessary, a vindictive blow struck by Mardus's necromancer, Vargûl Ashnazai. He'd killed the family, captured Alec, and left the cruelly mutilated bodies for Seregil to find. In his grief, Seregil had set the place ablaze as a funeral pyre.

At the top of the ridge Alec reined in and whistled shrilly through his teeth. An answering call came from off to their left, and they followed it to a pond.

"It reminds me of the one below Watermead," she said.

"It does, doesn't it?" said Alec, smiling again. "We even have otters."

None of them saw Seregil until he stood up and waved. He'd been sitting on a log near the water's edge and his drab tunic and trousers blended with the colors around him.

"Micum? And Beka!" Feathers fluttered in all directions as he strode over to them, still clutching the wild goose he'd been plucking.

He was thin and weathered, too, but every bit as handsome as Beka remembered—perhaps more so, now that she saw him through a woman's eyes instead of a girl's. Though slender and not overly tall, he carried himself with a swordsman's grace that lent unconscious stature. His fine-featured Aurënfaie face was sunbrowned, his large grey eyes warm with the humor she'd known from childhood. For the first time, however, it struck her how old those eyes looked in such a young face.

"Hello, Uncle!" she said, plucking a bit of down from his long brown hair.

He brushed more feathers from his clothes. "You picked a good time to come visiting. There've been geese on the pond and I finally managed to hit one."

"With an arrow or a rock?" Micum demanded with a laugh. Master swordsman that he was, Seregil had never been much of a hand with a bow.

Seregil gave him a crooked smirk. "An arrow, thank you very much. Alec's been paying me back for all the training I've put him through. I'm almost as good with a bow as he is with a lock pick."

"I hope I'm better than that, even out of practice," Alec muttered, giving Beka a playful nudge in the ribs. "Now will you tell us what brings you and a decuria of riders clear up here?"

"Soldiers?" Seregil raised an eyebrow, as if noticing for the first time that she was in uniform. "And you've been promoted, I see."

"I'm here on the Queen's business," she told him. "My riders know nothing of what I'm about to tell you, and I need to keep it that way for now." She pulled a sealed parchment from her tunic and handed it to him. "Commander Klia needs your help, Seregil. She's leading a delegation to Aurënen."

"Aurënen?" He stared down at the unopened document. "She knows that's impossible."

"Not anymore." Dismounting with practiced ease, Micum pulled his stick from the bedroll behind his saddle and limped over to his friend's side. "Idrilain squared things for you. Klia's in charge of the whole thing."

"There's no time to lose, either," Beka urged. "The war's going badly—Mycena could fall any day now."

"We get rumors, even here," Alec told her.

"Ah, but there's worse news than that," Beka went on. "The queen's been wounded and the Plenimarans are pushing their way west every day. Last we knew, they were halfway to Wyvern Dug. Idrilain's still in the field, but she's convinced that an alliance with Aurënen is our only hope."

"What does she need with me?" asked Seregil, handing the unread summons to Alec. "Torsin's dealt with the Iia'sidra for years without my help."

"Not like this," Beka replied. "Klia needs you as an additional adviser. Being Aurënfaie, you understand the nuances of both languages better than anyone, and you certainly know the Skalans."

"Given all that, I could end up with neither side trusting me. Besides which, my presence would be an affront to half the clans of Aurënen." He shook his head. "Idrilain actually got the Iia'sidra to let me return?"

"Temporarily," Beka amended. "The queen pointed out that since you're kin to her through Lord Corruth, it would be an affront to Skala to exclude you. Apparently it was also made clear that it was you who solved the mystery of Corruth's disappearance."

"Alec and I," he corrected absently, clearly overwhelmed by this news. "She told them about that?"

Before Nysander's death he, Alec, and Micum had been part of the wizard's network of spies and informers, the Watchers. Even the queen had not known of their role in that until he and Alec had helped uncover a plot against her life. In the process, they'd discovered the mummified body of Corruth í Glamien, who'd been murdered by Lerans dissenters two centuries earlier.

"I don't suppose it hurt that your sister is a member of the Iia'sidra now," said Micum. "Word is that the faction favoring open trade is stronger than ever."

"So you see, there's no problem with all that," Beka broke in impatiently. If she had her way, they'd be riding back down the mountain before sunset.

Her heart sank when Seregil merely stared down at his muddy boots and mumbled, "I'll have to give it some thought."

She was about to press him when Alec laid a hand on Seregil's shoulder and gave her a warning look. Clearly, some wounds hadn't healed.

"You say Idrilain is still in the field?" he asked. "How badly was she hurt?"

"I haven't seen her. Hardly anyone has, but my guess is it's worse than anyone is letting on. Phoria is War Commander now."

"Is she?" Seregil's tone was neutral, but she caught the odd look that passed between him and her father. The "Watcher look," her mother called it, resenting the secrets that lay between the two men.

"The Plenimarans have necromancers," Beka added. "I haven't met up with any yet, but those who have claim they're the strongest they've been since the Great War."

"Necromancers?" Alec's mouth tightened. "I suppose it was too much to hope that stopping Mardus would put an end to all that. You and your people are welcome to make camp in the meadow tonight."

"Thanks," said Micum. "Come on, Beka. Let's get your people settled."

It took her a moment to realize that Alec wanted time alone with Seregil.

"I expected him to be happy about going home, even if it is only for a little while," she mused, following her father down the trail. "He looked as if he'd received a sentence."

Micum sighed. "He did, a long time ago, and I guess it hasn't really been changed. I've always wanted to know the story behind what happened to him, but he never said a thing about it. Not even to Nysander, as far as I know."

A pair of otters was frisking on the far bank, but Alec doubted Seregil saw them, or that it was news of the war that had left him so pensive. Joining him at the water's edge, Alec waited.

When they'd finally become lovers, it had done much more than deepen their friendship. The Aurënfaie word for the bond between them was *talímenios*. Even Seregil couldn't fully interpret it, but by then there'd been no need for words.

For Alec, it was a unity of souls forged in spirit and flesh. Seregil had been able to read him like a tavern slate since the day they'd met; now his own intuition was such that at times he almost knew his friend's thoughts. As they stood here now, he could feel anger, fear, and longing radiating from Seregil in palpable waves.

"I told you a little about it once, didn't I?" Seregil asked at last.

"Only that you were tricked into committing some crime, and that you were exiled for it."

"And for once you didn't ask a hundred questions. I've always appreciated that. But now—"

"You want to go back," Alec said softly.

"There's more to it than that." Seregil folded his arms tightly across his chest.

Alec knew from long experience how difficult it was for Seregil to speak of his past. Even talímenios hadn't changed that, and he'd long since learned not to pry.

"I better finish plucking this goose," Seregil said at last. "Tonight, after the others are settled, I promise we'll talk. I just need time to take this all in."

Alec clasped Seregil's shoulder, then left him to his thoughts.

· · ·

Alone at last, Seregil stared blindly across the water, feeling unwelcome memories rising like a storm tide.

the solid finality of the knife's bloody handle clenched in his fist—choking, suffocating in the darkness—angry faces, jeering—

Bowing his head, he pressed his hands over his face like an eyeless mask and sobbed.

3

OLD GHOSTS STIRRING

An early half-moon was already rising in the evening sky when Seregil returned. Beka's riders had set up camp and had cook fires going. He looked for familiar faces, wondering which decuria she'd brought, and was surprised at how few people he recognized.

"Nikides, isn't it?" he asked, approaching a small group gathered around the nearest fire.

"Lord Seregil! It's good to see you again," the young man exclaimed, clasping hands with him.

"Are you still with Sergeant Rhylin?"

"I'm here, my lord," Rhylin called, coming out of one of the little tents.

"Any idea what all this is about?" asked Seregil.

Rhylin shrugged. "We go where we're told, my lord. All I know is that we head back down toward Cirna from here, to meet up with the rest of the turma. The captain's waiting for you over at the cabin. Just so you know, she's in one hell of a hurry to move on."

"So I gathered, Sergeant. Rest well while you can."

Beka was sitting with Alec and Micum by the front door. Ignoring her expectant look, Seregil tossed Alec the goose and went to wash his hands in a basin by the rain barrel.

"Supper smells good," he noted, giving Micum a wink as he sniffed the pleasant aromas wafting from the open doorway. "Lucky for you Alec's the cook tonight, and not me."

"I thought you looked thin," Micum said with a chuckle as they went in.

"Not quite your Wheel Street villa, is it?" Beka remarked, gesturing around the cabin's single room.

Alec grinned. "Call it an exercise in austerity. The snow got so deep this past winter we had to cut a hole in the roof to get out. Still, it's better than a lot of places we've been."

The place was certainly a far cry from the comfortably cluttered rooms he and Seregil had shared at the Cockerel, or Seregil's fine Wheel Street villa. A low-slung bed took up nearly a quarter of the floor. A rickety table stood near it, with crates and stools serving as chairs. Shelves, hooks, and a few battered chests held their modest belongings. Squares of oiled parchment were nailed over the two tiny windows to keep out the drafts. In the stone fireplace a kettle bubbled on an iron hook over the flames.

"I looked in at Wheel Street last month," Micum remarked as they crowded around the table. "Old Runcer's been ailing, but he still manages to keep the place just as you left it. A grandson of his helps out around the place now."

Seregil shifted uncomfortably, guessing that his friend had meant the statement as more than a casual remark. The house was his last remaining tie in Rhíminee. Like Thryis, old Runcer had kept his master's secrets and covered his tracks, enabling Seregil to come and go as he pleased without arousing suspicion.

"Where does he say we've been all this time?" he asked.

"By last report, you were at Ivywell, watching over Sir Alec's interests and providing horses to the Skalan army," Micum said, giving Alec a wink. Ivywell was the fictitious Mycenian estate bequeathed to Alec by his bucolic and equally fictitious father. This obscure squire had supposedly made Lord Seregil of Rhíminee the guardian of his only son. Seregil and Micum had concocted both tale and title over wine one night to explain Alec's sudden appearance in Rhíminee. Given the insignificance of the title and locale, no one had ever questioned it.

"What's said of the Rhíminee Cat?" asked Seregil.

Micum chuckled. "After six months or so, rumors began to go round that he must be dead. You may be the only nightrunner ever mourned by nobility. I gather there was a significant lapse of intrigues among that class in the wake of your disappearance."

Here was one more reason not to return. Seregil's clandestine work as the Cat had made his fortune. His work as one of Nysander's Watchers had given him purpose, while the public role he'd played as foppish Lord Seregil, the only one left him now, had become increasingly burdensome.

"I suppose I should sell the place off, but I don't have the heart to put Runcer out. It's been more his home than mine. Perhaps I'll deed the house over to your Elsbet when she finishes her training at the temple. She'd keep him on."

Micum patted Seregil's hand. "It's a kind thought, but won't you be needing it again, one of these days?"

Seregil looked down at the big freckled hand covering his own and shook his head. "You know that's not going to happen."

"How is everyone out at Watermead?" Alec asked.

Micum sat back and tucked his hands under his belt. "Well enough, except for missing the pair of you."

"I've missed them, too," Seregil admitted. Watermead had been a second home to him, Kari and her three daughters a second family. They'd claimed Alec as one of their own from the first day the boy had set foot in their house.

"Elsbet's still in Rhíminee. She took sick in the plague that swept through last winter, but came through it whole," Micum went on. "Temple life suits her. She's thinking of becoming an initiate. Kari has her hands full with the two babes, but Illia's old enough to help now. It's a good thing, too. Ever since Gherin learned to walk he's been trying to keep up with his foster brother. That Luthas has the gift of mischief. Kari found them halfway down to the river one morning."

Seregil smiled. "Shades of things to come, I'd say, with you for a father."

They chatted on for a while, exchanging news and stories as if this were some casual visit. Presently, however, Seregil turned to Beka.

"I suppose you'd better tell me more. You say Klia's in charge of this delegation?"

"Yes. Urgazhi Turma's been assigned as her honor guard."

"But why Klia?" Alec asked. "She's the youngest."

"A cynical person might say that makes her the most expendable," Micum remarked.

"She or Korathan would be whom I'd choose, in any case," Seregil mused. "They're the smartest of the pack, they've proven themselves in battle, and they carry themselves with authority. I assume Torsin will go, along with a wizard or two?"

"Lord Torsin is in Aurënen already. As for wizards, they're as hard to spare in the field as generals these days, so she's taking only Thero," Beka replied, and Seregil knew she was watching him for a reaction.

And with good reason, he thought. Thero had succeeded him as Nysander's pupil after Seregil had failed in that capacity. They'd disliked one another on sight and bickered like jealous brothers for years. Yet they'd ended up in each other's debt after Mardus had kidnapped Thero and Alec. From what Alec had told him afterward, they'd kept each other alive through a horrific journey, long enough for Alec to escape before the final battle on that lonely stretch of Plenimaran coast. Nysander's death had laid their rivalry to rest, yet each remained a living reminder to the other of what had been lost.

Seregil looked hopefully at Micum. "You're coming, aren't you?"

Micum studied a hangnail. "Not invited. I'm just here to convince you to go. You'll have to make do with Beka this time out."

"I see." Seregil pushed his dish aside. "Well, I'll give you my answer in the morning. Now, who's for a game of Sword and Coin? It's no fun playing with Alec anymore. He knows all my cheats."

For a time Seregil was able to lose himself in the simple enjoyment of the game, the pleasure made all the more precious by the knowledge that this moment of peace was a fleeting one.

He'd enjoyed their long respite. He often felt as if he'd stepped from his world into the one Alec had known before they'd met: a simpler life of hunting, wandering, and hard physical work. They'd found enough mischief to get into along the way to keep up their nightrunning skills, but mostly they'd done honest work.

And made love. Seregil smiled down at his cards, thinking how many times he and Alec had lain tangled together in countless inns, by countless fires under the stars, or on the bed Micum was currently using as a seat. Or on the soft spring grass beneath the oaks down by the stream, or in the sweet hay of fall, or in the pool on the ridge, and once, floundering half-dressed in deep new snow under a reckless waxing moon that had broken their sleep for three nights running. Come to think of it, there weren't too many spots around here where the urge hadn't overtaken them one time or another.

They'd come a long way from that first awkward kiss Alec had given him in Plenimar, but then, the boy had always been a fast learner.

"Those must be some good cards you're holding," said Micum, giving him a quizzical look. "Care to show us a few? It's your turn."

Seregil played a ten pip and Micum captured it, cackling triumphantly.

Seregil watched his old friend with a mix of sadness and affection. Micum had been about Beka's age when they first met—a tall, amiable wanderer who'd happily joined Seregil in his adventures, if not in his bed. Now silver hairs outnumbered the red in his friend's thick hair and mustache, and in the stubble on his cheeks.

Tírfaie, we call them: the short-lived ones. He watched Beka laughing with Alec, knowing he'd watch silver streak her wild red hair, too, while his was still dark. Or would, Sakor willing, if she survived the war.

He quickly kenneled that dark thought with the others baying somewhere in the back of his mind.

They burned two candles to stumps before Micum threw down his cards. "Well, I guess that's enough losing for one night. All that riding's finally caught up with me."

"I'd put you up in here, but—" Seregil began.

Micum dismissed his apology with a knowing look. "It's a clear night and we have good tents. See you in the morning."

Seregil watched from the doorway until Beka and Micum had disappeared among the tents, then turned to Alec, belly already tight with dread.

Alec sat idly shuffling the cards, and the flickering light of the fire made him look older than his years. "Now?" he asked, gentle but implacable.

Seregil sat down and rested his elbows on the table. "Of course I want to go back to Aurënen. But not this way. Nothing's been forgiven."

"Tell me everything, Seregil. This time I want it all."

All? Never that, talí.

Memories surged again like a dirty spring flood bursting its banks. What to pluck out first from the debris of his broken past?

"My father, Korit í Solun, was a very powerful man, one of the most influential members of the Iia'sidra." A dull ache gripped his heart as he pictured his father's face, so thin and stern, eyes cold as sea smoke. They hadn't been like that before his wife's death, or so Seregil had been told.

"My clan, the Bôkthersa, is one of the oldest and most highly respected. Our *fai'thast* lies on the western border, close to the Zengati tribal lands."

" 'Fade as'?"

"Fai'thast. It means 'folk lands'; 'home.' It's the territory each clan owns." Seregil spelled the word out for him, a comfortingly familiar ritual. They'd done it so often that they scarcely noticed the interruption. Only later did it strike him that of all the words he'd poured out in his native tongue over the past two years, that one had not been among them.

"The western clans always had more dealings with the Zengati—raids out of the mountains, pirates along the coast, that sort of thing," he continued. "But the Zengati are clannish, too, and some tribes are friendlier than others. The Bôkthersa and a few other clans traded with some of them over the years; my grandfather, Solun í Meringil, wanted to go further and establish a treaty between our two countries. He passed the dream on to my father, who finally convinced the Iia'sidra to meet with a Zengati delegation to discuss possibilities. The gathering took place the summer I was twenty-two; by Aurënfaie reckoning that made me younger than you are now."

Alec nodded. There was no exact correlation between human and Aurënfaie ages. Some stages of life lasted longer than others, some less. Being only half 'faie himself, he was maturing more rapidly than an Aurënfaie would, yet he would probably live as long.

"Many Aurënfaie were against a treaty," Seregil went on. "For time out of mind the Zengati have raided our shores—taking slaves, burning towns. Every house along the southern coast has a few battle trophies. It's a testament to the influence of our clan that my father got as far with his plan as he did.

"The gathering took place beside a river on the western edge of our fai'thast, and at least half the clans there had come to make sure he failed. For some, it was hatred of the Zengati, but there were others, like the Virésse and Ra'basi, who disliked the prospect of western clans allying with the Zengati. Looking back now, I suppose it was a justifiable concern.

"You recall me saying that Aurënen has no king or queen? Each clan is governed by a khirnari—"

" 'And the khirnari of the eleven principal clans form the Iia'sidra Council, which acts as a meeting place for the making of alliances and the settling of grievances and feuds,' " Alec finished, rattling it off like a lesson.

Seregil chuckled; you seldom had to teach him anything twice, especially if it had to do with Aurënen. "My father was the khirnari for Bôkthersa, just as my sister Adzriel is now. The khirnari of all the principal clans and many of the lesser ones came together with the Zengati. The tents covered acres, a whole town sprung up like a patch of summer mushrooms." He smiled wistfully, remembering kinder days. "Entire families came, as if it were a festival. The adults went off and growled at each other all day, but for the rest of us, it was fun."

He rose to pour fresh wine, then stood by the hearth, swirling the untasted contents of his cup. The closer he came to the heart of the story, the harder it was to tell.

"I don't suppose I've ever said much about my childhood?"

"Not a lot," Alec allowed, and Seregil sensed the lingering resentment behind the bland words. "I know that, like me, you never knew your mother. You once let slip that you have three sisters besides Adzriel. Let's see: Shalar, Mydri, and—who's the youngest?"

"Ilina."

"Ilina, yes, and that Adzriel raised you."

"Well, she did her best. I was rather wild as a boy."

Alec smirked. "I'd be more surprised to hear that you weren't."

"Really?" Seregil was grateful or this brief, bantering respite. "Still, it didn't much please my father. In fact, I don't remember much about me that did, except my skill at music and swordplay, and those weren't enough most days. By the time I'm speaking of, I mostly just stayed out of his way.

"This gathering threw us back together again, and at first I did my best to behave. Then I met a young man named Ilar." Just speaking the name made his chest tighten. "Ilar í Sontír. He was a Chyptaulos, one of the eastern clans my father hoped to sway to our side. My father was delighted—at first.

"Ilar was . . ." The next part came hard. Just speaking the man's name aloud brought him back like a summoned spirit. "He was handsome, impetuous, and always had plenty of time to go hunting or swimming with my friends and me. He was nearly man grown, and we were all terribly flattered by his attention. I was his favorite from the start, and after a few weeks the two of us began to go off on our own whenever we could."

He took a long sip from his cup and saw that his hand was trembling. For years he'd buried these memories, but with a single telling the old feelings surfaced, raw as they'd been that long ago summer.

"I'd had a few flirtations—friends, girl cousins, and the like—but nothing like this. I suppose you could say he seduced me, though as I recall it didn't take much effort on his part."

"You loved him."

"No!" Seregil snapped, as memories of silken lips and callused hands against his skin taunted him. "No, not love. I was passion-blind, though. Adzriel and my friends tried to warn me about him, but by then I was so infatuated I'd have done anything for him. And in the end, I did.

"Ironically, Ilar was the first to recognize and encourage my less noble talents. Even untrained, I had clever hands and a knack for skulking. He'd devise little challenges to test me—innocent at first, then less so. I lived for his praise." He glanced guiltily at Alec. "Rather like you and me, back when we first met. It's one of the things that made me keep you at arm's length for so long; the fear of corrupting you the way he did me."

Alec shook his head. "It was different with us. Go on, finish this and be done with it. What happened?"

Older than his years, Seregil thought again. "Very well, then. One of my father's most vociferous opponents was Nazien í Hari, khirnari of Haman clan. Ilar convinced me that certain papers in Nazien's tent would aid my father's cause, that I alone had the skill to sneak in and 'borrow' them." He grimaced, disgusted at the green fool he'd been. "So I went. Everyone else was off at some ritual that night, but one of Nazien's kinsmen came back and caught me at it. It was dark; he must not have seen that it was a boy he was drawing his dagger against. There was just enough light for me to see the flash of his blade and the angry glint in his eyes. Terrified, I drew my own and struck out. I didn't mean to kill him, but I did." He let out a bitter laugh. "I don't suppose even Ilar expected that when he sent the Haman back."

"He *wanted* you to be caught?"

"Oh, yes; that's what all his attentiveness had been leading to. The 'faie seldom stoop to murder, Alec, or even to outright violence. It all comes down to *atui,* our code of honor. Atui and clan are everything—they define the individual, the family." He shook his head sadly. "Ilar and his fellow conspirators—there were several, as it turned out—had only to manipulate me into betraying the atui of my clan to accomplish their end, which was the disruption of the negotiations. Well, they certainly got that! What followed was all very dramatic and tawdry, given my reputation and my all-too-obvious relationship with Ilar. I was found guilty of complicity in the plot, and of murder. Did I ever tell you what the penalty is for murder among my people?"

"No."

"It's an ancient custom called *dwai sholo*."

" 'Two bowls'?"

"Yes. Punishment is the responsibility of the criminal's clan. The wronged clan claims *teth'sag* against the family of the guilty person. If that clan breaks atui and does not carry out their duty, the wronged family can declare a feud and any killing that follows is not considered murder until honor is restored.

"Anyway, for dwai sholo, the guilty person is shut up in a tiny cell in the house of their own khirnari and every day they are offered two bowls of food. One bowl is poisoned, the other not. The condemned can choose one or refuse both, day after day. If you survive a year and a day, it's considered a sign from Aura and you're set free. Few manage it."

"But they didn't do that to you."

"No." —*the choking heat, the darkness, the words that flayed*— Seregil gripped the cup. "I was exiled instead."

"What about the others?"

"The small cell and two bowls, as far as I know. All except for Ilar. He escaped the night I was caught. And he'd accomplished his purpose. The Haman used the scandal to wreck the negotiations. Everything my family and others had worked decades to accomplish was swept aside in less than a week's time. The whole plot had hinged on duping the son of Korit í Solun into betraying the clan's honor. And you know what?"

His voice was suddenly husky, so husky that he had to take another gulp of wine before he could finish. "The worst of it wasn't the killing or the shame, or even the exile. It was the fact that people I should have trusted had tried to *warn* me, but I was too vain and headstrong to listen." He looked away, unable to bear Alec's look of sympathy. "So there you have it, my shameful past. Nysander was the only other person I ever told."

"And this happened over forty years ago?"

"By Aurënfaie reckoning, it's still last season's news."

"Has your father ever forgiven you?"

"He died years ago, and no, he never forgave me. Neither did my sisters except for Adzriel—did I mention that Shalar was in love with a Haman? I doubt very many of my clan who've borne the burden of the shame I brought on our name will be in any hurry to welcome me back, either."

Talked out, Seregil knocked back the last of his wine as images from that final day in Virésse harbor flashed unbidden through his mind: his father's furious silence, Adzriel's tears, the scathing jeers and catcalls that had propelled him up the gangplank of a foreign ship. He hadn't wept then and he didn't now, but the crushing sense of remorse was as fresh as ever.

Alec waited quietly, hands clasped on the table in front of him. Stranded in silence by the fire, Seregil suddenly found himself aching for the reassuring touch of those strong, deft fingers.

"So, will you go?" Alec asked again.

"Yes." He'd known the answer since Beka had first told him of the journey. Framing the question he hadn't yet dared to ask, Seregil forced himself across the bit of floor that separated them and extended a hand to Alec. "Are you coming with me? It may not be very pleasant, being the talímenios of an exile. I don't even have a proper name there."

Alec took his outstretched hand, squeezing it almost to the point of pain. "Remember what happened the last time you tried to go off without me?"

Seregil's relieved laugh startled them both. "Remember? I think I've still got some of the bruises!" Tightening his own grip, he pulled Alec out of his chair and onto the bed. "Here, I'll show you."

Seregil's sudden demand for lovemaking surprised Alec less than the wildness of what followed. Anger lurked just beneath his lover's frenzied passion, anger not meant for him, but that still left a scattering of small bruises across his skin to be discovered by tomorrow's sun.

Alec didn't need the heightened senses of the talímenios bond to tell him that Seregil was trying to somehow burn all memory of that hated first lover from his own skin, or that it hadn't worked.

Locked sweaty and breathless in Seregil's arms afterward, Alec listened as the other man's ragged breathing slowed to normal and for the first time felt empty and uneasy instead of sated and safe. A black gulf of silence separated them even as they lay heart against heart. It frightened him, but he didn't pull away.

"What became of Ilar? Was he ever found?" he whispered at last.

"I don't know."

Alec touched Seregil's cheek, expecting to find tears. It was dry. "Once, just after we met, Micum told me that you never forgive betrayal," he said softly. "Later, Nysander told me the same. They both believed it was because of what happened to you in Aurënen. It was him, wasn't it? Ilar?"

Seregil took Alec's hand and pressed the palm to his lips, then moved it to his bare chest, letting him feel the quick, heavy beat of his heart. When he spoke at last, his voice was thin with grief.

"To give someone your love and trust—I hate him for that! For robbing me of innocence too early. Spoiled and silly and willful as I was, I'd never had to hate anyone before. But it taught me things, too: what love and trust and honor really are, and that you can never take them for granted."

"I suppose if we ever met I'd have to thank him for that, at least—" Alec murmured, then froze as Seregil's hand suddenly tightened around his.

"You wouldn't have time, talí, before I cut his throat."

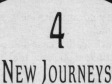

4

New Journeys

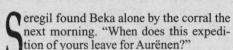

Seregil found Beka alone by the corral the next morning. "When does this expedition of yours leave for Aurënen?"

"Soon." She turned and gave him an appraising look. Damn, she looked like her father. "Does that mean you're coming?"

"Yes."

"Thank the Flame! We're to meet Commander Klia in a little fishing town below the Cirna Canal, by the fifteenth of the month."

"What route is she taking to Aurënen?"

"I don't know. The less information she gives out ahead of time, the less there'll be for Plenimaran spies to pick up."

"Very wise."

"If we push, we can be in Ardinlee in three days. How soon can you be ready?"

"Mmmm, I don't know." He looked around the place as if taking stock of some vast holding. "Is a couple of hours soon enough?"

"If that's the best you can do."

Watching her stride briskly off toward the tents, he decided she had a good deal of her mother in her, too.

Alec slipped his black-handled dagger into his boot and settled his sword belt more comfortably against his left hip.

"Don't forget this." Seregil took their tool

rolls from a high shelf and tossed Alec's over to him. "With any luck, we'll be needing them."

Alec unrolled the black leather case and checked the slender implements stored in its stitched pockets: lock picks, wires, limewood shims, and a small lightstone mounted on a knurled wooden handle. Seregil had made everything; these weren't the sort of tools you found in the marketplace.

Satisfied, Alec slipped it inside his coat, where it lay against his ribs with a comfortably familiar weight. That left only his bow, some clothes, a bedroll, and a few personal effects to pack. He'd never had much in the way of belongings; as Seregil was fond of saying, the only things of real value were those you could take away with you in a hurry. That suited Alec and made packing a simple matter.

Seregil had finished with his own gear and was looking rather wistfully around the room. "This was a good place."

Coming up behind him, Alec wrapped an arm around his waist and rested his chin on Seregil's shoulder. "A very good place," he agreed. "But if it hadn't been this moving us on, there would have been something else."

"I suppose so. Still, we're spoiled with privacy," Seregil said, pressing back against him with a lewd grin. "Just wait until we're trapped aboard some ship, cheek by jowl with Beka's soldiers. You'll wish we were back here and so will I."

"Hey in there, are you ready yet?" Beka demanded, appearing suddenly in the doorway. Seeing them together, however, she halted uncertainly.

Alec jumped back, too, blushing.

"Yes, we're ready, Captain," Seregil told her, adding under his breath, "What did I tell you?"

"Good." Beka covered her own embarrassment brusquely. "What about all this?" She gestured around the little room. Except for their clothes and gear, the cabin looked much as it had last night. The fire was banked, and clean dishes lay drying on a shelf by the window.

Seregil shrugged and headed for the door. "It'll be of use to someone."

"He's still not wearing a sword?" Beka asked Alec when Seregil was gone.

"Not since Nysander's death."

She nodded sadly. "It's a shame, a great swordsman like that."

"There's no point in arguing with him," Alec said, and Beka guessed from his tone that this was a battle he'd lost with Seregil more than once.

They set off at midmorning, following the road south.

Despite Seregil's misgivings, it felt good to be riding with Micum again. Every so often the two of them would find themselves out ahead of the others, and for a while it was like old times: the two of them off on a mission for Nysander, or pursuing some harebrained quest of their own for the sheer hell of it.

But then the sun would strike silvery glints in his old friend's hair, or he'd catch sight of Micum's crippled leg, stiff in the stirrup, and Seregil's exhilaration evaporated again into a twinge of guilty sadness.

Micum's was not the first generation he'd outlive, but it didn't get any easier with experience. In Skala, among these Tír he loved, only the wizards endured, and even they could be killed.

Now and then he caught Micum watching him with a bemused expression that suggested he was having similar thoughts, but he seemed to accept the situation. It was Seregil who'd quietly drop back to find Alec, like a cold man seeking a fire.

The roads grew drier as they turned west the next day, and the rolling plains were already thick with crocus and yellowstar. Trusting the clear nights, they rode long and slept rough, letting the horses forage as they went.

Except for the number of troops they met, Seregil found it hard to imagine the terrible war that was being waged on land and sea. Talking with Beka's riders soon brought the reality of the situation home to him, however. He recognized only four of Rhylin's ten riders: Syra, Tealah, Tare, and Corporal Nikides, who'd aged into a man since they'd met, as well as acquiring a jagged white scar down his right cheek. The other six were new to the turma, replacements for those who'd fallen in battle.

"Well, Beka, I always knew you'd amount to something," Seregil said as the group sat around the fire their second night on the road. "Right hand to Commander Klia? That's a mark of real favor."

"It gets them out of harm's way for a bit, too," Micum added.

Beka shrugged noncommittally. "We've earned it."

"We've lost a lot of people since you last saw us, my lord," Sergeant Rhylin remarked, stretching the day's stiffness from his legs. "You recall the two men who were planked? Gilly lost a hand and went home, but Mirn healed up fine; he and Steb are in Braknil's decuria now."

"We lost Jareel at Steerwide Ford a day after we got back," Nikides put in. "And remember Kaylah? She died scouting an enemy camp."

"She had a lover in the turma, didn't she?" asked Alec, and Seregil smiled to himself.

Alec had been more taken with the idea of soldiering than he'd ever let on and had formed quite a bond with Beka's riders in the short time they'd known one another in Rhíminee, and later during the dark days in Plenimar.

Nikides nodded. "Zir. He took it hard, but you have to go on, don't you? He's Mercalle's corporal now."

"Sergeant Mercalle?" Seregil looked up in surprise. Mercalle was an experienced old soldier, one of the sergeants who'd helped train Beka and then requested the honor of serving with her when she was given a command. "I thought you lost her in the first battle of the war?"

"So did we," replied Beka. "She went down under her horse and broke both arms and a leg, along with a few ribs. But she tracked us down again before the snow flew that fall, ready to fight."

"We were lucky to get her back," said Corporal Nikides, "She fought with Phoria herself in their younger days."

"She and Braknil have seen us through some dark days," Beka added. "By the Flame, their lessons have saved us a time or two!"

Never one to waste valuable time, Seregil spent much of the journey drilling Alec and anyone else who cared to listen on the clans of Aurënen: their emblems, customs, and most importantly, their affiliations. Alec took in the information with all his usual quickness.

"Only eleven principal clans?" he'd scoffed when someone else complained at the complexities of Aurënfaie politics. "Compared to dealing with Skalan nobility, that's no worse than your mother's market list."

"Don't be too certain," warned Seregil. "Sometimes those eleven feel more like eleven hundred."

Beka and the others also saw to it that Alec brushed up his swordplay. He was soon bruised but happy to be reclaiming his hard-won skills.

Seregil pointedly ignored the hopeful glances they cast in his direction during these sessions.

They met with columns of soldiers more frequently as they neared the coast and from them learned that Plenimaran ships now controled much of the Inner Sea's northeastern waters, and that raids on eastern Skalan were increasing. Skala still held crucial control of the isthmus and canal, but the pressure was mounting.

News of the land battles was more encouraging. According to an infantry captain they met just north of Cirna, Skalan troops held the Mycenian coastline as far west as Keston, and had pushed east to the Folcwine River. As Seregil had long ago predicted, however, the Plenimaran Overlord had extended his influence into the northlands and was gradually seizing control of the trade routes there.

"Have they taken Kerry?" Alec asked, thinking of his home village in the Ironheart Mountains.

"Don't know Kerry," the captain replied, "but I've heard rumors that Wolde's gone over to them."

"That's bad," Seregil muttered.

Wolde was an important link in the Gold Road, the caravan route between Skala and the north. If the Plenimarans captured the north's iron, wool, gold, and timber at their source, it wouldn't matter if Skala held the Folcwine; there'd be no more goods coming downriver.

They reached the isthmus on the third day and crossed the echoing chasm of the great Cirna Canal. Following the Queen's Highroad west, they came in sight of the little village of Ardinlee just before sunset.

Micum reined in to take his leave where the road branched and Seregil felt again that gulf of change and distance.

Beka leaned over to hug her father. "Give my love to Mother and the others."

"I will." Turning to Alec and Seregil, he grinned ruefully. "Since I can't come with you, I'll just have to trust you three to keep each other out of trouble down there. I hear the 'faie are persnickety about foreigners."

"I'll keep that in mind," Seregil replied dryly.

With a final wave, Micum turned his horse south and galloped away.

Seregil remained for a moment, watching his old companion disappear into the evening's dusty haze.

Klia was camped at a prosperous estate just south of the village. Riding through a vineyard, they found Sergeant Mercalle on guard at the front door of the house. She saluted Beka smartly as they rode up, then gave Alec a welcoming wink. Despite her injuries she stood as straight at fifty as the young soldiers on duty beside her.

"Well met, my lords," she greeted them as they dismounted. "I haven't seen you since that fancy send-off you gave us back in Rhíminee."

Seregil grinned. "I remember the early part of the evening, but not much later on."

"Ah, yes." She feigned disapproval. "Thanks to you, most of my riders were carrying sore heads the next morning. Tell me, Sir Alec, do you recall the blessing you gave us when we were all pissed as newts?"

"Now that you mention it, I do seem to remember standing on a table, saying something pretentious as I poured wine on people."

"I wish you'd gotten a few more drops of it on me. It might have saved me a few broken bones," Mercalle said, rubbing her left arm. "Of those you splashed, only one's been killed. The rest are all still with us. You're a luckbringer, and no mistake."

Seregil nodded. "I've always thought so."

They found Klia in a library on the first floor, poring over reports and charts with several uniformed aides.

"Tell him we can't wait for his shipment," she was saying when Seregil entered with Alec and Beka. "There'll be dispatch ships every few days. He can send it along with one of them."

Seregil studied her profile as he waited for her to finish. Klia had always looked more the commander than the princess, but war had left its mark on her all the same. Her uniform hung loosely on her slender frame, and faint worry lines bracketed her mouth when she frowned. A new sword scar cut across the tiny faded burn marks that peppered one cheek.

When she looked up at last and smiled, however, he saw that a little of the girl he'd known lived on in her bright blue eyes.

"So you talked them into it, Captain?" she said to Beka. "Well done. We sail the day after tomorrow. Any trouble on the road?"

Beka gave her a crisp salute. "Just a sore ear from traveling with Seregil, Commander."

Klia chuckled. "I don't doubt it. I expect you want to see your sergeants, eh? You're dismissed."

Saluting again, Beka and the aides withdrew.

Klia watched Beka go, then turned to Seregil. "I'm in your debt for wrangling that commission for her. She's saved my life more than once."

"I hear her turma spends more time behind the enemy than they do in front of them."

"That's what comes of growing up under your influence, and her father's." Klia came around the table to clasp hands with them. "I was afraid you wouldn't come."

"Beka made it clear that the queen had gone to some trouble to smooth my way with the Iia'sidra," Seregil replied. "Under the circumstances, it would've been most ungrateful of me to ignore your request."

"And for that I thank you," she replied with a knowing look. Loyal kinsman he might be, but as an Aurënfaie, exile or not, he was not hers to command. "By the Flame, it's good to see you both! I take it you mean to come with us, Alec?"

"If you'll have me."

"I will, and gladly." She waved them to seats near the window and poured wine. "Aside from my respect for your talents, it may prove favorable to have a second 'faie in my entourage."

Seregil noted Alec's quiet flicker of amusement; Klia had never mentioned his 'faie heritage before.

"Who else is going? Is Captain Myrhini with you?" he asked.

"She's Commander Myrhini now, promoted to take my place in the field," Klia replied with poorly concealed regret. "As for an entourage, it will be a small one. We've done our best to keep word of our journey from getting out, since we're still not sure what Plenimar's intentions are regarding Zengat. The last thing we need is them stirring up trouble for Aurënen just when we want the Iia'sidra's full attention.

"Lord Torsin is already there. Urgazhi Turma will be my honor guard and household; Beka will serve as aide-de-camp. I suppose she's told you that Thero's coming as my field wizard?"

Like Beka, she stole a quick glance at him as she said this; she'd spent enough of her girlhood underfoot at the Orëska House to know of the famous rivalry.

Seregil sighed inwardly. "A good choice. May I ask how you settled on him?"

"Ostensibly, because the more experienced wizards are needed in the field."

"And the real reason?"

Klia picked up an ornate map weight and tapped it absently against her palm. "You don't walk among swordsmen without a sword, but if your blade is too big, they're insulted and mistrust you. If it's too small, they scorn you. The trick is to find the right balance."

"And if you can make a large sword look smaller and less threatening, then so much the better? Nysander always claimed he was remarkable. A year with Magyana will only have enhanced his talents—perhaps even his personality."

Alec shot him a warning look, but Klia smiled.

"He's an odd duck, I admit, but I'll feel safer having him along. We're facing a great deal of opposition, not the least of which is the fact that there are plenty of Aurënfaie who don't want us going anywhere except Virésse."

"You mean that's not where we're going?" Seregil asked, surprised. No Tírfaie had been allowed to land anywhere except the eastern port since Aurënen had closed its borders.

"There's not much choice," Klia told him. "You can practically walk across the Strait of Bal on the decks of enemy ships these days. We're to land at Gedre. Do you know the place?"

"Very well." The name was tinged with bittersweet memories. "So we're to meet the Iia'sidra there?"

Klia's smile intensified. "No, over the mountains, at Sarikali."

"Sarikali?" Alec gaped. "I never thought I'd see Aurënen, much less Sarikali!"

"I could say the same," Seregil murmured, fighting to retain his composure as a wave of conflicting emotions raged through him.

"There is one more thing you ought to know," she warned. "Lord Torsin has opposed including you."

The words took a moment to register. "Why?"

"He believes your presence will complicate negotiations with some of the clans."

Seregil let out a derisive snort. "Of course it will! Which means the queen must have some very pressing reason for sending me against the advice of her most experienced envoy."

"Yes." Klia turned the map weight over in her hands. "As envoy to Aurënen, Lord Torsin has served my family faithfully for three decades. There's never been any question as to his loyalty or wisdom. However, in all that time, outsiders have never been allowed beyond the city of Virésse, which means he's more familiar with that clan and their allies in the east. It would be—understandable if his long association with certain khirnari might unconsciously predispose him in their favor. The queen and I believe your westerner's point of view will prove a very valuable balance."

"Perhaps," Seregil said doubtfully. "But as an exile, I have no connections, no influence."

"Exile or not, you're still Aurënfaie, still the brother of a khirnari. As for influence—" She gave him a knowing look. "You know better than most in how many directions that can work. You'll certainly be seen as having my ear. I'm betting that some Aurënfaie will see you as a sympathetic conduit. Alec, too, for that matter."

This was familiar ground. "We'll do what we can, of course."

"Besides which," Klia continued earnestly, "there's no one else in all Skala I'd rather have at my back than the pair of you if things get complicated. I'm not asking you to spy on them, but you do have a talent for ferreting out information."

"Why do you think they're letting you come there, after all these years?" asked Alec.

"Self-interest, I suppose. The prospect of Plenimar controlling Mycena and perhaps striking a bargain with Zengat to the west has made at least some of them reexamine their alliegences."

"Has there been more news of the Zengat situation?" asked Seregil.

"Nothing certain, but there are enough rumors flying around to make the Iia'sidra nervous."

"It should. The world's a smaller place than it once was; it's time they realized that. So, what is it that Idrilain wants?"

"Ideally? Wizards, fresh troops, horses, and open trade. The northlands and Virésse are already all but lost to us and it's likely to get worse. At the very least, we need Gedre as an open port. The establishment of an armorers' colony at the outer Ashek iron mines would be even better."

Seregil ran a hand back through his hair. "By the Light, unless things have changed significantly from what I remember, we've got a hard task ahead of us. The Virésse will oppose anything that threatens their monopoly on Skalan trade, and everyone else will be horrified at the thought of a Skalan colony on Aurënfaie soil."

Flexing her shoulders wearily, Klia returned to the paper-strewn table. "Diplomacy is a lot like horse trading, my friends. You have to set your price high so they can beat you down to what you really want and still believe they got the best of the bargain.

"But I've kept you long enough and Thero is anxious to see you. A room's been made ready for you upstairs. By the way, I took the liberty of asking your manservant in Wheel Street to send down some necessities. Beka said you two had been living rough up there in your hideaway." She took in their plain, mud-spattered clothing with a comic grimace. "I see now she rather understated the situation."

Sarikali. The Heart of the Jewel.

Alec repeated the magical name silently as he and Seregil climbed the stairs. He'd listened carefully to all Klia had said, but that one detail, and Seregil's shocked reaction, had captured his imagination.

They'd spoken of Sarikali only once that Alec could recall. "It's magical ground, Alec, the most sacred of all," Seregil had told him in the depths of a long winter night. "An empty city older than the 'faie themselves; the living heart of Aurënen. Legend says that the sun pierced the heart of the first dragon with a golden spear, and that the eleven drops of blood which fell from its breast as it flew over Aurënen created the 'faie. Some of the stories say that Aura took pity on the dying dragon and placed it in a deep sleep beneath the city until it heals and wakens again."

Alec had all but forgotten the tale, but now a hundred images sprang up before his mind's eye, like the first 'faie from the blood in the legend.

They found Thero at work at a small desk in the first bedchamber at the top of the stairs. Of all of them, the wizard had changed the most. The scruffy black beard was gone, and his curly hair was pulled back in a short queue. His thin face had filled out a bit, and he'd lost his bookish pallor. His customary reserve was still in place, but a hint of warmth in his pale green eyes made his gaunt features somewhat less imposing. He'd even shed his immaculate robes in favor of the simple traveling garb Nysander had always favored.

It suits him, Alec thought. He'd seen glimpses of this side of the man during the dark days of their captivity in Plenimar and was glad that Magyana had found a way to cultivate it. Perhaps the sense of compassion Nysander had always hoped would balance Thero's great potential was finally emerging.

Seregil was the first to clasp hands with him. The two stood a moment, regarding each other without speaking. The rivalry that divided them for so many years had died with Nysander; what would fill that void remained to be seen.

"You've prospered," Seregil said at last.

"Magyana's a remarkable mentor. And the war—" Thero shrugged expressively. "Well, it's been a harsh but efficient training ground." Turning to Alec, he smiled. "I ride like a soldier now, if you can imagine that. I've even lost my seasickness."

"That's a lucky thing, crossing the Osiat this time of year."

"Klia said you've brought more information regarding my return?" asked Seregil.

"Yes." Thero's smile faltered. "The Iia'sidra has laid down certain conditions."

"Oh?"

"As you know, the ban of exile has not been lifted," Thero replied with a briskness that undoubtedly masked discomfort. "You're being allowed a special dispensation at the queen's request."

"I understand that." Seregil sat down on the edge of the bed, hands clasped around one up-drawn knee. "What's it to be then? Branding me on the cheek, or just a placard around my neck reading, 'Traitor'?"

"No one's branding him!" Alec exclaimed, alarmed.

"I'm joking, talí. All right, Thero, lay out the terms."

The wizard clearly took no pleasure in his task. "Your name is still forfeit; you'll be known as Seregil of Rhíminee. You're forbidden to wear Aurënfaie clothing or any other clan marks, including the *sen'gai*."

"Fair enough," said Seregil, but Alec saw a muscle tighten in his jaw. The sen'gai, a traditional Aurënfaie head cloth, was an integral part of Aurënfaie identity. Its color, patterns, and how it was wrapped denoted both clan and status.

"You are banned from all temples, and from participating in any religious ceremony," Thero went on. "You will be accepted as a voice of council on behalf of Skala but have none of the common rights of a 'faie. Finally, you are not allowed outside Sarikali except to accompany the Skalan delegation. You will lodge with them, and carry no weapons. Violate any of these and teth'sag will be declared against you."

"Is that all? No public flogging?"

Thero leaned forward with a look of genuine concern. "Come now, what did you expect?"

Seregil shook his head. "Nothing. I expect nothing. What does Idrilain think of all this?"

"I'm not certain. These details arrived after I'd left her in Mycena."

"Then you have seen her since she was wounded?" Seregil pressed.

Thero wove a spell in the air before continuing. The change was so subtle that at first Alec couldn't figure out what had happened. An instant later, he realized he could no longer hear sounds from outside the room.

"Between us as Watchers, I can tell you that we need to accomplish the queen's purpose as quickly as possible."

"Idrilain is dying, isn't she?" asked Seregil.

Thero nodded grimly. "It's only a matter of time. Tell me, what's your impression of Phoria?"

"You've seen more of her than I have this past year."

"She's opposed to our course of action."

"How could she be?" asked Alec. "If Klia's right, Skala isn't strong enough to defeat Plenimar."

"Phoria refuses to accept that. Prince Korathan and a number of generals support her view, refusing to admit that magic is as important a weapon as bows or swords. No doubt you've heard about the Plenimaran necromancers?" The wizard's mouth set in a hard line. "I've faced them in the field. The queen is quite correct, but Magyana's convinced that Phoria will abandon the plan as soon as her mother dies. That's why she sent Klia rather than Korathan. He's an honorable man, but loyal to his sister."

"Phoria's been in the middle of things from the start," mused Seregil. "How could she not understand what she's up against?"

"At first the necromancers didn't seem much of a threat. Their numbers have grown, along with their power."

"Just imagine if they had the Helm," Alec said.

A chill seemed to pass over the room as the three men recalled the glimpse they'd had of the power embodied by the Helm of Seriamaius.

"Nysander didn't die in vain," Thero said softly. "But even without the Helm, the necromancers are strong and without mercy. Phoria and her supporters simply haven't seen enough of them to believe yet. I fear it may take a tragedy to sway her."

"Stubbornness can be a dangerous trait in a general."

Thero sighed. "Or a queen."

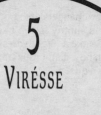

5

VIRÉSSE

So, they are coming, and not by way of your city, Khirnari," said Raghar Ashnazai, turning his wine cup idly on the polished surface of the balcony table.

The gaunt Plenimaran's nails were smooth and clean, Ulan í Sathil noted, watching his guest from his place by the balustrade; this was a Tírfaie whose tools were words. Three centuries of trade with such men had taught Ulan to be wary.

"Yes, Lord Torsin left to meet them yesterday," he replied, turning his attention to the harbor spread out below the balcony. Silently he counted the foreign vessels moored there—more than two dozen today in spite of the war. How empty the harbor would be without them.

"If the Bôkthersa and their allies have their way, your great marketplace will not be so full of northern traders," the Plenimaran envoy went on, as if reading his thoughts.

He wasn't, of course; Ulan would have sensed any magic and countered it with his own. No, this man's power lay in astuteness and patience, not magic.

"It's true, Lord Raghar," he replied. His old knees ached badly today, but standing allowed him to look down at the Plenimaran, a position worth the discomfort. "It would be a great blow to my clan and our allies if the present routes of trade were changed. Just as it might be a serious blow to your country if Aurënen joined forces with the Skalans."

"Then our concerns are similar, if not our interests."

Ulan acknowledged the truth of this, glad that he had not underestimated whom he was dealing with; as khirnari of Virésse, he'd dealt with five Tírfaie generations from the Three Lands and beyond. The Ashnazai were one of the oldest and most influential families in Plenimar.

"And yet I am curious," he countered, keeping his voice neutral. "There are rumors suggesting that Plenimar needs no assistance from anyone in their war against the Skalans—something to do with necromancy, I believe?"

"You surprise me, Khirnari. The practice of necromancy was outlawed centuries ago."

Ulan shrugged graciously. "Here in Virésse we take a more pragmatic view of such things. Magic is magic, no? I'm sure your cousin, Vargûl Ashnazai, would say the same. Or would have, had he not already given his life in the service of your Overlord's half-brother, the late Duke Mardus."

This time Raghar's surprise was genuine. "You are well informed, Khirnari."

"I think you will find most of the eastern clans are." Ulan smiled, his silver-grey eyes narrowing like an eagle's. "Your country has very long arms; we know better than to underestimate such a neighbor."

"And the Skalans?"

"As allies, they would pose a different sort of threat."

"Far beyond a threat to Virésse's port monopoly, I think. Bôkthersa clan's blood ties to the Skalan throne, for instance?"

Ah, yes, very astute indeed. "You have a better grasp of Aurënfaie politics than most, Raghar Ashnazai. Most outsiders think of us as a single, united land ruled by the Iia'sidra in place of a queen or overlord."

"Overlord Estmar understands that the eastern and western clans have different concerns. And that clans such as Bôkthersa and Bry'kha are looked on by many as troublemakers, too ready to mix with foreigners."

"The same has been said of the Virésse. But there is a difference. The Bôkthersans are fond of foreigners, while we in Virésse . . ." He paused and looked directly at the Plenimaran for the first time, letting a hint of his power travel along the thread of their gaze. "We merely consider you—useful."

"Then we are of similar minds, Khirnari." Ashnazai smiled coldly through his beard as he pulled a sealed document tube from his sleeve and laid it on the table. "According to my sources, Queen Idrilain is dying, though few outside the royal circle know of it. I do not think she will live long enough for Klia to complete her mission."

Ulan eyed the tube. "I understand Phoria is a worthy successor."

The envoy tapped the tube meaningfully with a ringed finger and smiled again. "So one might think, Khirnari, and yet there are certain rumors suggesting a rift between her and the queen. Rumors that even now my people in Skala are allowing to seep out into certain well-placed ears. Even without this information, there are some Skalans who do not welcome the idea of a barren queen. There are few enough rightful heirs as it is. Just the second sister, Aralain, and her daughter. And Klia, of course."

"That would seem sufficient," remarked Ulan.

"In time of peace, perhaps, but in war? So much death and uncertainty. Let us hope for Skala's sake that their four gods guard these women lovingly, eh?"

"I pray Aura may watch over their lives," Ulan retorted, turning away to hide his revulsion; how easily these Tír turned to the expediency of assassination and outright murder. The brevity of their lives seemed to engender a brutal impatience abhorrent to the Aurënfaie mind.

"I am grateful as always for your information and support," he went on, still gazing out over the harbor. His harbor.

"You honor me with your trust, Khirnari."

Ulan heard the scrape of the chair and the rustle of a cloak. When he turned at last, Ashnazai was gone, but the sealed tube still lay on the table.

Avoiding the chair the Plenimaran had occupied, Ulan eased painfully into the one opposite and stretched his aching legs. At last he opened the tube and shook out its contents: three parchments. One was a Plenimaran affidavit of sorts signed by someone named Urvay. The other two were Skalan court documents apparently having to do with the treasury. Each bore the signatures of Princess Phoria and the late Skalan Vicegerent, Lord Barien. One of these also carried the Queen's Seal.

Ulan read them all carefully, then again. When he'd finished he set them down with a sigh, wishing not for the first time that it was Skala or Mycena lying so close across the Strait of Bal, rather than Plenimar.

· · ·

That night Ulan sat again on the balcony, this time entertaining three other members of the Iia'sidra. The meal had been cleared away and the wine poured. As was the custom, they sat in silence for a while, watching the waning moon climb the canopy of stars. Two of Ulan's guests were there at his invitation. The third had surprised them all with her unexpected arrival.

A fragrant breeze fluttered the ends of their sen'gai against their faces and lifted Lhaär ä Iriel's thin silver hair, revealing the tracery of Khatme clan marks on her wizened neck behind her heavy jeweled earrings.

Her arrival that afternoon was a mixed blessing. Because of her, Raghar Ashnazai's scrolls remained tucked away out of sight in Ulan's study. The fact that the Khatme khirnari would travel so far to meet with him might be interpreted by some as a sign of support, yet who could guess what any of that strange clan was thinking behind their painted eyes and elaborate tattoos?

The others were a different matter. Elos í Orian, khirnari of nearby Goliníl, was husband to Ulan's daughter. Malleable, and transparent as water, Elos understood how intertwined the interests of the Goliníl were with those of Virésse.

Old Galmyn í Nemius, who'd come east from Lhapnos bearing messages of support from his own clan and the Haman, was another matter. The interests of those two clans were more complex, and more obscure, yet they had both voted against the impending delegation from Skala. What would have happened, Ulan wondered, if the Skalans had not insisted on bringing the Bôkthersan exile, Seregil í Korit, with them? No matter, really. It would work to his favor at Sarikali.

"We meet under a propitious moon," Elos í Orian observed cheerfully.

Lhaär ä Iriel spared him a cold glance. "The same moon shines on all. As I recall, it was under Aura's Bow that the vote went against you at the Iia'sidra."

"Only that the delegation could come, nothing more," Galmyn í Nemius reminded her tersely. No doubt his thoughts echoed Ulan's: *"Went against you," she'd said, not "us." What is the woman doing here?*

"Just fifty years ago the Skalans would have been given a flat refusal," Elos observed. "Now we agree to parley with them—and at Sarikali! That most certainly means *something*."

"Perhaps that the western clans are gaining influence," Ulan said. "Their interests are not necessarily compatible with our own."

"One might say the same of Lhapnos and Virésse," Galmyn í Nemius put in dryly. "Yet here I am."

"Lhapnos stands with the Haman, and the Haman stand against Bôkthersa and the other border clans. There's no mystery there," Lhaär ä Iriel stated bluntly.

Ulan smiled. "I enjoy plain speech among friends. Perhaps you would explain where Khatme stands?"

"In the mind of Aura, as always. The Khatme have no love for Tírfaie of any sort, but the Skalans honor Aura, under the name of Illior. Although they blaspheme by placing the Lightbearer with other gods, their wizards are descendants of our own Orëska and continue to thrive. It presents us with a great quandary, one which neither the Lightbearer nor the dragons have yet clarified to our priests."

Galmyn í Nemius arched one greying brow. "In other words, you still have a leg on either side of the stile."

The clan marks on Lhaär ä Iriel's face seemed to subtly rearrange themselves as she turned to him. "That is not at all what I said, Khirnari."

The Lhapnosan's self-important smile died on his lips. For a long moment the others found it more comfortable to return their attention to the moon.

"Who can we be sure of, then?" asked Elos.

"Besides ourselves and Haman, with due respect to you, Lhaär, I think we may also depend on the Ra'basi," replied Ulan. "The Akhendi remain uncertain, but have more to gain from supporting open borders. A few others must be swayed."

"Indeed," the Lhapnosan murmured. "And who better than you to sway them?"

6
LEAVING HOME, GOING HOME

The following day was filled with final preparations for Klia's voyage. A steady stream of baggage carts and dispatch riders raised clouds of dust along the vineyard road all morning.

Alec went with Seregil and Klia down to the shipyard to inspect the three vessels anchored there. Dressed in plain riding clothes and mounted on scrub horses, they passed unnoticed through waterfront crowds and onto a long quay where a high-prowed carrack was moored. Sailors swarmed over her like ants on a sweetmeat, wielding ropes and tools.

"This is the *Zyria*. She's a beauty, isn't she?" Klia said, leading them aboard. "And those two out there are our escorts, the *Wolf* and the *Courser*."

"They're huge!" Alec exclaimed.

Over a hundred feet long, each ship was easily twice as large as any he'd been on. Their aft castles rose like houses in the stern. The rudders behind were as high as an inn. Square-rigged with two masts and a bowsprit to carry the red sails, their bulwarks were lined with shields bearing the flame and crescent moon crest of Skala. These shields were bright with new paint and gilt work that did not quite hide the scars of recent battles.

The captain, a tall, white-haired man

named Farren, met them on deck wearing a naval tunic stained with
pitch and salt.

"How goes the loading?" Klia asked, looking around with approval.

"Right on schedule, Commander," he replied, consulting a tally
board at his belt. "The hold ramp for the horses needs a bit of work,
but we'll have her ready for you by midnight."

"Each ship will carry a decuria of cavalry and their horses," Klia
explained to Alec. "The soldiers will double as ship's archers if the
need arises."

"Looks like you're prepared for the worst," Seregil remarked,
peering into a large crate.

"What are those?" asked Alec. Inside were what looked like large
pickle crocks sealed with wax.

"Benshâl Fire," the captain told him. "As the name implies, it was
the Plenimarans who discovered how to make it years ago. It's a
nasty mix: black oil, pitch, sulfur, nitre, and the like. Launched from
a ballista, it ignites on impact and sticks to whatever it hits. It burns
even in water."

"I've seen it," Seregil said. "You have to use sand or vinegar to
douse it."

"Or piss," added Farren. "Which is what those barrels under the
aft platform are for. Nothing goes to waste in the Skalan navy. But
we won't be looking for battle this time out, will we, Commander?"

Klia grinned. "We won't, but I can't vouch for the Plenimarans."

Excitement left a hollow void in Alec's belly as he and Seregil
joined the others for a final supper in Skala that night. They were
dressed once more as Skalan nobility and Klia arched an appreciative eyebrow. "You two look better than I do."

Seregil made her a courtly bow and sat down beside Thero.
"Runcer's shown his usual foresight."

Opening their trunks the night before, they'd found the best of the
garments they'd worn in Rhíminee: fine wool and velvet coats, soft
linen, gleaming boots, doeskin breeches smooth as a maid's throat.
Alec's coats were a bit tight through the shoulders now, but there
was no time for tailoring.

"Will you be meeting the 'faie as Princess Klia or Commander
Klia when we arrive in Gedre?" asked Alec, seeing that Klia was
still in uniform.

"It's gowns and gloves for me once we get there, I'm afraid."

"Any news from Lord Torsin?" asked Beka, noting a stack of dispatches at Klia's elbow.

"Nothing new. Khatme and Lhapnos are as insular as ever, although he thinks he senses a hint of interest among the Haman. Silmai support is still strong. Datsia seems to be turning in our favor."

"What about the Virésse?" asked Thero.

Klia spread her hands. "Ulan í Sathil continues to hint that they and their allies in the east would just as soon trade with Plenimar as Skala."

"With the Plenimaran Overlord openly supporting the resurgence of necromancy?" Seregil shook his head. "They suffered more at the hands of the Plenimarans during the Great War than any other clan."

"The Virésse are pragmatists at heart, I fear." Klia turned to Alec. "How does it feel, knowing we set sail at dawn for the land of your ancestors?"

Alec toyed with a bit of bread. "It's hard to describe, my lady. Growing up, I didn't know I had any 'faie in me at all. It's still hard to comprehend. Besides, my mother was Hâzadriëlfaie. Any Aurënfaie I meet in the south will be distant relatives at best. I don't even know what clans my people came from."

"Perhaps the *rhui'auros* could divine something of your lineage," suggested Thero. "Couldn't they, Seregil?"

"It's worth looking into," Seregil replied with no great enthusiasm.

"Who are they?" asked Alec.

Thero shot Seregil a look of pure disbelief. "You never told him of the rhui'auros?"

"Apparently not. I was only a child when I left, so I hadn't had much to do with them."

Alec tensed, wondering if anyone else noticed the edge of anger in his friend's voice. Here were more secrets.

"By the Light, they're the—the—" Thero waved a hand, at a loss for words and too caught up in his own enthusiasm to notice the cool reception he was getting from the one person among them who might have direct knowledge. "They stand at the very source of magic! Nysander and Magyana both spoke of them with reverence, Alec, a sect of wizard priests who live at Sarikali. The rhui'auros are similar to the oracles of Illiór, aren't they, Seregil?"

"Mad, you mean?" Seregil looked down at the food he was not eating. "I'd say that's a fair assessment."

"What if they tell me I'm related to one of the unfriendly clans?" Alec asked, trying to draw Thero's attention.

The wizard paused. "That could create difficulties, I suppose."

"Indeed," mused Klia. "Perhaps you should be circumspect in your inquiries."

"I always am," Alec replied with a smile only a few at the table fully understood. "But how could the rhui'auros tell who my ancestors were?"

"They practice a very special sort of magic," Thero explained. "Only the rhui'auros are allowed to travel the inner roads of the soul."

"Like the truth knowers of the Orëska?"

"The Aurënfaie don't have that magic, exactly," Seregil interjected. "You'd do well to keep that in mind, Thero. The punishment for invading another's thoughts is severe."

"My skills in that direction are not particularly strong. As I was saying, the rhui'auros believe they can trace a person's *khi,* the soul thread that connects us all to Illior."

"Aura," Seregil corrected.

"Being a full half 'faie, Alec, yours should be strong," said Beka, following the conversation with interest.

"I'm not sure that makes any difference," said Thero. "I'm generations away from my 'faie ancestors, yet my abilities are equal to those of Nysander and the other old ones."

"Yes, but you're one of the few younger ones left who possess such power," Seregil reminded him.

"If all wizards have some Aurënfaie blood, do they know which clans they're related to?" asked Beka.

"Sometimes," said Thero. "Magyana's father was an Aurënfaie trader who settled in Cirna. My line goes back to the Second Orëska at Ero, with generations of intermarried mixed-bloods. Nysander's teacher, Arkoniel, was from the same line.

"Speaking of rhui'auros, Seregil, have you thought of visiting them yourself? Perhaps they could discover why you have such trouble with magic. You've got the ability, if only you could master it."

"I've managed well enough without it."

Was it his imagination, Alec wondered, or had Seregil actually gone a bit pale?

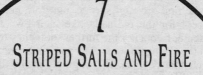

7

STRIPED SAILS AND FIRE

By dawn, the *Zyria* and her escorts were already well out to sea.

Much to Alec's disappointment, Beka had sailed aboard the *Wolf* with Mercalle's decuria. He could see her striding around the deck, red hair shining in the sun. They exchanged shouted greetings, but the distance and rushing sea made conversation difficult.

Thero accompanied Klia on their ship, and although Alec was happy to renew their acquaintance, he soon began to suspect that the wizard had changed less than he'd originally thought. Thero was less abrupt, to be sure, but still a bit distant—a cold fish, as Seregil liked to say. Forced together in close quarters, he and Seregil were soon sparring again, if not quite so bitterly as before.

When Alec remarked on this, Seregil merely shrugged. "What did you expect, for him to somehow turn into Nysander? We are who we are."

They followed the coastline all day, sailing a few miles outside the scattered islands that edged the western shore.

Standing at the rail, Alec scanned the distant sea cliffs and thought of his first journey here aboard the *Grampus,* when Seregil lay dying in the hold. The steep land between cliff and mountains showed the first green of spring, and from here it all looked peaceful—except for the red sails like their own that began to appear with greater frequency the further south they traveled.

Alec was at the rail again when they passed the mouth of Rhíminee harbor later that day. Gazing longingly at the distant city, he could make out scores of vessels at anchor on both sides of the moles. Beyond them, atop her towering grey cliffs, the upper city glowed like gold in the slanting afternoon light. The glass domes of the Orëska House and its four towers gave back a burning glare like points of flame, leaving black spots in front of his eyes when he looked away. Blinking, he searched the deck for Seregil and found him leaning against the aft castle wall, arms folded across his chest as he gazed up at the city he'd forsaken. Alec took a hesitant step in his direction, but Seregil walked away.

As Rhíminee slowly slipped from sight behind them, the three ships struck south east across the Osiat with a fresh following wind. A growing air of tension hung over the three vessels as sailors and soldiers alike kept watch for striped Plenimaran sails. As darkness fell, however, conversation grew freer. A waning moon rose above them, spangling the waves with silver.

Seregil and Torsin retired to the bow with Klia to discuss negotiation tactics. Left to their own devices, Alec and Thero paced the deck. They could make out the dark shapes of the escort ships sailing abreast of the *Zyria* a few hundred feet to either side. It was a calm night, and voices carried easily across the water. Some unseen musician aboard the *Courser* struck up a tune on a lute.

Braknil and his riders had gathered around the hatchway lantern on the foredeck. Spying Alec and the wizard, the old sergeant waved them over.

"That'll be young Urien strumming away," he said, listening to the distant music.

When the song ended, someone aboard the *Wolf* answered with the first verse of a popular ballad.

A pretty young maid strolled down the shore, with naught but her shadow beside her.
Over in the bushes hid the farmer's lad and lustfully he eyed her.

One-eyed Steb produced a wooden flute, and his comrades bawled the melody across the water.

Steb's lover, Mirn, gave Alec a playful jab with his elbow. "You too good to sing with us tonight? You're the closest thing to a bard here."

Alec made him an exaggerated bow and took up the next verse:

"Oh, come with me, my sweet pretty maid," the farmer's lad said he.
"I'll make you my wife and keep you for life if only you'll lie with me."

Mirn and young Minál hoisted Alec onto a hatch cover and helped lead the interminable randy verses. Thero hung back by the rail, but Alec could see the wizard's lips moving. When the song was done, cheers and catcalls echoed from the other ships.

"Well now, isn't this a hard life?" Sergeant Braknil chuckled, lighting his pipe. "We're like a bunch of nobles off on a pleasure voyage."

"I don't suppose it'll be much harder once we get to Aurënen," a veteran named Ariani agreed. "As honor guard, we're just along for show."

"You've got that right, girl. After a few weeks of standing about on guard duty, we'll be happy enough to get back to the fighting. Still, it's something to be the first to see Aurënen after all these years. Lord Seregil must've told you something of it, Alec?"

"He says it's a green place, warmer than Skala. There was a song he sang—"

Alec couldn't recall the tune, but some of the words had stayed with him. " 'My love is wrapped in a cloak of flowing green, and wears the moon for a crown. And all around has chains of flowing silver. Her mirrors reflect the sky.' There's more to it, all very sad."

"Magic is more common there, as well," Thero added with mock severity. "You'd all better mind your manners; the 'pretty young maids' might answer an insult with more than clever words."

A few of the riders exchanged worried looks at this.

"A strange land with strange folk in it," Braknil mused around his pipe stem. "As I hear it, they're handy with their swords and bows, too. But you only have to look at Lord Seregil to see the truth in that. Or did, anyway. And perhaps it's what makes you such a fine archer, eh, Alec?"

"More like having an empty belly if I didn't shoot true."

Someone brought out dice, and Alec joined in a friendly game. The soldiers were a gregarious lot and even managed to pull Thero into the circle despite his initial reticence. There was much joking about the wisdom of dicing with a wizard, but Thero managed to allay their worries by losing every toss. Eventually people began to wander off to find their beds for the night—some alone, some in pairs.

Alec felt a pang of envy as Steb slipped an arm around Mirn on their way below. Seregil had been distracted by other concerns lately, and the lack of privacy here hadn't helped matters. Stretching out on the hatch cover, he resigned himself to a few more days of abstinence.

To his surprise, Thero joined him. Crossing his arms behind his head, the wizard hummed a few bars of the song, then said, "I've been watching Seregil. He seems apprehensive about returning to Aurënen."

"There are plenty of folks who won't welcome him."

"I felt the same, going back to the Orëska House that day we all returned from Plenimar," Thero said softly. "Nysander saw to it that my name was cleared before he left that last time, but there'll always be doubts in some people's minds as to how much my—" He paused, as if the words were as distasteful as the memory. "How much my affair with Ylinestra had to do with the attack on the Orëska House that night. Even I'll never be certain."

"Better to look forward than back, I guess."

"I suppose so."

They fell silent again, two young men gazing into the infinite mystery of the night sky.

The next few days passed quietly enough. Too quietly, in fact. Bored and at loose ends, Alec found himself missing their lost solitude, just as Seregil had predicted.

Quarters belowdecks were too close for Seregil's taste, the air too pungent with the smell of oil and horses. Curtained alcoves had been hastily knocked together for the passengers of rank, but these afforded little more than the illusion of privacy. Taking advantage of the fair weather, he and Alec claimed a sheltered section of deck beneath the overhang of the forward castle. It was comfortable enough there—for sleeping.

Not one to stand on rank, Klia lolled about with the rest of them, sharing tales of the war.

"I don't suppose you two would consider joining the Horse Guard?" she asked, giving Seregil and Alec a pointed look as they sat in the shade of the sail with Thero and Braknil. "Men with your talents are in short supply these days. I could use you."

"I never expected it to last this long," Alec said.

"Something's changed since the new Overlord took over," Klia said, shaking her head. "His father kept the treaties."

"This one's been fed on tales of lost glories," Braknil said around the stem of his pipe.

"By his uncle Mardus, no doubt," Seregil agreed. "Still, it was bound to happen."

"What makes you say that?" asked Thero.

He shrugged. "Peace follows war. War follows peace. Necromancy is suppressed, only to grow in secret, until it bursts like a boil. Some things are eternal, like the pattern of the tides."

"Then you don't think a lasting peace can ever be achieved?"

"It depends on your point of view. This war will end, and maybe there'll be peace through Klia's lifetime, perhaps even that of her children. But wizards and Aurënfaie live long enough to see that sooner or later it all starts again—the same old pull and haul of greed, need, power, and pride."

"It's like a great wheel, always turning, or the changes of the moon," mused Braknil. "No matter what things look like today, change is always coming, for good or ill. When I was a lad, new to the regiment, my old sergeant used to ask us if we'd rather live a short time in peace or a long time in war."

"What did you say?" asked Seregil.

"Well now, as I recall I always wanted more choices than that. Thank the Flame, I think I got 'em. But it's true what you said, though I often forget it. You and these two young fellows will see more turns of that wheel than any of us. Someday when you look in the mirror and see as much grey in your hair as I've got, drink a pint to my dusty bones, won't you?"

"I forget sometimes, too," Klia murmured, and Alec saw her study Seregil's face, and then his own, an indefinable expression in her eyes that was neither sadness nor envy. "I'll do well to keep it in mind once we get to Aurënen, won't I? I understand negotiating with them is something of a challenge."

Seregil laughed softly to himself. "Well, their concept of hurrying will certainly be different than ours."

Alec was pacing the deck their third afternoon out when a lookout suddenly shouted down, "Plenimaran ship to the southeast, Captain!"

Seregil was up on the aft castle with Klia and Captain Farren, and Alec hurried up to join them. Everyone was scanning the horizon. Shading his eyes, Alec squinted across the water and found an ominous shape against the late-afternoon glare.

"I see her," Captain Farren said. "She's too far off yet to tell if she's spotted us."

"Is it the Plenimarans?" Thero asked, joining them at the rail.

"Time to earn your keep," Klia told him. "Can you keep them from seeing us?"

Thero thought a moment, then plucked a loose thread from his sleeve and held it up. Alec recognized the trick; he was testing the wind's direction.

Satisfied, Thero raised both hands in the direction of the enemy vessel and chanted in a high, faint voice. Drawing a wand of polished crystal from the folds of his coat, he flung it toward the distant ship. Glittering like an icicle, it spun end over end and disappeared below the grey-green waves. Tendrils of mist immediately curled up where it fell.

Thero snapped his fingers; the wand sprang out of the water and into his hands like a live thing, trailing a thick rope of mist in its wake. Pulled by the wizard's spell, heavy fog spread with supernatural speed into a thick bank that shielded their vessel from sight.

"Unless they have a wizard of their own aboard, they'll think we're just a bit of weather," he said, drying the wand with the edge of his cloak.

"But we can't see them, either," said the captain.

"I can," Thero replied. "I'll keep watch."

The ruse worked. Within half an hour Thero reported that the Plenimaran ship had disappeared over the horizon. He ended the spell and the fog bank fell behind them like a hank of wool torn from a distaff.

The sailors on deck let out a cheer, and Klia gave Thero an approving salute that brought a flush to the young wizard's cheeks.

"That's as nice a bit of magic as I've ever seen," Farren called from the stern.

From across the deck, Alec saw Seregil stroll over to the wizard. He was too far away to hear what passed between them, but Thero was smiling when they parted.

·   ·   ·

Shouts of landfall woke Alec at dawn the next day.

"Aurënen already?" he said, scrambling from beneath the blankets. Seregil sat up and rubbed his eyes, then rose to join the crowd already gathered at the port rail. They could just make out a distant line of low islands on the western horizon.

"Those are the *Ea'malies*, the 'Old Turtlebacks,' " Seregil said, stifling a yawn.

Klia eyed the close-lying islands distrustfully. "A likely place for an ambush."

"I've sent up extra lookouts," Farren assured her. "We should reach Big Turtle by this afternoon. We'll put in there for fresh water, then it's just another day to Gedre."

This day seemed longer to Alec than all the rest put together. Bows slung ready over their shoulders, he and Seregil took their turn on watch, scanning the surrounding water. In spite of Klia's concerns, however, they reached the outlying islands without incident and set a course toward the largest.

Sitting atop the forecastle with Thero and Seregil, Alec studied the islands for signs of life. But they were arid, little more than domed masses of pale, sun-baked stone scattered over with patches of sparse vegetation.

"I thought you said Aurënen was green," said Thero, clearly less than impressed.

"This isn't Aurënen," Seregil explained. "No one claims them, really, except sailors and smugglers. Gedre is dry, too, as you'll soon see. The winds sweep up from the southwest across the Gathwayd Ocean and drop their rain as they go over the mountains. Across the Ashcks the green will hurt your eyes."

"Sarikali," Thero murmured. "What do you remember of it?"

Seregil leaned his arms on the rail. Though his gaze was on the passing islands, Alec could tell that his friend was seeing another place and time.

"It's a strange, beautiful place. I used to hear music there, just coming out of the air. When it was over I couldn't remember the tunes. Sometimes people hear voices, too."

"Ghosts?" asked Alec.

Seregil shrugged. "We call them *Bash'wai*, the Ancients. Those who claim to have seen them always describe them as tall, with black hair and eyes, and skin the color of strong tea."

"I've heard there are dragons there, too," said Thero.

"Just fingerlings, mostly, but they're common as lizards. The larger ones keep to the mountains. A lucky thing, too. They can be dangerous."

"Is it true that they're magical from the start, but that they don't develop speech and intelligence until they're quite large?"

"That's right, which means you're more likely to be killed by one the size of a hound than those bigger than houses. Only a few of the fingerlings survive and they move up into the mountains as they grow. If you do happen to meet one of any size, always treat it with respect."

"Then there's the *khtir'bai*—" Alec began, but was interrupted by another warning cry from the lookout.

"Enemy vessels off the port bow!"

Jumping to their feet, they spotted two sets of striped sails rounding a point of land no more than a mile ahead. Alec's hands tightened around his bow; the sight of those sails brought back ugly memories.

"Something tells me they knew we were coming," Seregil muttered.

"Are they showing the battle flag?" Farren called up to the lookout.

"No, Captain, but they've got fires lit."

"Run up the battle standards!"

Sleek and fast as lion hounds, the great ships cleared the point and wheeled in their direction. Plumes of black smoke trailed in their wakes.

"Too late for tricks," said Thero, halfway to the castle ladder already.

"At least we outnumber them," said Alec.

Seregil shook his head. "They're bigger, faster, and more heavily armed than our ships. And probably crawling with marines."

"Marines?" Alec's mouth set in a hard line. Dodging through the throng of sailors and soldiers scrambling to their posts, he led the way to the port rail and joined the line of archers already positioned.

Sailors struck the mizzen, slowing the *Zyria* to allow the other ships to engage the enemy first. As the *Wolf* sailed past, Alec saw Beka among those hurrying around the deck with weapons and jars of Benshâl Fire. Busy shouting orders, she didn't see the luck sign he made in her direction.

The *Wolf* was the first to attack, striking one of the enemy vessels amidships with canisters of Benshâl Fire. Oily smoke billowed up, but the ship held its course and sent a volley of arrows in return as it swept past to bear down on the *Zyria*.

On Alec's left, Minál shifted nervously. "We're in for it now."

"Archers at the ready!" Klia shouted from the forecastle deck. "Shoot at will!"

Alec chose a man on the foredeck of the enemy vessel, drew the Black Radly's bowstring to his ear, and released the first shaft. Not pausing to see if it struck home, he drew one arrow after another and sent them speeding across the water. Beside him, Seregil and the archers of Urgazhi Turma did the same, each setting their own grim rhythm as the great ship closed in on them.

Enemy shafts were flying around their ears now, thudding into the deck and the wooden shields mounted on the rail. The hissing song of string and shaft was soon joined by the first cries of the wounded.

As the ship loomed ever closer, Alec spotted what appeared to be the bronze heads of some sort of monster mounted below her forecastle rail. The placement seemed too strategic to be mere decoration, but he couldn't imagine what they could be.

He was about to point them out to the others when Seregil let out a startled curse and staggered back, struck in the right shoulder by a blue-fletched Plenimaran arrow.

"How bad?" Alec demanded, pulling him to shelter against the rail.

"Not so bad," Seregil hissed through gritted teeth, yanking the shaft out with surprising ease. The thick leather strap of his quiver and the mail beneath his coat had prevented the head from piercing his shoulder, but the arrow had struck hard enough to drive the metal rings of the mail through the shirt below, leaving a bloody dent in his shoulder mere inches from his throat.

He handed the enemy shaft to Alec with a wry grimace. "Send this back to its owner for me, will you?"

Standing up, Alec nocked the shaft and raised his bow to take aim at the vessel looming over them now. Before he could draw, however, the bronze heads on the Plenimaran's port side suddenly spewed streams of liquid fire. It struck the rigging overhead and fresh screams burst out. A sailor fell to the deck, neck snapped like an oat stalk. Another hung tangled and screaming in the yards, sheathed in flame. Fire crews clambered up with buckets of sand and urine to douse smoking holes in the sails.

Aboard the Plenimaran ship, marines jeered and waved.

"What's *that*?" cried Alec, ducking down in alarm again.

"Bilairy's Balls!" gasped Seregil, grey eyes wide with astonishment."The Fire. They've learned to pump it, the clever bastards!"

The two ships were nearly parallel now, and Alec felt a jolt go through the deck boards as the *Zyria*'s aft ballistas launched their loads of canister. One struck the enemy's mast; another exploded near her far rail, engulfing men in a spreading sheet of flame. Alec quickly looked away, but as the huge ship swept past he saw more men burning in her wake. Taking careful aim, he put three out of their misery before the ship carried him out of range. Taking advantage of the momentary lull in battle, he joined the other archers gathering enemy arrows to refill their quivers.

"Down, Alec!" Steb yelled, jerking him sideways just in time to avoid a strip of burning canvas. The headsail was in flames and coming to pieces as it burned. Overhead, sailors worked frantically to cut it free before the mast caught fire, while others on deck slapped flames out with wet sacking. The mingled stinks of oil, piss, and burning flesh settled over the vessel in a pall of stinging smoke.

Coughing, Alec gave the one-eyed soldier a quick nod of thanks. "You know, I believe I'd rather fight on land."

"So would I," Steb agreed.

Aboard the *Wolf,* Beka and the ship's captain, Yala, were having similar misgivings. The first Plenimaran ship had slipped past too easily and was heading for Klia's vessel. The *Courser* turned in pursuit, leaving *Wolf* to block the second man-of-war alone.

Standing atop the aft castle, they watched as the Plenimaran's striped sails filled the sky and heard the sharp groan of her forward catapults. A sack of quicklime struck the forward castle, bursting to engulf a knot of riders in a choking grey cloud; a second struck the mainsail, blinding several sailors and archers perched in the yards.

The screams of the maimed were terrible. Some of the archers positioned in the waist started in their direction, but Beka barked out, "Tell your riders to hold their positions, Sergeant Mercalle. Stand and shoot!"

"Stand and shoot!" Mercalle yelled, pushing men and women back into place.

But the Plenimaran ship was still coming at them bow on, presenting a limited target. The *Wolf*'s ballistas sent jars of fire into her rigging and prow, but she still came on.

"She's got a ramming prow!" someone yelled from the shrouds.

"Hard about!" shouted Captain Yala.

The helmsmen threw themselves against the tiller, and the ship yawed, sending archers tumbling across the deck.

The enemy catapults sang again, and spiked iron balls splintered the *Wolf*'s forward mast and tore a gaping hole in the headsail. The ship shuddered and slowed, her fallen mast dragging over the side.

The man-of-war swept past, close enough for Beka to see the fierce, grinning faces of the black-clad marines sighting down their arrows. Mercalle's riders howled out their war cries and returned a hail of arrows, aiming skyward to arch their shafts onto the higher deck. The forward ballista crews launched more fire jars, but these missed their mark.

As the crew of the *Wolf* watched in horrified wonder, bronze lion heads mounted under the Plenimaran vessel's rail vomited streams of liquid fire that streaked the *Wolf*'s torn sails with flames. From belowdecks came the screams of panicked horses and the cries of the wounded.

"By the Four!" Beka gasped. "What the hell was that, Captain?"

Before Yala could answer, a shaft buzzed past Beka's cheek and struck the woman in the eye. Clutching at it, Yala sank to the deck with an agonized groan.

"She's rounding on us, Captain," a lookout warned. "And she's running up fresh canvas!"

"Prepare—" Yala slumped slowly forward, blood flowing down her cheek. "Prepare to repel—"

Trailing smoke from one smoldering sail, the man-of-war closed on them again with a thick volley of arrows. Pinned down in the shelter of the rail shields, the remaining Skalan defenders shot back as best they could. A dozen or more bodies littered the deck, and Beka's heart sank as she counted three green tabards among them. Spotting Mercalle and Zir near the aft castle, Beka raced across the deck to them.

"Yala's dead. Have you seen the mate?"

The sergeant jerked a thumb at the forecastle. "That first load of quicklime got him."

"They're fixing to ram!" the remaining lookout shouted down to them.

"To what?" called Beka in alarm.

Everyone on deck had heard the warning, but there was little that could be done about it now. Marten and Ileah hurried over, supporting Ileah's brother Orineus between them. The young rider's tabard was stained dark around the broken arrow shaft in his chest. Beka could tell by his color that he was dying. Kallien brought up the rear.

The enemy vessel was almost upon them now, aiming straight for the *Wolf*'s waist. Another burst of fiery liquid shot from the bronze heads as she bore down on the doomed carrack.

"Sakor's Eyes, the horses!" gasped Zir, face pale beneath his thick beard.

"Come with me," ordered Beka, starting for the main hatch.

"No time, Captain!" Mercalle warned.

The last thing Beka remembered before the whole world heaved under her feet was the muffled screams of the horses.

Searching the deck for Seregil, Alec caught sight of Thero for the first time since the battle began. Standing calmly on the forecastle deck, he raised his hands palms outward at the oncoming enemy vessel. A bright corona of light flashed around him, obscuring him from sight for a moment. Alec was still blinking when a great shout went up from the crew.

The enemy ship was foundering crazily off course, her fallen sails sagging over her spars and deck. Fires broke out and quickly spread, driving men overboard into the sea. The *Courser* swooped down to finish her off.

Alec scaled the forecastle ladder and found Thero sitting on a crate surrounded by grinning sailors.

"What did you do?" Alec asked, elbowing his way in to him.

"Turned their ropes to water," Thero said hoarsely, looking quite pleased with himself. "And relieved them of this."

At his feet lay a heavy metal rod nearly six feet in length.

"Their rudder pin!" Farren exclaimed. "Even with their rigging, they wouldn't get far without that."

But their triumph was short-lived. The *Wolf* was sinking.

Clambering down the ladder again, Alec joined Seregil and Klia at the starboard rail. Ahead of them, the *Wolf* listed in the shadow of the second man-of-war. The Plenimarans were showering the vessel with arrows and liquid fire. The carrack's sails and masts were in flames, sending a great column of smoke slanting across the water. They could all make out figures falling or leaping into the sea from the tilting deck.

"They've broken her back," Klia gasped.

"Hoist what sails we've got," Farren shouted to the mate. "Prepare the attack!"

The battle call traveled the length of the ship as the *Zyria* headed for the embattled craft. The *Wolf* was going down fast.

"Beka's there," Alec cried, staring helplessly across at the foundering vessel. "Thero, can't you do something?"

"Quiet. He is," said Seregil. "Give him time."

Thero stood a little apart from them, eyes squeezed shut. Sweat poured down the wizard's face as he clenched his hands together in front of him. Then his thin lips curved up in a smile and he let out a small grunt of satisfaction. Without opening his eyes, he chanted softly under his breath and wove a series of symbols on the air.

"Ah, good choice, that," Seregil murmured approvingly.

"What? What is it?" demanded Alec.

Seregil pointed across to the enemy vessel. "Watch. This should be impressive."

An instant later a huge ball of fire erupted from the belly of the Plenimaran ship. Flames far fiercer than those aboard the doomed *Wolf* burst from every hatch, quickly engulfing everything above the waterline.

"Beautiful!" Seregil crowed, thumping Thero on the back. "You've always had a way with fire. How did you do it?"

The wizard opened his eyes and expelled a pent-up breath. "Her hold was full of Benshâl Fire. I merely concentrated on that until it exploded. The rest took care of itself."

Leaving the *Courser* to her work, the *Zyria* sailed on for the *Wolf*. The broken carrack was rolling slowly onto its side, wallowing in the swells. Sheets of oily flame spread out from her smashed hull.

"Come on, come on!" Seregil hissed, hanging over the rail to scan the debris surrounding the wreck. Beside him, Alec did the same, praying to find Beka among the living. All too quickly, dark forms resolved into bodies, some charred beyond recognition, others fighting to stay afloat and crying out for help. A few horses—too few—churned in circles, screaming in panic.

"All boats away," the captain ordered. "Quick now, before the sharks get them."

Seregil and Alec ran for the nearest longboat being lowered over the side. When it smacked own in the water with a jolt, they took the prow seats, searching the waves while the sailors pulled the oars.

"There's someone, over there to the right," Alec called to the oarsmen, pointing the way. The boat leaped forward, closing the distance between them and a struggling Skalan sailor.

They were within ten feet of him when a huge shape broke the surface and dragged the man under. For one awful instant, Alec looked into the doomed man's wild eyes, and the shark's soulless black one. Then they were gone.

"Maker's Mercy!" he gasped, rocking back on his heels.

"Poor old Almin," someone said behind him, and the sailors rowed harder.

Leaving the dead to the sea, they rounded the *Wolf*'s stern and found several people clinging to a broken spar.

"That's Mercalle!" Alec exclaimed.

The sergeant and two of her riders were supporting another between them. Alec recognized the sodden mass of red hair even before they had her all the way into the boat. Beka's face was white as milk except for a gash across her right temple.

"O Dalna, let her be alive," he muttered, feeling for a pulse at her throat.

"She is," Mercalle told him through chattering teeth. "She needs a healer, though, and soon."

The other riders looked only slightly better. Ileah was weeping silently, her face a mask of grief. Sitting close on either side of her in the bottom of the boat, Zir and Marten were chilled but apparently unhurt.

"It's her brother," Zir told him, putting an arm around Ileah. "He was dead before the bastards rammed us. How's the captain?" He looked anxiously at Beka.

Bent over Beka's still form, Seregil did not look up as he replied, "Too soon to tell."

Aboard the *Zyria*, they carried Beka below to one of the little cabins. Groans and screams came up from the hold, where the wounded sailors had been laid out. The stink of blood and Benshâl Fire hung strong on the stale air.

While Alec went in search of the ship's drysian, Seregil stripped off Beka's sodden clothes. He'd done the same when she was a child, but she was a child no more. For once, he was glad of Alec's absence. Surprised at his own embarrassment, he finished as quickly as he could and wrapped her in blankets. It hadn't been only her brief nakedness that was discomforting but the number of battle scars marring her pale freckled body.

That sort of thing had never bothered him before, not even with Alec. Sitting on the floor beside Beka now, though, he rested his head in his hands, fighting down guilt and grief. He'd been the first after Micum to hold Beka in his arms at her birth; he'd carried her on his shoulders, carved toy swords and horses for her, helped teach her to ride and how to fight dirty.

And got her the commission that put her here, unconscious, scarred, and bloody, he thought dismally. *Thank the Light I never had any children of my own.*

The drysian arrived at last, Alec on his heels with a basin of steaming water.

"She was thrown when the enemy ship rammed hers," he said, watching as the healer set to work.

"Yes, yes, Alec's told me all about it," Lieus said impatiently, sponging blood from the ragged wound. "She took a bad knock, all right. Still, the cut didn't go deep, thank the Maker. She'll wake up in a while with quite a headache, and probably some sickness. There's nothing for it now but to clean her up, keep her warm, and let her sleep. You two clear out; you're just in my way here." He jerked a thumb at Seregil. "I'll see to your shoulder later. Arrow, was it?"

"It's nothing."

The drysian grunted, then tossed Alec a small jar. "Wash his wound and keep some of this on it until the scab dries. I've seen wounds like that go putrid a week later. You don't want to lose your sword arm, now, do you, my lord?"

On deck, they found Klia busy taking stock of the situation. The *Courser* had finished with the other Plenimaran vessel and now rode at anchor nearby.

"You heard him," Alec ordered, mimicking the drysian's gruff tone. "Let me see what that arrow did to you."

The cuts from the mail rings were still oozing, and the whole area was dark and swollen. Now that the excitement of the crisis was over, Seregil was surprised at how much it hurt. Alec helped him remove the mail shirt and set about dressing the wound, his touch as sure and gentle as any healer's.

Those same hands were drawing a bow not so long ago, Seregil reflected with another stab of guilt. Alec had never killed a man before they'd met, and probably never would have if he'd been left to his trapping and wandering.

Life changes, he mused, *and life changes us.*

The soft afternoon breeze off the islands carried a sun-warmed mingling of scents he hadn't known for nearly forty years: wild mint and oregano, footcatch cedar, and fragrant powder vine. He'd last visited these islands a few months before his banishment. Looking across the water to Big Turtle, he could almost see his younger self jumping across the rocks, diving fish-naked in the coves with his friends—a silly, self-involved boy who'd had no idea what immensity of pain lay just over the horizon of his short life.

Life changes us all.

Klia climbed on a nearby hatch, still wearing her filthy green battle tabard. Braknil and Mercalle's riders gathered on the deck in front of her as she began to take stock.

"Who do you have left, Sergeant Mercalle?" Seregil heard her ask.

"Five riders and my corporal, Commander," the woman replied, betraying no emotion. Behind her, Zir and the other looked bedraggled and dispirited. Most appeared unhurt, although the lute player, Urien, was cradling a bandaged hand against his chest. "We've lost most of our weapons, though, and the horses."

"Those can be replaced. Riders can't," Klia replied brusquely. "And you, Braknil?"

"No deaths, Commander, but Orandin and Adis were badly burned by those damned fire streams."

Klia sighed. "We'll leave them in Gedre if the khirnari is agreeable."

Spotting Seregil, she waved him over. "What did you make of that?"

"That they were expecting us," he told her.

Klia scowled. "And I thought we'd been so careful."

The information didn't necessarily come from Skala, he thought, but kept the thought to himself for the time being.

"Can we make Gedre without stopping for water?" she asked the captain.

"Yes, Commander. But it will be dark by the time we've run up the new sail. Plenty of time to send landing crews over to fill some casks."

Klia rubbed the back of her neck wearily. "If those ships were waiting to ambush us, then they knew why we were going to the island. They could have ambushers waiting at the spring. I've had enough surprises for one day. I say we push on to Gedre."

No one slept that night, or spoke above a whisper as they sailed on under the dark new moon. Every lantern was extinguished, and Thero stood guard on the rear castle with the captain and Klia, ready to weave whatever magic they needed to evade notice.

The groans of the wounded came up from belowdecks like the voices of ghosts. Alec and Seregil ventured down every hour or so to check on Beka. When she woke at last, she was so ill that she ordered them to go away and leave her in peace.

"That's a good sign," Seregil noted as they made their way up to the bow. "She'll be well enough in a day or two."

Perched on a large coil of rope behind the bowsprit, they settled in to scan the starlit waters ahead for any sign of enemy lights or sails.

"She's lucky she wasn't burned," Alec said as another agonized cry floated up to them over the rush of the water.

Seregil said nothing, his face lost in shadow. At last he pointed up to the dark moon, just visible over the western horizon. "At least the moon's on our side tonight. Most 'faie call the dark moon *Ebrahä Rabás,* the Traitor's Moon. Where we're headed, she's called *Astha Nöliena.*"

" 'Lucky black pearl,' " Alec translated. "Why's that?"

Seregil turned to give him a humorless grin. "Smuggling's a common sideline where I'm from, ever since the Edict closed Gedre as a legal port. Virésse is a long way off from landlocked Bôkthersa; much simpler to head up to Gedre for the 'fishing.' My uncle, Akaien í Solun, used to bring my sisters and me along with him sometimes. On nights like this we'd sail out in fishing boats with our goods hidden under the nets to meet Skalan trade ships."

"I thought you told me he is a swordsmith?"

"He is, but as he used to say, 'Bad laws make good rogues.' "

"So you're not the first nightrunner in your family after all."

Seregil smiled. "I suppose not, though smuggling's practically an honorable trade here now. Gedre was a thriving trade port once, but when the Iia'sidra closed the borders she began to die. She's been slowly withering ever since—along with Akhendi—the fai'thast on the other side of the mountains. For centuries the northern trade routes were their life's blood. Klia's mission represents a great hope for them."

And for you, talí, Alec thought, sending up a silent prayer to the Four for their mutual success.

8

GEDRE

The next morning, Seregil watched the port town of Gedre appear out of the thin mists like a familiar dream just remembered. Her white domes shone in the bright morning light. Beyond them, brown hills patched with green rose like mounting waves to the feet of the jagged Ashek peaks—the Wall of Aurënen, Dragon Home. He was probably the only one aboard who noted the scattering of ruins above the town, like a line of dried foam left in the tide's wake.

A land breeze swept the scent of the place across the water: tender spring sweetgrass, cooking smoke, sun-warmed stone, and temple incense.

Closing his eyes, he recalled other dawns, skimming into this harbor in a little skiff laden with foreign goods. He could almost feel his uncle's big hand on his shoulder, smell the salt and smoke and sweat on the man's skin. It had been Akaien í Solun who'd given him the praise he never seemed to merit in his own father's house. *"You're a good bargainer, Seregil. I never thought you'd talk that merchant up to such a price for my swords"* or *"Well steered, my boy. You've learned your stars since our last voyage."*

His father was gone, but so was his claim on this land. Reaching up, he touched the lump Corruth's ring made, hanging inside his somber grey surcoat. Only he and Alec knew it was there; the rest of the world saw only the flame and crescent emblem on a heavy silver chain on his breast, signifying his rank among Klia's entourage. For now, it was best that this be all that they see, these strangers who were once his people.

He knew the others were watching him and kept his face to shore, letting the wind cool the stinging behind his eyes as he watched the boats of Gedre put out from shore to welcome them.

Alec's heart beat faster as he watched the little vessels skimming across the waves under their colorful lateen sails to greet the *Zyria* and her remaining escort.

He leaned over the rail, waving to the half-naked sailors. They wore only a sort of short kilt around their slim hips, regardless of age or gender. Skimming in past the larger ships' prows, they laughed and waved, their long dark hair streaming in the breeze.

Several of Beka's riders let out appreciative whistles.

"By the Light!" murmured Thero, eyes widening as he saluted a lithe, sun-browned girl. She gestured back, and a fragrant purple blossom appeared behind the young wizard's left ear. Other boatmen followed her lead and more flowers materialized to adorn or shower the Skalan visitors.

"Sort of makes you want to reconsider that wizard's vow of celibacy, doesn't it?" asked Alec, giving him a teasing nudge in the ribs.

Thero grinned. "Well, it *is* strictly voluntary."

"It's a better welcome than we've had anywhere for a long while," said Beka, joining them. Someone had magicked a wreath of blue and white flowers around the brim of her burnished helmet, and more blossoms were tucked into her long red braid. She was still pale beneath her freckles, but no one had been able to convince her to lie low once land came in sight.

Standing nearby, Klia was clearly as excited as any of them. Today she wore a gown and jewels worthy of her royal status. Freed from its usual military braid, her thick chestnut hair fell in waves about her shoulders. Some Aurënfaie admirer had decked her with a girdle and wreath of wild roses.

Alec had put on his best, as well, and the neck of his cloak was fastened with a heavy silver and sapphire brooch. Klia had smiled when she caught sight of it; it had been a gift from her own hand, an unspoken gesture of gratitude for saving her life.

Looking around, he saw with a sudden twinge of guilt that Seregil was standing alone. He held a single white bloom, absently twirling it by the stem between his long fingers as he watched the boats.

Going to him, Alec stood close enough to touch shoulders and took Seregil's free hand in his beneath the cover of their cloaks. Even after all their months of intimacy, he was still painfully shy about public gestures.

"Don't worry, talí," Seregil whispered. "Gedre holds good memories for me. The khirnari is a friend of my family."

"I'll have to learn who you are all over again," Alec sighed, rubbing his thumb across the back of Seregil's hand, loving the familiar play of bone and tendon beneath the skin. "Do you know the town well?"

Seregil's thin lips softened into a smile as he tucked the white flower behind his ear. "I used to."

The *Zyria* and the *Courser* glided into harbor like two storm-battered gulls and dropped anchor at two of the town's remaining quays. Tumbled piles of stones stretching out into the water were all that remained of several others.

Alec studied the crowd at the waterfront in awe. He'd never seen so many Aurënfaie in one place, and from a distance they all looked distressingly alike, even in their varying states of dress. Everyone seemed to have Seregil's dark hair, light eyes, and fine features. They weren't identical, of course, but the similarities threatened to blur into an indistinguishable whirl.

Most wore a simple tunic and breeches and colorful red and yellow sen'gai. Seregil had spent a good deal of the voyage schooling the Skalans on the various combinations, but this was the first time he'd seen the actual headdress. They added a bright, exotic note to the scene.

As he came nearer, however, differences began to emerge: He saw blond and ruddy hair scattered among the crowd, a man with a great wen on his cheek, a child missing a leg, a woman with a hunched shoulder. Still, they were all Aurënfaie, and beautiful in Alec's eyes.

Any of them could be blood kin to me, he thought, and in that moment felt the first true stirrings of understanding. In this foreign place he saw faces that resembled his own more than any he'd seen in Kerry.

The *Zyria* docked beside the quay and the crowd fell back as the Skalan sailors ran out the plank for Klia. Following her with the others, Alec saw a bearded old man in Skalan robes awaiting them with several important-looking 'faie.

"Lord Torsin?" he asked, pointing him out to Seregil. He'd met the envoy's niece several times in Rhíminee; she was a regular in Lord Seregil's circle. Torsin, however, he'd seen only at a distance at a few public assemblies.

"Yes, that's him," said Seregil, shading his eyes. "He looks ill, though. I wonder if Klia knows?"

Alec craned his neck for a closer look at the old man as their two groups converged on the quayside. Torsin's skin was sallow, his eyes sunk deeply beneath his thick white brows. The skin of his face and neck hung in folds, as if he'd recently lost weight. Even so, the man still cut an imposing figure, austere and dignified. The close-cropped hair showing beneath his plain velvet hat was snowy white, his long face creased with solemn furrows that seemed to sag with the weight of his years. As he approached Klia, however, his stern expression gave way to a surprising smile that immediately disposed Alec in the man's favor.

The principal members of the Aurënfaie contingent were easily distinguished by their fine tunics of ceremonial white. Foremost among these were a Gedre man with thick streaks of white in his hair, and a young, fair-haired woman wearing the green-and-brown-striped sen'gai of Akhendi clan. Of the two, she was the more heavily jeweled, denoting higher status. Smooth gems set in heavy gold glowed in the sunlight on her fingers, wrists, and at her throat.

The man was the first to speak. "Be welcome in the fai'thast of my clan, Klia ä Idrilain Elesthera Klia Rhíminee," he said, clasping hands with Klia. "I am Riagil í Molan, khirnari of Gedre. Torsin í Xandus has been extolling your virtues to us since his arrival yesterday. I see that, as usual, he speaks without exaggeration."

Removing a thick silver bracelet from each wrist, he presented them to her. Among the 'faie, Alec had learned, one gained honor by being able to make a lavish gift to one's guests as if it were only a trifle.

Smiling, Klia slipped the bracelets onto her wrists. "I thank you for your welcome, Riagil í Molan Uras Illien Gedre, and for your great generosity."

The woman stepped forward next and gave Klia a necklace of

carved carnelians. "I am Amali ä Yassara, wife of Rhaish í Arlisandin, khirnari of Akhendi clan. My husband is in Sarikali with the Iia'sidra, so it is my great pleasure to welcome you to Aurënen and to accompany you on your remaining journey."

"So lovely," Klia said, placing the necklace around her neck. "Thank you for your great generosity. Please allow me to present my advisers."

Klia introduced her companions one by one, rattling off the lengthy strings of patronymics or matronymics with practiced ease. Each Skalan was greeted with polite attention until they came to Seregil.

Amali ä Yassara's smile disappeared. She gave no direct insult but instead treated Seregil like so much empty air as she stepped quickly past. Seregil pretended not to notice, but Alec saw the way his friend's eyes went hard and blank for a moment, shutting away the pain.

The Gedre khirnari regarded Seregil thoughtfully for a long moment. "You are greatly changed," he said at last. "I would not have known you."

Alec shifted uneasily; this was not the greeting of an old friend.

Seregil bowed, still betraying neither surprise nor disappointment. "I remember you well, and kindly, Khirnari. Allow me to present my talímenios, Alec í Amasa."

The Akhendi still kept her distance, but Riagil clasped Alec's hand between his own with evident delight. "Be welcome, Alec í Amasa! You are the Hâzadriëlfaie Adzriel ä Illia told us of when she returned from Skala."

"Half, my lord. On my mother's side," Alec managed, still rocked by their treatment of Seregil. He hadn't expected anyone to know of him, much less care.

"Then this is a doubly happy day, my friend," Riagil said, patting his shoulder kindly. "You will find Gedre a welcoming clan for *ya'shel*."

He moved on, greeting the lesser aides and servants. Alec leaned closer to Seregil and whispered, "Ya'shel?"

"The respectful word for 'half-breed.' There are others. The Gedre have the most mixed bloods of any clan in Aurënen. See that woman with fair hair? And that fellow there by the boat, with black eyes and dark skin? Ya'shel. They've mixed with Dravnians, Zengati, Skalans—anyone they trade with."

"Word of your arrival has already been sent to Sarikali, Klia ä

Idrilain," Riagil announced when the introductions were finished. "Please be my guests tonight, and we will begin the journey tomorrow. The clan house lies in the hills above town, only a short ride."

While the nobles exchanged their greetings, Beka oversaw the unloading of their remaining horses and riders.

Rhylin's decuria had fared better than the others, despite the fighting they'd done. Counting them over, Beka was relieved to see that all were accounted for and none seriously wounded. There were long faces among the survivors of the ill-fated *Wolf,* however. Less than half of Mercalle's decuria had escaped unscathed.

"Bilairy's Balls, Captain, I haven't understood a word since we got here," Corporal Nikides muttered nervously, eyeing the crowd. "I mean, how would we know whether someone wanted a fight or was offering us tea?"

Before Beka could answer, a deep, amused voice just behind them drawled, "In Aurënen, the brewing of tea does not involve weapons. I am certain you would soon discern the difference."

Turning, she saw that the speaker was a dark-haired man dressed in a plain brown tunic and worn riding leathers. His thick brown hair was tied back beneath a black-and-white-patterned sen'gai. By his stance, Beka guessed him to be a soldier.

He's as handsome as Uncle Seregil, she thought.

The man was taller than Seregil, and perhaps a bit older, too, but had the same wiry build. His face was darkly tanned and wider through the cheekbones, giving it a more angular cast. He met her questioning look with a disarming smile; his eyes, she noted for no good reason, were a particularly clear shade of hazel.

"Greetings, Captain. I am Nyal í Nhekai Beritis Nagil of Ra'basi clan," he said, and something in the lilting timbre of his voice stirred a warm flutter deep in Beka's chest.

"Beka ä Kari Thallia Grelanda of Watermead," she replied, extending a hand as if they were in some Rhíminee salon. He took it, his callused palm warm and familiar against her own for the instant the handclasp lasted.

"The Iia'sidra has charged me to act as your interpreter," he explained. "Am I correct in assuming that most of your people do not speak our language?"

"I think Sergeant Mercalle and I know enough between the two of us to get into trouble." She felt a self-conscious grin threatening and quickly quelled it. "Please give the Iia'sidra my thanks. Is there someone I can speak to about horses and weapons. We ran into some trouble on the way across."

"But of course! It wouldn't do for Princess Klia's escort to enter Sarikali riding double, no?" Giving her a conspiratorial wink, he strode off toward a group of Gedre nearby, speaking rapidly in his own tongue.

Beka watched him for a moment, caught by the way his hips and shoulders moved beneath his loose tunic. Turning back, she caught Mercalle and several riders doing the same.

"Now, there's a long-legged bit of joy!" the sergeant exclaimed appreciatively under her breath.

"Sergeant, see that your people get their gear packed for riding," Beka snapped rather more sharply than she'd intended.

The Ra'basi was as good as his word. Though many of Mercalle's decuria still lacked proper weapons, they set off for the khirnari's house on horses each worth half a year's pay back home.

Klia's famous black stallion had weathered the voyage well and pranced proudly at the head of the procession, shaking its white mane.

"That's a Silmai horse," Nyal noted, riding at Beka's side. "The moon-white mane is their gift from Aura; it occurs nowhere else in Aurënen."

"He's carried her through some fierce battles," Beka told him. "Klia cares as much for that horse as some women do for their husbands."

"That is clear. And you handle an Aurënfaie mount as if you were born to it."

His slight, musical accent sent another odd little shiver through her. "My family has Aurënfaie stock in our herd, back home at Watermead," she explained. "I was riding before I could walk."

"And here you are, in the cavalry."

"Are you a soldier?" She'd seen nothing that looked like a uniform, but Nyal had the air of someone used to command.

"When necessary," he replied. "It is the same with all the men of my clan."

Beka raised an eyebrow. "I didn't see any women among the honor guard. Are they not allowed to be soldiers?"

"Allowed?" Nyal considered this for a moment. "There is no allowance necessary. Most simply choose not to. They have other gifts." He paused, lowering his voice. "If I may be so bold, I had not expected Skalan soldier women to be so pretty."

Normally Beka would have bristled at such a statement, but the words were said with such earnestness and obvious goodwill that it took the edge off. "Well—thanks." Anxious to change the subject, Beka looked around at the white buildings that lined the streets. They were topped with low domes instead of a pitched roof; the shape reminded her of a bubble clinging to a block of soap. None were more than two stories high and most were unadorned, except for a piece of dark, greenish stone set into the wall by the front door. "What are those?" she asked.

"Sacred stone from Sarikali, a talisman to protect whoever lives within. Hasn't anyone ever told you that you are pretty?"

Facing him this time, Beka pursed her lips into a stern line. "Only my mother. It's not the sort of thing that matters much to me."

"Forgive me, I meant no offense." Nyal's eyes widened in dismay and the way the slanting light struck the irises made Beka think of pale leaves lying at the bottom of a clear forest pool. "I know your language, but not your ways. Perhaps we can learn from each other?"

"Perhaps," Beka told him, and to her credit, her voice did not betray the undisciplined pounding of her heart.

The Gedre horsemen formed an honor guard for Klia and the Aurënfaie dignitaries as they rode out from the town and up into hills scattered with farms, vineyards, and deep-shaded groves. Drifts of fragrant purple and red flowers grew thickly in the coarse, pale grass along the roadside.

Alec and Seregil rode with Thero and the other aides just behind Lord Torsin. It felt good to have Windrunner under him again after so many days at sea. The glossy Aurënfaie gelding tossed his head, scenting the wind as if he recognized his homeland. Seregil's black mare, Cynril, was doing the same. Both horses drew admiring glances, and Alec, who seldom gave thought to such things, was suddenly glad of the impression they made.

"Who's the Ra'basi, I wonder?" he murmured, nodding toward a man riding beside Beka at the head of the column. What Alec could see of the fellow's face from this angle made him curious to see the rest.

"He's a long way from home," said Seregil, who'd also taken note of the stranger. "Beka seems rather taken with him, don't you think?"

"Not really," Alec replied. The Ra'basi was obviously trying to make conversation, but her responses came mostly in the form of terse nods.

Seregil chuckled softly. "Wait and see."

In the distance ahead, snow-covered peaks gleamed against the flawless blue of the spring sky. The sight brought Alec an unexpected pang of homesickness; "The Asheks look a lot like the Ironheart Range around Kerry. I wonder if the Hâzadriëlfaie felt the same when they first saw Ravensfell Pass?"

Seregil pushed a windblown lock of hair out of his eyes. "Probably."

"Why did those Hâzad folks leave Aurënen?" asked Sergeant Rhylin, riding on his left. "Even if this is the dry edge of the place, it's better country than anyplace I've seen north of Wyvern Dug."

"I don't know much about it," Seregil replied. "It happened over two thousand years ago. That's a long time, even for the 'faie."

The Ra'basi stranger appeared out of the press and fell in beside them.

"Forgive me for intruding, but I could not help overhearing," he said in Skalan. "You are interested in the Hâzadriëlfaie, Seregil í Korit?" He paused, looking abashed. "Seregil of Rhíminee, I meant to say."

"You have me at a disadvantage, Ra'basi," Seregil replied with a sudden coldness that sent a warning shock through Alec. "You know the name taken from me, but I don't know the one you carry."

"Nyal í Nhekai Beritis Nagil Ra'basi, interpreter for Princess Klia's cavalry. Forgive my clumsiness, please. Captain Beka ä Kari speaks so highly of you that I wished to meet you."

Seregil bowed slightly in the saddle, but Alec could tell he still had his guard up. "You must have traveled. I hear the accents of many ports as you speak."

"I hear the same in yours," Nyal replied with an engaging smile. "Aura gifted me with an ear for languages and restless feet. Thus, I've spent most of my life as a guide and interpreter. I am most honored that the Iia'sidra considered me worthy of this commission."

Alec watched the handsome newcomer with interest. From what he'd heard, the Ra'basi clan had everything to gain if the borders were reopened, yet they were also closely tied to their northern neighbors, Virésse and Golanil, who opposed any altering of the Edict of Separation. So far, their khirnari, Moriel ä Moriel, did not openly support either side.

It was a moment before Alec realized the man was also studying him.

"But you're not a Skalan, are you?" he said. "You have neither

the look nor the accent—ah, yes, I see it now! You are the Hâzadriëlfaie! What clan are you descended of?"

"I never knew my people, or that I was one of them until quite recently," Alec told him, wondering how often he'd have to give this
explanation. "It seems to mean a great deal here, though. Do you
know anything of them?"

"Indeed I do," Nyal replied. "My grandmother has told me their
story many times. She's a Haman, and they lost many people to the
Migration."

Seregil raised an eyebrow. "You're related to the Haman?"

Nyal grinned. "I'm from a wandering family. We're related to
half the clans in Aurënen one way or another. It's said to make us
more—what's the word—forbearing? Truly, Seregil, even with a
Haman grandmother, I bear you no ill will."

"Or I you," Seregil replied rather less than convincingly. "If
you'll excuse me?"

Without waiting for reply, he wheeled his horse and rode toward
the rear of the column.

"It's a bit overwhelming for him, being here," Alec apologized. "I
would like to hear what you know of the Hâzad. Tomorrow,
perhaps?"

"Tomorrow, then, to pass the time during our long ride." With a
juanty salute, Nyal rejoined the line of Skalan riders.

Alec rode back to rejoin Seregil. "What was that all about?" he
demanded under his breath.

"He'll bear watching," Seregil muttered.

"Why, because he's part Haman?"

"No, because he overheard what we were talking about from
twenty feet away, over the noise of the horses."

Looking back over his shoulder, Alec saw the interpreter chatting
with Beka and her sergeants. "He did, didn't he?"

"Yes, he did." He lowered his voice and said softly in Skalan,
"Our long holiday is truly over now. It's time to start thinking like . . ."
Lifting his left hand, Seregil briefly crossed his thumb over his ring
finger.

A chill ran up Alec's backbone; it was the hand sign for "Watchers." This was the first time since Nysander's death that Seregil had
used it.

The clan house Riagil had spoken of turned out to be more like a
walled village. White, vine-raddled walls enclosed a sprawling

maze of courtyards, gardens, and houses decorated with painted designs of sea creatures. Flowering trees and plants filled the air with heavy fragrances, underscored by the smell of fresh water close at hand.

"It's beautiful!" Alec exclaimed softly, though that hardly came close to expressing the effect the place had on him. In all his travels, he'd never seen anything so immediately pleasing to the eye.

"A khirnari's home is the central hearth of the fai'thast," Seregil told him, clearly delighted with his reaction. "You should see Bôkthersa."

By the Four, I hope we both do someday, Alec thought.

Leaving the escort riders in a large courtyard inside the main gate, Riagil led his guests to a spacious, many-domed house at the center of the compound.

Dismounting, he bowed to Klia. "Welcome to my home, honored lady. Every preparation has been made for your comfort and that of your people."

"You have our deepest thanks," Klia replied.

Riagil and his wife, Yhali, led the Skalan nobles through cool, tiled corridors to a series of rooms overlooking an inner courtyard.

"Look there!" Alec laughed, spying a pair of small brown owls roosting in one of the trees. "They say owls are the messengers of Illior—Aura, that is. Is it the same here?"

"Not messengers, but a favored creature all the same, and a bird of good omen," Riagil replied. "Perhaps because they are the only predatory bird that does not feed on the young of the dragons, Aura's true messengers."

Alec and Seregil were given a small, whitewashed room to themselves at the end of the row of guest chambers. The rough-textured walls were inset with numerous well-blackened lamp niches. The furnishings were elegantly simple, made of pale woods with little ornamentation. The bed, a broad platform surrounded by layers of an airy cloth Seregil called gauze, was a particularly welcome sight after their cramped public quarters at sea. Looking around, Alec felt urges held firmly at bay during the sea crossing making themselves known and regretted they were only spending one night here.

"Our bath chamber is being prepared for you and your women," Yhali told Klia as she and Riagil took their leave. "I'll send a servant to escort you."

Riagil spared Seregil a cool glance. "The men will use the blue chamber. You remember the way, I'm certain?"

Seregil nodded, and this time Alec was certain he saw a flicker of sadness in his friend's grey eyes.

If the khirnari saw it, he gave no sign. "My servants will conduct you to the feast when you have refreshed yourselves. And you, Torsin í Xandus?"

"I will remain here for now," the old man replied. "I'm not acquainted with some of our party, it seems."

As the khirnari and his lady withdrew, Torsin turned and addressed Alec directly for the first time since his arrival. "I have heard many times how you saved Klia's life, Alec í Amasa. My niece Melessandra also speaks most highly of you. I am honored to make your acquaintance."

"And I yours, honored sir." Alec managed to keep a straight face as he accepted the man's outstretched hand. After a lifetime of complete obscurity, such widespread notoriety was going to take getting used to.

"I will join you momentarily, if you will excuse me?" Torsin said, entering his chamber.

"Come along, you two," Seregil said to Alec and Thero. "I believe you'll enjoy this. I certainly intend to."

Crossing the flower-filled courtyard, they entered a vaulted chamber, the walls of which were painted blue and decorated with more of the whimsical sea creatures Alec had seen on the exterior walls. Sunlight streamed in through several small windows set near the ceiling, the rays dancing off the surface of a small, steaming pool sunk into the floor. Four smiling men of varying ages stepped forward with murmured greetings to help them out of their clothing.

"Leave it to the Aurënfaie to make a guesting custom of bathing," Alec remarked to cover his initial discomfort with such attentions.

"It doesn't do to tell your visitors that they stink," Seregil murmured with a chuckle.

Before Alec had met Seregil, a bath was something undertaken only as an absolute necessity, and then only in the heat of high summer. Daily ablutions struck him not only as absurd but downright unsafe until he'd been won over in Rhíminee by the amenities of heated water and tubs without splinters. Even then, he'd considered Seregil's devotion to such physical comforts to be just another of his friend's forgivable quirks. Later, Seregil had explained that bathing was an integral part of Aurënfaie life and the heart of hospitality.

And now at last, he was going to experience it firsthand—if in a slightly altered version. Separate bathing for men and women was a Skalan custom; Alec wasn't sure how he could have gotten through a communal bath with Klia.

Clay pipes brought heated water into the bath chamber from somewhere outside. The steamy air was redolent with sweet herbs.

Surrendering the last of his clothes to the attendant, Alec followed the others into the bath. After so many days at sea, it was a delicious sensation and he soon relaxed, watching the play of reflected light across the ceiling as the embracing water drew out all the tensions and bruises of their journey.

"By the Light, I've missed this!" Seregil sighed as he stretched lazily, resting his head against the side of the pool.

Thero's eyes narrowed as he caught sight of the arrow wound on Seregil's shoulder. The skin was still swollen, and an ugly purple bruise had spread darkly across his fair skin, reaching halfway to the small, faded circular scar at the center of his chest.

"I didn't realize it was that bad," he said.

Seregil flexed the shoulder nonchalantly. "It looks worse than it feels."

After a proper soak and scrub, the servants dried them and led them to thick pallets on the floor, where they massaged them from head to toe, kneading aromatic oils into every joint and muscle. Seregil's attendant took special care with his bruised shoulder and was rewarded with a series of appreciative groans.

Alec did his best to relax as skilled hands worked inexorably down his back toward portions of his anatomy he generally considered off-limits to anyone but Seregil. None of the others seemed to have any qualms about it, though, not even Thero, who lay growling contentedly on the next pallet.

Take what the Lightbringer sends and be thankful, Alec reminded himself, still striving to adopt Seregil's avowed philosophy.

Torsin joined them during the massage, lowering himself slowly into a chair beside them.

"And how are you enjoying our host's hospitality?" he asked, smiling down at Alec and Thero. "We Skalans may consider ourselves a cultured people, but the 'faie put us quite to shame."

"I hope they offer it everywhere we stay," the wizard mumbled happily.

"Oh, yes," Torsin assured him. "It's considered a great disgrace for host or guest to neglect such niceties."

Alec groaned. "You mean if I don't wash or use the proper tableware I'll cause a scandal?"

"No, but you will bring dishonor on yourself and the princess," Torsin replied. "The laws governing the behavior of our hosts are even stricter. If a guest is harmed, the entire clan carries the dishonor."

Alec tensed; there was no mistaking the veiled reference to Seregil's past.

Seregil rose on one elbow to face the old man. "I know you didn't want me here." His voice was level, controlled, but the knuckles of his clenched fists were white. "I'm as sensitive as you to the complications of my return."

Torsin shook his head. "I'm not certain you are. Riagil was your friend, yet you cannot have misread his reception today." He broke off suddenly and coughed into a linen napkin. The fit went on for several seconds, bringing a sheen of sweat to the old man's brow.

"Forgive me. My lungs aren't what they once were," he managed at last, tucking the napkin into his sleeve. "As I was saying, Riagil could not bring himself to welcome you. Lady Amali will not even speak your name, despite her support of Klia's cause. If our allies cannot bear your presence, what will our opponents make of it? If it were up to me, I would send you back to Skala at once rather than risk jeopardizing the task our queen has set us."

"I'll bear that in mind, my lord," Seregil replied with the same false composure that had worried Alec earlier. Rising from the pallet, he wrapped himself in a clean sheet and left the room without a backward glance.

Swallowing his own anger, Alec followed, leaving Thero to sort things out as best he could. He caught up to Seregil in the garden court and reached to halt him. Seregil shook off his hand and strode on.

Back in their chamber, he tugged on a pair of doeskin breeches and used the sheet to dry his hair. "Come along now, make yourself presentable, my ya'shel," he said, face still obscured.

Alec crossed the room and grasped his wrist, pulling the cloth away. Seregil glared at him through a tangled mass of hair, cold fury burning in his eyes. Pulling roughly away again, he grabbed a comb and yanked it through his hair hard enough to pull out several strands.

"Give me that before you hurt yourself!" Shoving Seregil down into a chair, Alec took the comb and set to work more gently, working out the knots, then settling into a soothing rhythm as if currying a high-spirited horse. Anger radiated from Seregil like heat, but Alec ignored it, knowing it was not directed at him.

"Do you think Torsin really intended—?"

"It's exactly what he *intended*," Seregil fumed. "For him to say that, and in front of those attendants—as if I need to be reminded why I have no name in my own country!"

Alec set the comb aside and drew Seregil's damp head back

against his chest, cupping his friend's thin cheeks in his hands. "It doesn't matter. You're here because Idrilain and Adzriel want you here. Give the rest time. You've been nothing but a legend here for forty years. Show them who you've become."

Seregil covered Alec's hands with his own, then stood and drew him close. "Ah, talí," he growled, hugging him. "What would I do without you, eh?"

"That's nothing you ever have to worry about," Alec vowed. "Now, we've got a feast to get through. Play Lord Seregil for all you're worth. Confound them with your charm."

Seregil let out a bitter laugh. "All right, then; Lord Seregil it is, and if that's not enough to win them, then I'm still the talímenios of the famous Hâzadriëlfaie, aren't I? Like the moon, I'll hang close to you through the night, reflecting your brilliance by virtue of my own dark surface."

"Behave yourself," Alec warned. "I want you in a sweeter temper when we get back here tonight." He brought his mouth to Seregil's to underscore his meaning and was gratified to feel the tight lips soften and open beneath his own.

Illior, patron of thieves and madmen, lend us the guile to survive this evening, he thought.

Torsin was not in evidence when a young woman of the household arrived to guide them to the feast. Thero was, however, and Alec saw that the wizard was out to make an impression; his dark blue robe was embroidered with silver vine work, and the crystal wand he'd used aboard the *Zyria* was tucked into a belt embossed with gold. Like Alec and Seregil, he also wore the flame and crescent medallion of Klia's household.

The feast was held in a large courtyard near the center of the clan house. Ancient trees overhung the long tables set there, their gnarled trunks and lower branches studded with hundreds of tiny lamps.

Looking over the assembled company, Alec was relieved to see that the Gedre didn't stand on ceremony. People of all ages were already gathered there, laughing and talking. Growing up in the northlands, the 'faie had been creatures of legend for him, magical and awesome. Standing here in the midst of a whole clan of them, Alec felt like he was back at Watermead, sharing a communal meal at day's end.

Spotting Beka at a table near the gate, he cast Seregil a hopeful look, but their guide was already ushering them toward the khirnari's table beneath the largest tree. Klia and Torsin sat to Riagil's right, Amali ä Yassara to his left. Alec was chagrined to find himself furthest from the others, seated between two of Riagil's grandchildren.

All the same, he found the food and etiquette involved in dining considerably less complicated than what he'd encountered at Skalan banquets.

Poached fish, a rich venison stew, and pastries stuffed with cheese, vegetables, and spices were served with baskets of bread shaped into fanciful animals. Platters of roasted vegetables, nuts, and several kinds of olives soon followed. Attentive stewards kept his cup filled with a spicy drink his dining companions called *rassos*.

No formal entertainment had been arranged; instead, various guests of the feast simply stood up on their benches and started a song or performed some colorful magical trick. As the meal progressed and the rassos flowed, these impromptu exhibitions grew more frequent and more boisterous.

Too far from the others to participate in their conversation, Alec looked with envy toward Beka's table. The riders of Urgazhi Turma were mingling sociably with those of the Aurënfaie honor guard. The interpreter, Nyal, was seated beside Beka, and the two looked to be sharing some joke.

Seregil also seemed to be making the best of things. Amali was still ignoring him, but he'd managed to strike up a conversation with several other 'faie. Catching Alec watching, Seregil gave him an amused wave, as if to say, "Be charming and make the best of things."

Alec turned again to his young dining companions.

"You really knew nothing of your 'faie blood?" asked the boy, Mial, after quizzing him pointedly about his family background. "Don't you have any magic?"

"Well, Seregil did teach me a trick with dogs," Alec said, showing him the left-handed sign. "But that's about it."

"Anyone can do that!" scoffed the girl, Makia, who appeared to be about fourteen.

"It's still magic," said her brother, though Alec had the impression he was merely being polite.

"I always just thought of it as a trick," Alec admitted. "None of the wizards we know seem to think I have any real magic in me."

"They're Tírfaie," Makia scoffed. "Watch this."

Furrowing her brow, she scowled down at her plate. Three olive pits slowly rose into the air and hung unsteadily in front of her face for a moment before clattering back to the table. "And I'm only twenty-two!"

"Twenty-two?" Alec turned to Mial in surprise. "And you?"

The young Aurënfaie grinned. "Thirty. How old are you?"

"Almost nineteen," Alec replied, suddenly feeling a bit strange.

Mial stared at him a moment, then nodded. "It's the same with some of our half-breed cousins; you mature much faster at first. You might want to keep your age to yourself once you get over the mountains, though. The purer clans don't understand ya'shel the way we do here. The last thing your talímenios needs is another scandal."

Alec felt his face go warm. "Thank you. I'll keep that in mind."

"You are to advise Princess Klia on the western clans, I understand?" Amali ä Yassara remarked, addressing Seregil directly for the first time.

Seregil looked up from his dessert to find her studying him coolly. "I hope to be of service to both our lands."

"And you do not think their request was in part motivated by the possibility that your presence would elicit strong reactions in certain quarters?"

Klia smiled at Seregil over the rim of her cup; blunt speech was considered a sign of goodwill in Aurënen. After all his years of intrigue in Skala, however, it was going to take some getting used to.

"The thought did occur to me," Seregil replied, adding pointedly, "However, as Lord Torsin opposed my inclusion for the very same reasons, I doubt that was their aim."

"Despite the errors of his youth, I can assure you that Seregil is a man of honor," Klia interjected calmly. He kept his eyes on his dessert dish as she went on.

"I've known him all my life, and he's been invaluable to my mother. No doubt you have heard that it was he and Alec who found the remains of Corruth í Glamien while uncovering a plot against the Skalan throne? I'm sure I don't have to explain to you the effect that discovery has had on relations between our two countries. If not for that, I might not be sitting here with you now, nor would Skalan ships be riding at anchor in this harbor again after all these years."

Riagil saluted her with his cup. "I begin to see why your mother entrusted you with this mission, Klia ä Idrilain.

"I do not doubt what you say of him, or disparage his good works," Amali said, apparently content to speak again as if Seregil were not there. "But if he is still 'faie in his heart, then he knows that one cannot change the past."

"Yet may not one's past be forgiven?" Klia countered. When the question went unanswered, she turned to Riagil. "What do you think his reception will be at Sarikali?"

The khirnari gave Seregil a thoughtful look, then replied, "I think that he should keep his friends close by."

A warning or a threat? wondered Seregil, unable to discern the sentiment behind the man's bland words. As the evening wore on, he often looked up to find Riagil watching him with that same enigmatic look—not smiling, but not cold, either.

After the meal people wandered among the tables, sharing wine and conversation.

Seregil was just looking about for Alec when he felt an arm around his waist.

"Torsin was right about her, wasn't he?" Alec muttered, nodding slightly in Amali ä Yassara's direction.

"It's atui," Seregil replied with a loose shrug.

"She also fears the effect you'll have on the Iia'sidra," Nyal said behind them.

Seregil rounded on the eavesdropper with poorly concealed annoyance. "It seems to be the prevailing attitude."

"Princess Klia's success means a great deal to the Akhendi," the Ra'basi observed. "I doubt she would judge your past so harshly if it did not pose a threat to her own interests."

"You seem to know much about her."

"As I told you, I am a traveler. One learns much that way." Bowing politely, he wandered off into the crowd.

Seregil watched him go, then exchanged a dark look with Alec. "Remarkable hearing that man has."

The gathering gradually tapered off as restless children disappeared into the shadows beyond the trees and their elders made their farewells to the Skalans. Released from social obligations at last, Alec had retreated to the company of Beka and her riders. When Seregil rose at last to take his leave, however, Riagil stayed him with a gesture.

"Do you remember the moon garden court?" asked the khirnari. "As I recall, it was a favorite haunt of yours."

"Of course."

"Would you care to see it again?"

"Very much, Khirnari," Seregil replied, wondering where this unexpected overture would lead.

They walked in silence through the warren of dwellings to a small courtyard at the far side of the enclosure. Unlike the other gardens, where colored blossoms contrasted vividly against sun-baked walls, this place was made for the meditations of the night. It was filled with every sort of white flower, medicinal herb, and silvery-leafed plant, banked like drifted snow in beds along paths paved with black slate. Even under the waning crescent that rode the stars tonight, the blossoms glowed in the darkness. Overhead, tubular paper kites with calligraphy-covered streamers rustled on wires, breathing their painted prayers on the night breeze.

The two men stood quietly awhile, admiring the perfection of the place.

Presently Riagil let out a long sigh. "I once carried you sleeping to your bed from here. It seems not so long ago."

Seregil winced. "I'd be mortified if any of my Tír companions heard you say that."

"We are not Tír, you and I," Riagil said, his face lost for a moment in shadow. "Yet I see now that you've grown strange among them, older than your years."

"I always was. Perhaps it runs in the family. Look at Adzriel, a khirnari already."

"Your eldest sister is a remarkable woman. Akaien í Solun was glad enough to hand the title to her as soon as she was of age. But be that as it may, the Iia'sidra will still perceive you as a stripling, and the queen as a fool for employing you as an emissary."

"If I've learned anything among the Tír, it's the value of being underestimated."

"Some might interpret that as a lack of honor."

"It's better to lack the semblance of honor but possess it than to possess the semblance and lack the honor."

"What a unique point of view," Riagil murmured, surprising Seregil with a smile. "Still, it has its merits. Adzriel brought favorable news of you from Rhíminee. Seeing you today among your companions, I believe her hopes are justified."

He paused, his face serious again. "You are a sort of two-edged blade, my boy, and as such will I employ you. Gedre has slowly withered since the Edict was imposed, like a vine whose roots are cut. It is the same for Akhendi, who shared in the trade through our port. Klia must succeed if we are to survive as we are. Trade with the north must be reestablished. Whatever the Iia'sidra decides, let your princess know what Gedre will support her cause."

"She has no doubt of that," Seregil assured him.

"Thank you. I shall sleep more peacefully tonight. Let me leave you with this." Riagil drew a sealed parchment from his belt and handed it to him. "It is from your sister. Welcome home, Seregil í Korit."

Seregil's throat tightened painfully at the sound of his true name. Before he could reply, Riagil tactfully withdrew, leaving him alone with the soft rustle of the kites.

He rubbed a thumb over the tree and dragon imprint in the wax, imagining his father's heavy seal ring on his sister's slender finger. Prying the wax up with a thumbnail, he unfolded the sheet.

Adzriel had tucked a few dried wandril flowers into the letter. Crushing the faded red petals between his fingers, he inhaled their spicy scent as he read.

"Welcome home, dear brother," the letter began, "for so I address you in my heart even if it is forbidden elsewhere. My heart breaks that I cannot yet claim you openly as kin. When we meet, know that it is circumstance that prevents me, not coldness on my part. Instead, I thank you for undertaking this most painful and dangerous task.

"Asking for your inclusion was no sudden inspiration. The first glimmer of it was already in my mind during our all-too-brief reunion that night in Rhíminee. Aura's blessings on Nysander's poor *khi* that he told me of your true work. Take care for the safety of our kinswoman, and may Aura guard you until we embrace again at Sarikali. I have so much to tell you, Haba.—Adzriel"

Haba.

The tightness in his throat returned as he reread the precious letter, committing it to memory.

"At Sarikali," he whispered to the kites.

9
INTO AURËNEN

The sound of small wings woke Seregil the next morning. Opening his eyes, he saw a chukaree perched on the windowsill, its green plumage shining like Bry'kha enamel work as it preened its stubby tail. He willed it to drop a feather, but it had no gift for him today; with a liquid trill, it fluttered away.

Judging by the brightness of the window, they'd overslept. The distant jangling of harness warned that Beka's riders were already making ready to go.

Yet he lay quiet a moment longer, savoring the feeling of Alec's warm body still wound contentedly around his own, and the comfort of a proper bed. They'd made good use of it, he thought with sleepy satisfaction.

His fragile sense of peace slipped away all too quickly. The coat thrown carelessly over a chair caught his eye like an accusation, bringing with it the memory of Torsin's words and those of Riagil. As the khirnari had so succinctly pointed out, life among the Tír had forced him to grow up far more quickly than the friends he'd left behind. He'd known more of death and violence, intrigue and passion than most 'faie twice his age. How many of the youngsters he'd played with had killed anyone, let alone the uncounted numbers he had in his years as Watcher, thief, and spy?

He stroked the arm draped over his chest, smoothing the fine golden hairs. Most 'faie his age hadn't even left the family hearth yet, much less made such a bond with anyone.

Who am I?

The question, so easy to ignore all those years in Rhíminee, was staring him in the face now.

Sounds of morning activity grew louder outside their window. Sighing regretfully, he ran a finger down the bridge of Alec's nose. "Wake up, talí."

"Morning already?" Alec mumbled blearily.

"There's no fooling you, is there? Come, it's time to move on."

The central courtyard was filled with people and horses. Urgazhi and Akhendi riders were busy loading a string of packhorses; others were gathered around smoking braziers where Gedre cooks were serving a hasty breakfast. Nyal clearly had his hands full, Seregil thought, watching the man with growing dislike.

"It's about time!" Beka called, seeing them. "Klia's looking for you. You'd better grab something to eat with us while you can."

"No one woke us," Seregil muttered, wondering if the slight had been intentional.

Begging fry bread and sausage at the nearest brazier, he and Alec ate as they wandered among the riders, picking up details.

Two of Mercalle's six remaining riders, Ari and Marten, were remaining behind with Corporal Zir to serve as dispatch couriers, carrying messages that would come by ship from Skala. The others would do the same from Sarikali.

Braknil was short a few riders as well; Orandin and Adis had been too badly burned at sea to continue and had remained aboard the *Zyria* for the return voyage.

The remaining members of Urgazhi Turma seemed out of sorts.

"Did you hear?" Tare grumbled to Alec. "We have to ride *blindfolded* parts of the way, for hell's sake!"

"It's always been that way for foreigners, even before the Edict," Seregil told him. "Only the Aurënfaie and Dravnian tribesmen who live in the mountains can pass over freely."

"How are we supposed to get over a mountain pass blind?" Nikides muttered.

"I'll just move my patch over to my good eye," Steb offered with a grin.

"He won't let you come to any harm, Corporal," Seregil assured Nikides, pointing to the Akhendi clansman sitting his horse nearby. "It would blemish his honor."

Nikides glowered at his escort. "I'll be sure to beg his pardon when I'm falling to my death."

"He's worried about falling," Alec explained to the Akhendi.

"He can ride double with me," the man offered, patting his horse's rump.

Nikides scowled, needing no interpreter. "I'll manage."

The man shrugged, "He can suit himself, but at least get him to accept this." Pulling a piece of wild gingerroot from a belt pouch, he tossed it to Nikides, who examined it distrustfully. "And tell him my name is Vanos."

"Some get queasy riding blind," Seregil explained. "Chew this if you do. And you might thank Vanos here for the consideration."

"The word is 'chypta'," Alec added helpfully.

Nikides turned rather sheepishly to his escort and held up the root. "Chypta."

"You welkin," Vanos replied with a friendly grin.

"Looks like they'll have lots to talk about," Alec chuckled. "Hope you brought some of that root for me."

Seregil took a piece from a wallet at his belt and presented it to him. "A disgrace to one talímenios is a disgrace to both. It would reflect poorly on me if you showed up covered in puke. And don't worry, most of the time you'll ride with your eyes open."

Riding to the head of the column, they fell in behind Klia and her hosts.

"My friends, we now begin the last leg of your long journey," Riagil announced. "It's a well-traveled route, but there are dangers. First among these are the young dragons, those larger than a lizard but smaller than an ox. Should you meet with one, be still and avert your eyes. Under no circumstances must you hunt or attack them."

"And if they attack first?" Alec whispered, recalling what Seregil had told them aboard the *Zyria*.

Seregil motioned him to silence.

"The youngest ones, fingerlings we call them, are fragile creatures," Riagil continued. "If you kill one by accident, you must undergo several days purification. To willfully kill one invokes the curse of its brethen, and brings that curse on your clan unless your people see to it that you are punished.

"Any animal that speaks is sacred and must not be harmed or

hunted. These are the *khtir'bai,* inhabited by the khi of great wizards and rhui'auros."

"If we're not supposed to harm anything, why are you all armed?" Alec asked one of their escort, who carried bows and longswords.

"There are other dangers," he told him. "Rock lions, wolves, sometimes even *teth'brimash.*"

"Teth' what?"

"People cut off from their clan for some dishonor," Seregil explained. "Some of them turn outlaw."

"I'm honored to guide you," Riagil concluded. "You are the first Tír to visit Sarikali in centuries. Aura grant that this be the first of many journeys shared by our people."

The road into the mountains started out broad and level, but as it left the foothills and twisted along the edge of a jagged precipice, Alec began to share Nikides's doubts about riding blind. Looking up, he could see the gleam of snow still clinging to the sides of peaks.

Seregil had other concerns.

"I'd say a bond was forming there, wouldn't you?" he asked under his breath, his expression neutral as he nodded slightly toward Beka and the interpreter.

"He's a handsome man, and a friendly one." Alec rather liked the garrulous Ra'basi, in spite of Seregil's reservations. For Beka's sake, he hoped that his friend's celebrated intuition was off its mark this time. "How old would you say he is?"

Seregil shrugged. "Eighty or so."

"Not so old for her, then," Alec observed.

"By the Light, don't go marrying them off yet!"

"Who said anything about marriage?" Alec teased.

Beka waved and rode over to them. "I've been bragging up your archer's skills all morning, Alec."

"Is this the famous Black Radly?" Nyal asked.

Alec passed the bow to him, and Nyal ran a hand over its long limbs of polished black yew.

"I've never seen a finer one, or such wood. Where does it comes from?"

"A town called Wolde, up in the northlands beyond Mycena." Alec showed him the maker's mark scrimshawed on the ivory arrow plate: a yew tree with the letter *R* woven into its upper branches.

"Beka tells me you destroyed a dyrmagnos with it. I've heard legends of these monstrous beings! What did it look like?"

"A dried corpse with living eyes," Alec replied, suppressing a shudder of revulsion at the memory. "I only struck the first blow, though. It took more than that to destroy her."

"To harm such a creature at all is a wizard's task," Nyal said, handing the bow back. "Perhaps someday you will tell me of it, but I believe I owe you a tale today. A long ride is a good time for a story, no?"

"A very good time," Alec replied.

"Beka tells me you did not know your mother or her people, so I'll begin at the beginning. Long ago, before the Tír came to the northern lands, a woman named Hâzadriël claimed to have been given a vision journey by Aura, the god you call Illior in the north."

Alec smiled as he listened. Nyal sounded just like Seregil, launching into one of his long tales.

"In this vision a sacred dragon showed to her a distant land and told her she would make a new clan there. For many years Hâzadriël traveled Aurënen, telling of her vision and calling for followers. Many dismissed her as mad, or chased her off as a troublemaker. But others welcomed her until eventually she and a great army of people sailed from Bry'kha; they were never heard from again and given up as lost until many generations later when Tír traders brought tales of 'faie living in a land of ice far north of their own. It was only then that we learned they had taken the name of their leader, Hâzadriël, as their own. Until then, they were simply referred to as the *Kalosi*, the Lost Ones. You, Alec, are the first to ever come to Aurënen claiming kinship with them."

"Then I can't trace my family to any one Aurënen clan?" Alec said, disappointed.

"What a pity not to have known your own people."

Alec shook his head. "I'm not so sure. According to Seregil, they didn't take much of Aurënfaie hospitality with them."

"It's true," Seregil told him. "The Hâzadriëlfaie have a reputation for enforcing their own isolation. I had a brush with them once, and almost didn't live to tell about it."

"You never told me that!" Beka exclaimed indignantly.

Nor me, Alec thought in surprise, but held his tongue.

"Well, it was a very brief brush," he admitted, "and not a pleasant one. The first time I traveled to the northlands, before I met Beka's father, I heard an old bard telling tales of what he called the Elder Folk. Alec here grew up hearing those same stories, never suspecting it was his own people they were talking about.

"I hounded the poor fellow for all he knew, along with every other storyteller I met for the next year or so. I suppose that was the beginning of my education as a bard. At any rate, I finally got enough out of the tales to trace them to a place in the Ironheart Mountains called Ravensfell Pass. Hungry for the sight of another 'faie face, I struck off in search of them."

"That's understandable," Nyal threw in, then gave Beka an embarrassed look. "I mean no insult."

Beka gave him a wry look. "None taken."

"I'd been in Skala for over ten years and was terribly homesick," Seregil continued. "To find other 'faie, no matter who they were, became an obsession. Everyone I talked to warned that the Hâzadriël-faie killed strangers, but I figured that only applied to Tírfaie.

"It was a long, cold journey and I'd decided to go alone. I started through the pass in late spring, and a week or so later finally came out in a huge valley and saw what looked like a settled fai'thast in the distance. Certain of a warm welcome, I headed for the closest village. Before I'd gotten a mile down the valley, though, I ran into a group of armed horsemen. All I saw at first was that they were wearing sen'gai. I greeted them in Aurënfaie, but they attacked and took me prisoner."

"What happened then?" Beka demanded as soon as he paused.

"They held me in a cellar for two days before I managed to escape."

"That must have been a bitter disappointment," Nyal remarked kindly.

Seregil looked away and sighed. "It was a long time ago."

The column had slowed steadily as they talked, and now came to a complete halt.

"This is the first hidden stretch," Nyal explained. "Captain, will you trust me as your guide?"

Beka agreed just a tad too readily, Alec noted with amusement.

Skalan riders paired off with Aurënfaie, handing over their reins and tying white cloth blindfolds over their eyes.

A pair of Gedre riders approached Alec and Seregil.

"What's this?" asked Seregil as one of the men sidled his horse up next to Seregil's and held out a blindfold.

"All Skalans must ride blind," the man replied.

Alec choked down a hard knot of resentment, almost grateful when his own blindfold hid the scene. How many more little ways would the 'faie find to underline the fact that Seregil was returning as an outsider?

"Ready, Alec í Amasa?" his own guide asked, clasping his shoulder.

"Ready." Alec gripped the saddlebow, feeling off balance already. Renewed grumbling among the Skalans came from all sides, then a brief chorus of surprise as a peculiar sensation came over them, a tingle on the skin. Unable to resist, Alec lifted a corner of the blindfold just enough to peek out from under it, then pulled it hastily back into place as his eye was assaulted by a stinging burst of swirling color that sent a bolt of pain through his head.

"I wouldn't do that, my friend," his guide chuckled. "The magic will hurt your eyes, without the covering."

To make amends to their guests, or perhaps to drown out the complaining, someone began to sing and others quickly joined in, voices echoing among the rocks.

Once I loved a girl so fair, with ten charms woven in her hair.
Slim as the tip of the newborn moon,
Eyes the color of a mountain sky.
For a year I wooed her with my eyes
And a year with all my heart.
A year with tears unshed,
A year with wandering feet,
A year with silent songs unsung,
A year with sighs replete.
A year until she was the wife of another and my safety was
   complete.

The play of sun and shadow across Alec's skin told him that the trail twisted sharply and it wasn't long before he dug in his pouch for the root Seregil had given him. It smelled of moist earth, and the pungent juice made his eyes water, but it did settle his stomach.

"I didn't think I'd be sick," he said, spitting out the stringy pith. "It feels like we're riding around in circles."

"That's the magic," said Seregil. "Whole miles of the pass are like this."

"How are you doing?" Alec asked softly, thinking of Seregil's frequent difficulties with magic.

Warm, ginger-scented breath bathed his cheek as Seregil leaned close and confessed, "I'm managing."

The blind ride went on for what seemed like a dark, lurching eternity. They traveled beside rushing water for a time, and at others Alec sensed walls closing in around them.

Riagil finally called a halt, and the blindfolds were removed. Alec rubbed his eyes, blinking in the afternoon brightness. They were in a small meadow bounded on all sides by steep cliffs. Looking back, he saw nothing but the usual terrain.

Seregil was bathing his face at a spring that bubbled up among the rocks a few yards away. Joining him, Alec drank as he studied the stunted bushes and clumps of tiny flowers and grasses clinging in clefts of rock. A few wild mountain sheep clattered among the rocks overhead.

"Would fresh meat be welcome tonight?" Alec asked Riagil, who was standing nearby.

The khirnari shook his head. "We have food enough with us for now. Leave these creatures for someone who needs them. Besides, I think you'd have a hard time making such a shot. They are a good distance off."

"I'd bet a Skalan sester he can shoot that far," Seregil told him.

"An Akhendi mark says he can't," Riagil countered, producing a thick, square coin seemingly out of thin air.

Seregil gave Alec a mischievous wink. "Looks like it's up to you to defend our honor."

"Thanks," Alec muttered. Shading his eyes, he looked up at the sheep again. They were still on the move, at least fifty yards away now, and the breeze was uncertain. Unfortunately, a number of people had heard the challenge and were watching him expectantly. With an inward sigh, he went back to his horse and pulled an arrow from the quiver slung behind his saddle.

Ignoring his audience, he took aim in the general direction of the hindmost sheep and released purposefully high. The shaft glanced off the rocks just over the large ram's head. The creature let out a bleat and sprang away.

"By the Light!" someone gasped.

"You'll make a living for yourself with that bow in Aurënen," Nyal laughed. "Archery's a betting sport here."

Objects of some sort were changing hands around the circle of onlookers.

Several men showed Alec their quivers, where masses of small ornaments strung on thongs hung from bosses set into the sides. Some were carved from stone or wood, others cast in metal or fashioned from animal teeth and bright feathers.

"These are *shatta,* betting trophies, used only by archers," Nyal explained, plucking one made of bear claws from his own considerable collection and tying it onto Alec's quiver strap. "There, that shot of yours should earn you something. This marks you as a challenger."

"You may not be able to lift that quiver of yours before we head home again, Sir Alec," said Nikides. "If they let us bet for drinks, I'll be laying my luck on you every time."

Alec accepted the praise with a shy grin. His shooting was one of the few things he'd been proud of growing up, though more for the success it had brought him as a hunter.

As he returned to the spring to drink, he felt glad of those skills again. In patches of soft ground around the spring he saw the marks of panther and wolves, together with several larger tracks he didn't recognize.

"Just as well we missed him," Seregil remarked.

Looking where his friend pointed, Alec saw a splayed, three-toed print twice the length of his foot.

"A dragon?"

"Yes, and of the dangerous size."

Alec placed his hand in the track, noting the deep imprint of talons at the end of each toe. "What happens if we meet one of these while we're blindfolded?" he asked, frowning.

Seregil's impassive shrug was less than reassuring.

The trail grew narrower still from here, barely wide enough in places for a horse to pass. Alec was pondering what it must be like to venture through here in the winter when something landed on the turned-back hood of his cloak. He reached back, expecting to find a clump of dirt. Instead, something slithered elusively beneath his fingertips.

"There's something on me," he hissed, praying to Dalna that whatever it was wasn't poisonous.

"Hold still," Seregil cautioned, dismounting.

Easier said than done, Alec thought as whatever it was scrambled up through his hair. The tickle of tiny claws assured him that it wasn't a serpent. He kicked a foot free of the stirrup, and Seregil stepped in and pulled himself up for a closer view.

"By the Light!" he called out in Aurënfaie, clearly delighted by what he'd found. "First dragon!"

The cry was taken up by the Aurënfaie, and those that could crowded around to see.

"A dragon?" Alec turned his head to see.

"A fingerling. Careful now." Seregil gently disentangled it and placed it in Alec's cupped hands.

The little creature looked like a manuscript illustration come to life. Perfectly proportioned in every respect, it was scarcely five inches long, with batlike wings so delicate he could see the shadow of his fingers through the stretched membranes. Its golden eyes had slitted pupils. Spiky whiskers fringed its narrow jaws. The only disappointment was the color; from snout to tail, it was mottled brown like a toad.

"You're the luckbringer today," Riagil told him, emerging from the crowd of soldiers with Amali, Klia, and Thero.

"It is a custom we have, going over the pass," Amali told him, smiling. "The first traveler to be touched so by a dragon is the luckbringer, and anyone who touches you before it flies away shares the luck."

Alec felt a bit self-conscious as the others crowded around to touch his leg. The fingerling seemed in no hurry to go. Wrapping its whip-end of tail around his thumb, it poked its bristly head under the edge of his sleeve as if investigating a potential cave. Its soft belly was fever-hot against his palm.

Klia reached up to stroke the dragon's back. "I thought they'd be more colorful."

"The laws don't extend to hawks and foxes," said Seregil. "These little ones take on the color of their surroundings to hide. Even so, only a few survive, which is probably a good thing. Otherwise we'd be hip deep in dragons."

Alec's little passenger rode with him for over an hour, exploring the folds of his cloak, burrowing through his long hair, and resisting all efforts to be passed to anyone else. Suddenly, however, it scrambled around to his left shoulder and bit him on the earlobe.

Alec let out a yelp of pain and it fluttered away, clutching a few strands of his hair in its claws.

Their Aurënfaie escorts found this highly amusing.

"It's off to make itself a golden nest," Vanos declared.

"A kiss to welcome you home, Kalosi!" said another, thumping him on the shoulder.

"It stings like snakebite!" Touching his ear, Alec felt the first signs of swelling and swore.

Vanos produced a glazed vial from a pouch slung from his belt and tapped out a few drops of viscous blue liquid.

"Don't worry, the venom's not much worse than a hornet's at that size," he said, holding out his finger. "This is *lissik*. It takes away the pain and heals the wound faster."

"It's also pigmented to permanently color the teeth marks, like a tattoo," Seregil said behind him. "Such marks are highly prized."

Alec hesitated, thinking of the ramifications of such an unusual distinguishing mark for someone in his profession.

"Should I?" he asked Seregil in Skalan.

"It would be an insult not to."

Alec gave a slight nod.

"There you are," Vanos said, dabbing lissik on the wound. It was oily and smelled bitter, but it cooled the burning instantly. "That'll be a real beauty mark once it heals."

"Not that he needs one," said another 'faie, giving Alec a friendly wink as he showed him a similar mark at the base of his right thumb.

"Your earlobe looks like a grape," Thero observed. "Odd that the creature took such a dislike to you."

"Actually, a fingerling's bite is considered a sign of Aura's favor," said Nyal. "If that little one survives, it will know Alec and all his descendants."

Other riders showed off their own marks of honor on hands and necks. One named Syli laughed as he proudly displayed three on each hand. "Either I am greatly loved by Aura, or I taste good."

"Known to a dragon, eh?" Beka let out a whistle of admiration. "That could be useful."

"To the dragon, perhaps," Seregil remarked.

They made camp at a way station that stood at the meeting of two trails. It was unlike any structure Alec had seen in Aurënen so far. The squat, round tower was at least eighty feet in diameter and had been built into the uneven rocks that rose around it like a mud swallow's nest. It was topped with a conical roof of thick, dirty felt and entered by a sturdy wooden ramp leading up to a door halfway up the tower. A few dark-eyed children watched their approach from the top of a low stone wall that fronted it. Others could be seen behind them, laughing as they chased black goats and each other up the tower ramp. A woman appeared at the door, then came out accompanied by two men.

"Dravnians?" asked Thero.

"They are, aren't they?" said Alec, who'd recognized them from Seregil's stories. Shorter than the 'faie, and more heavily built, they had black, almond-shaped eyes, bowlegs, and coarse black hair slicked back with grease. Their sheepskin clothing was richly decorated with colorful beading, animal teeth of various types, and painted designs. "I didn't expect to see them this far east."

"They wander the whole Ashek range," Seregil told him. "These mountains are their home; no one knows more about how to survive the snows. This traveler's lodge has stood here for centuries and probably will forever, with the occasional new roof. The 'faie share the use of it with the local tribes."

Though Alec couldn't understand their language, there was no mistaking the welcoming smiles the Dravnians gave Riagil and the others. Tethering their horses in the stone enclosure, they all trooped up the ramp.

The upper floor was a single large room with a smoke hole in the center of the floor. Stone stairs followed the curve of the wall down to the lower room, which doubled as hearth room and byre. More Dravnians were at work down there, mucking out from the winter. One of the younger woman waved up at them, flashing a shy smile.

"That custom you told us about, of having to sleep with their daughters—?" Thero asked nervously, wrinkling his nose at the pungent odors wafting up from below. Seregil grinned. "Only at a home hearth. It's not expected here, though I'm sure they'd be flattered if you offered."

The girl waved again, and Thero retreated quickly, his wizard's celibacy evidently safe for the moment.

The evening passed in relative comfort, though the frequent howls that drifted to them on the night wind made Alec and the others doubly grateful for the tower's thick walls and stout door. The Dravnians, he learned, called this time of year the end of the hungry season.

Though stark by Aurënfaie standards, the tower was warm and the company good. They traded some of their bread for Dravnian cheese and ended up making a communal meal of it. The evening was passed trading tales and news, with Nyal and Seregil interpreting for the Skalans.

After several hours, the Ra'basi excused himself and went outside for a breath of air. A few moments later Seregil did the same, giving Alec the surreptitious signal to follow in a moment. Assuming he was offering a brief moment of privacy, Alec counted to twenty, then slipped out after him.

But Seregil had something else in mind. Just outside the door he touched Alec's arm and motioned toward two dark figures barely visible up the trail. "Nyal and Amali," he whispered. "She went out a few minutes ago and he followed."

Alec watched the pair disappear around a bend in the trail. "Should we follow them?"

"Too risky; no cover and these rocks echo every sound. We'll just sit here and see how long they're gone."

Walking down the ramp, they sat down on a large flat rock by the enclosure wall. Above them, sudden laughter rang out from the doorway.

They must have found themselves another interpreter, thought Alec. A moment later he heard Urien strike up a soldier's ballad.

Staring out into the darkness, Alec tried without success to gauge his companion's mood. The further they ventured into Aurënen, the more distant Seregil became, as if he were listening ever more closely to some inner voice only he could hear.

"How come you never told me about getting captured by the Hâzadriëlfaie?" he asked at last.

Seregil laughed softly. "Because it never happened, at least not to me. I heard the story from another exile. The bit about collecting the legends was true, and I was homesick enough to consider making the journey, but the man to whom the tale belongs talked me out of it, just as I did you once, if you recall."

"So you do think Nyal's a spy?"

"He's a listener. And I don't like how quickly he's cozied up to Beka. If you were a spy, what better place to be than at the side of Klia's protector?"

"So you gave him a false story?"

"And now we wait to see if it resurfaces, and where."

Alec sighed. "Will you say anything to Klia?"

Seregil shrugged. "There's nothing to report yet. I'm more worried about Beka just now. If he does turn out to be a spy, it will reflect badly on her."

"All right then, but I still think you're wrong." *Hope you're wrong,* he amended silently.

They'd kept watch for perhaps half an hour when they heard the sound of returning footsteps in the darkness. Moving into the deeper shadow below the ramp, they watched as Nyal reappeared supporting Amali with one arm. Their heads were close together in conversation, and neither seemed to notice Alec and Seregil in the shadows.

"Then you'll say nothing?" Alec overheard her whisper to Nyal.

"Of course not, but I must question the wisdom of your silence," he replied, sounding worried.

"It is my wish." Releasing his arm, she walked up the ramp.

Nyal watched her go, then wandered back up the trail alone, apparently lost in thought.

Seregil's hand closed over Alec's. "Well, well," he whispered. "Secrets in the dark. How interesting."

"We still have nothing. The Akhendi support Klia."

Seregil frowned. "And the Ra'basi may not."

"I still say you're jumping at shadows."

"What? Alec, wait!" Seregil hissed.

But Alec was already gone, ambling noisily up the trail. Stones crunched and tinkled under his boots. He hummed aloud for good measure.

He found the interpreter sitting on a rock beside the trail, looking up at the stars.

"Who's that?" Alec called out, as if startled to find someone there.

"Alec?" Nyal jumped to his feet.

Guiltily? Alec wondered, unable to make out the man's expression at this distance.

"Oh, there you are!" Alec said lightly, striding up to him. "Did the Dravnians wear you out already? There are stories going untold for lack of you."

Nyal chuckled, his voice deep and rich in the darkness. "They'll go on all night whether we understand them or not. Seregil's throat must be raw by now, left alone with them so long. What are you doing out here all alone?"

"Had to tap the hogshead," Alec said, patting the lacings of his breeches.

Nyal looked blank for a moment, then broke into a broad grin. "Piss, you mean?"

"Yes." Alec turned aside to make good his claim.

Nyal chuckled behind him. "Even when you speak my own tongue, you Skalans are not always easy to understand. Especially the women." He paused. "Beka Cavish is your friend, isn't she?"

"A good friend," Alec replied.

"Has she a man of her own?"

Still facing away, Alec heard the hope in the man's voice and felt an irrational twinge of jealousy.

His own fleeting attraction to Beka in the early days of their friendship had been no match for her determination to follow a military career. No doubt the difference in their ages had played a larger part in her mind than his, too. Nyal, on the other hand, was man-grown and handsome besides. There was no faulting Beka's choice on that account.

"No, no man of her own." Tugging his breeches closed, Alec turned to find Nyal still smiling at him. The man was either a consummate actor or more guileless than Seregil cared to believe. "Don't tell me you fancy her?"

Nyal spread his hands, and Alec suspected he was blushing. "I admire her very much."

Alec hesitated, knowing Seregil would disapprove of what he was about to do. Stepping closer to the 'faie, he looked him in the eye and said gravely, "Beka admires you, too. You asked if I'm her friend. I am, and her almost-brother as well. You understand? Good, then as her almost-brother, I'll tell you that I like you, too, though I don't know you well. Are you a man she can trust?"

The Ra'basi squared his shoulders and made him a respectful bow. "I am a man of honor, Alec í Amasa. I would bring no harm to your almost-sister."

Alec stifled an undignified chortle and clapped Nyal on the shoulder. "Then why don't you go and keep her company?"

Grinning, Nyal strode off toward the tower. Alec hoped the man's celebrated hearing wasn't acute enough to hear his own strangled snort of laughter. Another of a more nervous variety escaped as he stopped to think what his fate would likely be if Beka ever learned that he'd appointed himself the defender of her honor. He hoped the talkative Ra'basi had enough discretion to keep his mouth shut about their little chat. He'd just started back when Seregil emerged from the shadows.

"I thought you said it was too risky to sneak up on people out here?" Alec gasped, startled by his sudden appearance.

"Not with all the noise you were making," Seregil retorted curtly.

"Then you heard?"

"Yes, and you're either brilliant or a damn fool!"

"Let's hope it's the former. I don't know what he was up to with Amali, but if he's not really love-struck for Beka, then I am a fool."

"Ah!" Seregil held up an accusing finger. "But he didn't happen to mention the good lady Amali, now did he?"

"He wouldn't, would he? We heard him promise to keep silent about something."

"Clearly a man of honor, your Ra'basi friend," Seregil observed dryly. "To his credit, I think you're right, at least about his feelings for Beka. Let's go keep an eye on him."

It was clearly Beka who occupied the interpreter's thoughts that night and the following morning, although she continued to greet his attentions with apparent bemusement.

The second day was much the same as the first. The air grew colder, and when the breeze shifted, Alec felt the chill kiss of glacial air on the back of his neck. Just after midday, the pitch of the trail begin to drop. Riding blind, Alec found it hard not to doze off. His chin was slowly sinking on his breast when a sudden warm gust of damp, acrid mist brought him awake.

"What is that?" he asked, wrinkling his nose.

"Dragon breath!" an Aurënfaie exclaimed.

He was already grasping the edge of the blindfold when someone gripped his wrist. Laughter broke out around them.

"A joke, Alec," his escort assured him, sounding like he was sharing in it. "It's just a hot spring. There are lots of them on this side of the mountains, and some smell even worse than this."

Alec smelled the strange odor again just as the hated blindfolds finally came off later that afternoon.

A few miles ahead, an ice field hung in a valley high between two peaks. The pass was wider here, and in places along its sloping sides clouds of white steam boiled from the ground, or wafted off the faces of little pools between the rocks.

Below lay a small tarn, its brilliant blue surface shimmering like a shard of Ylani porcelain beneath a shifting pall of vapor. Deep azure at its center, the waters gradually lightened to a pale turquoise toward the shore, where the rocks were a dull yellow. Rocky ground surrounded it, devoid of vegetation. A line of darker stone ran down the slope to the water's edge and beyond, like a stain.

"One of your 'mirrors of the sky'?" asked Alec.

"Yes," said Seregil. "It's the largest hot spring along this trail, a very sacred spot."

"Why is that?"

Seregil smiled. "That's Amali's tale to tell. We're in Akhendi fai'thast now."

They made camp upwind of the tarn. It was warm in the little vale; the ground gave off heat they could feel through the soles of their boots. The foul odor was stronger here, too, like eggs gone bad. The yellow coloration Alec had noted earlier turned out to be a crusty rime built up just above the waterline.

"Sulfur," Thero said, taking a pinch between his fingers and igniting it in a puff of orange flame.

Despite the smell, most of the 'faie were already stripping off to bathe in it. Amali ä Yassara dipped up a cupful and presented it to Klia.

"Odd sort of spot to call sacred, don't you think?" asked Alec, eyeing the gently roiling water distrustfully. "It can't be poison, though. Everyone's drinking it."

Testing the water, he found it hot as a bath. He scooped up a small amount in one cupped palm and took a sip. It was an effort to swallow; the flat, metallic flavor was not something that invited deep drinking.

"A mineral spring!" Thero noted, wiping his lips—though not discreetly enough to escape Amali's notice.

"You are perhaps wondering why we revere such a place?" she asked, laughing at the wizard's expression. "I will show you in a little while. In the meantime, you all should bathe, especially you, Alec í Amasa. The waters are healing and would do that ear of yours good."

"Is my talímenios welcome, as well?" Alec asked, keeping his tone respectful even as his gut tightened.

Amali colored, but shook her head. "That I cannot grant."

"Then I thank you for the offer." He gave her a slight bow and strolled off to the cluster of tents nearby. Seregil followed.

"You didn't have to do that!"

"Yes, I did. I can't stand them all fussing over me while they slap you down at every opportunity."

Seregil pulled him to a halt. "They aren't doing it to insult me, you damn fool!" he whispered angrily. "I brought this on myself a long time ago. You're here for Klia, not me. Any insult you offer to our hosts reflects on her."

Alec stared at him a moment, hating the resignation that underlay his friend's hard words. "I'll try to keep that in mind," he mumbled, pulling his pack down from the saddle and carrying it into the tent assigned to them. He waited, expecting Seregil to come in. When he didn't, Alec looked out through the tent flaps and saw him back at the water's edge, watching the others swim.

. . .

Seregil kept up his air of cordial distance, speaking little but making no effort to retreat from the main company. When Amali invited the Skalans to walk along the shore that evening, he joined in without comment or apology.

She led them up to the outcropping of dark stone. Bulging up from the surrounding stone and skree, it spread like an ink stain to the edge of the lake.

"Look closely," she told them, running her hand over a curving slab.

Examining it, Alec saw nothing out of the ordinary except the peculiar smoothness of the weathering in places.

"It's skin!" Thero exclaimed from the other side of an upthrust slab. "Or at least, it was. And here's the ridge of a spine. By the Light, was this a dragon? It must have been over three hundred feet long, if we're seeing all that there was of it."

"Then it's true what I've read," Klia mused, climbing around to where the crumbling edge of what might have been a wing bone jutted from the ground. "Dragons do turn to stone when they die."

"This one did," Amali replied. "But it is the only one of this size ever found. How they die, just as how they are born, remains a mystery. The little ones appear; the great ones disappear. But this place, called Vhadä'nakori, is sacred because of this creature, so drink deeply, sleep well, and attend carefully to your dreams. In a few days, we will be in Sarikali."

Seregil knew the Akhendi woman had not meant to include him in her invitation at the Vhadä'nakori; she'd been unfailingly distant since Gedre. Perhaps her ill will accounted for his poor sleep that night.

Curled beside Alec in the tent they shared with Torsin and Thero, he tossed restlessly through a dream of uncommon vividness, even without aid of the waters.

It began like so many of his nightmares had over the past two years. He stood again in his old sitting room at the Cockerel, but this time there were no mutilated corpses, no heads gummed in their own blood on the mantelpiece chattering accusations at him.

Instead, it was as he remembered it from happier days. The cluttered tables, the piles of books, the tools laid out on the workbench beneath the window—everything was just as it should be. Turning to the corner by the fireplace, however, he found it empty. Alec's narrow cot was gone.

Puzzled, Seregil walked to the door of his bedchamber. Opening it, he found himself instead in his childhood room at Bôkthersa. The details here were equally clear and achingly familiar—the cool play of leaf shadow on the wall above his bed, the rack of practice swords near the door, the rich colors of the corner screen in the corner—painted by the mother he'd never known. Toys long since lost or packed away were there, too, as if someone had collected all of his most treasured belongings and laid them out for his return.

The only discordant element were the delicate glass orbs strewn across the bed. He hadn't noticed these when he'd first come in.

He was taken by their beauty. Some were tiny, others the size of his fist, and they gleamed like jewels, multihued and translucent. He didn't recognize them, but in the strange way of dreams, knew that these, too, were his.

As he stood there, smoke suddenly seeped up through the floorboards around him. He could feel heat through the soles of his boots and hear the angry crackle of flames from below.

His first thought was to save the orbs. Try as he might, though, a few always slipped away and he had to stop and pick them up again. Looking around frantically, he knew that he couldn't save everything; the fire was bursting up through the floor in earnest now, licking at the corners of the room.

He knew he should run and warn Adzriel. He longed to save familiar mementos but could not decide what to take, what to sacrifice. And all this time, he was still trying to gather the glistening spheres. Looking down, he saw that some had turned to iron and threatened to smash the more fragile ones. Others were filled with smoke or liquid. Confused and frightened, he stood helpless as smoke boiled up around him, blotting out the light—

Seregil woke drenched in sweat, with his heart trying to hammer its way out of his chest. It was still dark, but he had no intention of sleeping again in this place. Finding his clothes, he slipped out.

The stars were still bright enough to cast faint shadows. Dressing quickly, he climbed up to the dragon stones overlooking the water.

"Aura Lightbearer, send me insight," he whispered, stretching out on his back to wait for dawn.

"Welcome home, Korit's son," a strange little voice replied, close to his ear.

Seregil looked around in surprise. No one was there. Leaning over the edge of the rock, he peered underneath. A pair of shining yellow eyes looked back at him, then tilted as the creature moved its head.

"Are you khtir'bai?" asked Seregil.

The eyes tilted in the other direction. "Yes, child of Aura. Do you know me?"

"Should I, Honored One?" Seregil had encountered only one such being, the khtir'bai of an aunt who'd taken the form of a white bear. This creature was far too small.

"Perhaps," the voice told him. "You have much to do, son of Korit."

"Will I ever be called that again?" Seregil asked as it finally sank in that the khtir'bai had addressed him by his true name.

"We shall see." The eyes blinked and were gone.

Seregil held his breath, listening, but no sound came from under the rock. He lay back again, staring up at the stars as he pondered this new turn of events.

A few minutes later he caught the soft scuff of bare feet on stone. Sitting up, he saw Alec climbing up to join him.

"You should have come sooner. There was a khtir'bai under there, one who knew my name."

Alec's look of disappointment was almost comical. "What did it look like?"

"It was just a voice in the dark, but it welcomed me home."

Alec sat down next to him. "At least someone has. Couldn't you sleep?"

Seregil told Alec all he could recall of his dream: the glass balls, the flames, the childhood memories. Alec listened quietly, gazing out across the mist-covered water.

"You've always claimed to have no magic, but your dreams—!" Alec said when he'd finished. "Remember those visions you had before we found Mardus?"

"Before he found us, you mean? The warnings I didn't understand until it was too late? A lot of good that did us."

"Maybe you're not supposed to do anything about them. Maybe you're just supposed to be ready."

Seregil sighed, thinking again of the khtir'bai's words. *You have much to do, son of Korit.* "No, this was different. Just a dream. What about you, talí? Any great revelations?"

"I wouldn't call it that. I dreamt about being aboard Mardus's ship with Thero, only when Thero turned around, he was you and you were weeping. Then the ship sailed over a waterfall and into a tunnel and that was the end of it. I don't think I'd make much of an oracle."

Seregil chuckled softly. "Or a navigator, from the sound of it. Well, they say all answers can be found at Sarikali. Perhaps we'll turn up a few there. How's the ear?"

Alec fingered the swollen skin and winced. "My whole neck hurts. I should have brought the lissik."

"Come on, I know something even better." Rising, Seregil pulled Alec to his feet and led him down to the water's edge. "Get in and give it a good soak."

"No. I already told you—"

"Who's to know?" Seregil challenged with a wink. "Go on now, before I toss you in. The ride ahead of us will be uncomfortable enough. Take what healing you can get."

"Well, did anyone else dream last night?" Klia asked as they stood around the morning fire a few hours later. "I couldn't recall a thing when I woke up, but I never do."

"Neither did I," said Beka, clearly disappointed.

None of the Skalans had anything to report, as it turned out.

"Perhaps the magic doesn't work for Tír?" Alec offered, still pondering his own strange dream.

When Thero emerged at last from the tent, however, he knew he was going to have to reevaluate his theory. The young wizard looked too dark under the eyes to have rested well.

"Bad dreams?" asked Seregil.

Thero gazed out over the pool, looking rather perplexed. "I dreamed of drowning here, with the moon shining in my eyes so brightly it hurt, even through the water. And all the while I could hear someone singing 'home, home, home.' "

"You're a wizard," Amali said, overhearing. "Your magic came from Aurënen, so perhaps you are home, in a sense."

"Thank you, lady," Thero said. "That is a more positive interpretation than I was able to come to. It felt very much like a dream of death to me."

"And yet does not water also signify birth among your people?" she asked, strolling away.

Below the Vhadä'nakori, the trail grew steeper and the Skalans had to ride most of the morning blindfolded. Chewing doggedly on a slice of ginger, Alec clung on with thighs and hands; at times it felt as if the horse were about to walk out from under him.

After a few miles of this torture, he swallowed his pride and let an Akhendi named Tael mount in front of him and take the reins. Judging by the muttered epithets he heard on all sides, he wasn't the only one to give in. Even with this help, however, his back and thighs were soon aching again as he clung on behind his guide.

Luckily, his torment was short-lived. Reaching a level patch of ground, the column halted and the hated blindfolds were removed.

Alec blinked, then let out a whistle.

Far below, a rolling green vista dotted with scattered lakes and netted with rivers stretched toward lowlands on the southern horizon.

"So green it hurts your eyes," Thero murmured.

They came down into the foothills through groves of flowering trees so dense it seemed as if they were riding through clouds. Beyond this, a packed-earth road led through the thick forests of Akhendi fai'thast.

Alec's fingertips ached for the pull of a bowstring. Sunlight slanted through the towering trees, illuminating little glades where herds of deer grazed. Flocks of game birds called *kutka* darted across the trail like startled chickens.

"Doesn't anyone hunt here?" he asked Tael.

The Akhendi shrugged. "Aura is bountiful to those who take only what they need."

The trail met a broader road that led through small, scattered villages. People gathered by the road, staring and waving at the Skalans and calling out to Amali, who was clearly well loved. Men, women, and children alike wore various versions of the familiar tunic and trousers, which some had augmented with colorful openwork shawls or sashes fashioned like fisherman's nets, but elaborate as lace.

"I can't tell the men from the women," said Minál.

"I assure you, rider, those who need to can tell the difference!" Nyal told him, eliciting a round of laughter from his companions.

The dwellings here were similar in design to those at Gedre, but built of wood instead of stone. Many had open-sided sheds nearby, where their owners plied their trades. From what Alec could make out from the road, woodworking was a common occupation in this part of the country.

Many of the byways that branched off from the main road looked disused and overgrown, he noticed. In the larger villages, many houses stood empty.

Riding up beside Riagil and Amali, he asked, "My lady, this was a trade road once, wasn't it?"

"Yes, one of the busiest. Our marketplaces saw goods from every corner of Aurënen, the Three Lands, and beyond. Our inns were always filled with traders. But now those same traders go downriver to Bry'kha, or overland to Virésse. Many of our people have moved closer to the routes, even gone to other fai'thasts."

She shook her head sadly. "The village I grew up in stands empty now. It is a shameful thing for any 'faie to be forced against her will to leave the place her family lived in for generations out of mind, to walk away from the house of her ancestors. It has brought our clan ill luck.

"It is even more difficult for my husband, both as our khirnari and as one who has lived so long and remembers what the Akhendi once were. I assure you, he will do all in his power to support your lady's mission, as will I."

Alec bowed, wondering again what she and Nyal had been doing together on that dark trail in the mountains.

Anxious as she was to see Sarikali, Beka found herself wishing they could stay longer in Akhendi. This country reminded her of the rolling forests she'd roamed as a girl, and of the peaceful life she'd taken for granted.

They stopped for the night in one of the larger villages, and their arrival created quite a stir, if a quiet one at first. A few at a time, villagers gathered to greet Amali and gawk at the Tírfaie visitors. Before long, the Skalans were surrounded by a silent, staring throng.

"We're as much creatures of legend here as the 'faie are in the northlands," Beka told her riders. "Come on. Give them a smile!"

A small girl was the first to approach. Pulling free of her mother's hand, she marched up to Sergeant Braknil and stared with unabashed curiosity at his grizzled beard. The old veteran returned the stare with amusement, then presented his chin for closer inspection. The girl dug her fingers into it and burst out giggling. At this, other children came forward, touching beards, clothing, and weapon hilts with delighted wonder. The adults followed, and anyone who spoke both languages soon had their hands full translating questions back and forth.

Beka's hair and freckles were the focus of especially intent curiosity. Pulling her braid loose, she shook out her hair and sat grinning as children and adults gently lifted the strands to see the coppery play of sunlight through them. Looking up, she saw Nyal watching her over the heads of the others, his leaf-and-water eyes tilted up at the corners with silent amusement. He winked and she looked quickly away as her cheeks went warm. Turning, she found herself face-to-face with the little girl who'd walked so boldly up to Braknil, who was now accompanied by a young man about Alec's age.

The child pointed to Beka and said something about "making."

Beka shook her head, showing that she didn't understand.

The young man held out his hand, showing her a bundle of colorful leather thongs. He covered them with his other hand, rubbed his palms together, then presented her with an intricately braided bracelet with loose strands at each end for tying.

"Chypta," she said, delighted. She'd watched Seregil do this sort of sleight of hand most of her life.

He gestured that he was not finished. Taking it back from her, he held it by one end and pulled it slowly through the fingers of his other hand. When he was done, a small wooden frog dangled from the middle of the weave.

The little girl tied it around Beka's left wrist, then touched a hand to her scabbard and the bruise on her forehead, talking excitedly.

"It's a charm to help wounds heal," explained Seregil, who'd wandered over with Alec. "She says she's never seen a woman soldier before, but she can tell you are very brave and so probably get hurt a lot. She's not old enough to make charms herself yet, so her cousin here obliged, but the gift was her idea."

"Chypta!" Beka said again, touched by the gift. "Hold on a minute, I want to give her something, too. Damn, what have I got with me?"

Rummaging in her pouch, she found a sack of fancy gaming stones she'd bought in Mycena, jasper lozenges inlaid with silver. "For you," she said in Aurënfaie, placing one in the child's hand.

The little girl clasped the piece in her fist and gave Beka a kiss on the cheek.

"And thank you." Beka looked up at the cousin, doubtful that he'd be impressed by such a reward.

He leaned down and touched a finger to his cheek. Beka took the hint and gave him a kiss. Laughing, he led the little girl away.

"Did you see that performance?" Beka asked Seregil, admiring the bracelet. "It reminds me of tricks you used to do for us after supper."

"What you just saw was magic, not sleight of hand. So is the charm, though not a very powerful sort. The Akhendi are known for their skill with charm making and weaving."

"I thought it was just a trinket! I should have made her a better gift."

Seregil grinned. "You saw her face. She'll be showing that bakshi stone to her great-grandchildren, a gift from a sword-carrying Tír-faie woman with hair the color of—let's see, what would the proper poetic simile be? Ah, yes, bloody copper!"

Beka grimaced comically. "I hope she comes up with something better than that."

Just then a young woman touched Alec on the sleeve and performed a similar trick, producing a bracelet with three red beads worked into it. He thanked her, asked some questions, then laughed and pointed to Seregil.

"What was that all about?" asked Beka.

"It's a love charm," Seregil explained. "He told her that he doesn't really need one of those."

The girl gave some teasing answer, arching a brow coyly in Seregil's direction, then passed the bracelet through her hand again. The beads disappeared, replaced by a dangling wooden bird carved from pale wood.

"That's more like it," Alec said. "This one warns if someone's having evil thoughts about me."

"Perhaps I should get one of those before I face the Iia'sidra again," Seregil murmured.

"What's this?" Beka asked, noticing what appeared to be a polished cherry pit hanging from a beaded thread in Seregil's hair.

"It's supposed to keep lies from my dreams."

Alec exchanged an odd look with his friend, and Beka felt a twinge of envy. There were secrets between these two she knew she'd never share, just as there were between Seregil and her father. Not for the first time, she wished regretfully that Nysander had lived long enough to induct her as a Watcher, too.

Meanwhile, her riders had gotten into the spirit of things. With

Nyal's help, gifts and questions were still being exchanged and everyone was sporting a charm or two. Nikides was flirting with several women at once, and Braknil was playing grandfather to a circle of children, shaking his beard and pulling coppers from their ears.

"It won't all be this easy, will it?" Beka said, watching one of the village elders present Klia with a necklace.

Seregil sighed. "No, it won't."

10
THE HEART OF THE JEWEL

"Lady Amali seems to have taken quite a liking to Klia," Alec observed, watching the two women laughing over some shared exchange as they set out again the next morning.

"I've noticed that," Seregil replied quietly. He glanced around quickly, no doubt making certain that Nyal was safely out of earshot. "They're of an age to be friends. She's much younger than her husband. She's his third wife, according to our Ra'basi friend."

"So you find him useful after all?"

"I find everyone useful," Seregil said with a sly grin. "That doesn't mean I trust them. I haven't seen him sneak off with her again, though. Have you?"

"No, and I've been watching. She's civil to him, but they seldom speak."

"We'll have to keep an eye on them in Sarikali, see if they seek each other out. The young wife of an aging husband, and Nyal such a handsome, entertaining fellow—it could be interesting."

Reaching a broad, swift river, they followed it south through ever deepening forest for the rest of the day. Villages grew scarcer, and game more plentiful—and at times peculiar.

Herds of black deer no bigger than dogs were common in marshy bends of the river, where they grazed on mallow shoots and water lilies torn from the mud.

There were bears as well, the first Alec had seen since leaving his mountain homeland. But these were brown rather than black, and bore the white crescent of Aura across their breasts. Strangest and most pleasing of all, however, were the little grey tree-dwellers called *pories*. The first of them appeared just after midday, but soon they seemed to be everywhere, common as squirrels.

About the size of a newborn child, the pories had flat, catlike faces large, mobile ears, and long, black-ringed tails that gyrated wildly behind them as they leapt among the branches with clever, grasping paws.

A few miles later, the pories disappeared as abruptly as they'd come. Midafternoon shadows were weaving themselves beneath the trees when the travelers reached a wide fork in the river. As if sundered by the parting of the waters, the forest opened up to either side, affording a clear view across a broad, rolling valley beyond.

"Welcome to Sarikali," Seregil said, and something in his voice made Alec turn to look at him.

A blend of fierce pride and reverence seemed to transform the man for an instant, making the Skalan coat he wore look as ill suited as mummer's garb.

Alec saw the same expression mirrored in other Aurënfaie faces, as if their very souls shone in their eyes. Exile or not, Seregil was among his own. Ever the wanderer, Alec envied him a little.

"Welcome, my friends!" cried Riagil. "Welcome to Sarikali!"

"I thought there was a city," Beka said, shading her eyes.

Alec did the same, wondering if some magic like that guarding the high passes in the mountains was at work. There were no signs of habitation that he could see within the embrace of the two rivers.

Seregil grinned. "What's the matter, don't you see it?"

A broad stone bridge arched across the narrower of the two branches, allowing riders to cross four abreast.

The steel helmets of Urgazhi Turma shone like chased silver in the slanting afternoon light, and steel and chain mail glinted beneath their embroidered tabards. Riding at their head, Klia was resplendent in wine-dark velvet and heavy jeweled ornaments. Polished rubies glowed in the large golden brooches that pinned her riding mantle at the shoulders and in the golden girdle of her gown. She also wore all the Aurënfaie gift jewelry she'd received, even the humble warding charms. Though she'd put aside armor for the occasion, her sword hung at her side in a burnished scabbard worked with gold.

Once across the river, Riagil led them toward a dark, rambling hillock several miles off. There was something odd about the shape of it, thought Alec. As they drew nearer, it looked stranger still.

"That's Sarikali, isn't it?" he said, pointing ahead. "But it's a ruins."

"Not exactly," said Seregil.

The city's dark tiered buildings and thick towers appeared to draw themselves out of the ground. Masses of ivy and creepers growing thickly up the stonework reinforced the illusion that the place had not been built by hands but erupted from the earth. Like a great stone in the river of time, Sarakali stood steadfast and immutable.

The closer Seregil came to Sarikali, the more the long years in Skala seemed to fade away. The one dark memory he had of the city, ugly as it was, could not efface the joy he'd always associated with this place.

Most of his visits had been in festival times, when the clans gathered to populate its streets and chambers. Banners and strings of kites festooned the streets of every *tupa,* the section of the city each clan traditionally used when visiting. In the open-air marketplaces one could find goods from every corner of Aurënen and beyond. Outside the city, colorful pavilions would sprinkle the level ground like great summer flowers; bright flags and painted poles marked out racetracks and archery lists. The air would be filled with magic and music and the smells of exotic foods to be tracked down and sampled.

Today the only signs of habitation were a few flocks of sheep and cattle grazing on the plain.

"You'd think the Iia'sidra would come out to meet the princess," Thero remarked disapprovingly in Skalan.

"I was just thinking the same." Alec eyed the place dubiously.

"That would give status," said Seregil. "They retain it by having her come to them. It's all part of the game."

.   .   .

Their Aurënfaie escort dropped back when they reached the city's edge, and Urgazhi Turma formed up into two mounted ranks, flanking Klia.

Turning to Riagil and Amali, Klia bowed in the saddle. "Thank you both for your hospitality and guidance."

Amali nudged her mount forward and clasped hands with Klia. "I wish you success. The blessings of Aura be with you!"

She and Riagil rode off, disappearing from sight with their respective riders among the dark buildings.

"Well, then," Klia said, squaring her shoulders. "It's up to us to make an entrance, my friends. Let's show them the queen's best. Seregil, you're my guide from here."

No curtain walls shielded the city; it had no gates, no guards. Instead, open ways paved with springy turf cut into the jumbled mass of the place like rambling fissures weathered through a mountain by a thousand years of rain. Its street were empty, the arched windows of it towers blank as dead eyes.

"I didn't expect it to be so empty," Alec whispered as they continued along a broad, winding concourse.

"It's different when the clans gather for the festivals," Seregil told him. "By the Light, I'd forgotten how beautiful it is!"

Beautiful? Alec thought. Eerie was more like it, and a little oppressive.

Evidently he was not the only one to feel it. Behind him, he could hear the Urgazhi plying Nyal with questions, and the steady murmur of the interpreter's replies.

Smooth walls of dark green stone etched with bands of complex designs rose on all sides. There were no recognizable figures; no carved animals, gods, or people. Instead, the intricate patterns seemed to fold and knot themselves into greater interconnected patterns that drew the eye to a single central point or away along lines of rhythmically repeated shapes and symbols.

The turf gave beneath their horses' hooves, sending up the scent of crushed herbs and deadening the sound of their passing. The deeper they rode into the city, the more muted sounds became, underscoring the strangeness of the place. The wind brought the occasional distant crowing of a cock or the sound of voices, but just as quickly whipped them away.

Alec gradually became aware of an unsettling sensation creeping

over him, a sort of tingling on his skin and the hint of a headache between his eyes.

"I've come over all strange," said Beka, feeling it, too.

"It's magic," Thero said in an awed voice. "It feels like it's seeping from the very ground!"

"Don't worry; you'll get used to it soon," Seregil assured them.

As they rounded a corner, Alec saw a lone robed figure watching
them gravely from the lower window of a tower. Beneath the red-
and-black sen'gai and facial tattoos that marked him as a Khatme,
the man's expression was aloof and unwelcoming. Alec uneasily recalled a favorite saying his father had had: *How you come into a
place is how you go out.*

Seregil's initial joy at seeing Sarikali did not entirely cloud his perception. Clearly the isolationists still held the upper hand. Nonetheless, his pulse quickened as he felt the quicksilver play of exotic
energies across his skin. Childhood habit made him peer into the
shadows, hoping for a fleeting glimpse of the fabled Bash'wai.

Rounding a familiar corner, they came into the open again, at the
center of the city, and the breath caught in Seregil's throat.

Here lay the *Vhadäsoori,* a clear pool several hundred yards wide
and so deep that its waters remained black at high noon. The magic
was said to radiate from this spot, the most sacred ground in Aurënen. Here, at the heart of the Heart, oaths were given, alliances
forged, wizardly powers tested. A pledge sealed with a cup of the
pool's clear water was inviolable.

The pool was ringed by one hundred and twenty-one weathered
stone statues that stood a hundred yards or so back from the water's
edge. Neither the reddish-brown stone nor the carving style was to
be found anywhere else in the city, or in Aurënen beyond. Thirty
feet tall, and vaguely man-shaped, the statues were said to be a relic
of some people older than the Bash'wai. They towered and tilted
now above the crowd gathered outside the circle. Expectant faces
and sen'gai of every description formed a colorful mosaic against
the muted backdrop of dark stone.

"That's him," he heard someone whisper loudly, and guessed
they were talking of him.

The crowd parted quietly as he led Klia and the others to the edge
of the stone circle. Inside, he saw the eleven white-clad members of
the Iia'sidra waiting for them at the water's edge, flanking the Cup of
Aura on its low stone pedestal. Its long, crescent-shaped bowl,

carved from milky alabaster and set on a tall silver base, glowed softly in the late-afternoon sunlight.

With a sudden sharp pang, he recalled his father bringing him here as a small child; it was one of the few positive memories he had of the man. Legends differed as to the Cup's origins, Korit had explained. Some said it was the gift of Aura's dragon to the first Eleven; others claimed that the first wandering band of 'faie to discover the city had found the Cup on its pillar already. Whatever the case, it had been here time out of mind, unmarred by centuries of use and weather, a symbol of Aura's connection to the 'faie, and of their connection to one another.

A connection I was cut away from like a diseased branch from a tree, Seregil thought bitterly, focusing at last on the faces of the Iia'sidra. Nine of this Eleven had spared his life, but they had also sealed his humiliation.

His father had been khirnari then, and ready enough to see atui served by his only son's execution. Adzriel stood in his place now, though Seregil could not meet her eye yet. The other new member of the council was the khirnari of Goliníl, Elos í Orian. Ulan í Sathil stood nearby, dignified and staid, his lined, angular face betraying nothing.

Beside Adzriel stood Rhaish í Arlisandin of Akhendi. His long hair was whiter than Seregil recalled, his face more deeply lined. Here was one dependable ally, at least, if not a powerful one.

With an effort, Seregil forced himself to look back at his sister, who stood closest to the Cup. She saw him but looked quickly away. *—know that it is circumstance that prevents me, not coldness on my part.* As he stood here, outside the circle, the assurance she'd sent him could not fill the void in his chest. Fighting down the choking sensation that suddenly gripped him, he hastily looked away.

At Klia's signal, Seregil and the others dismounted. Unbuckling her sword belt, Klia passed it to Beka and strode into the stone circle with the assurance of a general. Seregil followed a few paces behind with Thero and Torsin.

The magic of Sarikali was strongest here. Beside him, Seregil saw Thero's pale eyes widen slightly as palpable waves of it enfolded them. Klia must have felt it as well, but did not hesitate or break her stride. Halting before the Iia'sidra, she spread her hands, palms up, and said in perfectly accented Aurënfaie, "I come to you in the name of great Aura the Lightbearer, revealed to us as Illior, and on behalf of my mother, Idrilain the Second of Skala."

Ancient Brythir í Nien of Silmai stepped forward, thin and dry as a dead willow branch. As the eldest member of the Iia'sidra, he spoke for all.

"Be welcome, Klia ä Idrilain Elesthera Corruthesthera Rhíminee, Princess of Skala and descendent of Corruth í Glamien of Bôkthersa," he replied, lifting a heavy necklace of gold and turquoise from his own neck and placing it around hers. "May the wisdom of the Lightbearer guide us in our endeavors."

Klia returned the gesture, giving him her girdle of golden plaques enameled with the Dragon of Illior. "May the Light shine in us."

Adzriel took up the Cup of Aura and filled it at the water's edge. Graceful in her white tunic and jewels, she raised it toward the sky, then presented it first to Klia, then Lord Torsin, Thero, and finally, to Seregil.

Seregil's fingers brushed his sister's as he accepted the Cup and raised it to his lips. The water was as cold and sweet on his tongue as he'd remembered. As he drank, however, his eyes met those of Nazien í Hari of Haman, grandfather of the man he'd killed. There was no welcome for him here.

Alec sat on his horse and listened as Nyal quietly named the various khirnari; all eleven wore white clothing and sen'gai for the ceremony, making it impossible to distinguish one clan from another.

There was one face Alec knew without being told, however. He'd met Adzriel once, just before the war, and watched with a thrill of excitement as she offered her brother the moon-shaped cup. What must they be feeling, he wondered, being so close at last, yet having to maintain such reserve?

Others were not so careful to guard their expressions. Several people exchanged dark glances as Seregil drank; a few others smiled. Among the latter was the first truly ancient Aurënfaie Alec had seen. The old man was thin to the point of gauntness, his eyes deeply sunk beneath sagging lids, and he moved with the caution born of frailty.

"That's Brythir í Nien of Silmai," Nyal told him. "He is four hundred and seventy if he's a day, an uncommon age even for us."

Still wrestling with the ramifications of his own heritage, Alec found the prospect of such a life span vaguely alarming.

Turning his attention to the nearest bystanders, he noted the sen'gai of several principal clans, as well as a scattering of minor ones. Though many wore tunics, others wore robes and long, flowing coats. The sen'gai were also diverse in style. Some were simple strips of loose-woven cloth; others were fashioned of silk and edged with small tassels or metal ornaments. Each clan had its own manner of wrapping them, as well, some simple and close to the head, others piled into elaborate shapes.

He was most pleased to discover a small group wearing the modest dark green of Bôkthersa. One of them, a young man with an incongruous streak of white in his hair, suddenly looked his way, as if he'd sensed Alec's gaze. He regarded Alec with friendly interest for a moment, then turned to whisper to an older couple. The man had a long, homely face. The woman was dark-eyed, with a thin, severe mouth that tilted into a warm smile as she looked Alec's way. She had facial tattoos, as well, though nothing as elaborate as those of the Khatme; just two horizontal lines beneath each eye. She nodded a greeting. Alec returned it, then looked away, suddenly self-conscious. It seemed they'd already guessed who he was.

"That woman who just greeted you is Seregil's third sister," Nyal murmured.

"Mydri ä Illia?" asked Alec, surprised. This woman bore little resemblance to Adzriel or Seregil. "What do those marks on her face mean?"

"She has the healer's gift."

"What about the other people. So you know them?"

"I don't recognize the younger man, but I believe the elder is Adzriel's new husband, Säaban í Irais."

"Husband?" Alec looked at the Bôkthersans again, then back at Nyal.

Nyal arched an eyebrow at him in surprise. "You did not know of this?"

"I don't think Seregil knows," said Alec. He hesitated a moment, then asked, "Are there any Chyptaulos here?"

"Oh, no. Because of Ilar's escape, theth'sag has never been settled between them and the Bôkthersans; the bad blood between the two clans is still very bitter. For the Chyptaulos to come here would also be seen as insulting Klia's lineage."

"Lord Torsin said Seregil's presence may have the same effect."

"Perhaps," replied Nyal, "but Seregil has the more powerful allies."

When the ceremony of greeting was over, the khirnari dispersed, disappearing with their kin down one of the many streets that fanned out into the city.

Adzriel accompanied Klia from the circle. As soon as they were outside the stones, however, she and Mydri embraced Seregil, clutching the back of his coat with both hands as if fearing he'd be spirited away. Seregil returned the embrace, his face hidden for a moment in their dark hair. The other Bôkthersans joined them, and for a moment he was lost from sight in the happy, chattering group. Säaban was introduced, and Alec watched as a look of amazement came over his friend's face, followed at once by a grin of delight. It appeared that Seregil approved of the match.

Klia caught Alec's eye and grinned. Beka and Thero were trying not to be too obvious as they strained for their first glimpse of Seregil's family.

"To see you here again!" said Adzriel, holding her brother at arm's length. "And you, too, Alec *talí*." Extending a hand, she drew him close and kissed him soundly on both cheeks. "Welcome to Aurënen at last!

"But I'm forgetting my duty," she exclaimed, hastily wiping at her eyes. "Princess Klia, allow me to present the rest of the Bôkthersan delegation. My sister, Mydri ä Illia. My husband, Säaban í Irais. And this is Kheeta í Branín, a great friend of Seregil's youth who has kindly offered to serve as your equerry in Sarikali."

This last was the young man who had stared so openly at Alec during the ceremony. A great friend, indeed, it seemed. Seregil grabbed the younger man in a rough hug, grinning like a fool.

"Kheeta í Branín, is it?" he laughed. "I seem to remember getting into trouble with you a time or two."

"Two? You were the cause of half the beatings I ever received," Kheeta chuckled, hugging Seregil again.

Was this fellow one of the "youthful flirtations" Seregil had spoken of? Alec wondered.

"You'd better close your mouth before something flies into it," Beka whispered, poking him in the ribs.

Ducking his head self-consciously, Alec prayed that his thoughts hadn't been quite so obvious to anyone else.

Releasing Seregil, Kheeta gave Klia a respectful bow. "Honored kinswoman, quarters have been prepared for you in Bôkthersa tupa. Whatever you need there, just ask me."

"Your house stands next to my own," Adzriel told her. "Will you dine with us tonight?"

"I'd like nothing better," replied Klia. "I can't tell you what a comfort it is to know that there is at least one khirnari of the Iia'sidra in whom I can place my complete trust."

"And here's another!" Mydri said as Amali ä Yassara joined them, walking arm in arm with a white-garbed khirnari.

By the Four! thought Alec. He'd known that Amali's husband was older than she, but this man could have been her grandfather. His face was deeply lined around the eyes and mouth, and the scant hair showing beneath his white sen'gai was the color of iron. If his wife's proud smile and glowing eyes were anything to go by, however, age was no barrier to affection.

"Klia í Idrilain, this is my husband, Rhaish í Arlisandin, khirnari of Akhendi clan," Amali said, positively beaming.

Yet another round of introductions ensued, and Alec soon found himself clasping hands with the man.

"Ah, the young Hâzadriëlfaie himself!" Rhaish exclaimed. "Surely it is a sign from the Lightbearer that your princess comes to us with such a companion!" Without releasing Alec's hand, he raised his other to touch the dragon bite on Alec's ear. "Yes, Aura has marked you for all to see."

"You're embarrassing poor Alec, my love!" Amali said, patting her husband's arm as if he were her grandfather after all.

"I'm grateful to be here, whatever the reason," Alec replied.

The conversation mercifully turned to other things and Alec retreated back among the Urgazhi. Nyal was there, too, but had not come forward to greet the Akhendi. Instead, he watched from a distance, his face somber as he followed Amali with his eyes.

"My wife speaks most affectionately of you, dear lady," Rhaish was saying to Klia. "It is a great event, having Skalans on Aurënfaie soil after so long an absence. Pray Aura we may see more of your people here in the future."

"You and your family must feast with us tonight, Khirnari," Adzriel offered. "Both in thanks for your kind escort of my kinswoman and her people, and because Klia can have no better ally than you."

"The hospitality of Bôkthersa is always an honor, my dear," Rhaish replied. "We will leave you now to settle your guests in. Until tonight, my friends."

Leaving Seregil to his family, Alec rode beside Beka.

"What do you think of it all so far?" he asked in Skalan.

She shook her head. "I can still hardly believe we're really here. I expect any minute for one of those dark-skinned ghosts of Seregil's to pop into sight."

Rounding a corner, Alec glanced up and saw someone watching

them, but it wasn't Bash'wai spirits. Several white-clad khirnari stood on a balcony high above the street. He couldn't see faces clearly at this angle, but he had the uneasy feeling that they were not smiling.

"The Skalan queen sends a child led by children!" Ruen í Uri of Datsia declared as he stood with Ulan í Sathil and Nazien í Hari, watching the Skalans ride past.

Ulan í Sathil allowed himself the hint of a smile. Ruen had supported this parley with Skala; the introduction of a little doubt suited his purposes nicely.

"You must not be deceived by their apparent youth," he warned. "The celadon fly hatches, mates, and dies in a day, but in the narrow space of that same day, it breeds hundreds of its kind, and its sting can kill a horse. So it is with the short-lived Tír."

"Look at him!" Nazien í Hari muttered, glaring down at the hated Exile riding freely through the streets. "Queen's kin or not, it's an affront to bring my grandson's murderer here. Can the Tír be such fools?"

"It's an affront to all Aurënen," Ulan agreed, never letting on that he had voted in favor of Seregil's temporary return.

Rhaish í Arlisandin slipped an arm about his young wife's waist and kissed her as they walked slowly toward Akhendi tupa.

"Your journey has agreed with you, talía. Tell me your impressions of Klia and her people."

Amali toyed with the amber amulet lying against his chest. "The Skalan princess is intelligent, forthright, and honest. Torsin í Xandus you know. As for the others?" She sighed. "As you saw, poor Alec is a child playing at being a man. Ya'shel or not, he is so innocent, so open, that I fear for him. Thank Aura he is of no real importance. But the wizard—he's a strange, deep fellow. We must not underestimate him, in spite of his youth. He will not show his true powers."

"And the Exile?"

Amali frowned. "He's not what I expected. Under that respectful manner lies a proud, angry heart. He's grown too wise for his years among the Tír, and from what my men picked up among the Skalans, there's more to him than meets the eye. It's fortunate that his goals are the same as our own, but I don't trust him. What does the Iia'sidra say of him? Will his presence here present an obstacle?"

"It's too soon to say." Rhaish walked on a moment in silence, then asked blandly, "And what of young Nyal í Nhekai? Such a long ride must have given you opportunity to renew your acquaintance."

Amali colored. "We spoke, of course. It seems he's quite taken with Klia's red-haired captain."

"Is that jealousy, talía?" he teased.

"How can you ask such a thing?"

"Forgive me." He pulled her closer. "Besotted with a Tírfaie, you say? How extraordinary! That could prove useful."

"Perhaps. I think our hope is well placed in Klia, if she can impress the Iia'sidra as she has me. She must!" Amali sighed, pressing a hand to the slight swell of her belly where their first child was growing. "By Aura, so much depends on her success. May the Lightbearer's favor lie with us."

"Indeed," he murmured, smiling sadly at the strong faith of youth. Too often it was the god's will that men make their own favor in the world.

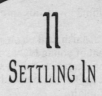

11
SETTLING IN

Alec's heart sank a little when Adzriel pointed out their guest house. Tall, narrow, and topped with some sort of small, open-sided structure, the house loomed ominously against the late-afternoon sky.

Inside, he found little to alter his opinion. Though well appointed and staffed by smiling Bôkthersans, the place had a shadowed, oppressive feel—not at all like the airy comfort of Gedre.

What in the world makes them think this place is beautiful? he wondered again, but kept his opinions to himself as Kheeta guided them through the house. The warren of dimly lit rooms were stacked at odd levels and connected by narrow corridors and galleries that seemed to all slant to some disconcerting degree. Interior rooms had no windows, while the outer ones opened onto broad balconies, many without the privacy of draperies or screens.

"Your Bash'wai had an interesting concept of architecture," Alec grumbled to Seregil, stumbling over an unexpected rise in a passageway.

The interior walls were crafted of the same patterned stone as the outer ones. Accustomed to the rich murals and statuary of Skala, it struck Alec as odd that a people would leave no pictorial record of their daily life.

A large reception hall took up much of the ground floor. Smaller rooms behind it were appointed for private use. At the back lay several bathing chambers and an enormous kitchen that overlooked a walled stable yard. This was flanked on the right by the stables, and to the left by a low stone building that would serve as a barracks for Beka's turma. A back gate let out onto an alley between this house and Adzriel's.

Klia, Torsin, and Thero had rooms on the second floor. Alec and Seregil had a large room to themselves on the third. Cavernous despite the colorful Aurënfaie furnishings, its high ceiling was lost in shadow.

Alec discovered a narrow staircase at the end of the hallway and followed it up to a flat roof and the octagonal stone pavilion that stood there.

Arched openings on each of its eight walls afforded pleasant views of the valley. Inside, smooth blocks of black stone served as benches and tables. Standing there alone, he could easily imagine the house's original inhabitants sitting around him, enjoying the cool of the evening. For an instant he could almost hear the lost echo of voices and footsteps, the rise and fall of music played on unknown instruments.

The scuff of leather against stone startled him and he jerked around to find Seregil grinning at him from the doorway.

"Dreaming with your eyes open?" he asked, crossing to the window that overlooked Adzriel's house.

"I guess so. What's this thing called?"

"A *colos*."

"It feels haunted."

Seregil draped an arm around Alec's shoulders. "And so it is, but there's nothing to fear. Sarikali is a city dreaming, and sometimes she talks in her sleep. If you listen long enough, sometimes you can hear her." Turning Alec slightly, he pointed across to a small balcony near the top of his sister's house. "See that window up there, to the right? That was my room. I used to sit there for hours at a time, just listening."

Alec pictured the restless grey-eyed boy Seregil must have been, chin propped on one hand as he listened for alien music seeping from the night air. "Is that when you heard them?"

Seregil's arm tightened around his shoulders. "Yes," he murmured, and for one brief moment his face looked as wistful as that lost child's. Before Alec could do more than register the emotion, however, Seregil was his old bantering self again. "I came to tell you that the baths are prepared. Come down as soon as you're ready."

And with that he was gone.

Alec lingered a bit, listening, but heard only the familiar bustle of his fellow travelers settling in.

Beka declined a room in the main house in favor of a small side room in the barracks.

"I haven't seen a decent fortification since we got here," Mercalle grumbled, looking the place over.

"Makes you wonder what happened to those Bash'wai folks," Braknil observed. "Anyone could ride in and take the place."

"I'm no happier about it than you are, but it can't be helped," said Beka. "Get watch fires started, give the place a thorough inspection, and set guards at all entrances. We'll rotate everyone between guard duty here, escort detail for Klia, and free time. That ought to keep them from getting bored too quickly."

"I'll keep those off duty to standard city drill," said Mercalle. "No less than three in a group, old hands watching out for the new ones, and keep them close to home for the first few days until we see how warm our welcome really is. Judging by some of the Aurënfaie I saw today, there's likely to be a bit of chest thumping."

"Well said, Sergeant. Pass the word, all of you; if there is any trouble with the 'faie, Commander Klia doesn't want steel drawn unless life is about to be lost. Is that clear?"

"As spring rain, Captain," Sergeant Rhylin assured her. "It's better politics to take a punch than to give one."

Beka sighed. "Let's hope it never comes to that. We've got enough enemies back over the sea."

Entering the long main room of the barracks, she found Nyal stowing his modest pack next to one of the pallets.

"You're bunking in with us, then?" she asked, feeling another odd little flutter below her breastbone.

"Shouldn't I?" he asked, reaching uncertainly for his pack again.

From the corner of her eye she saw Kallas and Steb exchange knowing grins. "We still need you, of course," she replied tersely. "I'll have to consider how to assign you, now that we'll be splitting into details. Perhaps Lady Adzriel can find me another interpreter or two. We can't expect you to be everywhere at once, can we?"

"I shall do my best to be, nonetheless, Captain," he replied with a wink. But his smile faltered as he added, "I think it might be best if I don't attend the feast tonight, though. You and your people will be well looked after by the Bôkthersans."

"Why not?" asked Beka, surprised. "You're living here in Adzriel's tupa. I'm sure she'd welcome you in her house."

The Ra'basi hesitated. "May we speak privately?"

Beka ushered him into her side room and closed the door. "What's the problem?"

"It is not the Bôkthersans who would not welcome me, Captain, but the Akhendi. More specifically, their khirnari, Rhaish í Arlisandin. You see, Amali ä Yassara and I were lovers for a time, before she married him."

The news sank in like a kick in the gut. *What's the matter with me? I barely know the man!* Beka thought, struggling to remain dispassionate. Instead, she suddenly recalled with merciless clarity how Nyal had kept his distance from Amali during the journey from Gedre when he had been so friendly with everyone else, and how he had faded into the background when her husband appeared at the Vhadäsoori.

"Are you still in love with her?" She wished the words back as soon as she spoke them.

Nyal looked away with a sad, shy smile. "I regret the choice she made, and will always consider myself her friend."

Yes, then. Beka folded her arms and sighed. "It must have been uncomfortable—being thrown together again this way."

Nyal shrugged. "She and I—it was a long time ago, and most agreed that she made a wise choice. Still, her husband is jealous, the way old men are. It's best that I stay in tonight."

"Very well." On impulse, she laid a hand on his arm as he turned to go. "And thank you for telling me this."

"Oh, I think it would have been necessary sooner or later to say something," he murmured, and was gone.

Sakor's Flame, woman, are you losing your mind? Beka berated herself silently, pacing the tiny room. *You barely know the man and you're mooning over him like a jealous kitchen maid. Once this mission is over you'll never see him again.*

Ah, but those eyes, and that voice! her mutinous heart replied.

He's a Ra'basi, for all his traveling, she countered. By all reports that clan was expected to support Virésse. And Seregil obviously distrusted Nyal, though he hadn't come out and said so.

"Too many months without a man," Beka growled aloud. That

was easy enough to remedy, and without all the bother of falling in love. Love, she'd learned through harsh experience, was a luxury she could not afford.

Freshly bathed and brushed, Alec and Seregil headed downstairs to meet the others in the main hall.

Reaching the landing at the second floor, however, Seregil paused. "I'd feel better if we were down here, closer to Klia," he noted, walking the length of the crooked corridor where the other guest rooms lay. At the far end was another stairway, with a window overlooking the rear yard. "This goes down to the kitchen, as I recall," said Seregil, following it down.

Wending their way past baskets of vegetables, they greeted the cooks and were directed down a passageway to the main hall at the front of the house. Klia, Kheeta, and Thero were there already, sitting next to a cheerful blaze on the hearth.

"It's too bad, having Akhendi there his first night with—" Thero was saying to Kheeta, but broke off when he caught sight of them.

"Hospitality must be served," Kheeta murmured tactfully, giving Seregil a knowing look that sent a niggling little jolt through Alec's gut. The two men may not have seen each other for forty years, but an undeniable rapport remained between them.

"Of course," Seregil agreed, brushing the matter aside. "Waiting for Lord Torsin, are we?"

And changing the subject as quickly as ever, too, thought Alec.

"He should be down in a moment," Klia said. The sound of cheers echoing down the back corridor just then.

"Ah, yes, and Captain Beka, too," Klia added with a knowing wink.

A moment later Beka strode in dressed in a brown velvet gown. Her unbound hair had been brushed until it shone and she even had on golden earrings and a necklace. It suited her, but if her expression was anything to go by, she didn't agree. Sergeant Mercalle came in just behind her, grinning broadly at her captain's unease.

"No wonder your riders were cheering," Kheeta exclaimed. "For a moment there I scarcely recognized you."

"Adzriel sent word that I was included among the guests," Beka explained, blushing as she flicked an imaginary bit of lint from her skirts. She looked up in time to catch Alec and Thero staring and bristled. "What are you gawking at? You've seen me in a dress before."

Alec exchanged a sheepish glance with the wizard. "Yes, but not for a long time."

"You look very—pretty," Thero hazarded, and got a dark look for his trouble.

"Indeed you do, Captain," chuckled Klia. "An officer on the rise has to know how to carry herself in the salon as well as in the field. Isn't that right, Sergeant?"

Mercalle came to attention. "It is, my lady, though this war hasn't given the younger officers much opportunity for anything except fighting."

Torsin came down the main stair and gave Beka an approving nod. "You do your princess and your country honor, Captain."

"Thank you, my lord," Beka replied, softening a bit.

Adzriel had included Klia's entire entourage in her invitation, and everyone was in high spirits as they walked over, even Seregil.

"It's about time I brought you to meet my family," he said, grinning crookedly as he slipped an arm around Alec and Beka.

Adzriel greeted them, flanked by her husband and sister. "Welcome, welcome at last, and Aura's light shine on you," she cried, clasping hands with each in turn as they entered. Seregil and Alec were soundly kissed on both cheeks. The word "brother" was not spoken but seemed to hover on the air like a Bash'wai spirit.

"The Akhendi and Gedre are here already," Mydri told them as they walked through several elegant chambers to a large courtyard beyond. "Amali is very taken with you, Klia. She's talked of nothing else since she got here."

This house was larger, but seemed to Alec to be more welcoming, as if centuries of habitation by this family had imbued the harsh stone with something of their own warmth.

Low, two-person couches for the highest ranking guests had been set out on a broad stone platform above an overgrown garden, positioned so that the members of the dinner party could watch the moon rise over the towers of Sarikali. Alec counted twenty-three people wearing the colors of Bôkthersa, and half again as many Akhendi and Gedre. The riders who'd accompanied Klia over the pass were seated at long tables in the garden among banks of fragrant, funnel-shaped white flowers. They called out happily to the Urgazhi, making space for them among their ranks.

Amali was already stretched prettily beside her husband. She had not warmed to Seregil during the long ride, and showed no signs of thawing now. Alec was glad to be seated several couches away from her, near Adzriel and the Gedre khirnari.

Sitting down next to Seregil, however, he studied the Akhendi khirnari with interest. Rhaish í Arlisandin sat with one arm clasped loosely around his wife, clearly pleased to be with her after a long absence. Looking up at Alec, he smiled. "Amali tells me you were the luckbringer of the journey?"

"What? Oh, this." Alec raised a hand to the dragon bite on his ear. "Yes, my lord. It was a bit of a surprise."

Rhaish arched an eyebrow at Seregil. "I would have thought you'd have told him all about such things."

Alec was close enough to feel Seregil tense, though he doubted anyone else noticed. "I've been very remiss, but I've always found it painful to—remember."

Rhaish raised a hand in what appeared to be some benediction. "May your time here be one of healing," he offered kindly.

"Thank you, Khirnari."

"You must sit with me as a most honored guest, Beka ä Kari," Mydri invited, patting the empty place beside her. "Your family took our—took Seregil in. The Cavish clan will always be welcome at the hearths of Bôkthersa."

"I hope we can offer your people the same hospitality one day," Beka returned. "Seregil has been a great friend to us, and saved my father's life many times."

"Usually because I'd gotten him into trouble in the first place," Seregil added, drawing laughter from many of the other guests.

Servants brought in trays of food and wine as Adzriel made introductions. Alec quickly lost track of the names but noted with interest the various Bôkthersans. Many were referred to as cousins; such terms often indicated ties of affection rather than blood. One of these people turned out to be Kheeta's mother, a dark-eyed woman who reminded Alec of Kari Cavish.

She shook a finger sternly at Seregil. "You broke our hearts, Haba, but only because we loved you so." The stern look gave way to a tearful smile as she embraced him. "It is so very good to see you in this house again. Come to the kitchen anytime and I'll bake spice cakes for you."

"I'll make you keep that promise, Aunt Malli," Seregil replied huskily, kissing the backs of her hands.

Alec knew he was seeing glimpses of a history he did not share. As the old familiar ache threatened to close around his heart, however, he felt long fingers close over his own. For once, Seregil understood and offered silent apology.

The meal began informally with several courses of finger foods: morsels of spiced meat or cheese wrapped in pastry, olives, fruit, fanciful nosegays of edible greens and flowers.

"*Turab,* a Bôkthersan specialty," a server murmured, filling Alec's cup with a frothy reddish ale.

Seregil clinked his cup against Alec's, murmuring, "My talí."

Meeting his friend's gaze over the rim of his cup, Alec saw an odd mix of joy and sadness there.

"I'd like to hear of this war from you, Captain," said Adzriel's husband, Säaban í Irais, as a course of meats was served. "And from you, as well, Klia ä Idrilain, if it is not too upsetting to speak of it. There are many Bôkthersans who will join your ranks if the Iia'sidra allows." Judging by the worried frown that crossed Adzriel's face, Alec guessed that Säaban might be one of them.

"The more I see of your people, the more I wonder why they would risk themselves in a foreign conflict," Beka replied.

"Not all would, or will," he conceded. "But there are those who would rather meet the Plenimarans now than fight them and the Zengati on our own soil later."

"We can use all the help we can get," said Klia. "For now, however, let's keep the darkness away and speak of happier things."

As the evening progressed and the *turab* flowed, conversation turned to reminiscences of Seregil's childhood exploits. Kheeta í Branín figured in a good many of these tales, and Alec was surprised to learn that the man was actually a few years older than Seregil. Seregil had moved to Kheeta's couch to share some story, and Alec studied the pair and those around them, trying yet again to get his mind around the long 'faie life span that he himself shared. Adzriel and her husband, he knew, were in their twelfth decade, a youthful prime among the Aurënfaie. The oldest guest, a Gedre named Corim, was in his third century and looked no older than Micum Cavish, at least at first glance.

It's the eyes, Alec thought. There was a stillness in the eyes of the older 'faire, as if the knowledge and wisdom of their long lives left its mark there—one that Kheeta did not yet show. Seregil, though—he had old eyes in a young face, as if he'd seen too much too soon.

And so he has, just in the time I've known him, Alec reflected. By the time they'd met, Seregil had already lived a human lifetime and seen a human generation age and die. He'd made a name for himself while the friends of his youth were still finishing out their long childhoods. Seeing him here, among his own kind, Alec realized for the first time just how young his friend actually was. What did his own people see when they looked at Seregil?

Or at me?

Seregil threw his head back, laughing, and for a moment he looked as innocent as Kheeta. It was good to see him like that, but Alec couldn't keep away the darker thought that this was how he might have been if he'd never gone to Skala.

"You're as solemn as Aura's owl, and as quiet," Mydri observed, sitting down next to him and taking his hand.

"I'm still trying to believe I'm really here," Alec replied.

"So am I," she said, and another of those unexpectedly warm smiles softened her stern features.

"Can the ban of exile ever be lifted?" Alec asked, keeping his voice low.

Mydri sighed. "It happens, especially with one so young. Still, it would take a petition from the Haman khirnari to begin the debate, and that doesn't seem very likely. The Haman are an honorable people, but they are proud in a way that breeds bitterness. Old Nazien is no exception. He still grieves at the loss of his grandson and resents Seregil's return."

"By the Light, you're a grim pair," Seregil called over, and Alec realized that he was drunk, a rarity for Seregil.

"Are we?" Mydri shot back, a gleam of challenge in her eyes. "Tell me, Alec, does Seregil still have his fine singing voice?"

"As fine as any bard's," Alec told her, giving Seregil a teasing wink.

"Sing for us, talí!" Adzriel urged, overhearing. At her signal, a servant came forward with something large and flat wrapped in patterned silk and placed it in Seregil's hands.

He unwrapped it with a knowing smile. It was a harp, its dark wood polished with use.

"We kept it for you, all these years," Mydri told him as he settled it against his chest and ran his fingers across the strings.

He plucked out a simple tune that drew tearful smiles from his sisters, then moved on to a complex tune, fingers flying across the strings as melody followed melody. Even drunk and out of practice, he played beautifully.

After a moment he paused, then began the exile's lament he'd sung the first time he'd spoken to Alec of Aurënen.

My love is wrapped in a cloak of flowing green
and wears the moon for a crown.
And all around has chains of flowing silver.
Her mirrors reflect the sky.
O, to roam your flowing cloak of green
under the light of the ever-crowning moon.

Will I ever drink of your chains of flowing silver
  and drift once more across your mirrors of the sky?

"A bard's voice, indeed," said Säaban, dabbing at his eyes with
the edge of his sleeve. "With such power to move the emotions, I
hope you know happier tunes."

"A few," Seregil said. "Alec, give us the harmony on 'Fair Rises
My Lover.' "

The Skalan song was warmly received, and more instruments appeared as if on cue.

"Where's Urien?" Seregil demanded, squinting out into the garden at the soldiers. "Someone give that boy a lute!"

This broke through the Urgazhi's reticence. The young rider's
friends all but carried the blushing musician forward, demanding
favorite ballads as if they were at a crossroads tavern.

"For the pride of the decuria, rider!" Mercalle ordered with mock
severity.

Urien accepted an Aurënfaie lute and smoothed an admiring
hand over its round back.

"For the pride of the turma," he said, striking a chord. "This is
from before my time with the Urgazhi."

Ghost wolves they call us, and Ghost Wolves we are.
Drawn to the enemy by a plague star
Fighting and burning, deep in their lines
Our Captain was fearless, we followed behind.

Death and dark magic, demons she faced,
Under the black sun, in that dread lonely place.
The black shields of Plenimar, rank upon rank
Until their Duke Mardus, in his blood sank.

Alec watched in dismay as Seregil's smile froze and Thero went
pale. One of several ballads that extolled the Urgazhi's early exploits, this one spoke of Nysander's death. Fortunately, Beka caught
on at once.

"Enough, enough!" she begged, masking her concern with a
comic grimace. "By the Four, Urien, of all the grim, threadbare ballads to choose! Give us 'Illior's Face Upon the Waters' to honor our
good hosts."

The chagrined rider nodded and commenced the tune, playing
each flourish flawlessly. Seregil moved to sit by Alec again.

"You looked as if you'd seen a ghost. Are you all right?" he whispered, as if the previous song had not affected him.

Alec nodded.

The song ended and Kheeta held a harp out to Klia.

"What about you, my lady?"

"Oh, no! I have the voice of a crow. Thero, didn't I hear you sing a passable ballad after our victory at Two Horse Crossing?"

"I'd had a bit more to drink then, my lady," the wizard replied, thin cheeks coloring as all eyes turned his way.

"Don't be shy!" Sergeant Braknil called out. "We heard you sing sober aboard the *Zyria*."

"All the same, perhaps our hosts would prefer a small demonstration of Third Orëska magic?" Thero countered.

"Very well," laughed Mydri.

Thero produced a pouch of fine white sand and sprinkled it in a circle on the ground in front of the couches. Using his crystal wand, he wove a series of glowing sigils over it. Instead of the tidy configurations he usually produced, however, they swelled and bulged, then exploded with enough force to scatter the sand and knock wine cups in all directions. Thero dropped the wand with a startled yelp and stuck his fingers in his mouth.

Alec stifled a laugh; the normally reserved wizard looked like a cat that had just slipped on a patch of ice, chagrined and determined to regain his dignity before anyone noticed. Seregil shook with silent laughter beside him.

"My apologies!" Thero exclaimed in dismay. "I—I can't imagine what happened."

"The fault is mine. I should have warned you," Adzriel assured him, clearly fighting down a smile of her own. "Magic must be performed with great care here. The power of Sarikali feeds into our own, making magic sometimes unpredictable. All the more so in your case, evidently."

"So I see." Thero retrieved his wand and tucked it in his belt. After a moment's thought, he sprinkled more sand and tried the spell again, drawing the sigils with his fingers this time. The patterns hung in the air a few inches above the ground, then coalesced into a flat disk of silvery light as big around as a serving platter. He added another sigil, and the smooth surface took on a mottled array of sun-washed colors, then resolved itself into a miniature city set high above a miniature harbor.

"How wonderful!" exclaimed Amali, leaning forward to admire his creation. "What place is it?"

"Rhíminee, my lady," he replied.

"That sprawling black-and-grey monstrosity is the queen's Palace, my home," Klia remarked dryly. "While this lovely white structure over here, the one with the sparkling dome and towers, is the Orëska House."

"I visited it during my time in Rhíminee," said Adzriel. "As I recall, the wizards of Skala were originally scattered around your land, some solitary, others serving various noble houses."

"Yes, my lady; what we called the Second Orëska. After the old capital, Ero, was destroyed, Queen Tamír founded Rhíminee and forged an alliance with the greatest wizards of her day, the Third Orëska. They helped build her city and other wonders; in return she gifted them with her patronage and the land for the Orëska House."

"Then it is true that those among you with magic are kept apart from others?" an Akhendi asked.

"No, not at all," Thero replied. "It's just that we are so different by virtue of that magic and its effect on us—life spans comparable to your own, and the barrenness that is its price—that it was good to have a haven, a place where we could live and share our learning among ourselves. Wizards are not required to live there, but many choose to. I spent most of my life there, in the tower of my master, Nysander í Azusthra. Wizards are highly honored in Skala, I assure you."

"Yet do you not find it sad, to be cut off from the natural flow of life among your own kind?" the same Akhendi asked.

Thero considered this and shrugged. "No, not really. I've never known any other life."

"Rhaish and I visited your city as boys," Riagil í Molan told Klia. "We went to attend the wedding of Corruth í Glamien to your ancestress, Idrilain the First. We were taken to visit this Orëska House of yours. Rhaish, do you recall that wizard who did tricks for us?"

"Oriena, I think her name was," the Akhendi khirnari replied. "It was a beautiful place, with gardens where it was always springtime, and a great mosaic on the floor showing Aura's dragon. The queen's Palace was much darker, with thick walls like a fortress."

"Which only goes to prove that my ancestor, Queen Tamír, should have included more wizards among her builders," Klia said, smiling.

"I should like to see this Third Orëska," said Amali.

"With pleasure, my lady, though it is a less happy place now than it once was." Thero uttered a quick command, and the city's image was replaced with a view of the Orëska gardens. A few robed figures were visible there, but the place looked strangely deserted. The scene shifted, and Alec recognized the view of the central atrium from the balcony by Nysander's tower door. Sections of the dragon mosaic still showed the damage caused by the attack of Mardus and his necromancers. Here, too, there were fewer people than Alec remembered from his time there.

"This is how it looks now?" Seregil asked softly.

"Yes." Thero changed the image again, showing them Seregil's Wheel Street villa.

"My Skalan home," Seregil said with a hint of irony.

What would they see if Thero conjured up their true home? Alec wondered. Was the blackened cellar hole still there, or had some new establishment been built over the ruins?

"I know a similar magic," said Säaban. A servant brought him a large silver basin mounted on a tripod. Filling it with water, he blew gently across it. Ripples ridged the surface for an instant, then cleared, leaving in their wake a view of green forests below snow-capped peaks. On a hill overlooking a broad lake lay a white sprawl of interconnected stone buildings similar to the khirnari's house at Gedre, but much larger and more elaborate. A town spread down the hill from it to the water's edge. At the forest's edge, a pillared temple stood in a grove of white birches, its domed roof gleaming in the brilliant sunlight that bathed the scene.

"Bôkthersa!" breathed Seregil. "I've forgotten so much."

The image faded and more turab was poured. Seregil drank deeply.

"We saw a bit of Akhendi magic as we passed through your fai'thast, Khirnari," Klia told Rhaish í Arlisandin, holding up her left wrist to show him the carved leaf hanging there.

"They're periapts, aren't they?" asked Thero, who wore a similar one.

"Very good," the khirnari said, acknowledging him with a nod. "It is the knots as much as the amulet itself that hold the magic. Either by itself does not work."

"I'd like to learn how they're made, if that's allowed. We have nothing quite like them in Skala."

"But of course! It's quite a common skill among my folk, though some are better at it than others." Rhaish turned to his wife. "Talía, you have a way with such things. Have you the makings with you?"

"I'm never without them." Amali moved to sit next to the wizard and produced a hank of thin leather laces from a purse at her belt. "It's simply a matter of knowing the patterns," she explained. With

one smooth gesture, she pulled the laces through her hand and produced a short band of intricate weave, far more complex than any
the Skalans had seen so far. "The second pass sets the amulet, according to the needs of the intended wearer." She took out a small
pouch and spilled a collection of little wooden carvings onto her
lap. She gazed at Thero a moment, then chose a simple, tapered
plaque carved with an eye symbol. "For wisdom," she told him, setting the charm into the weave and tying it around his wrist.

"One can never have enough of that," laughed Klia.

Amali quickly created another and presented it to her, this one
with a bird charm very similar to ones Alec and Torsin wore. "It's
just a simple binding spell. It warns if someone is ill-wishing you."

"I've found those to be of use many times," Torsin remarked, showing her his. "I only wish the Orëska wizards had the knack for them."

"Can you tell me what these are?" asked Klia, showing her the
carved leaf charm and another made from an acorn strung on a few
twisted strands. "I couldn't understand a word of what the woman
who made them said."

Amali examined them and smiled. "These are more trinkets or
luck pieces than charms, but given with a loving heart. The leaf is
for good health; the acorn symbolizes a fertile womb."

"I'll take the health, but I'd best save this other for later." Klia un-
tied the acorn charm and tucked it away.

"And you say this magic is possessed only by Akhendi?" asked
Thero, examining a charm on his own wrist with interest.

"Others can sometimes learn a few tricks, but it's our clan's gift—
magic using knots, weaving, or bindings." Amali handed him a few
laces. "Care to try?"

"But how?" he asked.

"Just think of someone here and will the laces to weave for them."

After several unsuccessful tries, Thero managed to knot two
strands into an uneven tangle.

Rhaish chuckled. "Well, perhaps with practice. Allow me to
show you something rather more sophisticated."

He walked down into the garden and returned with a handful of
flowering vines. Taking a gold ring from his finger, he threaded
some of the vine through it, then pressed both between his hands.
The vine turned to gold before their eyes, each delicate blossom and
leaf gleaming like fine jeweler's work. Rhaish wove it into a wreath
and presented it to Klia.

"It's lovely!" she exclaimed, placing it on her head. "How wonderful it must be, to create such beauty with such ease."

"Ah, but nothing is ever as easy as it seems. The real magic is in hiding the effort."

The conversation rambled on over the wine, as if they'd all gathered for an evening of simple pleasure. Presently, however, Klia gently brought them back to business.

"Honored friends, Lord Torsin í Xandus had describe to me his impressions of the Iia'sidra's stand regarding our arrival. I would be most interested to hear your thoughts."

Adzriel tapped a long finger against her chin as she considered the question, and Alec was again struck by the strong resemblance she bore to her brother.

"It's too soon to tell," she replied. "While you may be certain of the support of Bôkthersa and Akhendi, or the opposition of Virésse, there are still many who remain undecided. Your goal is to gain aide for your embattled country. Yet what you ask requires us to violate the Edict of Separation, thus embroiling you unwittingly in a debate that has been festering here for years."

"It doesn't have to," Klia countered. "One more open port—that's all we're asking for."

"One port or a dozen; it's all the same," said Riagil. "The Khatme and their supporters want to bar all foreigners from Aurënen soil. Then you have the Virésse; Ulan í Sathil will oppose any change that challenges his monopoly on northern shipping."

"And those who have come to rely on his good favor to market their own wares are being cowed with subtleties not to oppose him," the Akhendi khirnari added, his face darkening with anger. "Whatever you do, never underestimate Ulan í Sathil."

"I remember him well, from the negotiations with the Zengati," said Seregil. "He could charm the stones from the earth, but behind that silky manner lurks the will and the patience of a dragon."

"I've come up against that will many times over the years," Torsin said with a rueful chuckle.

"Who are his surest allies?" asked Thero.

Adzriel shrugged expressively. "Goliníl and Lhapnos, without question. Goliníl because of blood ties."

"And Lhapnos because they stand to lose valuable trade routes if Gedre opens and northern goods no longer must be shipped down Lhapnos's great river and up the coast to Virésse instead of the short way over our mountains," Rhaish í Arlisandin added.

"That is true, but I still say it is the Edict itself which creates the greatest opposition," said Mydri.

"But that came about because of the murder of Lord Corruth,

didn't it?" asked Alec. "Seregil and I proved who killed him. Hasn't honor—atui—been served?"

She shook her head sadly. "That was not the reason for the Edict, only the catalyst. From the time of the first contact between the Tír and the Aurënfaie, many of our race have resisted mingling with Tír of any sort. For some it is a matter of atui. Others, like the Khatme, claim it is the will of Aura. What it comes down to, however, is the simple drive to preserve our kind."

"Against the making of ya'shel like me, you mean?" said Alec.

"Yes, Alec í Amasa. As much as you resemble the 'faie, the years run differently in your blood—it shows already in the fact that you are almost man-grown at nineteen. That will slow as you get older, but look at Seregil, and Kheeta; three times your age, but not so far ahead. You are neither Aurënfaie nor Tírfaie, but a mingling of both. There are those who feel that more is lost than gained by such a breeding.

"But I think it's the Skalan wizards who concern them most of all," she went on, looking at Thero. "The wizards of Skala call themselves the Third Orëska. The First Orëska is my own race. The mingling of blood gave your people magic, but it also changed that magic over the years. The barrenness of your kind is only part of that change. You can move objects, even people, over great distances, some of you, and read thoughts, a practice strictly forbidden here. You have lost the power of healing, as well." Mydri touched the marks on her cheeks. "This is left to priests of other gods."

"The drysians," Seregil said.

"Yes, the drysians. The only vestiges of that gift seem to exist among the Plenimarans, who took the gift of Aura and mingled it with the black cults of Seriamaius to create necromancy, the perversion of healing."

"This was all being debated generations ago," Adzriel explained. "Corruth's disappearance was only the final puff of wind that caused the smoldering tinder to ignite. Our people still trade with lands to the south and west of Aurënen. The reason they were not included in the ban is that there is no magic among the ya'shel bred of their kind."

Thero blinked in surprise. "No magic?"

"None that they did not already possess," Säaban amended. "Thus, the existence of the Third Orëska itself remains an impediment in the minds of some, no matter how persuasive your argument. But to answer your original question, those who stand now against you are Virésse, Goliníl, Lhapnos, and Khatme, four of the Eleven already."

"What about Ra'basi?" asked Alec, thinking of Nyal. "They border Virésse to the south, don't they?"

"Moriel ä Moriel has not stated her clan's position openly, nor have the Haman, for whom the opening of Gedre would almost certainly work to advantage. They have withheld support out of loyalty to their allies in Lhapnos."

"And to spite Bôkthersa," Seregil said quietly.

Säaban nodded. "That, as well. Ill will still clouds their judgment. The Silmai, Datsia, and Bry'kha are also elusive; as far west as they are, with trade to the west and south and blood ties mostly among themselves, they have little to gain or lose."

"Who among those three has the most influence?" asked Klia.

"Brythir í Nien of Silmai is the Elder of the Iia'sidra, greatly respected by all," said Mydri, and others nodded agreement around the circle.

"Then perhaps Aura is smiling on our endeavors, after all," said Klia. "We dine with him tomorrow."

The gathering moved indoors as the night air cooled. Alec overheard Thero, Mydri, and Säaban comparing spells and would have joined them, but found himself cornered by a succession of well-intentioned Bôkthersans. Across the room, Seregil was just visible in a small crowd of well-wishers.

On his own for the moment, Alec soon gave up trying to keep track of the intricate family connections each new acquaintance listed off to him.

"If the ban of exile is ever lifted, you can be initiated into our clan as his talímenios, you know," a woman informed him in the course of one such conversation.

"That would be a great honor. I was also hoping to trace who my mother's people were."

The faces around him grew solemn. "Not to know your family line, that is a great tragedy," the woman said, patting his hand kindly.

"How long have you been talímenios?" asked Kheeta, coming over to join them.

"Two years," Alec told him, watching for a reaction.

But Kheeta merely nodded approvingly as he looked across at Seregil. "It's good to see him happy at last."

"Where are Seregil's other sisters?"

Kheeta made a sour face. "Adzriel brought only Bôkthersans who accept Seregil's return. Don't be misled by what you see here.

There are a great many who don't. Shalar and Ilina count themselves among that group. I suppose it's understandable with Shalar; she was in love with a Haman and the match was forbidden after— well, the trouble. As for Ilina, she and Seregil were closest in age, but they never got on."

More discord; no wonder Seregil never spoke of his past.

"What about Säaban? Seregil didn't know that he'd married Adzriel, but he seems quite happy with her choice."

"They knew one another before Seregil was sent away. Säaban and Adzriel have been friends for years. He's a man of great honor and intelligence, as well as possessing a keen gift for magic."

"He's a wizard, you mean?"

"As I understand your use of the word, yes. Quite a good one."

Alec was just beginning to mull over the possibilities this new insight presented when they were interrupted again and he was drawn away to answer the same few questions over and over: No, he had no memory of the Hâzadriëlfaie; yes, Seregil was a great man in Skala; yes, he was happy to be in Aurënen; no, he'd never seen any place like Sarikali. He was scanning the room for escape routes when he felt a hand on his arm.

"Come with me. There's something I need to do and I need your help," Seregil whispered, guiding him through a doorway and up a back staircase.

"Where are we going?"

"You'll see."

Seregil smelled strongly of turab, but his steps were steadier than Alec would have expected. They climbed three sets of stairs, pausing on each level to inspect a room or two. Seregil could usually be counted on to hold forth at length, telling him more than anyone needed to know about the history of a place or thing. Tonight, however, he said nothing, just stopped to touch an object here and there, reacquainting himself with the place.

Alec had a talent for silence. Hands clasped behind his back, he followed Seregil down a winding third-floor corridor. Plain wooden doors opened off the passage at irregular intervals, each one no different from the last as far as he could tell. A small village could easily have put up in the place, or an entire clan.

Seregil halted in front of a door next to a sharp turning of the passage. He knocked, then lifted the latch and slipped into the darkened room.

It had been a long time since they'd burgled a house, but Alec automatically took stock of the place: no light, no smell of hearth or candle smoke, no coverlet on the bed. The room was a safe one, not in use.

"Over here."

Alec heard the creak of hinges, then saw Seregil's lean form framed against an arch of night sky across the room. Drunk or not, he could move silently when he chose.

The arch let onto a small balcony overlooking the guest house.

"That's our room," Seregil told him, pointing out a window there. "And this room was yours."

"Ah, yes. I told you, didn't I?" Seregil leaned on the stone parapet, face inscrutable in the moonlight.

"This is where you sat listening to the city dream," Alec murmured.

"I did considerable dreaming of my own. Wait here." Seregil went back inside and returned with a dusty feather tick from the bed. Wadding it against the wall, he sat down and reached for Alec, pulling him down between his legs with his back to Seregil's chest.

"There." He nuzzled Alec's cheek, holding him close. "Here's one dream come to pass, anyway. Aura knows, nothing else has turned out the way I thought it would."

Alec leaned back against him, enjoying their shared heat. "What else did you dream about, sitting here?"

"That I'd leave Bôkthersa and travel."

"Like Nyal."

Alec felt rather than heard Seregil's ironic chuckle. "I suppose so. I'd live among foreign people, immerse myself in their ways for years and years, but always return here, and to Bôkthersa."

"What would you do on your travels?"

"Just—search. For places no Aurënfaie had seen, for people I'd never meet by remaining at home. My uncle always said there's a reason for every gift. My skills with languages and fighting—he guessed that all added up to someone who was meant to wander. Looking back now, I suppose deep down I was hoping I'd find a place where I was something more than my father's greatest disappointment."

Alec considered this in silence for a moment. "It's difficult for you, isn't it? Being here, the way things are."

"Yes."

How could a single quiet word convey such pain, such longing?

"What else did you wish for, sitting here?" Alec asked quickly, knowing there was nothing he could do to assuage that wound; better just to move on.

A hand slid slowly under his jaw, cupping his cheek as lips

brushed his cheek. The touch spread a tingle of anticipation down his whole right side.

"This, talí. You," Seregil said, breath warm on his skin. "I couldn't see your face back then, but it was you I dreamed of. I've had so many lovers—dozens, hundreds maybe. But not one of them—" He broke off. "I can't explain it. I think some part of me recognized you that first night we met, battered and filthy as you were."

"In that distant foreign land." Alec turned to meet the next kiss with one of his own. How long before someone missed them and came looking?

Time enough.

But Seregil only pulled him closer, cradling him without any of the usual playful groping that preceded their lovemaking. They sat like that for some time, until Alec finally realized that this was what Seregil had come here for.

They fell silent again, and Alec felt himself slipping into a doze. He snapped awake again when Seregil shifted his legs.

"Well, I suppose we should go back down," Seregil said.

Alec rose awkwardly, still sleep dazed. The night air felt cold against his right side where he'd lain against him. The sudden loss of physical contact left him disoriented and a little melancholy, as if he'd absorbed Seregil's sorrow through his skin.

Seregil was looking at the guest house again. "Thank you, talí. Now when I look over here from there, I can remember this as more than just a place that isn't mine anymore."

They replaced the tick and were almost out the door when Seregil paused and turned back, muttering something to himself.

"What is it?" asked Alec.

Instead of answering, Seregil pulled the bedstead to one side and disappeared behind it.

Alec heard the scrape of stone against stone, followed by a triumphant cackle. Seregil popped into view again, holding up a grappling hook and rope.

"Where did that come from?" Alec asked, amused by his friend's obvious delight.

"Come see for yourself."

Alec climbed onto the dusty bed and peered over the edge. Seregil had pried up one of the polished stone floor tiles, revealing a dark space underneath.

"Did you make that hole?"

"No, and I wasn't the first to use it, either. The grapple was mine, a later addition, and this." He lifted out a clear quartz crystal as long as his palm. "I found the loose tile by accident. These other things were already here. Treasures." A pretty box of Aurënfaie inlay work followed the crystal, and inside Alec found a child's necklace of red and blue beads and a falcon's skull. Seregil placed a painted wooden dragon with gilded wings beside it, then a small portrait of an Aurënfaie couple painted on ivory. Finally, with great care, he lifted out a fragile wooden doll. Its large black eyes and full-lipped mouth were painted on, but the hair was real—long, tightly curled ringlets of shining black.

"By the Four!" Alec touched a finger reverently to the hair. "Do you think this is Bash'wai?"

Still kneeling behind the bed, Seregil touched each object with obvious affection and nodded. "The doll is, and perhaps the necklace."

"And you never told anyone?"

"Just you." Seregil carefully replaced everything except the grapple. "It wouldn't have been special if anyone else had known."

Standing, he tilted Alec a crooked grin. "And you know how good I am at keeping secrets."

Alec uncoiled the grapple rope. It was still supple, and knotted every few feet for climbing. "It's too short to reach the ground."

"I'm disappointed in you, talí," Seregil chided, carrying it out to the balcony. With one easy toss, he threw the hook up and secured it on the edge of the roof above. Giving Alec a parting wink, he shimmied up and out of sight.

Knowing that he'd just been issued a challenge, Alec followed and found Seregil waiting for him in the large colos there.

"I used to sneak out of my room this way, then use the back stairs over there to get out of the house. Or Kheeta and I would meet up here and trade sweets we'd nicked from the kitchen. Later on it was beer, or turab. Actually, it's a wonder I didn't break my neck one of those nights on the way back down." He looked around a moment, then laughed outright. "One time six of us were up here, pissed as newts, when our lookout heard my father on his way up. We all went down the rope that night and hid out in my room until dawn."

Alec smiled but couldn't quite suppress another jealous pang, especially at the mention of Kheeta. Tagging along after his nomadic father most of his life, Alec hadn't had a real home or many friends. Thoughts of the rhui'auros flashed to mind, and he silently vowed that before this journey was over, he was going to learn whatever he could of his own missing past.

Seregil must have sensed this roil of emotion, for suddenly he was close beside Alec again, pressing a turab-scented kiss to his lips. "It's one of the few memories I have now that doesn't hurt," he offered.

"Shall we go down the same way we came up?" Alec asked, passing it off lightly.

"Why not? We're practically sober."

Back on the balcony, Seregil gave the rope a neat flick that unseated the hook. Coiling it up again, he returned the grapple to its hiding place with the other toys.

"Leaving it for the next child who discovers your secret cache?" Alec asked.

"It seems only right." Seregil set the tile back in place and pushed the leg of the bed over it. "It's good to know something around here hasn't changed."

Alec pondered the toys hidden in the dark as they returned to the gathering. Somehow, they seemed to fit into the strange, complex mosaic of Seregil's life, a tiny model of the treasure-strewn and equally hidden rooms they'd shared at the Cockerel, or the unexpected bits of his own past that Seregil doled out like precious relics.

Or perhaps precious wasn't the right term.

It's one of the few memories I have now that doesn't hurt.

You never told anyone?

Just you.

How many times had someone looked at him in surprise when he'd mentioned something Seregil had shared with him? *He told you about that?*

Humbled by this realization, he steered Seregil back to Kheeta and went off to find Beka.

12
The Great Game Begins

The first round of negotiations began the next morning, and from the outset Seregil could see that it was going to be a laborious process.

The Iia'sidra met in a stone pavilion overlooking the great pool at the center of the city. The original builder's purpose for the broad, octagonal building was not known; inside, it was one huge, two-story chamber with a sweeping stone gallery. A temple, perhaps, although no one knew what gods the Bash'wai had worshiped. The eleven principal khirnari were already seated in open booths arranged around the hall's central circle. The khirnari and their chief advisers sat in front; scribes, kin, and servants of various sorts were allotted seats behind them. Outside the circle and in the gallery above, members of the numerous minor clans had their own hierarchy. They might not vote in the Iia'sidra, but they did have a voice.

Seated with Alec just behind Klia in the Skalan booth, Seregil gazed around the vaulted chamber, studying faces. He'd wondered how he would feel, attending the Iia'sidra for the first time as an adult. As he caught sight of Adzriel and her small entourage he decided the experience was not an altogether pleasant one. Sääban, who also acted as adviser, sat at Adzriel's right, Mydri on her left. Seregil would have held a rightful place there, too. Instead, he sat on the opposite side of the council circle, wearing the clothes and speaking the words of strangers. Better not to dwell on that, he told himself sternly. He'd put himself here; now there was work to be done, honorable work for an honorable cause.

Klia had once again displayed a considerable talent for appearances. Today she'd ridden to the council hall in full dress uniform, with two decuria for escort. Torsin and Thero flanked her like some living tableau of aged wisdom and youthful intellect. Anyone expecting a supplicant from a dying nation was in for quite a surprise.

When everyone had settled, a woman stepped forward and struck a hollow silver staff against the floor. Its solemn chime reverberated around the stone chamber, commanding silence.

"Let no person forget that we stand in Sarikali, the living heart of Aurënen," she announced. "Stand in Aura's sight and speak the truth."

She struck the chime again and withdrew to a small platform. Brythir í Nien rose first to speak.

"Brothers and sisters of the Iia'sidra, and all people of Aura in this place," he began. "Klia ä Idrilain, Princess of Skala, seeks audience today. Are there any who object to her presence, or that of her ministers?"

There was a weighty pause; then the khirnari of Haman, Lhapnos, and Goliníl rose as one.

"We object to the presence of the exile, Seregil of Rhíminee," stated Galmyn í Nemius.

Alec and Thero both shot Seregil worried glances, but he'd expected as much.

"Your objections are noted," Brythir í Nien told the dissenters. "Any others? Very well, then. Klia ä Idrilain, you may speak."

Klia rose and made the assembly a dignified bow. "Honored Khirnari and people of Aurënen, I come before you today as a representative of my mother, Queen Idrilain. From her I bear greetings and a proposition.

"As you know, Plenimar is once more making war against Skala and our ally, Mycena. From your own agents we also know that they have courted the favor of your own enemy, Zengat. Aurënen has fought with us against Plenimar before. I stand before you today as a warrior who has faced this aggressor in the field, and they are as mighty now as in the days of the Great War.

"Already our trade routes with the northlands have been cut off. Mycena will almost surely fall. We Skalans are great warriors, yet without allies or supplies, how long can we stand come winter? If Plenimar lays claim to the Three Lands and their territories, how long will it be before their fleets and those of the Zengati pirates mass along your coast?

"Our two races stood against Plenimar through the dark days of the Great War. For many years we mixed our blood and called each other kin. In the face of this new crisis, Queen Idrilain proposes a renewed alliance between our two lands for our mutual defense and benefit."

Galmyn í Nemius of Lhapnos was the first to respond. "You speak of supplies, Klia ä Idrilain. You already have these from us, do you not? Aurënfaie goods are still carried north from Virésse by Tírfaie ships."

"But few of them are Skalan ships these days," she replied. "Few of our vessels can reach Virésse, and fewer still return. Plenimaran ships lurk behind every island. They attack without provocation, pillage the cargoes, kill the crew, and send the ships to the bottom of the Osiat Sea. Then they sail back to trade at your port. And their reach is growing. My own ship was attacked no more than a day's voyage from Gedre."

"What would you have of us, then?" asked the Khatme, Lhaär ä Iriel.

Klia motioned to Lord Torsin. "The list, please."

The envoy stepped forward and unrolled a parchment. Clearing his throat, he read: "Queen Idrilain asks first that the Iia'sidra Council grant Skala a second open port, Gedre, and leave to mass ships there and in the Ea'malie Islands for no longer than the duration of the present conflict. In return, she pledges increased payments for Aurënfaie horses, grain, and weapons.

"In addition, the queen proposes a military alliance for the mutual benefit and defense of our two lands. She asks that you commit to a levy of Aurënfaie warships, soldiers, and wizards, with her pledge in kind to provide the same in the event that Aurënen is attacked."

"A hollow pledge, from a land that cannot even defend itself," observed a Haman. Torsin pressed on as if he hadn't heard.

"Finally, she earnestly desires to reestablish the accord that once existed between our two peoples. In this dark time, she prays that the Iia'sidra will honor the call of blood to blood and once again treat Skala as her friend and ally."

Nazien í Hari was on his feet before Torsin finished rolling up his scroll. "Are the memories of the Tír so short, Torsin í Xandus?" he demanded. "Has your queen forgotten what sundered our peoples in the first place? I am not the only one present today who is old enough to recall the outcry of your people against Corruth í Glamien when he married the first Idrilain, or how he disappeared immediately after her death—murdered by Skalans. Adzriel ä Illia, how can you support those who ask us to embrace the murderers of your own kinsman?"

"Are the Skalans a single clan, that the action of one member brings shame to all?" Adzriel replied. "The Exile, once my brother, stands among us now in part due to his role in solving the mystery of Corruth's disappearance. Thanks to his efforts, the bones of my kinsman lie in Bôkthersa at last, and the clan of those who killed him has suffered disgrace and punishment. *Atui* had been served."

"Ah, yes!" sneered Nazien. "And what an advantageous discovery that was. It occurs to me that we have only the word of his murderers that the bundle of charred bones we saw was that of Corruth. What proof has been offered?"

"Proof enough for his kinswoman, the queen," Klia retorted. "Proof enough for me, who saw the body before it was burned. And proof remains. Seregil, if you would?"

Steeling himself, Seregil rose and faced Nazien. "Khirnari, did you know Corruth í Glamien well?"

"I did," Nazien snapped, then added pointedly, "in the days long before discord sundered the bonds of friendship between Haman and Bôkthersa."

Thanks so much for bringing that up here, Seregil thought. *But strike a bruise often enough and it goes numb.*

"Then you would recognize this, Khirnari." He pulled out the ring and carried it slowly around the circle for inspection.

Nazien's face darkened with suspicion as it came round to him. "This was Corruth's," he grudgingly acknowledged.

"I removed this and the consort's seal ring from the hand of his intact corpse before it was burned," Seregil told him, looking the man squarely in the eye. "As Princess Klia has stated, she herself saw the body." When all had seen and acknowledged the ring, he returned to his seat.

"The murder of Corruth is the concern of Bôkthersa and the Skalan queen, not of this assembly," Elos í Orian of Goliníl argued impatiently. "What Princess Klia has just proposed challenges the Edict of Separation. For more than two centuries we have lived peacefully within our own borders, trading with whom we choose without allowing foreigners and barbarians to roam our soil."

"Trading with whom Virésse chooses, you should say!" Rhaish í Arlisandin burst out angrily, prompting a groundswell murmur of agreement from many of the minor clans sitting in the outer circle. "It's all well and good for you eastern clans—you do not have to cart your goods past the ports you once used, and you profit from those who must. When is the last time the markets of Akhendi or Ptalos saw Tírfaie goods and gold? Not since your Edict of Separation closed its hold about our throats!"

"Perhaps Virésse would prefer to see Skala fall?" Iriel ä Kasrai of Bry'kha suggested. "After all, it has always been a shorter voyage to Benshâl than to Rhíminee!"

Ulan í Sathil remained conspicuously silent as the others of the council warmed to the familiar fight; evidently the khirnari of the Virésse knew when to let others fight his battles for him.

"There's your strongest adversary," Seregil told Klia, letting the surrounding uproar cover his words.

Klia glanced in Ulan's direction and smiled. "Yes, I can see that. I want to know this man better."

Silmai was the wealthiest of the western clans, and Brythir í Nien had spared nothing in the name of hospitality. Tense as he was from the day's business and the prospect of the evening still ahead, Seregil felt something loosen a little in his chest as he and the others entered the rooftop garden Brythir í Nien had prepared for them.

Flowering plants and trees in huge carved urns were thickly banked around three sides of the roofline, screening the rest of the city from view except for the broad avenue below, which had been cordoned off for displays of horsemanship. Bright silk banners and prayer kites rustled softly in the evening breeze overhead. In water-bowls decorated with sea creatures, tiny silver ships carried candles and smoking cones of incense on their decks. The sen'gai of the Datsians and Bry'khans who'd already arrived added to the illusion that they'd all been transported to Silmai itself.

"I thought the Haman were to be here?" Alec whispered, scanning the crowd warily.

"Not here yet. Or perhaps my presence scared them off?"

"Nazien í Hari doesn't strike me as someone easily frightened."

Dressed in a sen'gai and flowing festival robe of Silmai turquoise, Brythir í Nien leaned on the arm of a dark-eyed young woman as he welcomed Klia and her party.

"You honor our household with your presence," he said as he gently urged a little girl in a colorful embroidered tunic forward. The child bowed and presented Klia with a pair of heavy gold and turquoise bracelets. Watching her place them on her wrists with the Gedre bracelets and Akhendi charms, Seregil wondered if such gifts didn't eventually burden the arms. It was unlikely he'd ever find out for himself.

"I'm told that you have an uncommonly fine appreciation of horses," Brythir went on, giving Klia a knowing smile. "You ride a Silmai black, I understand?"

"The finest mount I've ever owned, Khirnari," she replied. "He's carried me through many a battle between here and Mycena."

"How I should like to show you the great horselands of my fai'thast. Our herds cover the hills."

"If my time here in Sarikali is productive, perhaps you shall," Klia replied with a subtle smile.

The old man recognized the unspoken implication. Offering her his frail arm, he gave her a mischievous wink that belied his years as he led her into the garden. "I believe tonight's entertainment will be very much to your liking, my dear."

"I understand Nazien í Hari will be joining us," said Klia. "Is he an ally of yours?"

The old man patted her hand as if she were one of his granddaughters. "We are friends, he and I, and I hope to make him one of yours. This Edict has worn sorely on me over the years, much as I loved Corruth í Glamien. He was a nephew of mine, you know. No, we Silmai are travelers, sailors, the best traders in Aurénen. We don't like being told where we may go and where we may not. How I miss lovely Rhíminee atop her high cliffs!"

"Your garden makes me long for the western coast," Seregil remarked as he and the others trailed along beside them. "I almost expect to see the green Zengati Sea shining beyond the rooftops."

Brythir clasped Seregil's arm for a moment with one frail hand. "Life is long, child of Aura. Perhaps one day you will see it again."

Surprised, Seregil bowed to the old man before moving on into the garden.

"That's encouraging!" Alec whispered.

"Or politic," Seregil muttered back.

His reception was somewhat cooler among the other guests. Datsia, Bry'kha, Ptalos, Ameni, Koramia—these clans had all supported his father's efforts with the Zengat, and thereby lost the most through Seregil's crime. He approached them with cautious civility and was greeted with the same by most, if only for the sake of Brythir's hospitality, or perhaps their interest in Alec.

If the weight of being a novelty was wearing on his companion, Alec gave no sign. Despite their long absence from the salons of Rhíminee, the lessons Alec had learned there still served him well. Modest, quiet, quick to smile, he moved among the guests as easily as water among stones. Trailing in his wake, Seregil watched with a mix of pride and amusement as various guests clasped Alec's hand a moment too long, or let their gaze wander a little too freely.

Stepping back, Seregil imagined seeing his friend, his talímenios, through their eyes: a slender, golden-haired young ya'shel utterly unconscious of his own appeal. It wasn't just his looks that struck people, either. Alec had a gift for listening to people, a way of focusing on whomever he was conversing with that made them feel like they were the most interesting person in the room. It didn't matter if that person was a tavern slopper or a lord, Alec had the touch.

Pride gave way to a wave of sensual hunger, reminding him that they hadn't done much more than fall asleep together since Gedre, and that it had been lean times for almost two weeks before that. Alec looked his way just then and smiled. Seregil hid his own grin behind the rim of a wine cup, suddenly glad of his full-skirted Skalan coat. Talímenios could be a tricky thing in public.

The tenor of the gathering changed subtly with the arrival of the Haman. Keeping to the background, Seregil watched as Klia greeted Nazien í Hari and his entourage. Surprisingly, the man greeted her cordially, clasping her hands and presenting her with a ring from his own finger. She did the same, and the two fell into conversation as Brythir looked on benevolently.

"What do you think of that?" Alec exclaimed softly, coming up behind him.

"Interesting. Perhaps even encouraging. After all, it's *me* the Haman hate, not Skala. Why don't you wander over for a listen?"

"Ah, there you are!" Klia smiled as Alec joined her. "Khirnari, I don't think you've met my aide, Alec í Amasa?"

"How do you do, honored sir?" Alec said with a bow.

"I have heard of him," Nazien replied, suddenly cool. Clearly, the man knew who he was and detested him on principle. With a single, subtle glance, the Haman dismissed him as thoroughly as if he'd ceased to exist. More amazing still, Klia seemed not to have noticed the slight.

Alec stepped back a pace, feeling as if the breath had suddenly been sucked from his lungs. It was his Watcher training that kept him there with Klia, listening, when every instinct counseled a hasty retreat.

So he hovered, studying the faces of the Haman beneath their yellow-and-black sen'gai as he pretended to listen to a nearby conversation. There were twelve Haman with Nazien—six men, six women, most of them close kin with the same dark, sharp eyes as their khirnari. Most chose to consider Alec invisible, though one, a broad-shouldered man with a dragon bite on his chin, spared Alec a challenging glare.

Alec was about to go when Nazien mentioned something about the Edict.

"It is a complex matter," the khirnari was saying to Klia. "You must understand, there was a great deal more to it than Corruth's disappearance. The exodus of the Hâzadriëlfaie centuries before was still fresh in the minds of our people—the terrible loss."

Alec inched closer; this was in line with what Adzriel had told them the night before.

"Then, as trade grew with the Three Lands, we watched as more 'faie disappeared to northern lands, mingling their blood with the Tír," Nazien continued. "Many of our clan mingled with yours, losing their ties with their own kind."

"Then you feel a 'faie belongs in Aurënen and nowhere else?" asked Klia.

"It is a common sentiment," Nazien replied. "Perhaps it is difficult for a Tírfaie to understand, as you find those like yourselves wherever you travel. We are a race apart, unique to this land. We are long-lived, it is true, but we are also, in Aura's great wisdom, slow to breed. I do not say that our lives are more sacred to us than those of the Tír are to you, but our attitude toward such things as war and murder is one of greater horror. I think you will be hard-pressed to convince any khirnari to send their people off to die in your war."

"And yet if you would only allow those who wish to go," Klia countered. "You must not underestimate our own love of life. Every day I am here more of my people die for want of the help you could so easily give. It is not honor we fight for, but our very lives."

"Be that as it may—"

They were interrupted by a call to the banquet. The light was failing quickly now, and torches were lit around the garden and in the street below. Klia and Nazien went to join their host. Alec moved off, looking for Seregil.

"Well?" asked Seregil as they took their seats on a couch near Klia's.

Alec shrugged, still smarting from the Haman's treatment. "Just more politics."

The entertainment began with the feast. A horn sounded and a dozen riders on Silmai blacks appeared from around the corner of a distant building. The horses' harnesses and girth straps were hung with tinkling gold and turquoise ornaments, and their streaming white manes and tails shone like combed milkweed silk.

The riders, men and women both, were equally exotic. Their long hair was bound tightly back into a club at the back of their necks, and each wore a silver crescent of Aura on their brow. The men wore short kilts dyed the turquoise blue of their clan and tightly belted with gold. The women wore tunics of similar design.

"They're ya'shel, too, aren't they?" Alec asked, pointing out several riders with golden-tan skin and curling black hair.

"Yes. Some Zengati blood, I'd say," Seregil told him.

Riding bareback at breakneck speeds, the performers leaped from one mount to another and rode standing on their horses' backs, their oiled limbs shining in the firelight. As one, they clapped their hands, and swirling masses of colored lights unfurled from their fingertips like banners, then were woven into patterns by the intricate drills they executed. The Skalans clapped and cheered. Standing guard behind Klia, Beka's riders cheered the loudest of all.

When the performers had finished and retired, a single rider took the field. Dressed like the others, he cantered out and saluted his audience, gripping his mount's sides with long, lean-muscled legs. His skin was a golden tan, his hair a cascade of long black curls.

"My youngest grandson, Täanil í Khormai," Brythir announced, beaming at Klia.

"And the banquet's main course, I suspect," murmured Seregil, nudging Alec with his elbow.

As Täanil set off on his first circuit of the grassy riding area, the khirnari leaned closer to Klia. "The skills of my grandson are not limited to riding. He is a fearless sailor, and a student of languages. He speaks your tongue quite flawlessly, I'm told. He would welcome the opportunity to converse with you."

I'll bet, thought Seregil, grinning behind his wine cup.

Coming down the field at a gallop, Täanil gripped his mount's girth strap and vaulted from side to side over its back, then went into a handstand, his lean body straight as a spear. The sight drew more than a few admiring sounds from the Skalan contingent.

The young Silmai joined Klia on her couch after his ride and charmed them all with his tales of sea trade and horsemanship.

When he left to perform again, Klia leaned over to Seregil and whispered. "Am I being courted?"

Seregil gave her a wink. "There's more than one way to forge an alliance. Marrying off a youngest grandson is a small price to pay for a new trade ally, wouldn't you say?"

"Are you saying I'm being offered second-rate goods?"

Seregil raised an eyebrow. "*I* certainly wouldn't call Täanil second rate. What I meant is that they wouldn't be losing a potential khirnari if he left."

Klia chuckled at this. "I don't think they have much to worry about on that score, but I suppose I can bear his company while we're here." She winked. "After all, we do need the horses."

13

GUIDES

Alec woke the following morning to find Seregil standing over him, dressed from head to foot in black: black leather breeches, black boots, long black velvet coat slashed with black silk. Above his gold badge of office, Corruth's ruby ring glowed on its silver chain. The overall effect was rather sinister. Seregil looked grim and tired.

"You were restless last night," Alec complained, yawning.

"I had that dream again, the one I had in the mountains."

"About going home?"

"If that's what it is." He sat down on the edge of the bed and laced his fingers together around one up-drawn knee.

Alec reached up to touch the Akhendi charm still braided into Seregil's hair. "It must be a true one, with this to guard your dreams."

Seregil gave a noncommittal shrug. "I think you'll be of more use behind the scenes today."

Changing the subject again, are you? Alec thought resignedly. Giving up for now, he settled back against the bolsters. "Where should I start?"

"You should learn your way around the city. I've asked Kheeta to guide you until you get used to the place. It's too easy to get lost when it's empty like this."

"How very tactful of you, Lord Seregil." Alec's sense of direction had a disconcerting way of deserting him in cities.

"Familiarize yourself with the area, make friends, keep your ears open." Leaning over, he ruffled Alec's already disheveled hair. "Look as simple and harmless as you can, even around our supporters. Sooner or later someone will let slip some interesting bit of information."

Alec affected a look of wide-eyed innocence and Seregil laughed.

"Perfect! And to think you used to say I'd never make an actor of you."

"What about that?" Alec said, pointing at the ring.

Glancing down in surprise, Seregil dropped it inside the neck of his coat, then headed for the door.

"Idrilain wouldn't have given it to you if she didn't think you were worthy of wearing it," Alec called after him.

Seregil gave him a last, thoughtful look and shook his head. "Good hunting, talí. Kheeta's waiting."

Alec lay back, thinking about the ring and wondering whose approval Seregil awaited. The Iia'sidra's? Adzriel's? The Haman's?

"Oh, well," he muttered, rolling out of bed. "At least I've got something to do today."

He washed with cold water from the pitcher and dressed for riding. He left his sword belt hanging with Seregil's over the bedpost. Most of the Aurënfaie he'd seen went unarmed except for belt knives. In the event of trouble, he always had the slender dagger in his boot. Their tool rolls were still hidden away for now, as well. According to Seregil, there were few locks in Sarikali, and most of those were magical in nature. That fact aside, it certainly wouldn't do for erstwhile diplomats to be caught carrying such a fine collection of lock picks.

Instead, he slung his bow and quiver over his shoulder and headed down in search of breakfast.

A cook gave him a pocket breakfast and news that Klia and the others had already left for the Iia'sidra. In the stable yard, he found Windrunner saddled next to another Aurënfaie mount.

"Feels like rain today, I'd say," Rhylin observed, on duty there.

Alec studied the hazy sky and nodded. The breeze had dropped and the clouds were already darkening ominously. "Have you seen Kheeta?"

"He went back to his room for something. He asked that you wait here."

The sound of voices drew Alec into the stable, where he found one of Mercalle's dispatch riders and her Akhendi guides trying to argue about liniments in two broken languages.

"Heading north?" he asked Ileah.

She patted the large pouch slung over her shoulder. "Maybe I can come by a few fancy dragon marks like yours along the way. Any letters you want carried to Rhíminee?"

"Not today. How long do you reckon it takes to get a message back through?"

"Less time than it took us to get here. We'll push harder over the unguarded sections of the pass, and we'll have fresh horses all along the way, compliments of our Akhendi friends."

"Good morning, Alec í Amasa!" said Kheeta, the fringed ends of his green sen'gai flying about his shoulders as he hurried in. "I'm to show you around, I'm told."

"Let us know if you find any decent taverns in this ghost city," Ileah implored.

"I wouldn't mind finding something like that myself," Alec admitted. "Where do we start, Kheeta?"

The Bôkthersan grinned. "Why, at the Vhadäsoori, of course."

Cloud shadows scudded across their path as they set off along the turf-muted avenue leading back to the center of the city.

It felt less deserted today. Riders galloped past, and there were people in the streets. Marketplaces had been set up at crossroads, with goods being sold on blankets or out of the backs of carts. Most of the people Alec saw looked like servants and attendants. Clearly, it took a sizable population behind the scenes to maintain the banquets and bathhouses that helped court alliances.

"It's difficult to believe a city like this just stands empty most of the time," Alec remarked.

"Not quite empty," said Kheeta. "There are the Bash'wai, and the rhui'auros. But as you say, Sarikali belongs mostly to itself and its ghosts. We are merely occasional lodgers, coming here for festivals, or to settle clan disputes on neutral ground."

He pointed to a stag's skull set on a post beside the street. It was painted red, with silvered horns. "See that. It's a boundary marker for Bôkthersa tupa. And that white hand with the black symbol on the palm painted on the wall across the street marks the tupa of Akhendi."

"Are people very territorial here?" Given the chances that he'd be nightrunning here sooner or later, it was a good idea to know the local customs.

"It depends on who is involved, I suppose. Violence is forbidden, but trespassers can be made to feel quite unwelcome. I stay clear of Haman tupa and you and your companions will do well to do the same, especially when you're alone. The Khatme aren't much for visitors, either."

At the Vhadäsoori they left their horses outside the circle of stones and entered on foot. Alec paused beside one of the monolithic figures, pressing a palm to its rough surface. He half expected to feel some magical vibration, but the stone was silent beneath the cool morning dew.

"You did not have a proper welcome the other day," Kheeta said, going to the moon-shaped chalice that still stood on its pillar. "All who come to Sarikali drink from the Cup of Aura."

"Is it left here all the time?" Alec asked, surprised.

"Of course." Kheeta dipped up water from the pool and presented it to him.

Alec took it in both hands. The narrow alabaster bowl was perfectly smooth, its silver base untarnished.

"Is it magical?" he asked.

The Bôkthersan shrugged. "Everything is magical in some way, even if we cannot perceive it."

He drank deeply, then handed it back to Kheeta. "Don't you have any thieves here in Aurënen?"

"In Aurënen? Of course. But not here."

A city without locks and without footpads and thieves? Alec thought skeptically. That would be magic indeed.

They spent the rest of the morning exploring. There were hundreds of tupas, counting those of the lesser clans, so Alec concentrated on those of the Eleven for the moment. Kheeta was a talkative guide, pointing out clan markers and points of interest. One hulking dark structure looked very much like another until he named it as a temple or meeting place.

Alec found himself studying his companion as well. "Does Seregil seem much changed to you?" he asked at last.

Kheeta sighed. "Yes, especially when he's dealing with the Iia'sidra or your princess. Then again, when he looks at you, or makes a joke, I see the same old haba."

"I heard Adzriel call him that," Alec said, pouncing on the unfamiliar word. "Is it like 'talí'?"

Kheeta chuckled. "No, haba are small black—" He paused, searching for the Skalan word. "Squirrels? Yes, squirrels, that live in the western forests. They're everywhere in Bôkthersa, feisty little creatures that can chew their way into the tightest bale, or will steal the bread from your hand when you're not looking. Seregil could climb like a haba, and fight like one when pushed to it. He was always trying to prove himself, that one."

"To his father?"

"You've heard about that, have you?"

"A bit." Alec tried not to sound too eager. This wasn't the sort of information he'd been sent to gather, but he wasn't about to let the opportunity pass.

"Well, you've met Mydri, so you can see the difference. Seregil and Adzriel were the only ones of the four who took after their mother. Perhaps things might have been different for Seregil if she'd lived." Kheeta paused, frowning at some unpleasant memory. "There are those in the family who say it was Korit's guilt that kept father and son at odds."

"Guilt? For what?"

"For Illia's death in childbirth. Most Aurënfaie women bear only one or two children, but Korit í Solun wanted a son to carry his name. Illia obliged him out of love, having daughter after daughter until she was past her prime. The last birthing was too much for her, or at least that's how I've heard it.

"The raising of Seregil fell to Adzriel, and a good thing, too. What finally happened with that bastard Ilar—" Kheeta spat vehemently over his horse's flank. "Well, there are those who laid the blame as much on his father as on Seregil. I tried to tell Seregil as much last night, but he won't listen."

"I know what you mean. It's best to leave certain subjects alone."

"And yet he became a great hero in Skala." Kheeta's admiration and affection for Seregil was evident. "And you, as well, from what I hear?"

"We got through some bad times with whole skins," Alec replied vaguely, not in the mood to extol their exploits like some bard's tale.

He was spared the trouble. As they came around a corner, they saw a woman dressed in a red robe and bulbous black hat standing in the shadowed doorway of a temple, apparently in the midst of an animated conversation with someone inside. As they drew closer, Alec could make out complicated patterns of black lines covering the woman's hands.

"What clan is she?"

"No clan. That's a rhui'auros. They give up their clan when they enter the *Nha'mahat*," Kheeta told him, making a sign of some sort in her direction.

Before Alec could ask what a nha'mahat was he came abreast of the rhui'auros and saw that she was talking to empty air.

"Bash'wai," Kheeta said, noting Alec's surprise.

A chill ran up Alec's spine as he looked back at the empty doorway. "The rhui'auros can see them?"

"Some do. Or claim to. They have some strange ways, and what they say is not always what they mean."

"They lie?"

"No, but they are often—obscure."

"I'll keep that in mind when we visit them. Seregil hasn't had a free moment since we—"

Kheeta stared at him. "Seregil spoke of going there?"

Alec thought back to that odd, tense conversation back in Ardinlee. Seregil hadn't spoken of the rhui'auros since.

"You mustn't ever ask him to go there," Kheeta warned.

"Why?"

"If he's not told you, then it's not for me to say."

"Kheeta, please," Alec urged. "Most of what I know about Seregil I've learned from other people. He gives away so little about himself, even now."

"I shouldn't have spoken. It's for him to tell you that tale, or not."

Being close-mouthed and stubborn must be a Bôkthersan trait, Alec thought, as they rode on in silence.

"Come," Kheeta said at last, relenting a bit. "I can show you where to find them for yourself."

Leaving the more populated tupas behind, they rode to a quarter at the southern edge of the city. The buildings here were overgrown and crumbling, the streets choked in places with tall grass and wildflowers. Weeds had claimed the courtyards. For all its strangeness, however, it appeared to be a popular destination; people strolled the ruined streets in pairs and small groups. Dragonlings, the first Alec had seen since they'd left the mountains, were as plentiful as grasshoppers, basking on the tops of walls like lizards or fluttering among the flowering vines with the sparrows and hummingbirds.

This place felt different, as well, the magic stronger and more unsettling.

"This is called the Haunted City," Kheeta explained. "It's believed that the veil between ourselves and the Bash'wai is thinnest here. The Nha'mahat lies just outside the city."

They rode past the last of the crumbling houses and out into the open. On a rise just ahead stood the most bizarre-looking structure Alec had seen here yet. It was a huge tower of sorts, built in a series of square tiers that diminished in size as they went up. It was topped with a large colos and Alec could see people moving in the archways there. Although different in design from anything he had seen in Sarikali, it was made of the same dark stone and had the same grown-from-the-earth look. Behind it, the white vapor of a hot spring billowed up, roiling on the slight breeze.

"The Nha'mahat," Kheeta said, dismounting well away from the building. "We'll go on foot. Be careful not to step on the little dragons. They're thick here."

Alec kept a nervous eye on the ground as he followed.

The ground level was bordered by a covered arcade. Prayer kites hung from the pillars, some new, some faded and tattered.

Entering, Alec saw that the walkways were lined with trays of food: fruit, boiled grains dyed yellow and red, and milk. Fingerlings seemed to be the main beneficiary of this bounty; masses of the little creatures vied for a meal under the watchful eye of several robed rhui'auros.

Strolling around to the back of the building, Alec saw that the ground fell away sharply. The vapor he'd seen issued from the dark mouth of a grotto beneath the tower. Steam belched from it like smoke from a forge. More rose in wisps from the stream that flowed down among the stones below.

Something happened to him here, Alec thought, suddenly picturing a much younger Seregil being dragged into the darkness below.

"Would you like to go in?" asked Kheeta, leading him back toward a doorway.

A gust of cold wind whipped across the open plain, carrying the first spattering of rain. Alec shivered. "No. Not yet."

If Kheeta sensed his sudden discomfort, he choose not to pry. "Suit yourself," he said amiably. "Since we have to go back through the Haunted City, how do you like ghost stories?"

The gash Beka had gotten during the sea battle was healing, but she still suffered from sudden headaches. The brewing storm had brought on another, and by midmorning its effects must have shown, for Klia sent her home with strict orders to rest.

Returning to the barracks alone, she retreated to her room and exchanged her uniform for a light shirt and tunic. Stretched out on the bed, she settled one arm over her eyes and lay listening to the soft clatter of gaming stones in the next room. She was drifting on the edge of sleep when she caught Nyal's voice outside. She hadn't exactly been avoiding him these past few days, she just hadn't had time to deal with the silly flux of emotions he provoked in her. The approach of booted feet warned that there was no avoiding it now except to plead illness. Not wanting to be caught at a disadvantage, she sat up quickly on the narrow bed, then choked down the wave of nausea the sudden move cost her.

"It's Nyal," Urien announced, peeking in around the door. "He's brought you something for your head."

"Did he?" How in Bilairy's name had he known she was ill?

To her horror, he entered carrying a little nosegay of flowers. What were the others going to make of that?

"I heard you were feeling unwell," he said. Instead of the flowers, however, he held out a flask. "I've picked up a fair bit of herb lore in my travels. This decoction works well for pains in the head."

"And those?" Beka asked with a wry grin, pointing to the flowers.

He passed her those as well, as if they'd been an afterthought. "I don't know all their names in Skalan. I thought you might wish to know what was in it."

Beka bent over the flowers, hoping he wouldn't notice her guilty blush. *Bringing you flowers, was he? And why are you so damned disappointed?* "I recognize a few of them. The little white ones are feverfew, and these branch tips are from a willow." She pinched a thick, dark green leaf, then took a nibble. "And this is mountain cress. I haven't seen these others before."

Nyal knelt in front of her and pushed her hair back to inspect the scabbed cut on her brow. "This is healing well."

"The Cavishes are a hardheaded bunch," Beka told him, pulling back from the light brush of his fingers against her face. Opening the flask, she took a swig and grimaced. There was honey in the mix, but not enough to mask the underlying bitterness.

"I didn't see any wormwood in that bouquet of yours," she sputtered.

He laughed. "That's the little pink blossom we call 'mouse ears.'" He poured a cup of water and handed it to her. "My mother used to hold my nose when she dosed me. I'll sit with you a moment until we see if it's going to do its work."

An awkward silence ensued. Beka wanted nothing more than to lie down and sleep, but not with him sitting there. The little room was stuffy; she could feel sweat trickling down her chest and back and regretted putting on the tunic.

After a few moments, however, she realized that the throbbing behind her eyes was nearly gone.

"That's quite a brew!" she said, sniffing the flask again. "I wouldn't mind keeping some of this on hand for the others. Sergeant Braknil does most of our healing for us in the field when there isn't a drysian handy."

"I'll see he gets the recipe." Nyal rose to go, then paused, eyeing her critically. "The air is so still today, perhaps a walk would do you good. I could show you some more of the city before the rain comes. There's so much you haven't seen yet."

It would have been a simple matter to plead illness. Instead, she smoothed her hair back and followed him out, telling herself that as the head of Klia's bodyguard, it was her duty to learn the lay of the land. In case of trouble.

They set off on foot as thunder wandered ever closer across the valley. Nyal headed south, pointing out tupas of various lesser clans as they went. He seemed to know a bit about all of them and shared a few amusing stories along the way. As they passed the outskirts of Akhendi tupa, she was tempted to ask more about the khirnari's wife but resisted the urge.

Most of the city was uninhabited, and the further they got from the center of it, the more overgrown the streets became. The grass grew longer here, and mud swallows had built nests in the corners of open windows.

One place looked very much like another to Beka, but Nyal seemed to have a particular destination in mind. This turned out to be a deserted neighborhood in the southern part of the city, one more silent and peculiar than any she'd seen so far.

"Here's a place I think you'll enjoy," he announced at last, leading her into a broad thoroughfare where scrubby bushes were taking back the open spaces.

She glanced around nervously. "I thought I'd gotten used to the feel of Sarikali, but this is different. Stronger."

"We call it the Haunted City," Nyal replied. "The magic works differently here. Can you feel it?"

"I feel *something*." Whether it was the magic of the place, the impending storm, or the way his arm occasionally brushed hers as they walked, she suddenly felt hot and restless. Pausing, she pulled the tunic off over her head, caring little that the loose linen shirt underneath was stained with sweat and metal tarnish. Tugging it free of her breeches, she undid the neck lacings to let the quickening breeze cool her skin. Like most of her female riders, she didn't bother with binding her breasts when not in the field. Glancing his way, she saw an enigmatic smile on his lips and knew that she had his attention. Alone with him here, she had to admit at last that she liked it.

"This is a very special place," he continued. "The Bash'wai who lived here simply walked away one day, leaving everything they owned behind."

They entered one of the houses and passed through an empty gallery to a fountain court. A stone table near the leaf-choked basin was set for six, complete with cups and cracked plates of fine red porcelain. A tarnished silver pitcher stood in the center, its interior still stained with the wine that had dried away countless years before. Beyond the courtyard lay a bedchamber. The furnishings were rotted with age, but a carved wooden tray on a chest still held a collection of gold jewelry, as if the woman who'd owned them had just taken them off before her bath.

"Why haven't thieves carried all this away?" Beka asked, picking up a brooch.

"No one dares rob the dead. One of my aunts loves to tell the story of a woman who found a ring here that was so beautiful she couldn't resist taking it. Her clan went home soon after and almost immediately she began to suffer nightmares. They became so powerful and terrifying that at last she threw the ring into a river. When she returned to Sarikali the following year, that ring was lying exactly where she'd found it."

Returning the brooch to the tray, Beka gave him a look of mock disapproval. "I think you brought me here to scare me, Ra'basi."

Nyal took her hand in his, stroking it with long fingers. "And why should I attempt such a thing with a brave Skalan captain?"

His touch sent a sensuous tingle up her arm, stronger than before.

"To test my bravery, perhaps?" she teased. "Or to create the opportunity to offer comfort?"

Looking into those clear hazel eyes, she felt another jolt of sensual anticipation; there was no mistaking the passion kindling there, or the open affection. It would be so easy to close the distance between her lips and his, she thought, as if gauging an arrow's flight. Without further thought, she kissed him.

She'd wanted this—wanted him—from the instant she'd laid eyes on him at Gedre. Now she let her hands roam, greedily exploring the hard, responsive body pressed to hers. His mouth was as sweet as she'd imagined, and when he pulled her close she buried her fingers in his hair, nipping his lower lip.

His hands slipped beneath the hem of her shirt, encircling her bare waist above her sword belt, working their way slowly higher.

"Lovely one, beautiful Tír," he murmured against her ear.

"Don't." She tensed and took a step back. Other lovers had used such blandishments and she'd let them pass; from Nyal they were unbearable.

"What is it?" he asked, concerned by the sudden shift. "Are you a virgin, or do you distrust me?"

Beka laughed in spite of the hot, resentful ache in her belly—or perhaps because of it. "I'm no virgin. But I'm not beautiful either, and don't need to fancy myself so. I'd rather we just be honest with each other, if it's all the same to you."

He stared at her in amazement. "Anyone who claims you are not beautiful is a fool. The first time I looked into your eyes I saw it, yet you have been denying it since we met."

He took her hand again. "I apologize for the clumsiness of my persistence, but I swear I will continue to say so until you believe me. You're unlike any woman I've ever met."

Trapped between doubt and arousal, Beka froze, unable to reply.

Misreading her hesitation, he brought her hand to his lips. "At least allow me to call you 'friend.' I promised your almost-brother I would never bring dishonor on you. I keep my word."

Perhaps he'd meant the gesture to be a chaste one; the warmth of his lips on her palm sent a wave of raw desire spiraling through her. Suddenly the light brush of her shirt against her skin was too much to bear. Freeing one hand, she pulled the shirt off, letting it drop to the dusty floor at her feet. Nyal's lips parted in a sigh as he traced the scars on her arms, chest, and side. "A true warrior."

"All my wounds are in the front," Beka managed, trying to sound flippant but shivering at the hot-and-cold touch of his fingers across her skin. By the time he reached her shoulders and breasts she was trembling.

"I like your spots," he murmured, bending to kiss her shoulder.

"Freckles," she corrected breathlessly, tugging up his tunic.

"Ah, yes. Freckles." He paused long enough to help her with his clothes, then pulled her close again. "So exotic."

That's a first, she thought, too far gone in the feel of his body warm against hers to care. His fingers traced burning patterns across her skin wherever he touched her, the sensation unlike anything she'd ever felt. Pulling back a little, she asked in wonder, "Are you using magic on me, Ra'basi?"

The hazel eyes widened, then tilted up at the corners as he laughed. The rich vibration of it against her chest and belly was a new and unprecedented pleasure.

"Magic?" he exclaimed, shaking his head. "By the Light, what sort of dolts have you let make love to you?"

Beka's laughter echoed around the ruined room as she pulled him closer. "Educate me!"

Nyal's expert tutelage lasted well over an hour, Beka guessed, seeing how the shadows had crept closer to where they lay. When it was over she was a good deal wiser, and happier than she'd been in recent memory.

The bed had proved too rickety, so they'd made do with a pallet of clothing on the floor. Unsnarling her breeches from the tangled mass, she reluctantly pulled them on, then leaned down to give her new lover a lingering kiss. Outside, thunder rumbled heavily in the distance.

Nyal's flushed face reflected her own elation. "Beautiful Tír," he said, gazing up at her.

"Beautiful Aurënfaie," she replied in his own language, no longer contesting his opinion.

"I did not think you would have me. Do all Tír hold back so?"

Beka considered this. "I have duties. What my heart and body want aren't what my head thinks I should do. And—"

"And?" he asked when she looked away.

"And I'm a little afraid of what you make me feel, afraid because I know it won't last. I lost someone, too. He died. Was killed." Beka closed her eyes against sorrow long denied. "He was a warrior, an officer in my regiment. I didn't have long with him, but we cared a great deal for each other. The pain I felt when he died was . . ." She stopped again, searching for words that wouldn't sound too cold but not finding them. "It was a distraction. I can't allow that sort of thing, not when I have people depending on me to lead them."

Nyal stroked her face until she opened her eyes again. "I won't hurt you, Beka Cavish, or cause you any distraction if it's in my power to avoid it. What we do—" He grinned, waving a hand around at the disordered room. "We are two friends sharing a gift of Aura. There's no pain from that. Whether you're here or in Skala, we are friends."

"Friends," Beka agreed, even as the little voice from her heart taunted, *Too late, too late!*

"It's early yet," she said, rising. "Show me more of your city. Seems I have an unquenchable appetite for wonders today."

Nyal sprawled limply and let out a comic groan. "Warrior women!"

They were nearly dressed when something he'd said earlier suddenly struck her. Turning to Nyal, she raised an eyebrow and demanded, "When exactly did you and my 'almost-brother' discuss what to do with me?"

Beka's sudden appearance in the doorway of one of the ruined houses startled Kheeta as much as it did Alec.

"Aura's Fingers!" the Bôkthersan laughed, reining in. "That's the first red-haired Bash'wai I've ever seen."

Beka froze for a moment, face reddening behind her freckles. An instant later Nyal stepped from the shadows behind her.

"Well, well, Captain," Alec said in Skalan, grinning mercilessly as he took in their disheveled hair and dust-streaked clothing. "Out reconnoitering?"

"I'm off duty," she retorted, and something in the look she gave him warned against further teasing.

"Have you shown her the House of Pillars yet?" Kheeta asked, apparently oblivious to the situation, or why his innocent question should draw such a loud and poorly suppressed snort of laughter from Alec.

"We were just heading there," Nyal replied, fighting to keep a straight face. "Why don't you come along with us?"

"Yes, *do* come!" Beka said, walking up to Alec and grasping his stirrup. In a low voice, she added, "You can keep a closer eye on me that way, Almost-Brother."

Alec winced. *Damn you, Nyal!*

The house in question lay several streets away. Thunder cracked again, much closer now, and a sudden gust of wind blew their hair into their eyes.

"There it is," Kheeta said, pointing out a sprawling, open-sided structure through the gloom. Just then the skies opened up in earnest. Lightning bleached the air white for an instant, then darkness closed down around them with a deafening roll of thunder. Gripping the reins of their nervous mounts, Alec and Kheeta dashed toward shelter through the pelting rain with Beka and Nyal close behind.

The House of Pillars was a pavillion with a flat, tiled roof set on ranks of tall, evenly spaced black columns. Shreds of faded cloth hung here and there, suggesting that walls of a sort had been created by hanging tapestries between the columns.

"Looks like we'll be here awhile," said Beka, raising her voice to be heard over the downpour.

A damp wind swept through the outer columns, and they retreated farther to avoid the soaking rain that blew in with it. Alec reached inside his coat for the lightstone in his tool roll, then remembered he'd left both back at his room. Kheeta and Nyal flicked their fingers, and small globes of light snapped into being at their tips.

"What was this place?" asked Alec, speaking Skalan for Beka's benefit.

"A summer retreat," said Nyal. "It gets terribly hot here in summer. The roof makes shade and there are bathing pools further in."

Occasional flashes from outside threw bars of light and shadow across their path as they walked deeper into the forest of pillars.

Alec had assumed they had the place to themselves, but soon heard the sound of water splashing and the echo of voices from somewhere ahead of them.

Emerging into a large chamber, they came to a large round bathing pool fed by underground springs. Channels fanned out from it to smaller pools and what appeared to have been water gardens or fish pools.

A few dozen people were swimming naked in the large pool. Others sat nearby playing some kind of game by the light of hovering light orbs. Alec noted with a twinge of unease that most of those who were dressed wore the sen'gai of Haman or Lhapnos. Judging by their age and clothes, they were young retainers of those delegations, taking their ease while their elders attended the council.

Nyal approached them with his usual openness, but Kheeta hung back warily.

"Nyal í Nhekai!" called a Lhapnosan youth. "It's been too long since I've seen you, my friend. Come join us."

His welcoming smile died, however, at sight of Alec and the others. Getting to his feet, the Lhapnosan let one hand rest near the hilt of the knife in his belt. Several of his companions did the same.

"But I forgot," he said, eyes narrowing. "You're not keeping the best company these days."

"He certainly isn't," one of the swimmers remarked, climbing from the pool. He strode up to them, his face set in a disdainful frown.

Alec tensed, recognizing him by the dragon bite on his chin. This was no servant. He'd been with the Haman khirnari last night at the Silmai banquet.

The Haman stood a moment, eyeing them with distaste. "A Bôk-thersan, a Tírfaie." His gaze came to rest on Alec. "And the Exile's *garshil ke'menios.*"

Alec understood only half the phrase—*garshil* meant "mongrel"—but that and the Haman's tone left no doubt that it was a calculated insult.

"This is Emiel í Moranthi of Haman, the khirnari's nephew," Nyal warned in Skalan.

"I know who he is," said Alec, keeping his tone neutral, as if he hadn't understood the insult.

Kheeta had no such reservations. "You should choose your words more carefully, Emiel í Moranthi!" he snarled, stepping closer.

Alec laid a hand on his arm, then said in Aurënfaie, "He can use what words he likes. It's of no concern to me."

His antagonist's eyes narrowed; none of the Haman had bothered chatting with him the night before and no doubt assumed he did not speak their language.

"What's going on?" Beka muttered, sensing trouble.

"Just a few insults between clans," Alec said evenly. "Best to walk away."

"Yes," Nyal agreed, no longer smiling as he urged the glowering Kheeta back the way they'd come. But Beka was still eyeing the naked man.

"It was nothing," Alec repeated firmly, snagging her by the sleeve and following.

"What's the matter, too frightened to join us?" Emiel jeered.

It was Alec who wheeled around and, against all better judgment, strode back to face him. With the same bravado he'd once used staring down back-alley toughs, he crossed his arms and cocked his head to one side, slowly scanning Emiel from head to foot until his would-be adversary shifted uncomfortably under the scrutiny.

"No," Alec replied at last, raising his voice for all to hear. "I see nothing here that frightens me."

He sensed the attack coming and jumped back as Emiel lunged for him. The Haman's companions caught at him, dragging him back. Alec felt hands on his arms, too, but shook them off, needing no restraint. Somewhere behind him, Beka was cursing pungently in two languages as Kheeta restrained her.

"Remember where you are, all of you," Nyal warned, shouldering in between them.

Emiel hissed softly between clenched teeth, but fell back. "Thank you, my friend," he sneered, though his gaze never left Alec. "Thank you for not letting me soil my hands with this little garshil ke'menios."

With that, he sauntered back toward the pool.

"Come away," Nyal urged.

The skin between his shoulder blades prickled and he tensed, expecting any moment for the Haman to change their minds and renew the fight. Aside from a few jeers and muttered insults, however, the defenders of the pool let them go in peace.

"What was that he called you?" Beka asked again as soon as they were out of earshot.

"Nothing that matters."

"Oh, I can see that! What did he say?" Beka demanded.

"I didn't get all of it."

"He called you a mongrel boy whore," Kheeta growled.

Alec could feel his face burning and was glad of the shadows.

"I've been called worse," he lied. "Let it go, Beka. The last thing Klia needs is the head of her bodyguard getting into a brawl."

"Bilairy's *Balls*! That filthy son of a—"

"Please, Beka, you mustn't say such things aloud. Not here," said Nyal. "Emiel's behavior is understandable. Seregil murdered his kinsman, and by our reckoning, Alec is kin to Seregil. Surely it's not so different among your own people?"

"Back home you can knock somebody's teeth in without starting a war," she snapped.

Nyal shook his head. "What a place this Skala must be."

Alec caught a hint of motion out of the corner of his eye just then and slowed, peering into the darkness between the pillars. Perhaps the Haman hadn't been put off so easily after all. He caught a hint of an unfamiliar scent, heavy with musk and spice. Then it was gone.

"What is it?" Beka asked softly.

"Nothing," he said, though instinct warned otherwise.

Outside, it was raining harder than ever. Curtains of mist anchored the clouds to the rooftops.

"Perhaps you should ride back with us," Kheeta suggested.

"I suppose so," Beka agreed. Accepting the Bôkthersan's outstretched hand, she swung easily up behind him.

Alec kicked a stirrup free for Nyal. The Ra'basi reached to accept a hand up, then stopped to examine the Akhendi charm dangling from Alec's wrist. The little bird carving had turned black.

"What happened to it?" Alec asked, peering at it in surprise. A tiny crack he hadn't noticed before marred the tip of one wing.

"It's a warning charm. Emiel ill-wished you," Nyal explained.

"A waste of good magic, if you ask me," Kheeta muttered. "It takes no magic to read the heart of a Haman."

Alec pulled out his dagger, intending to cut the charm free and toss it into the bushes.

"Don't," Nyal said, staying his hand. "It can be restored so long as you don't destroy the knots."

"I don't want Seregil seeing this. He'll know something happened and I hate lying to him."

"Give it to me, then," the Ra'basi offered. "I'll get one of the Akhendi to fix it for you."

Alec plucked the lacings free and handed it to him. "I want your word, all of you, that Seregil won't hear about this. He has enough to worry about."

"Are you sure that's wise, Alec?" asked Kheeta. "He's not a child."

"No, but he does have a temper. The Haman insulted me to get at him. I'm not going to play their game for them."

"I'm not so sure," Beka said, more concerned than angry now. "You keep your distance from them, especially if you're alone. That was more than bluff and bluster just now."

"Don't worry," Alec said, forcing a grin. "If there's one thing I've learned from Seregil, it's how to avoid people."

14

MYSTERIES

Thero envied Beka the headache that had
released her from the day's duties. As negotiations rambled on, the wizard grew
increasingly restless. Most of the day's
speeches were hollow posturing, currying favor with one side or the other. Stories and
grievances from centuries past were trotted
out and argued. Apparently there was no
shame in napping during these interludes; a
number of onlookers up in the gallery were
snoring audibly.

Thunderstorms descended on the city soon
after midday, throwing the Iia'sidra chamber
into lamp-lit gloom. Cold winds swept in
through the windows, carrying rain and
leaves. At times thunder drowned the voice of
the speaker on the floor.

Chin on hand, Thero watched the lightning
illuminate rippling sheets of rain lashing
down outside. It brought back memories of
his apprentice days in Nysander's tower. Sitting at the window of his chamber on summer afternoons, he'd watched the barbed
white bolts spike down over the harbor and
dreamed of capturing that power, channeling it
through his hands. To control something that
could destroy you in an instant—the thought
had made his pulse race. One day he'd blurted out his idea to Nysander, asking if it could
be done.

The older wizard had merely given him a look of kindly forbearance and asked, "If you could control it, dear boy, would it be as beautiful?"

The response had seemed nonsensical to him at the time, he thought sadly.

An especially long, bright flash lit the Iia'sidra just then, transforming the window he'd been staring at into an oblong of weird blue-white brilliance. Thero saw the black outline of a woman framed there, as if in a doorway.

The window went dark again, and a clap of thunder shook the building, driving in a fresh gust of wind. The figure had been no fleeting vision, however. A young rhui'auros stood there, resting one hand lightly against the stone frame as she stared across the chamber at him. Her lips moved and he heard a voice whisper in his mind, *Come to us afterward, my brother. It is time.*

Before Thero could even nod, she had faded away in a blur of color.

Thankfully, the council adjourned early that day. Thero doubted he could have told anyone what had been said. Following Klia and the others out into the storm, he found the woman waiting for him by his horse. She was very young, with grey-green eyes that seemed overly large beneath her ridiculous hat. Her soaked robe clung to her thin frame like a wrinkled second skin, and the wind had whipped her wet hair into lank strands against her cheeks. She should have been shivering, but she wasn't.

Klia gave her a surprised glance.

"With your permission, my lady, I would like to visit the rhui'auros," he explained.

"In this weather?" Klia asked, then shrugged. "Take care. I'll need you first thing tomorrow."

Thero's strange companion did not speak as they set out, nor would she accept his cloak or an offer to ride. He was soon glad to have a guide. In this weather, one broad, deserted street looked no different from another.

Reaching the Nha'mahat at last, the girl motioned for him to dismount, then led him by the hand along a well-worn path to the cave beneath the tower. Clouds of vapor issued from the low opening, crawling low across the ground to disappear in wisps on the wind. Mineral secretions coated the rock here, white and yellows shot through with wavering bands of black. Untold pairs of feet had worn a smooth path inside.

A sudden rush of wonder brought a lump to Thero's throat as he followed it into the large natural chamber beyond. If Nysander had been correct, this was the very womb of mysteries, the source of the magic that had come to his own people through the blood of Aurënen.

The place was humid and primitive, its rough walls unaltered except for a few scattered lamps and a broad staircase that curved like a ram's horn at the center of the room, its even stonework out of place in such a setting. Light shone down from some upper room, and Thero smelled the sweet reek of incense as they passed. Down here there was nothing of ritual or decoration. Steam curled up from a network of fissures and small pools in the floor. Rhui'auros and 'faie moved among the shadows, quiet as ghosts.

The girl gave him no time to get his bearings but continued down one of several passageways that branched off from the main chamber. There were no lamps here and she did not strike a light. The darkness posed no problem for Thero, either; when his eyes failed other senses took over, showing him his surroundings in muted shapes of black and grey. Was this a test, he wondered, or did she simply assume that, sharing a similar magic, Tír wizards could see in the dark?

Sweltering air closed in around them as they went on, and Thero was aware of the downward slant of the tunnel floor beneath his feet. Small, hive-shaped structures stood here and there along the way, large enough to hold a person or two. Brushing his fingers across one as he passed, he felt thick, sodden wool. Leather flaps covered a small door and an opening at its top.

"*Dhima,* for meditation," she told him, speaking at last. "You may use them whenever you like."

Evidently this was not the point of the current expedition. The passage took a sharp jog to the right and the air grew cooler, the way more steep and narrow. There were no dhima here.

In places they had to duck their heads as the overhanging stone dipped low. In others, they grasped thick ropes strung through metal eyelets driven into the stone, lowering themselves over short drops. He lost track of time in the darkness, but the feeling of magical energy grew stronger with every step.

At last they reached level ground again, and Thero heard a sound like wind in branches. After a few yards the tunnel curved again, and suddenly he was blinking in the relative brightness of clear moonlight. Looking around in surprise, he saw that they were standing at the edge of a forest clearing under a clear night sky. The ground sloped gently to the edge of a glassy black pool. The crescent moon's reflection floated motionless on its still surface, undisturbed by any ripple.

The light grew brighter as he stood there. Looking around, he could find no sign of his guide, but the pool was now surrounded by a great throng. Those he could make out wore the robes and hats of the rhui'auros. He knew by the lifting of the hair on his arms that at least some of them were spirits, though one looked as solid as another, even the ones with the curling black hair and dark skin of Bash'wai. Beyond them, in the thick, night-black forest, something moved—many creatures, and large ones.

"Welcome, Thero son of Nysander, wizard of the Third Orëska," a deep voice rumbled from the darkness. "Do you know where you are?"

Caught off guard by the misnomer, it took Thero a moment to grasp the question. As soon as he did, however, he knew the answer.

"The Vhadäsoori pool, Honored One," he replied in an awed whisper. How he knew it was a mystery—there was no sign of the statues, much less the city itself, but the magic that radiated from the black water was unmistakable.

"You see with the eyes of a rhui'auros, Nysander's son."

The girl who had been his guide stepped from the crowd and offered him a cup fashioned from a hollow tusk. It was as long as his forearm and wrapped in an intricate binding of leather thongs that formed handles on either side. Grasping these, Thero closed his eyes and drank deeply. Beneath his fingers, the cup vibrated with the touch of a thousand hands.

When he looked up again, he and the girl were alone in the clearing. Her face no longer looked so young, and her eyes were flat disks of gold.

"We are the First Orëska," she told him. "We are your forebears, your history, Wizard. In you we see our future, as you perceive your past in us. The dance goes on, and your kind will be made whole."

"I don't understand," he said.

"It is the will of Aura, Thero son of Nysander son of Arkoniel son of Iya daughter of Agazhar, of the line of Aura."

Gentle, unseen hands loosened the fastenings of Thero's garments and they fell away, shoes and all. A will other than his own guided him to the water's edge, and on, until he was up to his neck in the pool. The water was winter cold, so cold it robbed the breath from his lungs and burned his skin like fire. Turning back toward shore, he was surprised to see himself still standing there beside the woman. Then he was dragged under.

The water closed over him, filling his eyes and nose and mouth, and then his lungs, yet he felt no discomfort, no panic. Lost in the formless dark, he floated, waiting. And remembering. The night they'd slept by the dragon pool in Akhendi he'd dreamed of this place and of drowning. The dream itself had raveled to mere fragments since then, yet it resonated with the same surety he'd felt when he'd named this place as the Vhadäsoori.

"What is the purpose of magic, Thero son of Nysander?" the deep voice asked.

"To serve, to know—" Thero was unsure whether he spoke aloud or only thought the words; it made no difference, for the other heard him.

"No, little brother, you are wrong. What is the purpose of magic, son of Nysander?"

"To create?"

"No, little brother. What is the purpose of magic, son of Nysander?"

The darkness pushed in on him. He felt the pressure of it in his lungs, smothering him. The first cold stab of fear hit him then, but he forced himself to remain still. "I don't know," he replied, humbled.

"You do, son of Nysander."

Son of Nysander. Sparks danced in front of his sightless eyes, but Thero held on to the image of his first mentor, the plain, good-humored man he'd too often underestimated. He recalled with shame his own arrogance and how it had blinded him to Nysander's wisdom until it was too late to honor it. He recalled the bitterness he'd felt when Nysander kept him from spells his skill could master but his empty heart could not wisely employ. For an instant he heard his old teacher's voice, patiently explaining, "The purpose of magic is not to replace human endeavor but to aid it." How many times had he said that over the years? How many times had Thero ignored the importance of the words?

The crescent moon wavered into view in front of him, dancing gently over the water's surface far above. Still mired in darkness, Thero felt the power of it breaking in on him, and his mouth stretched wide with joy.

"Balance!"

Like a cork buoy suddenly released, he shot to the surface, shattering the moon's reflection.

"Balance!" he shouted up at it.

"Yes," the voice said approvingly. "Nysander understood better than any Tír the role of Aura's gifts. We waited for him to come to us, but it was not to be. The task falls to you."

What task? Thero wondered with a thrill of excitement.

"Balance was lost long ago between your people and our own, between the Tír and the Light. Light balances darkness. Silence balances sound. Death balances life. The Aurënfaie preserve the old ways; your kind, left to dance alone for a time, have forged the new."

Thero reached a tentative foot down and found solid ground in easy reach. Wading from the pool, he walked to the lone figure awaiting him, an ancient Bash'wai woman. Her face and skin were black in the moonlight, her hair silver.

Thero fell to his knees in front of her. "Is that why Klia was allowed to come here, and at this time? Did you make this happen?"

"Make?" She chuckled, and her voice was deep, too large for such a frail frame. She stroked his head like a child's. "No, little brother, we only dance the dance with whatever steps we can manage."

Confused, Thero pressed a hand over his eyes, then looked up again. "You said the wizards of Skala would be made whole. What does that mean?"

But the Bash'wai was gone. In her place sat a large dragonling with golden eyes. Before Thero could do more than register its presence, it darted forward between his bare thighs and bit him on the scrotum. Leaping up with a panicked shout, he felt his head connect with something hard and the moon spun away like a dropped ring.

When Thero came to again, he was sprawled facedown and fully clothed just inside the mouth of a tunnel leading off from the main cavern beneath the Nha'mahat.

A vision! he thought in dazed wonder. He shifted to stand up, then pressed flat again, squeezing his eyes shut as fiery talons of pain tightened around his balls. The memory of Alec's bitten earlobe, swelled three times its normal size, presented itself ungraciously, and he let out a groan.

The sound of movement against stone made him open his eyes again. Through a haze of pain, he saw a seated figure uncoil itself from the nearby shadows and resolve into his young guide.

"Lissik." She held a flask down for him to see before disappearing behind him.

A mark of honor, they call these bites! he thought helplessly as she went about her ministrations. *If I survive long enough to heal, how am I ever going to show it off?*

People came and went around him. If the sight of a Skalan wizard cackling hysterically on the ground with his robe tucked up around his waist struck any of them as odd, none were so ungracious as to say so in his hearing.

15

DISCOMFORT

W here's Thero?" Alec wondered aloud as they set off for a banquet in Bry'kha tupa that evening.

"Gone to visit the rhui'auros," Klia told him. "I'd expected him back by now."

The rain had slacked off to a warm, sullen drizzle. Everyone rode with hoods pulled up, in little clumps behind Klia and Torsin. Alec and Seregil brought up the rear, the closest semblance of privacy they'd had all day. Seizing the opportunity, Alec confided his encounter with Beka and Nyal in the Haunted City.

Seregil took the news more calmly than he'd expected. "According to Thero, Queen Idrilain herself encourages such unions as part of the mission," he said quietly.

Alec glanced around at their Urgazhi escort. "What? Marrying her soldiers off to Aurënfaie?"

Seregil smirked. "I don't think marriage is a priority, but one of the goals of our current mission is to get a healthy infusion of Aurën-faie blood to renew that stock."

"Yes, but—! You mean she hoped Beka and her female riders would come home pregnant?" Alec exclaimed. "I thought they got drummed out for that?"

"The rules have been relaxed for the time being. No one is talking openly about it, but

Thero heard rumors that a bounty has even been offered. I suppose the men are free to bring home any Aurënfaie bride who'll have them, too."

"Bilairy's Balls, Seregil, that's coldhearted, turning the best turma in Skala into breeding stock!"

"When it comes to the survival of a nation, there's not much that's considered beyond the pale. It's not even that unusual. Remember my sojourn among the Dravnians? I kept up my duties as guest, so to speak. Who knows how many of my own offspring are toddling around somewhere up in the Asheks as we speak?"

Alec raised an eyebrow at this. "You're joking."

"I'm not. As for our current situation, it's all for the greater glory of Skala, which makes it honorable enough. How patriotic are *you* feeling these days?"

Alec ignored the jibe, but found himself watching the Urgazhi more closely during the banquet that followed.

Seregil was eating breakfast with Klia and Torsin in the hall early the next morning when Thero came shuffling in. His face was grey and he held himself as if his insides were made of glass and poorly packed.

"By the Light!" Torsin exclaimed. "My dear Thero, shall I send for a healer?"

"I'm fine, my lord, just a bit under the weather," Thero replied, coming to a halt behind an empty chair and grasping the back of it.

"You're not fine," Klia retorted, turning to look at him.

"It could be river fever," Seregil offered, suspecting it was no such thing. "I'll send for Mydri."

"No!" Thero said quickly. "No, that's not necessary. It's just a slight distemper. It will pass."

"Nonsense. Take him back to his room, Seregil," Klia ordered.

Thero's skin felt hot and clammy, and he leaned heavily on Seregil's arm as he limped back upstairs. Reaching his room, he laid down but refused to undress.

Seregil stood over him, frowning. "So, what happened?"

Thero closed his eyes and ran a hand over his unshaven cheek. "A dragon bit me."

"Bilairy's Balls, Thero! Where in Sarikali did you find one big enough to make you this sick?"

The wizard managed a sickly smile. "Where do you think?"

"Ah, of course. You'd better let me have a look."

"I've used lissik on it already."

"Lissik won't do for large bites. Come on now, where is it? Arm? Leg?"

With a sigh, Thero pulled up the front of his robe.

Seregil's eyes widened. "You said Alec's ear looked like a grape when he got bitten by that little one. This looks more like—"

"I *know* what it looks like!" Thero snarled, covering himself.

"This needs attention. I'll get something from Mydri. No one has to know the details."

"Thank you," Thero rasped, staring up at the ceiling.

Seregil shook his head. "You know, I've never heard of anyone getting bitten on the—"

"It was an accident. Just *go!*" Thero pleaded.

An accident? Seregil thought, hurrying next door. *Not if the rhui'auros had anything to do with it.*

To his considerable relief, Mydri asked few questions. He described the injury in general terms, and she mixed several infusions and a bowl of poultice. Eyeing the latter, Seregil hoped Thero was up to treating himself.

16

AN EVENING'S ENTERTAINMENT

Thero kept to his bed through the next day. Having been bitten himself, Alec couldn't share Seregil's amused attitude and was happy enough to keep Thero's secret.

He was thankful when Klia decided that he was of more use wandering at large than at the Iia'sidra. Aurënfaie deliberation was conducted at a glacial pace, every issue seemingly tied to centuries of history and precedent. Except for occasional visits to stay abreast of developments, he found other ways to occupy himself.

As a result, he saw little of Seregil during the day, and the evenings were taken up by a seemingly endless number of banquets with clans major and minor, each fraught with unspoken undercurrents of influence and will.

When they finally did reach their room again, sometimes only a few hours before dawn, Seregil either fell asleep immediately or disappeared up to the colos to pace in the dark. Alec had seen enough already to know the rejection Seregil faced each day. In public, all but a few avowed friends kept their distance. Members of the Haman clan made no secret of their animosity. As always, however, Seregil preferred to battle his demons alone. Alec's love might be welcome; his concern was not.

Adzriel noted her brother's withdrawal

one night during a visit with Klia, and Alec's muted pain. Putting an arm about his shoulders, she hugged him and whispered, "The bond is there, talí. For now, let it be enough. When he's ready he will come to you."

Alec had no choice but to heed her advice. Fortunately, he had work of his own to do. As he became more familiar with his surroundings, he went more often alone and soon formed a few alliances of his own—and among the class he'd always been most at home with.

While the Iia'sidra and influential clan members spent their days in solemn debate, the lesser members of the various households frequented the city's makeshift taverns and gaming houses. Alec's bow was as good as a letter of introduction in such company. Unlike Seregil, most Aurënfaie were consummate archers and loved to argue makes and weights as much as any northland hunter. Some favored longbows; others carried gracefully reflexed masterpieces of wood and horn. But none had seen anything quite like his Black Radly, and curiosity almost always led to friendly shooting contests.

Alec had fashioned a few shatta from Skalan coins, and these were much sought after, but he generally won more than he lost and he soon had a respectable collection dangling from his quiver strap.

Such pastimes bore other fruit, giving him access to that most useful of resources, the careless chatter servants exchange out of their masters' hearing. Gossip was gold to any spy, and Alec quietly took note. In this way, he learned that the Khatme khirnari, Lhaär ä Iriel, had taken an interest in Klia's occasional evening rides with the young Silmai horseman, Täanil í Khormai. Alec even managed to sow a few rumors about that himself, though the truth was that Klia found the man something of a bore.

Alec also picked up reliable rumors that the khirnari of several key minor clans supposedly aligned with friendly Datsia had been seen visiting Ra'basi tupa under cover of night.

Perhaps his most important discovery, however, was that the khirnari of Lhapnos had quarreled with his supposed ally, Nazien í Hari, over support for Skala, and that several of the Haman's own people had taken the Lhapnosan's side. Principal among the dissenters was Alec's nemesis, Emiel í Moranthi.

"This is a new development," Lord Torsin remarked as Alec made his nightly report to Klia.

The princess gave Alec a wink. "You see, my lord? I told you he'd earn his keep."

. . .

Their tenth night in Sarikali brought a welcome respite. For the first time since their arrival they had no outside obligations, and Klia sent word for the evening meal to be a simple, communal affair in the main hall.

Alec was in the stable yard passing the time with some of Braknil's men when Seregil returned from the Iia'sidra alone.

"Had a good day, did you, my lord?" Minál called out.

"Not especially," Seregil snapped, not slowing as he disappeared into the house.

With an inward sigh, Alec followed him up to their chamber.

"Aura's Fingers, I was never meant to be a diplomat!" Seregil burst out as soon as they were alone. A button flew across the room as he yanked off his coat. He flung it into a corner and the sweat-soaked shirt beneath quickly followed. Grabbing the ewer from the washstand, he stalked out onto the balcony and emptied it over his head.

"You might have been a bit more pleasant to poor Minál," Alec chided, leaning against the doorframe. "He thinks a lot of you, you know."

Ignoring him, Seregil slicked the water from his eyes and pushed past him into the room. "No matter *what* Klia or Torsin says, someone manages to twist it around into a threat. 'We need iron.' 'Oh, no, you want to colonize the Asheks!' 'Let us use a northern port.' 'You would steal Ra'basi's trade routes?'

"Ulan í Sathil is the worst, though he seldom speaks. Oh, no! He just sits there, smiling as if he agrees with everything we say. Then, with a single well-chosen comment, he throws everyone into an uproar again and sits back to watch the fun. Later, you see him gathering the uncertain ones around him, whispering and wagging his finger. Bilairy's Balls, the man's smooth. I wish to hell he was on our side."

"What can you do?"

Seregil snorted. "If it were up to me, I'd challenge the whole damn lot of them to a horse race and settle the matter! It's been done before, you know. What are you laughing at?"

"You. You're raving. And dripping." Alec tossed him a cloth from the washstand.

Seregil gave him an apologetic grin as he toweled off. "And how did you do today? Anything new?"

"No. It seems I've gleaned all I can among the friendlier folk, and

I still haven't found a way to wiggle in among the Haman or Khatme." He decided not to share how often his presence had drawn challenging stares and whispers of "garshil" in certain quarters. "In Rhíminee, all I had to do was change clothes and blend into the crowd. Here they mark me as outlander and guard their words. I think it's time I did a little nightrunning."

"I've broached the subject to Klia but she says to wait, honorable woman that she is. Be patient, talí."

"*You* counseling patience? That's a first!"

"Only because I don't see any other choice just now," Seregil admitted. "At least we have a night off. However shall we pass the time?"

Most of the others were already seated by the time they came downstairs for supper. Long tables had been set up, Skalan style, in the main hall, and Beka waved them over to seats at the end of Klia's table.

"I wondered where she'd gotten off to all day," Seregil muttered, seeing Nyal at her side.

"Behave yourself," Alec warned.

"You can thank your captain for the fine desserts and cheese we're having tonight," Nyal announced as they sat down.

"Me?" Beka laughed. "He got word yesterday of a trader's caravan coming in from Datsia. We met it outside the city and haggled the best pickings out of them before anyone else was the wiser. You've never tasted such honey, Alec!"

"I thought you looked like you'd found something sweet," Seregil remarked blandly.

Alec used Thero's fortuitous arrival to mask the kick he dealt him under the table.

Klia stood and raised her wine cup, as if they were all comrades in a plain soldier's mess. "We've no priests among us, so I'll do the honors. By Sakor's Flame and Illior's Light. May they smile on our endeavors here." Turning, she sprinkled a few drops on the floor as a libation, then took a long drink. The others did the same.

"What's the word at the Iia'sidra, Commander?" Zir called from the next table. "Should we keep our packs tight, or settle in?"

Klia grimaced. "Given our reception so far, Corporal, I'd say you might as well get comfortable. Time seems to mean a great deal less to the 'faie than to us." She paused, saluting Seregil and Alec with her cup. "Present company excepted, of course."

Seregil returned the salute with an ironic chuckle. "If I ever had any Aurënfaie patience, I've long since lost it."

The windows and doors had been thrown open to let in the soft breeze; evening birdsong provided the meal's music as the shadows crept slowly across the floor. The only discordant notes were Torsin's occasional fits of coughing.

"He's getting worse," Thero murmured, watching the envoy dab at his lips with a stained napkin. "He won't admit it, of course— claims it's the climate here."

"Could it be that fever you had?" Beka asked.

Thero looked blank for an instant, then shook his head. "No, not that. I can see a darkness hovering about his chest."

"Will he survive the negotiations?" asked Alec, gazing over at the old man with concern.

"By the Light, the last thing we need is him dying in the midst of all this," muttered Seregil.

"Why wouldn't he let his niece come in his place?" Beka whispered. "Lady Melessandra knows as much of the 'faie as he does."

"This is the crowning achievement of a long and distinguished career," Seregil replied. "I suppose he couldn't bear not to see it through to its conclusion."

As the meal ended Klia wandered down to their end of the table. "We've been given the luxury of doing nothing tonight, my friends. Kheeta í Branín says the colos offers a pleasant view of the sunset. Anyone care to join us?"

"We'll make an Aurënfaie of you yet, my lady," Seregil said, rising to accompany her.

"Good. You and Alec can be our minstrels for the evening."

"If you will excuse me, my lady, I must retire early," Torsin said, still seated.

Klia laid a hand on the old man's shoulder. "Of course. Rest well, my friend."

Servants carried wine, cakes, and cushions up to the colos. Seregil made a quick detour to their room for his harp. By the time he joined the others, they'd settled in to enjoy the cool of the evening. The lingering green glow of sunset was fading quickly on the western horizon. To the east, a ruddy full moon was already rising over the city.

He and Alec were laughingly given the place of honor across from Klia. Beka and Nyal sprawled on the floor near the door, their backs to the wall.

A sudden lump rose in Seregil's throat as he struck the first notes

of "Softly Across the Water"; from where he sat he could see the colos on Adzriel's house, where he'd played for his family on so many
evenings like this. Before he could halt or falter, Alec took up the
melody, catching his eye with a small, questioning lift of an eyebrow. Fighting off the unexpected rush of sadness, Seregil focused
all his attention on the intricate fingering of the song and came in
with harmony on the refrain with the others, letting their voices
cover any lingering unsteadiness in his own.

It still amused Alec to find himself consorting with royalty. Not so
long ago he'd thought it a treat to sit next to a smoking hearth in
some filthy tavern, back in the days when the 'faie were still creatures of legend rather than his own kin.

Seregil cheered up as the evening wore on, and the two of them
acquitted themselves admirably as minstrels. When their throats
went dry, Thero took over with a pretty collection of illusions he'd
picked up in his travels with Magyana.

"The wine's run low," Kheeta announced at last.

"I'll lend a hand," Alec offered, wishing his bladder felt as light
as his head. He and Kheeta gathered the empty jugs and made their
way downstairs toward the servant's stair at the end of the second-
floor corridor. This took them past Torsin's chamber, and Alec saw
that the door was slightly ajar. The room beyond was dark. *Poor old
fellow,* he thought, gently pulling the latch shut. *He must have been
sicker than he let on to retire this early.*

"She's a great lady, your princess," Kheeta observed warmly as
they headed down to the kitchen. He'd had his share of the wine and
was slurring his words a little. "It's sad . . ."

"What's sad?"

"That the 'faie blood has run so thin in her," the Bôkthersan
replied with a sigh. "You don't understand yet how fortunate you
are, being ya'shel. Just you wait a few hundred years."

The cooks had propped the kitchen door open to catch the breeze
from the yard. Passing it, Alec caught sight of a cloaked figure hurrying out the postern gate. Something in the sloped set of the man's
shoulders made him pause; a familiar, muffled cough made him thrust
the still empty wine jugs into his companion's arms and follow.

"Where are you going?" Kheeta called after him.

"I need some air." Alec sprinted across the yard before the other
man could question him.

The guards by the watch fire took no more notice of him than they had of Torsin. Why worry about one of their own going out when it was folk creeping in they were set to guard against? Outside the gate Alec paused, letting his eyes adjust to the darkness. A cough nearby guided him to the left.

He'd acted on pure instinct until now, but suddenly he felt rather foolish ghosting along after Klia's most trusted adviser as if he were a Plenimaran spy. What was he going to tell her when he got back, or say to Torsin if the old man caught him tailing along behind him? As if in answer, a large owl—the first he'd seen since they'd left Akhendi—glided past, flying in the same direction Torsin had gone.

I can claim I had an omen, he thought.

Ill or not, Torsin moved as if he had a purpose more serious than taking the night air. The taverns were busier than ever, and music seemed to come from all directions. Aurënfaie were out in pairs and groups, enjoying the night. He stopped now and then to exchange a greeting with some person he knew but didn't linger to chat.

Leaving Bôkthersa tupa, he led Alec down a succession of streets that took them past boundary markers of Akhendi and Haman. When he slowed at last, Alec's heart sank. This street was marked with the moon symbol of Khatme. Thankfully, there were fewer folk abroad here, but Alec was careful to keep to the shadows of doorways and alleys. He wasn't nightrunning, he told himself, hoping he never had to justify that to anyone else. He was just keeping an eye on an ailing old man.

Torsin stopped at an imposing house Alec guessed rightly to be the house of Lhaär ä Iriel. A brief slice of candle glow from inside illuminated the old man's face as he entered, and Alec was close enough to read what looked like resignation on Torsin's haggard features.

There were no obvious ways into the house, even for Alec. The well-guarded villas of Rhíminee possessed a comforting symmetry of design by comparison. There might be walls to climb, dogs to avoid or charm his way past, but you could almost always find some aperture to wiggle through if you knew your business. Here there were only barred doors and windows out of reach.

He was further stymied by the fact that this building, whatever it was, abutted several others, all of which presented equally blank faces. He was about to give up when he caught the sound of several voices somewhere overhead.

Looking up, he made out the dark jut of a balcony. The voices

were too soft for him to catch the gist of the conversation, but the
erratic punctuation of Torsin's coughing left no doubt in Alec's
mind that he'd found his man again.

There were at least two others with him, a man and a woman—
Lhaär ä Iriel herself, perhaps.

The conference did not last long. The unseen conspirators soon
disappeared back into the house. Alec waited a few minutes to see if
they'd return, then headed back to the front of the building to wait.

Torsin emerged a few minutes later, but not alone. A man walked
with him for several minutes before turning in the opposite direction.

Alec was still trying to decide which one to follow when a familiar shape emerged from the shadows beside him.

"Seregil?"

"You take Torsin; I'll follow this other fellow. Watch out for
Khatme along the way. You won't be welcome here." With that,
Seregil disappeared as quickly as he'd come.

Torsin led Alec straight back to their own door, the front one
this time. After exchanging a few words with the sentries, he went
inside.

Looking up at the colos, Alec saw lights still burning there. Not
knowing what excuses had been made for his absence or Seregil's,
he went in through the stable yard and up the back stair. Halfway up,
he heard Klia's voice, and Torsin's.

"I thought you'd turned in already," Klia said.

"A short walk in the night air helps me sleep," Torsin replied. No
mention of where he'd been.

Alec waited until he heard two doors close, then continued on to
his chamber and settled in to wait for Seregil so they could get their
stories straight. That seemed a safe enough plan, far more attractive
than being the one to tell Klia that her trusted minister has just been
consorting with their opposition behind her back.

Seregil's man was not wearing a sen'gai, but he guessed from the
cut of his tunic that he was from one of the eastern clans. He was
soon proven right. The man led him to the house of Ulan í Sathil.

Lurking in a nearby doorway, Seregil pondered the possible connections. Intractable Khatme and worldly Virésse; the two clans
were divided as much by their ideology as they were by the spur of
mountains that lay between their ancestral lands. The only uniting
factor he knew of was their opposition to the Skalan treaty.

The greater question was whether Torsin knew of the connection.

He returned to the guest house to find the colos dark, the music stilled. Entering by the back gate, he found Korandor and Nikides on guard duty.

"Has anyone else come or gone this way tonight, Corporal?" he asked.

"Just Lord Torsin, my lord," Nikides replied. "He left a while back and we haven't seen him since."

"I thought he'd turned in for the night."

"Couldn't sleep, he said. Now, I say night air's the worst thing for weak lungs, but there's no telling these nobles anything—begging your pardon, my lord."

Seregil gave the man a knowing wink and continued on as if he'd just been out on a constitutional of his own.

He found Alec pacing impatiently in their room, every lamp blazing. Shadows still clung in the corners, resisting his superstitious efforts to banish them.

"Seems they can't carry on without us." Seregil grinned, pointing up toward the abandoned colos.

"Klia came down about half an hour ago," Alec told him, coming to a rest in the center of the room. "What did they say when I didn't come back?"

"Kheeta had some story about you feeling your wine, but he slipped me the nod. What happened?"

Alec shrugged. "Luck in the shadows, if you can call it that. I just happened to be there when Torsin left. He came straight back here from Khatme tupa after I saw you. Klia met him in the passage as he came up."

"Did she know where he'd been?"

"I couldn't tell. What about your man?"

"Care to guess?"

"Virésse?"

"Smart boy. Too bad we don't know what was said either place."

"Then you didn't learn anything, either." Alec sank into a chair by the hearth. "What do you suppose Torsin was up to?"

"The queen's business, I hope," Seregil replied doubtfully, sprawling in the chair opposite.

"Do we tell Klia?"

Seregil closed his eyes and massaged the lids. "That's the real question, isn't it? I doubt that spying on our own people was quite what she had in mind when she invited us along."

"Maybe not, but she did say she was worried that he might be too sympathetic to Virésse. This proves it."

"It proves nothing, except that he and someone with connections to Ulan í Sathil met at the house of Lhaär ä Iriel."

"So, what do we do?"

Seregil shrugged. "Bide our time a little longer, and keep our eyes open."

17

ALEC KEEPS BUSY

ide our time.

B To Alec, it seemed all they'd done since they arrived was wait, held impotent by the strictures of diplomacy and the plodding pace of Aurënfaie debate. The last thing he felt like doing was biding his time now that something interesting had finally happened.

He rose early the next morning and took himself out for a dawn ride around the city walls. The distant hills floated like islands above the thick mist rising from the rivers. The bleat of sheep and goats came from closer by. Reaching the Nha'mahat, he stopped to exchange greetings with a rhui'auros who was setting out fresh offerings for the dragons. At this hour the little creatures fluttered in swarms thick as spring swallows, circling the tower. Others scrabbled over the bowls in the arcade. Several lit on Alec and he froze, not relishing the thought of another painful bite, no matter how auspicious the marks might be.

Riding back through the Haunted City he passed the House of Pillars and was surprised to see Nyal's horse, a black gelding with three white stockings, grazing there next to a sturdy white palfrey. Alec had an eye for horses and recognized this little mare as the mount Lady Amali had ridden over the mountains from Gedre.

If it hadn't been for Beka, he might have ridden on. Instead, he tethered Windrunner out of sight and hurried inside.

Voices echoed from several directions, and he set off following those that sounded most promising to the pools at the center of the sprawling place. At last, he found his way to a small, weed-grown court some distance further on, where the comforting rise and fall of a man's voice sounded a counterpoint to a woman's soft weeping. Creeping closer, Alec slipped behind a tattered tapestry that still hung near the courtyard's edge and peered out through a hole.

Amali sat on the edge of an empty fountain, her face in her hands. Nyal stood over her, stroking her hair gently.

"Forgive me," Amali said through her fingers. "But who else could I turn to? Who else would understand?"

Nyal drew her close, and for an instant Alec scarcely recognized him. The Ra'basi's handsome face was suffused with an anger Alec had never seen in him before. When he spoke again, his voice was almost too low to hear. Alec could make out only the words "hurt you."

Amali raised her tear-stained face and clasped his hands beseechingly. "No! No, you must never think such a thing! He's in such distress at times I hardly know him. Word came that another village near the Khatme border has been abandoned. It's as if Akhendi is dying, too!"

Nyal murmured something and she shook her head again. "He cannot. The people would not hear of it. He won't abandon them!"

Nyal pulled away and walked off a few steps, clearly agitated. "Then what is it you want of me?"

"I don't know!" She reached out to him. "Only—I needed to know you are still my friend, someone I can open my heart to. I'm so alone there!"

"It's where you chose to be," Nyal retorted bitterly, then relented as she dissolved into tears again.

"I am your friend, your dear friend," he assured her, gathering her close and rocking her gently. "You can always come to me, talía. Always. Just give me this much: Do you ever regret your decision? Even just a little?"

"You mustn't ask me that," she sobbed, clinging to him. "Never, never, never! Rhaish is my life. If only I could make him well."

Amali could not see the despair that filled Nyal's eyes at her words, but Alec could. Ashamed of his eavesdropping, he waited until the pair had gone, then set off for home.

• • •

Seregil and the others had left for the Iia'sidra by the time Alec arrived. He checked at their room, in case Seregil had left any last-minute instructions, but found nothing. On his way down to the kitchen for breakfast, however, he found himself pausing outside Torsin's door, his heart beating just a little too fast. It seemed to be his day for opportunities; the door was ajar again.

The envoy's strange behavior the previous night was too much to ignore, given Seregil's concerns about the man's loyalties. And this—the open door was just too tempting to pass unexplored.

With a last guilty glance around and a quick prayer to Illior, he slipped inside and closed the door.

Torsin's room was a large one, with an alcove at the far side. A desk stood beneath a window there, dispatch box, writing materials, and a few sealed parchments arranged neatly on its polished top. The room was furnished with the usual accoutrements: gauze-hung bed, a washstand, clothes chests, all made in the simple Aurënfaie style— pale woods and clean, sweeping lines accented with darker inlay.

Feeling guiltier by the moment, he worked quickly, examining the desk and its contents, the clothes chests, and the walls behind the hangings, but found nothing of note. Everything was meticulous, orderly.

Picking up a daybook from a stand by the bed, he found a terse but detailed record of each day's developments written in Torsin's precise script. The first entry was dated three months earlier. As he moved to put it back it fell open to more recent entries, one dating a week or so before Klia's arrival in Gedre. The handwriting was still recognizable, but the letters were not as clearly formed, and words occasionally strayed from the careful lines or were marred by blots and smudges.

That's his illness doing that. Alec paged back through the book, trying to gauge how long Torsin had been failing, but was interrupted by the sound of brisk footsteps from the corridor.

Aurënfaie beds were low-slung affairs, yet he managed to wedge himself out of sight under it without too much trouble. It wasn't until he was hidden that he realized he was still clutching the book.

The latch lifted and he held his breath, watching from beneath the edge of the coverlet as the door swung open and a pair of boot-clad feet—a woman's, by the size—strode across the room to the desk. It was Mercalle; he recognized her limp. He heard the small squeak of the dispatch box's lid and the unmistakable rustle of parchments.

Turning his head, he looked out under the other side of the bed and could see the bottom of a dispatch pouch hanging against her thigh.

Seems I'm the only spy here, after all, he thought, letting out a pent-up breath when she'd gone out. She'd simply come to collect the day's dispatches.

He remained where he was a moment, and opened the daybook again. The first sign of weakness in Torsin's handwriting appeared several weeks before Klia's arrival. Pondering this, he turned to the latest entry, a summary of the previous day's debate.

U.S. remains subtle, letting the L. raise opposition—

Alec allowed himself a wry smirk. What had he expected? *"Met with the Virésse. Plotted against the princess"*?

His current position afforded him a different perspective on the room. From here, he could see the careful polish on the row of shoes lined up next to a clothes chest, and the crisply folded pleats in the hem of a robe hanging on the wall.

One glance into a person's private rooms will tell you more about him than an hour's conversation, Seregil had once told him. Alec had found the statement amusing at the time, considering the source; any space Seregil inhabited was soon in complete disarray. Torsin's room, on the other hand, shouted order. Everything was in its place, with nothing extraneous in evidence.

As he slid out from under the bed he noticed a flash of red in the ashes on the hearth, just beneath the metal bars of the grate. If he'd been standing, he'd have missed it.

Crawling over, he saw it was the half-charred remains of a small silk tassel, dark red with a few blue threads mixed in. He doubted Torsin owned a garment with such embellishments, but they were common enough on Aurënfaie clothing, edging cloaks and tunics.

And sen'gai.

He gingerly plucked it out, heart racing again. It was the right size and colors to have come from the edge of a Virésse head cloth. Someone had meant to destroy it, but it had fallen through the grate before the fire had completely consumed it.

No chance of it being missed, then, he reasoned, tucking it into the wallet at his belt.

He spent the rest of the morning loitering about the edges of Khatme tupa in hopes of striking up a profitable conversation.

Skilled as he usually was at such ploys, he had no luck here. Unwelcoming stares and whispers of *"garshil"* warned him off whenever he ventured too deeply into the area.

Perhaps I used up all my luck this morning, he thought, frustrated.

The few outlying streets he did manage to explore had none of the usual gathering spots. Unfriendly tattooed faces peered at him from windows and balconies, then disappeared from view. No one, it seemed, had time to drink or game here. Or perhaps, insular as they were, their taverns were located deeper in the tupa, far from prying impure eyes.

As midday approached he gave up and started for home. It took only a few turnings, however, to realize that he had once again gotten himself lost.

"Illior's Fingers!" he muttered, scowling as he scanned the anonymous walls and doorways.

"Blaspheming won't get you free, half-breed. You must use the Lightbearer's true name here."

A Khatme woman stepped into view a few yards away, her tattooed face impassive beneath her bulging red-and-black sen'gai. She wore none of the usual heavy jewelry Alec associated with the clan, but her tunic was stitched with rows of silver, pomegranate-shaped beads.

"I meant no disrespect," Alec replied. "And you can spare yourself the effort of magic; I get lost on my own without any help."

"I've been watching you all morning, half-breed. What is it you want here?"

"I was just curious."

"You're lying, half-breed."

Do the Khatme read thoughts after all, or do I just look as guilty as I feel? Putting on the bravest face he could, he replied. "My apologies, Khatme. It's a practice we Tír have when what we are doing is none of another person's business."

"There's an etiquette to duplicity, then? How interesting."

Alec thought he saw a hint of a smile shift the black tracery covering one cheek. "You say you've been watching me, yet I haven't seen you," he countered. "Were you spying on me?"

"Were you spying on Lord Torsin when he came here at our khirnari's request last night, half-breed?"

There was no use dissembling. "That doesn't concern you. And my name is Alec í Amasa, not half-breed."

"I know. Retrace your steps." Before he could respond, she was gone, disappearing like smoke on the air

"Retrace my steps?" Alec grumbled. "What else have I been doing?"

This time, however, it worked and he found himself back in familiar territory, near the Iia'sidra chamber. Having nothing better to do, he went in and settled in an inconspicuous corner, watching faces. He watched Torsin's most closely of all.

He managed to catch Seregil's attention when the council adjourned for the midday meal. Motioning him outside, Alec walked him quickly into an empty side street.

"Find out anything in Khatme tupa?" Seregil asked hopefully.

"Well, no. Not there." Steeling himself, Alec plunged into a hurried account of his findings in Torsin's room, what he'd seen between Nyal and Amali momentarily forgotten.

Seregil stared a him incredulously, then whispered, "You burgled *Torsin's* room? Bilairy's Balls, didn't I tell you to wait?"

"Yes, and if I'd listened to you we wouldn't have this, would we?" Alec showed him the Virésse tassel. "What's the matter with you? A member of Klia's own delegation sneaks out to talk to the enemy and you say wait? Back in Rhíminee you'd have been in there last night yourself!"

Seregil glared at him a moment, then shook his head. "It's not the same here. This isn't the Plenimarans we're dealing with. The Aurënfaie are Skala's allies in spirit if not in actual fact. It's not as if they're likely to be plotting her assassination. And Torsin?"

"But this could be the proof Klia was looking for, about his divided loyalty."

"I've been thinking about that. It's not sympathy that would make Torsin court Ulan's favor. He's worried that we could lose all by offending the Virésse: not get Gedre, and lose our port in Virésse in the bargain. Still, if he did go behind her back to do it—?"

"How did he seem at the Iia'sidra?"

"Any guilty glances or secret nods exchanged, you mean?" Seregil asked with a crooked grin. "None that I saw. The one possibility we haven't considered is that he was acting on Klia's behalf, and that it's the rest of us who aren't supposed to know."

"Well, that brings us right back to my original question. What do we do?"

Seregil shrugged. "We're Watchers. We'll watch."

"Speaking of watching people, I saw Nyal and Amali together again early this morning."

"Oh?" This clearly piqued Seregil's interest. "What were they up to?"

"She was upset about her husband and it was Nyal she turned to."

"They were lovers once. Clearly there's still a bond there," said Seregil. "What was it she was upset about?"

"I didn't hear everything, but it sounded like this debate is taking a toll on Rhaish."

Seregil frowned. "That's not good. We need him strong. Do you think Amali and Nyal are still secretly lovers?"

Alec thought back over the morning's scene: Amali clinging to the tall Ra'basi, the anger he'd seen in the man's face at the mere hint of abuse. "I don't know."

"I think it's time we found out, and not just for Klia's sake. Let's see if Adzriel knows more than she's been letting on."

They found Adzriel sitting with Säaban in her colos.

"Nyal and Amali?" Säaban chuckled when Seregil broached the subject. "Have you two been gossiping in the taverns?"

"Not exactly," Seregil hedged. "I've heard a few rumors, and Nyal's been showing a lot of attention to Beka Cavish; if he's leading her on, I mean to take steps."

"They were lovers before her marriage to Rhaish í Arlisandin," Adzriel said. "A sad story, the stuff of ballads."

"What happened?"

Adzriel shrugged. "She chose duty over love, I suppose, marrying the khirnari of her clan rather than an outsider. But I know she's grown to love Rhaish dearly; it's Nyal who carries the pain of that decision. He strikes me as the sort of man who does not stop loving even when his love is turned away. Perhaps Beka can heal his heart."

"Just so long as he doesn't break hers in the process. Rhaish is getting long in years. Is he well?"

"I've been wondering that myself. He doesn't seem himself; the strain of the negotiations, no doubt."

"He's known more than his share of sorrows, too," said Säaban. "He's seen two wives die, one barren, one in childbed, along with the child. Now Amali carries their first child. That's bad enough by itself, but to be khirnari and watch your people suffer as his do—I can only imagine how much this business weighs on his mind. I suspect Amali wanted nothing more from Nyal than a shoulder to cry on."

· · ·

"Try as I may to dislike the man, I hear nothing but good spoken of him," Seregil muttered as they walked back to their room.

"The Akhendi khirnari?" asked Alec.

"No, Nyal. Caring for the lover who threw you over shows more character than I have."

Alec allowed himself a smug grin. "See? I knew you were wrong about him."

Amali huddled in darkness by the bedchamber window, fighting back tears as Rhaish thrashed again in his sleep. He would not tell her what his dreams were, though they grew worse every night, making him sweat and groan. If she woke him he would cry out, glaring at her with mad, sightless eyes.

Amali ä Yassara was no stranger to fear; she'd seen her family skirt starvation, driven by it out of the lands they knew to live like beggars in the streets of successive towns and cities across Akhendi. She'd let Nyal heal her fears for a time, but he wanted to take her away, to wander like a teth'brimash again. It was Rhaish who'd saved her, lifted her up and made her proud again to wear the sen'-gai of her people. Her parents and brothers ate at the khirnari's table now, and she carried the khirnari's son under her heart. Before the Skalans had come, bearing hope, she had felt safe. Now her husband shouted madness in his sleep.

With a guilty shudder, she felt in the pocket of her nightdress for the warding charm Nyal had given her to mend. It wasn't his, but it was a link to him, an excuse to meet again when she'd finished with it. Her fingers stroked the crude knots of the wristband: a child's work, but effective. Nyal's fingers had brushed her palm as he'd given it to her when they first arrived at the House of Pillars. She let herself savor the memory of that touch, and those that followed; his fingers on her hair, his arms around her, shielding her for a little while from all her fears and worries. It wasn't the Ra'basi she ached for now, but the sense of peace he'd always been able to give her—just never for long enough.

She pushed the charm back into her pocket, her talisman to summon that comfort again if she needed it. Drying her tears, she found a soft cloth and went to wipe her beloved's brow.

18

MAGYANA

*C*ool mountain air against her face.
*Jagged peaks against a flawless sky. One
more pass to traverse and she'd be on the
high plains beyond. She closed her eyes
for a moment, savoring the mingled scents of
wet stone, wild thyme, and the sweat steaming from her horse's withers.*

*Freedom. Nothing ahead of her but end-
less days of exploration—*

Magyana jerked out of her doze as the
quill slipped from her fingers. Her mouth
was dry. The stale, overheated air inside the
queen's tent made her head ache. The dream
had been so clear—for just an instant a flash
of resentment overwhelmed her. *I never
asked for this!*

Retrieving the fallen pen, Magyana
trimmed it and settled resignedly back in her
chair. Freedom was an illusion she'd been
able to maintain too well for too many years.
The gifts that raised a wizard to the highest levels of the Orëska came with a price—
different for each, according to their talents.

The bill for her wandering years had come
due, and here she sat, unable to do more than
watch over the best of queens as Idrilain
fought death, her final adversary.

Being Idrilain, she had managed to rally, at
least for a time. Klia's departure for Aurënen
had somehow buoyed her. In the month since,

she clung doggedly to life, even putting on a little flesh as the infection in her lungs receded. Most days she hovered in a murky half-sleep, surfacing now and then into lucid conversation, catching up with a few questions on the progress of the war and Klia's mission, though of the latter there was still cruelly little to report. Neither strong enough nor willing to make the long journey back to Rhíminee, Idrilain was content to remain in what was now essentially Phoria's camp. As Queen's Wizard, Magyana remained with her, trapped in this stuffy tent, surrounded by medicine vessels and the heavy smell of illness and an old woman dying—

Magyana pushed away the guilty thoughts. Yet tied she was, by love, oath, and honor, until Idrilain saw fit to release her, or was released herself.

Leaving the queen to sleep, Magyana carried her chair and writing materials outside. Late-afternoon light bathed the sprawling encampment in a deceptively gentle light. Dipping her pen in the inkpot, she began again.

"My dear Thero, yesterday the Plenimarans drove a line of Mycenian troops back to within a few miles of where I sit. In Skala more towns have been burned along the eastern coast. Stories of a darker sort come in from all quarters—half a regiment of White Hawk archers stricken in one night, overwhelmed by evil vapors; dead men rising to strangle their own comrades; a dyrmagnos summoning ghostly terrors and fountains of fire in broad daylight. Some are mere soldiers' tales, but a few have been verified. Our colleague, Elutheus, himself witnessed a necromancer calling down lightning at Gresher's Ford.

"Even Phoria cannot discount such reports, but she stubbornly maintains that such attacks are so isolated as to be of little concern. In the short term, she may be right. With the destruction of the Helm, the Overlord's necromancers cannot command enough power to overwhelm us with mere magic, but the threat of it among our soldiers, fed by rumor and report, does great harm nonetheless.

"The news is not all bad, however. To Phoria's credit, she is a decisive leader, if not a diplomatic one, and the generals trust her. Over the past week she has organized significant strikes against enemy forces to the east, and has had several victories. Tell Klia that her friend, Commander Myrhini, captured fifty enemy horses. A great coup indeed, as many cavalry soldiers are afoot for lack of mounts to replace those killed in battle. Others are making do with whatever horses they can commandeer about the countryside, a situation that is not endearing them to the locals.

"The third of Klia's dispatches reached us here yesterday. Phoria said little, but her impatience is clear. Surely some small concession can be coaxed from the Iia'sidra? Otherwise, I fear she will recall you. With every new death of an able commander reported, Klia's presence on the field is more greatly missed."

Magyana paused, considering information she dared not entrust to writing, even in such a message as this. Like the fact that she, eldest of the remaining Orëska wizards, dared not openly translocate this parchment to her protégé lest Phoria hear of it. The Princess Royal made no secret of her distrust of wizards in general, and her mother's adviser in particular. Magyana had already been summoned once to explain her actions, and for nothing more than performing a scry at General Armeneus's request. In the weeks since Phoria had taken over as War Commander, a subtle shift had occurred. Watchful eyes and ears were at work for her in every quarter, including those of that handsome snake, Captain Traneus.

Klia has enough to occupy her mind, thought Magyana, obscuring the letter with a spell only Thero could unravel. She would put it in the hands of the dispatch rider herself later. Let Traneus make of that what he would.

19

ANOTHER EVENING'S ENTERTAINMENT

*T*he dream was less coherent this time, but more vivid. The burning room was still his old chamber in Bôkthersa, yet here were the heads of Thryis and the others glaring at him from the mantelpiece. There was no chance this time to choose what things to save, what to abandon. Fire raced up the hangings of the bed, the draperies, up his legs, but its touch was deadly cold.

The smoke boiling up through the floorboards thickened the band of sunlight spilling into the little chamber, blinding him with its bright glare. His throat was full, his hands useless.

Across the room, just visible through the smoke, a lean figure moved closer.

"No!" he thought. "Not here. Never here."

Ilar's presence made no more sense than that of the glass spheres he clutched so desperately in both hands. The flames cleared before Ilar as he approached, his smile warm and welcoming.

So handsome. So graceful.

Seregil had forgotten how the man moved, light and easy as a lynx. Almost close enough to touch now.

Seregil felt the cold flames eating into him, felt smooth glass slipping through his fingers.

*Ilar reached for him. No, he was offering him something, a
bloody sword.*

"No!" Seregil shouted, clutching frantically at the glass orbs.
"No, I don't want it!"

Seregil started up in bed, drenched in sweat and amazed to find Alec
still asleep beside hm. Hadn't he been shouting?

Shout? he thought in sudden alarm. He couldn't even get his
breath. The cold smoke from the dream still filled his lungs, making
even the slight weight of Alec's arm across his chest a stifling burden. He was choking, suffocating.

He slid out of bed as carefully as his rising panic allowed, still ir-
rationally concerned about waking Alec. Snatching up discarded
clothing, he blundered out into the dimly lit corridor.

Breath came easier once he was in motion. But when he paused to
drag on his breeches and boots, the smothering sensation overwhelmed him again. He hurried on, pulling on the surcoat—Alec's,
it turned out—as he went.

He was practically running now, past the second landing and on
down the broader staircase that led to the hall.

What am I doing?

He slowed, and as if in answer, the breath locked tight in his
chest. So he blundered on, praying he didn't meet anyone in his current state.

Raw instinct guided him down a side passage and out through the
kitchen to the stable court. The moon was down, the shadows thick.
A murmur of voices and a faint glow of firelight near the gate
marked where the sentries stood, just outside the gate. Scaling the
back wall unseen was a simple feat for the man once know as—

Haba

—the Rhíminee Cat.

The soft turf of the street muffled the sound of his boots as he
jumped down from the top of the wall and loped away, the unfastened
coat flapping loosely around his bare sides.

For a while the feel of his heart and breath and the long legs carrying
him along were enough to fend off thought. Gradually, however, he
grew calmer, and the panicked dash slowed to a walking meditation.

The confusion of the Cockerel with his childhood room—a
homecoming of sorts? he wondered, beginning to pick away at the
dream that had precipitated this headlong nocturnal perambulation.

But the rest: glass orbs, fire, smoke, Ilar. Try as he might, the dream's import still eluded him.

But then again, the images spoke of the past he'd mourned and here he was, alone under the stars, as he'd so often dreamed of being during the lonely years in Skala.

Alone with his own thoughts.

Introspection had never been a favorite pastime. In fact, he was quite skilled at avoiding it. "Take what the Lightbearer sends and be thankful." How many times had he quoted that, his creed, his catalyst, his bulwark against self-revelation?

The Lightbearer sent dreams—and madness. His thin mouth tilted into a humorless smirk: *better not to dwell too long on that.* Nonetheless, this dream had driven him out alone for the first time since their arrival in Sarikali. Goose flesh prickled his skin, and he fastened the coat, noting absently that it was a little loose in the shoulders for him.

Alec.

Seregil had been with him or others day and night without cease since their arrival, making it a simple matter to fill every waking moment with the business at hand—so many concerns, so much to do. So very easy to stave off the thoughts brewing since he'd set foot in Gedre—hell, since Beka had told him about this mission in the first place.

Exile
Traitor

Alone here in the haunted stillness of a Sarikali night, he was stripped of his defenses.

Murderer
Guest slayer

With hallucinatory clarity, he felt the hardness of a long-gone dagger's hilt clenched in his right fist, felt again for the first time the jar and give as the blade sank into the outraged Haman's—

You knew him. He had a name. His father's voice now, filled with disgust.

Dhymir í Tilmani Nazien
Guest slayer

—into Dhymir í Tilmani Nazien's chest all those nights and years and deaths ago. There was an obscene simplicity to that sensation. How was it that it took less effort, less strength, to stab the life from a person than to carve one's mark in a tavern tabletop?

With that thought came the old unanswerable question: What had made him draw steel against another when he could just as easily have run away? With a single stroke he'd taken a life and changed the entire course of his own. One stroke.

It had been almost nine years before he killed again, this time to protect himself and the Mycenian thief who'd taught him the first rudiments of the nightrunner's trade in the dark stews and filthy streets of Keston. That killing had been fraught with no such doubts. His teacher had been pleased, said she could make a first-class snuffer of him, but even under her questionable tutelage he had never killed unless driven to it.

Later still, when he'd killed a clumsy ambusher to protect a young, recently met companion named Micum Cavish, his new friend had assumed it was Seregil's first time and made him lick a little of the blood from the blade, an old soldier's custom.

"Drink the blood of your first kill and the ghosts of that and any other can't haunt you," Micum had promised, so earnest, so well-intentioned. Seregil had never had the heart to confess that it was already far too late, or that only one death had ever haunted him, one that galled enough to pay off all the others.

A glint of light ahead as he rounded a corner broke in on his thoughts. He'd been striding along without thought of direction, or so he'd imagined. A grim smile tugged at the corner of his mouth when he realized that his wandering feet had taken him deep into Haman tupa.

The light came from a large brazier, and in the compass of its flickering glow he saw the men gathered around it. They were young, and drinking. Even at a distance, he recognized a few of them from the council chamber, including several of Nazien's kin.

If he turned now, they'd never know he'd been there.

But he didn't turn, or even slow.

Take what the Lightbearer sends—

With a perverse shiver of excitement, he squared his shoulders, smoothed his hair back, and strolled on, passing close enough for the firelight to strike the side of his face. He said nothing, gave no greeting or provocation, but he could not suppress a small, giddy smile as a half dozen pairs of eyes widened, then tracked him with instant recognition and hatred. The tightness in Seregil's chest returned as he felt the burn of their gaze between his shoulder blades.

The inevitable attack was swift, but strangely quiet. There was the expected rush of feet, then hands grasped at him out of the darkness. They slung him against a wall, then threw him to the ground. Seregil raised his arms instinctively to cover his face but made no other move to protect himself. Boots and fists found him again, striking from all directions, finding his belly and groin and the still tender arrow bruise on his shoulder. He was picked up, shoved from one man to another, pummeled, spat on, flung down, and kicked some more. The darkness in front of his eyes lit up momentarily in a burst of white sparks as a foot connected with the back of his head.

It might have gone on for minutes or hours. The pain was crude, erratic, exquisite.

Satisfying.

"Guest slayer!" they hissed as they struck. "Exile!" "Nameless!"

Strange how sweet such epithets sounded when flavored with the dry lilt of Haman, he thought, floating dreamily near unconsciousness. He'd have thanked them if he could have drawn breath to speak, but they were intent on preventing that.

Where are your knives?

The beating stopped as abruptly as it had begun, though he knew without uncurling to look around that they were still standing over him. A muttered order was given, but he couldn't make out the words over the ringing in his ears.

Then a hot, stinging stream of liquid struck him in the face. Another fell across his splayed legs and a third hit his chest.

Ah, he thought, blinking piss from his eyes. *Nice touch, that.*

Giving him a few last disdainful kicks, they left him, tipping over the brazier as they went as if to deny him the comfort of its warmth. They could just as easily have emptied it onto him.

Noble Haman. Merciful brothers.

A low chuckle scraped out of his chest like a twist of rusty wire. Oh, it hurt to laugh—he had a few cracked ribs to remember the night by—but once he got started he couldn't stop. The breathless gasps grew to undignified giggles, then bloomed into raw, full-throated cackles that racked fresh pain through his sides and head. The sound would probably draw the Haman back, but he was too far gone to care. Red spots swirled in front of his eyes, and he had the strangest sensation that if he didn't stop laughing soon, his unmarked face would come loose from his head like an ill-fitted mask.

Eventually the whoops lessened to hiccups and snorts, then dwindled to whimpers. He felt amazingly light, cleansed even, though his dry mouth tasted bitterly of piss. Crawling a few feet to safer ground, he sprawled on the dew-laden grass, licking moisture from the blades beneath his lips. There was just enough moisture to torment him. Giving up, he staggered to his feet.

"That's all right," he mumbled to no one in particular. "Time to go home now."

Something twisted painfully in his chest as he whispered the word again.

Home.

Seregil wasn't sure afterwards just how he got back to the guest house, but when he came to he was curled up in a back corner of the bath chamber, dawn light streaming in softly around him through the open windows. It hurt to breathe. It hurt to move. It hurt to have his eyes open, so he closed them.

Hurried footsteps brought him around.

"How did he get there?"

"I don't know." That was Olmis, one of the servants. "I found him when I arrived to heat the water."

"Didn't anyone see?"

"I asked the guards. No one heard anything."

Seregil cracked an eyelid and saw Alec kneeling beside him. He looked furious.

"Seregil, what happened to you?" he asked, then recoiled, nose wrinkling in disgust at the rank odor emanating from Seregil's damp clothing. "Bilairy's Guts, you stink!"

"I went for a walk." Fire erupted in Seregil's side as he spoke, turning the words to gaps.

"Last night, you mean?"

"Yes. Just had to—walk off a bad dream." The ghost of a chuckle slipped out before he could stop it. More pain.

Alec stared at him, then motioned for Olmis to help strip off the filthy clothing. Both let out startled exclamations as they opened his coat. Seregil could guess what he must look like by now.

"Who did this to you?" Alec demanded.

Seregil considered the question, then sighed. "I fell in the dark."

"Down a privy, by the smell of him," muttered Olmis, wrestling off his breeches.

Alec knew he was lying, of course. Seregil could tell by the hard set of his lover's mouth as he helped Olmis lift him into a warm bath and wash away what they could of the night's debacle.

They probably tried to be gentle with him, but Seregil hurt too much to appreciate the effort. He didn't feel light anymore. The night's euphoric spell was broken; this pain was dull, nauseating, and constant—no brilliant flashes or crests. Closing his eyes, he endured the bath, endured being lifted out and swathed in a soft blanket. He let himself drift off, away from the massive throbbing in his head.

"I should fetch Mydri," Olmis was saying, his voice already faint in Seregil's ears.

"I don't want anyone else seeing him like this. Not his sisters, especially not the princess. This never happened," Alec told him.

Well done, talí, Seregil thought. *I don't want to have to explain it, either, because I can't.*

Seregil awoke propped up in a soft bed. Squinting up in confusion, he made out the play of firelight on rippling gauze hangings overhead.

"You slept all day."

Moving only his eyes, Seregil found Alec in a chair close beside their bed, a book open across his lap.

"Where—?" he rasped.

"So you fell, did you?"

Snapping the book shut, Alec leaned forward to place a cup of water to Seregil's lips, then one containing a milky sweet concoction that Seregil fervently hoped was either a painkiller or swift poison. He had to lift his head slightly to drink, and when he did, hot wires of pain drew taut in his neck and throat. He swallowed as quickly as he could and sank back, praying he didn't vomit it back up. That would involve far too much movement.

"I told everyone you came down with a fever in the night." This time there was no mistaking Alec's tightly reined anger.

Something fell into place in Seregil's addled brain. "I wasn't out spying without you." He longed for some of the previous night's hysteria to buoy him, but it was long gone, leaving him flat and depressed.

"What, then?" Alec demanded, pulling back the blankets. "Who did this to you, and why?"

Glancing down, Seregil saw that his ribs were expertly bandaged, the bands just tight enough to ease the pain and help the cracked bones to knit. The rest of his naked body was covered with a truly impressive array of bruises of varying sizes and shapes. The acrid stink of urine had been replaced by the cloying aroma of some herbal salve. He could see the greasy sheen of it on his skin.

"Nyal bound you up," Alec informed him, replacing the bed-clothes with hands far more gentle than his tone. "I waited until the others left for the day, then brought him up. No one else knows about this yet, except Olmis. I told them both to keep quiet. Now, who did this?"

"I don't know. It was dark." Seregil closed his eyes. It wasn't too great a lie, really; he'd known only one of them by name, the khirnari's nephew Emiel í Moranthi, and Kheeta had hinted at bad blood between him and Alec, though he'd refused to elaborate.

If it's vengeance you're after, talí, don't bother. The scales are still too heavily laden in the Hamans' favor.

Once his eyes were closed, he found it hard to open them again. The milky liquid evidently was a painkiller and he welcomed its dulling influence.

After a moment he heard Alec sigh. "The next time you feel the need to go out for a 'fall,' you *tell* me, understand?"

"I'll try," Seregil whispered, surprised by the sudden sting of tears behind his eyelids.

Warm lips brushed his forehead. "And next time, wear your own damn clothes."

At Alec's insistence, Seregil's "fever" lasted through the following day.

"I'll go keep an eye on Torsin and the Virésse," Alec told him, ordering Seregil not to stir from bed. "If anything of interest actually happens, I'll bring you every detail."

Truth was, Seregil was in no condition to argue the point. A short trip to the chamber pot had been an exercise in pain in more ways than he wanted to think about, though he'd managed it by himself. He was pissing blood, and thanked any gods still listening that Alec wasn't nursemaid enough to check. He'd have to speak to the slop boy, tell him to keep his mouth shut. Hell, he'd pay him if he had to. He'd survived worse treatment and there was no sense in worrying Alec any more than he was already.

Left alone for the day, Seregil lapsed back into sleep for a time, only to awaken in a panicky sweat to find Ilar bending over him. He braced to roll away, only to hit a solid wall of pain.

He fell back with a strangled moan and found himself looking up instead at Nyal. From the look on the Ra'basi's face, his waking expression hadn't been a welcoming one.

"I came to check your dressings."

"Thought you were—someone else," Seregil croaked, fighting down the hot nausea welling at the back of his throat.

"You're safe, my friend," Nyal assured him, not understanding. "Here, drink some more of this."

Seregil sipped gratefully at the milky draught. "What is it?"

"Crushed Carian poppy seed, chamomile, and boneset leaf boiled in goat's milk and honey. It should ease your pain."

"It does. Thanks."

Seregil could feel the effects already, just blunting the edges. He stared up at the ceiling while the Ra'basi gently checked the bindings around his chest, asking himself what the hell he had been thinking, handing himself over to the Haman like that. Mortification wrenched at his heart as he thought of what would be made of his absence from the Iia'sidra chamber. His attackers would have better sense than to brag about committing violence on sacred ground, but rumors might already be leaking out along the fretted network of gossip that underlay any large gathering. That aside, he'd virtually abandoned his responsibilities and left the burden on Alec.

"Madness," he hissed.

"Indeed. Alec is still very angry with you, and rightly so. I never took you for a stupid man."

Seregil managed a weak chuckle. "You just don't know me well enough."

Nyal frowned down at him, suddenly devoid of sympathy. "If that little night encounter had happened so much as a pace outside the boundaries of Sarikali, your talímenios might be *mourning* you right now."

Ashamed, Seregil looked away.

"What, no laughter at that? Good." Nyal produced a steaming sponge from somewhere below Seregil's line of vision and set about cleaning him.

"I didn't know you were a healer," Seregil said when he trusted himself to speak again.

"I'm not, really, but one picks up all sorts of skills, traveling."

Seregil studied the other man's profile. "We do, don't we?"

Nyal glanced up from his task. "That sounded almost friendly, Bôkthersa."

"You'll get into trouble calling me that."

Nyal gestured sloppily with the sponge. "Who's to overhear?"

Seregil acknowledged the barb with a grin of his own. "You're a nosy bastard, and an easterner. Not to mention the fact that you're the lover of a young woman who's the closest thing to a daughter I'll ever have. The combination makes me nervous."

"So I've noticed." Nyal gently turned Seregil over to spread fresh salve on his back. "A spy, am I?"

"Perhaps, or maybe just a balance to my presence."

Nyal eased him back down, and Seregil looked him in the eye. Incredible eyes, really, clear and seemingly guileless. Strange that he hadn't noticed them before. No wonder Beka—

He was wandering, he realized. "So are you?"

"A balancing factor?"

"A spy."

Nyal shrugged. "I answer to my khirnari, like anyone else. What I've told her is that what your princess says in private is no different than what she says to the Iia'sidra."

"And Amali ä Yassara?" Aura's Fingers, had he said that aloud? Nyal's potion must be having more of an effect than he'd thought.

The Ra'basi merely smiled. "You're an observant man. Amali and I were once lovers, but she chose to accept the hand of Rhaish í Arlisandin. But I still care for her and speak with her when I safely can."

"Safely?"

"Rhaish í Arlisandin loves his wife very much; it would be unworthy of me to be the cause of discord between them."

"Ah, I see." Seregil would have tapped the side of his nose knowingly if he could have raised his hand that far.

"There's nothing dishonorable between Amali and me, I give you that on my honor. Now come, you must get up and move before your muscles stiffen any more. I expect it will hurt."

Getting out of bed proved to be the worst of it. With Nyal's assistance and considerable cursing, Seregil managed to slip on a loose robe and stagger woozily around the room several times. On one pass he caught sight of himself in the mirror and cringed—eyes too large, skin too pale, expression too nakedly helpless to be the infamous Rhíminee Cat. No, here was the frightened, shame-laden young exile come home again.

"I can walk by myself," he growled, and pulled away from Nyal only to find that he couldn't, not by a long shot.

Nyal caught him as he staggered. "That's enough for now. Come, you can do with some fresh air."

Seregil surrendered himself back into the man's capable hands and was soon settled more or less comfortably in a sunny back corner of the balcony. Nyal was just tucking a blanket around him when a brisk knock sounded at the door.

Nyal went to answer it, but it was Mydri who returned. Seregil hastily checked the neck of his robe, hoping no telltale marks showed. It was a futile effort.

"A fever, is it?" she said, glowering down at him. "What were you thinking, Seregil?"

"What did Alec tell you?"

"He didn't have to tell me anything. I could see it in his face. You should tell that boy not to bother lying; he's got no skill for it."

He does when he wants to, Seregil thought. "If you're here to scold me—"

"Scold you?" Mydri's eyebrows arched higher, the way they always had when she was truly angry. "You're not a child anymore, or so I'm told. Do you have any idea what it would do to the negotiations if word got out that a member of Klia's delegation had been attacked by a Haman? Nazien is already expressing admiration for Klia—"

"Who said anything about the Haman?"

Her hand moved so fast it took him a second to register that he'd been slapped, and hard enough to make his eyes water and his ears ring. Then she was bending over him again, poking him painfully in the chest with one finger.

"Don't compound your stupidity with a lie, little brother! Did you think such a hollow act would make anything right? Did you *think* at all, or just hare off blindly like you always did? Have you changed so little?"

The words hurt far more than the blow. He probably hadn't changed all that much, though he knew better than to say so just now.

"Does anyone else know?" he asked dully.

"Officially? No one. Who would strut around bragging of breaking Aura's sacred peace? But there have been whispers. You must be at the Iia'sidra tomorrow, and you'd damn well better look like you've been ill!"

"That shouldn't be a problem."

For a moment he thought she was going to hit him again. Sparing him a last disgusted glare, she swept out. He braced to hear the door slam in her wake, but she refrained. *Mustn't give the servants anything to talk about.*

He pressed his head back against the cushions and closed his eyes, concentrating on the sounds of the birds and breeze and people passing by along the street below. The brush of cool fingers against his cheek a moment later startled him badly. He thought Nyal had gone when his sister had arrived, but here he was again, studying him with unwelcome concern.

"Are people so eager to hit you back in Skala?" the man asked, examining whatever new mark Mydri had left.

Seregil should have been angry at the intrusion, but suddenly he was too tired, too sick.

"Now and then," he replied, closing his eyes again. "But there it's usually strangers."

20

THE PASSING OF IDRILAIN

Midnight was long past by the time Korathan reached Phoria's camp. He'd outdistanced his escort some miles back, pressing on alone in the vain hope of catching his mother's dying words.

The pickets recognized his shouted greeting and cleared out of the road without challenge. Thundering into camp, he reined in at the tent showing his mother's banner, scattering a crowd of servants and officers gathered there.

Inside, the heavy odor of death assailed him.

Tonight only Phoria and a wizened drysian attended the queen. His sister's back was to him as he entered, but the drysian's solemn face told him that his mother was already dead.

"You're too late," Phoria informed him tersely.

From the state of her uniform, he guessed she'd been called in off the battlefield, too. Her cheeks were dry, her face composed, but Korathan sensed a terrible anger just held in check.

"Your messenger was delayed by an ambush," he replied, throwing off his cloak. Joining her beside the narrow field bed, he looked down at the wasted corpse that had been their mother.

The drysian had already begun the final ministrations for the pyre. Idrilain was dressed in her scarred field armor beneath the lavish burial cloak. That would please her, he thought, wondering if these considerations were Phoria's doing or the servants'. The strap of her war helm was cinched tight to hold her jaw shut, and her dimmed eyes were pressed open for the soul's journey. Her ravaged face had regained a certain dignity in death, but he saw traces of blood and dried spittle crusting her colorless lips.

"She died hard?" he asked.

"She fought it to the end," replied the drysian, close to tears.

"Astellus carry you soft, and Sakor light your way home, my Mother," he murmured hoarsely, covering Idrilain's cold hands with his own. "Did she speak much before she went?"

"She had little breath for talking," Phoria told him, turning abruptly and stalking out. "All she said was, 'Klia must not fail.' "

Korathan shook his head, knowing better than anyone the pain Phoria's anger hid. He'd watched for years in silence as the gulf between queen and heir had widened while Idrilain and Klia drew ever closer. Loyal to both, he had been able to comfort neither. Phoria had never spoken of what caused the final rift between herself and their mother, not even to him.

Whatever it was, you are queen now, my sister, my twin.

Leaving the drysian to complete his task, Korathan walked slowly to Phoria's tent. As he approached, he heard her voice raised sharply. A moment later Magyana emerged hastily from the doorway.

Seeing Korathan, she gave him a respectful bow, murmuring, "My sympathies, dear Prince. Your mother will be sorely missed."

Korathan nodded and continued in.

He found Phoria sitting at her campaign table, greying hair loose about her shoulders. Her soiled tunic and mail lay in a heap beside her chair. Without looking up from the map before her, she said tonelessly, "I'm appointing you as my vicegerent, Kor. I want you in Rhíminee. The situation here is too dire for me to leave the field, so we'll hold the coronation tomorrow as soon as you round up the necessary priests. My field wizard will officiate."

"Organeus?" Korathan took a seat across from her. "It's customary for the former queen's wizard to officiate. That would be—"

"Magyana. Yes, I know." Phoria looked up at last, pale eyes flashing dangerously. "But only because Nysander died. Who was she before that but a wanderer who spent more time in foreign lands than in her own? And what did she do while she served Mother except convince her to become dependent on foreigners?"

"The mission to Aurënen, you mean?"

Phoria let out an inelegant snort. "The queen's not cold an hour and Magyana is in here badgering me for a pledge to continue with Idrilain's plan! Nysander would have been no different, I suppose. Meddlers all, these old wizards. They've forgotten their place."

"What did you tell her?" Korathan asked quickly, hoping to circumvent another tirade.

"I informed her that as queen I do not answer to wizards, and that she would be informed of my decisions when I saw fit."

Korathan hesitated, choosing his words with care. One had to, when Phoria was like this. "Do you mean to abandon the negotiations? The way things have gone these past months, Aurënfaie aid might be of value."

Phoria rose and paced the length of the tent. "It's a sign of weakness, Kor. I dare say the surrender of the Mycenian troops along the northwestern border—"

"They surrendered?" Korathan groaned. Never in the history of the Three Lands had Mycena failed to stand with Skala against the incursions of Plenimar.

"Yesterday. Laid down their weapons in return for parole. No doubt they've heard that the Skalan queen sent her youngest daughter begging to the 'faie and it took the last of the heart out of them, exactly as I predicted it would. Southern Mycena is still with us, but it's only a matter of time until they turn coat, too. And of course, the Plenimarans know. I've had reports of raids on the western coast of Skala as far north as Ylani."

Korathan rested his face in his hands a moment as the enormity of the situation rolled over him. "I've been pushed back nearly ten miles in the past six days." The force we met above Haverford had necromancers in the front line. Powerful ones, Phoria, not the hedgerow conjurers you've met with back here. They killed an entire turma's horses beneath them as they charged, then sent the corpses galloping back among our ranks. It was a rout. I think—"

"What? That Mother was right?" Phoria rounded on him. "That we *need* the Aurënfaie and their magic to survive this war? I'll tell you what we need: Aurënfaie horses, Aurënfaie steel, and the Aurënfaie port of Gedre if we're to defend Rhíminee and the southern islands. But still the Iia'sidra debates!"

Korathan watched with wary fascination as his twin paced, left hand clenched over the pommel of her sword so tightly that the knuckles showed white.

Her old campaigning sword, he noted. She'd put aside the sword of Ghërilain for now so that she could be formally invested with it at her crowning, with all the power and authority it represented. He'd known all his life that this moment would come, that his sister would be queen. Watching her now, why did he suddenly feel as if the ground had given way under him?

"Have you sent word to Klia?" he asked at last.

Phoria shook her head. "Not just yet. I'm expecting fresh dispatches by tomorrow. We'll wait to see which way the wind's blowing down there. Strength, Kor. We must preserve a position of strength at all costs."

"Any news you get by dispatch, even if it comes tomorrow, will be at least a week old. Besides, Klia is sure to put the best light on things, especially once word reaches her that you've taken the throne."

Phoria gave him a strange, tight smile that narrowed her pale eyes like a cat's. Going to a table at the side of the tent, she unlocked an iron box and took out a sheaf of small parchments. "Klia and Torsin are not my only sources of information at Sarikali."

"Ah, yes, your spies in the ranks. What do they say? Will the Iia'sidra give us what we ask?"

Phoria's mouth set in a harsh, unyielding line. "One way or another, we shall have what we need. I want you in Rhíminee, my brother."

Going to him, she took one of his large hands in hers and tugged a ring from his finger, the one set with a large black stone carved with a dragon swallowing its own tail. Smiling, she slipped it on the forefinger of her left hand. "Be ready, Kor. When this dragon comes back to you, it's time to go after another."

It won't take much acting to play the recovering invalid, will it?" Alec said as he helped Seregil dress the third morning after the beating. His friend's body showed a shocking array of purple and green bruises where it wasn't bandaged, and he still wasn't eating much except broth and Nyal's infusions.

"The act will be to convince them that I *am* recovered." Seregil let out a strangled groan as he eased his arms into the sleeves of his coat. "Or to convince myself."

Seregil still refused to divulge what had really happened to him that night. The fact that he seemed in better spirits since the attack bothered Alec almost as much as his friend's stubborn silence on the matter.

No sooner do I rake a few old secrets out of him than he goes and takes on a load of new ones.

"I'll come with you today," he said. "It's almost gotten interesting. The khirnari of Silmai has been taking Klia's part openly, and she's convinced the Ra'basi are about to tumble our way. You missed the banquet with them last night; most cordial, and the Virésse noticeably absent. Do you think Nyal had a hand in that?"

"He claims not to have been asked his

opinion. It could be that Ra'basi is getting tired of being under Virésse's sway." Seregil limped to the small mirror over the wash-stand. Evidently satisfied with what he saw there, he stretched his arms tentatively and let out another pained gasp. "Oh, yes, I'm *much* better!" he muttered, grimacing at his white-faced reflection. "Help me downstairs, will you? I think I can manage after that."

The others were at breakfast in the hall. Klia sat poring over a stack of new dispatches.

"Feeling better?" she asked, glancing up.

"Much," Seregil lied. He eased into a chair next to Thero and accepted a cup of tea he had no intention of drinking. The wizard was frowning over a letter.

"From Magyana?" he asked.

"Yes." Thero passed it to him and Seregil skimmed the contents, holding it so Alec could see, too.

" 'The third of Klia's dispatches reached us here yesterday. Phoria said little, but her impatience is clear,' " Alec read aloud. " 'Surely some small concession can be coaxed from the Iia'sidra? otherwise, I fear she will recall you—' "

"Yes, we've already seen that," Torsin told him. "A small concession, she asks for. What else have we been laboring for all these weeks?"

Seregil saw the quick glance Alec shot the envoy and knew he was recalling the man's night visit to Khatme tupa.

"I get hints of the same threat from my honored sister," Klia growled, tossing aside the letter she'd been reading. "Let her come down and see what I'm up against. It's like trying to argue with trees!" She turned to Seregil with a grimace of frustration. "Tell me, my adviser, how to make your people hurry! Time's running short."

Seregil sighed. "Let Alec and I do what we're best at, my lady."

Klia shook her head. "Not yet. The risks are too great. There must be another way."

Seregil stared into the depths of his cup, wishing his head was clear enough to think of one.

The ride to the council chamber was a tense affair. Ignoring Seregil's muttered warnings, Alec helped him mount and dismount, claiming he looked faint. By the time Seregil was finally seated in his place just behind Klia, he was pale and sweating, but seemed to recover a little once he'd gotten his wind back.

Alec scanned the faces around the circle. Reaching the Haman contingent, he stopped, a sudden knot of tension tightening his belly. Emiel í Moranthi was grinning openly at Seregil. Catching Alec's eye, he gave him a slight, sardonic nod.

"It was him, wasn't it?" Alec grated under his breath.

Seregil merely glanced at him as if he didn't know what Alec was talking about, then motioned him to silence.

Alec looked back at Emiel, thinking, *Just let me and a few friends catch you in a dark street some night soon. Or just me alone, come to that.* He hoped the thought showed on his face, whatever the cost.

Seregil saw the Haman's appraising leer, but steadfastly ignored him. It was easier to carry on with the pretense that he had recognized no one in the darkness that night.

And just who are you trying to fool?

He pushed the thought aside with practiced ease. There were more important things to be dealt with right now.

Alec had been correct about a shift in the Ra'basi's stance. Moriel ä Moriel took it upon herself to contest a point being put forth by Elos of Goliníl about certain Skalan shipping practices. Whether it represented full support remained to be seen.

Satisfied that Seregil was back on his feet, Alec returned to his ramblings through the city the next day. At Klia's request, he commandeered Nyal and set out to ingratiate himself among the Ra'basi in the hope of gleaning both goodwill and useful information.

It proved an easy task. Alec soon found himself welcome at a makeshift tavern, known for its ready supply of strong beer and spiced eggs. Not only was it a popular meeting place for people of various clans, but Artis, the brewer who ran the place during the day, was a servant of one of the Ra'basi khirnari's closest advisers. He'd set up shop on the street level of a deserted house, serving his customers through an open window that overlooked a walled garden. Archery, dice, and wrestling were the sports of choice to pass the time.

The beer proved passable, the eggs inedible, and the results of Alec's spying meager. After three days of loitering and drinking, he'd added nearly a dozen shatta to his collection, lost his second-best dagger to a Datsian woman who outwrestled him, and learned only that the khirnari of Ra'basi had some sort of falling out with the Virésse a week before, though no one seemed to know the details.

Lounging there with Nyal and Kheeta after a shooting match, Alec decided that he'd probably learned everything there was to be learned among the Ra'basi. He was about to leave when he overheard Artis launch into a tirade against the Khatme. Evidently he'd had a run-in with a member of that clan the night before over a keg of beer he'd sold. Still smarting from his own failure among that strange clan, Alec sauntered over to hear more.

"Arrogant bunch of stargazers, that's what I say," Artis fumed as he served beer from his window perch. "Think they're closer to Aura than the rest of us."

"They don't take to outsiders much, I've found," Alec ventured. "Or ya'shel, for that matter."

"They've always been a strange, standoffish bunch," the brewer muttered.

"What do you know of the Khatme?" a Goliníl woman scoffed.

"As much as you do," he drawled, passing out cups of murky new beer. "They keep to themselves and they serve themselves, for all their talk of Aura."

"I hear they make fine wizards," Alec put in.

"Wizards, seers, rhui'auros," the brewer allowed grudgingly. "But magic is a gift meant to serve and that's something the Khatme don't do willingly. Instead, they stay up in their eagles' nest of a fai'thast, dreaming their strange dreams and handing down proclamations."

"You know, in all the time I've been here, I haven't seen much magic used. Where I come from, folks imagine the 'faie throwing it around left and right."

Several of Alec's companions snickered.

"Look around, Skalan," Artis said. "Do you see any need for magic? Should we fly through the air instead of using our own feet? Or knock birds out of the sky instead of learning archery?"

"This beer of yours could use a bit of magicking," a boy laughed.

Artis gave him a hard look, then wove a brief sigil over their cups. The beer foamed slightly, giving off a strong, malty odor.

"Taste that, then," he challenged.

The contents of Alec's cup were certainly clearer than before. Impressed, he took a drink, but immediately spat it out.

"It tastes like swamp water!" he sputtered.

"Of course," Artis declared, laughing now. "Beer has its own magic. It doesn't need any help, as any brewer knows."

"And so knowing, takes it too much for granted," said a new voice.

A grey, wizened little rhui'auros stepped from the shadows of a cul-de-sac next to the building.

Kheeta and the others raised their left hands and gave the man a respectful nod. In turn, he raised a tattooed hand in blessing.

"Welcome, Honored One," said Artis, coming out to offer him beer and food.

The others made room for the old man and he sat down, wolfing down the eggs and bread as if he hadn't eaten in days and dribbling his beer down the front of his already none-too-clean robes.

When he'd finished he looked up and pointed to Alec. "Our little brother asks about magic and you scoff, children of Aura?" Shaking his head, he picked up a bow lying near his feet and placed it in Alec's hands. "Tell me, what do you feel?"

Alec rubbed his palm over the smooth limbs. "Wood, sinew—" he began, then gasped as the rhui'auros touched a finger firmly to the center of his forehead.

A cool sensation swept the skin between his eyes, like the kiss of a mountain breeze. As it spread deeper, the bow seemed to subtly vibrate in his hands, reminding him of the time he'd touched a drysian's staff and felt the surge of power through the wood.

"I feel—I don't know. It's like holding a living thing."

"It is Shariel ä Malai's magic you feel, her khi," the rhui'auros replied, pointing to the Ptalos woman who owned the bow. He motioned for Kheeta to give Alec the knife from his belt.

Gripping it, Alec felt similar sensations from the metal. "Yes, it's there, too."

"Our khi suffuses us the way oil soaks a wick," the rhui'auros explained. "Everything we touch takes on a bit of it, and from it comes all our gifts. Shariel ä Malai, take up Alec í Amasa's bow."

She obeyed, eyes widening in surprise as the man touched her brow. "By the Light, the khi is strong as a storm wind in it!"

"You shoot well, do you not?" the rhui'auros asked, noting the collection of shatta on Alec's quiver.

"Yes, Honored One."

"Better than most?"

"Perhaps. It's just something I'm good at."

"Good enough to strike a dyrmagnos?"

"Yes, but—"

"*He* fought a dyrmagnos?" someone whispered.

"It was a good shot," Alec admitted, recalling the strange, dreamlike calm that had come over him when he took aim at his hated tormentor. His bow had trembled strangely in his hands as he'd let fly, but he'd always put those sensations, indeed even his success, down to the spells Nysander had woven around it.

"Little brother, when will you visit me?" the rhui'auros chided. "Your friend Thero comes to the Nha'mahat often now, yet for you I wait and wait."

"I'm sorry, Honored One. I—I didn't realize I was expected," Alec stammered, taken aback by this revelation about Thero. The wizard had never mentioned it. "I've been wanting to, but—"

"You must bring Seregil í Korit, as well. Tell him to come tonight."

"The Exile no longer bears that name," an Akhendi reminded him.

"Doesn't he?" the rhui'auros asked, turning to go. "How forgetful of me. Come tonight, Alec í Amasa. There is so much you must tell me."

Tell you? thought Alec, but before he could question the man further the rhui'auros blurred before his eyes, disappearing like a design of colored sand in a strong wind.

"Well, at least you can't complain of not seeing magic," said Artis. "Now what's this about you killing a dyrmagnos?"

Alec's first thought was to find Seregil and tell him about the rhui'auros's strange summons, but his drinking companions wouldn't let him go without hearing the tale of the battle against Irtuk Beshar and Mardus. Struck by a sudden inspiration, he played heavily on Seregil's role in the fight, reasoning that stories of the "Exile's" heroism could only do Seregil good in reclaiming his place among his people. As he recounted his own part that day, however, the rhui'auros's words kept coming back to him, making him wonder if there actually had been more than experience guiding his hand that day.

Afternoon sunshine lit the eastern half of the Iia'sidra chamber and threw the other half into near darkness. When Alec slipped in, a member of the Khatme delegation was pacing the open floor at the center of the room, haranguing the assembly with an extensive list of the historic depredations of outlanders.

Many in the audience were nodding approval. Just visible behind Klia, Thero appeared angry, Seregil bored and tired. Braknil and his honor guard loomed behind them, faces duty-blank. Wending his way through the minor clans, Alec took a seat beside Seregil.

"Ah, you've come at the most interesting part," his friend murmured, stifling a yawn.

"How much longer will you be?"

"Not long. Everyone's out of sorts today; I think most of them are ready for a jug of rassos. I know I am."

Torsin turned and shot them a pointed look. Seregil covered a smirk with his hand and sank a bit lower in his chair. With his other, he signed for Alec to stay.

The Khatme finished at last, and Klia stood to reply. Alec couldn't see her face, but from the set of her shoulders he guessed she'd had enough, too.

"Honored Khatme, you speak well and clearly of Aurënen's concerns, " she began. "You speak of raiders, and those who have betrayed the laws of hospitality, yet in all these tales, I hear no mention of Skala. I don't doubt that you have good reason to fear some foreigners, but why should you fear us? Skala has never attacked Aurënen. Instead, we have traded in good faith, traveled your land in good faith, and respected the Edict of Separation in good faith, although we believe it is unjust. Many here do not hesitate to remind me of the murder of Corruth; is that because it is the only transgression you can throw up at us?"

"You demand access to our northern coast, our port, our iron mines," a Haman declared. "If we let you bring miners and smiths to make settlements, how then can we expect them to leave when your need is gone?"

"Why do you think they will not?" Klia countered. "I have seen Gedre. I have ridden through the cold, barren mountains where the mines are. With all due respect, perhaps you ought to visit my land. Perhaps then you would understand that we have no desire for yours, only the iron to fight our war and save our own."

This response gained her a ripple of applause and a few poorly muffled laughs among her supporters. But Klia remained stern.

"I have listened to Ilbis í Tarien of Khatme recite the history of your people. Nowhere in that history did I hear of Skala acting as aggressor toward your land, or any other. Like you, we understand what it is to have *enough*. Through husbandry and trade and the blessings of the Four, we have never needed to take what was not freely offered. The same can be said of the Mycenians, who even now sway, driven to their knees by the onslaught of Plenimar. We fight to repel the aggressor, not to conquer. The previous Overlord of Plenimar was content within his own borders for many years. It is his son who has renewed the old conflict. Must I, youngest daughter of a Tírfaie queen, remind the Aurënfaie of their heroic role in the first Great War when we fought as one?

"My throat grows sore from giving the same assurances day after day. If you will not allow us to mine, then sell us your iron and let our ships come to Gedre to get it."

"And so it goes," Seregil muttered. "The war could be lost before we can get beyond whether or not Klia is personally responsible for Corruth's murder."

"Are there any plans for tonight?" Alec asked, glancing nervously in Torsin's direction.

"We're to dine in Khaladi tupa. I'm actually looking forward to this one. Their dancers are exceptional."

Alec settled back with an inward sigh. The shadows crept a few more inches across the floor as Rhaish í Arlisandin and Galmyn í Nemius of Lhapnos launched into a verbal battle over some river that divided their lands. The argument ended when the Akhendi stalked from the chamber in a rage. The outburst signaled the end of the day's debate.

"What did that have to do with Skala?" Alec complained as the assembly broke up.

"Balance of trade, as usual," Torsin told him. "At the moment Akhendi must depend on Lhapnos's goodwill to float goods down to port. If and when Gedre opens, then Akhendi will gain the advantage. That is only one of several reasons why Lhapnos opposes Klia's request."

"Maddening!" Klia muttered under her breath. "Whatever they decide in the end, it will have more to do with their troubles than ours. If we were dealing with a single ruler, things would be different."

Their host of the evening swept down on her, and Klia allowed herself to be led aside for a private conversation.

Seregil gave Alec a questioning look. "You've been waiting to tell me something, I think?"

"Not here."

The walk back to their lodgings seemed a long one. When they were finally alone in their room, Alec closed the door and leaned back against it.

"I met a rhui'auros today."

Seregil's expression did not change, but Alec detected a sudden tightness at the corners of his friend's mouth.

"He asked that we come to the Nha'mahat tonight. Both of us."

Still Seregil said nothing.

"Kheeta hinted that you have—bad feelings about them?"

"Bad feelings?" Seregil raised an eyebrow as if considering Alec's choice of words. "Yes, you could say that."

"But why? The one I met seemed kind enough, if a little eccentric."

Seregil folded his arms. Was it Alec's imagination, or was he trembling slightly?

"During my trial—" Seregil began, speaking so softly that Alec had to strain to hear. "A rhui'auros came, saying I was to be brought here, to Sarikali. No one knew what to think. I'd already confessed everything. . . ."

He faltered, and the hint of a dark memory traveled to Alec across the talímenios bond; his vision darkened as a burning stab of panic constricted his chest.

"They tortured you?" Memories of his own experiences added to the leaden weight settling in the pit of his stomach.

"Not in the way you mean." Going to a clothes chest, Seregil threw back the lid and rummaged in its depths. "It was a long time ago. It doesn't matter."

But Alec could still feel the sour tang of panic clinging to his companion. Going to him, he laid a hand on Seregil's shoulder. The man sagged a little under the light touch.

"I just don't understand what they want with me now."

"If you'd rather not go, I could make some excuse."

Seregil managed a lopsided grimace. "I don't think that would be wise. No, we'll go. Together. It's time you did, talí."

Alec was silent a moment. "Do you think they can tell me about my mother?" The words came hard. "I—I need to know who I am."

"Take what the Lightbearer sends, Alec."

"What do you mean?"

The strange, guarded look came into Seregil's eyes again. "You'll see."

22

DREAMS AND VISIONS

The minor clans had no official voice in the Iia'sidra, but they were not without influence. The Khaladi were among the most respected and fiercely independent; Klia considered them an important potential ally.

At Sarikali they occupied a small section in the eastern part of the city. The khirnari, Mallia ä Tama, met them at the head of what appeared to be her entire clan and led them on foot to the open land beyond the city's edge. Her blue-and-yellow sen'gai was made of twisted bands of silk intertwined with red cord, and she wore a voluminous silk coat over her tight-fitting tunic.

The Khaladi were taller and more muscular than most of the 'faie Alec had met, and many had bands of intricate tattoos encircling their wrists and ankles. They smiled readily and treated their guests with a mix of respect and warm familiarity that quickly put him at ease.

On a flat expanse of ground just beyond the city's edge, a circular area a few hundred yards in diameter had been covered with huge, multicolored carpets and ringed with bonfires. Instead of the usual dining couches, low tables and piles of bolsters were arranged around the perimeter. Mallia ä Tama and her family served Klia's party themselves, washing their guests' hands over basins to symbolize the customary bath and offering them wine and dried fruits dipped in honey. Musicians arrived carrying pipes and long-necked stringed instruments unlike any Alec had seen. Instead of plucking or strumming the latter, the players sawed at the strings with a short bow, producing a sound at once mournful and sweet.

As the sun sank and the feast progressed, it was not difficult for Alec to imagine himself transported to their mountain fai'thast. Under different circumstances, he would have been content to spend the entire night in such company.

Instead, he kept a watchful eye on Seregil, who often fell silent and glanced frequently at the progress of the moon.

Do you dread the night's destination so much? Alec wondered with a twinge of guilt at his own anticipation.

As the banquet neared its end, thirty or more Khaladi rose and shed their tunics, stripping down to short, tight-fitting leather breeches. Their lightly oiled skin shone like satin in the firelight.

"Now we'll see something!" Seregil exclaimed under his breath, looking happy for the first time that night.

"We are great dancers, the best in all Aurënen," the khirnari was telling Klia. "For in the dance we celebrate the circles of unity that make our world—the unity between our people and Aura, the unity of sky and earth, the unity that binds us one to another. You might feel the magic of it, but do not be alarmed. It is only the sharing of khi that unites the dancers with those who watch them."

The musicians struck up a dark, skirling melody as the performers took their places. Working in pairs, they slowly lifted and balanced each other with sinuous grace. Without the least hint of strain or tremor, their bodies twined into configurations at once disciplined and erotic, arching, folding, curving as they rose and fell.

Rapt, Alec felt the flow of khi the khirnari had spoken of; differing energies of each successive dance enfolded him, drawing him in although he never stirred from where he sat.

Some dances featured a single gender or male and female couples, but most involved all the varying groups at once. One of the most moving was a performance by pairs of children.

Klia sat motionless, one hand pressed unconsciously to her lips. Pure wonder showed on Thero's thin features, softening them to something approaching beauty. Beyond them, Alec could see Beka among the honor guard, the hint of tears glistening in her eyes. Nyal stood beside her, not quite touching as he watched her watch the dance.

One pair of men held Alec's attention for dance after dance. It was not simply their skill that moved him but the way they seemed to hold each other with their gaze, trusting, anticipating, working in perfect unison. His throat tightened as he watched them during one particularly sensual dance; he knew without being told that they were talímenios and that they had lived this dance, this mingling of souls, together most of their lives.

He felt Seregil's hand cover his own. Without the least embarrassment, Alec turned his hand, weaving their fingers together and letting the dance speak for him.

As the moon rose higher, however, Alec found himself increasingly distracted by the thought of the rhui'auros's summons.

Ever since Thero had first mentioned the rhui'auros and their abilities back in Ardinlee, he'd wondered what it would be like to have that missing piece added to the small mosaic of his life. Wandering with his father, knowing no kin, claiming no town as their own, he'd never questioned his father's silence. Only when he'd gone to Watermead and been embraced by Micum Cavish's family had he realized what he'd lacked. Even his formal name reflected that: plain Alec í Amasa of Kerry. Where there should be additional names to link him with his own history, there were only blanks. By the time he'd been old enough to ask such questions his father was dead, all the answers reduced to ash plowed into a stranger's field.

Perhaps tonight he would learn his own truth.

He and Seregil saw Klia home, then turned their horses for the Nha'mahat.

The Haunted City was deserted tonight, and Alec found himself starting at shadows, certain he saw movement in the empty windows or heard the whisper of voices in the sighing of the breeze.

"What do you think will happen?" he asked at last, unable to bear the silence any longer.

"I wish I could tell you, talí," Seregil replied. "My experience wasn't the ordinary sort. I believe it's like the Temple of Illior; people come for visions, dreams—the rhui'auros are said to be strange guides."

I remember that house, that street, Seregil thought, amazed at the power of memory.

He'd avoided this section of the city since their arrival, but he'd come here often as a child. In those days the Nha'mahat had been an enticingly mysterious place only adults were allowed to enter, and the rhui'auros just eccentric folk who might offer sweets, stories, or a colorful spell or two if you loitered long enough between the arches of the arcade. That perception had been shattered along with his childhood when he'd finally entered the tower.

The fragmented memories of what followed had haunted the farthest reaches of his dreams ever since, like hungry wolves hovering just outside the safe circle of a campfire's glow.

The black cavern.

The stifling heat inside the tiny dhima.

The probing magicks stripping him, turning him inside out, flaying him with every doubt, vanity, and banality of his adolescent self as the rhui'auros sought the truth behind the killing of the unfortunate Haman.

Alec rode beside him cloaked in that special silence of his, happy, full of anticipation. Some part of Seregil longed to warn him, tell him—

He gripped the reins so tightly that his knuckles ached. *No, never speak of that night, not even to you. Tonight I enter the tower a free man, of my own will.*

At the command of a rhui'auros, an inner voice reminded him, whispering from among the gaunt wolves of memory.

Reaching the Nha'mahat at last, they dismounted and led their horses to the main door. A woman emerged from the darkened arcade and took the reins for them.

Still Alec said nothing. No questions. No probing looks.

Bless you, tali.

A rhui'auros answered their knock. The silver mask covering his face was like those worn at the Temple of Illior: smooth, serene, featureless.

"Welcome," a deep male voice greeted them from behind it.

The tattoo on his palm was similar to those of the priests of Illior. And why not? It was the Aurënfaie who'd taught the ways of Aura to the Tír. For the first time since his arrival, it struck him how deeply intertwined the Skalans and 'faie still were, whether they realized it or not. There had been years enough for the Tír to forget, perhaps, but his own people? Not likely. Why then did some of the clans fear reclaiming the old ties?

The man gave them masks and led them into a meditation chamber, a low, windowless room lit by niche lamps. At least a dozen people lay naked on pallets there, their dreaming faces hidden by silver masks. The damp air was heavy with thick clouds of fragrant smoke from a brazier near the center of the room. Just beyond it, a broad, circular stairway spiraled down out of sight. Wisps of steam curled up from the cavern below.

"Wait here," their guide told Seregil, pointing to an empty pallet against the far wall. "Someone will come for you. Elesarit waits upstairs for Alec í Amasa."

Alec brushed the back of Seregil's hand with his own, then followed the man up a narrow staircase at the back of the chamber.

Seregil walked across to his assigned pallet. This took him past the round stairway, and his chest tightened. He knew where it led.

Alec resisted a look back at Seregil. When the rhui'auros had told him to bring Seregil, he'd assumed they would make their visit together.

They climbed three flights of stairs in silence, meeting no one in the dark corridors. On the third floor they followed a short hallway to a small chamber. A clay lamp flickered in one corner, and by its wavering light Alec saw that the room was empty except for an ornate metal brazier by the far wall. Not knowing what was expected of him, he turned to ask his guide, but he was already gone.

Strange folk, indeed, he thought, yet they held the key that could unlock his past. Too excited to sit still, Alec paced the little chamber, listening anxiously for the sound of approaching footsteps.

They came at last. The rhui'auros who entered wore no mask, and Alec recognized him as the old man he'd met at the tavern. Striding over to Alec, he dropped the leather sack he carried and clasped hands warmly.

"So you have come at last, little brother. Seeking your past, I think?"

"Yes, Honored One. And I—I want to know what it means to be Hâzadriëlfaie."

"Good, good! Sit down."

Alec settled cross-legged where the man indicated, in the center of the room.

Elesarit dragged the brazier to the center of the room, summoned fire there, then took two handfuls of what looked like a mix of ash and small seeds from the sack and cast them into the flames. Sharp, choking smoke curled up, making Alec's eyes water.

Elesarit pulled his robe over his head and threw it into a corner. Naked except for the tattooed whorls covering his hands and feet, he began to slowly circle Alec, bare soles whispering across the floor as he moved. Thin and wizened as he was, he moved gracefully, weaving his patterned hands and thin body through the smoke. Alec felt goose flesh break out on his arms and knew at once that, like the dances of the Khaladi he'd watched earlier, these movements were a form of magic. Faint music, strange and distant, hovered at the edge of his perception, perhaps magic, perhaps only memory.

It was unnerving, this ceremony: the old man's silence, the shapes that twisted themselves from the smoke and dissolved before he could quite make them out, the heady smell of the substances burning on the coals of the brazier. Lightheaded, Alec fought against a sudden wave of dizziness.

And still the rhui'auros danced, moving in and out of Alec's field of vision, in and out of the ever-thickening smoke that seemed to wind itself into denser coils in his wake.

The man's feet fascinated Alec. He couldn't look away from them as they whisper-shuffled past: long toes, brown skin, and branched ridges of veins beneath the shifting black tracery.

The smoke stung Alec's eyes, but he found he didn't have the strength to lift his hand and wipe them. He could hear the rhui'auros circling behind him now, yet somehow the feet stayed before him, filling his vision.

Those aren't his feet, Alec realized in silent awe. They were a woman's—small and delicate in spite of the dirt that edged the nails and darkened the cracks on the callused heels. These feet were not dancing. They were running.

Then he was looking down at them as if they were his own feet, flying beneath the edge of a stained brown skirt, running along a trail through a frost-rimed meadow just before dawn.

A misstep on a sharp stone. Blood. The feet did not stop running.

Fleeing.

There was no sound, no physical sensation, but Alec knew the desperation that propelled her on as clearly as if the emotions were his own.

Meadow gave way to forest with dreamlike speed, one landscape melting into another. He felt the burning in her lungs, the clenching ache deep in her belly where dark blood still flowed and the slight weight of the burden she carried in her arms, a tiny bundle wrapped in a long, dark sen'gai.

Child

The infant's face was still covered in birthing blood. Its eyes were open and blue

as his own.

Gradually his line of sight shifted upwards and he gazed through her eyes at a lone figure in the distance, standing on a boulder against the first pale wash of dawn.

The girl's desperation gave way to hope.

Amasa!

Alec had recognized his father first by the way he carried his bow across his shoulders. Now the wind whipped tangled blond hair back from that square, plain, bearded face in which Alec had tried so often without success to find himself. He was young, not much older than Alec himself, and racked with desperation as he glared back past the girl.

He loomed closer until he seemed to fill Alec's vision. Then came a wrenching lurch, and Alec was looking down into the face of a young woman with his own dark blue eyes, full lips, and fine-boned features, all framed by ragged clumps of dark brown hair, hacked cruelly short.

Ireya!

He didn't know if the voice was his own or his father's, but he felt the agony of that despairing cry. Helpless as his father had been, Alec watched in horror as she thrust the baby into his arms and dashed back the way she'd come, toward the horsemen who pursued her.

Then Alec was looking down at the small, bruised feet again as she ran at them, spreading her empty arms wide as if to gather the arrows speeding at her heart from the bows of

brothers

The force of the first shaft knocked Alec flat on his back and hot pain sliced the breath from his lungs. It passed as quickly as it had come, however, and he felt his life leaving like smoke from the wound, rising on the sparkling morning air until he could see the horsemen gathered around the still body below. He couldn't see their faces to know if they were pleased or horrified at their own deed. He saw only that they ignored the distant figure fleeing west with his tiny burden.

"Open your eyes, son of Ireya ä Shaar."

The vision collapsed.

Opening his eyes, Alec lay sprawled on the cold floor, arms flung wide.

Elesarit crouched next to him, eyes half closed, lips parted in a strange grimace.

"My mother?" Alec asked through dry lips, too weak to sit up. The back of his head hurt. In fact, he hurt all over.

"Yes, little brother, and your Tírfaie father," Elesarit said softly, touching Alec's temple with the fingertips of one hand.

"My father—he had no other names?"

"None that he knew."

The smoke closed in around him again, bringing another wave of dizziness. The ceiling overhead dissolved into a miasma of shifting color.

Stop! he begged, but his throat was numb. No sound escaped.

"You carry the memories of your people," the rhui'auros said, lost somewhere in the shifting blur. "I take these from you, but not without giving something back."

Suddenly Alec was standing on a rugged mountainside beneath a huge crescent moon. Barren peaks stretched out in front of him for as far as he could see. Far below, a torch-lit procession wended its way along a twisting track, hundreds of people, it seemed, or thousands. The chain of tiny, bobbing lights stretched back through the night like a necklace of amber beads tossed on rumpled black velvet.

"Ask what you will," a low, inhuman voice rumbled behind him, like rocks grinding together in an avalanche.

Alec whirled, reaching for a sword that wasn't there. A few yards from where he stood, a cliff rose into the darkness overhead, sheer except for a small hole near the bottom not much larger than the door of a dog kennel.

"Ask what you will," the voice said again, and the vibration of it sent loose pebbles clinking and pattering down around Alec's feet.

Sinking to his hands and knees, he looked into the hole, but there was only darkness beyond.

"Who are you?" he tried to ask, only somehow the words came out "Who am I?" instead.

"You are the wanderer who carries his home in his heart," the unseen speaker replied, sounding pleased with the question. "You are the bird who makes its nest on the waves. You will father a child of no woman."

A deathly chill rolled over him. "A curse?"

"A blessing."

Suddenly Alec felt weight and heat against his back. Someone placed a thick fur robe over him, one that had been warmed before a fire. It was so heavy that he couldn't lift his head to see who had covered him, but he glimpsed a man's hands and recognized them—strong, long-fingered Aurënfaie hands. Seregil's.

"Child of earth and light," the voice pronounced. "Brother of shadows, watcher in the darkness, wizard-friend."

"What clan am I?" Alec gasped as the warm robe pressed down on him.

"Akavi'shel, little ya'shel, and no clan at all. Owl and dragon. Always and never. What do you hold?"

Alec looked down at his hands, pressed to the rocky ground as he fought now to hold up the weight of the robe. Tangled in the fingers of his left hand was his Akhendi bracelet with the blackened charm. Wadded beneath his right was a bloodstained length of cloth—a sen'gai, though he couldn't make out the color.

The weight of the robe was too much for him. Falling forward, he was trapped by its smothering bulk.

"What name did my mother give me?" he groaned as the moon was blotted out.

There was no reply.

Exhausted, trapped, and aching in every muscle, Alec cradled his head on his arms and wept for a woman nineteen years dead, and for the silent, brooding man who'd stood helplessly and watched his only love die.

Seregil inhaled deeply as he waited, hoping the smoke of the strong herbs would take the edge off his fear. There were no meditation symbols in this chamber—no Fertile Queen, Cloud Eye, or Moon Bow. Perhaps the rhui'auros stood too close to the Lightbearer to need such things.

"Aura Elustri, send me light," he murmured. Folding his hands loosely in his lap, he closed his eyes and tried to find the inner silence necessary to free his thoughts, but it would not come.

I'm out of practice. How often had he entered a temple during all his years in Skala? Less than a dozen times, probably, and always with some ulterior need.

The even breathing of the dreamers around the room grated on his nerves, mocking his restlessness. It was a relief of sorts when a guide finally came and led him down the winding stairs to the cavern below.

Oh, yes, he remembered this place, with its rough stone and heat and the flat, metallic odor that tightened the knot of dread already cramping his gut.

Three passages branched from the main chamber, sloping down

into darkness. Seregil's guide waved a globe of light into being and set off down the one to their right.

The same? Seregil wondered, stumbling along behind him. Impossible to know for certain; he'd been so frightened that night, half dragged, half carried into total darkness.

It got hotter as they went. Steam curled thickly from seams in the rock. Condensation dripped from above. It was difficult to catch his breath.

drowning in darkness—

Small dhima stood at irregular intervals along this tunnel, but Seregil's guide led him far deeper into the earth before stopping beside one.

"Here," the man instructed, lifting the leather door flap. "Leave your clothes outside."

Stripping off everything but the silver mask, Seregil crawled inside. It was stifling and stank of sweat and wet wool; a small fissure emitted a steady flow of hot vapor. Seregil crawled to a rush mat next to the steam vent. His guide waited until he was seated, then dropped the flap back into place. Blackness closed quickly in around Seregil; the man's footsteps faded back in the direction they'd come.

What am I so scared of? he wondered, fighting down the panic that threatened to unman him. *They finished with me, passed sentence. It's over. I'm here now by Iia'sidra dispensation, a representative of the Skalan queen.*

Why didn't someone come?

Sweat drenched his body, stinging the scabbed abrasions on his back and sides. It dripped from the tip of his nose to pool in the contours inside the mask. He hated the feel of it, hated the darkness and the irrational sense that the walls were pressing in on him.

He'd never feared the dark, not even as a child.

Except here. Then.

And now.

He crossed his arms across his bare chest, shaking in spite of the heat. He couldn't fight off the wolves of memory here. They rushed at him, wearing the faces of all the rhui'auros who'd interrogated him. They'd woven their magic deep into his mind, pulling out thoughts and fears like so many rotten teeth.

Now, as he huddled trembling and sick, other memories followed, ones he'd buried even deeper: the sharp sting of his father's hand against his face when he'd tried to say farewell; the way friends had refused to meet his eye; the sight of the only home he'd ever known or hoped to dwindling to nothing in the distance—

Still no one came.

His breath whistled harshly through the mask. The dhima trapped the steam, searing his lungs. Stretching out his arms, he felt for the wooden ribs on either side of him to reassure himself that the sodden walls were not collapsing in on him. His fingers brushed hot wood and rested there. A moment later, however, he let out a sharp hiss of suprise as something hot and smooth skittered over his left hand. Before he could pull it back, the unseen creature had clenched itself around his wrist. Needle teeth pierced the fleshy part of his palm just below the thumb, spreading quickly to engulf his entire hand.

A dragon, and one at least the size of a cat, judging by the weight.

Seregil willed himself not to move. The beast released him, dropped to his naked thigh, and scrambled away.

Seregil held still until he was certain it was gone, then cradled his hand against his chest. What was a dragon that size doing so far from the mountains, and how venomous was such a bite? This made him think of Thero, and he choked back an hysterical laugh.

"That will leave a lucky mark."

Seregil jerked his head up. Less than a foot to his left squatted the glowing, naked form of a rhui'auros. The man's broad face looked vaguely familiar. He had thickly drawn markings on his large hands. His muscular chest was covered with others that seemed to move with a life of their own as he reached to examine Seregil's wound.

There was no light; Seregil couldn't even see his own hand, but he could see the rhui'auros as clearly as if they both sat in daylight.

"I remember you. Your name is Lhial."

"And you are called the Exile now, yes? The Dragon now follows the Owl."

This last phrase sounded familiar somehow, but he couldn't place it, though he recognized the two references to Aura: the dragons of Aurënen, the owls of Skala.

The rhui'auros cocked his head, regarding him quizzically. "Come, little brother, let me see your newest wound."

Seregil didn't move. This was one of those who'd interrogated him. "Why did you ask me to come here?" he asked at last, his voice hardly more than a hoarse whisper.

"You have been on a long journey. Now you have returned."

"You cast me out," Seregil retorted bitterly.

The rhui'auros smiled. "To live, little brother. And you have. Now give me your hand before it swells any more."

Baffled, Seregil watched as his hand became visible at the rhui'auros's touch. A soft glow spread out from the two of them, brightening the tiny chamber and making both of them visible. Lhial moved closer so that their bare knees touched.

Prodding gently at one of the bruises on Seregil's chest, he shook his head. "This accomplishes nothing, little brother. There is other work ahead for you."

Turning his attention to Seregil's hand, he inspected the bite. Parallel lines of punctures oozed blood on the lower palm and the back of his hand where the dragon's jaws had clamped around the base of his thumb. The rhui'auros produced a vial of lissik and massaged the dark salve into the wound. "You remember that night you were brought here?" he asked, not looking up.

"How could I not?"

"Do you know why?"

"To be tried. To be exiled."

Lhial smiled to himself. "Is that what you've thought, all these years?"

"Why then?"

"To tinker with your fate, little brother."

"I don't believe in fate."

"And you suppose that makes any difference?"

The rhui'auros looked up with an amused smile, and Seregil recoiled against the dhima wall. Lhial's eyes had gone the color of hammered gold.

An image leapt into Seregil's mind: the shining golden eyes of the khtir'bai gazing at him from the darkness that night in the Asheks.

You have much to do, son of Korit.

"I walk the banks of time," Lhial told him softly. "Looking at you, I see all your births, all your deaths, all the works the Lightbearer has prepared for you. But time is a dance of many steps and missteps. Those of us who see must sometimes act. Dwai sholo was not your dance. I made certain of that the night you were brought here, and so you were spared for other labors. Some you have already accomplished."

"Was Nysander's death part of this dance?"

The golden eyes blinked slowly. "What you and he accomplish together is. He dances willingly, your friend. His khi soars like a hawk from beneath your broken sword. He dances still. So should you."

Tears blurred Seregil's vision. He swiped at them with his free hand, then looked up into eyes again blue and full of concern.

"Does it hurt, little brother?" Lhial asked, patting Seregil's cheek.

"Not so much now."

"That's good. It would be a shame to damage such clever hands." Lhial settled back against the far wall, then snatched something from the shadows above his head and tossed it to Seregil.

He caught it and found himself clutching an all-too-familiar sphere of glass the size of a plum. He could see his own startled reflection on its dark, slightly roughened surface.

"They weren't black," he whispered, holding it in his cupped palm.

"Dreams," the rhui'auros said with a shrug.

"What is it?"

"What is it?" Lhial mimicked, and tossed him two more before he could put the first aside.

Seregil caught one but missed the last. It shattered next to his right knee, splattering him with maggots. He froze for an instant, then brushed them away in revulsion.

"There are many others," the rhui'auros said with a grin, pitching more of the orbs at him.

Seregil managed to catch five before another broke. This one released a puff of snow that sparkled in the air for an instant before melting away.

Seregil scarcely had time to consider this before the rhui'auros tossed him more. Another broke, releasing a brilliant green butterfly from a Bôkthersan summer meadow. And another, splashing him with dark, clotted blood flecked with bone. More and more flew from the rhui'auros's fingers, one after another, until Seregil was surrounded by a small pile of them.

"Clever hands, indeed, to catch so many," Lhial remarked approvingly.

"What are they?" Seregil asked again, not daring to move for fear of breaking more.

"They are yours."

"Mine? I've never seen them before."

"They are yours," the rhui'auros insisted. "Now you must gather them all and take them away with you. Go on, little brother, gather them up."

The same feeling of helplessness he had in the dreams threatened to overwhelm him now. "I can't. There are too many. At least let me get my shirt."

The rhui'auros shook his head. "Hurry now. It's time to go. You can't leave unless you take them all."

The rhui'auros's eyes shone gold again as he stared through the curling steam at him, and fear closed in around Seregil.

Standing as best he could in the low chamber, he tried to gather an armload, but like eggs, they slipped from his grasp and smashed, releasing filth, perfumes, snatches of music, fragments of charred bone. He couldn't move without crushing them, or knocking them out of sight into the shadows.

"It's impossible!" he cried. "They're *not* mine. I don't want them!"

"Then you must choose, and soon," Lhial told him, his tone at once kind and merciless. "Smiles conceal knives."

The light disappeared, plunging Seregil into darkness.

"Smiles conceal knives," Lhial whispered again, so close to Seregil's ear that he jumped and flung out a hand. It found nothing but empty air. He waited a moment, then cautiously reached out again.

The spheres were gone.

Lhial was gone.

Disoriented, angry, and no wiser than when he had entered, Seregil crawled to the door but couldn't find it. Feeling his way along the wall with his good hand, he made several circuits of the tiny chamber before giving up; the door was gone, too.

He returned to the mat and settled there miserably, arms wrapped around his knees. The rhui'auros's parting words, the strange glass spheres that now haunted his waking life as well as his dreams—there must be some meaning behind it all. He knew in his gut that there was, but Bilairy take him if he could find the pattern.

Tearing the mask off, he wiped the sweat from his eyes and rested his forehead against his knees.

"Thank you for the enlightenment, Honored One," he snarled.

Seregil woke in the public meditation chamber. His head hurt, he was dressed, and the silver mask was in place again. He held his left hand up and found it whole. No dragon bite. No lissik stain. He almost regretted it; it would have been a fine mark. Had he gone down to the cavern at all, he wondered, or had the dreaming smoke here simply carried him into a vision?

Getting up as quickly as the pounding behind his eyes allowed, he discovered Alec sitting on a nearby pallet. A mask still covered his face, and he seemed to be staring off across the room, lost in thought.

Seregil rose to go to him. As he did so, something slipped from the folds of his coat and rolled away toward the stairwell—a small orb of black glass. Before he could react, it rolled over the edge and was lost without a sound. Seregil stared after it for a moment, then went to rouse Alec.

Alec started when Seregil touched his shoulder. "Can we leave now?" he whispered, getting unsteadily to his feet.

"Yes, I think we've been dismissed."

Removing their masks, they left them on the floor beside the dozing doorkeeper and let themselves out.

Alec looked dazed, overwhelmed by whatever had happened to him in the tower. Leading his horse by the reins, he set out on foot. He said nothing, but Seregil sensed a weight of sadness pressing down on him. Reaching out, he pulled Alec to a stop and saw that he was crying.

"What is it, talí? What happened to you in there?"

"It wasn't—it wasn't what I expected. You were right about my mother. She was killed by her own people right after I was born. The rhui'auros showed me. Her name was Ireya ä Shaar."

"Well, that's a start." Seregil moved to put an arm around him, but Alec pulled away.

"Is there a clan called the Akavi'shel?"

"Not that I know of. The word means 'many bloods.' "

Alec bowed his head as more tears came. "Just another word for mongrel. Always and never—"

"What else did he tell you?" Seregil asked softly.

"That I'd never have any children."

Alec's evident distress took Seregil by surprise. "The rhui'auros are seldom that clear about anything," he offered. "What exactly did he say?"

"That I would father a child of no mother," Alec replied. "Seems clear enough to me."

It did, and Seregil kept quiet for a moment, working it around in his mind. At last he said, "I didn't know you wanted children."

Alec let out a harsh sound, half-laugh, half-sob. "Neither did I! I mean, I'd never given it a lot of thought before. It was just something I assumed would happen sooner or later. Any man wants children, doesn't he? To carry his name?"

The words went through Seregil like a blade. "Not me," he replied quickly, trying to make light of the matter. "But then, I wasn't raised a Dalnan. You didn't think *I* was going to bear you any babes, did you?"

The bond between them was too strong for him to mask his sudden flash of fear and anger. One look at Alec's stricken face told him he'd gone too far.

"Nothing will ever separate us," Alec whispered.

This time he didn't resist as Seregil embraced him, but instead clutched him closer.

Seregil held him, stroking his back and marveling at this fierce blend of love and pain.

"The rhui'auros—" Alec's voice was muffled against Seregil's neck. "I can't even explain what I saw, or how it felt. Bilairy's Balls, I see now why you hate that place!"

"No matter what you think they showed you up there, talí, you won't lose me. Not as long as I have breath in my body."

Alec clung to him a moment longer, then stepped back and wiped his eyes on his sleeve.

"I watched my mother die. I felt it." There was still a deep sorrow in him, but also awe. "She died to save me, but my father never spoke of her. Not once."

Seregil stroked a stray strand of hair back from Alec's cheek. "Some things are too hurtful to speak of. He must have loved her very much."

Alec's face took on a faraway look for a moment, as if he were seeing something Seregil couldn't. "Yes, he did." He wiped at his eyes again. "What did they want with you?"

Seregil thought again of the maddening glass balls, the snow and filth and the butterfly. Somewhere among those jumbled hints lay a pattern, a link of familiarity.

They are yours.

"I'm not sure."

"Did he say anything about the ban of exile being lifted?"

"It never occured to me to ask."

Or perhaps I didn't want to hear the answer, he thought.

A great lethargy settled over Seregil as they rode for home. By the time they reached the house and stabled their horses, his bones ached with it.

A few night lamps lit their way upstairs. Alec's arm stole around his waist and he returned the embrace silently, grateful for the contact.

Tired as he was, he barely took note of a sliver of light showing beneath a door on the second floor.

. . .

A whisper-gentle touch on Thero's chest had woken him in the middle of the night. Starting up in alarm, he scrutinized the corners of his chamber.

No one was there. The small warding glyphs he'd placed on his door when he'd taken up residence here were undisturbed.

Only after he'd made a complete circuit of the room did he notice the folded parchment lying among the disordered bedclothes.

Snatching it up, he broke the plain wax seal and unfolded it. The small square was blank, except for a tiny sigil in one corner—Magyana's mark.

He paused, hearing footsteps in the corridor outside. Casting a seeking spell, he saw it was only Alec and Seregil and returned his attention to Magyana's message.

Hands, heart, and eyes, he mouthed silently, passing his hand across the sheet. Ink seeped from the parchment, flowing into Magyana's cramped scrawl.

"My dear Thero, I send you sad news in secret and at my own risk. By your Hands, Heart, and Eyes. . . ."

A hard knot of dread crystallized in the young wizard's throat as he read on. When he'd finished he pulled on a robe and stole barefoot to Klia's chamber.

23

A Conversation

Ulan í Sathil rubbed Torsin's token—half a silver sester—between his fingers as he strolled beside the Vhadäsoori pool. It was quite dark, and he heard the Skalan before he saw him. The wracking cough was as distinctive as a halloo, echoing faintly over the water. It was always distressing when a Tír began to fail this way, especially one of such value.

Following the sound, Ulan stepped out onto the surface of the pool and glided across to where Torsin stood waiting. It was a good trick—one of many that had not come down to the Skalan wizards—and made a strong impression on the mind of any Tír who witnessed it. It was also much easier on his aching old knees than walking.

Torsin, of course, had seen the trick before and seemed only mildly surprised when Ulan stepped up onto shore.

"Aura's blessings on you, old friend."

"May the Light shine on you," Torsin replied, patting his lips with a handkerchief. "Thank you for meeting me on such short notice."

"A walk under the peace of the stars is one of the few pleasures left to old men like ourselves, is it not?" Ulan replied. "I'd suggest stretching out on the grass to watch the sky as we used to, but I fear neither of us would regain our feet without help or magic."

"Indeed not." Torsin paused, and Ulan thought he heard regret in the sigh that followed. When Torsin spoke again, however, he was his usual direct self. "The situation in Skala is shifting rapidly. I am now instructed to present you with a tentative counterproposal, one which will most assuredly be more palatable to you."

Instructed by whom, I wonder? thought Ulan.

Linking arms, the two men strolled slowly along the water's edge, speaking too softly now for the slender figure watching from the shadow of a standing stone to hear.

24

BAD NEWS

A brisk rap at the chamber door jerked Seregil awake just before dawn. Still half caught in a nightmare, he sat up mumbling, "Yes? What is it?"

The door swung open a few inches and Kheeta peered in at him. "Sorry to come so early, but it's by Klia's order. She wants you and Alec in her chamber at once."

The door closed and Seregil fell back among the pillows, trying to pull together the scattered images of his latest dream. Once again, he'd been trying to save the glass spheres from the rising fire, but each time he tried to gather them, there were more: a handful, a roomful, a dark, limitless vista of the cursed things beneath which unseen monsters burrowed, coming ever closer.

"O Illior, maker of dreams, give me the meaning of this one before it drives me mad!" he whispered aloud. Rolling out of bed, he fumbled in the dark for his boots. "Wake up, Alec. Klia's expecting us."

There was no answer. The other half of the bed was empty, the sheets cool. Alec had been too shaken to sleep after they'd returned from the Nha'mahat. He'd been sitting by the fire when Seregil fell asleep.

"Alec?" he called again.

His questing fingers found a taper on the mantel and he pushed it about in the banked ashes on the hearth until he found a live coal. The wick flared at last and he held it up.

Alec was nowhere to be seen.

Puzzled, he finished dressing and set off for Klia's room alone. He was halfway down the corridor when he heard footsteps on the stairs leading to the roof. Here was Alec at last, bleary eyed and still dressed in last night's clothes.

"Were you up there all night?"

Alec rubbed at the back of his neck. "I couldn't sleep, so I went up to the colos to think. I must have finally dozed off. Where are you off to so early? I was hoping for a few hours' sleep in a warm bed."

"Not just yet, talí. Klia's sent for us."

This woke him up. "Do you think the Iia'sidra has reached a decision?" he asked, following Seregil downstairs.

"Even if they had, I doubt they'd spring that on us at dawn."

As they walked down the second-floor corridor toward Klia's chamber they could hear familiar sounds echoing up from the kitchen: clattering of pots, hurried footsteps, the voices of some Urgazhi riders joking with the cooks in broken Aurënfaie as they came in for their breakfast.

"Sounds like a normal enough morning," Alec remarked.

Thero answered their knock and admitted them to Klia's sitting room.

The princess sat by a small writing table. Although she was dressed for a day with the council, one look at her pale, too-calm face left Seregil with a sinking feeling. No, this was no normal morning.

Thero moved to stand just behind her, as if she were queen and he her court wizard. Lord Torsin and Beka already occupied the room's only chairs, and they looked as uneasy as Seregil suddenly felt.

"Good, you're all here. The queen my mother is dead," Klia announced flatly.

The words sapped the strength from Seregil's legs. The others seemed equally affected. Alec pressed one hand to his heart, the Dalnan sign of respect for the dead. Beka sat with her hands clasped around the hilt of her sword, head bowed. Of them all, Torsin appeared most stricken by the news. Sagging in his chair, he coughed convulsively into the stained handkerchief.

"I will not see her like again," he gasped out at last.

Thero held up a letter for the others to see. "It's from Magyana, dated yesterday and written in evident haste. It reads: 'The queen died the night before last. Brave soul, she should not have survived this long, even with our magic and healing. The darkness seems already to be closing in around us.

" 'Northern Mycena has fallen to Plenimar. Phoria has already been crowned in the field. Korathan will replace Lady Morthiana as vicegerent at Rhíminee.

" 'Against all urging, Phoria has forbidden sending this news to Klia, so I risk all that you may not be taken by surprise.

" 'I am presently out of favor and have little influence. I have not been released from service, but am no longer consulted. Korathan has her ear, but is his sister's man, as is her wizard, Organeus.

" 'Phoria has not yet ordered Klia's return, which puzzles me. She and her supporters clearly have little faith in a propitious outcome. You must impress upon Klia that she is very much on her own now.

" 'I wish I could offer you more guidance, dear boy, but things are as yet too uncertain. Illior grant that I will not be sent from the royal camp before you are all safely on your way home again. —Magyana' "

"This couldn't have come at a worse time," said Klia. "Just when we were beginning to make progress among the Haman and some of the undecided clans. How will they respond to this?"

Another coughing fit shook Torsin, doubling him over in his chair. When it passed, he wiped his lips and wheezed out, "It is difficult to predict, my lady. They know so little of Phoria."

"I'd say our greatest concern is the fact that she didn't send word herself," said Seregil. "What do you suppose prompted that lack of sisterly consideration?"

"Does the Iia'sidra know of her opposition?" asked Alec.

"I suspect some of them do," Torsin replied bleakly.

"Two days!" Klia slammed a hand down on the polished desktop, making the others jump. "Our mother dead for two days and she sends me no word? What if the Aurënfaie already know? What must they think?"

"We can find out, my lady," Alec told her. "If this was Rhíminee, Seregil and I would have paid a few night visits to your opponents already. Isn't that why the queen wanted us here in the first place?"

"Perhaps, but I'm the one who makes those decisions here," Klia warned. "For *any* Skalan to be caught spying could destroy everything we've worked for. And consider Seregil's position. What do you think would happen to him if he were caught? No, we'll wait a bit longer. Come with me to the council today, both of you. I want your impressions."

Torsin exchanged an uneasy look with Seregil, then said gently, "You mustn't go to the Iia'sidra today, my lady."

"Don't be ridiculous. Now more than ever—"

"He's right," said Seregil. Going to her, he knelt and rested a hand on her knee. This close, he could see how red her eyes were. "Mourning is a deeply sacred rite among the Aurënfaie; it can last for months. You must at least observe the Skalan four-day ritual. The same applies to me, I suppose, considering how much we've made of my kinship to your family. Alec can be my eyes and ears."

Klia rested her head on one hand and let out a shakey sigh. "You're right, of course. But Plenimar presses closer to the heart of Skala every day I'm here without an answer. This delay is the *last* thing Mother would have wanted!"

"We may be able to wring some advantage from it, all the same," Seregil assured her. "According to Aurënfaie custom, the khirnari are expected to visit you. This could offer certain opportunities for, shall we say, private debate?"

Klia regarded him quizzically. "I can't appear publicly, yet I can scheme and intrigue from behind a veil of mourning?"

Seregil gave her a crooked grin. "That's right. I'll wager certain people will be watching quite closely to see who comes to you and how long they stay."

"Yet how are we to announce the queen's death?" Thero asked suddenly. "If it weren't for Magyana, we wouldn't even know."

"What am I supposed to do? Lie?" Klia asked, angry again. "Dissemble until our new queen sees fit to inform me of this turn of events? If lack of mourning would dishonor me in the eyes of the Iia'sidra, what would that do, eh? That could well be Phoria's purpose. By the Four, I won't be her dupe!"

"Quite right, my lady," Torsin agreed. "Your forthrightness has been our greatest asset."

"Very well, then. Lord Torsin, you'll go to the Iia'sidra today and announce the queen's passing. Let Phoria worry for herself where we came by the information. Alec and Thero will accompany you, together with a full honor guard. I want a detailed report of the day's proceedings. Captain, find black sashes for your riders and see that their cloaks are reversed and the horses' manes cropped. My mother was a Skalan warrior; she'll be accorded a warrior's honors."

Beka rose to attention. "Do you wish me to announce the queen's death to my riders?"

"Yes. You're dismissed. Now, Seregil, what else must I do to satisfy Aurënfaie convention?"

"You'll better talk to my sisters. I'll fetch them."

"Thank you, my friend. we aren't bested yet. Now if you'll excuse us, I need a moment with Lord Torsin."

It's time we learned whether she knows of his meeting with Khatme, Seregil thought, following the others out. As he turned to close the door, something on the floor next to the doorjamb caught his eye: a small, flattened clod of moist earth. Kneeling, he examined it more closely.

"What's that?" asked Thero, already halfway to the stairs.

"How old do you make this?" Seregil asked Alec.

Alec squatted down beside him and nudged at it with a forefinger. "Not more than a few minutes. The floor's still damp beneath it, and no sign of drying about the edges. It's come off somebody's boots." Picking it up, he sniffed it and took a closer look. "Horse manure, with bits of hay and oats stuck in it."

"Beka must have tracked it in," said Thero.

Alec shook his head. "No, she was already here when we arrived, and this is fresher than that. And I was standing near the door the whole time we were in there and would have heard if anyone walked by. This person didn't mean to be heard, and this bit of muck places him close to the wall next to the door—an eavesdropper for certain, one who came in through the stable yard."

"Or from it," Seregil muttered, inspecting the corridor floor and both stairways. "There are a few other smudges here, leading to the back stairs. Not an experienced hand, our visitor. I'd have taken off my boots, but our spy just clomped in trusting to luck."

"But how would anyone have known to come here just now?" asked Thero. "I went straight from my chamber to Klia's. No one could have known about Magyana's letter."

"Beka came in from the stable yard," Seregil pointed out. "Anyone taking note of the summons could have followed her in. The approach also suggests that whoever it was, he was either very bold, very foolish, or trusted that his presence in the house wouldn't be questioned if anyone saw him. Or her."

"Nyal!" Alec whispered.

"The interpreter?" Thero said incredulously. "You can't seriously think that the Iia'sidra would assign a spy to Klia's staff, especially one as inept as this one appears to have been?"

Seregil said nothing for a moment, recalling the conversation he and the Ra'basi had shared during his convalescence. Perhaps the painkilling draughts had skewed his judgment, but he hoped Nyal wasn't their spy; the irony of the realization forced a grin to his lips. Now it was Alec who seemed ready to believe Nyal guilty.

"This isn't the first time we've had cause to question his motives." Alec sketched out the details of the tryst they'd observed between Nyal and Amali outside the Dravnian way station.

"You didn't actually overhear what they were discussing?" asked Thero.

"No."

"That's unfortunate."

"Suspicion and conjecture," said Seregil. "We're still standing on smoke."

"Who else could it have been?" said Alec. "One of the guards or servants?"

"I don't think Beka or Adzriel would be pleased with that speculation."

"I'll add a few spells here," Thero said, glaring at the doorframe as if it had somehow betrayed him. "We'd better warn Klia."

"Later. She has enough to trouble her this morning," Seregil advised. "You and Alec attend the Iia'sidra as planned. I'll find out what our Ra'basi friend has been up to this morning."

Alec started upstairs to change, then turned back. "You know, Phoria trying to hide the queen's death like that makes me wonder just who our real enemies are."

Seregil shrugged. "I suspect we have plenty on both sides of the Osiat."

Alec hurried off, but Thero lingered a moment longer, his narrow face more serious than usual.

"Worried about Magyana?" asked Seregil.

"Phoria will know who sent us the news."

"Magyana understood the risks. She can look out for herself."

Thero turned in at his own door. "Perhaps."

Seregil stopped in the stable yard on his way to Adzriel's to inquire about Nyal's whereabouts and was relieved to find Beka nowhere in sight. Steb and Mirn were standing guard duty at the courtyard gate.

"How long have you been on duty?" he asked them.

"Since before dawn, my lord," Steb told him, rubbing at the patch over his blind eye as he stifled a yawn.

"Any visitors? Anyone go in or out of the house?"

"No visitors, my lord, and the captain was the first in the house this morning. Princess Klia sent for her. She told us about poor old Idrilain when she came back." The one-eyed rider paused, touching his hand to his heart. "Since then most of us have been in and out of the kitchen for our breakfast, but that's about all."

"I see. By the way, have you seen Nyal this morning? I need to speak with him."

"Nyal?" said Mirn. "He went out riding not long after Captain Beka was summoned to the house."

"Right after? Are you sure?" asked Seregil.

"Guess her moving around woke him up." Mirn smirked, earning a quick elbow and a dark look from his comrade.

Seregil brushed this aside. "This morning, though, he went riding as soon as she went to the main house?"

"Well, not just that minute," Steb explained. "He stayed on to breakfast with us, then headed out. We saw him leave."

"I expect he'll be back soon. He always is," Mirn added.

"Then this isn't the first dawn ride he's made?"

"No, my lord, though more often than not the captain goes with him. That's what makes some folks think—"

"You tell them to keep that sort of thinking to themselves," Seregil snapped.

In the barracks, he found Beka conferring with her three sergeants.

"Good, you're all here," Seregil said, joining them. "Seems we may have an eavesdropper in the house."

Mercalle looked up sharply. "What makes you think that, my lord?"

"Just a hunch," he replied. "Keep an eye on who enters the house. The upper floors are off-limits anyway, so there shouldn't be anyone going up there except Klia's people and the servants."

Beka gave him a look that said she suspected there was more behind his request than he was letting on, just the sort of quiet, questioning glance her father would have used.

Seregil gave her a nod, then let himself out the back gate and crossed to Adzriel's door.

Entering this early had a bittersweet familiarity about it. As a boy, he'd often slipped out to ride before dawn or stayed out all night with a gang of companions when he could get away with it. How many times, he wondered, had he and Kheeta sneaked in by a certain back door and crept like thieves up to their beds?

For a fleeting moment he was tempted to try it now and come sauntering down as if—

as if I belonged here.

Tucking this new bit of heartache away for later scrutiny, he knocked and was led to a room near the kitchen, where his sisters and their household were just starting an informal breakfast. Another twinge struck as he took in the cozy family tableau.

Mydri was the first to notice him. "What's the matter, Seregil? What's happened?"

Adzriel and the others turned, hands poised motionless over their torn bread and boiled eggs.

"Our—your kinswoman, Idrilain, is dead," he informed them, glad of a plausible excuse for what must have been a very long face.

Alec took his place behind Lord Torsin and Thero in the Iia'sidra circle and looked around, only to find himself being watched in turn by the Virésse khirnari.

Already seated among his delegation, Ulan í Sathil gave Alec a cordial nod as their eyes met. Alec returned it and hastily looked away, making a show of greeting Riagil í Molan. People were already taking note of Klia's empty chair, and Adzriel's.

Brythir í Nien of Silmai leaned forward in his chair and peered across at Torsin. "Will Princess Klia not attend today?"

The ambassador rose with melancholy dignity. "Honored Khirnari, I bring tragic news. We have just received word that Queen Idrilain of Skala is dead, felled by wounds received in battle. Princess Klia begs your patience while she mourns."

Säaban í Irais stood. "Adzriel ä Illia also sends her regrets. She and our sister Mydri must attend Klia to mourn the passing of our kinswoman."

Most registered regret or surprise at this news. Khatme was inscrutable, Virésse solemn. Rhaish í Arlisandin of Akhendi gazed stonily at the floor. Beside him, Amali looked stunned.

The Silmai khirnari pressed both hands over his heart and bowed to Torsin. "May Aura's light guide her khi. Please convey our great sorrow, Torsin í Xandus. Will the princess not return to Skala to mourn?"

"It was Idrilain's wish that her daughter stay until her mission among you here is accomplished. Princess Klia asks that you grant her four days to conduct the proper rites, after which she prays that our long debate may see a timely conclusion."

"Are there any objections?" the old Silmai asked the assembly. "Very well, then we will gather again at the end of the mourning period."

· · ·

Signs of mourning were already in evidence by the time Alec and the others returned to the guest house.

Following Skalan custom, the main entrance was sealed and hung with an inverted shield. Incense billowed up from a brazier set on the doorstep. Strings of Aurënfaie prayer kites also fluttered from poles set into the ground, and from the windows and roof.

A low, droning song greeted them as they entered the main hall by a side door; six rhui'auros stood in a circle at the center of the room, chanting softly.

Klia was with Seregil, Adzriel, and Mydri, putting the final touches on a large prayer kite. Nearby several Bôkthersan servants were busy constructing others. It looked as if they meant to festoon the whole house with them.

"What news?" Klia asked as they entered.

"All is well, my lady," replied Torsin. "The council will resume in five days."

Seregil dismissed the servants, then asked, "And what were your impressions?"

"That the Virésse already knew," Alec told him. "I can't explain it; it was just the way Ulan í Sathil watched us as we came in."

"I think he's right," Thero agreed. "I didn't dare chance brushing Ulan's mind, but I briefly touched that of Elos of Goliníl. There was no surprise, only thoughts of Ulan."

"You did what?" Seregil gaped at the wizard in dismay. "Didn't I tell you how dangerous that could be?"

Thero spared him an impatient glance. "You didn't think I was dozing through all those long sessions, did you? I've been making a study of the Iia'sidra members. Ulan í Sathil and the khirnari of Khatme, Akhendi, and Silmai have the strongest aura of magic about them. I'm not certain what the full extent of their skills may be, but I've sense enough to stay clear of them. Most of the others are far more limited—Elos of Goliníl in particular. If Ulan has a weak point, it's his daughter's husband."

"If they did know, then perhaps you're right about having a spy in the house," Klia noted, frowning.

Adzriel looked up sharply, her face as solemn as her brother's. "I chose the staff for this house myself. They are above reproach."

Seregil shook his head. "That's not who I was thinking of."

25

NIGHTRUNNING

Skalan mourning was an austere affair, and fires, hot food, alcohol of any sort, lovemaking, and music were all strictly abstained from. A single candle was allowed in each room at night. Should the soul of the departed visit any of its loved ones, there must be nothing to distract it from its journey.

This was new territory for Alec, whose Dalnan upbringing dictated a quick burning and ashes plowed into the earth. He'd seen death often enough since he'd come south with Seregil, but his friend was neither Skalan nor one to adhere to custom. When Thryis and her family had been murdered, Seregil had set the inn ablaze as a pyre and sworn vengeance on their murderer, a vow Alec had himself carried out when he strangled Vargûl Ashnazai. Seregil's grief for Nysander's death had been too deep and silent for mere ritual to encompass. For a time he'd almost stopped living himself.

This time, however, Seregil willingly observed the abstentions, sitting with Klia through the interminable visitations. Alec sensed genuine sadness in his friend, although Seregil said little.

It was Beka who finally drew him out. The three of them had gathered with Thero in the wizard's room on the second night, passing the time in desultory conversation.

Thero was weaving the shadows cast by the candle into fantastic shapes against the wall. Seregil remained unusually quiet as he sat slouched in his chair, legs stretched out before him, chin on hand. Alec studied his friend's pensive face, wondering if Seregil was watching Thero's shadow play or lost to his own inner phantoms.

Beka suddenly nudged Seregil's foot with her own and raised her eyebrows in mock surprise when he looked up.

"Oh, it's *you*," she said. "And here I'd been thinking it must be Alec sitting there. No one else I know can keep quiet for so long."

"I was just thinking about Idrilain," he replied.

"You liked her, didn't you, Uncle?"

Alec smiled, guessing that she'd used the familiar term to coax him out of his brown study; she called him "Uncle" only in private now.

Seregil shifted in his chair, clasping his hands over one updrawn knee. "Yes I did. She was queen when I came to Rhíminee, and did her best to find a place for me at court. It didn't work out, of course, but I might never have met Nysander if not for her." He sighed. "In a way, Idrilain *was* Skala to me. Now Phoria sits on the throne."

"Don't you think she'll rule well?" asked Beka.

Seregil's eyes met Alec's, acknowledging shared secrets. Then he shrugged. "I suppose she'll rule according to her nature."

The nature of the new queen proved to be a topic of prime interest to the Aurënfaie.

Adzriel had arranged a receiving room for Klia just off the main hall, mixing Skalan and Aurënfaie trappings. A tripod of headless spear shafts supported Klia's inverted shield. Censors clouded the air with the bittersweet vapors of myrrh and stop-blood weed, the soldier's field herb. Delicate Aurënfaie scrolls hung beside the room's three doors, painted with prayers directing the queen's soul onward should she come to visit her daughter and forget how to move on. An Aurënfaie screen of thin parchment blocked the window, except for a small hole by which the khi could come and go.

Another Aurënfaie touch was a small brazier by the door, where each guest cast a small bunch of cedar tips as they entered, an offering to the departed. The scent of it was said to be pleasing to the dead, but the living were soon well sick of it. By the end of each day a pall of smoke hung near the ceiling in a slow-roiling cloud. The odor of it clung to clothing and hair and followed them to their beds at night.

Sitting beside Klia each day, Seregil wondered what the dead queen would make of the conversation if she did choose to visit.

Each visitor, regardless of clan or stance, began with the usual expressions of condolence but soon maneuvered their way to subtle inquiries about Phoria.

Alec reported similar interest. Every member of the Skalan delegation, even the Urgazhi riders, were suddenly thought to be authorities on the new queen's character. People who had not deigned to speak to Alec since his arrival now cornered him on the street. "What is this new queen like?" they all wanted to know. "What is her interest here? What does she want from Aurënen?"

Braknil and Mercalle had the most to say in Phoria's favor; they'd both fought beside her in their younger days and praised her bravery in glowing terms.

Lacking Seregil's connection to the royal family, Alec made himself useful helping Thero and Torsin greet their visitors in the hall and seeing that each dignitary was properly attended to as they waited for an audience with Klia.

He was so occupied on the third day when Rhaish í Arlisandin and his young wife arrived. He withdrew as Torsin and the khirnari launched into a hushed discussion, but Amali followed him and laid a hand on his arm.

"There's something I must share with you in private," she murmured, casting a quick glance back at her husband.

"Certainly, my lady." Alec led her to an unused room just off the hall.

As soon as he'd closed the door she strode to the far end, clasping her hands in obvious agitation. Alec folded his arms and waited. She hadn't spoken directly to him more than twice since their arrival in Sarikali.

"Nyal í Nhekai advised me to speak with you," she confided at last. "He says you are a man of honor. I must ask that no matter what you say to the request I am about to make, what I say will go no further than this room. Can you give me your word on that?"

"Perhaps it would be better if you spoke to someone with more authority," Alec suggested, but she shook her head.

"No! Nyal said to speak only to you."

"You have my word, my lady, as long as whatever you have to say doesn't put me at odds with my loyalty to Princess Klia."

"Loyalty!" she exclaimed softly, wringing her hands. "You must be the judge of that, I suppose. Ulan í Sathil has summoned certain khirnari to meet with him tonight at his house. My husband is among those who will be there."

"I don't understand. I thought he and your husband were enemies?"

"There is no good feeling between them," Amali admitted, looking more distracted than ever. "That is why it worries me so. Whatever Ulan has to say, it cannot bode well for your princess, yet my husband will not tell me what the purpose of the meeting is to be. He has been so—so very upset by all this. I cannot imagine what would convince him to go to that man's house."

"But why tell me?"

"It was Nyal's idea, as I said. I spoke with him earlier. 'Bring this to Alec í Amasa as soon as you can!' he said. Why would he send me to you?"

"I can't say, my lady, but I give you my word that your secrets are safe."

Amali clasped his hands between hers for a moment, tears standing in her eyes as she searched his face. "I love my husband, Alec í Amasa. I wish no harm or dishonor to come to him. I would not have spoken if I did not fear for him. I cannot explain it—there's just been such a weight of dread on my heart since this whole dreadful debate began. Now more than ever, he is Klia ä Idrilain's best ally."

"She knows that. When are the khirnari to meet?"

"At the evening meal. The Virésse always wait until after sunset to dine."

Alec stored away this information. "Perhaps you should return to the hall now, before you're missed?"

She gave him a small, grateful smile and slipped out. Alec waited a few moments, then went out to the barracks to find Nyal.

The Ra'basi was playing bakshi with Beka and several of her riders. As soon as Alec appeared in the doorway, however, he excused himself and walked with him into the stable.

"I just spoke with Amali," Alec told him.

Nyal looked relieved. "I feared she would not go to you."

"Why, Nyal? Why me?"

The man gave him a wry look. "Who better than you to act on such information? Unless I'm mistaken, you and Seregil have certain—

talents, shall we say? But Seregil is bound at Klia's side by duty and blood ties, and by other concerns you are well aware of. You aren't."

"Concerns such as atui?"

The Ra'basi shrugged. "Sometimes honor is a matter of perspective, is it not?"

"So I've been told." Alec wondered if he'd just been insulted or shared a confidence. "What's the purpose of this meeting? Amali seems concerned for her husband's safety."

"I have no idea. I'd heard nothing of it until she came to me. Ra'basi was not included in the invitation."

Ah, so that's your angle! Keeping the thought to himself, Alec went on ingenuously, "That's odd. Moriel ä Moriel still supports Virésse, doesn't she?"

"Perhaps Virésse grows arrogant," said Nyal, arching a sardonic eyebrow. "Perhaps Ulan í Sathil forgets that Ra'basi is one of the Eleven and not some minor clan who owes him loyalty."

"And if I do make use of this information, what then? What do you want from me in return?"

Nyal shrugged. "Only to know of anything that affects my clan's interests. Or Akhendi's."

"Akhendi? You ask that on behalf of your khirnari?"

Nyal colored visibly. "I ask for myself."

Alec frowned. "Or for Amali ä Yassara? How many lovers do you have, Nyal?"

"One lover," he replied, meeting Alec's look without flinching, "but many that I love."

Alec was waiting for Seregil when he emerged from the receiving chamber late that afternoon. Drawing him aside, Alec quickly repeated what Amali and Nyal had told him, then held his breath, waiting for Seregil to come up with some reason for him not to investigate. Not that it would stop him from going, of course.

To his relief, Seregil finally gave a reluctant nod. "Klia must know nothing of it until you're back."

"Easier to apologize than to get permission, eh?" Alec grinned. "I suppose you can't—"

Seregil dragged the fingers of one hand through his hair, scowling. "I hate this, you know. I hate not being able to act, being so damned constrained by honor and law and circumstance."

Alec raised a hand to his friend's cheek, then let his fingers trail down to a fading bruise just visible above his collar. "I'm glad to hear it, talí. You haven't seemed yourself since we got here."

"Myself?" Seregil gave a mocking laugh. "Who's that, I wonder? You go, Alec. I'll stay here and behave myself like a good little exile."

They slipped into Klia's darkened receiving room just after nightfall. Alec felt a bit guilty, but elated, too. Beneath his cloak, he wore an Aurënfaie tunic, trousers, and loose sandals, filched by Seregil from some servant. His tool roll, rescued at last from the obscurity of the clothes chest, was secreted once more inside his tunic. It was a risk to bring it, which is why he hadn't bothered to tell Seregil, but he felt better having it along.

I'm doing this for Klia, whether she wants me to or not, he thought, quelling any doubts.

They lifted aside the screen covering the window and Alec threw one leg over the sill. A sudden rush of excitement left him a little giddy. Finally, after all these weeks, here was some useful work. A stray thought sobered him for a moment, however. "No sen'gai!" he whispered, raising a hand to his head.

"I didn't know if I could still wrap one properly," Seregil admitted. "Besides, going bareheaded will make you all the more anonymous in the dark—just another servant out for an evening stroll."

"I'm always a servant," Alec complained jokingly, trying to simultaneously whisper and whine.

"Breeding tells," Seregil shot back, clasping him by the back of the neck and giving him a playful shake. "Luck in the shadows."

"I hope so."

It was a short drop to the ground, and Alec managed it soundlessly. This side of the house stood perpendicular to the street and overlooked open ground. Following it back would take him to the wall of the stable yard. Either direction meant passing sentries. He could hear Arbelus and Minál talking somewhere out front. Waiting until they'd wandered back toward the door, he quickly crossed the grassy verge and blended into the shadows beyond.

Following Torsin weeks before had been an impulse, a fluke. This time, he had a mission and it felt as if he were seeing the place through different eyes, overlaid with memories of similar jobs carried out in Rhíminee. Here there were no cutpurses and footpads to avoid, no City Watch to evade. No whores of either sex called to him from the shadows. There were no lunatics, beggars, or drunken soldiers. The makeshift taverns had none of the disreputable reek of the raucous establishments of Skala.

Instead, the strange quiet that overlay the city tonight pressed in on him, and his imagination conjured ghosts in shadowed doorways. Never before had he been more aware that this was a city of the dead, tenanted only occasionally by the living. It was a relief to meet other people along the streets, though he kept his distance.

He had an uneasy moment as he passed Haman tupa. Movement in a side street to his left caught his eye. He continued on to the next building, then ducked around the corner and looked back, waiting for any potential stalkers to betray themselves. No one appeared. Nothing but the call of a night bird broke the silence.

Shrugging off a lingering sense of being watched, he continued on, running now to make up for lost time. It wouldn't do to arrive late even if he wasn't invited.

Ulan í Sathil's grand house stood on a small rise overlooking the Vhadäsoori. According to Seregil, who'd known the place in his youth, it was laid out around a series of large courtyards, not unlike the clan house at Gedre..As he surveyed its imposingly plain walls from the shelter of a nearby alleyway, he longed again for Rhíminee's villas, with their tall, well-tended trees and usefully ornate exterior carvings. If the Virésse house ran true to form, however, whatever it lacked in handholds was more than made up for by a scandalous lack of walls, dogs, sentries, and locks. At least this place had a few accessible windows.

Most were dark. The only visible signs of light were concentrated to the left of the main entrance. Alec kicked off his sandals and poised for a dash, but shrank back at the sound of approaching hooves. Four horsemen reined in and knocked for admittance. In the spill of light from the doorway Alec caught a brief glimpse of the visitors as they entered. He couldn't make out faces from this angle, but he saw that they wore the purple sen'gai of Bry'kha.

Looks like I'm just in time.

He waited until the door closed, then ran to a window to the right of the door that looked promising, unshuttered and dark. Alec slipped over the sill and went into a crouch, listening. Satisfied that the room was unoccupied, he pulled the lightstone from his tool roll and shielded it with his hand. By its light, he saw that he was in an empty room. He tucked the stone into his belt and crept out into an unlit corridor, his bare feet silent on the smooth stone floor.

He found his way to a passageway leading to the main hall. As he

watched from the shelter of a doorway, a servant crossed the room
and returned a moment later with several Lhapnosans. He caught
the words "welcome" and "garden."

Luck in the shadows indeed, thought Alec, retreating back the
way he'd come. Whatever the 'faie might think about thieves and
thought readers, it seemed their god had a favor or two to spare the
humble nightrunner. Now if his luck would just hold until he found
the right garden.

After several wrong turns, Alec ended up in a room with a low
balcony overlooking an illuminated courtyard. Creeping to the
archway, he peered out, then ducked quickly back, heart pounding
in his chest. Ulan í Sathil sat less than twenty feet away. Moving
more carefully, Alec chanced another look.

The large, lushly overgrown garden was lit by crescent-shaped
lanterns set on tall poles. Ulan faced his guests, most of whom were
hidden from view by the angle of the wall. Alec guessed by the murmur of conversation that there were no more than a dozen people
present. Those he could see included the khirnari of Lhapnos and
Bry'kha, together with some of their kin and members of minor
clans. Servants were circulating with wine and sweets.

He was about to belly-crawl to the opposite side of the archway
when a whiff of scent froze him on all fours. He'd smelled the same
spicy, musk only once before, in the shadows of the House of Pillars. It raised the hairs on the back of his neck and spread gooseflesh
up his arms.

Turning, he scanned the room for its source, glancing toward the
door in time to see a growing glimmer of light beneath it. He had
just time enough to scuttle behind the door before it swung open.
Through the crack between door and frame, he saw a bored-looking
watchman raise the lantern he held and peer around the room. Satisfied, he went out again, closing the door behind him.

Alec stayed where he was for nearly a minute, testing the air like
a hound as he waited for his heartbeat to slow. For an instant he
thought he smelled the perfume again.

"Who are you?" he whispered, realizing as he did so that he was
more fearful of receiving a response than not.

No one answered, and the scent did not return.

Don't be a fool, he berated himself as he crept back to the window. Someone wearing a strong scent had passed by in the corridor,
maybe even someone the watchman was looking for. It was probably a common scent. Then again, he'd been to endless gatherings
since his arrival in Aurënen and never smelled anything like it.

He shook off the disconcerting thoughts. He couldn't afford to linger.

Standing on the opposite side of the archway now, he peered around and with a sinking heart recognized Seregil's old friend, Riagil í Molan of Gedre sitting between Ruen í Uri of Datsia and Rhaish í Arlisandin. The khirnari of Bry'kha and Silmai were there, too, along with several minor khirnari.

It was clear from the level of conversation that more guests were expected. A few moments later several Haman entered, but Nazien í Hari was not one of them. These were all younger men, and it was Emiel í Moranthi who bowed in greeting to their host.

Alec's lip curled at the sight of him, his distaste tempered only by the pleasure of observing the arrogant bastard unaware.

This must have completed the company, for Ulan stood to address them. Alec sank down and settled his back against the wall to listen.

"My friends, my opposition to the Skalan's demands are no secret among you," Ulan began. "I am frequently accused of acting out of self-interest. I do not deny this, nor do I apologize. I am a Virésse, and the khirnari of my clan. My first duty is to my people. There is no dishonor in this."

He paused, perhaps to let his guests reflect on their own loyalties. "Until now my opposition has been based on my desire to preserve the prosperity of my clan. Like you, I had the greatest respect for Idrilain ä Elesthera. She was a Tírfaie of great atui and valor. Klia ä Idrilain is very like her mother and I hold her in equal esteem.

"But now Idrilain is dead, and it is not Klia who ascends that throne, but her half-sister, Phoria. I have called you here tonight not as a Virésse, or a khirnari, but as a fellow Aurënfaie who realizes that we must, in the affairs of the wider world, act as a single people. This new queen is not a woman of honor. Of this I have proof."

Alec scrambled to his feet and peered out. Ulan was holding up a handful of documents, the largest of which bore a large wax seal Alec knew only too well.

O Illior! Memories of secrets he'd all but forgotten he knew settled over Alec like a pall. It was a Queen's Warrant, no doubt the lost twin of a forged document used by Phoria five years earlier to reroute a shipment of gold destined for the Skalan treasury. On the surface it had been a foolish indiscretion, done to help protect a kinsman of the queen's vicegerent, Lord Barien, who'd also been rumored to be Phoria's lover. In fact, the whole business had been secretly engineered by enemies of the queen, a faction known as the

Lerans. He and Seregil had uncovered the plot by accident during their investigation of that same forger. Only Nysander had been privy to the resulting confrontation between Idrilain and her daughter. All Alec knew was that Phoria had remained heir.

He gnawed his lip in frustration as Ulan fitted the facts into a far more damning picture, depicting Phoria as a weak woman, led by passion rather than honor.

Risking another glance out into the courtyard, Alec saw the gloating satisfaction of the Haman and Lhapnosans. The Gedre khirnari was whispering anxiously to Rhaish í Arlisandin, who'd gone pale. The Silmai elder merely stared down at his hands, as if lost in thought.

Ulan í Sathil continued on, evincing nothing but an earnest desire to inform. Nonetheless, Alec was certain he caught a triumphant gleam in the man's eyes.

What a schemer you are, Alec thought, not knowing whether he should feel angry or awed.

Too restless for company, Seregil retired early and attempted to read by the fire, but one book followed another onto the untidy pile beside his chair. Soon he was up and pacing as he mulled various unhappy scenarios to account for Alec's prolonged absence.

Alec's foray into Torsin's room aside, it had been months since either of them had done any outright burgling. As the stars marched toward midnight, he found himself worrying as if Alec were still his green protégé.

Perhaps he'd been caught. Seregil could imagine Klia's reaction if Alec was brought home under Virésse guard, accused of spying. Or maybe he'd stumbled into the clutches of Seregil's Haman friends.

No, he thought, rubbing at the fading bruises on one forearm, Alec was too clever for that. Maybe he'd just gotten lost.

Seregil had nearly talked himself into going out to look for him when Alec slipped in.

"Well?" Seregil demanded.

Alec was frowning. "You're not going to like it. Ulan found out about Phoria and Barien: the whole business of the forged papers, the Leran gold, everything."

"Bilairy's stinking codpiece!"

"And he did a fine job of painting our new queen as an honorless liar," Alec went on as he changed into his own clothing. "You know what this means, don't you?"

"Yes." Seregil sighed. "Come on, let's find Thero and get this over with."

Klia entered Thero's room clad in a soft velvet robe, her hair loose and tousled about her shoulders. She looked anything but sleepy, however, as she noted the three of them standing uneasily by the hearth. Thero closed the door and wove a spell, sealing the chamber off from prying eyes and ears.

Klia raised an eyebrow at him, then took a seat in the room's only chair ."Well, out with it."

Seregil leaned an elbow on the mantel and launched into a tale he'd never intended to tell.

"It has to do with Phoria, and your mother's late vicegerent."

"Barien? The man's two years dead, and by his own hand. What on earth could—?"

Seregil held up a placating hand. "This will take some explanation. You know that your sister and Barien were lovers?"

"I'd always suspected, though I never understood why they kept it such a secret. She was devastated when he died."

"Were you aware of any new tension between your mother and Phoria after his death?"

"I suppose so, though neither of them would speak of the reason. Why are you dredging all that up now, and at this hour?"

Seregil sighed inwardly; so much for his hope that Idrilain had confided in her daughter before Klia's departure for Aurënen. Who'd have guessed there'd ever be reason to?

"My lady, Phoria and the vicegerent unwittingly betrayed the queen. Barien had a nephew, Lord Teukros. Several years before Barien's death, Teukros was duped into treason by the Lerans. This came out when we were tracking down the woman who nearly killed you and Alec."

"Kassarie." Klia touched the faded scars on her cheek, eyes darkening as angry disbelief set in. "Barien and Phoria were involved with *her*? With those filthy insurrectionists?"

"Unwittingly, I promise you."

"What we must tell you now was known only to Nysander, Seregil, Alec, and myself," Thero assured her. "Nysander had it from your mother and Phoria just after Barien died. He confided it to us because it directly impacted the work Seregil and Alec were carrying out for Nysander."

"Seregil was in prison when Barien died," said Klia.

Seregil gave her a sheepish grin, studiously not looking at Thero. "Not exactly. Thero here kindly gave me the loan of his body, and kept mine company while Alec and I looked into things—"

Klia held up a hand. "Just get on with it."

"We found the forger who'd made documents that led to my arrest and the execution of other Skalan nobles whose blood was less than pure. We also stumbled onto evidence of a deeper plot to discredit your mother. Three years earlier, certain Leran sympathizers had lured that young fool Teukros into accruing massive debts, knowing that the vicegerent could be manipulated into protecting him. Barien turned in desperation to Phoria, who aided him in the rerouting of a treasury shipment to cover the debt. They used forged copies of Queen's Warrants to do it, documents forged by the same man Alec and I tracked down. Neither Phoria nor Barien had any idea who was behind the plot, I assure you. Teukros had handled all that. The moneys were to be repaid as soon as possible and everyone thought they'd seen the end of it, never knowing that the misplaced gold had gone directly into the coffers of the Lerans. When Alec and I cornered this forger, it all came out. Barien couldn't bear the shame and killed himself. Phoria confessed all to your mother and Nysander."

Klia's hands clenched on the arms of her chair. "And no one thought *I* might need to know of this?"

"In all honesty, no, my lady," Seregil assured her. "The few of us who knew were sworn to secrecy by Idrilain and Nysander. We expected to take the story to our graves. What we hadn't counted on was someone among the queen's enemies knowing the secret."

"That's where I come in, my lady," Alec said, looking decidedly uncomfortable. "I got word today that Ulan í Sathil was holding a secret parley at his house, and that certain khirnari who support you or seem like they're leaning in that direction were the ones invited. Forgive me, but I disobeyed your orders and spied on them."

"With my permission," Seregil added quickly.

"Go on," Klia sighed.

"Somehow Ulan í Sathil came into possession of one of these forged warrants, and the secret about Phoria's involvement," Alec continued. "I saw the documents myself. He had some other papers, too, but I was too far away to tell what they were. At any rate, he used them to put Phoria in the worst possible light—you know what store the 'faie set by honor and family. He made Phoria out to be untrustworthy, a traitor almost, and a threat to deal with. He also suggested that your mother had lacked judgment in not casting her out of the line of succession."

"That's the least any khirnari would do, if not outright exile," added Seregil. "Hereditary rule makes no sense to my people. This isn't going to raise their opinion of it much."

"Who was there?" Klia asked, pinning Alec with an unfathomable glare.

Alec listed off those he'd seen.

"And what was their response to this revelation of Ulan's?"

"I couldn't see everyone, but from what I heard, confusion. Silmai argued in your favor; the Haman sounded pleased."

"Just what Ulan í Sathil intended, I'm sure," said Thero.

Klia nodded. "How do you think he came by this information?"

"I've been considering that," said Seregil. "There are several possibilities. He could have had it from the Plenimarans. They keep an ear or two among the Lerans. Perhaps someone involved in the Teukros debacle let something slip? Or Ulan may have known about this for years, and simply bided his time until he could make the best use of the information."

"I can well imagine," Klia said. "But you think there are other explanations?"

Seregil cast a quick glance at Alec, who nodded slightly and turned away.

"Lord Torsin, my lady—"

"Torsin?"

"Torsin met secretly with someone in Khatme tupa one night, about two weeks after our arrival," said Seregil. "At least one person at that meeting was a Virésse. There's evidence that Ulan summoned him to that meeting. It was only by chance that Alec discovered he'd gone out."

Klia gave Alec a dubious look that made the younger man color guiltily. "When I ordered you two not to spy without my permission, that included spying on our own people."

Seregil started to reply but she cut him off abruptly. "Hear me, both of you. You needn't concern yourself with Torsin. Wherever Ulan may have gotten this damaging information against my sister, I assure you, it did not come from Torsin. I suggest you concentrate on learning where it *did* come from."

She knows about her envoy's midnight meetings, or thinks she does, thought Seregil, smarting under the unexpected reprimand. It hadn't occurred to him that Klia might keep secrets from him. On the other hand, he was fairly certain Torsin knew nothing of his or Alec's true talents. If that were so, then Klia was playing a more complex game than he'd guessed. He glanced at the wizard, wondering how much Thero knew. He didn't appear much surprised by this exchange.

"If it came from Plenimar, then that might also explain those Plenimaran warships that ambushed us in the Ea'malies," Thero mused. "Perhaps the honorable khirnari paid for information with information."

Klia nodded slowly. "I'd very much like to know the truth of that. The negotiations have limped along too long. Every dispatch I get from Phoria is more impatient than the last. Today's all but accuses me of purposefully stalling."

"How could Phoria think that?" exclaimed Alec.

"Who can explain what my sister thinks these days, or why?" Klia rubbed wearily at her eyelids. "This business with Virésse might be just the thing to turn matters our way. Tell me, my Aurënfaie adviser, would it be safe to say that Ulan has acted dishonorably toward me?"

"An argument could be made," said Seregil. "Of course, if we had to explain to the Iia'sidra how you found out about it, it would put Alec on chancy ground."

"I'll leave it up to you to keep us from having to explain anything to anyone. Two days from now, we and the Eleven are to be the guests of Ulan í Sathil."

"Are you suggesting what I think, my lady?"

Klia gave an eloquent shrug. "What's the use of bringing fine coursing hounds to the hunt if you never slip the lead? First thing tomorrow I'll speak in private to Lord Torsin and Adzriel ä Illia of all you've told me tonight. My principal adviser and our best ally must not be taken by surprise, either."

"Will you tell Torsin that I spied on him?" Alec asked nervously.

"No, but I want your word that you won't do it again. Is that understood?"

"Yes, my lady."

Klia leveled a knowing look at Seregil. "That includes you, as well."

"You have my word. What about Nyal? If it hadn't been for him, we might have missed this altogether. He asked Alec to tell him what he learned."

Klia sighed. "Ah, yes, Nyal. He's served us well, and word is bound to spread, anyway, since that appears to be Ulan's intent. Tell him only what Alec heard. Nothing more."

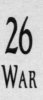

26
WAR

The flush of victory made Phoria feel younger than her years. For two days they'd fought under driving spring rains, forcing the Plenimarans from a pass west of the river. The cost had been high on both sides, but Skala had regained a few precious acres.

A cheer went up across the camp as she rode in at the head of what remained of the Horse Guard regiment. Mingled with the accolades were the wails of camp followers as the missing were noted. There'd be a more somber welcome for the fallen, who followed in carts somewhere back down the road.

Her route through the camp led the new queen past the tents of the guilds, and she caught sight of a potter standing with her hands on her hips, no doubt making a rough count of empty saddles, estimating how many urns would be needed to hold the ashes of the dead for that last journey home.

Phoria dismissed the thought for now. Victories had been hard enough to come by this spring and she meant to savor this one.

At her pavilion, she was greeted by more cheers from the soldiers and servants massed there.

"You showed 'em today, General!" a griz-

zled veteran called out, waving a regimental banner in one hand.
"Give us a chance tomorrow to do you proud!"

"You've done me proud every day you've been on the field,
Sergeant," Phoria called back, earning another roar of acclaim. The
soldiers still addressed her by her military title, and for now, that
was just how she wanted it.

Dismounting, she led her attending officers inside to the waiting
meal. Not a banquet, perhaps, but reward enough for honest soldiers.

They were still at table when Captain Traneus appeared at the
open flap of the tent. He was muddy to the knees and carried a
pouch over his shoulder.

"What word from Rhíminee, Captain?" Phoria called.

"Word from Prince Korathan, my lady, and fresh dispatches from
Aurënen," he said, handing over the pouch.

Inside she found three documents. The first, from Korathan,
robbed the day of its savor. Reading it through twice, she lowered it
slowly and looked around at the expectant faces turned her way.
"The Plenimarans have attacked Skala's southern coast. They've
burned three cities already: Kalis, Yalin, and Deep Trebolin."

"Yalin?" General Arlis gasped. "That's only fifty miles from
Rhíminee!"

Pain flared behind Phoria's eyes. She set her brother's dispatch on
the table before her, and opened the parchment bearing Klia's seal.
It brought the same news as ever—progress was slowly being made.
Now she thought perhaps the Haman clan was being swayed. But no
concessions. No end in sight.

Closing her eyes, she massaged the bridge of her nose as the pain
mounted to a throbbing ache. "Leave me."

When the scrape of feet and creak of leather had died away, she
looked up to find Traneus still there.

Only now did she reach for the third missive, this one sealed with
a few drops of candle wax. Like the others that had come to her in
the past weeks, it was careful in its phrasing. Klia was not lying, but
putting a more hopeful cast on events.

"Our informant tells me that the Virésse have increased their influence," she told Traneus. "The negotiations are at a standstill. She
does not share my sister's optimistic view of the outcome. There is
even talk that Virésse may prefer the gold of Plenimar to our own."

She handed the letter to Traneus, who locked it away in a nearby
casket with the others already neatly stacked there.

"What message shall I take back, my lady?"

Phoria tugged at a ring on her left hand. Her fingers were swollen from the day's battle, and she had to spit on it to work it loose. Wiping it on the hem of her tunic, she held it a moment, admiring the play of light over the dragon carved into the black stone. "Return this to my brother. I want it on his hand within two days. No one is to know of it but you. Go immediately."

Traneus had only just come from Rhíminee, a hard journey of several days by land or sea. The task she'd just set him meant no rest, but the man's face betrayed nothing but obedient devotion, just as she'd expected. If he survived this war, a ring of a different sort might just find its way onto his talented hand.

Alone in the great tent, Phoria sat back in her chair and smiled as she regarded the slightly lighter circle of skin where the ring had been.

Her headache was nearly gone.

27
More Ghosts

Seregil woke before daybreak on the final day of mourning, once again trying to grasp a dream before it faded. It had started out with the same familiar images. This time, however, he seemed to recall the rhui'auros, Lhial, standing in the corner of the room, trying to tell him something very important in a voice too low to make out over the crackling of the flames.

There was no panic this time, but he knew where he had to go; he could feel the pull of the place like a hook under his breastbone. With a sigh, he slipped out of bed, wondering if he could make it back before the day's visitors began to arrive.

Someone was singing a dawn song from an upper window of the Nha'mahat as Seregil approached on horseback. Flocks of tiny dragons whirled around the building, their drab bodies turned to dusky gold by the first rays of morning.

"Marös Aura Elustri chyptir," he whispered, not sure what the reason for the prayer was, except that he suddenly felt grateful for the sight before him and the fact that he was here in this blessed place to witness it.

Donning a mask at the door, he followed a guide into the main chamber. A few dreamers already lay there. "I'd like to speak with Lhial, if I may," Seregil told the girl.

"Lhial is dead," she replied.

"Dead?" he gasped. "When? How?"

"Almost forty years ago. It was a wasting illness, I think."

The floor seemed to shift subtly under Seregil's feet. "I see. May I use a dhima?"

She prepared a firepot for him and gave him a handful of the dreaming herb. He accepted these with a respectful bow and hurried down to the cavern below. Choosing one of the little huts at random, he stripped and crawled under the door flap, welcoming the steamy closeness this time. Settled on the rush matting, he threw the herbs onto the coals and waved a hand to mix the smoke and steam.

Taking deep, rhythmic breaths, he slowly relaxed as the mildly narcotic smoke took hold.

His first thought was the realization that he felt no fear, and had felt none from the moment he'd impulsively decided to come here. He was not choking. He'd come here of his own volition, without fear or resentment.

Seregil closed his eyes, pondering this as sweat collected inside the mask, tickling his nose. The smoke from the herbs seared his lungs, making him light-headed, but he welcomed the sensations and waited.

"You begin to understand, son of Korit," a familiar voice said.

Opening his eyes, Seregil found himself sitting on sun-washed stone overlooking the dragon pool in the mountains of Akhendi fai'thast. Lhial sat beside him, his eyes golden again.

"I'm not certain I do, Honored One," Seregil admitted, shivering a little as a chill mountain breeze blew across his bare skin.

The rhui'auros picked up a pebble and threw it into the pool below. Seregil followed it with his eyes, then looked back to find Nysander sitting there in Lhial's place. Somehow, the transformation didn't surprise him. Instead, he felt a rush of the same inexplicable gratitude the sight of the dragonling swarm had given him.

Nysander sat cross-legged, looking out over the water, his plain face serene. He wore one of his threadbare old coats, and the toes of his worn boots were wet, as if he'd been walking through dew-laden grass. The curling white hair that edged his bald pate stirred in the breeze, and Seregil could see a smudge of ink in his close-cropped beard. Not once since Nysander's death had Seregil dreamed of his old friend. When he remembered him waking, no matter how he tried, the sight of Nysander's bloody, dead face rose in his mind's eye to obscure any happier memory.

He looked away quickly, bracing for the vision to shift. A gentle hand cupped his chin, turning him back to face the wizard.

"Open your eyes, Seregil."

He did, and nearly wept with relief to find Nysander, unchanged.

"You have a stubborn mind sometimes, dear boy," he said, patting Seregil's cheek. "You can track a black cat on a moonless night, yet so much of your own heart is still unknown to you. You must pay better attention."

Nysander took his hand away, and Seregil saw that the wizard now held one of the mysterious glass orbs. With a careless flick of his wrist, he tossed it up into the air. It glittered a moment in the sunlight, then fell to shatter on the rocks at their feet. For one terrible instant Seregil was back on the windswept Plenimaran ledges, blood—Nysander's blood—dripping from his ruined blade. Just as quickly, the image was gone.

"Didn't it make a lovely sound?" the wizard asked, smiling down at the tiny shards.

Seregil blinked back tears, trying to make sense of what he was being shown. "The rhui'auros said I have to keep them."

But Nysander was gone, and Lhial sat in his place again, shaking his head. "I said they were yours, son of Korit. But you know that. You knew it before you ever came to me."

"No, I don't!" Seregil cried, but with less conviction now. "What am I supposed to do?"

The wind blew colder. He pulled his knees up and wrapped his arms around them, trying to warm himself. He felt movement next to him and saw that Lhial had been replaced this time by a young dragon the size of a bull. Its eyes were gold, and kind.

"You are a child of Aura, little brother, a child of Illior. The next step in your dance is at hand. Carry only what you need," the dragon told him, speaking with Lhial's voice. With that, it spread leathery wings with a sound like summer thunder and rose to blot out the sun.

Seregil was drowned in darkness. The hot, acrid atmosphere of the dhima closed around him like a fist. Fighting for breath, he found the door flap and scrambled out, then collapsed gasping on the warm, rough stone outside.

There was something beneath his left hand. Even without the faint light filtering down to him from the main cavern, he knew what it was; recognized the curve of cool, slightly rough glass under his fingers. Swaying to his feet, he weighed the sphere on his palm for a moment; it was heavy, too heavy for something no bigger than a raven's egg. It was precious, loathsome; his to do with as he wished.

Carry only what you need.

With sudden vehemence, he flung it against the far wall. There were no visions this time, just the sharp, satisfying *chink* of breaking glass.

The sun was still low over the eastern horizon when he emerged from the Nha'mahat. His body hurt and he was as tired as if he really had journeyed to the mountains and back on foot.

Back at the guest house, he found Alec still abed, a pillow over his head. He woke as Seregil closed the door, emerging sleep-tousled and yawning.

"There you are," he said, raising himself on one elbow. "Out early again? Where'd you go this time?"

No words would come. Seregil sat down on the edge of the bed and ruffled Alec's tangled hair. "Just wandering," he said at last. "Come on. We've got a busy day ahead of us."

The Haman were among the last to pay their respects to Klia. Warned of Nazien í Hari's arrival, Seregil tactfully withdrew with Alec to a side chamber, where they could watch the proceedings from behind the door.

The khirnari was accompanied by ten of his clan, including Emiel í Moranthi.

"Suppose Nazien knows where his nephew was last night?" whispered Alec.

Seregil found himself hoping in spite of himself that Nazien did not. Proud and arrogant the Haman might be, but Klia had clearly taken a liking to the man and it seemed to be reciprocated.

Nazien and the others laid their little cedar bundles on the brazier and bowed to Klia.

While Nazien chatted quietly with her, Seregil watched his nephew's face for some betraying expression. Emiel merely looked distant, and a bit bored.

When the initial greetings had been dispensed with, Klia leaned forward and regarded the old man earnestly. "Tell me, Khirnari, will the Iia'sidra vote soon on my petition? I long for my homeland, and to do proper honors at the grave of my mother."

"It is time," Nazien agreed. "You have been most patient, though I wonder if you will be pleased with the outcome."

"Then you think it will fail?"

Nazien spread his hands "I cannot speak for all the others. For myself, regardless of my feelings toward your kinsman, the Exile, I wish you to know that I have never supported the stringent measures the Edict of Separation have forced on us."

Standing behind his uncle, Emiel said nothing, but Seregil thought he saw him tense.

"I'm an old man, and perhaps a wishful one," Nazien went on. "Now and then I almost think I see a glimpse of my friend Corruth in you, my lady, as I last saw him. You are like him in many ways: patient, forthright, and quick of wit. I think perhaps you possess his stubbornness, as well."

"How strange," Klia said softly. "Corruth í Glamien is a figure of legend to me. His body, before it was destroyed, was a preserved relic of ancient days. Yet to you he will always be the friend of your youth, unchanged, as Seregil is to me. What is it like, I wonder, to be 'faie or wizard, to live long enough to span such memories? My life is so brief in comparison, yet it doesn't seem so to me."

"Because you use it well," Nazien replied. "But I fear your time in Sarikali grows short and I fear we may not meet again. I would be most honored if you would hunt with me before you depart."

"The honor would be mine," Klia replied warmly. "Virésse is hosting a great gathering tomorrow night; perhaps the following morning?"

"As you like, Klia ä Idrilain."

"Perhaps you should warn her that we Haman take the hunt most seriously," Emiel put in pleasantly. "Tradition dictates that the feast be made up of whatever is caught that day. There's always the chance you and your people will have to sup on bread and turab with the rest of us."

"You're fortunate in my choice of companions, then, Emiel í Moranthi," Klia laughed. "Alec í Amasa can probably supply us all with ample meat."

Seregil nudged Alec in the ribs as several Haman covered shocked looks. "Sounds like you're invited, at least."

28

BURGLARS AT THE BANQUET

Whether it was Klia's tacit approval for them to spy on her behalf, or simply the end of the enforced abstinence, Seregil surprised Alec with a burst of passion as soon as they were alone that evening.

"What's this?" Alec laughed as he was propelled none too gently onto the bed. Thanks to Seregil's frequent dark moods and the lingering effects of his mysterious "fall," they'd scarcely touched in days, weeks even.

"If you have to ask, then it *has* been too long," Seregil growled, yanking Alec's coat open and fumbling with his belt. He was wild, urgent, hungry to please. Alec responded in kind, neither of them noticing until much later that the door of their balcony was open to the world.

"We've probably got everyone from here to the kitchens blushing or cursing our names," Seregil laughed when he'd finally collapsed on the floor beside the bed.

Alec hung an arm over the side and toyed with a strand of his dark hair. "If they can still hear us, tell them to fetch a healer to re-string my joints."

Seregil grasped his hand and pulled him over the edge, grunting as Alec landed on top of him. "Bilairy's Guts, talí, you're all knees and elbows." Nuzzling Alec's neck, he in-

haled appreciatively. "You smell so good! How is it I always forget
how—"

Alec pulled back to look at him. "There's something I forgot to
tell you the other night when I got back from Ulan's. The business
about Phoria drove it right out of my head."

"Hmmm? You forgot—" Seregil murmured, hands roaming.

Alec caught one of them and pinned it against his chest. "Listen,
will you? While I was spying on Ulan, a strong smell like perfume
warned me that a watchman was coming to the room where I was
hiding."

This got Seregil's attention. "Warned you how?"

"It distracted me so that I saw the watchman coming. I'd have
been caught for sure if it hadn't. And it wasn't the first time I
smelled it, either."

"Oh?"

Alec rolled free and sat up. "It was just after we arrived in
Sarikali. Kheeta took me to the House of the Pillars and we ran into
Emiel í Moranthi. . . ." He faltered, seeing Seregil's eyes narrow
dangerously. "It was just some insults, that's all."

"I see. Then what?"

"As we were leaving I smelled that same sweet scent at about the
same moment I thought I heard someone following us. Maybe that
was a warning, too."

Seregil nodded thoughtfully. "Some people experience the
Bash'wai that way."

A superstitious chill spider-walked up Alec's spine. "You think
that's what it was?"

"I expect so. Interesting."

"That's one word for it," Alec replied. "Where I'm from, it's an
unlucky thing when the dead take an interest in you."

"And where I'm from, we say take what the Lightbringer sends
and be thankful." Seregil chuckled, rising to pull him into bed again.
"Keep your nose to the breeze and let me know if you smell it
again."

Corporal Nikides gave Seregil and Alec a knowing smirk the next
morning as they went through the kitchen passage. "Good to have
the mourning over with, eh, my lords?"

"Damn right," Seregil agreed jauntily.

"Oh, hell!" Alec growled beneath his breath, coloring hotly.

Seregil wrapped an arm around his friend's waist. "Oh, come

now, you didn't think it was any secret, did you? Or are you ashamed of me, my stiff-necked Dalnan prude?"

For a moment he feared Alec would pull away. Instead, he found himself pinned roughly against the wall of the now deserted hallway.

Pressing his hands to the stone on either side of Seregil's head, Alec leaned in for a bruising kiss. "Of course I'm not ashamed, but I *was* a stiff-necked Dalnan prude before you came along, so next time let's make certain the door's closed, all right?"

Seregil clucked his tongue in mock concern. "Dear me, I see there's a good deal more we have to work on with you." Laughing, he slipped under Alec's arm and continued on toward the hall. "At the solstice festival here, they—"

"I know what they do," said Alec. "I only pray we're back in Skala before then."

Klia and the wizard were there, waiting for the rest to join them before leaving for the council.

"You two are looking remarkably well rested this morning," Klia observed dryly.

"As are you, my lady," Seregil returned with gallant good humor, trying not to laugh as Alec cringed beside him. "We'll all be needing our wits about us today."

An air of expectation hung over the Iia'sidra chamber as the members gathered for the morning session. Seated with Alec in his usual place behind Klia, Seregil studied the faces around the council circle and read in many a subtle, collective tension that hadn't been there a week before. The Khatme were looking unusually sanguine, the Akhendi grim—both bad weather signs for Skala. Ulan's private cabal had certainly had an effect.

Elos í Orian was the first to speak. He paused a moment to tuck back the ends of his brown-and-white sen'gai, letting the others wait, then addressed the chamber with the ease of one who has had his speech laid out for him in advance.

"Klia á Idrilain, you have shown great patience," he began, acknowledging her with a nod. "Your presence here has done honor to your race, and brought new insight to our people." He turned to the assembly. "Are we of the Iia'sidra unaware of the pain such delay must have caused her and her people? Many things have been discussed in this chamber; all have had their say. What more is there to be done?" He paused for a murmur of approval. "The will of Aura and the people must be served. To that end, I propose that the vote be cast at the Vhadäsoori in seven days' time."

One by one, the khirnari signaled unanimous consent.

"That's the first thing they've agreed on since we've been here," muttered Alec.

The decision brought the council to an abrupt halt. Abandoning the orderly rote, people wandered freely, major and minor clans alike. Some, including the Akhendi, left quickly. Others lingered to cajole and harangue one another.

The Skalans and Bôkthersans withdrew and rode back to their tupa together.

"It was most tactful of Ulan to have his daughter's husband push for the vote," Adzriel observed sourly.

"You think he means to capitalize on the doubts he's sown?" asked Klia.

"Of course he does," said Seregil. "How long do you suppose he's been planning this maneuver? You notice he's one of the last to host a feast in your honor?"

"Ostensibly in my honor," Klia said. "He's invited everyone in Sarikali."

"I've been to Virésse banquets. They may throw us out of Aurënen empty-handed, but at least they'll show us a good time first. Wouldn't you agree, Lord Torsin?"

Caught coughing softly into his handkerchief, Torsin wiped his lips and smiled. "He cannot present his usual collection of foreign entertainments here, but I'm certain he will provide us with a most memorable evening."

"If he's so certain of the decision, why did he have Elos í Orian set a date a week off?" Alec asked. "Why not tomorrow?"

"It's the least time allowed before a vote," Säaban í Irais explained. "As you've all observed, the Aurënfaie prefer not to rush into anything. It's an auspicious number, seven; a quarter of the moon's cycle, and the time it takes for it to pass into each of the four phases."

"Auspicious for whom, I wonder?" asked Klia.

" 'The same moon shines on all,' " Mydri quoted.

"True," Seregil agreed. "And this isn't over yet; at least we have a little time to sway the undecided. This hunt of yours with the Haman tomorrow feels like a turn of luck to me. Nazien í Hari has already taken a liking to you. He could be a valuable advocate. If he comes around to our side, his vote could make the difference."

"Yet that would mean antagonizing both Lhapnos and many

members of his own clan," Torsin reminded him. "I hesitate to put too much stock in his support."

"To be honest, my lady, I'm not so sure I like the idea of you going off with them into the hills," said Beka.

Adzriel shook her head. "Whatever tensions may lie between my clan and his, I know Nazien to be a man of honor. He will watch over your princess as closely as if she were in his own fai'thast, no matter where they are."

"And I'll have you and Alec and a whole decuria of soldiers to protect me, Captain," Klia added cheerfully. "After all these weeks of formalities, I'm looking forward to a hard day's ride."

The waning moon hung low over the horizon as the Skalans and Bôkthersans strolled to Virésse tupa that evening. At Seregil's suggestion, the entire delegation had dressed in their richest clothes.

"We don't want to come in looking like poor relations," he warned, guessing what lay in store for them.

Consequently, Klia was decked out like a queen. Her satin gown rustled richly as she walked arm in arm with Torsin. Aurënfaie jewels sparkled at her wrists, throat, and fingers. The gold circlet on her brow bore a crescent set with diamonds that caught even the gentle light of the moon and stars and turned them to fire. She even wore the humble Akhendi charms.

The rest were equally resplendent. Alec could have passed for royalty on the streets of Rhíminee. Beka, who would act as Klia's personal aide, was elegant in her close-fitting tabard and burnished gorget and brimmed helmet.

By the time they reached the Vhadäsoori they could make out lights twinkling brightly outside the Virésse khirnari's house.

With Klia and Adzriel in the lead, they skirted the shore of the broad pool and emerged from between the stone guardians on the far side to find their host's house festooned with mage lights, artfully arranged by some talented hand in clusters among the columns of the long portico.

"It looks a bit different from the last time I was here," Alec murmured.

"At least this time you get to use the door," Seregil whispered back. "Where's the fun in that?"

They were met by Ulan's wife, Hathia ä Thana, and a gaggle of flower-bedecked children, who presented each guest with a small parchment lantern hung on a red-and-blue silk cord.

"What a pretty magic!" exclaimed Klia, holding hers up to admire the soft, shifting glow that came from within.

"It is but a *reosu,*" Hathia demurred, welcoming them in.

"No magic to it. It's a firefly lantern," Seregil explained. "I remember making these on summer evenings as a child. But I don't recall ever seeing fireflies here in Sarikali this early in the year."

"They're quite thick in the marshes of Virésse just now," their hostess replied, leaving it to her guests to guess the expense and trouble of importing enough of the tiny insects overland for the simple pleasure of a few lanterns.

They passed through the receiving hall and continued out onto a terrace overlooking the enormous garden court at the center of the house. The spectacle that greeted them drew gasps of appreciation from everyone.

Hundreds of reosu hung in the flowering trees that ringed the garden. Others swung gently from the lines of brightly colored prayer kites rustling overhead. The walls of the courtyard were covered by swaths of crimson silk and gauze that rippled voluptuously in the evening breeze beneath garlands of gilded seashells. The soft music of flutes and cymbals came from some shadowed corner. A large crowd had already gathered in the garden, with more still arriving by various doors.

Spices and incense from half a dozen foreign lands perfumed the air, mingling with the aromas of the feast laid out on long tables hung with colorful Skalan tapestries. Ulan í Sathil had opened his doors to all in Sarikali, and it looked like he had the provender to make good on the offer.

Great antlered stags roasted whole lay between platters of birds cooked and dressed in their own plumage. Fish and seafood from the eastern coast were laid out in enormous seashells. Jellies of all descriptions quivered and gleamed next to mounds of rosy wingfish roe, huge smoked eels, and other costly delicacies. Fragrant parsley bread trenchers were stacked man-high in great wooden trays on the ground.

Pastries the size of bed pillows dominated the display. A Virésse specialty, these were shaped into fanciful beasts and decorated with edible paints and gilt. Wines glimmered with limpid fire in huge, ornate bowls carved from blocks of mountain ice.

Ulan stepped forward as they stood admiring the display. "Welcome to you, dear ladies, and to your kin and people," he said, presenting Klia with a strand of black Gathwayd pearls the size of gooseberries.

"I am most honored, khirnari," Klia replied. Removing her diamond circlet, she placed it in Hathia's hands. The making of such a lavish gift to her host's wife caused no insult, but stated without words that Klia was Ulan's equal. Her manner was flawlessly gracious, betraying nothing of her knowledge of his clandestine maneuvering.

"For someone who opposes Klia's mission, Ulan certainly hasn't stinted on the welcome," Alec remarked in an awed whisper as they followed Klia down the steps.

"This display is more for his own benefit than Klia's," Seregil noted, recognizing a show of influence when he saw one. "She'll go home eventually. He'll still be here, a force to be reckoned with each time the Iia'sidra meets."

"I have heard much of you through our friend Torsin over the years," Hathia was telling Klia. "It's said the best of your ancestors lives again in you."

"The same is said of my sister, the queen," Klia replied, just loudly enough for her voice to carry to the curious onlookers nearby. "May Aura grant that we are both worthy of such praise. You have a unique perspective on my family, having lived through so many generations of them. Ulan í Sathil, I believe you visited Skala in the days before the Edict?"

The deep creases in Ulan's cheeks deepened as he smiled. "Many times. I remember dancing with your ancestor Gërilani before she was crowned. That would be—how many generations back?"

He paused in thought, though Seregil suspected the whole exchange had been carefully rehearsed.

"Eight Tír generations back, I think?" said Hathia.

"Yes, talía, at least that long. Gërilani and I were hardly more than children at the time. Fortunate for you," he added with a twinkle in his wife's direction. "She was most enchanting."

Klia's arrival signaled the start of the feast. There were too many guests for tables; each person loaded a trencher and sat where they could, on the grass and the rims of fountains, or spreading into the rooms off the courtyard itself. The mix of opulence and informality was the hallmark of Virésse hospitality.

A succession of entertainments commenced with the banquet: musicians, jugglers, tellers of tales, dancers, and acrobats.

Seregil and Alec remained by Klia at first, watching and listening as the crowd flowed around them. Nazien í Hari was among the first to come to her, and Seregil noted with relief that Emiel and his cronies were not in evidence. Perhaps their khirnari was tired of having his policies challenged in public. Or maybe rumors of Seregil's beating had reached the old Haman's ears at last and he was chancing no further transgressions against Sarikali law. Whatever the case, Seregil breathed a little easier without them there, and Nazien was all smiles.

"The weather promises fair. I hope we can show you good sport," Nazien said, slipping his arm through Klia's.

"A hard ride and the chance to explore a bit more of your country will be sport enough for me, Khirnari," Klia replied warmly.

Seregil signaled Alec with a discreet nudge and faded back into the surrounding crowd, leaving Klia to charm these potential allies. They had other work to do.

"This is the most people we've been around since we left Rhíminee," Alec remarked.

And I've missed this, Seregil thought, already straining his ears for interesting conversational tidbits. He suspected Alec felt the same. He'd already fallen into that unassuming manner that made him all but invisible in such gatherings, but his blue eyes were alert as those of a hound that sensed the chase at hand.

It was not difficult to linger unnoticed for a moment while Lhaär ä Iriel expressed her continuing opposition to any lessening of the Edict to a sympathetic Haman, or to watch one of their host's kinsmen gently interrogating a Bry'khan woman as to her feelings about Aurënfaie mercenaries joining the war in the north.

Alec drifted away for a while, returning with Klia and word that some of the guests were not above grumbling at the extravagance surrounding them.

"I was standing near Moriel ä Moriel a moment ago," he reported, pointing discreetly at the Ra'basi. Nyal was with her, gesturing animatedly in Beka Cavish's direction. "She told aLhapnosan that what we're feasting on are the spoils that Virésse keeps for itself under the protection of the Edict."

"I've heard others say the same," murmured Klia. "Still, she's one I still can't read. Ra'basi benefits from the trade coming up the eastern coast by ship, even if it is only Virésse's crumbs. Yet she's made it clear more than once that the Ra'basi do not like being treated like some dependent clan." Her expression brightened as she glanced toward the main entrance. "Ah, but here are the Akhendi at last! I'd feared they wouldn't come."

"Rhaish í Arlisandin doesn't look very pleased to be back here so soon," said Alec.

"He has reason enough not to be," Seregil agreed. The khirnari was pale and dour, though his greeting to their host and his wife seemed civil enough. His grey hair was windblown beneath his sen'gai, and he wore the same plain robe he'd had on at the morning's council.

"I'll sound him out," Klia said, going off to meet him. Seregil and Alec trailed behind her, picking up Thero along the way.

The crowd was thick. By the time they reached him, Rhaish had already been waylaid by Lord Torsin and the Gedre khirnari. Clasping hands with the envoy, Rhaish fumbled his reosu lantern, dropping it at Torsin's feet.

"Ah, the cost of age!" he groaned, shaking his head as he went stiffly down on one knee to retrieve it.

Klia and Thero both stepped forward, but the princess was quicker. Taking Rhaish's hand, she tried to help him up. The old man yanked his hand away with a gasp and staggered to his feet. Realizing it was Klia who'd tried to assist him, he bowed deeply. "Forgive me, my dear, I did not see you there," he said, embarrassment lending a little color to his cheeks.

"Where is your lady tonight?" Klia asked, looking around hopefully. "I've missed her."

"She's been weary these past few days and her women felt it would be best if she remained at home tonight," Rhaish replied quickly, still flustered. "She asked me to express her regards, and the hope of seeing you tomorrow if her condition permits. I won't be staying long myself."

"Of course not. It was good of you to make an appearance. I've been thinking Amali looked worn out these past few days. You know, there's a tea Skalan women drink back home to build them up during their pregnancy. My captain might know what's needed; her mother knows a good bit of midwifery." Chatting brightly, Klia slipped her arm through the khirnari's and drew him away in the direction of the iced wine.

"We have work to do," hinted Alec.

"I suppose so," Thero agreed.

Seregil raised an eyebrow at the wizard. "Anxious to throw your dignity to the wind, are you?"

Thero turned to study the banquet table. "I've been thinking about Nysander's old tricks. That flock of roast wrens has definite possibilities."

"Our host is a fastidious man, so try not to make too much of a mess."

In the early days of their acquaintance, Thero had been mortified by his mentor's penchant for amusing magical tricks at parties. Now the young wizard attempted the same silliness with a sense of showmanship Seregil would never have credited him with.

Leaving the food alone for the moment, Thero began instead with the reosus. Approaching a group of Virésse children, he summoned several dozen of the little lanterns down from the boughs of a nearby tree and set them spinning in a circle above the children's delighted faces. When he had their attention, and that of some of their elders, he brought the lights down into a man-shaped formation and set it capering like a demented acrobat.

When a sufficient number of bystanders had turned to watch these antics, Alec and Seregil slipped out a nearby door and set off in search of the khirnari's private quarters.

Beka saw them go and watched to see if anyone followed. Satisfied that they were safe for the moment, she turned her attention back to Thero, who was now surrounded by a small crowd.

"I think your friend has lost his mind," Kheeta chuckled as he joined her.

"You should have seen his old master when he had a drop in," Beka replied, thinking wistfully of the pretty spells Nysander had concocted.

Some of the older 'faie seemed to share Kheeta's opinion. The khirnari of Akhendi stood next to Klia, looking doubtfully from the wizard to the princess, who was laughing gaily, as if Thero played the mountebank on a regular basis.

Sending the lanterns back to their branches, he proceeded to pull flowers and colored smoke from the ears of the rapt children gathered around him. It was rare to see Thero smile; rarer still to see him playful.

A familiar muffled cough distracted Beka. Turning, she saw Lord Torsin pressing a pristine handkerchief to his lips as his shoulders heaved. Hurrying to his side, she took his arm and offered him her wine cup. He drank gratefully and patted her hand. His own were cold.

"Are you unwell, my lord?" she asked, noting the fresh stains on the white cloth as he tucked it away in his sleeve.

"No, Captain, just old," he replied with a rueful smile. "And like so many old men, I weary sooner than I'd like. I believe I'll have a little stroll, then make my way home to bed."

"I'll send an escort with you." Beka gestured to Corporal Nikides, who stood nearby.

"There's no need for that," Torsin said. "I much prefer to see myself home."

"But your cough—"

"Has been with me a good long time." Torsin shook his head firmly. "You know how I enjoy my quiet walks under the stars here. With today's decision . . ." He looked around sadly. "I shall miss Sarikali. Whatever the outcome, I doubt if any of us shall see it again."

"I'll be sorry if that is so, my lord," Beka said.

With a last bemused look at Thero, who was now coaxing a dragon-shaped pastry to life, the old envoy went to take leave of Klia and their host. Turning, Beka bumped into Nyal.

Weaving his fingers with hers, he raised her hand and pressed it to his lips. "I shall be very sorry to see you go. I've been thinking of nothing else since the vote was announced this morning. Our parting will be all the worse, knowing that you return to your war, talía."

It was the first time he had used the endearment, and the sound of it brought a rush of warmth to her heart and the sting of tears to her eyes.

"You could come with me." The words escaped before she could second-guess them.

"If they vote to lift the Edict, you could remain," he countered, still holding her hand.

The possibility hung between them for a moment, then Beka shook her head. "I can't abandon my command, or Klia. Not when every soldier is needed."

"This is what comes of loving a warrior." Nyal rubbed his thumb across her knuckles, studying the faded scars there.

"My offer stands." Searching those sad hazel eyes for an answer, she added in Aurënfaie, "Take what the Lightbearer sends and be thankful, talí."

Nyal chuckled softly. "That's a Bôkthersan proverb, but I will reflect upon it."

Seregil and Alec moved through the labyrinthine house with their usual caution, but were soon satisfied that most of the household was busy in the main courtyard. The few people they encountered along the way, servants and trysting lovers mostly, were easily evaded.

"Does any of this look familiar?" Seregil asked.

"No, I was in the other wing."

Seregil had once known this sprawling house well. Wandering through familiar corridors and courts, he found his way at last to the khirnari's living quarters. The rooms faced a small courtyard encircled by banks of peony and wild rose. A pool at its center was stocked with large, silver fish.

"If we don't find the papers here, and quickly, we give up and go back," Seregil said, trying a door and finding it unlocked. "We've got to return before we're missed." He squinted at Alec in the dim moonlight. "You haven't smelled anything, have you?"

"Just the flowers."

Their search was made easier by the spare furnishings Ulan and his lady favored. Each room had what it needed to make it habitable, no more. Thick carpets softened the sound of their feet, but there were no tapestries, just airy silk hangings around the bed.

"Odd," Alec whispered, keeping a lookout at the door. "This is all of the best quality, but after what we've seen so far tonight, I'd have expected Ulan's tastes to be more elaborate."

"What does that suggest?" Seregil asked, poking through a clothes chest.

"That he doesn't care about material goods? That it's the power he craves, and displays of wealth like this gathering tonight are simply manifestations of his power?"

"Very good. There's more to him than that, though. He lives for his clan. Not that he hasn't made himself a great man in the process, but the power, the goods, trade, reputation? It's all for Virésse. That's the mark of a great khirnari."

He broke off, bent over a drawer in a small chest. "Look at this."

He flipped something bright at Alec, a new Skalan sester coin that had been cut in two.

"I bet I know what this is," he whispered, tossing it back. "Ulan sends sen'gai tassels. Torsin sends these."

"If you're right, then they've met at least five times." Seregil showed him more of the tokens. "What do you suppose Ulan is doing, keeping these close to hand? Now, what was I saying?"

"That Ulan is a great khirnari."

"Ah, yes. One of the greatest. That's why he opposes Klia, not because he dislikes her, or the Tír. If it had somehow benefited his clan to give Klia what she wants, we'd be home in Skala by now with his blessings. Ah, here's something else! Looks like a dispatch box." Seregil held it up. It was the right size, but utterly smooth, with no sign of a lock hole.

"I'm guessing what we're after is in here, if it still exists at all.

Either way, we're not getting our hands on it. This is held shut with magic."

"We should have brought Thero—" Alec broke off, hearing the sound of approaching footsteps. Hissing a quick warning, he ducked out of sight behind the door. Seregil rolled silently under the bed and Alec made a mental note; if he ever suspected intruders in Aurënen, that was the first place to look. Their unseen visitor paused a moment in the courtyard, then walked back the way he'd come.

"So much for your Bash'wai protector," Seregil complained, brushing dust from his coat as he emerged. "Not a whiff of 'em, eh?"

"I'm afraid not. What do you suppose that means?"

"Who knows, with the Bash'wai."

He moved to the sitting room off the bedchamber. After a few moments he emerged with a wrinkled sheet of parchment held triumphantly aloft. "This just might be of use," he whispered, examining it with the lightstone. "It's the beginning of a letter, but a large splotch of ink has spoiled the page after a few lines. He's not so fastidious as I thought, to leave this lying about."

Alec craned his neck for a look. "That's not Aurënfaie lettering."

"Plenimaran." Seregil's brows shot up as he scanned the first lines. "Well now, how small the world is sometimes. The salutation is to one 'honored Raghar Ashnazai.' "

"Ashnazai? Kin to Vargûl Ashnazai?"

"Oh, yes. Plenimaran families are very close-knit, especially the powerful ones. Necromancers, spies, diplomats, influence peddlers; what a charming lot the Ashnazai must be around the supper table."

He replaced the parchment where he'd found it. "Well, it's better than nothing. At least we know whom he's dealing with. We'd better get back now. I imagine Thero's running low on tricks. They do require a sense of humor, after all."

Returning to the central courtyard, they parted ways and entered by different doors.

Apparently Seregil had been right about Thero, Alec thought, finding the wizard in conversation with a small group that included their host, Klia, and the khirnari of Khatme. Adzriel and Säaban were with them, too, and everyone looked decidedly tense. Lhaär ä Iriel was actually shaking a finger at Thero.

"There you are," Klia muttered as he stepped in beside her. "Poor Thero could do with a bit of support."

"But I've seen Aurënfaie themselves use magic for innocent entertainment," the embattled wizard was saying. "I assure you, I meant no offense."

"Fools and children, perhaps," Lhaär ä Iriel retorted sternly. "The power granted by Aura is a sacred thing, not to be toyed with."

"Is laughter not a gift of Aura, too, Lhaär ä Iriel?" Ulan í Sathil asked, coming to his guest's defense.

"Indeed, I've spent a good many rainy afternoons doing such tricks for the children of my own household," Säaban added.

Alec stifled a grin. "Dear me, Thero, whatever have you been up to?" The wizard pointedly ignored him.

"Come now, this is my house and I declare no harm done," Ulan said. "We must be tolerant of one another's differences, must we not?"

The Khatme gave him a dark look and glided away.

Ulan winked at Thero. "Pay her no mind, Thero í Procepios. The Khatme are of a different mind on so many things. I am honored that you should exercise your talents for the benefit of my guests. I pray you do not let her harshness reflect insult on my house."

Thero bowed deeply. "If I have in any way repaid your magnanimous hospitality, Khirnari, then I am satisfied."

Alec remained with Thero as the rest of the group dispersed.

"I was actually enjoying myself, until the Khatme took me to task," Thero admitted. "You remember that trick Nysander had of making the wine jugs sing? I believe I carried it off rather well." Pausing, he slipped Alec the hand sign for "any luck?"

Alec nodded, then froze as the hint of a familiar scent tickled his nostrils.

"What is it?" Thero asked.

"I—I'm not certain." The smell of the Bash'wai, if that is what it had been, was already gone. Alec turned, sniffing the air.

"What are you doing?" Seregil asked with a bemused smirk, coming over to join them.

"I thought I smelled it again, just for a second," Alec murmured.

"Smelled what?" asked Thero.

"Some people see the Bash'wai. Alec claims to smell them," Seregil explained.

"It's like a heavy perfume," Alec said, still sniffing.

"Really?" Thero glanced around. "I'd be hard put to pick out a ghost here, what with all the other aromas."

"It could have been a Ykarnan." Seregil pointed out several people wearing black tunics and sea-green sen'gai. "They favor a very distinctive scent."

"You're probably right," Alec said. "Say, have any of you seen Lord Torsin? I expected him to be with Klia, but I don't see any sign of him."

"He left," Thero told him.

"Left? How long ago?" Seregil asked.

"It was just after you two went, I think."

"Seregil, Alec!" Klia called, waving to them over the heads of the crowd. "Our host has asked you to play."

Alec grinned. "Singing for our supper again? Just like old times."

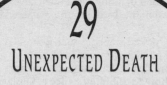

29

UNEXPECTED DEATH

Klia and the rest of the hunting party were already at breakfast by the time Alec reached the kitchen the next morning. Braknil's decuria had drawn the lucky straw, and Nyal was with them, chatting with Kheeta and Beka.

Heeding Nazien's advice, Klia had dressed in a military tunic and boots, a few Akhendi charms her only ornaments. Alec smiled to himself; in the soft light of the hearth, she looked like the carefree young soldier he'd first met beside a Cirna horse trader's corral.

"Have trouble finding your way out of bed again this morning, did you?" Beka chided good-naturedly, drawing a chuckle from a few of Braknil's riders, presumably those who'd been on sentry duty two nights earlier.

Alec ignored her, giving his full attention to a plate of bread and sausage one of the cooks handed him. He'd made certain the balcony door had been tightly shut last night.

"You should eat, my lady," Kheeta urged Klia, eyeing the barely touched plate balanced on her knee. "Old Nazien is likely to lead you halfway to Haman and back before dark."

"So I've been warned, but I'm afraid I haven't the stomach for food just yet," Klia replied, patting her belly ruefully. "It's a sorry thing for a soldier to admit, but I must have drunk a bit past the point of wisdom last night. I still haven't mastered the wines of your country."

"I thought you looked poorly," said Beka. "Perhaps we should put off this hunt? I could send word to Nazien."

"It will take more than a sour stomach and sore head to make me miss this hunt," Klia said, nibbling a slice of apple without much enthusiasm. "Nazien is as good as won over, I'm certain of it. Time's running short and this day can buy us more goodwill than a week's debating."

She reached out and ran a finger through the collection of shatta dangling from Alec's quiver. "You've gamed with them, Alec. What do you say? Which will gain us the greatest favor: shooting very well or very poorly?"

"If we were at Rhíminee, I'd say the latter, my lady. Here, though, I'd say a show of skill is best."

"That would be best, if you want Nazien's respect," Nyal concurred.

Alec paused, considering his next question. "Are you sure it's wise for me to go? The Haman have made it clear that they don't like me any more than they do Seregil, and I wouldn't want to get in your way if you think they're coming around."

"Leave that to me," she replied. "You're a member of this delegation and a friend. Let them accommodate me for a change."

"You're also our best hunter," Beka added with a wink. "Let Emiel and his friends chew that one over!"

"How is Lord Torsin feeling this morning?" asked Nyal.

"Still asleep, I think," Klia replied. "I've ordered the servants not to disturb him. It's just as well, really. Another day's rest will do the poor fellow good."

Kheeta finished his meal and left, returning a short while later with news of the Hamans' arrival.

"Is Emiel í Moranthi with the khirnari today?" asked Klia.

"Yes, along with a dozen or so of his supporters," Kheeta told her. "But Nazien has brought along a number of older kin, too."

Klia exchanged a bemused glance with Beka and Alec. "Shoot well, my friends, and smile nicely."

Nazien í Hari and a score of Haman awaited them on horseback in the street. Their black-and-yellow sen'gai looked fiercely vivid against the hazy morning sky, like the warning colors of a hornet.

All carried bows, javelins, and swords. The quivers of the young bloods of Emiel's faction were heavy with shatta.

We're outnumbered, Alec noted uneasily, wondering what Klia thought of this reception. A glance in Beka's direction told him she was having similar misgivings.

But Klia strode up to Nazien and clasped hands warmly with him.

Emiel sat his horse in a place of honor just behind his uncle, his expression carefully neutral. For the moment, at least, he seemed content to ignore Alec's presence.

Suits me fine, you arrogant bastard, just so long as you mind your manners, he thought, watching suspiciously as Emiel offered Klia his hand.

They were about to mount when the khirnari of Akhendi and several kinsmen came into view down the street, out for an early stroll. Amali was with him.

"Looks like the morning sickness is still with her," Beka remarked. "She's looking wan."

"It appears you'll have a pleasant day," Rhaish í Arlisandin called out, coming to greet Klia and the others. "I trust you rested well, Klia ä Idrilain?"

"Well enough," Klia replied, looking at Amali with concern. "You're the one who looks weary, my dear. What brings you out at this hour?"

Amali clasped Klia's hands, smiling. "Oh, I wake with the sun these days, and it's such a pleasant time to be out." She cast a quick glance in the Haman's direction. "I trust you'll take care today. The hills can be dangerous—for those not used to them."

Nazien bristled noticeably. "I'm sure we will keep her safe."

"Of course you will," Rhaish agreed coolly. "Good hunting to you all."

A warning, perhaps? wondered Alec, listening to this odd exchange of pleasantries.

The Akhendi continued on their way, but he saw Amali cast one final look back.

Bôkthersan servants brought out horses for Klia and her party. Once mounted, Alec found his position of rank threw him in next to Emiel. There was no avoiding him, it seemed. Emiel soon proved him right.

"Your companion is not joining us?" he asked.

"I think you know the answer to that already," Alec replied coldly.

"Just as well. He was never any hand with a bow. Blades, though—now that was another matter."

Alec forced a smile. "You're right. He's an able teacher, too. Perhaps you'd like to cross swords with me sometime in a friendly contest?"

The Haman's smirk widened. "I'd welcome the opportunity."

Nyal sidled his horse closer. "Even practice bouts are forbidden in the city. They fall under the proscription against violence." He gave the Haman a pointed look. "You of all people should know that."

Emiel reined his horse sharply away, followed by his companions.

Nyal watched them with evident amusement. "Touchy fellow, isn't he?"

Watching from an upstairs window, Seregil counted sen'gai unhappily. He hadn't liked the idea in the first place, and liked it even less seeing how outnumbered the Skalans were. Klia appeared unconcerned, laughing with Nazien and praising the horses.

You see it, too, don't you, tali? he thought, reading even at a distance Alec's attitude of quiet watchfulness.

The day ahead of him suddenly loomed very long indeed.

When the hunting party had ridden off at last, Seregil headed down to the bath chamber and found he had the place to himself.

"Shall I prepare a bath for you?" Olmis asked, rising from a stool in the corner.

"Yes, and as hot as you can make it." Keeping his still fading bruises secret had meant doing without proper baths for days. This man already knew his guilty secret, and had kept it, too.

Stripping down, Seregil slid into the hot, fragrant water and let it lull him as he floated limply just beneath the surface.

"You're looking much better this morning," Olmis observed, bringing him a rough sponge and soap.

"I'm feeling much better," Seregil said, wondering if he dared take the time for a proper massage. Before he could make up his mind, however, Thero rushed in. The normally fastidious wizard was unshaven and uncombed, his coat buttoned awry.

"Seregil, I need your help at once!" he said in Skalan, stopping just inside the doorway. "Lord Torsin has been found dead."

"Found?" Splashing up out of the tub, Seregil reached for a towel. "Found where?"

Thero's eyes widened perceptibly at the sight of Seregil's battered body, but thankfully he let it pass for the moment. "At the Vhadä-soori. Some Bry'khans—"

"By the Light!" Seregil hissed. The last thing Klia or the negotiations needed was another death. "Does anyone know when he went out this morning?"

"I haven't had time to ask."

Seregil tugged on his breeches and boots, hopping awkwardly from one foot to the other in his haste. "Tell whoever found him that he's not to be moved!"

"Too late for that, I'm afraid. The woman who brought the news says her kinsmen are already on their way with the body. They should be here any time now."

"Bilairy's Balls!" Seregil threw on his coat and followed.

The sound of raised voices guided them to the main hall. A middle-aged Bry'khan woman and two youths had just arrived, carrying a cloak-shrouded body on a shutter. The contorted angles beneath the makeshift pall already suggested that Torsin had not died peacefully. Escorted by Sergeant Rhylin and four riders, they set their makeshift litter down in the center of the room. The woman introduced herself as Alia ä Makinia. The young men with her were her sons.

"I found this beside him," one of the boys said, handing Seregil a bloody handkerchief.

"Thank you. Sergeant Rhylin, post a guard at the doors outside and send someone to inform my sisters of what's happened." He turned back to the Bry'khans. "The rest of you stay a moment, please."

A welcome sense of detachment settled over Seregil as he knelt by the litter, the body already reduced in his mind to a puzzle to be solved.

Drawing back the cloak, he found Torsin lying on his back, knees drawn up and twisted to the left. His right arm was extended stiffly above his head, the splayed hand white and swollen beneath a thin layer of drying mud. The left hand was clenched tightly against his chest. The robe was the same one Torsin had worn the night before, but soiled and damp now. Bits of dead grass were tangled in the old man's hair and in the links of his heavy gold chain.

Someone had tied a cloth around the dead man's face. Black blood had soaked through it by the mouth. More blood had dried on the front of his coat and the back of the fist clutched awkwardly to his chest.

"By the Light, his throat's been cut!" Thero exclaimed.

Seregil probed beneath the jaw pressed rigidly to the chest. "No, his neck's sound."

He pulled the cloth from the dead man's face, certainty already taking shape in his mind. The lips, chin, and beard were streaked with dried blood and flecked with bits of dead grass and mud. Death had cruelly transformed the dignified features, and insects had been busy in the open eyes and between the parted lips. The left side of the head had turned a mottled purple and was peppered with small indentations. The rest of the face and neck were a leaden hue.

Thero caught his breath sharply and made a warding sign.

"There's no need for that," Seregil told him. He'd seen more corpses than he cared to recall and knew the marks of death like an alphabet. He pressed a fingertip into the livid cheek and released it. "This side of his head rested against the ground. It's the settling of the blood after death that discolors the skin this way. See here, on the undersides of his arms and neck?" He pressed the darkened skin again, noting that it didn't blanch beneath his fingers. "He's been dead since last night."

He looked up at the Bry'khans again. "When you found him, he was lying on his face at the water's edge, wasn't he? With this hand outstretched in the water, the other curled under him?"

The Bry'khans exchanged startled looks. "Yes," Alia replied. "We went to the Vhadäsoori for blessing water this morning and found him lying just as you said. How did you know?"

Preoccupied, Seregil ignored the question. "Where was the Cup?"

"On the ground beside him. He must have dropped it while drinking." She made a blessing sign over the dead man. "We treated him with all respect and said the words of passing over him."

"You and your kin have my gratitude, Alia ä Makinia, and that of the princess," Seregil said, wishing they'd left Torsin where he lay. "Did you find anything else near the body?"

"Just the cloth."

"Where is the Cup now?"

The older boy shrugged. "I put it back on the stone."

"Go and fetch it at once!" Seregil ordered sharply. "Better yet, carry it to Brythir í Nien of Silmai and explain what has happened. Tell the khirnari I fear poison."

"Aura's Cup poisoned?" the woman gasped. "That's impossible!"

"There's no sense taking chances. If you can, learn if anyone has used it in the meantime. Hurry, please!"

The moment they were gone, he let out a snort of annoyance. "Thanks to their kindness, we may never pick up the trail now."

"No wonder no one saw him go out," Thero murmured, hunkering down beside the body. "These are the clothes he had on last night. He must not have come home at all."

"Beka said he refused an escort home from Ulan's house."

The wizard touched Torsin's face gingerly. "My experience with death is still quite limited, it seems. I've never seen a person turn blue like that. What can it mean?"

"Suffocation, most likely." Seregil held up the handkerchief. "His lungs finally gave out on him, drowning him in his own blood. Of course, he may have been strangled or smothered, too. We'd better have a look at the rest of him, just to be sure. Help me strip him."

And pray to Aura he wasn't murdered, he thought. There had never been a murder in Sarikali as far as he knew. Better that Skala didn't set the precedent. There was no telling how the 'faie would react to that.

Thero might be unversed in death, but the war had toughened him to its aftermath. In his sheltered days at the Orëska House, the young wizard had lacked the stomach for such things; now he worked with grim determination, mouth pressed into a tight line as they cut and pulled the clothes from the stiff limbs.

They found no obvious wounds or bruising, nor any evidence of theft. Torsin's skull and long bones were sound, and his right hand and wrists showed no wounds indicating he'd warded off an attacker; the left fist would have to wait until the rigor passed.

"So what do you think? Was it poison?" Thero whispered when they'd finished.

Seregil prodded at the rigid muscles of the dead man's face and neck, then pried back the wrinkled lips. "It's hard to say with the discoloration. Any feel of magic on him?"

"None. What was he doing by the pool?"

"It lies between here and Virésse fai'thast. He must have stopped there to wet his throat, then collapsed. He was staggering by the time he reached it."

"How do you know that?"

Seregil picked up a discarded shoe. "Look at the toe, how scuffed and stained it is. Torsin would never wear dirty shoes to a banquet; therefore, it happened after he left. And see how dirt is ground into the front of his robe about the knees and arms? He fell at least twice getting to the water, yet had the presence of mind to use the Cup instead of simply dipping it up with his hand. He was sick, all right, but I'd say death itself overtook him suddenly there at the water's edge."

"But the contortion of the body?"

"It hasn't the look of a death agony, if that's what you mean. He collapsed and fell over sideways. The death rigor hardened his limbs this way. It makes for a grisly corpse, I grant you, but there's nothing unusual about it. All the same, I want a look at where they found him."

"We can't just leave him lying here."

"Have the servants lay him out upstairs."

Thero looked down at his soiled hands and sighed. "First Idrilain and now him. Death seems to be dogging us."

Seregil sighed. "Both were sick and old. Let's hope Bilairy has had enough of us through his gate for a while."

Adzriel arrived in the hall just as Seregil and Thero were leaving for the Vhadäsoori.

"Kheeta sent word. Poor Lord Torsin!" she exclaimed. "He'll be greatly missed. Will there be another mourning period, do you think?"

"I doubt it," Seregil replied. "He wasn't royal kin."

"That's just as well," she mused, pragmatic despite her concern. "The negotiations are tenuous enough as things stand."

"We're off to see the place where he was found. Care to come along?"

"Perhaps I should."

The sun had cleared the tallest of Sarikali's towers by the time they reached the sacred pool. To Seregil's dismay, a small crowd of gawkers had gathered outside the ring of stones. Inside, old Brythir í Nien stood next to the Cup with Lhaär ä Iriel and Ulan í Sathil. Of these, the Virésse looked the most visibly shaken.

Here to test the wind, now that your principal advocate is gone? thought Seregil.

"Stay here a moment, please," he told Adzriel and Thero. "There have already been enough people trampling around."

Using the pedestal and Ulan's house as reference points, he went slowly over the area Torsin had most likely crossed, starting near the stone statues and working in.

There'd been a heavy dew the night before, and the grass was still moist. Here and there Seregil found the marks of what appeared to be Skalan shoes, overlaid with dew. The heels made a deeper im-

pression than the flat boots favored by the 'faie. The uneven spacing
and occasional small gouge or dent in the turf spoke of a man already unsteady on his feet.

He might have found more distinct signs near the water's edge if
his well-meaning predecessors had not in their zeal trampled over
the area. Even Micum would have been hard-pressed to make sense
of this mess, he fumed silently.

His persistence was repaid in part, however. At the water's edge
he found four long marks scored by grasping fingers. A flattened
patch of ground showed where the body had lain, a nexus for various sets of footprints. Here were a few uneven steps—Torsin's last.
Parallel marks of Aurënfaie boots were most likely those of the
Bry'khans who'd borne him away. At some point, someone had
knelt by the body. These tracks had been crossed by the Bry'khans.
All of them crossed Torsin's prints.

Straightening, he waved Thero and his sister over.

"We grieve for your loss," Brythir told him, his wizened face
somber. "No one has touched the Cup since I arrived."

"You imagined it poisoned, I suppose," Lhaär said acidly. "You
have lived too long among the Tír. No Aurënfaie would poison the
Cup of Aura."

"I spoke in haste, Khirnari," Seregil replied, bowing. "When I
heard that the Cup had been found by the body, I wished to chance
no mishap. Having looked the ground over, however, I'm reason-
ably certain that Torsin met his end alone, and that he was dying
before he reached the water."

"May I examine the Cup, Khirnari?" asked Thero. "It might be
possible to learn something of his state of mind if he touched it before he died."

"Aurënfaie law forbids the touching of minds," the Khatme
replied tersely.

Brythir placed a hand on her arm. "A guest has died while under
our protection, Lhaär ä Iriel. It is only right for his people to pursue
their own manner of inquiry to satisfy themselves as to the nature of
that death. Besides, the mind of Torsin has gone with his departed
khi. Thero í Procepios seeks only memories in stone. You may proceed, young wizard. What can you learn from this mute object?"

Thero examined the alabaster bowl closely, even going so far as
to dip up a little water and taste it.

"You let him dishonor us with his suspicions," the Khatme
muttered.

"The truth dishonors no one," said Ulan í Sathil.

Undeterred, Thero pressed the cup to his brow and mouthed a silent incantation. After several minutes he replaced it on its rough pedestal and shook his head. "This vessel has known only reverence until Torsin came here. He alone touched it with a discordant mind, and that was due to the extremity of his illness."

"You can feel his illness?" asked Adzriel.

Thero pressed a hand to his chest. "I felt some of what Torsin felt as he held it—a burning pain here, under the breastbone."

"What of his last thoughts?" challenged the Khatme.

"I do not possess such magic as that would take," Thero replied.

"Thank you for your patience, Khirnari, said Seregil. "There's nothing to be done now but await Klia's return."

Brythir shook his head sadly. "What a pity to spoil her fine day with such news."

30

THE HUNT

Alec's initial qualms had lessened somewhat by the time they forded the fog-shrouded river and headed up into the hills. The younger Haman were in high spirits and the mood soon spread among the Skalan riders. Alec was as glad as any of them to escape the dark walls of Sarikali for the day—especially on a day that promised as fair as this. The rising sun sent streaks of gold across a sky as flawlessly blue as Cirna turquoise.

Even this close to the city, game tracks were thick on the soft mould: stag, black deer, boar, and flocks of some large bird. There were also signs of other hunters—wolves, bears, and foxes.

Their guides didn't slow to hunt here but pressed on into the forest ahead, where fir and oak towered up to block the rising sun.

The Aurënfaie had no dogs for coursing. Instead, they dismounted when game was sighted, letting a few chosen hunters stalk it on foot while the rest waited. This was the sort of hunting Alec knew best, and he quickly earned his host's praise when he brought down a fat doe with a single shaft. Strangely, Klia did not fare as well.

"I hope you're not depending on me to round out tonight's feast," she remarked ruefully after letting fly too soon on a clear shot.

In spite of this, many of the younger Haman who'd been standoff-ish began to warm to her, if not to her entourage. Emiel grew particularly attentive, even lending Klia his own bow when hers failed her on another shot.

"Looks like she decided to play coy after all," Beka muttered, waiting for Klia and Emiel to return from a stag chase. "I've seen her shoot better than this in a driving rain at dusk!"

The day turned warm as the morning mist burned off. Beneath the trees the air grew heavy. The birds fell silent, and swarms of tiny flies plagued riders and mounts alike, buzzing about their heads and raising itching welts on any patch of exposed skin. Ears and noses seemed a favorite target.

They reached a large grassy glade on the crest of a hill just before midday, and Nazien called a halt. Poplars edged the clearing, their coin-shaped leaves rustling in the breeze. A wide stream cut along one edge of it, and a cool breeze drove off both heat and flies. Stacks of wood, old fire circles, and the evidence of several other trails leading off through the trees marked this as a popular destination.

"The game will sleep until the noonday heat passes," Nazien was saying to Klia. "We may as well do the same."

Fruit, bread, and wine were produced from various saddlebags. Several of Beka's riders helped clean and spit kutka for roasting. Alec stayed a little apart, keeping a surreptitious eye on Emiel and the khirnari as they sat with Klia in the shade.

After the meal, most of the hunters lay down to sleep. Settled comfortably with his back to a tree, Alec was just drifting into a doze when he sensed someone standing over him. A woman was regarding him with a guarded smile. *Orilli ä something,* he thought, trying to summon the rest of her name. Behind her, several of her companions stood watching.

"You shoot uncommonly well for a Tír," she said.

"Thank you," he replied, then added pointedly, "The rhui'auros say it's my gift from Aura, by my mother's blood."

She nodded politely. "My apologies, ya'shel. My friends and I were wondering if you would care to match that odd black bow against ours."

"I'd like that." Perhaps Klia had been right about the diplomatic value of this excursion after all.

A tree boll across the clearing served for the first target. It was an easy mark, and Alec outshot most of the Haman archers. By the end of it, he had five new shatta on his quiver.

"Would you care to try something a bit harder?" he asked.

The others exchanged amused glances as he cut a dozen straight young branches and trimmed them to wands. Setting these upright in a patch of soft ground, he paced back twenty feet and scratched a shooting line in the moss with his heel.

"And what are we to do with those? Split them down the middle?" a Haman youth scoffed.

"You could." Alec settled his quiver against his right hip. "But this is the way I was taught."

Drawing four shafts in smooth succession, he nipped off the tips of four wands, alternating high and low.

Turning, he saw a mix of admiration and dismay on his opponents' faces. "Master Radly of Wolde, who makes these bows, won't sell them to anyone who can't do that."

A man named Ura held up a carved boar-tooth shatta. "I wager you can't do that again!"

Side bets were exchanged. Alec took his time fitting an arrow to the bowstring, waiting for a puff of wind to die down. A familiar calm settled over him, as it always did when he gave himself up to the bow. Bringing his left arm up, he drew and released in one smooth flow of motion. The chosen wand shivered as his arrow nicked the tip neatly away. He nocked a second shaft, then a third and fourth, sending each unerringly to their targets. Amazed laughter and a few low grumbles burst out among his competitors.

"By the Lightbearer's own Eyes, you are as good as they claim!" Orilli exclaimed. "Come on, Ura, meet your bet."

Alec accepted the prize with a modest smile, but couldn't help looking around to see if Klia had witnessed his victory.

She wasn't there.

Nazien lay dozing on the moss now, but there was no sign of her anywhere in the glade. Or of Emiel, he realized with a stab of alarm.

Stay calm, he thought as he excused himself from the games and walked over to Beka, who was talking with Nyal. *Her horse is still here, so they can't have gone far.*

"She took a walk with Emiel over that way," Beka told him, pointing to a trail leading down through the trees. "Klia complained of the heat, and Emiel offered to show her some shady pools downstream. I tried to go along with an escort, but she

ordered us to remain here." The look in her eyes suggested that
she was much less happy about the situation than he'd first
supposed.

"How long have they been gone?"

"Since just after you began your archery contest," Nyal replied,
squinting up at the sun. "Half an hour, perhaps a little more."

Alec's sense of uneasiness returned in force. "I see. Perhaps I'd
enjoy seeing these pools."

"I'm sure you would," Beka replied, keeping her voice low. "See
that you keep out of sight."

The track led down a steep slope through wide-spaced trees. The
stream that watered the glade crossed it, then tumbled down through
a series of deep basins. Two sets of boot prints showed clear along
the soft bank, and Alec followed them, reading the story they told.
Two people had meandered along the water's edge, jumping across
the narrow watercourse several times and pausing at the larger
pools, perhaps looking for fish.

Rounding a bend in the stream, Alec caught a bright flash of
Haman yellow between the trees. He approached softly, intending to
ascertain Klia's whereabouts and discreetly withdraw.

What he saw as he came closer, however, made him abandon all
stealth. Klia was thrashing on the ground beneath Emiel, who
crouched over her, hands locked around her throat. Klia was tearing
at the man's hands, heels kicking up clods of damp moss as she
struggled to free herself. Water streamed from her hair, soaking the
upper part of her tunic.

Alec charged, knocking the Haman away from her. Emiel came
down hard on his back.

"What was your plan, then?" Alec snarled, bending over him, one
hand on his dagger hilt. "Were you going to dump her in the water
and claim she got lost? Or that some animal had killed her? Do you
have beasts that strangle here in your forests?"

Gathering a fistful of the Haman's tunic, Alec dragged him to his
feet with one hand and drove his other fist into Emiel's face twice, as
he let loose all the pent-up hate he felt for the humiliations and insults he and Seregil had endured. Blood spurted from the man's
nose and welled in a shallow gash above his right eye. Twisting in
Alec's grip, he swung back wildly, catching Alec on the side of the
head. The pain only fed his anger. Grabbing Emiel with both hands,
Alec slammed him into the nearest tree. Momentarily stunned,
Emiel collapsed in an awkward heap.

"So much for Haman honor!" Alec snarled, pulling off Emiel's sen'gai. Shaking the long strip of cloth loose, he bound the man's arms behind his back, then yelled for Beka.

Emiel groaned and tried to rise, and Alec kicked his feet out from under him. He drew back his fist again, welcoming an excuse to strike, but was stopped by a rasping croak behind him.

Klia was on her knees, one hand pressed to her throat, the other reaching out toward him.

"It's all right, my lady, I have him," Alec assured her.

Klia shook her head, then crumpled slowly to the ground.

Fear of a new sort shook him. Forgetting Emiel, he ran to her and gathered her in his arms. Half conscious, Klia writhed weakly against him, her breath coming in shallow, labored gasps. Tipping her head back, he found angry red scratches on her throat.

"Klia, can you hear me? Open your eyes!" Alec steadied her head between his hands. Her face was white, her skin clammy. "What's wrong? What did he do to you?"

Klia stared blearily up at him and slurred out, "So cold!"

He rolled her on her belly and pressed hard on her back, hoping to squeeze any water from her lungs. His efforts produced nothing but a dry, hacking wheeze. When he turned her over again, he found her insensible.

"What happened?" Beka yelled, racing down the trail with Nyal and a pack of armed Urgazhi on her heels.

"He attacked her!" Alec spat out. "He was strangling her or drowning her—I don't know which. She can hardly draw breath! We've got to get her back to Sarikali."

"Riders, keep the others back!" Braknil ordered, taking in the scene. "We've got to get to the horses."

"Keep who back?" Nazien demanded, arriving with several of his men. "What's happened?"

He halted in astonishment, looking first at his kinsman, bloodied and trussed with his own head cloth, then at Klia gasping in Alec's arms. "Emiel í Moranthi, what have you done?"

"Nothing, my uncle. By the Bow of Aura I swear it!" Emiel replied, rising awkwardly to his knees. Blood streamed from his smashed nose, and one eye was already swollen shut. "She paused to drink, then fell. I pulled her from the water, but she was choking. I was trying to help her when this"—he shot Alec a stony look—"this *boy* appeared and attacked me."

"Liar!" Alec tilted Klia's head back against his shoulder. "I saw his hands on her throat. Look for yourselves; you can still see the marks. No fall would stop her breath like this."

Nazien stepped closer to inspect Klia, only to be blocked by Beka and Braknil. Other Urgazhi flanked them, blades drawn in warning. Outrage warred with concern in the old Haman's face for an instant, then he sagged visibly. "Please believe me, my friends, I had no hand in this and will see that no one hinders your return to the city. You'll find your way faster with a guide. Will you trust me to lead you?"

"After this?" Beka exclaimed, standing over the princess. Her tone was menacing, but her freckles stood out starkly against the sudden pallor of her face.

Klia stirred in Alec's arms. Opening her eyes, she rasped, "Let him."

"Let the khirnari lead us?" Beka asked in dismay.

The princess fixed her with a look that brooked no argument.

"My lady accepts your pledge," Beka told Nazien grudgingly.

"We're losing time! Someone give me a hand here, damn it," snapped Alec.

"Sergeant, see to the horses. Corporal Kallas, you and Arbelus take charge of the prisoner," Beka ordered. "Mirn, Steb, you help Alec carry Klia back to the clearing. Someone will have to ride double with her."

"I will," said Alec. "Just give me an escort who can keep up."

Later Alec would recall little of that long, frantic ride except the flash of Nyal's sen'gai through the trees ahead of him and the feel of Klia's struggle for breath as he held her.

Somewhere behind them, Sergeant Braknil followed with the Haman prisoner under guard, but just now he didn't care if he saw any of them again, so long as he got Klia back to the city before it was too late.

He tightened his grip around her, trying to keep her upright without impeding her increasingly labored breathing. Her braid had come loose and the wind whipped her hair against his face. Shifting his hold, he pressed her head to his cheek, supporting her as best he could.

If Klia died, then everything they'd worked for was lost. Skala would fall, her brave fighters swept aside by the black tide of Plenimar's soldiers and necromancers—Rhíminee, Watermead, the few places he'd learned to call home, all crushed under the Plenimaran's unchecked onslaught. Words from his vision came back with new resonance: *You are the bird who makes its nest on the waves.*

Could that have been a portent of their failure? And what of Seregil? Sent to guide and protect, could there be redemption for him on either side of the Osiat Sea?

By the time the river came into sight Alec's muscles were cramped and his clothes were soaked through with sweat. Urging his horse across the ford, he pushed on, leaving all but Ariani behind. Swiftest of the pack, the Urgazhi scout whipped her foaming horse into a gallop and raced ahead as vanguard.

Seregil was helping Sergeant Mercalle treat a lame horse in the stable court that afternoon when the chilling wail of an Urgazhi battle cry rang out in the distance.

The sergeant looked sharply in the direction of the cry. "That's Ariani!" Whirling to face the startled riders lounging in front of the barracks house, she barked, "Raise the alarm! There's trouble!"

The cry came again, closer now, and the sound of it raised the hair on the back of Seregil's neck as he ran for the street. Kheeta, Rhylin, and the men of the current watch stood on the upper steps, shading their eyes.

"Here she comes!" Rhylin shouted.

Ariani came into sight down the street, her blond braid flying. Reaching them, she reined in sharply. "A Haman attacked Klia!" she cried as her lathered horse wheezed and sidled. "Alec's bringing her. They're right behind me. By the Four, send for a healer!"

Kheeta dashed off.

"How bad?" Seregil demanded.

"One of the Haman tried to strangle her."

"Which Haman?"

"I'm not sure, my lord, but Alec caught the son of a whore at it."

"Where was the captain?" asked Mercalle.

"Never mind that now!" barked Seregil. "There's a shutter there in the hall. Fetch it, quickly!"

A small group of riders had come into sight down the street and he saw Alec in the forefront, clutching a limp body against him one-armed. Beka, Nyal, and the Haman khirnari trailed behind him.

Reaching the house, Alec reined in, his face white with anger or exhaustion. From the looks of his bloodied right hand, he'd fought for her.

"Is she alive?" Seregil asked, gripping Windrunner's head stall.

"I think so," Alec rasped, still clasping her. "Seregil, it was Emiel. He did this."

"Bastard!" Memories of surrendering himself to the hands of that man hit Seregil like a fresh kick in the gut. He fought them down and helped Mercalle lift Klia down onto the shutter, thankful that the others knew nothing yet of the use it had already seen that day.

Mercalle and Beka hovered just behind Seregil as he knelt over Klia and pushed the tangled hair back from her face. She was cold and her breath came in tortured gasps. The delicate skin beneath her eyes was tinged an ominous blue. Examining her hands, Seregil saw that some of the nails were thinly edged with dried blood.

Good for you! he thought. With any luck, he'd leave a few marks on Emiel himself before the day was over.

She gave a choked gasp and opened her eyes.

"It's all right," he said, clasping her hand.

Klia's fingers closed over his in a punishing grip. Her mouth moved, forming soundless words.

"What is she saying?" asked Alec, crouched beside him.

Seregil leaned down, ear close to her lips.

"No—no vengeance," she managed. No teth—"

"No teth'sag?"

She nodded. "My order. The treaty—all that matters."

"We understand, Commander," Beka grated out. "I'll bear witness to it."

"And so will I," Mercalle rasped, tears coursing down her lined cheeks.

Unable to move or say more, Klia searched each of them out with despairing eyes, as if to impress her will on them.

Seregil had once seen a fellow traveler swept beneath the ice of a river. It had been clear but too thick to break through. Still alive, the man had stared up into Seregil's eyes with the same burning desperation for an instant before the current dragged him away.

Klia went limp, and he felt anxiously at her throat for a pulse.

"Her heart is still strong," he told the others, reluctantly letting go of her hand. "Where's Emiel? Teth'sag or not, he's going to answer for this."

"Just behind us, under guard," Beka replied.

Seregil drew Klia's dagger from its sheath. "She didn't have time to defend herself."

"I noticed that." Alec dismounted and leaned unsteadily against his horse's side. "He must have taken her by surprise."

Beka bowed her head. "I failed her."

"No, Captain, the guilt lies on my clan," Nazien í Hari told her, his voice hollow with grief. "Your princess should have needed no protection among my people."

"There'll be time enough for all that later. Get her inside!" Seregil ordered.

Thero met them in the hall and took charge. "Here, lay her on the table. There's no time to be lost. The rest of you, get back. Give her air." He bent over Klia and pressed his hands to her temples, throat, and chest.

Meanwhile, Seregil opened the front of her tunic to inspect the wounds there more closely. The skin between her chin and the breast band she wore beneath her linen shirt was scored with shallow scratches.

Braknil came to the door, helmet in hand. "How is she?"

"Alive," Alec told him.

"Ah, thank the Four! We've got the Haman under guard in the stable yard."

"I'll be out shortly," said Seregil, still focused on Klia.

Mydri hurried in with Kheeta on her heels. "By the Light, what's happened?"

"Alec will explain," Seregil told her. Leaving Klia to those who could best help her, he headed for the yard.

Good for you, Alec, he thought again, seeing Emiel's battered face. The young Haman sat on a low stool, ignoring the armed soldiers surrounding him. The rest of the Haman hunting party stood dourly behind him. Braknil's riders had their swords drawn and looked as if a single word from their sergeant would be all the orders they needed to cut the accused to pieces.

Nazien stood a little apart, grey with shame.

You've worn your hatred for me like a mark of honor, Seregil thought with satisfaction. *Perhaps now you'll savor my family's shame a bit less.*

The accused was another matter. Emiel showed his usual contempt as Seregil came to a halt just in front of him.

"Alec í Amasa says he saw you attack Princess Klia," Seregil said.

"Must I speak to this exile, Khirnari?"

"You will, and truthfully!" Nazien snarled.

Emiel turned back to Seregil with distaste. "Alec í Amasa is mistaken."

"Take off your tunic and shirt."

Standing, Emiel undid his belt with exaggerated slowness, then pulled off the two garments together and tossed them down on the stool. For all his bravado, however, he flinched at Seregil's touch as he examined Emiel's hands and arms. There were a few fresh scratches on the backs of his hands. Otherwise, the callused fingers and palms showed only the soil of a long day's hunt. His chest, neck, and throat were also unmarked.

"He was seized immediately after the attack?" Seregil asked.

"Yes, my lord," Braknil assured him. "Alec said this man was still choking her when he found them."

"She fell. I was trying to help her," Emiel retorted. "Perhaps it was a fit of some sort. The Tír are prone to disease, or so I hear. You'd know more about that than I."

Seregil resisted the urge to slap the arrogant sneer off the man's face. The arrival of Alec and Kheeta at the kitchen door provided a welcome distraction.

"What does he say?" Alec demanded, striding over to them.

"That he was trying to help her."

Alec lunged for Emiel, but Seregil wrestled him back. "Don't do this," he muttered, close to his ear. "Go back inside and wait. We have to talk." Alec quit struggling, but didn't back off.

"If she dies, Haman, there'll be no dwai sholo for you!" Alec hissed.

"Enough. *Go!*" Seregil nodded to Kheeta, and the Bôkthersan took Alec by the arm, drawing him back inside.

"Do you have anything more to say?" Seregil asked Emiel.

"I've nothing to say to you, Exile."

"Very well. Sergeant, search this man and his saddlebags." He paused, then without looking at Nazien í Hari, added, "Search all the Haman who went today and bring me whatever you find. They're to be held here until you hear differently."

Silence followed him back into the house. Kheeta had Alec cornered in what had been the mourning chamber.

"Klia has been moved to the women's bath," Kheeta told him. "Mydri ordered that a small dhima be set up for her there."

"Say nothing of what you saw out there for now, all right?"

Kheeta nodded and slipped out.

Finally alone, Seregil summoned what little patience he had left and turned his attention to Alec. "I need you to calm down."

Alec glared at him, eyes dark with fear and anger. A soul-deep pain radiated from him; Seregil could feel it tightening his own throat. "Maker's Mercy, Seregil, what if she dies?"

"That's out of our hands. Tell me exactly what you saw. Everything."

"We stopped at a clearing in the hills at midday. We ate a meal and waited for the heat of the day to pass. Emiel offered to show Klia some pools along a stream."

"You heard the invitation?"

"No, I was—distracted," Alec admitted, shamefaced. "Some of his friends challenged me to a shooting match. Klia and Emiel were sitting in the shade talking the last I noticed. After the match they were gone. Beka had seen them, knew where they'd gone. She'd offered to go with them, but Klia said no. She must have been hoping to win Emiel over. Anyway, they couldn't have been alone more than half an hour when I found him wrestling with her on the ground. Her hair and tunic were wet and she was fighting hard. By the time I'd gotten him off her she was having trouble breathing. I got her on a horse and we came here as quickly as we could."

Seregil considered all this, then shook his head, the words he was about to speak already bitter ashes in his mouth. "There's a chance he's telling the truth."

"I *saw* him! And you've seen the marks on them both."

"The marks on her neck aren't right. There should be bruises, finger marks, but there aren't."

"Damn it, Seregil, I know what I saw!"

Seregil ran a hand back through his hair and sighed. "You know what you think you saw. How did Klia's face look when you first reached her? Was it pale or dark?"

"Pale."

"Damn. There's no bruising on her neck, and the bones here—" He touched a finger to his larynx. "They're undamaged. If she was being strangled, her face would have been dark. I'm not saying he's innocent, just that he didn't choke her. You've got to let go of that, or you'll be no use to me at all."

"But those scratches on her neck?"

"There's blood under her nails, but not his. She did that to herself, clawing at her throat in panic. It's a common reaction to choking. Or poison."

"Poison? We all ate from the same bowls. I shared a wineskin with her myself. It still comes back to Emiel doing something to her down by the water."

"So it would seem. Are you certain no one else was there with them?"

"The ground was so soft in places mice had left tracks. If there'd been anyone else down there in the past two days, I'd have seen signs of them."

"Then let's hope Braknil finds something for us to hang an accusation on, although Emiel doesn't strike me as the type to leave empty poison flasks in his pockets. In the meantime, we've got to be careful what we say."

Alec sank his head into his hands. "Beka's right. We failed. Hell, how could I have been so stupid? An archery contest!"

Kheeta opened the door and looked in. "Alec, Mydri needs you. You're to come right away."

Four riders of Rhylin's decuria were on guard at the bath-chamber door. Beka and Rhylin stood just inside. A scene of quiet chaos lay beyond, but at first all Alec could focus on was the sight of Thero and Seregil's two sisters at work over Klia.

The princess was wrapped in a clean linen robe and lay on a pallet next to one of the small sunken tubs, which had been converted into a fire pit. An iron tripod had been set over the flames, supporting a large, steaming kettle. Thero knelt motionless beside her, eyes closed, holding one of her hands between his.

Mydri was supervising half a dozen servants around the room.

"Is the infusion steeped yet?" she called to a woman working over a nearby brazier. "Morsa, Kerian, finish with that dhima and get it heated!" This last was directed at several men who were struggling to stretch a thick felt cover over a wooden frame.

Kneeling beside Klia, Alec listened to the faint, steady whistle of breath in her throat. Her face had taken on a bluish pallor, and the dark circles around her eyes had deepened alarmingly.

"Look at this," said Seregil, lifting Klia's free hand. The flesh beneath her fingernails had turned a dusky blue. Her bare feet showed the same discoloration up to the ankles, and were icy to the touch.

"She shows signs of poisoning," Mydri said doubtfully, "yet it's like none I've ever seen. None of the usual remedies alleviate her stupor, but still she lives."

Alec looked at Thero again. The wizard was sweating and drawn. "What's he doing?"

"I tried a divining trance," Thero said without opening his eyes. "Some magic blocked my vision, which suggests that whoever did this covered his tracks. Now I'm just lending her strength. Magyana and I did the same for her mother."

The woman at the brazier brought over a cup and began patiently spooning its contents between Klia's lips, a few drops at a time. The workmen finished with the dhima and lifted it to cover Klia, the woman, and the makeshift fire pit.

"From the time you first met with Klia this morning, what did you see her eat?" Mydri asked Alec.

"Almost nothing before we left," Alec replied. "She complained of being wine sick."

"So Beka said, but she did eat later. Just list it off. Whatever you saw the whole day."

"A little bread, an apple. I picked some wintergreen leaves for her in the woods to settle her stomach. I think she nibbled a bit of that. And I'm sure that's what it was. I tasted it myself to be sure.

"By the time we stopped for the midday meal she seemed better. She shared part of a roast kutka with Beka and me, drank a little wine—" Alec closed his eyes, picturing the meal. "Nazien offered her cheese and bread. But I saw him eat from the same portions."

"The poisoning could have been accidental," said Mydri. "Did she eat anything wild besides the wintergreen? Berries, mushrooms? The scent of caramon buds is tempting, but they're dangerous even in small amounts."

Seregil shook his head. "She knows better than that."

The sound of retching came from inside the dhima and went on for several minutes. When it subsided the woman nursing Klia handed a basin out to Mydri. She inspected the contents closely, then passed it to another servant to carry away. "It appears you are correct, Alec."

"What about snakebite?" suggested Thero.

"There are no snakes in Aurënen, only dragons," Seregil said.

Mydri shrugged. "The sweating and purges should help. That and some strengthening magic are all we can do for now. She's survived this long. Perhaps this will pass."

"Perhaps?" Alec rasped.

Sergeant Mercalle entered hesitantly, dispatch pouch in hand. "Captain? I was about to send this when we got the news about Lord Torsin, so I held it for the Commander's return." She cast a mournful look at the dhima. "It's sealed and ready to go, but shouldn't someone write Queen Phoria about what's happened?"

Beka looked over at Seregil and the others. "Who do I take orders from now?"

"That would be you, Thero," said Seregil. "You're the last Skalan standing with any noble blood in him. The Iia'sidra certainly won't deal with me."

Thero nodded gravely. "Very well. Send it as it is, Captain. We'll inform the queen of her sister's illness when we have determined the cause. It's unwise to risk spreading rumor without facts."

Mercalle saluted. "And the Haman, my lord?"

Thero looked to Seregil. "You're my adviser now. What do we do with them?"

"Hold Emiel, but let Nazien and the rest go back to their tupa under pledge of honor. Don't worry. He won't go anywhere, and if any of his people make a dash for it, we'll know who our poisoner is. Beka, station some of your people to keep an eye on them, but discreetly."

"I'll see to it myself," she assured him.

31
DEATHWATCH

A sense of foreboding enveloped the household. All through the night the servants went quietly on about their business, cooking food that went uneaten, turning down beds no one slept in. Lord Torsin lay forgotten for the moment.

Leaving Klia in Mydri's care, Seregil enlisted Alec, Thero, and Adzriel to go over every flask, knife, and piece of jewelry confiscated from the Haman. Neither sharp eyes nor magic turned up any evidence of poison.

"You said yourself they wouldn't keep anything that would give them away," Alec insisted. "I want to go back to that clearing. There wasn't time to look around properly before."

"If Klia touched the object that contained the poison, I could locate it," offered Thero.

"You're needed here," Seregil told him.

"Säaban has the gift," said Adzriel. "He knows the way to the clearing, as well. Shall I ask him to make arrangements?"

"If we leave before dawn, we'll be back by midday," Alec added.

"I suppose you'd better," said Seregil. "Where's Nyal, by the way?"

"I haven't seen him since you got back," said Thero. "Perhaps he's with Beka?"

"The one time I want the man and he's nowhere to be found," Seregil grumbled, suddenly weary beyond words. "Fetch him. He may have heard something of use."

The night wore on. The three of them sat on the floor beside the dhima, listening to Mydri's soft songs of healing through the felt walls; now and then each took a turn inside.

Sitting by Klia, hair and clothes plastered damply against his skin, Seregil allowed his mind to wander back to the dhimas beneath the Nha'mahat and the rhui'auros's words to him there: *Smiles conceal knives.* The Haman had certainly been smiling when they rode out that morning.

He didn't know he was dozing until Mydri touched his arm.

"You should rest," she said, yawning herself.

Thero and Alec were asleep where they sat just outside the dhima. Seregil passed them silently and went to the window to cool his face. Looking out, he saw the dwindling moon disappearing behind the western towers.

Almost Illior's Moon, he thought. *Or rather, Aura's Bow.* He was back among his people at last; it was time he started thinking like a 'faie.

"You're a child of Aura, a child of Illior," Lhial had told him. Aura Elustri, creator of the 'faie, mother of dragons. Illior Lightbearer, patron of wizards, madmen, and thieves. Light and darkness. Male and female. Wisdom and madness.

Different faces for all comers, thought Seregil, smiling as he slipped out the window and set off for the stable yard. *Just like me.*

The barracks were heavily guarded, but the long building itself was empty except for Kallas, Steb, and Mirn standing guard over their sullen prisoner. Emiel sat on a pallet in the corner furthest from the door. A clay lamp hanging overhead cast an uncertain light across the prisoner's face. Emiel didn't look up at Seregil's approach but sat staring out a tiny window under the eaves, watching the moon.

"Leave us," Seregil ordered the guards. When they hesitated, he added impatiently, "Lend me a sword, and stay by the door. I promise you, he won't get past me."

Steb gave Seregil his sword and moved off with the others.

Seregil walked slowly over to the prisoner.

"Here to murder another Haman, Exile?" Emiel asked, as calmly as if inquiring about the weather.

"I have one too many of your people on my conscience as it is." Seregil rested the blade point on the floor. This was the first time since Nysander's death that he'd allowed himself to touch a sword; it felt awkward in his hand. "However, teth'sag is not murder, is it?"

The Haman's gaze did not waver. "To kill me here would be murder."

"But for you to kill my kinswoman, Klia ä Idrilain, was that teth'sag?"

"She's dead?"

"Answer my question. If a Haman killed Klia ä Idrilain, would it be teth'sag against Bôkthersa? Against me?"

"No, the tie is too distant." Emiel rose to his feet and faced him. "Even if it weren't, I would never bring shame on my clan for the likes of you. You are dead to us, Exile, a ghost come to haunt a little while. You disturb the khi of my murdered kinsman with your presence, but you'll soon be gone. I can be patient."

"Patient as you were the night you and your friends met me in Haman tupa?"

Emiel returned to his contemplation of the moon, but Seregil heard him chuckle.

"Answer me this, then."

"I told you before, Exile, I have nothing to say to you."

Seregil gauged the man before him, then slid the sword away. It clattered and spun across the uneven boards, drawing startled looks from the guards.

"Stay there unless I call for you," Seregil told them, waving Steb and the others away. He moved closer to Emiel, stopping just inches away and lowering his voice. "The Haman are great bargainers. Here's an even trade for you. Answer my question and earn another taste of teth'sag. Right here. Right now."

Emiel turned away slightly, and Seregil mistook the move for a refusal. An instant later, he found himself flat on his back with blood in his mouth. Black spots danced in front of his eyes, and the entire left side of his head had gone numb where Emiel's fist had caught him.

Steb and the others were nearly on Emiel by the time Seregil had gathered his wits. "No! S'all right. Go 'way," he managed, staggering to his feet. The look the corporal gave him warned that he'd be explaining himself to Beka later. Or worse yet, to Alec, who'd probably offer to even up the two sides of his head for him. No time to worry about that now.

Emiel's arrogant sneer was firmly in place again. "So ask your question, Exile. Ask as many as you like. The price is the same for each."

"Fair enough," Seregil replied, feeling with his tongue for loose teeth. "I know about the secret meeting Ulan í Sathil held a few nights back, and what he told you there. I know that you don't share your uncle's sympathy for Skala. How did he react when you told him what you'd learned?"

Emiel let out a derisive snort, then lashed out again, backhanding Seregil hard enough to make him stagger. "You're wasting that handsome face of yours on that? He was shocked, of course, and dismayed. Klia ä Idrilain has great atui. So did her mother. This new queen of yours, though?" He shook his head. "Even my uncle wonders if we should wait another generation before lifting the Edict. So do many of the other khirnari."

"You're generous with your answers," Seregil muttered, almost managing a crooked grin.

"Ask another."

Seregil took a breath and braced his feet, determined not to be caught off guard this time. "All right—"

But Emiel surprised him again, going for his belly instead of his face. Seregil doubled over, gasping for air. When he could breath again, he asked, "Did you know of Lord Torsin's private chats with Ulan í Sathil?"

"The Virésse? No."

Seregil leaned back against the wall, one hand pressed to his belly. His ears were ringing and his head hurt, but he didn't miss how that last question had shaken his opponent.

He considered pressing further on the Torsin angle but decided against it, not wanting to give too much away in case Emiel was telling the truth about not knowing. Instead, he let out a hollow chuckle. "So you think my face handsome, do you?"

Emiel took a menacing step toward him. "Is that another question, Exile?"

Seregil side-stepped hastily. "I withdraw it."

"Then I'll answer you for free." Grinning, Emiel raised his voice loud enough for the others to hear. "You were always a handsome little slut, Exile, more handsome even than the Chyptaulos traitor you played the whore for that summer."

The words froze Seregil where he stood.

"You don't remember it, but I was there, too. I remember you and Ilar í Sontír—that was his name, wasn't it? The man you killed my kinsman for? Too bad it wasn't just your ass Ilar was after, eh, guest killer? Perhaps we'd all have been friends. He could have passed you around. Did you like it rough back then, too?"

The words hit harder than any blow. Shame welled like bile in

Seregil's throat. How many of the Urgazhi in earshot had understood? Emiel's scornful gaze seemed to scorch his skin as Seregil retrieved the sword and headed for the door.

"I don't speak much 'faie, my lord, but I didn't like the sound of that," Steb growled as Seregil handed him back his weapon.

Emiel í Moranthi has just confessed. He tried to murder Klia. Kill him. That's all it would have taken.

Locking the words away behind a bloodied smile, Seregil shook his head. "See that no harm comes to our guest, riders. Not so much as a harsh word."

As he'd feared, news traveled fast among the Urgazhi. Alec was waiting for him just outside.

"Now what have you done?" he demanded, turning Seregil's face toward the watch fire to inspect the latest damage.

Seregil pulled away and continued on into the house. "Don't worry, it was my own doing."

"That's what I'm worried about."

"It wasn't like last time. I goaded him to see what he'd say. It was atui that made him swing at me."

"So it's honorable for him to hit you?"

"Absolutely. While he was at it, however, he let slip a few valuable bits of insight." He stopped just short of the great hall and lowered his voice. "As we'd feared, Ulan has done us a great deal of harm. Phoria's honor is in question, and some of those who supported us while Idrilain lived are wavering. But from what Emiel said just now, Torsin's secret meetings with Ulan aren't common knowledge." He fingered a tender spot next to his eye, hoping it wasn't going to swell. "Maybe we can use that to cast doubt back on Virésse. If we do, and prove that Klia was poisoned, perhaps we can sway some clans back to our side. I have to talk to Adzriel."

"She's in the hall."

Seregil clapped him on the shoulder. "See what you can find back in the hills. We need to know what Haman's role in all this is."

"It's going to take some doing," Alec admitted. "If they threw away something during the ride, chances are we'll never find it."

"We have to try. Otherwise, we can just stick our heads up our backsides and let it all fall to pieces."

Adzriel was talking with Rhylin and Mercalle beside the hall hearth. Drawing her into the mourning chamber, Seregil and Alec outlined the evening's findings.

"You can't believe the Haman are innocent?" she asked, searching Seregil's face.

"I'm not ready to say that yet, but something isn't right. I think Emiel is capable of it, but if he was going to go to the extreme of murder to get his way, wouldn't his uncle be a more logical target?"

"What about Nazien?" asked Alec. "He could have played us all for fools."

Seregil shrugged. "That seems even less likely. As much as I hate to admit it, he strikes me as an honorable man."

Adzriel touched Seregil's bruised cheek, frowning. "What will you do now?"

"Keep searching. Am I correct in guessing that anyone who falls under reasonable suspicion can be excluded from the vote?"

"Yes, the Haman must prove themselves innocent, or you must prove them guilty within a moon's span."

"We don't have that long," said Alec.

"Perhaps not," Adzriel replied. "Please, Alec, I'd like a moment alone with Seregil before he goes."

Alec cast a worried look at Seregil, then bowed. "Of course, my lady."

Adzriel gave him a wink. "Don't worry, I'll send him back to you soon, talí."

She watched Alec fondly out of sight, then turned and touched a finger to Seregil's swollen lip.

"You must stop this," she said softly. "It's wrong to seek this out from them."

"What do you mean?" he asked, folding his arms.

"You know exactly what I mean! Do you think Mydri kept the last occurrence from me? What is it you expect from such behavior? Justice? Atonement?"

"It wasn't like that this time," Seregil countered. "Sometimes you have to fool your enemy into doing what you want them to do. By letting Emiel think—"

"And what will everyone else think when they look at you tomorrow?" she demanded angrily. "For once in your life, listen to good counsel. Hear me, if not as your elder, then as the khirnari of the clan I pray you will one day rejoin. To allow a Haman to lay hands on you dishonors the princess you serve and the clan you sprang from. It dishonors Alec. Have you considered that?"

"That was pointed out to me, actually. But tonight—"

"Tonight you let a Haman put his hands on you again, as if it were his right."

Seregil knew it had been different tonight. He knew that whatever the cost, it had been worth the information he'd gotten. Any Rhíminee footpad or noble intriguer would have applauded him for it. At the same time, he knew with equal certainty that there was no way his sister would ever understand.

"Forgive me, talía. Bringing pain and dishonor to those I love best seems to be a particular talent of mine."

She cupped his chin. "Self-pity is a weakness you cannot afford to indulge. You know my hopes for you, talí. I want my brother back. I want you to be Aurënfaie again."

Tears stung his eyes as he pulled her close. *I want that, too, more than you know. I just have my own ideas on achieving the impossible.*

Alec paced slowly around the hall. He had the place to himself for the moment, the first time since Klia's mysterious collapse that he'd had a quiet moment to think. When he tried to make sense of the day, however, he was overwhelmed by the confusion of events. Klia's illness and Torsin's untimely death. Bad enough that they might be returning to Skala empty-handed and in the middle of a lost war. He'd stood by and allowed Klia to be poisoned right under his nose. Now Seregil was acting like a madman. Perhaps they'd both been too long away from Rhíminee, after all.

Seregil came out of the mourning room looking subdued.

"Well?"

"Go back up to that clearing at first light. Find whatever you can."

Alec opened his mouth to reply but succumbed to a jaw-creaking yawn instead.

"Get some sleep," Seregil advised. "There's nothing else you can do tonight, and tomorrow is shaping up to be a very long day."

"Are you coming up?"

"Maybe later."

Alec watched Seregil cross the darkened hall toward the bath chamber. "I still think Emiel did something to her."

Seregil paused but didn't look back. "Find me some proof, talí," he rasped. "Find me proof."

32

SNAKES AND TRAITORS

Seregil woke groggily to the sounds of an argument. He'd been dreaming of the Cockerel Inn again, but this time he'd been sitting on the roof.

Stiff and disoriented, he sat up and looked around the dim hall to get his bearings. He'd stayed with Klia until Mydri had chased him off, then made a makeshift bed out of two chairs out here. He hadn't expected to sleep, yet here he was with a stiff neck and one leg numb to the hip. The night lamp was guttering, and faint light was showing at the windows.

The argument in question was being carried on in Skalan outside the front door. Limping over, he looked out to find Nyal facing several Urgazhi sentries. Corporal Nikides and Tare were resolutely blocking the door. A few steps below, the Ra'basi interpreter looked tired and apologetic, but determined.

"It's Captain Beka's orders," Nikides was saying. "No Aurënfaie except Bôkthersans are to be let in. When she comes back—"

"But the rhui'auros said Seregil sent for me!" Nyal insisted.

"Which rhui'auros?" Seregil demanded, sticking his head out.

"Elesarit."

It wasn't the name Seregil was expecting,

but he played along. "Of course. It's all right, Corporal. I'll take charge of him."

As soon as the door had swung shut behind them, he grasped the Ra'basi by the arm and pulled him to a halt.

"What did this rhui'auros say, exactly?"

Nyal shot him a surprised look. "Only that you required my services."

"And that I'd sent for you?"

"Well, no, now that I think of it. I just assumed—"

"We'll sort that out later. Where have you been?"

"Ra'basi tupa. With all the confusion here, I thought it best to stay out of the way. I left word for Beka with Sergeant Mercalle, in case I was needed."

"She's still out keeping an eye on the Haman."

"Of course. Is Klia—?"

"As far as I know. Let's go see."

They met Säaban í Irais coming out of the bath chamber. He was dressed for riding, and looked as if he hadn't slept much, either.

"A bad night," he told them. "Alec is with her now. My riders and I can leave as soon as he's finished."

The dhima lay like an upended turtle against the far wall. Klia had been moved next to the central bathing pool, and wet cloths were draped across her forehead and wrists. Mydri and Adzriel sat next to her, each grasping one of her hands. Alec and Thero stood over them, hollowed-eyed and solemn.

"Sweating only made her breathing worse," Mydri explained worriedly. "I've purged her, given her herbs, sang the six songs of purification; nothing seems to help."

"By the Light!" Nyal went down on one knee beside Klia and inspected her hands and feet. The discoloration was darker and had spread up her limbs.

"Has she opened her eyes at all, or moved?" asked Nyal.

"Not for hours."

"Then I think you must be wrong about when she was poisoned." Seregil gave the Ra'basi a sharp look. "What do you know about it?"

Nyal shook his head wonderingly. "I don't know how it could be, but this has all the signs of an apaki'nhag bite."

"A what?" asked Mydri.

"It's a snake," said Nyal.

"I thought there weren't any snakes in Aurënen!" Alec exclaimed.

"Not on the land. Apaki'nhags are sea snakes. There are a number of different types."

"Apaki'nhag. 'Gentle assassin?' " Seregil translated.

Nyal nodded. "So called because its bite is painless, and because the effects of the venom don't appear for hours in most cases, sometimes not even for days. Shellfish divers often grab them by mistake among the weeds, not realizing they've been bitten until they fall ill later. I've seen it often enough among sailors and fishermen to know the signs. It's good you removed that." He gestured toward the dhima. "Sweating only drives the poison deeper into the body."

"A water snake? She was wet when I found her," Alec told him. "Emiel said she'd stopped to drink—"

"No, Alec. Apaki 'nhag are saltwater creatures."

"Where are they found?" asked Seregil.

"Along the eastern coast. I've never heard of any south of Ra'basi."

"Ra'basi, Gedre, Virésse, Goliníl," Seregil said, ticking likely places off on the fingers of one hand. "And let's not forget Plenimar."

"Plenimar?" said Alec.

"I'm not ready to rule them out just yet. Whether or not they did the actual poisoning, they've raised it to an art and wouldn't be above selling both the poison and the means of best using it. They have as much reason as anyone for wanting Klia to fail."

"If you're right, then she may not have been poisoned by something she ate but by something she touched," said Thero, concentrating on more immediate issues.

"Something that touched her, more likely," Seregil corrected, examining Klia's cold hands. "It's the mark of a two-legged serpent we're looking for. You say the victim doesn't feel the bite, Nyal?"

"That's right. The snake's teeth are quite small, and the venom deadens feeling. Ra'basi healers sometimes use a very dilute form of it in salves."

"A needle or small blade concealed in a ring is a favorite toy among Plenimaran assassins." Seregil pushed the sleeves of Klia's gown back to inspect her arms.

"This venom, Nyal, would it affect someone who's already ill more quickly?" Thero asked.

"Yes, with the old or infirm, it's nearly always fatal within—"

"Torsin!" Seregil exclaimed, looking up at the wizard. "Alec, keep looking for marks."

He and Thero took the stairs two at a time to the envoy's chamber. Cold lamps sparked to life at the wizard's command.

The dead man's face had lost its leaden hue, darkening already to the mottled greenish pall of dissolution. The rigor had passed and someone had straightened the limbs, bound up the slack jaw and eyes, and blanketed the corpse with fragrant herbs. Neither these nor the resinous smoke from the incense pot could mask the heavy stench. A round, salt-glazed urn with a cover of fitted leather had been left on the clothes chest, ready to receive the dead man's ashes for the journey home.

"A not-so-subtle hint that my people don't let their dead linger," Seregil noted, pointing at the jar. "We're lucky he hasn't already been carted out to a pyre somewhere."

"I'm not sure 'lucky' is the word I'd have chosen," Thero replied, recoiling at the smell.

"Damn this warm weather, eh?" Seregil muttered, wrinkling his nose. "Let's get it over with."

He spread the fingers of Torsin's right hand and inspected them. He heard Thero suck air and hold it as he pried open the clenched left fist. Perhaps he wasn't as hardened to all this as Seregil had supposed.

An excited gasp quickly followed, however. "Look at this!" Thero exclaimed, pulling a tangled clump of fine threads free of the wrinkled palm.

Seregil took it and smoothed the strands out on his palm: red and blue silk, knotted into a small tassel identical to the one Alec had found on the envoy's hearth two weeks earlier. "It's from a sen'gai. See here? There's a bit of cloth still attached above the knot."

"A sen'gai? But those are the colors of Virésse!"

"So they are." Seregil returned to his inspection of Torsin's other hand with a sardonic grin. It was still bloated from lying in the water, but with the aid of a lamp he finally located a small puncture wound on the fleshy part of the palm just below the base of the thumb. He pressed the skin, and a globule of dark blood oozed out.

Thero drew a silver knife from his belt and gently scraped it up.

"Think there are any apaki'nhags slithering about in the Vhadä-soori?" asked Seregil.

"I very much doubt it. That doesn't look like snakebite."

"More like a needle or thorn puncture. Nyal must be right about the numbing effect of the poison. This went deep."

"So the poisoner followed him to the Vhadäsoori when he left

Ulan's house," Thero speculated. "Judging by this, they struggled. Torsin grasped at his attacker, pulling that bit of fringe from his sen'gai in his death throes."

They were interrupted by Alec's noisy entrance. "We found it!" he announced triumphantly. "There's a tiny mark on her left hand, between the first and second fingers."

"But I looked there," Seregil exclaimed. "How did you find it?"

Alec touched the dragon bite on his ear. "This gave me the idea. When we couldn't find anything, I tried rubbing lissik on her skin to bring out any breaks and there it was. It's marked for good now. The flesh is beginning to go white around it, too. Nyal says that's a sure sign."

"Well, we just found something similar on Torsin. And this." Seregil passed Alec the tassel. "Thero's speculated that Torsin's murderer followed him from the banquet, and that Torsin grappled with him and tore this from his head cloth. What do you think?"

Alec picked at the shred of cloth, then shook his head. "This was cut, not ripped. See how the weave is still straight? With this loose-woven cloth, the threads would be all ragged if anyone pulled on it hard enough to tear it. I'd say this was sent as a token, like the last one. Maybe Torsin went to the Vhadäsoori to meet someone. A Virésse."

"Possibly," said Seregil. "But if Nyal is right about how the poison works, he was dying before he got there. Then again, judging by the difference in the symptoms he and Klia have shown, it was probably his lungs that killed him, after all. The poison just hastened the inevitable."

"What I felt from the Cup of Aura bears that out," Thero agreed. "Still, he couldn't have known how ill he really was, or he'd have asked for help getting home."

Alec held up the tassel. "If we're right about this being a signal, he may have had reasons for wanting to go out alone."

Seregil examined the puncture again. "If this is apaki'nhag venom, then he was most likely poisoned at the banquet. If he and Klia were poisoned at roughly the same time, which seems likely, then perhaps our poisoner miscalculated its effects, given Torsin's condition."

"Maybe they even intended for suspicion to fall on the Haman the way it did," Alec speculated. "It was no secret that we were hunting with them."

"And yet here we have evidence of the Virésse," said Thero, indicating the tassel.

"And they traffic with Plenimar," said Alec. "I'll bet you a gold sester that if we find the device our murderer used, it will be Plenimaran."

"I'd back your side of that wager," Seregil said. "I'll ask Adzriel if she can smooth my way to searching the house of Ulan í Sathil. Thero, if I do find the object used, you might be able to divine who used it."

"Or the missing warding charm," said Alec.

"What?" asked Seregil, eyes narrowing.

"He's missing a warding charm," Alec told him, pointing at the dead man's left wrist. "Torsin had a warding charm just like mine, remember?"

"It was to warn of ill-wishing, wasn't it? I see yours is gone, too."

"It's a long story, but I know Torsin still had his a day or two ago. I remember seeing him fiddle with it when we were greeting visitors on the final day of mourning."

"If we could find that, it could tell us who poisoned him," Thero said hopefully. "I've been talking with our Akhendi friends. People of that clan can sometimes sense details from the spent charms."

"He could have taken it off, in which case it's probably here somewhere," said Seregil.

A thorough search of the room turned up nothing, however.

"Maybe he lost it," Alec suggested, giving up. "Or someone took it. I say we look for it at Ulan í Sathil's house." He held up the tassel again. "They certainly have reason to want Klia out of the way, they had her and Torsin in easy reach, and they'd know about that snake poison."

Seregil tapped a finger against his lips, frowning as another thought occurred. "The same might be said of most of the eastern clans. The Ra'basi, for instance."

Alec groaned. "Oh, Illior, are we back to that again?"

"Back to what?" asked Thero.

"Maybe nothing, except that I haven't quite trusted Nyal since we met," Seregil explained, taking little pleasure in the thought. "The Ra'basi aren't exactly neutral parties in the negotiations, and as Alec just pointed out, they'd have knowledge of the poison in question."

"Anyone could have known," Thero pointed out.

"Yes, but who else has come and gone here freely from the start? With the exception of the Bôkthersans, what Aurënfaie has had closer contact with Klia and Torsin?"

"And Beka," Alec added unhappily.

"But he's the one who alerted you to the poison!" Thero exclaimed.

Seregil shrugged. "He wouldn't be the first murderer to cover his tracks by bustling in helpfully after the damage is done. He's been everywhere Klia has the past day or so. He knew Torsin was ill, and how the poison worked."

"But that seems like all the more reason not to tell us what it was," Alec insisted. "Go slowly with this, Seregil. Accusing him falsely won't hurt just him. Think of Beka."

"Yes, but what about his tragic romantic attachment to Amali ä Yassara? You once said you thought I disliked him because he was too much like myself. If you're right, we have good reason to distrust him. How many times do you suppose I've ingratiated myself with a mark, or gotten into a place to spy by way of the bedchamber?"

Alec gave him a humorless smirk. "More often than I want to know about, obviously."

"The Akhendi could be his next targets for all we know," mused Thero.

"I say we keep quiet until we have more proof," Alec warned, still doubtful. "Beka's already given orders to keep out anyone but Bôkthersans. Can't we let it go at that for now?"

"We're a long way from making any accusations yet," Seregil admitted, running a hand back through his tangled hair. "In the meantime, I don't want him to guess we suspect him. Just make certain he's not left alone with Klia."

"All the same, there are still too many other possibilities," said Thero. "If Klia and Torsin were both poisoned at the Virésse banquet, which seems as good a theory as any, then it narrows our field of suspects down to—"

"Just about everyone in the whole damn city," Alec finished for him. "There were hundreds of people there."

"Except Emiel í Moranthi," said Seregil.

"We're standing on smoke," Alec muttered.

"Yes, we are," Seregil agreed. "But this is a start toward something more solid." He took a last look at Torsin's hand; with the dark blood cleaned away, the puncture mark was practically invisible again. "I want you to keep this discovery to yourselves for a while. Act as if you think his death was a natural one."

"What about Nyal?" asked Thero.

"Tell him we found nothing. If he or someone else knows otherwise, sooner or later they may let it slip." Arranging the dead man's hands on his chest, Seregil turned for the door. "Let's go see what our helpful Ra'basi is up to now."

They didn't have far to go. Emerging from Torsin's room, they met Nyal and Mydri in the hall, accompanying Klia as she was carried to her bedchamber on a litter.

Dread washed over Seregil, seeing the pallor of death in her face. Only the slight rise and fall of her chest showed she still lived.

"An infusion of black tea steeped in brandy may help her breathing," Nyal advised. "Otherwise, there's little to do but keep her warm and wait for it to run its course."

Looking up at Seregil, he raised an expectant eyebrow. "Was Torsin poisoned, do you think?"

"No. It's as we thought, a failure of the lungs."

The Ra'basi seemed to accept this. Even as he surreptitiously watched him, however, Seregil felt a twinge of regret, thinking again of Nyal's kindness to him after his ill-fated walk in Haman tupa. In spite of everything else he might suspect, somewhere along the way, he'd begun to like the man.

When Klia was settled in bed, Alec showed them a tiny spot of blue between her fingers. Even with the lissik, it was just a pinprick surrounded by a patch of bleached flesh.

"It's spreading," Nyal said, frowning as he pressed at the white skin.

"This is what apaki'nhag bites look like?" asked Seregil.

"Yes, but not until after the person has already sickened. The venom slowly kills the flesh around the bite. This area will turn black soon and may have to be cut away, if she survives."

No wonder they'd missed the bite on Torsin, thought Seregil. Not only was the hand bloated from being in the water, but Torsin had died too quickly for the telltale signs to appear.

"If?" Alec croaked. "But she's made it this long—"

Nyal placed a hand on his shoulder. "There are many kinds of apaki'nhag, some more venomous than others. The symptoms are the same, only the result differs. Some victims survive unscathed. Others are left blind or crippled."

Seregil pressed a hand to Klia's moist brow, then bent close to her ear. "No matter what happens, I'm not leaving Aurënen until I know who did this to you, and why."

He straightened and looked at Nyal a moment without speaking.

"What is it?" the older man asked.

"This is a dangerous time for us here. Your own clan may fall under suspicion before I'm finished. Will you stand by us?"

"As long as I can act with honor," Nyal assured him earnestly. "What of Beka's order, though? I'm not even supposed to be here."

"Keep to the barracks for now. I'll sort it out when she gets back. If you need to go out, be sure to let someone know in case Mydri needs you."

"I'll do whatever I can." With a last sad look at Klia, Nyal went out. Seregil counted to three, then peered around the doorframe in time to see the Ra'basi meet Sergeant Mercalle and several of her riders on the back staircase. They spoke briefly, then Nyal continued down.

Seregil stepped out to meet Mercalle.

"We're here to relieve Rhylin," she told him.

Mydri came out to join them. "Seregil, would you ask one of the cooks to send up a honey poultice, hot water, and clean rags? I'm going to do everything I can to save that hand."

Kheeta hurried up the front stairs. "Is Alec here? Säaban and the others are waiting out front."

"I'm here," Alec said, coming out to join them. "I'll be there in a moment."

"You'd better wear your sword," Seregil said.

Alec glanced down in surprise. "I've gotten out of the habit. It's upstairs."

Seregil clasped him by the shoulder. "Good hunting, talí, and be careful."

Alec smiled slightly. "I was about to say the same to you. I've got the easier task, I think."

"Probably. I doubt Ulan will be glad to see me again so soon."

He watched Alec out of sight, then went out the back way toward his sister's house.

Alec retrieved his sword belt from the bedpost and buckled it on as he hurried back down. In his haste, he nearly fell over Beka, who was sitting alone on the stairs just below the second-floor landing. She shifted closer to the wall but remained where she was, the picture of exhaustion.

"When did you get back?" he asked.

"Just now. I'm on my way up to see her, but I needed a moment alone. This seemed as good a place as any."

"There's no change."

"So I heard. It's good news in its way, I guess."

"Have the Haman done anything interesting?"

"Not a thing. Steb told me about Seregil's run-in with Emiel last night. Is he all right?"

"Oh, yes. Seems more his old self than he has for days, in fact." Alec hesitated, then said quietly, "About Nyal—"

"You think he has something to do with all this, don't you?" She looked down at her clasped hands.

"Seregil does, but so far it's just a hunch."

She sighed. "I've asked him to come back to Skala with me."

Alec blinked in surprise. "What did he say?"

"He asked me to stay. I can't."

"Are you—I mean, I heard—" Alec broke off, feeling himself blushing.

"Pregnant?" Beka favored him with a dark look. "Heard about the bounty, did you? It wasn't an order, just an opportunity. Kipa and Ileah think they may be. It's not the road for me." She yawned suddenly, pressing a hand over her mouth. "You'd better get moving."

"And you'd better get some rest." Alec started down, then paused a few steps below her and reached to grip her by the knee. "Just— well, be careful."

She gave him a sour scowl. "I'm not love blind, Alec. I just hope Seregil's wrong."

"So do I."

A sizable entourage awaited Alec in front of the house. Säaban and Kheeta had half a dozen kinsmen with them, all with swords and bows. Braknil and his decuria flanked them, dressed for battle.

"Have you something of Klia's for me?" asked Säaban, his long face graver than usual beneath his dark green sen'gai.

Alec handed him the tunic Klia had worn to the hunt, still stained with dirt and blood. Säaban held it between his hands for a moment, then nodded. "Good. The feeling of her khi is strong. I can even sense her illness. If she touched some object that caused her harm and it is there, I should be able to sense it. It does take great concentration, however. I can't just ride along picking things out of the air."

"But if I show you where she fell, you could check the immediate area, couldn't you? Emiel may have dropped the ring or whatever it was into the stream."

Säaban shrugged. "It is possible."

Possible. Alec sighed, doubting they'd come back anything but empty-handed. "All right, then. Let's get going."

• • •

They followed the same route as before, riding hard for stretches, stopping when Alec recognized places they'd halted the previous day.

This was the first time since his arrival that he'd had the opportunity for any extended conversation with Säaban, and it occurred to Alec as they rode that if not for the standing ban against Seregil, he and Säaban would be calling each other kin.

The man's quiet demeanor made him easily overlooked at banquets. Today, however, he proved to be a valuable companion, a skilled and patient tracker. He reminded Alec of Micum Cavish, and the similarity was underscored by the sword at Säaban's side. The hilt was worn with use, the scabbard scarred and weathered.

"I've been meaning to ask you something," Alec said as they combed a site together on foot. "Killing is forbidden, and murder is rare among the 'faie, yet your sword has clearly seen some use."

"As has yours," Säaban replied with a knowing look at Alec's scabbard. "We fight Zengati raiders, mostly. The slavers grow bolder by the decade."

"I thought Seregil's father made peace with them?"

"With some, not all. They're a tribal people, not controlled by any one ruler. Rather like the Aurënfaie, I suppose," he added with a fleeting smile.

"And there are bandits in the mountains, too," said Kheeta, whose scabbard showed considerably less wear. "There's a troublesome band of them who range north of Bôkthersa—a real mongrel pack: teth'brimash, mostly, with some Zengati and Dravnians mixed in. They steal, slave, whatever takes their fancy." He tugged proudly at his lock of white hair. "That's how I got this. The first time I went out to fight them, one of the faithless bastards tried to take my head off. I dodged just in time to get away with a nick, then returned the favor, but lower."

"We may abhor fighting, but those of us who live on the coasts and borders must train our children to the bow and sword as soon as they can hold them," said Säaban.

"Then it wasn't just life in Skala that made Seregil so good?"

Kheeta snorted. "No, he comes from a long line of swordsmen: his father, his uncle, their father before them."

"That's the way it is with our people, too," said Sergeant Braknil, who'd been following the conversation.

"I've watched you Skalans at your practices," said Kheeta. "I would rather fight beside you than against you."

"We should put on a demonstration for the Iia'sidra," Alec joked. "Maybe that would sway them to helping us."

"The final outcome of the vote will have little to do with Skala." Säaban told him.

"What about what's happened to Klia and Torsin? I thought the harming of a guest was a great crime, especially at Sarikali," said Alec.

"It is a grievous offense, but it is a matter of atui, not unlike what happened when Seregil committed his unfortunate act. Bôkthersa was banned from the Iia'sidra until the matter was tried and teth'sag satisfied, just as the Haman are now."

"It was only out of respect for the rhui'auros that the matter was settled as it was," said Kheeta.

"The rhui'auros?" Alec looked at the two men in surprise.

Säaban exchanged a look with Kheeta. "Then it is true. Seregil has not told you what happened."

"Not much." Alec shifted uncomfortably. "Just that the Iia'sidra spared his life after he was questioned by a rhui'auros."

"It was the rhui'auros who saved Seregil from execution, not the Iia'sidra," Säaban explained. "His guilt was clear and the Haman demanded the two bowls in spite of his youth. Korit í Solun did not contest the sentence. Before it could be carried out, however, a rhui'auros intervened, asking that Seregil be brought to Sarikali. He was in the Nha'mahat for three days. At the end, the rhui'auros themselves ordered his banishment. Seregil was transported directly to Virésse and sent to Skala."

"Three days?" Alec recalled how uneasy Seregil had been that night they'd gone there. "What did they do to him?"

"No one knows exactly, but I was there when he came out afterward," Kheeta replied, suddenly grim. "He wouldn't look at any of us, and wouldn't speak. The ride to Virésse took over a week, and he hardly said a word the whole way. The one time I got close enough to talk to him, he said he wished they'd just killed him."

"Some say the rhui'auros took part of his khi from him," Säaban murmured.

"I think it was Ilar who did that," said Alec. "But you said that what's happened here now is somehow the same?"

"In some ways," the older Bôkthersan replied. "As a descendant of Corruth í Glamien, Klia may be able to claim teth'sag. In the meantime, a clan under suspicion cannot vote."

"And if guilt is not proven?"

Säaban spread his hands. "Then teth'sag cannot be carried out. How do you mean to proceed, if you do not find what you are looking for in the forest?"

"I suppose we begin with anyone who had the most reason to hurt Klia. The way I see it, that brings in the Virésse first of all, since they're the ones with the most to lose. Then there are the Khatme, who hate us because we're Tír, outsiders."

Säaban considered this. "There's sense in what you say, yet you are thinking with the mind of a Tír. This outrage was committed by an Aurënfaie. Their reasons might not be what you suppose."

"You're saying I should think like an Aurënfaie?"

"As you are not one, I doubt that's possible, any more than I could think like a murderer. It's madness to kill another. How can one think like a madman unless you are mad yourself?"

Alec smiled. "Seregil claims that Aurënfaie have no talent for murder. Where I'm from, it comes a bit easier to most—whether they're doing it or just thinking of it."

They reached the clearing at midmorning and found everything as it had been the day before. The ash in the fire circles was damp and undisturbed. Flies buzzed lazily over the piles of offal left where hunters had cleaned their kill.

Alec could still make out Klia's footprints beside the cascading series of pools. "It was here that I found her and Emiel," he told Säaban, showing him the spot.

The Bôkthersan draped Klia's tunic over one shoulder and began a tuneless humming.

The pool Alec had found her beside yielded nothing. However, a few yards downstream Säaban halted suddenly and plunged his hand into the water, bringing up a sodden arrowhead pouch. An ivory plaque on one of the drawstrings showed the flame and crescent device of the Skalan royal house.

"It's Klia's, all right," Alec said, examining it. "It must have come loose during the struggle."

Säaban held the pouch in one hand, concentrating. When he spoke again, his voice had a high, singsong timbre. "Yes. Her legs gave way and she fell, choking on water. Her face—her eyelids were heavy, stiff."

"Emiel?" Alec asked hopefully.

Säaban shook his head. "I'm sorry, Alec. It is only Klia I feel on this."

They spent the next hour searching but turned up nothing but a few lost buttons and a Skalan amulet.

Searching the edges of the main clearing, Alec looked up to see Säaban on the far side, rubbing wearily at his forehead. He'd made no complaint, but Alec guessed that even for the 'faie magic took a toll on the user.

He slowly retraced the way Klia and Emiel had taken down to the stream, poking into clumps of dead leaves and bracken along the way. Reaching the spot where he'd overtaken them, he looked around again. The only other marks were those left by the soldiers who'd carried Klia up the slope to her horse, a steeper but more direct route than the path. Following this, he cast back and forth as he worked his way up the hillside. The ground here was covered with dead leaves and fresh new undergrowth; an easy place to lose a small item. Säaban followed, humming softly to himself as he searched in his own fashion.

Reaching the top, Alec turned and started down again, knowing that things always looked different with a change of direction. Halfway down, his patience was rewarded with a glimpse of something in a clump of tiny pink flowers.

Alec went down on one knee, heart suddenly beating faster. It was an Akhendi bracelet, half trampled into the soft ground. Pulling it free, he saw that it was the one he'd watched Amali make for Klia that first night in Sarikali; there was no mistaking the complicated pattern on the band. The ties had broken, but the bird-shaped charm still hung from it, coated in mud. Alec used the hem of his shirt to clean it, then let out a low whistle of triumph.

The pale wood had gone a telltale black.

"Ah, no wonder I missed this," Säaban said, though he looked a bit chagrined. "The magic on it interferes with my own. Are you certain it is Klia's?"

"Yes, I saw it on her yesterday morning." He touched the charm. "And this was still white. I don't suppose you can tell anything from it?"

"No. You'd best take it to an Akhendi."

For the first time that day, Alec smiled. "I know just the Akhendi for the task."

Kheeta's grin mirrored his own. "Let's hope Seregil is as lucky with his search."

34
Investigations

Seregil paced impatiently around his sister's hall, waiting for her to rise and dress. Adzriel appeared at last, looking anything but rested. Declining her offer of breakfast, he quickly outlined his intentions.

"Must it be you?" she asked. "The Iia'sidra must approve such a search, and having you involved will not sit well with most of them."

"I have to get in there. Thero will be in charge, of course, but I have to be there. By the Light, I'd have done it my own way long before now if we were anywhere else but here. If Ulan is our poisoner, he's already had too much time to do away with any evidence."

"I'll do what I can," she said at last. "There must be no soldiers, though."

"Fine. I assume the other khirnari will insist on being there?"

"Brythir í Nien, at least. Any accusations at Sarikali must be made before him. Give me time to call the assembly. An hour at the very least."

Seregil was already halfway to the door. "I'll meet you there. There's someone else I need to speak with first."

I'm getting to be a regular visitor here, he thought as he came in sight of the Nha'mahat. Dismounting at a safe distance, he crossed the dew-laden grass, keeping an eye out for fingerlings. There were plenty about at this hour, frisking and flapping over the morning offerings in the temple porch.

"I wish to speak with Elesarit," he told the masked attendant who met him at the door.

"I am he, little brother," the old man replied, ushering him inside.

To Seregil's considerable relief, the rhui'auros bypassed the stairs to the cavern, taking him instead up to a small, sparsely furnished room. On the open terrace Seregil saw breakfast laid for two on a little table. Several fingerlings had worried a loaf of dark bread to bits across its polished surface. Laughing, the rhui'auros shooed them away and tossed the crumbs after them.

"Come, you have had nothing to eat in almost a day," he said, uncovering dishes containing Skalan cheeses and hot meats. He filled a plate and set it before Seregil.

"You were expecting me?" Seregil's belly growled appreciatively as he speared a sausage with a knife and wolfed it down. The food suddenly seemed to stick in his throat, however, as he noticed a platter of oat cakes dripping with butter and honey. Nysander had always served them at his extravagant morning meals.

"You miss him a great deal, do you not, little brother?" asked Elesarit, his own food untouched before him. He'd removed his mask, revealing a lined face both kindly and serene.

"Yes, I do," Seregil replied softly.

"Sometimes sorrow is a better guide than joy."

Nodding, Seregil took a bite of oat cake. "Did you send Nyal to me this morning?"

"He came, did he not?"

"Yes. If it hadn't been for him, we might not have figured out what was wrong with Klia, or how to help her."

The rhui'auros's brows arched dramatically. Under different circumstances, the effect would have been comical. "Someone has harmed your princess?"

"You didn't know? Then why did you send Nyal?"

The old man eyed him slyly and said nothing.

Seregil fought back his impatience. Like the Oracles of Illior, the rhui'auros were said to be possessed by the madness that came of being touched by the divine. This fellow was clearly no exception.

"Why did you send him to me?" he tried again.

"I did not send him to you."

"But you just said—" Seregil broke off, too tired to deal with subtle games and riddles. "Why am I here, then?"

"For the sake of your princess?" the man offered, seeming equally mystified.

"Very well, then. Since you were expecting me, you must have had *something* to say to me."

A dragon the size of a large cat crawled out from under the table and leapt into the rhui'auros's lap. He stroked its smooth back absently for a moment, then looked up at Seregil with vague, unfocused eyes.

Pinned by that strange gaze, Seregil felt an uneasy chill crawl slowly up his back. The dragon was watching him, too, and there was more intelligence in its yellow eyes than in those of the man who held it.

Elesarit suddenly thrust his clenched fist across at Seregil, who recoiled instinctively.

"You'll be needing this, little brother."

Hesitantly, Seregil held out his hand, palm up, to receive whatever the man was offering. Something smooth and cool dropped into his hand. For an instant he thought it was another of the mysterious orbs from his dreams. Instead, he found himself holding a slender vial fashioned of dark, iridescent blue glass and capped with a delicate silver stopper. It was exquisite.

"This is Plenimaran," he said, recognizing the workmanship with a thrill of anticipation, even as another part of his mind piped in, *too easy.*

"Is it?" Elesarit leaned over for a closer look. "He who has two hearts is twice as strong, ya'shel khi."

Only half listening to the man's nonsensical ramblings, Seregil uncapped the vial and took a cautious sniff, wishing he'd thought to ask Nyal what apaki'nhag venom smelled like. The acrid aroma was disappointingly familiar. Tipping out a drop, he rubbed it between a thumb and finger. "It's just lissik."

"Did you expect something else?"

Seregil replaced the stopper without comment. He was wasting his time here.

"A gift, little brother," Elesarit chided gently. "Take what the Lightbearer sends and be thankful. What we expect is not always what we need."

Seregil resisted the urge to sling the bottle across the room. "Unless that dragon of yours is about to bite me, I'm not certain what to be thankful *for*, Honored One."

Elesarit regarded him with a mix of pity and affection. "You have a most stubborn mind, dear boy."

Cold sweat broke out across Seregil's shoulders; Nysander had said these very words to him during his last vision. Seregil glanced at the oat cakes again, then back at the rhui'auros, half hoping to catch another glimpse of his old friend.

Elesarit shook his head sadly. "Seldom have we seen one fight his gifts as you do, Seregil í Korit."

Disappointment shot through with vague guilt settled in Seregil's gut like a bad dinner. He missed Nysander terribly, missed the old wizard's quick mind and clarity. He might have kept secrets, but he never spoke in riddles.

"I'm sorry, Honored One," he managed at last. "If I do have some gift, it's never worked for me."

"Of course it does, little brother. It is from Illior."

"Then tell me what it is!"

"So many questions! Soon you must begin to ask the *right* ones. Smiles conceal knives."

The right questions? "Who murdered Torsin?"

"You already know." The old man gestured at the door, no longer smiling. "Go now. You have work to do!"

The dragon spread its wings and bared needle-sharp fangs at him, hissing menacingly. The unsettling sound followed Seregil as he beat a hasty retreat into the corridor. Glancing back over his shoulder, he saw with alarm that the creature was in fact chasing him. A peal of laughter rang out behind him from the open doorway.

Getting down three flights of stairs with a dragon, even a small one, slithering after you was not a pleasant experience. On the second landing Seregil turned to shoo it away and the creature flew at him, snapping at his outstretched hand.

Admitting defeat, he fled. More laughter, eerily disembodied now, sounded close to his ear.

His fiesty pursuer gave up somewhere between the last stairway and the meditation chamber. He stole frequent glances over his shoulder all the same until he was outside again. Fingerlings frisked around his feet, chirping and fluttering. Picking his way gingerly past them, he hurried to his horse. It wasn't until he reached to undo the hobble that he realized he was still clutching the vial of lissik.

Did I really expect the rhui'auros to hand me the murderer's weapon? he thought derisively, pocketing it.

Cynril's steady pace calmed him. As his mind cleared, he slowly began combing Elesarit's ravings for whatever message lay concealed there. In his heart, Seregil knew better than to dismiss the words of any rhui'auros as nonsense; their madness masked the face of Illior.

"Illior!" he murmured aloud, realizing that Elesarit had used the

Skalan name for the god rather than Aura. It was like finding the free end in a tangled skein—knots began to unravel as he followed it.

He who has two hearts is twice as strong, ya'shel khi.

Ya'shel khi. Half-breed soul. The words filled him with an odd mix of dread and elation.

He returned to the guest house to find the place in an uproar.

"Klia's awake!" Sergeant Mercalle told him as he hurried in. "She can't move or speak, but her eyes are open."

Seregil didn't wait to hear more. Bounding upstairs, he found Mydri, Thero, and Nyal bending anxiously over the bed.

"Thank Aura!" he exclaimed softly, taking her hand in his. It was bandaged, he noticed, and smelled of herbs and honey. She looked up at him, her eyes aware and full of pain.

"Can you hear me, Klia? Blink if you understand."

Klia's discolored eyelids slowly raised and lowered. The left moved more than the right, which sagged alarmingly.

"Does she know all that's happened, what we've learned so far?" he asked Thero. "Can you tell who did this?"

"Her thoughts are still too confused."

"I'm going to find out," Seregil promised, stroking her cheek. "I swear I'll see teth'sag invoked against them in the Iia'sidra."

Klia gave a small, hoarse groan and her eyes closed.

He motioned the others into the corridor and closed the door. "Does this mean she'll live?"

"It's a hopeful sign," Nyal replied, clearly still cautious. "It could be days before she can speak."

"What about her hand?"

"The area around the wound is spreading," Mydri said.

"You think she could lose it?"

"If the flesh rots, as Nyal expects, then yes. But we must give the poultice time to work."

"Do whatever you have to, short of amputation," Seregil pleaded. "Thero, I need you. Can you come with me to Ulan's?"

The wizard looked at Mydri, who nodded. "Yes, Thero, you've done all you can for now. Go do what you must."

Seregil and Thero arrived at the Iia'sidra to find a solemn gathering awaiting them. It was the right of any khirnari not directly involved to witness the questioning of another, and close to a dozen had opted to claim the right, among them Khatme, Akhendi, Lhapnos, Golinfl, and Ra'basi, Bry'kha, and several lesser clans. Escorted by a small honor guard of Silmai, they proceeded on foot to Virésse tupa. From the outset, Seregil was careful to be seen deferring to Thero.

Ulan greeted them with surprising cordiality. "I would offer you a meal, but given the circumstances, the usual gestures seem inappropriate."

Prepared in advance by Adzriel, Thero bowed slightly and gave the expected response. "Your offer of hospitality is understood, Khirnari. Aura grant that you be proven innocent."

"My house is a large one, as you know," Ulan said, leading them to the garden where the banquet had been held. "Do you mean to search the entire place?"

"Seregil will assist me as I scry," Thero replied.

"Scry?" said Elos. "How do you mean to do that?"

"I shall employ this." The wizard produced a square of stained linen. "This is blood from the wound on Klia's hand," he explained, not adding that some of Torsin's was there, as well.

"Blood magic? Necromancy!" Lhaär ä Iriel hissed, making a sign in Thero's direction.

The Khatme was not alone in her disapproval, Seregil noted, watching the others uneasily.

"Brythir í Nien, how can you allow such an abomination?" Moriel ä Moriel exclaimed.

"The use of blood is only incidental. It's not necromancy of any sort," Thero assured them. "If Klia was stuck with a sharp object, as we suspect, then some of her blood and the poison remains on it, as it does on this cloth. It's nothing but a finding spell, like calling to like."

"The 'faie have similar magicks," Brythir said, leaning on Adzriel's arm. "Unless my fellow khirnari intend to demand a vote, I say you may do so, Thero í Procepios."

"I pray you, grant him leave to proceed," Ulan added. "I have nothing to hide."

"Thank you, Khirnari," said Thero. "First, was an Akhendi charm found anywhere in your tupa after the banquet?"

"No, nothing of that sort."

"Very well." Going to a stone bench that stood nearby, Thero spread the stained cloth out and wove a spell over it with his wand. The others watched with growing interest as the colored patterns twisted in and out of existence at his command.

Seregil quietly turned his attention to the immense garden. The trappings of the banquet had been cleared away, of course. Recalling how the various tables had been set up, he began a methodical search of the area, hoping to find the lost charm, if nothing else.

Unfortunately, Ulan's servants had been thorough in their tidying up. He didn't find so much as an overlooked mussel shell or lost knife.

"I have the sense of something lying in that direction," Thero announced at last, motioning vaguely to the wing of the house where the khirnari's rooms lay.

They moved on, passing along the same corridors Seregil and Alec had walked a few nights earlier. Seregil guided Thero, who walked with eyes half closed, his wand held out before him between his upraised palms.

The wizard's face registered nothing but detached concentration until they reached the garden court where Ulan's private chambers lay. Suddenly his eyes snapped open and he looked around, brow furrowed. "Yes, there's something here, but it's still very faint."

Too easy, Seregil thought again, rifling his way once more through the bedchamber and sitting room. It was a bit distracting, doing this in broad daylight with an audience that included the owner of the room. It felt indecent, really, like having someone watch you take a crap. The day had turned warm, and sweat trickled down his back and sides as he worked.

Again, he found nothing. "Are you certain about this?" he muttered, coming back to Thero, who was standing by the fish pool.

Thero nodded. "It's unclear, I admit, but it's here."

Pondering what corners he might have missed, Seregil stared down at the fragrant white water lilies floating on the pool's dark surface. Fish darted below the round, green leaves like half-glimpsed inspirations. A single dead fish floating in a far corner of the pool was the only jarring element; no doubt the usually fastidious khirnari had more pressing things on his mind since Klia's collapse than the care of his fish pool.

The others were watching his every move with varying degrees of interest or hostility. Doing his best to ignore them, Seregil looked around the courtyard again. If Thero said there was something here, then something was here. It was just a matter of looking in the right place.

Or asking the right questions.

The masses of white peonies and roses caught his eye; he didn't much relish the idea of uprooting them without good cause. Red

damsel flies darted around the blooms. One strayed to land on the
lip of a lily pad. A fish flashed up and swallowed it.

"They are always hungry," Ulan murmured, lifting the cover
from a bowl set into the rim of the pool. He scattered a handful of
crumbs, and the calm water churned as more fish rose to snatch up
the morsels.

The dead fish reclaimed Seregil's attention. It was a large one,
longer than his hand, and its scales were still bright. That, and the
fact that its hungry companions hadn't begun picking at it yet, suggested that it hadn't been dead long.

Curious, he walked around to where it floated and scooped it
up for closer inspection. Its dark eyes were still clear. Yes, freshly dead.

"May I borrow a knife?" Seregil asked, careful to keep the rising
excitement out of his voice.

This violated the terms of his return, but the Silmai elder himself
handed Seregil a dagger.

He slit the belly with a single stroke and was rewarded with a
glint of steel among the guts. With the tip of the dagger, he extracted
a plain ring. Not so plain after all, though, he thought, discovering a
tiny barb protruding from its outer rim.

The others crowded around, muttering excitedly. Seregil looked
over their heads at Ulan í Sathil, who stood unmoved near the roses.
His face betrayed no guilty blanch, no panicked admission.

I wouldn't like to play cards against you, Seregil thought with a
certain grudging respect.

"A clever piece of work, this," he remarked, showing the others
how the barb could be extended and retracted by means of a lever
set inside the band. "The Plenimarans rather poetically call this a
kar'makti. It means 'hummingbird's tongue.' With some, the barb is
dipped in poison. Others have a reservoir inside the ring. We'd better handle it carefully until I figure out which sort it is. It could still
be dangerous."

"But how could such an odd-looking ornament go unnoticed?"
asked Adzriel.

"See these?" Seregil showed her several traces of gold on the
ring's edges. "It was fitted inside a larger ring, which would in turn
have a hole for the barb to fit out through."

"Can you produce this other ring?" the old Silmai asked Ulan.

"I cannot, because I own no such ring, nor have I ever," the
Virésse replied. "Anyone could have dropped this thing here."

"You seem to know quite a lot about such devices, Exile," the Khatme khirnari observed, turning on Seregil.

"In Skala it was my business to know," Seregil replied, letting her make of that what she would. "Have you ever seen this object before, Ulan í Sathil?"

"Certainly not!" Ulan said, bridling at last. "I give my oath before Aura and the khi of my father. Violence may well have been done under my roof; I accept the dishonor of that. But it was not done by me."

Seregil made certain the barb was fully retracted before passing it to Thero. "Can you divine anything from this?"

The wizard pressed the ring between his palms and muttered a quick spell. "It will take a more concentrated effort."

"May I?" asked Adzriel. After a moment, however, she shook her head as well and gave it back to Thero.

"Either it was too long inside the fish or someone has purposefully masked it," he said. "Given the difficulty I had finding it in the first place, I'd guess the latter."

They'd have done better to retract the barb, thought Seregil. "You sense nothing else in the house?"

"No. There's little more to be learned here."

"Except that our poisoner was a man," Seregil said, fitting the ring easily onto his forefinger. "And that he had a knowledge of eastern sea snakes and Plenimaran poisoning tricks."

"All of which points to a Virésse, I suppose?" said Elos í Orian, standing protectively by Ulan.

"Not conclusively," Seregil replied. He turned to go, then paused, as if he'd just remembered something. "There was one other thing I meant to ask about, Khirnari." He took the Virésse tassel from his pouch and held it up for the others to see. "This was found in Lord Torsin's hand after he died. Was someone of your clan in the habit of sending these to him to signal a secret assignation?"

The khirnari's eyes narrowed slightly, and Seregil sensed he'd at last managed to take the man by surprise. "I did so," Ulan admitted. "But not that night. Why would I, when the man was in my own house?"

"Yet who else but a Virésse would have such a token to send?" asked the Silmai. "I fear Virésse must remain under interdiction, Ulan. Until we have cleared this matter up to the satisfaction of the Skalans, you may not vote with the Iia'sidra."

Ulan í Sathil bowed to the elder khirnari. "So it must be. I will do all in my power to bring justice to the Skalans for the injuries they have suffered beneath my roof."

"What was the reason for your secret meetings with Torsin?" asked Seregil.

"That has nothing to do with this!" Ulan objected.

That definitely struck a nerve.

Thero stepped in smoothly. "For the time being, Khirnari, I speak for Princess Klia and must know of any dealings between the two of you, no matter what they relate to."

Ulan looked to the Silmai khirnari, but found no help there. "Very well, but I must insist we speak privately."

Ulan had clearly intended to exclude Seregil, but Thero motioned for him to follow, as if he could not imagine being denied his adviser.

Smothering a grin of admiration, Seregil squared his shoulders and followed the two men into Ulan í Sathil's inner chamber. Once alone with the khirnari, however, his amusement quickly died.

"May I see the tassel?" Ulan asked. He maintained the semblance of respect, but his eyes were cold as he examined the hank of silk. "This was certainly cut from a Virésse sen'gai, but not one of mine. As khirnari, mine have a thread of darker red woven in among the others. This one does not.

"As for the death of Torsin í Xandus, it is as great a loss to me as it is to you. He has been a great friend of mine for many years. He understood the workings of the Iia'sidra better than any Tírfaie I have known."

"And he was sympathetic to the plight of Virésse," Thero put in.

Seregil watched in amazement. Young as he was, Thero appeared to consider himself a match for this venerable intriguer. There was not the least show of hesitancy as he met the khirnari's appraising stare.

"What were you discussing with him, those times you met?" the wizard asked. "A separate deal of some sort, one that would protect the interests of your clan?"

Ulan gave a condescending nod. "But of course. We were working toward a compromise, one your Princess Klia was quite aware of: open trade through Gedre for the duration of the Skalan's war, but with the understanding that when the need was gone, control of shipping would return to Virésse. Many of my fellow khirnari have grave misgivings about Klia's original proposal, given the character of your new queen."

"And you made certain they knew of her flaws," Seregil said quietly.

Ulan inclined his head as if accepting a compliment. "Gedre is too remote, too unguarded, and too weak a clan to protect itself, should Phoria renege on her agreements. Who is to say that a woman who would betray her own land, her own mother, would not seek to possess the riches Aurënen can offer, once she has seen how to get at them?"

And what was your plan, before Phoria was queen? Seregil wondered with grudging admiration. How many different scenarios had the man prepared for to protect his clan's interests? He'd held his secrets about Phoria in reserve, to be played like a winning hand of cards. What would he have done with them if Idrilain were still hale and hearty on the throne?

"It's Plenimar's capture of the northern trade routes that's put Skala in need," Thero was saying.

"I'm aware of that, as it was Skala's rather possessive control of that same route which cemented the bonds of trade between Plenimar and the eastern clans these past few centuries," Ulan replied. "Win or lose, Plenimar remains the more attractive suitor for Aurënen's affections."

"Despite the fact that they have been courting Zengati support against Aurënen in the event that the Iia'sidra votes in Skala's favor?" asked Seregil.

Ulan gave him a condescending look. "You haven't heard? The Zengati have troubles of their own just now. Tribal war has broken out again, as it does periodically among that excitable race."

"You're certain of this?" Thero gasped.

"My spies there are most reliable. I cannot give them credit by name, of course, but I suspect Seregil would recognize one or two of them."

"Ilar?" Seregil rasped as a bolt of sick apprehension tore through him. "He's alive?"

The khirnari smile was inscrutable. "I have had no communication with that man since his disappearance, but even if it were he, surely you of all people must admit that exiles may have their uses?"

Since his disappearance? Why would the khirnari of Virésse know a young Chyptaulos at all, unless he had good reason to? Meeting Ulan's cool gaze, Seregil knew in his bones what the answer to that question would be. He knew with equal certainty that

Ulan would never reveal that truth unless it were in his own interest to do so.

"The timing of this tribal war was very fortunate," Thero observed. "It would have been disastrous for Aurënen if the Zengati and Plenimar forged a bond."

"Luck can be an expensive thing," Ulan replied with a meaningful look. "Yet who can put a price on the security of one's homeland? But that need not concern you, as it may work to your benefit one day."

"You believe Plenimar will win this time, don't you?" asked Seregil, controlling himself with an effort.

"Yes. Why sacrifice Aurënfaie lives, Aurënfaie magic, to a lost cause?"

"How could Torsin agree to such an arrangement?" Thero demanded angrily.

"He is a Tírfaie, measuring the future in his own short spans. The same can be said of Klia and her line, clever though they undoubtedly are." Ulan waved a dismissive hand at them. "The two of you are still too young to see how slowly the tides of history turn. It is not that I wish to see Skala suffer; I am determined that Virésse shall not. Daughter of Idrilain or not, Phoria will not prove a worthy ally."

"But the Overlord of Plenimar and his necromancers will?" Seregil exclaimed. "The name of Raghar Ashnazai is not unknown to you, Khirnari. I knew the man's kinsman, a necromancer."

"And you overcame him, as well as a dyrmagnos," Ulan returned indifferently. "If you were able to accomplish that with a handful of Tír, what should the Aurënfaie fear from them?"

"It was only one dyrmagnos, and a handful of necromancers, but it took the life of the great Nysander í Azusthra to defeat them," Thero said softly, and something in his voice made Seregil glance nervously at his friend. For an instant Seregil thought he saw the wizard's eyes flash gold. Probably a trick of the light. "Beware what you trade away for prosperity, Ulan í Sathil," Thero went on. "There are those with vision even longer than yours."

Ulan went to the door and opened it. "Torsin was my friend and I grieve his loss. There is nothing more to be said. As for what happened to Klia beneath my roof, it is a most grievous offense, but one she perhaps brought upon herself. She's sown discord in a city that has known only peace for time out of mind. Perhaps this is Aura's punishment."

Thero blanched at this but held his tongue.

Seregil felt less restraint. "The Lightbearer had nothing to do with this," he growled. "Mark my words, Khirnari, the truth of this will come out. I'll see to it."

"You?" Ulan made no effort to hide his contempt. "What do you know of truth?"

A lec saw Seregil waiting for him on the front steps when he and his search party returned.

"Any luck?" he called.

Alec swung down from the saddle and presented him with the Akhendi charm. "It's Klia's, all right. It must have come loose in the struggle."

"Illior's Fingers!" Seregil exclaimed, examining the blackened carving.

"Kheeta's gone to fetch Rhaish," Alec told him. "Säaban claims he should be able to use it to tell us who caused this. It was still white before the hunt. Care to lay any bets on who changed that?"

Seregil took the poisoner's ring from a pouch. "Not just yet, I think."

"Where did you find that?"

"In the fish pond outside Ulan's bedchamber. So far, Thero hasn't been able to divine anything from it, though. He says it's masked."

Alec cocked an eyebrow. "How hard is that to do?"

"Hard enough to make me think that we're dealing with someone powerful."

"Damn! Then this charm may be, too."

"It may be useful to learn that it is," said Seregil, examining the bracelet again. "That would suggest that whoever masked one masked the other, as well. Chances are they'd have to be there to do so after Emiel had attacked her."

"So we find out who in the hunting party was also at the Virésse banquet?"

Seregil shrugged. "If this turns out to be masked, then yes."

Kheeta arrived with the Akhendi khirnari, and Seregil ushered him into the sitting room off the main hall, where Alec and Thero were waiting.

"You found something in the forest?" Rhaish asked.

"This," said Alec, giving him the blackened charm. "Can you tell us who did this?"

The khirnari held it a moment. "Ah, yes, this is my wife's work. It would be best if I took it to her. I'll send you word of what she finds. She is not well enough today to go out."

"If you don't mind, Khirnari, we'll save you the trouble and come along now," Seregil interrupted.

"Very well," Rhaish replied, clearly taken aback by such presumption. One did not demand access to the home of a khirnari.

"Forgive my rudeness," Seregil quickly added, hoping to smooth it over. "But time is of the essence, for Klia's sake."

"Of course. I was not thinking. Akhendi will do all in its power to ensure her recovery."

"Thank you, Khirnari." Motioning for Alec to accompany them, Seregil led the man out.

Akhendi tupa was modest in comparison to the Virésse, and the faded appointments spoke of better days.

They found Amali resting on a silken couch in one of the garden courts, picking listlessly at a dish of dried kindle berries while she watched several of her women play at dice.

She brightened a bit at the sight of her husband. "Back so soon, talí? And with company for me!"

"Forgive an unforgivable intrusion," Seregil said gallantly. "I would not disturb you if it were not of the utmost urgency."

"Think nothing of it," she replied, sitting up. "What brings you here?"

Seregil showed her the bracelet. "My lady, your gift to Klia was well thought of. I believe it can lead us to her attacker."

"How wonderful!" she exclaimed, taking the soiled bracelet gingerly between two fingers. "But what's happened to it?"

"Klia lost it during the hunt," Alec explained. "I found it when I went back this morning."

"I see." Pressing the charm between her palms, she murmured a spell over it. A moment later she let out a gasp and slumped back against the cushions, face drained of color. "A Haman!" she said faintly. "I see his face, contorted with anger. I know this man: He is here in the city. The nephew of Nazien í Hari."

"Emiel í Moranthi?" asked Alec, shooting Seregil a victorious look.

"Yes, that is his name," Amali whispered. "Such anger and contempt. Such violence!"

"Can you tell us anything more, my lady?" Seregil asked, leaning forward.

"Enough!" Lips tight with anger, Rhaish tore the bracelet from her grasp as if it were a poisonous snake. "Talía, you are not well enough for this." Turning to Seregil, he said sternly, "You see her condition. What more do you need?"

"If she could tell us more of the nature of this attack, Khirnari, it would be of great value."

"Leave this with us for now, then. When she has recovered her strength, perhaps she can see more in it."

"I'd prefer to keep this with me," Seregil told him. "When your lady is well I'll bring it back."

"Very well." Rhaish looked thoughtfully at the bracelet, then handed it back. "How odd, for so much to depend on such a simple object."

"In my experience, it is often the simplest things that yield the greatest insights," Seregil replied.

"Well?" Alec demanded as they walked home with Thero. "I told you he attacked her. There's your proof!"

"I suppose so," Seregil mused absently.

"You suppose so? By the Four, Seregil, she was working with her own magic."

Seregil lowered his voice to a whisper. "But why, Alec? Klia and Torsin were poisoned at Virésse tupa, of that I'm certain. If it was done by the Haman, then it was someone other than Emiel, because he wasn't there."

"If the Haman are behind it, then it was planned by a fool," added Thero. "Everyone knew they were hunting the next morning.

Why choose a poison that would affect her while she was in their company?"

"And why go to the trouble of attacking her if she was already dying?" Seregil pointed out.

"Unless Emiel didn't know about the poison," Alec said. "He's a violent bastard, Seregil. He went after me once, right in the city in front of witnesses, not to mention what he did to you!"

"That was different. Attacking Klia was madness. Based on what Amali just told us, he could face dwai sholo." He handed the poisoner's ring to Thero. "Keep at this. I'll bet you my best horse if you do find out who used it, it won't be a Haman."

"You think these could be separate events, then?" the wizard asked, staring down at the deadly little circle of steel.

"You mean more than one clan wanted Klia dead?" Alec felt the beginnings of a headache behind his eyes. "Perhaps Sarikali is more like Rhíminee after all."

It was a depressing thought.

Rhaish í Arlisandin dismissed the women as soon as their Skalan visitors were gone, then knelt beside Amali. Her air of quiet triumph sent a chill through him; for a moment he could scarcely feel the ground beneath his knees.

"By the Light," he gasped, clutching at her wrist. "Amali, what have you done?"

She raised her chin proudly, though he saw tears standing in her eyes. "What had to be done, my husband. For Akhendi, and for you. The Haman is no man of honor; the violence is his."

She reached out to him, but Rhaish shied away. The terrible mix of sorrow and adoration in his wife's face scorched him like wildfire, even as the world grew darker around him. Staggering to a nearby chair, he covered his eyes with his hands.

"You would not confide in me, my husband!" she said imploringly. "Yet I could see your anguish. When Aura placed the means in my hands, I knew what I must do."

"The Lightbearer had no hand in this," he mumbled.

Alec and Seregil went straight to Klia's chamber. Though she had not yet regained full consciousness, it seemed right to be in her presence as much as possible, as if they could lend her their life force through sheer proximity

It was also the most securely guarded room in the house. Two Urgazhi were stationed outside her door. Inside, Beka sat dozing at the bedside. She jerked awake as they entered, one hand flying to the hilt of her knife.

"It's just us," Seregil whispered, approaching the bed.

Klia was asleep, but there was a hint of color in her pallid cheeks. A sheen of sweat stood out on her brow and upper lip.

"She still can't speak, but Mydri got a little broth into her," Beka told them. "She's been like this most of the day, though she opens her eyes now and then. It's hard to know if she understands what's said to her yet."

Alec caught his breath as a sickly odor assaulted his nostrils. Klia's left hand was bandaged from fingertips to wrist, and angry red lines of infection arced up the inside of her forearm. Those hadn't been there at dawn.

"Amali says Emiel definitely attacked her," Seregil told Beka.

She closed her eyes wearily. "I knew it. Did she say why?"

"No. I think I'd better have a talk with Nazien, though I'm not looking forward to it."

"What about the Virésse?" she asked.

Seregil scrubbed a hand through his hair and sighed. "Finding the ring in Ulan's fishpond should be pretty damning evidence."

"Should?"

"Well, dropping the ring right outside his own bedchamber door is either the most daring or the most stupid thing I've seen in a while. I haven't decided which yet."

"If the Haman are our poisoners, they could have dropped it there to make Ulan look guilty," said Alec.

"That begs the question of whether they support the repeal of the Edict. Nazien might want to see Ulan dishonored, if he was serious about supporting Klia after all. Otherwise, he would have supported him. As for Emiel, he was on the side of the Virésse, so it's unlikely he'd have been behind such a ruse."

"We might have just missed seeing the murderer," Alec said glumly, thinking of the unseen visitor who'd interrupted their tossing of Ulan's chambers.

Thero slipped in just then, and the others greeted him with hopeful looks.

"Nothing yet," the wizard told them, leaning over Klia's bed to pass Seregil the ring. "If only I could question her about that night."

"Our assassin chose his moment well, whoever he was," Alec

muttered. "If we do clear Haman or Virésse, that still leaves most of Sarikali suspect."

"Even if I were free to go about reading minds, it would take months," added the wizard.

Beka took the poisoner's ring. "A lot of good this does us, if you can't divine any more than you have of it."

"I told you, I wasn't meant to. Someone has masked it so that I can't trace it to its owner," Thero snapped. "This is a real wizard we're dealing with, not some hedgerow conjurer."

"Then for all we know, the man we're looking for has escaped already," she fretted, handing it back to him. "People come and go all the time here. Our man could be miles away already. By the Flame, Seregil, can't these rhui'auros of yours do something?"

He sighed, resting his face in his hands. "According to the one I spoke with this morning, I already know who did it, whatever that means."

Beka paused beside Seregil and rested a hand on his shoulder. "Tell us what he said, word for word."

Seregil glanced down at Klia and found her eyes open and focused on him. He lifted her good hand and held it gently. "Let's see. He fed me breakfast and we spoke of Nysander. He admitted that he sent Nyal but claimed that he didn't send him to me." He looked at Thero and shook his head. "You know how they can be. Anyway, then he gave me the Plenimaran bottle of lissik. When I recognized the workmanship, he told me 'He who has two hearts is twice as strong,' and called me 'ya'shel khi.' "

"Half-breed soul," Alec translated for Beka's benefit.

Seregil nodded. "I've been turning that around in my mind all day, along with his talk of my so-called gift. Whatever that is."

"And he said you fight it," Alec prompted.

Seregil shrugged again. "A gift for magical ineptitude? A gift for picking pockets and lying well? The only thing he said that makes any sense to me yet is that somehow or other we've missed asking the right questions."

"Or the right people," Beka said. "What did Adzriel say about the vote? Will it go forward as things are now?"

"Nothing's been changed, so far as she knows."

"Both Virésse and Haman are still under interdiction," said Alec. "Doesn't that give us an advantage? I mean, we know that Virésse would have voted against us, and Haman might have."

"Haman would have been the keystone," Seregil said. "With just

Virésse out of the picture, Nazien's vote would have broken any tie vote, for good or ill. Things are as uncertain as ever now. Of the nine left, we know Goliníl, Khatme, and Lhapnos are against us. Ra'basi and the rest? Who can say, now that everyone's so leery of Phoria? Ulan may win without having to vote at all. Beka, I'd like you to fetch Nazien í Hari. Don't say why, just that I have information regarding his nephew."

"Maybe it's time I went back to the taverns," Alec offered. "Short of going into housebreaking as a full-time occupation, I don't see how else we can find much more than we already have. Whoever left that ring meant for us to end up right where we are now, mired solid."

"You might as well—"

He was interrupted by Mydri's arrival with fresh infusions for Klia.

"But not alone," he continued. "Take Kheeta with you, and a rider or two. No one goes out alone, not anymore."

"Then you think our murderer is still here?" asked Beka.

"We have to be prepared for the possibility, and that he's not done with us yet," Seregil replied.

"Do take care," Mydri warned, picking up the thread of the conversation. "Adzriel has had people out listening around the city; word of what you found has already spread, and tempers are ugly. Akhendi is the worst, accusing Virésse outright of murder. There's talk of banning Goliníl, and even the Khatme seem to be under suspicion. It's rumored that Lhaär ä Iriel and Ulan í Sathil were meeting secretly to plot against Klia."

"Any news from the Nha'mahat?" Seregil asked.

Mydri gave him a surprised look. "You know they don't mix in Iia'sidra business."

"Of course." Seregil bent to pat Klia's hand one last time, then motioned for Alec to come with him.

On the way out they nearly collided with Sergeant Mercalle in the corridor.

"Begging your pardon, my lords," she said, giving them a quick salute. "I need to speak with Captain Beka regarding orders."

"What is it, Sergeant?" Beka asked, stepping out to join them.

"It's about the prisoner, Captain. His people are at the front door, asking what we mean to do with him."

"Well, well, Nazien has saved us the trouble," Seregil murmured. "Tell him we'll speak with him at once, Sergeant. Put them in the sitting room off the main hall."

Mercalle nodded to one of the Urgazhi on guard at the door, and the man hurried off. "There is one other thing, as well," she added. "The house servants wish to know what's to be done with Lord Torsin."

Beka grimaced. "Sakor's Flame, it's been a couple of days, hasn't it? He'll have to be burnt, and his remains sent home to Skala."

"It will have to be done outside the city," Seregil told her. "Nyal can probably find the materials we'll need. Have it done tonight; the priests can deal with the proper rites back in Rhíminee. You'd better bring Emiel into the hall now. I want him there when I give his uncle the bad news."

"I can't wait to see their faces," Beka said, striding off toward the back stair with Mercalle.

Thero waited until the two women were gone, then lowered his voice. "I've been thinking about what you said of the rhui'auros. Whatever your sister may think, I believe they see more than mere politics in all this. I'm convinced they want this alliance."

"I know," Seregil replied. "What puzzles me is why they don't seem to be making that clear to their own people."

"Maybe the Aurënfaie aren't listening," Alec suggested.

Nyal was loitering in the stable yard when Beka came out with Mercalle. Her heart gave an unruly leap at the sight of him. He'd been out riding, judging by the dust on his boots and cloak. Coming closer, she smelled beer and green herbs on his breath, the scent of a fresh breeze in his hair. She'd have given a month's pay for five minutes alone in his arms.

"We need materials for a funeral pyre, a fast, hot one," she told him, keeping her tone neutral.

His hazel eyes widened in alarm. "Aura's Light, not Klia—"

"For Lord Torsin," she told him.

"Ah, of course. The proper materials are kept in the city for such contingencies," he replied. "I'm sure they'll be made available to you, but it might be best if someone of Bôkthersa clan made the request on Skala's behalf. Shall I find Kheeta í Branín?"

"Thank you," Beka said gratefully. "I want his ashes ready for tomorrow's dispatch rider, if possible."

"I'll see to everything," he said, already on his way.

"He's been a good friend to us, Captain," Mercalle said with evident affection.

By the Four, how I want to believe that! Beka thought, watching her lover out of sight. "Get an honor guard together for me, Sergeant. Have them in the main hall in five minutes. Lord Seregil is meeting with the Haman and we want to make the proper impression."

Mercalle winked knowingly. "I'll make sure they're all tall and mean, Captain."

"Mean shouldn't be too difficult to come by, considering who our guests are," Beka replied, clapping her on the shoulder.

She'd been too distracted by Klia's condition and her own guilt to pay very much attention to the unwelcome "guest" in the barracks. As she headed in to fetch Emiel, she reflected that it couldn't have been a comfortable few days for him, with Klia's own guard looking daggers at him every waking hour. There wasn't one of them who wouldn't cheerfully cut the Haman's throat.

Half a dozen riders were taking their ease inside. Two more kept watch at the back of the room, where Emiel sat on his pallet, the remains of a recent meal on a plate beside him. He looked up at her approach, and she was pleased to see a flicker of apprehension cross his face.

"On your feet. You're wanted in the house," she ordered.

Outside, Emiel blinked as his eyes adjusted to the slanting afternoon sun. He betrayed no fear, but she did catch him stealing a quick glance at the stable yard gate, which stood tantalizingly open.

Go on, try to run for it, Beka thought, loosening her grip a little, wondering if he knew how much she'd welcome the opportunity to take him down.

The man knew better, of course, and kept up a disdainful front until he entered the hall and saw his uncle and a half dozen kinsmen standing tensely before Thero's makeshift tribunal. Alec and Sääban flanked the wizard, with Mercalle's guard in a line behind them. Seregil entered a moment later, escorting Rhaish í Arlisandin.

"Is there anyone else you wish to have present?" Thero asked Nazien.

"No one," the old Haman answered. "You claim to have proof of my kinsman's guilt. Show it to me and let's be done with the matter."

The Akhendi stepped forward, and Seregil handed him Klia's warding charm.

"You know of my people's skills with such magic," said Rhaish. "Your kinsman's guilt is written here, in this little carving. You recognize what it is, I think."

Nazien took the charm and clasped it, closing his eyes. After a moment his shoulders sagged. When he looked at Emiel, there was disgust in his eyes. "I brought you to Sarikali to learn wisdom, nephew. Instead, you have brought disgrace on our name."

Beka felt the young Haman go rigid. "No," he rasped out. "No, my uncle—"

"Silence!" Nazien ordered, turning his back on Emiel and facing Thero. "I vow atonement to avert teth'sag between our people. If evidence of my kinsman's innocence cannot be found within the next moon cycle, he will be put to death for the attempted assassination of the queen's sister."

Nazien regarded Emiel stonily for a long moment. "Did you know," he said at last, "that during the hunt I pledged my support to Klia and her cause?"

"No, Khirnari, we did not," Thero replied. "The princess has been unable to speak since her collapse."

"Who heard you give this pledge, I wonder?" Rhaish í Arlisandin asked harshly.

The Haman eyed him levelly. "We spoke in private, but I'm certain Klia will verify my words when she recovers. Good day. May Aura's light illuminate the truth for all."

None of the Haman spared Emiel a glance as they filed out. He watched his kinsmen leave, then turned on Rhaish í Arlisandin.

"I might have known the Akhendi would use their paltry trinkets to sell their honor!" he snarled, twisting out of Beka's grasp and lunging at the khirnari, hands outstretched to throttle the man.

Beka grappled him to the ground but needed the help of three strong riders to hold the man down as he thrashed and cursed. Beka got an elbow in the eye for her trouble but held on blindly until the Haman suddenly jerked and went limp.

Peering up blearily, Beka found Alec standing over him, rubbing his fist.

"Thanks," she grunted, getting up. "Tie this madman up, Sergeant, and clear out one of the storerooms for a cell. If we've got to hang on to him, I want him behind a locked door!"

Mercalle motioned to her men, who dragged the unconscious Haman none too gently out the door.

Beka bowed to the Akhendi. "My apologies."

"Not at all," the older man replied, apparently shaken by what he'd just witnessed. "If you will excuse me, I must return to my wife. She's still not well."

"Thank you, Khirnari," Thero said, holding up the bracelet.

"Your help has been invaluable. I hope to learn more from this, as well."

"I'm unfamiliar with your methods, Thero í Procepios, but I caution you not to undo any of the knots. Once the magic of the object is so broken, no one will be able to tell anything from it."

"That shouldn't be necessary," Seregil replied, taking it and tucking it away for safekeeping. "Captain, see that the khirnari gets home safely."

It was just as well that Beka went with the Akhendi. There was something different in the air today and tension hung over the formerly placid streets. It was nothing overt, just a sense she picked up as they passed too quiet taverns and small knots of people.

Nyal was waiting for her on the front steps when she returned. "You are exhausted, talía," he said, taking her hand and pulling her down beside him.

"I don't have time to be tired yet," she returned sourly, though she knew he was right. She ached with weariness, and the world was taking on a surreal glow.

"I hear Emiel did not exactly confess?"

For an instant, Beka saw the Ra'basi through Seregil's eyes—an outsider who asked too many questions. "That's not for me to discuss," she said curtly, and quickly changed the subject. "Our troubles have upset the general population, I think."

Nyal gave her a slanting smile. "Perhaps the Khatme have been right all these years. Let the Skalans into Sarikali and suddenly we have fistfights in the streets."

"Well, we'll be gone soon enough."

"Leaving havoc in your wake. This simple request of yours has brought a good many simmering clan disputes to a boil. Now, with the deaths, everyone suddenly has new reasons for distrusting their enemies."

"Have the clans ever gone to war among themselves?" Beka asked. Such a thing hardly seemed possible, even with all she'd seen lately.

Nyal shrugged. "They have, though not for a long time. It's not murder, to kill in war, but lives are cut short nonetheless. For a 'faie to shed 'faie blood—ah, Aura forbid! It's the worst thing imaginable."

Perhaps if she hadn't been so tired his words would not have rankled so. As it was, they burned like salt in a fresh wound.

"What do you know of war?" Beka snapped. "Your people sit

here, clucking their tongues at us, but when we try to get help saving a few hundred of our short lives, you sit on your hands, debating whether we'll pollute your blessed shores! Never mind that you've murdered one of our people and maimed Klia so that she may—"

She broke off abruptly, seeing the sentries nearby shifting in embarrassment. She was practically shouting.

It wasn't Nyal's fault, not any of it, but right now he seemed to stand for every slow-talking, law-spouting, way-blocking Aurën-faie in the land.

"I'm tired, and there's so much left to do," she said, squeezing her eyes shut.

"Rest awhile," Nyal said softly. "Sleep if you can."

She sighed. "No, we've got a pyre to build."

The confrontation with the Haman left
Seregil oddly pensive.

"Do you think Nazien was telling the
truth when he said he'd support Skala?"
Alec asked when the others had left the hall.

"It's plausible. We'll go have a listen
around town, see how the wind blows once
word of all this gets around."

"If we split up—"

"No," Seregil shook his head, frowning.
"I still don't want any Skalan out alone
anywhere."

Alec grinned. "Suddenly cautious, are we?"

Seregil chuckled. "Let's just say even I can
learn from my own poor example."

That evening, they wandered the city's taverns and squares, picking up threads of outraged opinion.

They went openly among the friendlier
clans and heard Virésse alternately de-
nounced and defended. Less was said against
the Haman; word of Alec's discovery had not
yet spread.

Later, they ventured into enemy territory,
going so far as to scale the wall of Nazien í
Hari's garden to see how the Haman were
conducting themselves in the wake of the ac-

cusations. The house lay in darkness, with no smell of an evening meal.

"A sign of humility and atonement," Seregil whispered to Alec as they crept away. "Nazien's taking his nephew's actions hard."

By contrast, Virésse tupa was ablaze with light well past midnight. Keeping to the shadows, they spotted the sen'gai of half a dozen clans among the people out on the streets. The house of Ulan í Sathil was too risky to burgle, but lurking nearby, they saw the khirnari of Khatme enter, accompanied by Moriel ä Moriel of Ra'basi.

Despite this apparent show of support, bands of Virésse watchmen patrolled the boundaries of the tupa, where angry supporters of Klia roamed looking for a fight. Many wore the green-and-brown sen'gai of Akhendi.

"Do you suppose that's a spontaneous show of support, or is our friend Rhaish í Arlisandin making certain his greatest rival is made uncomfortable?" asked Seregil.

"Perhaps we should pay Akhendi tupa one last visit."

The whole of the Akhendi delegation seemed to have taken to the streets for the night, and Seregil and Alec were hailed as friends, commiserated with, and plied with liquor and questions.

News of the poisoner's ring had sealed Ulan's fate in the minds of most, and some were convinced that the Haman were in collusion with him. All agreed that it was a great coup for Akhendi, having their most hated opponent besmirched with even the hint of scandal.

"We knew they'd do anything to protect themselves, but assassination!" a taverner exclaimed, treating them to mugs of her best. "Maybe the Khatme are right about too much contact with outsiders. No offense to present company of course. I'm talking of the Plenimarans."

"You won't hear us defending them," Seregil assured her.

Stopping in at another tavern, they met Rhaish í Arlisandin, accompanied by several younger kinsmen. The khirnari seemed surprised to see them.

"With all the unrest in the city tonight, we thought we'd stop by and see that you and your people are safe," Seregil explained, joining him at a long table and accepting a mug of ale.

"I thank you for that," Rhaish replied. "These are uncertain times indeed when the insidious weapons of Plenimar are found in Sarikali."

"It chills my heart," Seregil agreed. "I thought you'd be at Torsin's funeral."

Rhaish shook his head sadly. "As you say, the mood of the city is so uncertain tonight, I thought it would be better if I remained with my own people."

As if to underscore this, the sound of angry shouting broke out suddenly in the direction of Khatme tupa.

"Aura protect us!" Rhaish groaned, sending men to investigate. "See that none of our people are doing violence!"

"Perhaps you're wise to remain close to home," Seregil observed. "Those who struck at us may strike at our closest allies, too."

"Just as you say," Rhaish acknowledged wearily. "But surely the guilt of the Virésse is clear? Why hasn't Klia declared teth'sag against them?"

"Skalans." Seregil shrugged and spread his hands, as if that explained everything.

"I must attend my people," Rhaish said, rising to go. "I trust you'll keep me informed of any new discoveries?"

"Of course. Aura's Light shine on you."

"And you." The khirnari's escort closed ranks behind him as he continued on his way.

Alec watched the stooped figure fade into the night. "Poor fellow. Except for Gedre and us, no one else stands to lose as much when everything goes to pieces. And it's going to, isn't it?"

Seregil said nothing for a moment, listening as the distant shouting took on a more dire tone. "I didn't come home for this, Alec. Not to watch the two lands I've called home bring each other down. We've got to uncover the truth of all this, and soon."

A moment later a tiny point of bluish light flickered into being just in front of them, one of Thero's message spheres. The wizard's voice issued softly from it, drained of emotion: "Come back at once."

37
WORSE NEWS

The arrangements for Torsin's funeral came together quickly, thanks to Nyal. He'd even turned up a bundle of spices somewhere, and with these Kheeta's mother had skillfully overseen the preparation of the corpse. By the time she and her helpers had sewn it into layers of canvas and patterned silk, the odor was almost tolerable.

Unwilling to spare too many soldiers from guarding the house, Beka took only Nyal, Kheeta, and her three corporals as torchbearers. A cart draped with cloaks and prayer scrolls served as catafalque, bearing Torsin out to a site on the plain outside the city. Adzriel and Säaban accompanied them, each with a painted prayer kite honoring the dead man. It was fully dark now, but the soft gleam of massed wizard lights was guide enough.

"Well, look at that, would you?" Nikides exclaimed softly.

In spite of the general unrest, at least a hundred Aurënfaie had gathered on the moon-washed plain. The pyre, a rectangular stack of cedar and oak logs fifteen feet high, was surmounted by a pair of carved dragon heads. Dozens of prayer scrolls fluttered against its sides.

"You'd think he was one of their own," said Corporal Zir.

"He was a good man," Nyal said.

Beka hadn't known Torsin well, but sensed a rightness in this final moment; the man had spent his life, and perhaps given it, trying to bring the two races together.

Kallas and Nikides slid the body into a shelflike opening near the top of the pyre. Adzriel made a few prayers in the dead man's behalf, then stepped back. Beka and her riders were about to light the tinder when another rider galloped out to join them. It was Sergeant Rhylin, and even in the warm glow of the torches, the tall sergeant's face looked grey.

"Thero sent this—to be put on the pyre," he whispered hoarsely, thrusting a small, canvas-wrapped parcel into Beka's hands.

"What is it?" she asked, already dreading the answer. The stiff cloth was tied up with a knotted thong and weighed almost nothing.

"Klia—" he began, as tears rolled down his cheeks.

"Sakor's Flame!" Beka's fingers felt numb and clumsy as she yanked the thong free and unrolled the cloth. The smell gagged her, but she went on, unable to stop.

Two black, swollen, fingers—first and middle—were packed in fresh cedar tips and rose petals. They were still joined by a sizable wedge of discolored flesh; the white tips of two neatly severed bones poked out from the raw lower edge.

"Mydri saved the hand, then?" she asked, spilling petals as she hurriedly tied the bundle up again.

Rhylin wiped at his eyes. "She isn't sure yet. The rot was spreading too fast. Thero worked a spell over Klia. We didn't even have to hold her down."

Beka's mind skittered away from the images that summoned, wondering instead if her commander would ever hold a bow again. "Thank the Maker it wasn't her sword hand," she mumbled. Climbing up the side of the pyre, she reached in and laid the little bundle on Torsin's breast, above his heart.

On the ground again, she knelt and thrust a torch into the thick bed of tinder and kindling packed under the logs. The Urgazhi sang a soldiers' dirge as flames fueled by beeswax and fragrant resins leaped up to engulf it.

The song ended, leaving only the crackle of the flames in its wake. As the thick white smoke went dark, a sorrowful keening started somewhere among the 'faie. It spread through the crowd and swelled to an uncanny, full-throated wail that rose and fell wordlessly and without cease. Her riders tensed, shooting Beka worried looks.

She shrugged and turned back to watch the roaring blaze.

The keening went on for hours, until the blaze had reduced itself to smoldering embers. Sometime during the night, hardly realizing what they did, the Skalans joined in.

Beka and the others returned to the guest house through a hazy red dawn, hoarse, light-headed, and covered in soot. The quiver holding Torsin's ashes hung warm against her thigh as she rode. In the end, they'd had to break the longer bones to fit them in.

Mercalle was standing by the stable with the day's courier, Urien, and his guide. The Akhendi had a nasty-looking bruise over his right cheekbone.

"What happened to you, my friend?" Nyal asked, squinting at him with smoke-reddened eyes.

The man gave him a cool stare and shrugged. "A slight disagreement with some of your kinsmen."

"Some of the Ra'basi support Virésse," Mercalle told Beka, not looking at the interpreter.

"I'm sure we'll get it all sorted out by the time the vote comes around," Beka replied.

"Captain!" a rider called out from the kitchen doorway. "Captain Beka, are you there?"

Beka turned and saw Kipa looking anxiously around the yard.

"Oh, there you are, Captain," she called, spotting Beka. "I've been watching for you. Lord Thero said I was to bring you as soon as you came in."

"Is it Klia? Has she—?" Beka asked, following the younger woman inside.

"I don't know, Captain, but it sure feels like bad news."

Beka could hardly breathe as she ran up to Klia's room. Mydri met her in the doorway, balancing a basin full of bloody water and rags against one hip.

"She took a bad turn last night," she told Beka. "She's sleeping again. For now."

The bedchamber's window was shuttered, the room lit only by the glow of a sizable bed of coals on the hearth. The stench of blood and seared flesh still hung heavily on the air. Thankfully, all other evidence of the amputation had been cleared away.

Klia lay pale and still, thick new bandages swathed around her hand. Seregil and Alec slept awkwardly in chairs beside the bed. Judging by their plain, rumpled clothing, they'd been about their own business most of the night.

Beka took a step toward the bed, then tensed as movement in a far corner caught her eye. Her hand flew to her knife.

"It's me," Thero whispered, coming far enough into the light for her to make out his swollen, red-rimmed eyes.

"I suppose it's best that it's over with," Beka said, pushing away the image of those severed fingers.

"I only hope she survives the shock of it," said Thero. "She's shown no signs of waking and it worries me, and Mydri, as well."

Seregil opened his eyes, then nudged Alec's knee. The younger man jerked awake and looked around blearily.

"Any trouble at the funeral?" he asked, voice raw with exhaustion.

"No. The 'faie who showed up gave him a good send-off. Were you here?" She gestured at Klia's bandaged hand.

"No. We just got back a little while ago," said Alec.

Seregil hooked a chair her way, then passed her a half-full flask of wine. "Here, you'll need this."

Beka drank deeply, then looked around at the others. "So, now what's happened?" Her heart sank when Thero sealed the room, then pulled a letter folded in Magyana's characteristic fashion from the air.

"Something none of us thought possible," he told her. "This is hard to make out. I'll read it for you. It begins, 'My friends, I write you as I flee Mycena and the queen's displeasure. Phoria has ordered an attack against Gedre to secure the port.' "

Beka let out a gasp of disbelief. "An attack!"

Seregil motioned her to silence.

" 'There is a spy in your midst,' " Thero continued. " 'Someone has been sending reports of the Iia'sidra's reluctance to act. I have seen these with my own eyes. In this way the queen also learned that it was I who sent you word of the old queen's death. I am banished.

" 'Make no mistake; Phoria was preparing for such a strike in any case. Recent attacks on Skala's western shores have given her the excuse she needed to secure the support for this madness. Her recent victories in Mycena have cemented the loyalty of most. Generals who a month ago would have questioned such an action now support her. Those who don't keep silent in the wake of the execution of General Hylus.' "

"Hylus?" said Beka. "Why in the world would she execute him? He was a brilliant tactician, and a loyal soldier."

"Loyal to Idrilain," Seregil observed with a cynical frown. "Go on, Thero."

" 'Prince Korathan left Rhíminee harbor with three fast warships yesterday at dawn. I believe he means to approach under the flag of a messenger ship and take the port by surprise. The surprise is more likely to be his. He might be reasoned with, if only you can find some way to prevent his arrival! Even if he is able to secure Gedre, whatever brief advantage this might afford will never offset the loss of Aurënen as an ally. If the 'faie turn against us now, what hope have we for Skala and the Orëska?' That's all she says." Thero folded the letter, and it vanished between his fingers.

Beka rested her head in her hands, feeling ill. "Bilairy's Balls. Does the Iia'sidra know?"

"Not yet, as far as we can tell," Alec replied. "Everyone is still busy accusing everyone else of poisoning Klia."

"It's only a matter of time before news leaks out," Seregil cautioned. "This will undo everything. Not only is it an act of war, but it proves every suspicion Ulan has raised about Phoria's motives."

"How could Phoria do this?" asked Alec. "Doesn't she understand what this means? Klia could be killed, or held hostage."

"Phoria's a general," Beka told him. "In war generals spend the lives of a few to gain advantage for the rest. She's decided we're expendable. Still—her own *sister*?"

Seregil let out a bitter laugh. "Klia's always been the people's darling, and the cavalry's. Now, with Korathan being promoted and their other brothers dead, she's next in line as High Commander of the Queen's Cavalry. It's her right by birth, unless Aralain is forced into it. I don't think Phoria wants her youngest sister quite so powerful."

"Phoria is using what's happened here to double advantage," said Thero. "Klia is gotten out of the way, and Phoria gains justification for taking what she wants from Aurënen."

Shock was already giving way to anger. Beka rose, pulse racing the way it did before a raid. "We have to get Klia away to safety before the 'faie find out."

Thero shook his head. "She's far too ill to move."

"What about by magic?"

"Especially not by magic," Thero replied. "Even if we could find someone to do a translocation, the flux would kill her."

"She's safe here," said Seregil.

"How can you say that? Beka snapped, rounding on him. "Take a good look at her! This is what all their talk of guest laws and sacred ground amounts to. Now they're fighting each other in the streets!"

"I wouldn't have thought it possible, not in Sarikali," Seregil admitted. "But now we know the danger, and we're guarded by your riders and by the Bôkthersans."

"I've put protections in place around the grounds," Thero added. "No one will get in or visit any magicks on us without my knowing about it."

"That still leaves us trapped here when word of Korathan's mission gets out," Beka growled.

"I know," said Seregil. "That's why we've got to do as Magyana's asked—try to head him off before anyone's the wiser."

"How do you suggest we manage that? I doubt sending him a polite note is going to do it, even if it got to him in time."

Seregil exchanged a veiled look with Alec. "I think it's time I prove Idrilain right in sending me along."

"There's a traitor's moon tonight," Alec told her, as if that explained everything.

Seregil chuckled. "How's that for an omen, eh?"

"What the hell are you talking about?" Beka demanded. "We've got to find a way to stop Korathan—" Breaking off, she stared at him. "You're not saying you mean to go?"

"Well, Alec and I."

Alec grinned. "Know anyone else you trust with this information who can pass as Aurënfaie?"

"But the proscriptions! If you're caught they'll kill you. And maybe Alec, too!"

Suddenly it wasn't a spy or coconspirator she was looking at but the man who'd been friend and uncle to her since her birth, who'd carried her on his shoulders, brought exotic presents, and taught her the finer points of fighting. And Alec— Tears stung her eyes and she turned quickly away.

Seregil clasped her shoulders, turning her to face him again. "Then we'd damn well better not get caught," he told her. "Besides, we'll be in Akhendi territory, then Gedre. They may haul me back, but they won't hurt me. I know it's risky, but there's no other way. Your father would understand. I'm hoping you will, too. We need your help, Captain."

The subtle rebuke stung just enough to clear her head. "All right, then. What's the soonest Korathan will reach Gedre?"

"With a good following wind? Four or five days. We can reach the coast in three and sail out to meet him before he comes in sight of the port."

"Time enough, barring accidents," she said, frowning. "But I still say it's suicide for you to go. Perhaps Alec and I could pull it off, or Thero."

Seregil shook his head. "Korathan is going to take a lot of convincing to cross his sister, and with all due respect, I think I'm the one who can best carry that off. He knows me, and he knows the regard his mother had for me. Loyal as he is to Phoria, he's the more reasonable of the pair. I think I can sway him."

"How do you plan to reach Gedre without getting caught? I assume someone will go after you as soon as they find out you're missing."

"They'll have to find us first. There are other routes over the mountains. The one I have in mind is tough going in places, but shorter than the trail we came over. My uncle used to bring us down that way on smuggling runs."

"Are those passes protected by magic, too?" asked Thero. "If anything happens to you, what will Alec do? He can't get through that any more than we could."

"We'll worry about that when we need to," Seregil replied. "Right now we need to figure out a way to get out of the city without being seen."

"The moon's in our favor, at least," said Alec. "With Aurënfaie clothes and horses, we shouldn't attract much attention. It could be morning before we're missed."

"Perhaps longer, if I can manage a few tricks," said the wizard.

"You could go out as escorts with one of my dispatch riders," Beka mused. "Steal different horses once you're well away from the city, while the rider takes yours with her and leaves a false trail."

"Sometimes I forget whose daughter you are," chuckled Seregil. His smile faded as he continued, however. "We have to keep this among ourselves. Except for the rider, no one else can know, not even our own people, since anyone who does will be forced to lie sooner or later.

"Play up Klia's illness, Beka. Keep the Iia'sidra away from her as long as you can. If you do get trapped here, Adzriel will protect you, even if it means claiming you as hostages." He shrugged. "Who knows? Maybe you'll see Bôkthersa before I do."

"That still leaves us penned in here with a spy." Thero shook his head in disgust. "Ever since I read that letter, I've been wondering how someone could have been spying on us under our very noses. If they'd used magic, I swear I'd have sensed it!"

"Torsin managed to carry on his business without our tumbling for quite some time," Seregil reminded him. "That didn't take any magic."

"But with Klia's knowledge," the wizard countered.

"When I find out who it is, they'll wish for poison!" hissed Beka, clenching a fist against her thigh. "There must be some way of flushing them out."

"I was thinking about that earlier," Alec said. "You're not going to like this, but what about the dispatch riders? It would be easy enough for them to slip a message through, since they're the ones carrying them. They're also the last ones to handle the pouch before it's sealed."

"Mercalle's decuria?" Beka snorted. "By the Flame, Alec, we've been through Bilairy's gate and back together!"

"Not all of them. What about the new ones? Phoria could have turned one of them."

"Or had them placed in Urgazhi Turma before this ever started," added Seregil. "In her place, that's what I'd have done. Knowing Phoria, she'd want eyes and ears anywhere she could get them—especially among Klia's troops."

Beka shook her head stubbornly. "We lost half of Mercalle's decuria during the battle on the way over here. Ileah, Urien, and Ari are all that are left of the new recruits, and they're just pups. As for the rest, Zir and Marten have been with me since the turma was formed. I know them. They've saved my life a dozen times over and I've done the same for them. They're loyal to the marrow of their bones."

"Just let me speak with Mercalle," Alec persisted. "She's closer to them than anyone. Maybe she's seen something, something she didn't even know was suspicious."

But Beka still hesitated. "Do you know what even the hint of this could do to the others? I need them united."

"It won't go beyond this room," Alec promised. "If anything does come up, Thero can deal with it with total secrecy. But we have to know."

Beka cast an imploring look at Seregil but found no help there. "All right, then, send for Mercalle." She looked down at Klia. "But don't question her here. Not here."

"We can use my room," said Thero. He flicked a tiny message sphere into being and sent it skittering through the wall with a wave of his hand.

The cooler air in the wizard's chamber seemed to clear Seregil's head, enough for him to feel chagrin at not having arrived at Alec's conclusions himself.

Alec had been right all along—and the rhui'auros, too. Since he'd come back to Aurënen, he'd been too wrapped up in his own past, his own demons, to be of much use to anyone. Perhaps it went back even further than that. In rejecting Rhíminee, had he buried the man he'd been there, the Rhíminee Cat? *I'd have been dead a hundred times over, or starved for lack of trade, if I was like this all the time.*

He sat down in the chair next to Thero's neatly made bed; the others remained standing.

Mercalle entered a few moments later and came to attention in front of Thero, oblivious to the tension in the room. "You sent for me, my lord?"

"It was me, Sergeant," Alec told her, and Seregil could see him rubbing a thumb nervously over the fingers of one hand. Alec admired the Urgazhi and had always been a bit in awe of them. To bring such an accusation against them was a difficult duty, and no less so for being self-imposed.

Once committed, however, he didn't hesitate. "We have reason to believe that there's a spy in the household," he told her. "Someone who's able to get messages back to Queen Phoria. I'm sorry to say this, but it could be someone in your decuria."

The greying sergeant stared at him in shocked silence, and Seregil felt a cold jolt of certainty. *Oh, hell, she does know something.*

"This is hard, I know," Alec went on. "The idea of any Urgazhi putting Klia in danger—"

Mercalle wavered a moment, then sank to her knees in front of Beka. "Forgive me, Captain, I never thought it would come to this!" Eyes averted, she drew the dagger from her belt and offered it hilt foremost.

Beka made no move to accept the offered weapon. Her face had gone blank, but Seregil recognized the pain in her eyes and fought down the impulse to grab the sergeant by the hair and shake her. Mercalle and Braknil had trained Beka when she'd first joined the regiment. Both had requested to serve under her when she earned her lieutenant's gorget. Between the three of them, they'd forged Urgazhi Turma.

That first betrayal—it's always the worst, the one that never quite heals.

"Stand and explain yourself," Beka ordered.

Mercalle rose slowly to attention. "I'm glad it's come out, Captain. I offer no excuses, but on my honor I hoped it would be for the best. I swear it by Sakor's Flame."

"Just get on with it."

"General Phoria summoned me the night Queen Idrilain gave Klia this mission," Mercalle said. "She believed her mother wouldn't survive to see this out. As heir, she wanted her own informant on the scene."

"But why *you*?" Beka demanded, and this time there was no mistaking the grief behind the words.

Mercalle stared at the far wall, not looking at her. "Phoria was the first officer I ever served under. With respect, Captain, I came up through the ranks under her before you were born. We saw dark times together—and good ones, too. She was there when I married both my husbands, and when I buried them. I'm not proud of what she's asked of me here, but orders are orders and she was in her rights as High Commander. I thought, 'If not me, then she'll find someone who doesn't feel the loyalty I do to Klia,' and to you, Captain. All I was asked to do was to send observations. That's all I did. I never opened any letters entrusted to me, or mislaid any. If what I wrote contradicted them, it's on my head. I only told the truth as I saw it, and tried to put the best light on it that I could for Commander Klia's sake. If I'd ever thought it would come to this—" A tear rolled slowly down her cheek. "I'd cut off my sword hand before I'd willingly bring harm to any of you."

"Did you send word that we knew of the queen's death?" asked Seregil.

"I sent my respects, my lord. I thought you all had."

"Then it was you, listening outside the door of Klia's room when we learned of it," said Alec.

Mercalle shot him another startled look. "Just for a bit. Those were orders, too."

Seregil recalled the bit of stable muck they'd found in the corridor outside and shook his head. Bilairy's Balls, it was a good thing one of them had retained some sense.

"Are any of the other riders involved?" asked Beka.

"On my honor, Captain, none of them. How could I order them to do something I found so repugnant myself?"

"Have you sent Phoria word of what's happened to Klia?" Seregil demanded.

"No, Lord Thero ordered me not to, the day she fell ill."

Seregil snorted. "A spy with honor. I just hope you're telling us the truth, Sergeant. You may have doomed us all as it is."

"When did you last send a report?" asked Alec.

"The day before Klia collapsed."

"And what did you say?"

"That the date of the vote had been set, and that no one seemed very hopeful about the outcome."

"We'll speak more of this later," Beka growled. Going to the door, she called in the two sentries on duty, Ariani and Patra. "Riders, keep Sergeant Mercalle under guard. She's relieved of duty until you hear differently from me."

To their credit, the riders didn't hesitate, though they both looked thunderstruck by the order. When they were gone, Beka rounded on Alec. "You *knew* it was her?"

"I didn't," he assured her. "Not until just now."

"Oh, Alec," Seregil muttered. His own reputation as a clever intriguer was founded on more fortuitous discoveries of this sort than he liked to admit, but he'd always been careful to capitalize on them by making it look intentional after the fact.

"There's a certain logic in what she said," Thero offered. "Perhaps it was better having a friend doing the spying than an enemy."

Beka stalked angrily to the window. "I'm aware of that. If Phoria had given me the same order—" She slammed her hand against the sill. "No! No, damn it! I'd have found a way to tell Klia, protect her. By the Flame, how could Phoria do this? It sounds as if she was counting on her mother's death."

Thero shook his head sadly. "My friends, I believe we are seeing the beginnings of a new era for Skala, one we may not like very much."

"We can worry about that later," Seregil said. "Right now we have enough problems. We'll leave as soon as it's dark."

Beka turned to look at him. "What are we going to tell your sisters?"

"Let me speak to them." Seregil ran a hand back through his hair and sighed, not relishing the prospect of such a farewell.

38
TRAITOR'S MOON

Seregil put off going to his sisters until nightfall, though they were never far from his thoughts. He and Alec had made most of their stealthy preparations separately, ostensibly to avoid notice. The truth was, he'd needed some small part of this leave-taking to himself.

Alone in the bedchamber that afternoon, he found himself working too quickly as he gathered what little he needed for the journey: his mail shirt, warm Aurënfaie clothes, a water skin, his tools.

Corruth's ring bumped gently against his chest as he worked. He paused a moment and pressed a hand over it, knowing he'd thrown away any chance he might have had to wear it with honor. He was already an outlaw.

A sudden wave of dizziness forced him down on the edge of the bed. It had been easy enough to keep up a front for the others; dissembling was one of his greatest talents. But alone now, he felt something inside break, sharp and hurtful as one of the shattered glass orbs from his visions. Pressing a hand over his eyes, he fought back the tears seeping beneath his tightly closed lids.

"I'm right. I know I'm right!" he whispered. He was the only one Korathan would listen to.

But you're not so certain as you've let on that he'll agree, are you?

Shamed by his momentary weakness, he wiped his face and pulled his poniard from his bedroll, savoring the familiar weight of its hilt against his palm. Beka had kept this and his dagger for him since they landed in Gedre. He tested the edges of the slender blade with a thumbnail, then slipped it into the knife pocket in his boot; another proscription broken.

If he failed? Well then, his failure would be gloriously complete. He hadn't protected Klia. He hadn't caught the assassins. Now he was probably throwing away his life, and Alec's in the bargain, to forestall Phoria's insane act of aggression.

Even if they did succeed, what awaited them in Skala? What sort of a queen ruled there now, and how glad would she be to see her sister safely home?

Another question lurked below all the others, one he had no intention of examining until he was well away from Aurënen—
forever
—a question he planned to spend the rest of his life avoiding.
what if—?
No!

Tossing his pack on the bed, he made a quick circuit of the room, focusing on its remaining contents. Whatever he left behind he wasn't likely to see again. No matter. He was about to go when the soft glint of silver caught his eye amid a pile of clothing next to the bed. Bending down, he fished out the vial of lissik the rhui'auros had given him.

"Might as well have something to show for my troubles," he mumbled, slipping it into a belt pouch.

The first lamps were being lit when he finally slipped next door. Alec hadn't offered to come, bless him, just given him a quick, knowing embrace.

Both Adzriel and Mydri were at home. Taking them aside into a small sitting room, he shut the door and leaned against it.

"I'm leaving Sarikali tonight."

Mydri was the first to recover. "You can't!"

Adzriel silenced her with a glance, then searched her brother's face with sorrow-filled eyes. "You do this for Klia?"

"For her. For Skala. For Aurënen."

"But it's teth'sag if you leave the city," Mydri said.

"Only for me," he told her. "I'm still outcast, so Bôkthersa can't be held accountable."

"Oh, talí," Adzriel said softly. "With all you've done here, you might have won your name back in time."

There it was, that question he'd buried alive.

"Perhaps, but at too high a price," he told her.

"Then tell us why!" Mydri pleaded.

He gathered the two women close, suddenly needing their arms around him, their tears hot against his neck.

O Aura! he cried silently, clinging to them. It was so tempting to let them convince him, to take it all back and simply wait out the inevitable here, as close to home as he was ever likely to get in this life. If Klia were taken hostage, perhaps he'd even be allowed to stay with her.

It hurt. By the Light, it hurt to leave that embrace, but he had to, before it was too late.

"I'm sorry, but I can't explain," he told them. "You couldn't maintain atui if you had to keep my secret. All I ask is that you say nothing until tomorrow. Later, when everything's sorted, I'll explain, I swear. But I promise you now, by the khi of our parents, that what I'm doing is honorable and right. A wise man warned me that I'd have to make choices. This is the right one, even if it's not what I'd hoped."

"Wait here, then." Adzriel turned and hurried from the room.

"You little fool!" Mydri hissed, glaring at him again. "After all it took to bring you here, you do this to her? To me?"

Seregil caught her hand and pressed it over his heart. "You're a healer. Tell me what you feel," he challenged, meeting her anger with his own. "Is it joy? Betrayal? Hatred for you or my people?"

She went still, and he felt heat spread slowly across his skin beneath her palm. "No," she whispered. "No, Haba, I feel none of that. Only resolve, and fear."

Seregil laughed a little at that. "More fear than resolve just now."

Mydri pulled him close again, hugging him hard. "You're still a fool, Haba, but you've grown into a fine, good man in spite of it. Aura watch over you always and everywhere."

"Our other sisters will hate me for this."

"They're bigger fools even than you," she said with a tearful laugh, pushing him away. "Adzriel's the only one of the five of us worth a peddler's pot."

Laughing outright, he thanked her with a kiss.

Adzriel returned with a long, slender bundle in her arms. "We meant to give you this when you left. It seems the time has come, if a bit sooner than I'd anticipated." Folding back the cloth wrappings at the upper end, she presented him with the hilt of a sword.

Seregil reached without thinking, closing his hand around the leather and wire-wrapped grip. With a single smooth motion he pulled the blade free of its scabbard.

Polished steel caught the light like dark silver. A grooved fuller ran down the center of the blade, making it both strong and light. Tapered cross guards curved gracefully toward the blade, good for catching an opponent's sword.

Seregil's breath caught in his throat as he hefted it. It moved perfectly in his hand, just heavy enough, and balanced by the weight of its round, flat pommel.

"Akaien made this, didn't he?" he asked, recognizing his uncle's hand in the sword's clean, strong lines.

"Of course," Adzriel replied. "We knew that you wouldn't want Father's, so he made this for you. After seeing how you lived in Rhíminee, I suspected you wouldn't want anything too ornate."

"It's beautiful. And this!" He smoothed a thumb over the unusual pommel, a large disk of polished Sarikali stone set in a steel bevel. "I've never seen anything like it."

No sooner had he said it, however, than he had the strongest sense that he had seen something very much like it, though he wasn't certain where.

"He said it came to him in a dream, a talisman to keep you safe and bring you luck," Mydri explained.

"Luck in the shadows," he murmured in Skalan, shaking his head.

"You know Akaien and his dreams!" Mydri said fondly.

Seregil looked up at her in surprise. "I'd forgotten."

He sheathed the blade and ran his fingers over the fine leather scabbard and long belt, fighting the temptation to put it on. "I'm not supposed to carry a weapon here, you know."

"You're not supposed to be leaving, either," Adzriel said with a catch in her voice. "With all Alec and Beka have told me, I was worried that you would not accept it."

Seregil shook his head, bemused. His hand had known this weapon from the instant he'd touched it; it hadn't occurred to him to refuse it.

"I promise you this." Unsheathing it again, he put the hilt in Adzriel's hand and set the point against his heart, leaning into it until it dented the front of his coat. "By Aura Elustri, and by the name I once had, this blade will never be drawn in anger against an Aurënfaie."

"Then keep your temper and protect yourself," Adzriel advised, handing it back. "What shall I say when they find you gone?"

Seregil smiled crookedly. "Tell them I got homesick."

He hid the sword in the stable, then took the back stairs two at a time. Resisting the urge to look in on Klia one last time, he hurried to his room, taking care to inform several servants he met along the way that he and Alec were retiring for the night.

The bedchamber was in near darkness, lit only by one small lamp. The balcony shutters were closed tight. The tunic and trousers he'd stolen earlier lay on the neatly made bed, together with an Akhendi sen'gai.

"Alec?" he called softly, hastily changing his clothes.

"Over here. I'm just finishing up," a voice said from somewhere beyond the bed.

Alec stepped into the light, still toweling his wet hair. Seregil halted, unexpectedly moved by the sight of his friend wearing Aurënfaie clothing. It suited Alec, making him look more 'faie than ya'shel. He'd always had the slender build and carriage—Seregil had recognized that the first time he'd laid eyes on him—but somehow it was more apparent now. As Alec removed the towel, the resemblance became that much stronger. Thanks to a walnut-shell concoction they'd brewed up earlier, his yellow hair and brows were now as brown as Seregil's.

"Did it work?" Alec asked, running a comb through the wet strands.

"It certainly did. I hardly recognize you myself."

Alec pulled something from his belt—another sen'gai. "I hope you know how to wrap these things. I haven't had much luck and didn't dare ask anyone for help."

"A good thing, too. Where'd you get these?" Seregil fingered the brown-and-green-patterned cloth with misgivings. Wearing false colors was a crime.

Alec shrugged. "Off a laundry line this afternoon. I just happened to be in the right place with no one else in sight. 'Take what the god sends and be thankful,' right? What are you waiting for? We've got to get moving!"

Seregil smoothed the cloth between his fingers again, then placed the midpoint across Alec's brow and began weaving the long ends around his head to form as good an approximation as he could manage of the Akhendi style. Tying the long ends off over Alec's tattooed ear, he stepped back and looked him over with approval. "The

Akhendi have enough ya'shel among them that you shouldn't draw much notice anyway, but you could pass for pure just as easily."

Even in this light, Seregil could see the faint blush of pleasure that darkened his friend's cheeks.

"What about you?" Alec asked, belting on his sword.

Seregil glanced down at the remaining sen'gai lying untouched on the bed. "No. If I ever do put on one again, it will be one I have a right to."

Thero slipped in and closed the door behind him. "I thought it must be time. Are you ready?"

Seregil exchanged a quick look with Alec, then nodded. "You go ahead and make sure the way is clear. We'll be right behind you."

The unlit stable yard appeared deserted. Thero stood a moment, then motioned for Seregil and Alec to follow. Sending a silent thanks to Beka, Seregil strode across to the stable.

Inside, a lone woman was saddling a horse with Aurënfaie tack by the glow of a lightstone. Two other horses, one Aurënfaie, one Skalan, were ready to go. She heard them come in and turned, pushing back the brim of her helmet.

"Bilairy's Balls!" Seregil growled.

It was Beka. She'd traded her captain's gorget for a dispatch pouch and wore the worn tabard of a common rider. Her long red hair was bound up tightly at the back of her neck.

"What are you doing?" Thero hissed, equally surprised.

"Going with them as far as need be," she whispered back, handing Alec and Seregil the reins of the Aurënfaie horses.

"You're needed here!"

"I've been wresting with that all day," she said. "This is a command decision. Right now, nothing is more important than stopping Korathan. Rhylin and Braknil can manage here until we get all this sorted out. And if we don't—well, it may not matter."

Seregil laid a hand on the wizard's arm, forestalling further argument. "She's right."

Frowning, Thero gave in. "I can shield you until you're out of the city," he offered, drawing his wand.

"No, you'd better not. There are too many folk around who'd smell your magic on us. We'll manage, with two of us—" He gave Thero the quick, subtle sign for "Watcher."

Alec saw and nodded at Beka. "Perhaps it's time we made it three? I think Magyana would approve."

"I believe she would," Seregil agreed. "A bit sooner than we'd planned, perhaps, but there's no doubt of her worth."

"You mean it?" Beka breathed, wide-eyed.

He grinned. The Watchers were a strange, fractured group—even he did not know who all the members were—but Beka had seen too much growing up not to have formed some ideas of her own.

"Do you understand what it means, Beka, to be a Watcher?" asked Thero.

"Enough," she replied, confirming Seregil's suspicions. "If it means serving Skala as Seregil and my father have, then I'm in."

"There's a great deal more to it than that, but we'll deal with that later," Seregil said, hoping she wouldn't have cause to regret this hasty decision during the dark days ahead. "Do it, Thero."

Thero pulled an ancient ivory dagger from his belt and set it spinning inches from Beka's face. This was the test of truth, and one that allowed for no mistakes. Beka stood unflinching, her gaze fixed on Thero.

The sight brought a lump to Seregil's throat. This same knife had belonged to Nysander. It had spun in front of his own face when he took the oath as a very young man. Years later, Alec had felt its threat and passed the challenge.

"Beka, daughter of Kari," Thero whispered. "A Watcher must observe carefully, report truthfully, and keep the secrets that must be kept. Do you swear by your heart and eyes and by the Four to do these things?"

"I do."

The knife tumbled harmlessly into Thero's outstretched hand. "Then welcome, and luck in the shadows to you."

Only then did she betray relief. "That wasn't so bad."

"That's the easy part," Alec told her, grinning as broadly as she was. "Now you're really in the middle of it."

Seregil felt his heart skip a beat as she turned to him, eyes full of quiet triumph. "Whatever comes, I'm with you."

"First the commission; now this. Your poor mother will never speak to me again." Seregil gave her shoulder a quick squeeze, then went to retrieve his sword from its hiding place in the hay.

"Where did you get that?" Alec asked.

"A gift from my sisters." Seregil tossed the sword belt to him and went to sling his pack over his saddlebow.

Alec drew the blade. "It's a beauty."

Seregil took the belt back, wrapping it twice around his waist. Alec gave him the sword and he sheathed it, fiddling with the scabbard lacings until it hung at the proper, low-slung angle against his left hip. His hands remembered each movement without the need for thought; the off-centered weight of the weapon at his side felt good and right. "Let's go."

"Luck in the shadows," Thero murmured again, walking them to the gate.

"And in the light," Seregil replied. He clasped the wizard's thin shoulder a moment, wondering what else to say. If this all went wrong, this would be their last parting.

Thero covered his hand with his own for a moment. The silence between them was charged with sentiments neither knew quite how to express.

Alec spared them the necessity. "We'll see that your rooms at the Orëska House are aired out for your return," he joked.

Thero's smile flashed in the darkness, then he was gone, barring the gate behind them.

Mounting his horse, Seregil looked up at the black disk of the new moon, just visible among the blazing stars.

Ebrahä rabás.
Astha Nöliena.

Nyal watched Beka and the others out of sight, then slipped away in the opposite direction, unaware of the rhui'auros who watched him.

Though it seemed a foolish risk, Seregil stopped one last time at the Vhadäsoori. Across the dark span of water he could see a few people gathered around the Cup for some ceremony, but this side of the pool was deserted. Driven by some half-formed desire, he dismounted and went to the water's edge. Kneeling, he drew his sword and plunged it into the sacred pool, hilt and all.

"Aura Elustri, I accept your gift," he whispered, too low for the others to hear.

Reversing his grip on the hilt, he stood and offered the weapon to the moon, then let out a soft laugh.

Alec joined him, scanning the surrounding shadows nervously. "What's so funny?"

"Look at this." Seregil held the pommel up; the round, dark stone looked like a second new moon against the stars. "My uncle and his dreams."

"So that runs in the family, too, does it?"

"Apparently." Sheathing his sword, Seregil scooped up a handful of water and drank. He felt edgy, light, a little giddy, the way he used to, just before a job.

It was time to go.

They set off to the north, anxious to get away from the populated streets. The unrest was worse tonight. Angry voices rang out in all directions around them. Alec thought he caught a fleeting hint of the Bash'wai's mysterious scent and remained vigilant, expecting pursuit at any moment.

But most of the people they met paid them little mind, until they reached the edge of the Goliníl tupa, where a half dozen youths emerged from a side street to follow them.

"Off to serve your foreign queen, Akhendi?" one of them shouted after Alec. The insult was followed by a hail of thrown rocks. One bounced off Beka's helmet. Another struck Seregil in the middle of the back. The horses shied, but Seregil kept a slow, steady pace.

"Aura bring you peace, brothers," he said.

"Peace! Peace!" came the jeering reply, together with more rocks. One grazed Beka's cheek when she unwisely looked back. Alec reined in angrily, ready to retaliate, but she blocked him with her horse.

"Come on; there's no time for this!" she warned, kicking her horse into a gallop.

The Goliníl soon gave up the chase, but the riders didn't slow until they burst out onto the open plain. *How far do we have to go before he's breaking the law?* Alec wondered as they slowed to a canter under the star-studded sky.

Just then the Bash'wai scent closed in around him again, strong enough to take his breath away. Reeling in the saddle, he felt rather than saw a dark force surround him, blinding him and roaring in his ears. Then the stars were back, brighter than ever, but sliding sideways.

He landed hard and gave thanks later that he hadn't flung out his arm in time to break or dislocate it. As it was, his ribs took a nasty jar. He lay still for a moment, gasping and tingling strangely all over.

Then Seregil was there, cursing fiercely under his breath as he ran his hands over Alec's face and head. "I didn't realize—I don't feel any blood. Where did they hit you?"

"Hit me?" Alec struggled up. "No, it was just the Bash'wai. That's the strongest I've ever felt them."

Beka loomed over Seregil's shoulder, drawn sword in hand. "What did they do to you? You just swooned over."

"Must have been their idea of saying good-bye," Alec said, grimacing as Seregil helped him to his feet.

"Or a warning," Beka put in darkly, scanning the darkness around them.

"No, this was different." He shivered, recalling the sense of being engulfed.

"You're chilled through," Seregil muttered, pressing a hand to Alec's cheek.

"I'm fine. Where's my horse?"

Beka handed him his reins. "We better go slowly for a few minutes. We don't need you keeling over at a gallop."

Alec glanced back at the city as they set off again, half expecting to see mysterious shapes drifting after him. Sarikali looked deceptively peaceful from here, a dark, jumbled sprawl against the sky touched here and there by the yellow gleam of a watch fire.

"Good-bye," he whispered.

The starlight was enough to see by as they crossed the bridge and rode into the shelter of the forest beyond, following the main road.

As the night wore on Alec reached tentatively out across the talí-menios bond, seeking answers to the questions there had been neither the time nor the privacy to ask earlier. Seregil glanced back at him and smiled, but his thoughts were wrapped in silence.

Tall fir and oak massed darkly on either side of the road, leaning over it in places to form an oppressive tunnel. Bats chirped and swooped around them, chasing huge moths with wings like dusty handprints. An owl flew along beside Alec for a moment, some long-tailed prey dangling from its talons. Other creatures marked their passing with a golden flash of eyes or startled yip.

They reined in briefly where a stream cut close to the road and watered the horses. Thirsty himself, Alec dismounted and walked a little way upstream to drink. He'd just bent down when a rank odor hit him. The horses smelled it, too, and blew nervously.

"Get back!" Alec hissed to the others, knowing this was no Bash'wai.

"What is it?" Beka asked behind him.

The horses shied again, then fought the reins as an enormous bear burst from the alders and splashed across the stream toward Alec.

"Don't move," he warned the others, mind already racing down well-known paths. It was a sow bear, thin from the winter's cub bearing. If they'd somehow gotten between her and her young, then he'd reached his journey's end for certain.

The bear had stopped a few feet away, swinging her massive head from side to side as she watched him. Seregil and Beka were still mounted, able to break for it. With one eye on the bear, he gauged the distance to the nearest climbable tree.

Too far.

The bear let out a loud grunt and lumbered forward to sniff his face. Alec gagged on the hot, fetid breath, then felt himself knocked backwards. Sprawled on his back, he looked up at the bear silhouetted against the sky, its eyes glowing like molten gold.

"You'd better not linger, little brother," she told him. "Smiles conceal knives."

With a last deep grunt, the sow wheeled around and splashed away upstream. Alec lay where he'd fallen, too stunned to move.

"By the Flame, I've never seen a bear act like that!" Beka exclaimed.

"Did you hear it?" he asked faintly.

"Not until you gave the warning," she replied. "It came out of nowhere."

"No, did you hear what she *said*?" he asked, getting shakily to his feet.

"She spoke to you?" Seregil asked excitedly. "By the Light, Alec, that was a khtir'bai. What did it say?"

Alec bent down and placed his hand easily inside one clawed paw print. It had been no apparition. "Same thing the rhui'auros told you," he replied in wonder. " 'Smiles conceal knives.' "

"At least they're consistent in their obscurity," grumbled Beka.

"I suspect we'll find out what it means soon enough," said Seregil.

Fog seeped up from the ground as they rode, collecting beneath the dark boughs and dripping coldly from the ends of long evergreen needles. Spiderwebs were woven across narrow places in the trail; they were all soon coated in sticky wet strands.

Just after midnight they reached a sizable village next to a small lake.

"The first change of horses for the dispatch riders is here, in a byre just beyond town," Beka whispered. "Do we dare make a change here, or cut around?"

Seregil slapped absently at a spider on his thigh. "We need the horses. Dressed as we are, and at this hour, we should be safe enough. I doubt there's even a guard posted."

Just past the last small house they found a sagging lean-to, its cedar-shake roof thick with moss. Three sturdy horses were stabled inside. Dismounting, they shifted their saddles over, working by the light of Seregil's lightstone.

As they led the new mounts out, however, a sleepy young face appeared out of a pile of hay at the back of the byre. Beka grabbed quickly for Seregil's light, waving the others outside. Holding the light high to keep her face in shadow below the brim of her helmet, she faced the boy. He was sitting up now, regarding her with groggy interest; not a guard, just someone left to tend the horses.

He mumbled something, and she recognized the word for "messenger."

"Yes, sleep again," Beka replied in her broken Aurënfaie. Her knowledge of the language had improved, but she still understood more than she could say back. "Ours we leave."

"Is that you, Vanos?" the boy asked, craning his head for a look at Alec.

Alec whispered something back and quickly disappeared.

The boy squinted back up at Beka as she turned to go. "I don't know you."

Beka shrugged apologetically, as if she didn't understand, then pocketed the light and led her horse out.

The hay rustled behind her and she heard the boy mutter, "Cheap Skalan."

Just like home, Beka thought with amusement. Pulling a coin from her wallet, she flipped it in his direction.

"Now we've been seen," Alec muttered as they set off up the road again.

"Couldn't be helped," Seregil said. "He mistook us for the usual riders, and we'll be long gone before anyone comes looking for us."

"I hope you're right," Beka replied doubtfully.

Thero prowled the halls after Seregil and the others left. Only Braknil and Rhylin shared his vigil; as far as the others knew, Beka was on duty with the princess. Klia remained unconscious, mercifully oblivious as Mydri checked her mutilated hand repeatedly through the night, debating whether or not to cut more away.

From the beginning, their little delegation had rattled about the cavernous place like seeds in a dry gourd. Now, with so many missing or dead, the sense of emptiness was palpable. Thero strengthened the warding spells he'd laid about the place, then retreated to the colos. The fragrant night breeze across the back of his neck felt good as he took a lump of candle drippings from his pocket and set about warming it between his fingers. When it was soft, he divided it in two and took out his wand. Slipping off the two long strands of hair—one Seregil's, one Alec's—knotted around it, he kneaded each into one of the wax balls until it disappeared. Speaking the appropriate spells, he covered them with netted designs he made with the tip of his dagger. A red glow flared briefly at the center of each soft lump when he finished. Satisfied, he tucked them away for future use.

It was well past midnight now; a few scattered pinpricks of firelight glimmered in the distance. Imagining groups of friends or lovers awake together in the glow of those lights, he was suddenly overcome by a wave of loneliness. The people he trusted most were already miles away. Those whose trust he needed, here in this strange land, he must lie to, breaking honor to serve his princess.

Shaking off the dark thoughts, he settled himself more comfortably on the stone seat to meditate. Instead, his unruly imagination took him back to the mysterious vision he'd experienced during his first visit to the Nha'mahat. He absently smoothed the lap of his robe; the dragon bite had healed, but the marks left behind remained as an impressive reminder of that night's half-realized enlightenments.

Something landed on the back of his hand, startling him badly. Looking down, he saw that it was a little dragon no longer than his thumb. It clung to his knuckle with tickling claws and regarded him curiously.

He sat very still, wondering if the creature would bite. Instead, it folded its delicate wings against its sides and went to sleep, its smooth belly radiating welcome heat against his skin.

"Thank you," he murmured to it. "I can use the company."

The dragon's warmth spread up from his hand, warming him through. Smiling, he settled into a quiet meditation. When the inevitable uproar began, whatever form it took, he would need his wits about him.

39

PATHS DIVERGING

Clouds had rolled down out of the mountains during the night, and dawn brightened slowly behind a fine veil of rain. Beka licked at a sweet drop that spattered against her cheek, grateful for a taste of fresh water.

They'd ridden steadily all night, keeping to the main road to preserve the illusion of being routine couriers. Along the way, however, they had paused long enough to steal four extra horses. When the time came to part, not too long from now, she'd take the way-station horses with her to confuse the trail.

It was a good plan—she'd carried out similar ruses often enough against the Plenimarans—but for the past hour or so Seregil had been quiet, and spent too much time staring off into the thick forest along the roadside for her liking. Alec was watching him, too, sensing trouble.

Seregil reined in again so abruptly that her horse barreled into his.

"Damn it, what is it now?" she asked, pulling her horse's head around sharply as Seregil's spirited sorrel lashed out with its back hooves.

He said nothing, just gentled his mount and scanned an overgrown byway on their left. His expression was not encouraging.

"We've missed the side road you're looking for, haven't we?" Alec asked, and Beka heard the undertone of worry in his voice. There was good reason for alarm. Seregil was their only guide here, and it had been over half a lifetime since he'd traveled these roads.

Seregil shrugged. "Maybe. Or perhaps it's been abandoned since I last saw it, given what Amali said about villages dying out here." He glanced up at the brightening sky, and his tight-lipped frown deepened. "Come on, we've got to get off the main road soon. There are other ways to the trail."

The khirnari of Akhendi woke to the sound of someone lifting the latch of his chamber door. Heart pounding, he reached for the knife beneath his pillow and flung an arm out to protect Amali, only to find the other half of the bed empty.

His steward, Glamiel, slipped in with a candle and padded softly to his bedside.

"Where is my wife?" Rhaish demanded, clutching his aching chest.

"In the garden, Khirnari. She rose a little while ago."

"Of course." Sleep visited him so seldom these days and left him muddled when he woke. "What is it, then? It's not dawn yet."

"It is, Khirnari. Amali gave orders that your rest not be disturbed, but there's been strange news this morning." Glamiel went to the tall windows and pulled back the hangings. Grey light filled the room, and the smell of rain. Looking out through the flowering boughs that framed the casement, Rhaish saw his wife sitting alone beneath an arbor. She'd wept last night, imploring him again to explain his silence and his anger. What could he have told her?

Distracted, he missed the first part of Glamiel's news and had to ask him to repeat it.

"The Skalans sent out a dispatch rider last night," the man told him.

"What of it?"

"As you say, Khirnari, no one thought anything of it, until word came in just now from the first way station that neither of the Akhendi escorts gave the usual signal, and that the Skalan rider was one the boy had never seen before. One of the escorts claimed to be Vanos í Namal, but he's still at the Skalan barracks. I've spoken with him myself. So are all the others assigned to guide the Skalans. What should we do?"

"How long ago did you get word of this?"

"Just now, Khirnari. Should Brythir í Nien be informed of this?"

"No. Not until we learn what our Skalan friends are up to." After a moment's consideration, he added, "Send for Seregil. I wish to speak with him at once."

Alone again, Rhaish sagged back against his pillows as an image rose to his mind's eye: Seregil skillfully slitting the dead fish, extracting the ring with as much certainty as if he'd known it was there all along. And earlier, in the garden, he'd searched so intently, so efficiently. At the time it had been gratifying, astonishing. Now the memory filled him with unease.

The cold kiss of a rain-laden breeze woke Thero. Outside the colos, a morning shower pattered down on the roof tiles and voices drifted up to him from the street below. Catching Seregil's name, he sent a sighting spell that way and discovered Mirn and Steb speaking with an Akhendi man he didn't recognize.

"I haven't seen Lord Seregil yet this morning," Mirn was saying. "I'll tell him Lord Rhaish is looking for him as soon as he comes down."

"It's a matter of some urgency," the Akhendi replied.

Here we go, then, Thero thought. Hurrying down to Seregil's abandoned room, he latched the door after him. None too soon, either, as it turned out. The latch lifted, then jiggled against the lock pin.

"Seregil, you're wanted downstairs." It was Kheeta, damn the luck. A servant could be put off with a curt response. "Are you awake? Seregil? Alec?"

Thero passed his hand quickly over the bed, willing a memory, any memory, from it. The bed let out a rhythmic creaking, accompanied by a throaty masculine moan. The wizard fell back a pace, annoyed. He'd expected snoring, but supposed he should have known better.

The sounds had the desired effect, however. There was a meaningful silence on the far side of the door, then the tactful retreat of footsteps.

Wasting no time, Thero took out the wax balls he'd prepared the night before, pinched them man-shaped, and placed them beneath the edge of the coverlet. Weaving shapes on the air with his wand, Thero hummed tonelessly under his breath, remembering faces, limbs, the shapes of hands and feet. The wax simulacra swelled and lengthened beneath the blankets. By the time he finished they had a fair likeness of Seregil and Alec but were still stiff and expressionless. Laying a finger on Seregil's cold brow, Thero blew into his nostrils. Color suffused the pallid cheeks, and the features relaxed into something like sleep. He did the same with Alec's double, then arranged the pair into a sleeping pose. Summoning more memories from shared nights on the road, he added the steady rise and fall of breath, with the lightest of snores from Alec. With any luck and a bit of delicacy on the part of servants, this might buy them a few more precious hours.

He left the door unlatched and made his way down to the main hall, where Kheeta was making excuses to their Akhendi visitor.

"Good morning," Thero said, coming forward to greet their guest. "What brings you here at this hour?"

The man bowed. "Greetings, Thero í Procepios. Amali ä Yassara wishes to examine the Akhendi charm Seregil brought her. She is feeling quite strong this morning."

The charm! Thero reached for the pouch at his belt, then frowned. Seregil had had it last; in all the confusion caused by Magyana's letter, Thero hadn't thought to get it back from him.

"You should have said so!" exclaimed Kheeta, already halfway to the stairway again. "I'm sure they won't mind being disturbed for that."

"Let me," Thero said quickly, regretting his own ruse. "I'll send him to you as soon as he's"—here he gave Kheeta a hard look—"awake."

"There; this is the one," Seregil called out happily, squinting down yet another unremarkable side road.

Beka stifled a groan. Except for the flock of kutka pecking morning grit in the tall grass, it looked just like all the other sidetracks he'd halted for this morning.

"The last one you were this sure of cost us half an hour's ride in the wrong direction," Alec pointed out, far more patiently than Beka could have managed.

"No, this is the one," he insisted. "See that boulder there?" He pointed to a large grey rock a few yards down the road on the right. "What does that look like to you?"

Beka gripped the reins more tightly. "Look, I'm hungry and I don't remember when I last slept—"

"I'm serious. What does it look like to you?" He was grinning madly now, and she wondered how long it had been since he'd had any rest himself.

Alec met her questioning look with his usual shrug, then turned his attention to the rock in question.

It was about six feet long, four high, and roughly oval in shape. The end facing them narrowed sharply into a pair of even concave depressions that made it look almost like—

"A bear?" she ventured, wondering if she was losing her mind, too. The narrowed end did have the look of a low-set head, with the smooth curve of a bear's back rising up behind it.

"I see it," chuckled Alec. "We seem to be haunted by bears. This is your landmark?"

"Yes," Seregil replied, clearly relieved. "Damn, I'd forgotten about it until I saw it just now. If you look closely, you can still make out where someone painted eyes on it. But this used to be a well-traveled route. There were several villages up in the hills, and a Dravnian trading camp beyond."

"It can't be seeing much traffic these days," Beka said, still doubtful. Foot-high saplings choked the narrow, weed-grown track.

"That's good," said Seregil. "The fewer people we run into, the better I'll like it. Thero isn't the only one who can send messages by magic, you know." He glanced up at the sun. "It's getting late. We should be further along by now."

Without dismounting, he and Alec shifted their saddles and gear to two of the stolen horses and climbed across. It took some managing, and Beka's help with the girths, but this way they left no telltale footprints for a tracker to read.

Beka fixed the reins of their cast-off mounts to her saddle with long lead ropes, letting the horses move with some independence. If anyone was tracking them, the signs would show that the "traveling companions" they'd joined up with the previous night had gone their own way while the three dispatch riders went on down the main road.

"Keep out of sight as long as you can," Seregil warned, clasping hands with her. "You can't get through the mountains without a guide, so you're trapped on this side."

"You worry about yourselves," she replied. "I'll just keep on this way as far as I can go, then strike off wherever seems best. I'll stay out another two days. After that, no matter what, I head back to Klia. The worst anyone will do if they do catch me is haul me back to Sarikali anyway. What will you do, after you've talked to Korathan?"

Seregil shrugged. "Stay with him, I expect, though it may be in chains. If I have my way, he'll set sail back to Skala directly."

"Then I'll see you both there," she said brightly, fighting back a surge of foreboding.

Alec gave her a wry smile. "Luck in the shadows, Watcher."

"And to you both." She sat her horse as they started up the road. Seregil disappeared around the first bend without a backward glance. Alec paused to wave, then followed.

"Luck in the shadows," she whispered again. Leading her string of horses on up the main road, she set her face for the mountains.

The road got no better as Alec and Seregil went on, but it was open enough for them to canter single file. Several miles on, they came to the remains of the first village, and Seregil paused to make a quick circuit.

Some of the cottages had burned down; the rest were slowly falling apart. Small trees and weeds were encroaching rapidly on the broad clearing, sprouting up in disused garden plots and doorways.

Looking inside one of the houses, Alec found only a few bits of broken crockery. "Looks like the villagers picked up and left."

Seregil rode over and passed him a dripping water skin. "No trade, no livelihood. At least the well's still clear."

Alec drank, then rummaged in his pack for a strip of dried meat. "I wonder if we'll be able to find fresh horses along the way?"

"We'll manage," Seregil said, studying the clouds. "If we hurry, we can make the second village before nightfall. I'd rather spend the night under a roof, if we can manage it. It's still early enough in the year for it to be damn cold at night up here."

Just beyond the village they struck a broad outcropping, steep and treacherous with loose rock and threaded with little rivulets from a spring above it. A few cairns still marked the way to several trails that continued on from here.

They gave their horses their heads, letting them pick their way carefully up the slope. Looking back over his shoulder, Alec saw that the animal's unshod hooves left almost no marks in passing. It was going to take one fine tracker to catch them, he thought with satisfaction.

"I don't have it! I destroyed it, burned it up in the fire," Amali sobbed, cowering back against the bed. She'd started out defiant but quickly dissolved into tears. It made her seem even younger than she was, and Rhaish hesitated, wondering if he had the resolve to strike her if it came to that.

"Don't lie to me! I must have it," he said sternly, looming over her. "If my fears are correct, you may already be found out. Why else would Seregil not have come by now?"

"Why won't you tell me what this is about?" she sobbed, instinctively shielding her belly with both hands.

The gesture broke his heart, and he slumped down on the bed beside her. "For the sake of Akhendi, and for our child, you must give me the rest of it if you still have it. I know you too well, my love. You would never destroy another's handiwork." He fought to keep the rising desperation from his voice. "You must let me protect you, as I always have."

Amali stifled another sob as she crawled off the bed and went to a workbox on her dressing table. Opening it, she lifted out a tray of charm-making goods and reached beneath it. "Here, and may you make better use of it than I did!" She threw the woven bracelet at his feet.

Rhaish bent to pick it up, recalling a similar moment four nights earlier. He pushed the thought away with a shudder, knowing himself damned.

The knot work on this bracelet was simple but well done; some magic still lingered despite the loss of the charm, strong enough to hold both the memory of its maker, a peasant woman from one of the mountain villages, and that of the young man it had been made for. Alec í Amasa's khi had permeated the fibers as surely as his sweat.

Amali was still weeping. Ignoring her for the moment, Rhaish sat down in a chair by the bed and pressed the bracelet between his hands, speaking a spell. The bracelet throbbed against his palms. Closing his eyes, he caught a glimpse of Alec and his surroundings, saw dripping boughs close overhead, distant peaks just visible through a break in the trees. Saw Seregil riding beside him, gesturing at something—a large, oddly shaped boulder that Rhaish recognized immediately.

Realization knocked the breath from his lungs, and he fell back in his chair. They did know! Klia must know, or why else would she have sent them, of all people, for the northern coast?

Cold hands clasped his, and he looked down into Amali's tear-streaked face as she knelt before him. "You must return home, talía. Say nothing of any of this, and go home."

"I only meant to help," she whispered, picking up the fallen bracelet and looking at it in horrified wonder. "What have I done, my love?"

"Nothing the Lightbearer has not ordained." Rhaish stroked her cheek gently, glad of her warmth against his thighs. He was cold, chilled to the bone despite the sunlight that had broken through the clouds. "Go on now, and prepare our house for my return. Your wait will not be long."

His legs shook as he stepped out into the deserted garden, heedless of how the wet grass soaked his slippers and the hem of his robe. Sitting down in Amali's arbor, he pressed the bracelet between his hands again, stealing glance after glance at the runaways as long as his strength allowed, until he'd seen enough to guess where they were headed.

Folding his hands, he rested a moment, feeling the comforting power of Sarikali seeping into him from the ground and air, replenishing him. He cupped his hands, picturing a distant village and the men he trusted there, while an orb of silvery light formed in the cage of his fingers. When he'd thought his message into it, he touched it and it whisked way, carrying what he hoped were the right words to the right ears.

Watching him from behind the window hangings, Amali dried her tears and prepared to send out a similar spell. "Aura protect us," she whispered when she finished, praying that this time shc acted rightly.

40

GAMBIT

Despite all Thero's precautions, the storm broke far sooner than he'd hoped. He was helping Mydri change Klia's dressings at midmorning when Corporal Kallas hurried in, looking worried.

"There's trouble next door, my lord. I think you'd better come."

A small crowd had gathered outside Adzriel's house. She stood in the doorway with Säaban as she faced the Haman khirnari. Beside him stood the formidable Lhaär ä Iriel, her face a mask of righteous indignation behind her tattoos.

"He would never have left without speaking to you!" Nazien í Hari said, leveling an accusing finger at her.

"You know as well as I that the ban of exile cut him off from clan and family," Adzriel retorted coldly. "There is no claim of atui on Bôkthersa in this. Even if there were, I can tell you nothing of where he's gone or why, for I do not know. I swear it by Aura's own light."

"There's the wizard!" someone else shouted, and the unfriendly crowd turned its collective glare on Thero.

"Where is Seregil of Rhíminee?" Lhaär demanded, and he could see a faint corona of power glinting around her. His heart sank;

she might not read thoughts, but no simulacrum of his was going to fool those sharp eyes.

"He's left the city," he replied tersely. "I don't know where he's gone." That was true enough after a fashion. Seregil had purposely not revealed his route.

"Why did they leave?" demanded the Akhendi khirnari, stepping into view for the first time accompanied by the Silmai and Ra'basi khirnari. Thero quailed inwardly, all his precautions useless. How could they all have found out so quickly?

He scanned the crowd, seeking one more familiar face beneath a Ra'basi sen'gai. Nyal was nowhere to be found.

"I cannot tell you why he left, Khirnari. Perhaps the strain of his situation here took more of a toll than any of us realized."

"Nonsense!" snorted Brythir. "Your queen and your princess both vouched for him as a man of character. I have judged him to be the same. He would not simply run off! You must answer to the Iia'sidra regarding this. I'll expect to see you and your household there at once!"

"Forgive me, Khirnari, but that is not possible." An ugly murmur spread through the crowd, and Thero was glad suddenly for the soldiers at his back. "Princess Klia lies close to death, poisoned by an Aurënfaie hand. We now have reason to believe that Torsin's death was not a natural one, either. I will attend the Iia'sidra as soon as they can be assembled, but I cannot in good conscience allow any other member of this household to leave here as long as she remains in danger."

"Torsin murdered?" The old khirnari blinked up at him. "You said nothing of this before."

"We believed the murderer might reveal himself by his own guilty knowledge."

"Do you know who this murderer is?" the Khatme khirnari demanded, looking skeptical.

"I can say nothing of that, as yet," Thero replied, letting the others take that as they would, and hoping it would deflect attention from Seregil's disappearance.

"Come then, Wizard," Brythir told him, motioning for Thero to follow.

"You don't mean to go alone?" Sergeant Braknil whispered, moving in beside him.

"Stay here, all of you," Thero told him calmly. "Klia's safety is all that matters now. Send the Bôkthersans back to Adzriel with my thanks, and then set siege guard." He paused, halfway down the stairs. "Release Sergeant Mercalle back to duty, too. We need everyone we can get."

"Thank you, my lord. She's loyal to Skala, whatever else you may think of her actions." Raising his voice, Braknil added, "Take care, my lord. Send word if you need us—for anything."

"I'm sure that won't be necessary, Sergeant." Going down the stairs, Thero joined the khirnari. Adzriel lingered with the others in front of her own door, but gave him a small smile as he passed. Encouragement, perhaps, or complicity?

Most of the Iia'sidra were waiting in the great chamber when they arrived. For the first time, Thero took the seat of honor in the circle, marooned in silence. Those around him spoke in low tones or behind their hands, casting occasional glances in his direction.

Ulan í Sathil was there but appeared uninterested in the whole affair. A great crowd of Haman had accompanied Nazien, and Thero recognized a good many of Emiel's companions among them. They looked to be out for blood.

Adzriel entered last with a contingent of twenty, taking her place in the circle with her husband at her side.

There was no ceremony or ringing of chimes today; this was a private matter between Skala and Haman. The others had gathered only to witness.

Nazien í Hari stepped forward as soon as the last of the khirnari had taken their seats, and to his credit displayed little satisfaction as he announced, "Before this body, I claim teth'sag against Seregil the Exile, formerly Seregil of Bôkthersa, and against all those who aid and abet him. He has violated vows given for his return and I claim the vengeance that is Haman's right."

"How convenient for you," sneered Iriel ä Kasrai of Bry'kha. "Seregil might have found proof of your nephew's guilt if he'd stayed around a bit longer."

"Silence!" snapped Brythir. "It is as Nazien í Hari says. The Iia'sidra itself could not deny them this right. Seregil knew this. He has made his choice and his former clan must make good their vow of atui."

"The guilt or innocence of Emiel í Moranthi has no bearing on this," Nazien proclaimed. "As khirnari of Haman, and as the grandfather of the man the Exile murdered, I have no choice. I demand that the Bôkthersans administer justice under the law."

Adzriel stood, pale but unbowed. "Justice shall be yours, Khirnari." Mydri and Säaban remained stoic, but behind them, Kheeta and several others covered their faces.

The Silmai turned next to him. "Now, Thero í Procepios, I demand that you explain Seregil's disappearance. Why did he leave, and who helped him?"

"I regret that I can tell you nothing," Thero said again, and took his seat amid the expected outcry.

A lone figure detached itself from the shadows near the door and entered the circle. Here was Nyal at last.

"I think you will find it was Alec í Amasa and the Skalan captain who accompanied Seregil," he announced, not looking in Thero's direction.

You skulking cur! the wizard thought, sick with rage. So that was how the Haman had gotten word so quickly.

Ulan í Sathil rose, and a hush fell over the chamber. Tarnished as his honor might be, he still commanded respect. "Perhaps the more immediate question we should be asking is why he left," he said. "This sudden and inexplicable flight makes no sense. Though I have no great love for the man, even I must admit that the Exile has acquitted himself well since his arrival here. He has won the respect, perhaps even the support, of many and enjoyed the company of his former kin. Why then, in the midst of his own investigations against my clan and the Haman, should he suddenly commit so gross an act of disloyalty?" He paused, then added, "Why, indeed, unless he or the Skalans have something to hide?"

"What are you implying?" demanded Adzriel.

Ulan spread his hands. "I merely speculate. Perhaps Seregil knows of something that takes precedence over the outcome of his current mission here."

For an instant, Thero forgot to breathe. Had Ulan's Plenimaran spies found out so soon of Korathan's ill-timed attack, or had Nyal somehow managed to betray them in this, as well? Rising, he said, "I can assure you, Khirnari, nothing is more important to Seregil or any of us than the success of our labors here." Even in his own ears, this scrap of truth sounded far less convincing than any lie he'd told so far.

"I do not mean to impugn Thero í Procepios's honor when I point out that we have only his word for that," Ulan said smoothly. "Nor when I also point out that it was Seregil himself, a proven traitor and murderer, who possesses the greatest knowledge of the device he claims was used to poison Klia. It was he himself who so easily and fortuitously found the ring in my house, thereby discrediting Skala's staunchest opponent."

"Are you suggesting that *he* poisoned Klia?" asked Brythir.

"I suggest nothing, yet she is not dead, is she? Perhaps a man who knows so much about poisons would also know how to administer them so as to not quite kill, thereby creating the semblance of a botched murder attempt?"

"That's ridiculous!" Thero retorted, but his protest was drowned out by the renewed burst of exclamations from all sides. People were out of their seats, shouting and arguing, crowding out onto the chamber floor. Even Brythir í Nien could not make himself heard over the din.

Thero shook his head, marveling at the ease with which the Virésse khirnari could manipulate an audience. Still, there was more than one way to get people's attention. Climbing up on his chair, he clapped his palms together over his head, forgetting, in his haste, to make allowances for the strange energy of the city.

Daylight failed for an instant, then a deafening clap of thunder rocked the chamber, rumbling around the room for the space of several heartbeats.

The result was nearly comical. People clutched at each other, clapped hands over their ears, or fell dumbstruck back into their seats. Ears ringing, Thero groped for the chair's back to keep his balance.

"Whatever Seregil has done, for whatever reasons, the matter of teth'sag lies between him and the Haman," he declared. "The greater wrong remains that done to Princess Klia, who lies insensible at the heart of a city she believed held no violence. Hunt him down if you must, but do not let the actions of one man destroy all we have worked toward during these long weeks! By all the sacred names of the Lightbearer, Klia has acted with nothing but honor, and been rewarded with injury, yet she demands no vengeance. I pray you remember that when the vote is cast—"

"How can you speak of a vote?" Lhaär ä Iriel demanded, gathering herself up from the floor and shaking off anyone who tried to assist her. "You see what comes of oaths made by the Tír. Cast them out and be done with it!"

"The vote will go forward," Brythir declared. "In the meantime, let the Exile be found and returned to face judgment."

Adzriel took the floor. "My fellow khirnari, Klia has labored long and honorably among us, as did Lord Torsin. They have been wronged; to cast the vote while she is unable to speak for herself would wrong her further. Until she recovers and the confusion that enfolds us has been lifted, I call upon the Iia'sidra to show mercy and postpone their decision. A few more days or weeks, what is that to us compared to what it may mean for Skala?"

"Let the Exile be brought back!" Elos of Goliníl called out, casting a dark look Thero's way. "I say we postpone the vote until he has answered for his actions. Only then will any doubts regarding Skala's true intentions be resolved."

"You speak wisely, Khirnari, as does Nazien í Hari," said Nyal, speaking up again. "I know the Exile and his companions better than any of you and would not see them brought to harm. They're most likely on their way north to Gedre, or west to Bôkthersa. You all know that I'm accounted a skilled tracker, and I know that country well. With the Iia'sidra's consent, I will lead a search party."

An angry outcry went up from the Bôkthersans, but Brythir stilled them with one upraised hand. "I accept your offer, Nyal í Nhekai, assuming Nazien í Hari has no objections."

"He may do as he likes," the Haman retorted. "I sent searchers west and north as soon as I learned of Seregil's escape."

Bowing, Nyal left the floor without looking in Thero's direction, and the wizard's fingers itched for magic to strike the man down.

Glaring at the Ra'basi's back, Thero vowed silently, *I'll give you teth'sag. If any harm comes to my friends through you, no law or magic will be enough to protect you!*

The Skalan guest house had become a fortress in Thero's absence. Armed guards stood at every door, and others paced the roof. Hurrying inside, he managed to make it to a chair near the door before his legs gave out. The sergeants and a handful of Urgazhi were waiting for him in the hall, together with several of the servants.

"What are you still doing here?" he asked the Bôkthersans.

Kheeta's mother shrugged. "Klia is still Adzriel's kin, and her guest. We do not desert our guests."

The wizard gave her a grateful nod, then quickly sketched out the debacle he'd just witnessed.

"Nyal's gone against us?" asked Corporal Nikides, stunned. "How can he do that to the captain? I'd have sworn—"

"What, that he loved her?" Sergeant Braknil let out a snort. "It's the oldest trick in the book, damn him! And he was good at it, too. He fooled me, and I've been out of the barn a time or two."

"He fooled us all," Thero admitted sadly. "I just hope Seregil and the others have had enough of a start to get through."

Gathering what strength he had left, he climbed the stairs to Klia's chamber.

41

REVELATIONS IN THE RAIN

A gentle drizzle dogged Alec and Seregil through the day, growing heavier and mixing with brief spates of sleet as afternoon slowly wore toward evening.

"This is a useless sort of rain," Seregil griped, shivering as he pulled his damp cloak around him. "It's not coming down hard enough to wash away our tracks."

"It's easier to stay warm in a snowstorm than in this," Alec agreed, chilled himself. His cloak and tunic had already soaked through at the shoulders and across the tops of his thighs. Now he could feel the wetness spreading. Waterlogged clothing wicked heat away from the body; even this late in the spring a man could take a killing chill from it. To make matters worse, the route Seregil had chosen ascended into the mountains sooner than the main road. The peaks in the distance ahead showed patches of white where snowfields still blanketed the summits. The dull outline of the sun, just visible through the mist, was sinking steadily in the west, stealing back the scant warmth of the day.

"We're going to have to stop soon," he said, chafing his arms with his hands. "Somewhere we can make a fire."

"We can't risk it yet," Seregil replied, scanning the road ahead.

"Dying of the chills will slow us down worse than getting captured, don't you think?"

Seregil urged his horse up a steep stretch of trail. They were still in the trees, but a wind was rising, adding to their discomfort. When the ground leveled out enough for them to ride abreast again, he turned to Alec, who knew at once by his slight frown and distant expression that he hadn't been thinking of rain or shelter.

"Even if Emiel is out to supplant Nazien, killing Klia would almost certainly work against him, don't you think? Emiel's a violent bastard, and no mistake, still—" He broke off, rubbing ruefully at the latest bruise on his jaw. "It's just a gut feeling, but after talking with him in the barracks that night, I can't imagine him risking the loss of honor."

"After all he did to you?" Alec growled. "I still say he's the most likely one. What about Ulan í Sathil?"

"Do you really think that man would make such a silly botch of the whole business? Would a man who knows how to foment civil war in another country have hidden the ring in his own courtyard like some common blackmailer keeping his dirty little collection of letters under his mattress?"

"No, he's too smart for that. If he had done it, we'd never have found him out. Besides, why would he do such a thing if Torsin was attempting some compromise in Virésse's favor. Which leaves us looking elsewhere. You recall what I said about the 'faie?"

Alec grinned. "That they're no good at murder because they don't do enough of it to keep in practice?"

"Ask the right questions," Seregil murmured, wandering off into his own thoughts again. "We're approaching this as if we're tracking some practiced assassin—it's what we're used to." He let out an exasperated sigh. "Amateurs! They're the worst."

"The Ra'basi have been cagey about which side of the fence they're on," Alec said, though he was more reluctant than ever to suspect Nyal after all his help with Klia. "The poison is one they're familiar with, and they had a man inside our house. And what about the Khatme? If I were going to pick anyone out for sheer malice, Lhaär and her lot would be it. It's clear they don't regard Tírfaie as equals. Perhaps they wouldn't count killing one or two as any great crime."

"An interesting thought," said Seregil. "And their religious zeal seems to have grown in my absence. I've seen that wreak more havoc than magic when it comes to war." Still, he didn't sound convinced.

. . .

They spent the night in a ruined hut, huddled miserably together under damp blankets as they ate a cold supper of dried venison, cheese, and rainwater. A wind came up soon after sunset, finding its way through every hole and chink of their paltry shelter, stirring the soaked clothing that lined the hut's one sound wall.

Pressed shoulder to shoulder with Alec, Seregil rested his head on his knees and tried to ignore the fits of shivering that shook him, and the way the slightest movement sucked cold air in around the edges of the blankets. He wasn't dangerously cold, just miserably uncomfortable.

As usual, Alec warmed faster. "Come here," he said presently, pulling Seregil to sit between his legs, back to Alec's chest. He rearranged the blankets into a better cocoon around them and wrapped his arms around him. "Better?"

"A bit." Seregil jammed his hands under his armpits to warm them.

Alec chuckled next to his ear. "I don't think you'd have survived where I grew up."

Seregil snorted softly. "I could say the same about you. I had some lean times and harsh lessons, wandering around Skala."

"The Rhíminee Cat."

"I was a lot of things before that. Ever wonder why I was so generous to whores, back when you first met me?"

"Not until just now." Alec's voice carried a note of weary resignation.

Seregil stared out a hole in the roof, watching the dark shapes of branches tossing in the wind. "Being back there, in Sarikali—it's like—I don't know, like being there clouded my mind. Considering the shambles we've left behind, I'm not sure how useful I've been to Idrilain, or to Klia." He took a deep breath, fighting down a surge of guilt. "We should have been able to learn more, do more."

Alec's arms tightened around him. "We would have, but Phoria cocked it up for us. And you're right about us being the only ones who could get to the coast. You're probably right about Emiel."

"Maybe, but I feel as if I've been sleepwalking since we arrived."

"I believe I pointed that out to you, not so long ago," Alec noted wryly. "It wasn't just you, though. Aurënen's a damn hard place for nightrunners. Too much honor."

Seregil chuckled. "Whatever happened to that honest Dalnan lad I took up with?"

"Long gone, and good riddance." Alec shifted his legs to a more comfortable angle."Do you really think Korathan will listen to you?"

"Would I be here if I didn't?"

"That's no answer."

"I'll have to make him listen."

They fell silent, and presently Alec's even breathing told Seregil that he'd fallen asleep. He shifted against Alec's shoulder, mind still racing.

Perhaps he had needed to get clear of Sarikali's powerful aura. The rhui'auros's convoluted words, his own strange dreams, his pathetic efforts to prove himself worthy—where had it all gotten him, except deeper into confusion? He was sick to death of the whole business and longed for the dangerous, straightforward life he'd left behind in Skala. Something Adzriel had said to him, when they'd seen each other so briefly in Rhíminee just before the war, came back to him. *Could you ever be content to sit under the lime trees at home, telling tales to the children, or debating with the elders of the council whether the lintel of the temple should be painted white or silver?*

His new sword lay close at hand, and he reached out, running his fingers over the hilt, thinking of how he'd felt, grasping it for the first time. Whatever the rhui'auros or Nysander or his family or even Alec thought, he was good at one thing, and one thing only— being a nightrunner. Courtier, wizard's apprentice, diplomat, honorable clan member, son—failed efforts, all.

Sitting here, with a sword at his side, Alec at his back, a dangerous journey ahead, and who knew how many of his former countrymen seeking his blood, he felt at peace for the first time in months.

"So be it," he murmured, drifting off at last.

The dream had altered again. He was in his old room, but this time it was cold and dingy, full of dust. The shelves were empty, the hangings tattered, the plastered walls peeling and streaked with grime. A few toys and his mother's painted screen lay broken on the floor. This was worse, he thought, overwhelmed with a grief that outweighed any fear. Weeping, he fell to his knees beside the sagging bed, waiting for the flames to come. Instead, the silence and chill increased around him as the light began to fail. Somehow, he knew the rest of the house would be just as empty and didn't have the heart to investigate. He sobbed on, so cold that his teeth chattered. Ex-

hausted at last, he wiped his nose on the hem of the rotting com-
forter and heard the familiar clink of glass.

The glass orbs, he thought with a flash of rage that outmatched
his earlier grief. Springing up, he raised his arm to sweep them off
the bed, then stopped, stunned to see them arranged in an intricate
circular pattern, like a sunburst. Some were black; others glowed
like jewels. The whole pattern was several feet across, and at its cen-
ter a sword had been driven to the hilt into the mattress. He hesi-
tated, fearful of disturbing the design, then pulled the blade free and
watched in awe as it began to shift form. One moment it was the
sword he'd sacrificed the day he'd slain Nysander, the next it had a
pommel like a dark new moon. But others followed, other swords,
and strange steel tubes with bent handles of bone or wood, each one
streaked with blood. It ran down onto his hand in an ever increasing
flow, staining the lines of his palm, dripping onto the bed.

Looking down, he saw that the orbs were gone; in their place lay
a square black banner stitched with the same intricate design. The
blood droplets still falling from his hand clung to the material and
turned to ruby beads where they fell.

"It is not complete, son of Korit," a voice whispered, and sud-
denly he was engulfed in searing pain and darkness—

Alec woke with a strangled curse when something hit him hard in
the face. Momentarily blinded by the pain, he struggled frantically
against the weight pressing down on his chest and legs. It disappeared,
replaced by a blast of cold air against his sweaty skin. The bright,
hot taste of blood at the back of his mouth made him gag. Touching
his nose gingerly, he felt wetness. "What the hell—?"

"Sorry, talí."

It was still too dark to see Seregil, but Alec heard scuffling in the
darkness, then felt a tentative touch on his arm.

He spat in the opposite direction, trying to get the blood out of his
mouth. "What happened?"

"Sorry," said Seregil again. Alec heard more fumbling, then
blinked at the sudden brightness of a lightstone. Seregil held it in
one hand and was rubbing the back of his head with the other.
"Looks like my nightmare woke us both up."

"You can keep yourself warm next time," Alec growled, trying
with limited success to pull the remaining blanket around him.

Seregil picked up the other and used a corner of it to staunch

Alec's nosebleed. His hands were shaking badly, though, and Alec pulled back to avoid further damage. "How long were we asleep?"

"Long enough. Let's move on," Seregil replied, widened eyes betraying some of the confusion Alec could feel radiating from him.

They dressed in silence, shivering at the unpleasant feel of damp wool and leather. Outside, the wind was still blowing, but Alec felt a change in the weather. Emerging from the hut, he saw stars showing through long rents in the scudding clouds. "Only an hour or two before dawn, I think."

"Good." Seregil mounted and looped the lead rein of his spare horse around the saddle horn. "We should reach the first guarded pass about then."

"Guarded?"

"Magicked," Seregil amended, sounding more himself now. "I could get through it in the dark, but I wouldn't want you doing it blindfolded. It's a bit tricky in places."

"There's something for me to look forward to," Alec grumbled, dabbing at his nose with his sleeve. "That, and a cold breakfast on horseback."

Seregil raised an eyebrow at him. "Now you're starting to sound like me! Next thing you know, you'll be wanting a hot bath."

Nyal had made a show of checking the Skalan's stables and searching out hoofprints, though he already had a fair idea of where Seregil and the others were headed. He'd shadowed them long enough to see them change horses at the way station and continue up the main road. Later, at the Iia'sidra, he'd overheard the Akhendi khirnari warn Nazien í Hari of a certain pass Seregil was likely to head for, one Nyal knew well for reasons of his own.

He took twelve riders with him for the chase, young bloods from some of the more neutral clans, including several of his own kin. He'd chosen carefully, wanting only youngsters who could be counted on to do as they were told.

Reaching the way station again before nightfall, he questioned the lad who watched the horses and learned that a certain signal had not been given by the last trio of dispatch riders, a fact that had raised suspicion almost before they'd ridden out of sight. That, and the fact that the Skalan rider had apparently understood more Aurënfaie than she let on.

The trail from here was not difficult to follow; the mare Beka had taken had a notch in her left rear hoof. Some miles on, though, Nyal was surprised to see that they'd fallen in with several other riders. Seregil and Alec must be more brazen than he'd guessed, passing themselves off as Akhendi here. They were certainly taking no pains to cover their tracks, keeping to the main road instead of splitting up and losing themselves in the network of side roads that branched off from it. There were streams they could have ridden up to cover their trail, byways that doubled back on themselves. Then again, Seregil had no way of knowing most of these routes.

"Perhaps these other horsemen are conspirators?" said one of the Silmai with him as they paused at a roadside spring where the fugitives had dismounted to drink.

"If so, then they aren't being much help," Nyal said, studying the footprints in the soft earth at the spring's edge: two sets of Aurënfaie boots, one Skalan. The others had remained mounted.

"They can't know the area, or they'd have shown him ways of getting away from the main road and putting us off the scent," a Ra'basi kinsman named Woril noted.

"Not yet," Nyal murmured, wondering again what Seregil could be up to. It wasn't until the following day, when he finally found where the two groups of riders had parted, that he began to understand.

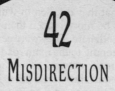

42

MISDIRECTION

Beka rode steadily through the night, avoiding the few Akhendi villagers she encountered along the way. She made no effort to cover her trail, counting on misdirection to protect her friends.

The rain continued, a cold, inexorable mist that seemed to seep right down to her bones. As the mountains loomed closer ahead, she finally gave up the ruse and turned aside onto a side road that twisted away to the east through the forest. By late the next day she was exhausted and utterly lost.

Ambling along, she spotted a game trail leading up a slope and followed it, hoping to find some shelter for the night. Just before dark, she found a dry patch of earth beneath a fallen fir tree and made camp there. Lightning had struck the tree sometime recently, shattering the trunk but not severing it, so that the thick top hung to the ground at an angle, creating a sheltered den among the lower boughs. After dragging in her pack, she dug a pit with her knife and built a little fire to stave off the chill.

Just for a few hours, she told herself, huddling close to the flames. The heat quickly baked the damp from her tunic and breeches. Wrapping herself in her blanket, she leaned against the rough bark behind her. A thin waxing moon showed itself between torn shreds of clouds, a reminder that in just two days the Iia'sidra would decide the success or failure of all their work here.

"By the Four," she whispered. "Just let us get Klia home alive and I'll be satisfied."

As she drifted off to sleep, however, it was Nyal who filled her thoughts, tingeing her dreams with an uneasy mix of longing and doubt.

The grip of a strong hand on her shoulder startled Beka awake at dawn. There was just light enough to make out Nyal kneeling beside her, face inches from her own.

"What are you doing here?" she gasped, wondering if she was still dreaming.

"I'm sorry, talía," he murmured, and Beka's heart sank as she saw the armed men behind him.

She pulled back, berating herself bitterly for being so easily caught.

"Beka, please—" Nyal tried again, but she shoved him away and scrambled to her feet. How had they gotten so close without her hearing them?

"Their horses are here, but there's no sign of them," a Ra'basi told Nyal.

"You son of a bitch!" Beka snarled, rocked to the core as realization sank in. "You led them here!"

"Where are they, Beka?" he asked.

She searched his eyes for some sign of hope but found none. Leaning closer, as if to confide in him, she spat in his face. "Garshil ke'menios!"

Nyal's mouth set in an angry line as he wiped his cheek with his sleeve. "There are others out looking for them, Captain, Haman among them."

Beka turned her back on him, saying nothing.

"We'll get nothing out of her," Nyal told the others. "Korious, you and your men get her back to the city. Akara, you wait until it's light enough, then scour the surrounding area for signs of them. I'll backtrack, then catch up with you."

"Very efficient, Ra'basi," Beka muttered as they stripped her of weapons and tied her hands.

"I assure you, Captain, you'll be treated with respect by these men," Nyal assured her. "As for your friends, it would be better for everyone concerned if I'm the one to find them. They're both in danger: Seregil and your almost-brother."

Beka sneered at him, not allowing him to play on her fears. "Go to hell, traitor."

The mountain road grew worse as Seregil and Alec went on. Bare stone peaks loomed ever closer, stark against the cloudy sky.

They reached the second village just before noon and found it as deserted as the first. No people meant no fresh horses, and Seregil's mare was limping badly.

Dismounting in the overgrown square, he ran a hand over the back leg she was favoring and found an angry swelling at the hock.

"Shit!" he hissed, gentling her as she shied. "She's bog spavined."

"The gelding is still sound," Alec told him, inspecting Seregil's other horse. One of Alec's horses, a bay mare, was cow hocked and probably wouldn't cover much rough country without coming up lame sooner or later, too.

Seregil shifted his saddle onto the gelding, then pointed up toward a distant notch between two crags. "We should hit the trail I want a few miles further on, inside the magicked area. You can't see it yet from here, but our pass is right up there. There's a Dravnian tower near the top. If these nags hold out, we might just make it. I don't want to be sleeping in the open tonight. There are wolves up there, and bandits."

"And smugglers?"

"If so, I hope they're smuggling horses. I suspect the war's put an end to that, though. Not much point in hauling goods to the coast if there aren't any Skalan night ships waiting for them."

"Too bad. I was hoping to meet that uncle of yours I keep hearing about. What are you going to do about that lame horse?"

In answer, Seregil smacked her hard on the rump and watched as she trotted awkwardly out of sight between the deserted houses. "Come on. Let's see how far we get before we lose that bay of yours."

A mile or so past the village Seregil spotted a carved post half hidden by twining creeper and brush. "This is where you get blind-folded, my friend."

Alec took out a strip of cloth and tied it over his eyes. "There, I'm in your hands, Guide."

"Not in quite the fashion I like," Seregil smirked, taking Alec's reins and setting off again.

. . .

Alec leaned forward and braced himself against the stirrups as the ground grew steadily steeper. He knew by the smells around him that they were still in the woods, but the echoes of the horse's hooves spoke of a narrow gap. From time to time he heard the rattle of loose stone, and for one heart-stopping moment his horse stumbled, scrabbling wildly for purchase. He clawed at the blindfold, terrified of being thrown off or crushed under a fallen horse.

"It's all right." Seregil's hand locked around his wrist, drawing his hand away.

"Damn it, Seregil, how much longer?" Alec gasped.

"Another mile or so. It levels out soon, I think."

The riding did get easier, but presently Alec noticed that he was hearing echoes only on their left. A cold wind sighed steadily against his right cheek. "Are we by a cliff?" he asked, tensing again.

"Not too near," Seregil assured him.

"Then why aren't you talking?"

"I'm looking for the cutoff to the pass. Keep quiet and let me concentrate."

After another small eternity he heard Seregil let out a pent-up breath. "I found our trail. It won't be long now, I promise."

The air grew cooler around them, and Alec smelled the spicy resin of pines and cedar. "Can I take this blindfold off?" he asked, as his earlier fears gave way to outright boredom. "I'd like to see what it looks like, with the magic."

"It will make you sick," Seregil warned. "Just hang on a bit longer. We're nearly—oh, Illior! Alec, get your head down!"

Before Alec could obey, his horse wheeled sharply and he heard a sharp buzz close to his ear. Then something struck him hard in the chest and thigh, knocking the breath from his body in a startled grunt. Seregil yelled something and Alec's horse reared. Then he was falling, falling—

The moment Seregil spotted the ambushers, he knew it was already too late.

Rounding a bend between two large outcroppings, he and Alec had come out into a narrow stretch of trail cut into a steep, sparsely wooded slope that slanted down to a riverbed several hundred feet below. Just ahead, the narrow cut up the mountainside that lead to the pass was gone, obliterated by a massive rock slide. The archers had taken positions up among the rocks, where they had a clear view of the killing floor below. Unable to go right or left, Seregil could only retreat the way he'd come and hope to get around the bend before they both got an arrow in the back. But as he wheeled his mount, dragging Alec's around by the head rein, he saw more men standing on the stones he'd just passed. The trap was sprung.

"Get your head down!" he shouted again, but it was too late for that, too.

Alec's bay reared, screaming, with an arrow protruding from its chest. Still blindfolded, Alec was thrown off, falling toward the downhill slope. Seregil just had time to register the shafts embedded in his friend's shoulder and leg before Alec disappeared from view.

"Alec!" Seregil threw himself off his horse to follow but four more ambushers leaped from the scant brush just above him and wrestled him to the ground. He fought wildly, desperate to escape, to find Alec and get him away—

If he were still alive

—but he was overmatched. His captors pinned him on his belly, grinding his face into the dirt, then flipped him onto his back. Someone grasped him roughly by the hair and yanked his head back. A grey-haired man leaned over him, dagger in hand, and Seregil closed his eyes, waiting for the inevitable slash across his throat.

Instead, the man sliced open the front of Seregil's tunic, the tip of the knife scraping across the steel rings of the mail shirt beneath. Reaching in, he yanked the chain free and held up the Corruth's ring. A younger man leaned into view, but before Seregil could get a proper look at him, the side of his head exploded in pain and the world went black.

Fear blotted out all else as Alec hit the ground and continued falling, tumbling head over heels. He'd always had a horror of falling, and doing it blind drove him into a panic. He fetched up at last against something that crushed the air from his lungs. Only then, as he lay sprawled on his side, bruised all over and gasping for air, was he able to give proper attention to the fiery pain lancing through his left thigh and right shoulder, and to a stabbing sensation just under his ribs. This last proved to be the hilt of his sword, caught underneath him at an awkward angle.

Thank the Four for that, at least, he thought, shifting the weapon a little so he could breathe.

Somewhere above he heard the sounds of men calling back and forth to one another, apparently looking for him.

Magic or no magic, he couldn't stand waiting like some blind, wounded animal. Tearing off the hated blindfold, he blinked at the sudden brightness and saw—ferns.

He could see perfectly well, after all, though the slight prickle of magic across his skin told him he was not clear of the guarded zone yet.

Shouts from up the slope warned that there was no time to ponder the matter further. Raising his head a little, he found himself lying in a dense patch of tall, feathery fern at the base of an ancient birch tree. From here, he could make out the trail several hundred yards above him and a few men moving about there. Outlaws, he guessed, seeing that they wore no sen'gai. As he'd feared, a few others were making their way down in his general direction.

His right shoulder throbbed again as he ducked down. Freshly scarred chain showed through a rent in the arm of his tunic where an arrow had scored a glancing blow.

The wound in his leg was more serious. A shaft had pierced his thigh and lodged there. Sometime during his fall the feathered end had snapped off, but the steel head still protruded a scant few inches below his lower trouser lacing. Not giving himself time to think, he grasped the shaft just below the head and yanked it out.

Then he fainted.

When he came to, someone was dragging him over rough ground by his bad shoulder. The pain in his leg had risen to exquisite intensity and he greyed out again. When his mind cleared, he was lying mercifully still, cradled in strong arms against a hard chest.

"Seregil, I thought—" But the eyes close above his were hazel green, not grey.

"Stay quiet," Nyal ordered, peering up over the edge of the gully where they lay. He was bareheaded and wore dull-colored clothing that blended in with the evening shadows lengthening across the forest floor.

Footsteps crunched over dead leaves nearby, then faded away in the opposite direction.

After a moment Nyal crouched down beside him and checked the wound on Alec's leg. "It's clean, but it needs binding. Stay here and keep your eyes shut if you can."

"I can see," Alec told him.

The Ra'basi blinked in surprise, but there was no time for

explanations. Bent low, he hurried off down the gully, vanishing quickly in the shadowy underbrush.

The ambushers seemed to have given up on finding him for the moment. Looking up the slope, Alec saw no sign of movement. A few moments later Nyal was back with his bow and a large wayfarer's pouch.

"It's not bleeding too badly," he muttered, pulling out a flask and a plain sen'gai. "Here, have a pull on this," he ordered, handing Alec the flask.

The strong spirit burned Alec's throat, and he took a second gulp, then craned his neck, nervously keeping watch while Nyal bound hasty compresses over the arrow holes.

"There, that should hold you for now." Nyal clapped him on the shoulder. "Now, let's see if you can walk on it. Seregil needs us." Standing, he extended his hand.

Alec grasped it and pulled himself up. His leg still hurt like hell, but the drink, together with the pressure of the bandage, made it just bearable. "Who tracked us, besides you?"

"No one but me," the Ra'basi replied, supporting Alec with a hand under his arm. "No other tracks cross yours. They were waiting for you. I'm only sorry I didn't catch up with you sooner. They were probably trying to kill your horse when your leg got in the way."

"And this?" Alec said doubtfully, showing him the tear in his tunic.

"Not everyone is as good a shot as you, my friend."

Alec was sweating with pain by the time they reached the ground just below the level of the trail. Lying on their bellies, they peered up over the edge and found it deserted.

"Stay here," Nyal whispered. Keeping low, he darted up over the edge of the bank, heading for Alec's dead horse. A man sprang from a low clump of brush and rushed at the Ra'basi.

"Look out!" Alec called.

Nyal whirled and threw himself sideways, rolling clear. The other man dove at him again, only to catch a sharp blow to the face that felled him like an ox. He went down without a sound.

Nyal tied and gagged the man, then coolly returned to his task, pulling Alec's bow and quiver free of the saddle. The bowstring had snapped in the fall and swung uselessly from one tip as Nyal scrambled back down to where he waited.

"I hope you have an extra," he said, thrusting the Radly into Alec's hands. "Mine won't fit this."

Alec took a fresh string from his belt pouch and stood to bend the bow. Bracing one limb tip against his foot, he pushed down on the upper one and let out a grunt as pain flared in his shoulder again. Nyal took the bow and fitted the string into place.

"Can you draw?"

Alec flexed his arm again. "I think so."

"And you can see?" Nyal said, shaking his head in amazement.

"It's something to do with the Bash'wai, I think," Alec offered, thinking of the strange farewell they'd given him.

"They certainly must have taken a liking to you. Come on. Let's find Seregil."

Dusk was coming on quickly now, and they spotted the yellow gleam of firelight high above the slide area choking the pass. Skirting the ruined trail, Nyal led him up a winding track that brought them out on a shelf of rock overlooking the top of a cliff. Eight men stood on a level stretch of ground near the edge. Several held torches, giving Alec enough light to shoot by. Behind them Seregil slumped on his knees and elbows, hands bound in front of him. His head was down, hair in his face. A man stood over him with his own sword while the others argued among themselves.

"It's not right!" one man said angrily.

"It's not your place to question," a younger man retorted, speaking with the authority of a leader. "There's no dishonor in it."

So even Aurënfaie bandits fretted over atui? Alec eased an arrow from his quiver and set it to the string. Beside him, Nyal did the same. Just then, several of the men threw up their arms and walked a few paces off. Seregil fought weakly as two others grabbed him by the shoulders and pulled him toward the cliff, clearly meaning to throw him over.

Alec brought his bow up and let fly, praying the shaft didn't find Seregil instead. He needn't have worried. His aim was off and it struck the ground harmlessly just in front of Seregil's would-be killers. Startled, they jumped back and Seregil twisted free, scrambling back from the edge. Most of the ambushers scattered, ducking for cover. Nyal hit two of them before they'd gotten ten feet. The leader grabbed for Seregil and Alec shot again, this time hitting his mark square in the chest. Seregil saw his chance and dashed away into the shadows.

Alec managed to take down one more man before the rest disappeared.

"This way." Nyal led him down another rock-strewn track, supporting him when Alec's bad leg gave out. The sound of horses came to them on the quiet night air as they reached the cliff, echoing up from the direction of the main trail.

"Damn, they got away!"

"How many?" wondered Nyal.

"Enough to be trouble if we don't get out of here fast," said a familiar voice overhead.

Alec looked up to find Seregil half hidden behind a boulder. He emerged and slid down the loose slope to join them, hands still tied but clutched now around the hilt of his sword.

"I take it that you can see?" he asked, giving Alec a thoughtful look.

Alec shrugged.

"How many were there?" Nyal asked.

"I didn't have a chance to take a count before they knocked me out," Seregil replied, leading them back to where the dead lay. There were five bodies.

"Just our luck, running into bandits," Alec muttered.

Seregil rubbed at a new bruise developing over his right cheekbone. "They did have the good grace to debate about killing me. Some of them didn't like the idea. They thought they'd killed you, though, Alec, and so did I, for that matter. When I saw you go off your horse like that—" Extending a hand to Nyal, he said almost grudgingly, "I guess I should be glad to see you. It seems we owe you our lives."

Nyal clasped hands with him. "Perhaps you'll repay me by speaking to Beka on my behalf. I imagine she's still cursing my name."

"So you found her, too?" Alec groaned, feeling a fool to be so easily tracked after all their planning. "Where is she?"

"Not as far away as she thought. We caught up with her at dawn this morning, less than ten miles from here."

"We?" Seregil's eyes narrowed.

"The Iia'sidra sent me with a search party," Nyal replied. "I volunteered, actually. When it became clear that others suspected where you might go, I thought it would be better if I found you first. Tracking her, I saw where you parted ways and guessed that you might make for this smuggler's pass, not knowing it was blocked. I made certain that my compatriots were occupied with her, then came looking for you."

"Our little ruse didn't fool you?"

Nyal grinned, "Fortunately for you, my companions don't have quite the eye for tracking that I do. An unladen horse walks a bit differently than one carrying a man. You won't get through this way, you know."

"So I see," Seregil said, shaking his head. "I should have guessed about the pass. I just assumed the villages had died for lack of trade."

He bent over one of the bodies and pulled his poniard free from the dead man's chest. "I've managed to keep my promise, Adzriel," he muttered, wiping the blade clean on the dead man's tunic and slipping it back into his boot. Bending over another, he emptied the man's purse onto the ground.

"Ah, here it is!" he exclaimed, holding up Corruth's ring. "The chain's gone. Oh, well, what wisdom forbids, necessity dictates." He slipped it onto his finger and went on with his task.

Leaving the bodies for the crows, they made a circuit around the area and found three horses tethered in a stand of trees up the slope from the trail, still saddled.

"You take these," said Nyal. "Mine is hidden down near where I found you, Alec. There's another trail a mile or so back down the trail that will take you over to the coast. I'll set you on it, then head back to report that I found no sign of you. I don't suppose that will win me any favor with Beka, but it's a start."

Seregil laid a hand on his arm. "You haven't asked why we're out here."

The Ra'basi gave him an unreadable look. "If you wanted me to know, you'd have told me. I trust enough in your honor, and in Beka's, to know that you must have good reason for risking your life like this."

"Then you really don't know?" asked Alec.

"Even my ears aren't that long."

"Can you trust the men who have Beka?" Alec asked, anxious for Nyal to be off.

"Yes. They'll keep her safe. Hurry now! There are others hunting you."

"You're really letting us go?" Seregil asked again, unable to believe it.

The Ra'basi smiled. "I told you, I never intended to capture you. I came to protect Beka if I could, and for her sake I help you now."

"What about atui? Where's your loyalty to your clan, to the lia'sidra?"

Nyal shrugged, his smile now tinged with sadness. "Those of us who travel far from our fai'thasts see the world differently than those who don't, wouldn't you say?"

Seregil gave the man a last, searching look, then nodded. "Show us this trail of yours, Nyal."

The night was clear and cold, with enough of a moon to travel easily by as they rode back the way they'd come.

Seregil knew of no other trails in the area, but presently Nyal reined in and led them on foot through a seemingly untouched stretch of woods to a little pond. Just past a jumbled pile of rocks on its far bank, they struck a trail that disappeared up the hillside.

"Be careful," Nyal advised. "It's a good route, well marked once you've followed it for a few miles, but treacherous in places, and home to wolves and dragons. Aura watch over you both."

"And you," Seregil returned. "I hope we meet again, Ra'basi, and under happier circumstances."

"As do I." Nyal pulled a flask from his pouch and handed it to Alec. "You'll be needing this, I think. It's been an honor to know you, Alec í Amasa of the Hâzadriëlfaie. I'll do all I can to keep your almost-sister safe, whether she wants me to or not."

With that, he melted away into the shadows. Soon they heard the beat of his horse's hooves fading rapidly away down the road.

The trail was as bad as Nyal had warned. Steep and uneven, it wound through gullies and across streams. There was no place to go if they were ambushed here.

It made for hard riding, and though Alec made no complaint, Seregil saw him take several quick swigs from the flask Nyal had given him. He was about to suggest stopping for the night when Alec's horse suddenly lost her footing and stumbled down a rocky slope, nearly going down on top of her rider.

Alec managed to stay on, but Seregil heard his strangled cry of pain.

"We'll make camp there," Seregil said, pointing to an overhang just ahead.

Tethering their mounts on a loose rein in case of wolves, they crawled in under the overhang and spread their stolen blankets.

It was a cold vigil, watching the moon arc slowly to the west. They could hear the hunting cries of wolves in the distance, together with occasional sounds nearer by.

Tired as he was, Seregil couldn't sleep. Instead, he pondered the ambush, wondering how a force of that size could have outflanked them in this country.

"Those weren't bandits, Alec," he muttered, fidgeting restlessly with his belt knife. "But how could anyone track us down fast enough to set up an ambush?"

"Nyal said they didn't track us," Alec replied drowsily.

"What?"

"That's what I thought, too, but he claims he didn't see any signs of anyone else chasing us. They were there already, waiting for us."

"Then someone sent word! Someone who knew exactly where we'd be, except that I'm the only one who knew which pass we were heading for. I didn't even tell you. Your lightstone, Alec. Do you have it?"

With the aid of the light, he stripped the saddlebags from their stolen mounts and emptied them into a pile. There were several packets of food, including fresh bread and cheese.

"Soft fare, for bandits, wouldn't you say?" he noted, carrying some up to Alec. Returning to the pile, he sorted through the oddments there: shirts, clean linen, a jar of fire chips, a few simples.

"What's that?" asked Alec, pointing to something among the tangle of clothes. Hobbling out of the shelter, he pulled a wad of cloth free and held it to the light.

"Bilairy's Balls!" gasped Seregil. It was an Akhendi sen'gai.

"It could be stolen," Alec said. Stirring through the clothes, he found no others.

Seregil went back to the horses and found a second one concealed under the arch of a saddle, just where he might have hidden such a thing.

"But they were going to kill you!" Alec gasped in disbelief. "Why would the Akhendi do that? And how did they find us?"

"By the Four!" Seregil tore a pouch from his belt and emptied it out beside the rest. There among the coins and trinkets lay Klia's Akhendi charm, still flecked with dried mud.

"I forgot I had this," he growled, clutching it. "I was going to take it back to Amali, then Magyana's letter came—"

"Damn. Someone could have used it to scry where we are."

Seregil nodded grimly. "But only if they knew I had it."

Alec took it and turned it over on his palm, holding it closer to the light. "Oh, no."

"What?"

"Oh, no no no!" Alec groaned. "This bracelet is the one Amali made for Klia, but the charm is different."

"How do you know that?" Seregil demanded.

"Because it's mine, the one that girl gave me in the first Akhendi village we stopped at. See this little crack in the wing?" He showed Seregil the fissure marring one wing. "That happened when I had the run-in with Emiel that turned it black. It's the same sort of carving as Klia's, though, and it was covered in mud when I found it. It never occurred to me to look more closely at it."

"Of course it didn't!" Seregil took it back. "The question is, how did it come to be white again for a while, and on Klia's bracelet? We saw Amali make this for her, and you still had yours then."

"Nyal must have given it to her," Alec told him, once more thrown into doubt about the Ra'basi.

"What was he doing with it?"

Alec told him of the day he'd met Emiel in the House of the Pillars and what had followed. "I got rid of it so you wouldn't find out. You were already upset enough and I didn't think Emiel was anyone who mattered. I was going to throw it away, but Nyal said it could be restored, and that he'd have an Akhendi see to it. I'd forgotten all about it."

Seregil scrubbed a hand over his face. "I can just guess which Akhendi! You've seen how these are made, and how the Akhendi can change one charm for another."

"The morning of the hunt, Amali and Rhaish came to see us off," Alec said, recalling that morning with jarring clarity. "I thought it was odd, since she'd been too ill to go out just the night before."

"Did he touch Klia?" Seregil asked. "Think, Alec. Did he get close enough to her to switch the charms somehow?"

"No," Alec replied slowly. "But she did."

"Amali?"

"Yes, she clasped hands with Klia. She was smiling."

Seregil shook his head. "But she wasn't at Virésse tupa that night."

"No, but Rhaish was."

Seregil clapped a hand to his forehead. "The rhui'auros said I already knew who the murderer is. That's because we saw it happen. You remember when Rhaish stumbled as he greeted Torsin? Torsin was dead a few hours later, and there was no charm on him. Someone had removed it. Rhaish must have seen the charm and known it could give him away. Knots and weaving, Alec. He must have taken the bracelet as soon as he'd poisoned him."

"And Klia helped Rhaish up when he stumbled," added Alec. "He left soon after, so it must have been then that he poisoned her." He paused. "But wait. Klia had on the same sort of charm. Why take Torsin's, and not hers?"

"I don't know. You're certain it was unchanged that morning?"

"Yes. I noticed it on her wrist at breakfast. So why change it for mine?"

"I don't know, but someone obviously changed it at some point, and they wouldn't have done so without reason." He stopped as realization struck.

"It could have been the husband and the wife together! 'Smiles conceal knives,' isn't that what we were told? Bilairy's Codpiece, I've been blinder than a mole in a midnight shit hcap. Rhaish didn't expect the Iia'sidra to vote his way. He never did. And if he'd learned of Torsin's secret negotiations, and what that meant for Akhendi—he needs to discredit the Virésse, and what better way than to show Ulan í Sathil to be a guest murderer? I, of all people, should have seen through that one!" He clasped his head in both hands. "If I'm ever, *ever* this stupid again, will you please boot me in the ass?"

"I haven't been any better," Alec said. "So Ulan is innocent, and Emiel, too?"

"Of murder, at least."

"Damn it, Seregil, we've got to warn Klia and Thero! After your own family, the Akhendi are the ones they're most likely to trust!"

"If we don't stop Korathan, it won't make much difference. We have to find him first."

Alec stared at him in disbelief. "Beka's heading right back into it, and we still don't know whose side Nyal is really on. Anyone who knows she was with us may assume that she knows whatever we know."

Seregil stared at the Akhendi charm. "I suspect she's in less danger now than we are. They found us with this once. They can again. Yet it's the one real piece of evidence we have against the Akhendi, so we can't afford to destroy it or throw it away. We'll just have to go on as fast and as cautiously as we can. Once we've dealt with Korathan, we'll figure out what to do."

"You mean we just leave her?" Alec kicked angrily at a loose stone. "This is really what it means to be a Watcher, isn't it?"

"Sometimes." For the first time in a very long time, Seregil felt the gulf of age and experience that lay between them, decp as the Cirna Canal. He gripped Alec gently by the back of the neck, knowing there was nothing he could say that would ease his friend's pain or his own. It was only the long years he'd spent with Nysander and Micum that allowed him to fend off visions of Beka dead, captured, lost.

"Come on," he said at last, helping Alec back to their makeshift shelter. "Thero chose her with good reason. You know that. Now get some sleep if you can. I'll keep watch."

He draped their blankets around Alec, settling him as comfortably as he could against the rough stone. Alec said nothing, but Seregil again sensed an unspoken welter of emotion.

Leaving him to his grief, he went out to keep watch. Duty was a fine and noble thing, most days. It was only at times like this one, when you noticed how it wore away at the soul, like water over stone.

43

DIRE SIGNS

Nyal rode all night and picked up the trail of Beka and the others just after dawn. They'd returned to the main road and pushed on at a gallop. Spurring his lathered mount, Nyal hurried on, hoping to catch up.

As he rode, he went over in his mind what he could say to Beka that would reassure her without giving away his own complicity in her friends' escape. At last he was forced to admit that, barring Seregil's own testimony on his behalf, there was little he could do for the moment except ensure her safe return to the city. Not that this should be such a difficult task. They were in Akhendi territory, after all.

Caught up in his thoughts, he galloped around a curve and was nearly thrown when his horse suddenly shied and reared. He clung on, yanking the gelding's head around and reining it to a standstill, then turned to see what had spooked it.

A young Gedre lay in the middle of the road, his face covered in drying blood. A chestnut mare grazed nearby.

"Aura's mercy! Terien," Nyal croaked, recognizing both man and horse. This was one of Beka's escorts.

Dismounting, he went to him and felt for a pulse. There was a nasty gash over the boy's eye, but he was still breathing. His eyes fluttered open as Nyal examined the wound.

"What happened?" Nyal asked, pressing his water skin to the boy's lips.

Terien drank, then slowly sat up. "Ambush. Just after sun up. I heard someone yell, then I went down."

"Did you see anyone?"

"No, it all happened so quickly. I've never heard of bandits this far south on the main road."

"Neither have I." Nyal helped him onto his horse. "There's a village not too far from here. Can you get yourself there?"

Terien grasped his saddle horn and nodded.

"How was the Skalan when you last saw her?"

Terien let out a faint snort. "Sullen."

"Was she tied?"

"Hand and foot, so she wouldn't fall off if her horse bolted."

"Thank you. Find a healer, Terien."

Sending him on his way, Nyal strode into the trees and looked for signs of the ambushers. He found the prints of at least six men, and where they'd hobbled their horses.

Leading his horse, he walked on down the road, reading the marks of an ambush and chase in the trampled earth. Around another bend he found three more of his men. Two Gedre brothers were supporting his cousin, Korious, as they headed back in his direction. There was blood on the Ra'basi's arm.

"Where are the others?" he asked, heart hammering in his chest.

"An ambush, not an hour ago," Korious told him. "They came out of nowhere, with their faces covered. Teth'brimash, I think. They killed two of the Silmai, back down the road. We lost some others in the initial attack."

"What happened to Beka?"

Korious shook his head. "I don't know. She was with us until the second group jumped us here, then she was gone."

"And you haven't found her horse?"

"No."

"Terien's coming your way. Be sure he gets to a healer."

He found the marks of Beka's horse a little further on. It appeared she'd broken away in the confusion and burst past the ambushers, chased by two other riders.

The tracks turned up a disused sidetrack, and for a moment Nyal couldn't get his breath. He knew this road. It came to a dead end in an abandoned stone quarry. He pictured her, bound and defenseless, clinging to her horse's mane as armed horsemen bore down on her. Her sword and daggers were still lashed behind his own saddle.

"Ah, talía, forgive me!" he whispered. Drawing his sword, he spurred his horse on, dreading what he would find.

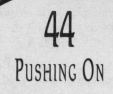

44

PUSHING ON

Seregil heard the first telltale sounds of pursuit just before dawn. At first it was only the distant tinkle of dislodged stones that could have been nothing more than a large animal on an early hunt. Sound traveled in this rocky country, however, and he soon made out the occasional scrape of boots over stone, then the echo of voices. Judging by the amount of noise they were making, they were searching blind, not realizing how close they were to their quarry.

He couldn't see them yet but knew it would be impossible to get the horses away without being heard. With Alec wounded, fighting was not an attractive option, especially since he couldn't tell how many men there were. What he didn't hear were more horses.

Crawling over to Alec, Seregil gently covered his friend's mouth. Alec came awake silently.

"How's the leg?"

Alec flexed it and grimaced. "Stiff."

"Company's on the way. I'd rather run than fight, if you can ride."

"Just help me up into the saddle."

Grabbing the blankets and sen'gai, Seregil wrapped his free arm around Alec's waist and helped him down to the horses. He could feel the younger man wince with every step, but

Alec made no complaint. By the time Seregil had mounted his own horse, Alec had his bow and quiver slung ready over his shoulders.

By now they could both hear snatches of their pursuers' conversation.

"Go!" Seregil ordered.

Alec kicked his horse into a gallop and sprang away. Close behind, Seregil hazarded a backward look and made out a few dark shapes down the trail, men on foot.

They got away clean, but soon had to slow down again. As Nyal had warned, the trail skirted precipices and in places was just wide enough for a single horse to pass. Fresh blood was seeping through Alec's trouser leg, but there was no time to stop.

They left their pursuers behind but kept a sharp eye out for another ambush ahead. By the time they reached the summit, just before midday, both were tense and sweating. From here, the land fell away sharply, affording them a clear view of the patched and rumpled sweep of Gedre fai'thast and the pale expanse of sea beyond.

"I'd better have a look at that leg before we go on," Seregil said, dismounting. "Can you get down?"

Alec leaned heavily on his saddlebow, breathing raggedly. "If I do, I may not be able to get back on."

"Stay there, then." Seregil found the flask of painkiller in Alec's saddlebag. Pressing that and the last of the bread into his hands, Seregil set about cutting away the bandage Nyal had put on.

"You're lucky," he muttered, rinsing away the crusted blood. "It's just seeping. The wound seems to be closing up on its own."

He tore strips from his shirt and bound the leg up again.

"How much longer?" Alec asked, finishing off the bread as Seregil worked.

"By late afternoon, if we don't meet any more trouble along the way." Seregil scanned the distant coast, searching for a familiar bend in the shoreline and finding it. "That's where we're headed. This trail of Nyal's has brought us out closer than mine would have."

He squinted at the horizon, wondering if Korathan's vessels were faster than he'd guessed, or if the following wind blew stronger—

Alec shifted his leg in the stirrup, looking worried again. "I know Riagil is a friend of your family, and I like the man, but he's also the Akhendi's ally. What if he's looking for us, too?"

Seregil had been avoiding that thought all morning, remembering instead that first bittersweet night in Aurënen, when he'd stood with Riagil in the moon garden, sharing good memories of the past. "We'll keep out of sight as much as we can."

. . .

Thero glanced up from the scroll he'd been reading, then threw it aside and jumped to his feet. Klia's eyes were open.

"My lady, you're awake!" he exclaimed, bending anxiously over her. "Can you hear me?"

Klia stared dully at the ceiling, giving no sign that she understood.

O Illior, let this be a sign for the better and not the worse! he prayed, and sent a summoning to Mydri.

Coming down out of the mountains, Seregil and Alec avoided the roads and skirted well clear of the scattered villages.

Shadows were lengthening toward nightfall by the time they came within sight of the sea again. Chancing the road at last, Seregil led the way to the edge of a little fishing village called Halfmoon Cove. The locals had always done a thriving trade with smugglers, including a good many Bôkthersans, and didn't bother the boats hidden in the surrounding forest. Seregil hoped that things hadn't changed too much in his absence.

Abandoning their exhausted horses, they made their way into the woods, looking for trails Seregil recalled from childhood. Alec was limping badly but refused Seregil's supporting arm in favor of a makeshift walking stick.

Aurënfaie might change little in fifty years, but forests did. Familiar as certain stretches of ground felt beneath his feet, Seregil couldn't seem to locate any specific landmarks.

"We're lost again, aren't we?" Alec groaned as they came to a stop in what had turned out to be a blind gully.

"It's been a long time," Seregil admitted, wiping the sweat from his eyes. He could hear the sigh of the sea in the distance and struck out in that direction, praying that something came to hand. He was about to admit defeat when they stumbled across not one but two little boats hidden beneath a blowdown. They had been stored upside down, with masts and sails lashed to the thwarts below. Choosing the stronger-looking of the two, they dragged it through the trees to the water's edge and set about rigging it to sail.

Alec knew little of boats or sailing but followed instruction readily enough. Stepping the mast, Seregil wedged it solid and sorted out the single sail. It was a simple craft, the same sort that had greeted them when they sailed into Gedre harbor. Even so, it was tricky, securing everything by the glow of a lightstone.

When it was ready, they hauled it out into the water and poled it away from the shore to deeper water with Alec's stick.

"Let's see how much I remember," Seregil said, settling at the tiller. Alec hauled the sail up and it caught the breeze, bellying out with a musty creak. The little craft came around nicely and plunged forward, cutting a V-shaped path across the smooth surface of the cove.

"We did it!" Alec laughed, collapsing in the bow.

"Not yet, we haven't." Seregil scanned the dark expanse of sea spread out before them, wondering if Korathan would follow the usual sea-lanes and turn up where he was expected. They had no food and only enough water for a day or two if they drank sparingly. The only thing they had in abundance was time, and that would hang heavy on them indeed if they didn't spot Skalan sails by tomorrow night.

Beka crouched in the brambles, ignoring the sharp thorns scraping her hands and face. She'd heard the horse coming in time to duck out of sight and wasn't too choosy about the hiding place.

Daylight was dying fast now. If she could elude her pursuer until nightfall, she might just manage to slip away, find another horse somewhere, and get back to Sarikali on her own terms.

The ambush that morning had taken her captors completely off guard. After Nyal had left them at dawn, they had settled down for a leisurely breakfast, then tied her hand and foot on a horse and set off for the city.

They'd treated her with respect—kindness, even—making certain her bonds were not cutting her wrists and offering her food and water. Playing along, she'd accepted their attentions, keeping her strength up and pretending not to understand their language.

The leader, a young Ra'basi named Korious, did his best to reassure her in broken Skalan.

"Back to Klia," he said, pointing in what must be the direction of Sarikali.

"Teth'sag?" she asked, pointing to herself.

He shrugged, then shook his head.

She went quietly to work on the wrist bindings as they rode, complaining repeatedly about them being too tight. After one or two adjustments Korious had refused to loosen them any more, but by now she had slack enough to surreptitiously twist her wrists, getting her fingers close enough to one of the knots to pick away at it.

It was a lucky thing she had. They hadn't been more than two hours on the road when one of the other riders toppled from his saddle, blood streaming from his head. Horsemen burst from the trees just behind them, followed by men on foot with swords and clubs.

Her escorts froze, too startled to react. Taking advantage of the momentary confusion, Beka gripped the saddlebow and gave her mount a hard kick in the sides. The horse leapt forward, finding its own way as it broke from the press and galloped wildly down the road. Arrows sang around her and she bent low, fighting at the ropes that still bound her hands.

One hand came free, then the other, and she snatched up the flapping reins. Over the thunder of pursuing hooves, she heard Korious shouting wildly, trying to rally his men.

Undisciplined fools! she thought in disgust, wondering how Nyal had managed to lumber himself with such a sorry bunch of green fighters. A handful of Urgazhi could have had that lot trussed up in no time.

The men who'd attacked them were another matter, however. Looking back over her shoulder, she saw two of them in close pursuit.

She hunched low over her horse's neck and plunged onward. There was no way she was going to elude them on the open road, so when a sidetrack appeared to the left, she reined hard in that direction, ducking overhanging branches.

Giving her mount its head, she clung on and tried to yank her right leg out of her boot. Muscles up and down her side protested, but she pulled free, nearly unseating herself in the process. Steadying herself, she reached down and pulled at the knot securing her other leg.

Her pursuers had faltered a moment, perhaps caught off guard by her sudden swerve. She couldn't see them at the moment, but she could hear them calling out to each other not far behind.

Shielded for the moment by a bend in the road, she reined in, jumped free of the horse, and slapped it hard on the rump, sending it on with her right boot still lashed in the stirrup. She just had time to dive for cover in a bramble patch before the men thundered past, unaware as yet that they were now chasing a riderless horse.

If they were as smart as she guessed they were, it wouldn't be long before they figured it out. Crawling from the brambles, she scrambled up the slope.

She ran until her lungs burned, using the sun as her guide. When she was satisfied that she'd left her pursuers behind, she paused to wash her bleeding foot in a stream, then slowly circled back to the place where the ambush had occurred, hoping to find some sign of who their attackers were.

Someone had been there before her, doing the same. A single set of footprints led from the road to the place where the ambushers had lain in wait, crossing their tracks and meandering in a way that spoke of a thorough search. The shape of the bootprint was familiar.

"Nyal," she whispered, resting her fingers a moment in one long footprint. The ground in front of her blurred, and she dashed the tears away angrily. She'd be damned if she'd weep for that traitor like some jilted dairy maid.

Following the tracks back to the road, she saw that he'd come back alone.

"Good for you, my friends!" she whispered, refusing to admit any other possibility than that Seregil and Alec had eluded him.

What she found next closed the dark fist of anger tighter around her heart. From here, Nyal had dashed off to track her.

Look for me in Sarikali, you son of a bitch! she thought, limping back into the trees.

46
A COLD WELCOME

Alec woke to the sound of waves slapping wood close to his head. Rising from his cramped place in the bow, he looked back past the sail and found Seregil at the tiller, scanning the horizon. He was a sorry sight, with his bruised face and filthy tunic. In this early light, he looked pale, drained of life.

Ghostly.

Alec secretly made a warding sign on his friend's behalf. Seregil glanced his way just then and gave him a tired grin.

"Look there," he said, pointing ahead. "You can just make out the Ea'malies there on the horizon. Keep an eye out for sails."

And so they did, through the morning and into the long afternoon. Their eyes burned from the glare, and their lips cracked from the salt and sun. They kept to a northeast course, using the distant islands as their guide as they tacked back and forth. Alec spelled Seregil at the tiller now and then, urging him to sleep, but he refused.

At last, as the sun slanted down toward the western horizon, Alec caught sight of a dark spot against the silver face of the sea.

"There!" he croaked, hanging over the side in his excitement. "Do you see it? Is that a sail?"

"A Skalan sail," Seregil confirmed, swinging the tiller hard. "Let's hope we get to her before nightfall. They'll never spot us in the dark, and we're too slow to chase them."

Over the next two hours Alec watched as the speck of color grew into the distant outline of a red-sailed Skalan warship. The vessel was taking the usual route used by the dispatch couriers.

"That's all it may be," Seregil fretted as they neared the vessel. "She's alone, not another ship in sight. By the Four, I hope we haven't been chasing the wrong one!"

Any fears they might have had about missing the ship in the dark were quickly allayed. The other vessel shifted course, heading directly for them.

"Looks like our luck is holding after all," Alec said.

As soon as they were within shouting distance they hailed the vessel and heard their greeting returned. Skimming in close to her side, they found a rope ladder hanging ready and the rail above lined with expectant faces.

"Take this," Seregil said, handing him a line. "I'll make this end fast. We don't want to lose this boat until we're sure this other is the right one."

The ladder swung crazily with the roll of the larger vessel, and Alec was dizzy and bruised by the time he'd fought his way up to the rail. Strong hands grasped him, pulling him the rest of the way. Then, to his considerable surprise, he was thrust forward and dragged to his knees.

"Hold on, just let me get—" He tried to rise, only to be pushed down again, harder this time. Looking around, he found himself hemmed in by armed sailors.

Seregil tumbled down beside him and was kicked flat when he tried to rise. Alec reached for his sword, but Seregil stopped him with a sharp look.

"We come in the name of Princess Klia and the queen!" he announced, keeping his own hands well clear of his weapons.

"Sure you do," someone growled.

The crowd parted for a black-haired woman wearing the salt-crusted jerkin of a Skalan naval commander.

"You're a long way from shore in that little bean pod of yours," she said, not smiling.

"We were sent by Princess Klia to intercept her brother, Prince Korathan," Seregil explained, clearly mystified by their hostile reception.

The commander folded her arms, unmoved. "Oh, were you? And where did you learn to speak Skalan so prettily?"

"At the court of Queen Idrilain, may Sakor welcome her spirit," Seregil retorted. He tried to rise and was shoved down again. "Listen to me! There isn't much time. I'm Lord Seregil í Korit, and this is Sir Alec í Amasa of Ivywell. We're aides to Princess Klia. There's been trouble and we must speak to Korathan."

"Why would Prince Korathan be on my ship?" she demanded.

"If not yours, then one close behind," Seregil said, and Alec was dismayed to sense his friend faltering. He looked around quickly, seeking an escape route and finding none. They were still hemmed in by the crew, and there were archers armed and ready along the rail, watching with obvious interest. Even if they did break free, there was nowhere to run.

"Let's see your proofs, then," the woman demanded.

"Proofs?"

"Letters of passage."

"Our journey was too dangerous to risk carrying anything written," Seregil retorted. "The situation in—"

"How convenient," she drawled, drawing an ugly laugh from the others. "It looks like we've caught ourselves a couple of dirty 'faie spies, lads. What do you say, Methes?"

The blond sailor at her side favored Alec and Seregil with an unfriendly look. "These fish are mighty small, Captain. Best to gut 'em and throw them back unless they can tell us a better story." He drew a long knife from his belt and signaled to several other men, who pinned Seregil's and Alec's arms. The one called Methes grabbed Seregil by the hair and yanked his head back to bare his throat.

"For hell's sake, listen!" snarled Seregil.

"We are who we say. We can prove it," Alec cried, struggling now for his life.

"No one knows Prince Korathan is coming," the captain told him. "No one could know, except spies. What are you doing here, Aurënfaie? Who sent you?"

"By the Light, stop this at once!" a man shouted from down the deck.

A middle-aged man dressed in the frayed robes of an Orëska wizard elbowed his way through the press. His long hair was touched with grey, and he had a burn scar on his left cheek. Alec couldn't recall the fellow's name but remembered seeing him around the Orëska and at court.

"Here's help at last," Seregil grunted.

"Stop, you fool!" the wizard cried again. "What are you doing?"

"It's just a couple of 'faie spies," the captain snapped.

The wizard stared hard at Seregil and Alec, then rounded on the captain. "This man is Lord Seregil í Korit, a friend of the Royal Family and of the Orëska House! And this, if memory serves, is his ward, Sir Alec."

The captain threw Seregil a dubious look, then motioned her men back. "Yes, those are the names they gave."

Seregil rose and dusted himself off. "Thank you, Elutheus. I'm relieved to find one sane person aboard. What are they up to, slaughtering Aurënfaie out of hand?"

"The queen's orders, I'm afraid," the wizard replied. "Captain Heria, I wish to question these men in my cabin. Please send down some food and drink. They look like they've had a hard time of it."

The wizard's cabin was a cramped, dark little kennel belowdecks, but he soon made them comfortable, clearing the cluttered bunk and sending for the ship's drysian to tend Alec's leg. Slumped on a stool, Seregil allowed himself to relax a little. Elutheus was a decent fellow who'd been a friend of Nysander's.

"What other wizards are with the prince?" he asked, accepting a cup of wine gratefully as he watched the healer work.

"Just the prince's field wizard, Wydonis."

"Oh, yes, I remember him. One arm. A bit stuffy at banquets. He didn't think much of Nysander's entertainments."

"No, but he respected his abilities. He's been given Nysander's old tower since you left."

Seregil clenched his cup, fighting down the sudden lump that rose in his throat at the thought of those familiar rooms being occupied by anyone else. Looking up, he saw Alec watching him over the drysian's shoulder, understanding in his blue eyes.

"How did he wrangle that, I wonder?" Seregil asked, trying to make light of it.

"He's wizard to the vicegerent now," said Elutheus.

Seregil finished his wine and accepted more, impatient for the drysian to finish. When the man was gone, Seregil took out the Akhendi bracelet. "Can you seal this away from prying eyes without disturbing the magic it contains?"

"Someone keeps using it to find us and we don't want to be found, especially not here," Alec put in. "Nysander used to seal things up in jars."

"Of course." Elutheus rummaged in a small trunk and came up

with a small clay bottle sealed with a cork. Placing the bracelet inside, he replaced the plug, secured it with a bit of string, and spoke a spell over it. Bluish light flickered around it for an instant. When it died away, he handed it to Seregil.

"Not elegant, perhaps, but this should keep you safe until you open it again. Now then, what are you doing here?"

"We're here on Klia's behalf," Seregil replied, cautious again. "What was all that talk about spies?"

Elutheus shook his head. "Phoria has been busy in her sister's absence. Even before the queen died, Phoria was using the Iia'sidra's inaction to stir up bad feeling against Aurënen, no doubt in preparation for taking what she needs by force. Hence Korathan's presence here now. Plenimar is pressing hard on our eastern borders, and she's grasping at straws."

Seregil shook his head. "I can understand her impatience, but to start a second war against a race that can fight you for centuries, and with magic—it's madness! Where are her mother's old advisers? Surely they've tried to talk her out of it?"

"Phoria listens only to her generals and sycophants. Even Orëska wizards can find themselves open to charges of treason if they're not careful. Lady Magyana has already been banished."

"Magyana? What for?" Seregil counterfeited surprise with his usual ease.

Elutheus studied him for a moment. "It was she who sent word to you, was it not?"

Chagrinned, Seregil said nothing.

"That's all right." The wizard shrugged, smiling. "We keep the secrets that must be kept, those of us who watch."

Alec gave Seregil a startled look behind the wizard's back, then made the sign for "Watcher?"

Seregil stared at the wizard, trying to gauge the man's expression, then said noncommittally, "What would you swear by?"

"Heart, hands, and eyes."

Relief washed through Seregil. "You? I had no idea."

"I was only guessing about you," the wizard replied with a wry smile. "There were always rumors, given your close association with Nysander. I must say, you've concealed yourself well all these years; you've been sorely missed at the gaming tables and pleasure houses since you disappeared this last time. Half of Rhíminee thinks you're dead."

"They were almost right. Now, where's Korathan? The message we carry is for his ears only."

"He should be catching us up very soon," the wizard told them, conjuring up a message sphere. "My lord Korathan," he said, speaking to the little point of light. "We have messengers aboard from your sister, bearing most urgent news."

"There," he said, sending it on its way and rising to go. "Rest now, my friends, and don't let the prince scare you. He's not a bad fellow, so long as you're direct with him."

Seregil chuckled. "I knew him in his younger days. He didn't laugh much, but he was always good for a loan."

Elutheus shook his head. "Luck in the shadows, boys."

"And in the light, wizard," Seregil replied.

"Things are looking up," Seregil remarked when the wizard had left them. "If we can get Korathan to Sarikali, we'll go along with him. It's as safe a ploy as I can think of, given the circumstances."

"Wait a minute," Alec said, frowning. "*You're* not thinking of going back?"

"I have to, Alec."

"But how? You've broken every law they laid down for your return—leaving the city, carrying a weapon, not to mention the fact that you killed a few people during the ambush."

"So did you, as I recall."

"Yes, but I'm not the one Nazien í Hari and the entire Iia'sidra invoked teth'sag against."

Seregil shrugged. "There's no other way."

"Horse shit, there isn't! I'll go. I'm just a stupid Skalan. They won't go as hard on me."

"No, and they won't listen to you, either." Seregil pulled his stool closer and clasped Alec's hand. "It's not just about the poisonings for me anymore, or explaining Korathan's sudden arrival."

"What then?"

"Honor, Alec. I broke teth'sag and left Sarikali because circumstance required it. If we can convince Korathan to play things our way, act as if he's come on Klia's account, then our journey's been worth the risk. But I need to finish that job properly. We have to clear Emiel and the Virésse. We have to find out which Akhendi were involved, and why. We might even get Phoria what she needs, whether she wants us to or not."

"And prove to them that you're not the Exile who ran away?" Alec asked.

"Yes. Because that's all I'll ever be in the minds of my kin forever, unless I go back and make things right."

"They could sentence you to death this time."

Seregil gave him a lopsided grin. "If they do, I'll need your help to make another dazzling escape. But this way it's my choice and, for once, I'm choosing honor. I need you to understand, talí." He paused, thinking of that last strange dream and all the other visions he'd been given since his return. "It's something the rhui'auros have been trying to tell me since we arrived."

"Honor, or atui?"

"Atui," Seregil admitted. "To act as a true Aurënfaie, whatever the consequences."

"You picked a hell of a time to start caring about that again."

"I always cared," Seregil said softly.

"All right then, we go back. How?"

"We'll surrender in Gedre and let them take us back."

"And if Riagil is in league with the Akhendi after all?"

"We'll find out soon enough."

Alec looked down at their clasped hands and rubbed his thumb over Seregil's knuckles. "You really believe this will all work?"

For a moment Seregil could almost feel the oppressive heat of the dhima, hear the clink of glass against glass. "Oh, yes. I have a gift for this sort of thing."

Four warships appeared from the northeast at sunset, dark outlines against the fading sky. Watching them approach, Alec made out the banner of the Skalan royal house flying from the mast of the foremost ship. This vessel drew in alongside their own, and sailors swung weighted boarding lines across for them.

"I haven't done this in a while," Seregil said, balancing precariously on the rail to grasp the rope.

"I never have," Alec muttered, forcing himself not to look down into the narrow, surging channel between the two ships. Following Seregil's lead, he clutched the rope high, wrapped its loose end around the ankle of his good leg, and pushed bravely off, letting the motion of the other vessel help swing him across to the far deck. He even managed to land on his feet once he got there.

Alec had seen Prince Korathan only from a distance a few times, but there was no mistaking the man. He was plain and fair-skinned like his sister and mother, and had the same sharp, appraising eyes. His black coat and close-fitting trousers were of military cut, but he wore the heavy gold chain of the vicegerent on his breast.

A wizard stood with the prince. He was a

portly, balding man, unremarkable except for the pinned-up sleeve of his ornate green robe.

"Wydonis?" Alec whispered.

Seregil nodded.

"Seregil? Sakor's Flame, man, what are you doing here?" the prince demanded, sounding none too pleased.

Perhaps Seregil had overestimated the man's fond memories of their younger days after all, Alec thought uneasily.

Seregil managed a courtly bow despite his bruises and filthy clothes. "We've gone to considerable trouble to reach you, my lord. The news we bring must be shared in private."

Korathan raked them both with a bleak glare, then gestured curtly for them to follow.

"Who's this?" he asked, jerking a thumb at Alec as they entered his cabin.

"Alec of Ivywell. A friend, my lord," Seregil told him.

"Ah, yes." Korathan spared Alec a second glance. "I thought he was blond."

Seregil's lips twitched the tiniest bit. "He usually is, my lord."

The cabin was as austere as the man who occupied it. Korathan seated himself at a small table and motioned curtly for Seregil to take the room's only other chair. Alec settled on the lid of a sea chest.

"All right, then, out with it," said Korathan.

"I know why you're here," Seregil told him, no less blunt. "I thought you were a wiser gambler than that. This is a fool's errand."

The prince's pale eyes narrowed. "Don't presume too much on our past association."

"It's for the sake of that, and my love for your family, that I'm here at all," Seregil retorted. "This plan to capture Gedre can only end in disaster. And not just for Klia and the rest of us trapped there. For Skala as well. It's insane! You must know that."

To Alec's surprise, Korathan appeared to consider Seregil's harsh words. "How do you know my mission?"

"Your sister's not the only one with spies in other camps," Seregil replied.

"Old Magyana, was it?"

Seregil said nothing.

Korathan tapped a finger on the tabletop. "All right then, we'll sort that out later. Phoria has the backing of the generals in this venture. As vicegerent, I'm obligated to obey."

"Clearly, the generals don't know what the Aurënfaie are capable of if they feel sufficiently threatened or insulted," Seregil replied, earnest now. "They trusted your mother, and many of them still trust Klia. She's a skillful diplomat, this half-sister of yours. She'd already swayed some of the opposing clans to our favor before news arrived of Idrilain's death. Phoria is another matter, though. Within days of the news, the Virésse were spreading the story that she'd betrayed her own mother and collaborated with the Lerans. Ulan í Sathil has the documents to prove it. Did you know of this?"

The prince eyed him levelly. "You seem to know quite a lot of things you shouldn't. How does that happen?"

"Do you recognize this?" Seregil held out his hand, showing him the ring.

"So you have it!"

"A gift from your mother, for certain services rendered. Alec and I both know the whole story, never mind how for the moment. Ulan í Sathil cast the whole business in the most damning light to a number of other khirnari—men and women he wanted to sway to his side. To the Aurënfaie, such an act demonstrates a shocking lack of honor. Even khirnari who were set to vote in Skala's favor are having second thoughts. If you cap it with this ill-considered raid, the next Skalans they deal with will call you ancestor."

"It's suicide, my lord," Alec added, tired of being ignored. "You'll get us all killed and accomplish nothing."

Korathan threw him an annoyed look. "I have my orders—"

"Orders be damned!" Seregil said. "You must have advised her against this?"

"She's queen now, Seregil." Korathan frowned down at his folded hands. "You know Phoria; you're either her ally or her enemy. There's no middle ground. That goes for me as much as anyone else."

"I don't doubt it, but I believe we can offer you a way out with honor served on all sides," Seregil told him.

"And what would that be?"

"Play the injured party and put honor on your side. Is Phoria aware that Klia and Torsin were poisoned by someone in Sarikali?"

"No, by the Flame! They're dead?"

"He is. Klia was hanging on when we left three nights ago, but she's deathly ill. You can use this, Korathan. When we left, no one else in Aurënen appeared to know that you're coming. If they've learned of it since, then we can argue that they had the purpose wrong. Sail into Gedre tomorrow with all flags flying and send word announcing that you've come seeking justice against the murderers. Play injured honor to the hilt and demand entrance to Sarikali."

"Who are these assassins?" asked Korathan. "Surely the Iia'sidra hasn't brushed such an act off lightly?"

"No, my lord, they haven't."

With Alec's assistance, Seregil explained the events of the past few days. They showed him the Akhendi sen'gai they'd found, and the bottle containing the bracelet. By the time they were finished, Korathan was staring at Seregil again.

"So you're not the wastrel you pretend to be. I wonder now if you ever were."

Seregil had the good grace to look embarrassed. "Anything I have done, my lord, I've done for the good of Skala—though there are few enough left who can vouch for my good character, and fewer still whom you have reason to trust. Your mother knew of some of my efforts on her behalf, as this ring attests. So did Nysander. If you have a truth knower among your wizards, Alec and I will happily submit ourselves to the test."

"A brave claim, Lord Seregil, but you always were a daring gambler," Korathan said with a sly smile. Raising his voice, he called out, "Doriska, what do you say to that?"

A side door opened and a woman in Orëska robes came in. "They speak the truth, my prince."

Korathan raised an eyebrow at them. "And a good thing, too. You've brought yourself close to a charge of treason just by coming here."

"Nothing could be further from our minds, my lord. Your mother sent me along to advise Klia on Aurënfaie customs. Let me do the same for you.

"Honor and family are everything here. You're well within your rights to land and demand Klia's return. If we play our cards right, I may even be able to salvage something of her mission here. But be warned; you'll accomplish nothing by force. If anyone guesses that you've come with an attacking force, your ships will be in flames before you sight land. So you see, we may well be saving your life, as well."

"So you mean to negotiate on my behalf, do you?"

"In Gedre, at least. I think Riagil's a man we can trust. He may be able to get you admitted to Sarikali, but he doesn't have the power you need to deal with the Iia'sidra, and no one is going to listen to me, after what I've done. You'll need Adzriel for that."

"I can damn well speak for myself," Korathan growled. "I'm the Vicegerent of Skala, and blood kin to the woman they tried to murder."

"Without a claim to Bôkthersan kinship, none of that will matter," Seregil told him. "That blood tie is your trump card, my lord, and Klia's. Let Adzriel help you use it to your best advantage. Of course, they may not allow you in at all. Whatever happens, though, Alec and I have to get to Sarikali and present the evidence we've found against Akhendi."

"They'll listen to you, but not to me?" asked Korathan. "Is this another of your risky gambles?"

"Yes, my lord, it is," Alec interjected. "He could face a death sentence by going back. If you still have any doubts as to our loyalties—"

Seregil cut him short with a warning look. "I think who our evidence clears and who it implicates will be proof enough of our good faith, my lord."

Korathan gave Alec another of those dismissive glances, making it clear he considered him little more than a servant, and one who would do well to hold his tongue. "I know of the terms of your return, Seregil, and what it meant to defy them. It strikes me as quite a sacrifice for a man to make for a country he abandoned two years ago, and for a queen he clearly does not trust."

Seregil bowed. "Meaning no disrespect, my lord, but we're doing this for Klia's sake, and for our own. And if Alec and I had abandoned Skala, as you put it, we wouldn't have undertaken this mission in the first place. Just so we understand one another."

"We do," Korathan replied with a tight smile that sent a ripple of unease up Alec's back. "Your declaration of loyalty is most appreciated."

"I don't trust him," Alec whispered when they were safely above decks again and out of the prince's hearing. "And you weren't much help. You practically insulted the queen to his face!"

"That truth knower of his was still lurking outside the door. Besides, I doubt I told him anything he hasn't already guessed. He knew it was foolish to try an attack; I've shown him a way to come out of this a winner."

"If we can get back to the city," muttered Alec, ticking his doubts off on his fingers. "If the Gedre or Akhendi don't execute you on Haman's behalf before we get there. If the Iia'sidra believes us, and if we're right about the Akhendi at all."

Seregil draped an arm over Alec's shoulders. "One problem at a time, talí. We've gotten this far, haven't we?"

48

An Uneasy Truce

Beka waited for nightfall before coming out onto the main road again. Cold, hungry, and footsore, she hummed ballads under her breath to keep her spirits up and her mind clear of questions she had no answers for.

Just before midnight she reached a village and helped herself to a horse. She hadn't seen a dog since she'd arrived in Aurënen. *A good thing, now that I'm turning thief,* she thought, grinning wryly to herself as she led the horse away.

When she was out of earshot, or at least bowshot, she mounted it bareback, wrapped her hands in the mane, and urged it into a trot, hoping it would respond to leg pressure since she had no reins. When it did, she kicked it into a gallop, laughing with relief.

Further down the road, she snagged a clean tunic and sen'gai from a washline and attempted to make herself a bit less conspicuous, binding her long red hair out of sight and making the best job of the sen'gai that she could.

By dawn she guessed she might be within a day's ride of the city, barring trouble. It was a chancy thing, staying on the road, but a growing sense of urgency drove her on. Her place was at Klia's side.

The bay mare was as good as any she'd ever ridden. Horse thieving would be a profitable profession here, she thought, if every nag stolen hastily in the dark proved as fine as one you'd have to raid a noble's stable for in Skala.

She encountered more people on the road as the morning wore on, but most were intent on business of their own and didn't waste a second glance on a poor, barefoot stranger. When there were more than a few people together, she turned aside and waited behind the shelter of the trees for them to pass. She kept a lookout to the rear, as well, but no one seemed in any hurry to overtake her.

This plan worked well enough until just past midday, when she struck a stretch of road that wended through a deep cut. Rounding a bend, she found herself faced with a pack of armed riders less than a hundred yards away, coming on at a canter. There was nowhere to go but back, and that was bound to attract notice.

At least they wore the colors of Akhendi, she noted with relief. Keeping to the side of the road, she continued on at a steady pace, praying that they'd go single file and keep their distance.

She was nearly past when one of them suddenly reached out and snatched the sen'gai from her head. Her red hair tumbled down over her shoulders, damning as any uniform.

"It's the Skalan!" the man shouted. Dropping the sen'gai, he drew his sword and raised it to strike.

Ducking low over her horse's neck, Beka grasped its mane and kicked hard. The mare bolted forward, then reared as two horsemen angled to block her escape.

Hands snatched at her tunic. For an instant all she could see was a circle of leering faces and glinting steel. Another man struck at her with a cudgel, bruising her arm through her mail shirt.

Suddenly a fierce yell sounded from somewhere overhead, followed by the sound of falling rock. Still wheeling her horse, Beka caught a glimpse of another horseman plunging down the steep slope to her right. Then he was among the Akhendi, laying about with the flat of his sword.

"Go!" he shouted, urging his horse forward to block one of her attackers. "Break out, damn it. Ride!"

Beka knew that voice. "Nyal?"

"Go!"

Looking around, she spotted a young rider who'd been startled by

Nyal's sudden appearance. Screaming an Urgazhi war cry, she barreled into him, knocking him off his horse as she surged past to the
open road beyond. It was the wrong direction, but it would have to
do for now.

She heard another wild whoop behind her, then the sound of pursuit. Looking back over her shoulder, she saw Nyal galloping after
her with the Akhendi close behind.

He caught up with her and thrust something at her: her sword, hilt
first. She wrenched it free, letting the scabbard fall away, and
slapped the flat of the blade across her mount's rump, urging it on.

"This way," Nyal shouted, pointing to a side road ahead.

Caught up in the moment, she followed without question.

"It's no use. They're still with us!" she cried, looking back to see
the Akhendi still in full cry behind them. "We can't outrun them.
Turn and fight! There are only five of them now."

"Beka, no!" Nyal cried, but she was already slowing.

Turning her horse, she let out another yell and galloped back,
sword held high. As she'd expected, the sudden turnabout startled
her pursuers. Three veered off, but the others charged her. The road
was narrow here, so she aimed her mount between them. Ducking
the leader's swing, she came up in time to catch the second a blow to
the head with her hilt. He toppled off his horse and she rode on
toward the remaining three. One turned tail and ran, but the other
two closed in on her.

Fighting on horseback without a saddle or stirrups to brace
against was dangerous at best. Instead, she slid off the far side, using the horse as a momentary shield, and ducked under its neck to
slash at the hocks of her closest opponent's mount. She managed to
nick it, and the animal reared, throwing the rider. Then she was turning to block a blow from his companion, who'd outflanked her.
Caught between two horses, she threw herself under the belly of her
attacker's mount and rolled to her feet on the other side. She slashed
him across the thigh, then smacked his horse on the rump, sending it
hurtling into the man she'd knocked from the saddle.

Another horseman bore down on her, and she braced for an attack, but it was Nyal, yelling for her to get up behind him. Grabbing
his outstretched hand, she thrust her foot over his in the stirrup and
let him haul her up behind his saddle. He wheeled about and took
off at a gallop, leaving their wounded ambushers in the dust.

Beka had no choice but to wrap her free arm around his waist,
clinging to him as they galloped further down the overgrown track.
Some part of her mind registered how good he felt, pressed against

her, but she pushed the thought away angrily, recalling instead the coldness in his eyes when he'd captured her.

They rode on in silence for a few miles, then stopped to let the horse drink at a stream. Beka slid quickly off, still grasping her sword, and took a few steps back.

Nyal dismounted but didn't try to approach her. He just stood there, sword sheathed, arms folded across his chest.

"Where did you come from?" she demanded. "Were you tracking me down again?"

"After a fashion," he admitted. "I saw where you'd been ambushed. I was certain I'd find you dead, but instead picked up your trail where you eluded the others. I figured you wouldn't be happy to see me, so I kept back, shadowing you to make sure you were safe. You did well, until the Akhendi jumped you. I wasn't expecting that, either."

Beka ignored the compliment. "If you wanted me safe, then why track me down in the first place?"

He gave her a rueful grin. "It seemed the best way to distract my fellow searchers from following your friends, whom I guessed rightly had business over the mountains."

"You found them?"

He nodded. "So did a gang of bandits, but we dealt with them. I sent Seregil and Alec on their way and came back to make certain you reached Sarikali safely."

"So you say," she growled.

"Talía." He stepped closer, and she spotted a dark stain on the front of his tunic, near the lower hem. It was blood, but too dry to have come from today's fighting.

"So you let them go, did you?" she said, pointing.

"Alec was wounded, shot through the leg," Nyal told her, rubbing at the stain. "I bound the wound for him."

This was agony. She wanted to believe him, even had some reason to do so, but caution still held her back. "Why did the Akhendi attack me?"

Turning away, Nyal sat down on a large stone next to the stream. "I don't know," he said, and she knew then that he was lying.

"It has something to do with Amali, doesn't it?"

This time there was no mistaking the guilty flush that suffused his face. *Seregil was right about him all along,* she thought miserably. "You're in league with her, aren't you?"

"No," he said, resting his elbows on his knees and hanging his head wearily.

She stared down at him, and her traitorous heart summoned memories of how his bare skin felt beneath her hands. She'd told Alec she wasn't love-blind; now was the time to prove it. "Give me your weapons," she ordered.

Without a word, he unbuckled his sword belt and tossed it at her feet, then did the same with the knife at his belt. She hung them over her shoulder, and checked his boots and tunic for hidden blades.

He was so patient, so passive, that she began to feel guilty. Before she could stop herself, she'd reached to brush a hand against his smooth cheek. He turned his head toward it, making the touch into a brief caress. She pulled back as if she'd been burned.

"If I've wronged you, I'm sorry," she said through clenched teeth. "I have my duty."

He looked away again. "So you've always said. What do you want to do now?"

"I have to get back to Klia."

"At least in that, we are in agreement," he replied, and she was certain she saw him smile as he turned away to mount his horse.

Somehow, she doubted whether the ride would be any easier from here.

49

SURRENDER

Lulled by the motion of the ship, Seregil slept deeply in spite of what lay ahead. He'd half hoped, half feared to dream again, but when he woke before dawn the following morning, he remembered nothing. Beside him, Alec frowned and muttered in his sleep, then came awake with a startled gasp when Seregil brushed his cheek.

Glancing out the tiny window at the end of the bunk, Alec settled back on his elbows. "Feels like we're still under sail."

Seregil shifted for a better look. "We're a mile or two out. I can see lights in Gedre."

They said little as they dressed in borrowed clothes. With a pang of regret, Seregil took off Corruth's ring and hung it around his neck on a string. The Akhendi bracelet was at the bottom of his old pack, wrapped in the Akhendi sen'gai they'd taken from the ambushers.

"What about our weapons and tools?" Alec asked.

"Wear your sword," Seregil said, buckling his own on. "Leave the rest here; I doubt we'll be allowed anything more dangerous than a fruit knife after today."

No one sailed out to meet them this time. Leaving his escort at the harbor's mouth,

Korathan anchored out beyond the piers and was rowed ashore in a longboat with the two wizards. Seregil and Alec followed in a second boat, hooded and anonymous among Korathan's guard.

"Riagil must suspect something," Alec whispered, scanning the distant crowd waiting for them on the shore.

Seregil nodded. It appeared that most of the city had turned out for their arrival, but there were no signs of welcome: no singing, no boats, no flowers strewn on the water. He rubbed his palms nervously on the legs of his leather trousers, knowing every pull of the oars brought them closer to what might prove a very disheartening moment of truth.

His sense of foreboding grew as they ground to a halt in the shallows, greeted only by the rough sigh of the wind and the slap of waves along the beach. They waded in behind Korathan and his entourage but hung back out of sight.

Following Seregil's instruction, Korathan stopped just above the water's edge, waiting to be summoned onto forbidden soil.

A man stepped from the crowd, and Seregil saw with relief that it was Riagil í Molan. He must have headed home as soon as their disappearance was discovered. The khirnari approached Korathan unsmiling, hands clasped in front of him rather than extended in welcome.

Alec shifted restlessly, knee-deep in the surf.

"Be patient," whispered Seregil. "There are forms to be observed."

"Who are you, to come to my shores with ships of war?" Riagil demanded in Skalan.

"I am Korathan í Malteus Romeran Baltus of Rhíminee, son of Queen Idrilain and brother of Queen Phoria. I do not come for battle, Khirnari, but seeking teth'sag for the attack on my sister, Klia ä Idrilain, and for the murder of her envoy, Lord Torsin. By my blood tie to the Bôkthersa, I claim that right."

The tension broke as Riagil smiled and walked down to meet him. "You are welcome here, Korathan í Malteus." Riagil removed a heavy bracelet from his wrist and presented it to the prince. "When I left Sarikali your sister still lived, though she remains ill and in seclusion. Her people protect her well. I will send word of your arrival to the Iia'sidra."

"I wish to speak with them myself," Korathan told him. "I demand an audience in the queen's name."

"This is most irregular, to say the least," Riagil said, taken aback by the man's abrupt manner. "I do not know if they will allow you to cross the mountains, but rest assured your claim of honor will be heard."

"The atui of Gedre is well known," Korathan replied. "To prove my own good faith, I honor the teth'sag of the Haman against my own kinsman."

On cue, Seregil waded forward, eyes averted. Splashing up to the beach, he drew his sword and drove it point first into the wet sand. "You know me, Riagil í Molan," he said, pushing back his hood. "I acknowledge that I have broken teth'sag and of my own free will surrender myself to the judgment of the Haman and the Iia'sidra." Dropping to his knees, he prostrated himself facedown, arms extended at his sides in a gesture of abject submission.

A moment of eerie quiet followed. Seregil lay absolutely still, listening to the water trickling between the grains of sand beneath his cheek. Riagil could by rights slay him with his own sword for breaking the decree of exile. If he were in league with Akhendi, it would be a most convenient tactic.

He heard muffled footsteps approach, then, from the corner of his eye, saw the sword blade shift slightly as someone grasped the hilt.

Then a firm hand closed over his shoulder.

"Rise, Exile," said Riagil, drawing him to his feet. "In the name of the Haman, I take you captive." Lowering his voice, he added, "The Iia'sidra are awaiting your return before the vote is taken. You have much to explain."

"I'm anxious to do so, Khirnari."

Alec splashed up beside them, planted his sword, and assumed the ritual posture.

"As a Skalan, you must be judged by your own people, Alec í Amasa," Riagil said, lifting him up. At his signal, one of his kinsmen collected their swords. Several others fell in beside Seregil.

"I must ask two things of you that may strain your patience, Khirnari," said Korathan. "These two must be allowed to speak on my behalf, regardless of the sentence passed against them. They came to me at great peril to their own lives to bring news of who has attacked my family."

"I have to speak to the Iia'sidra. Emiel í Moranthi's life and the honor of three clans depend on it," Seregil told him. "I swear it by Aura's name."

"This is why you left?" Riagil asked.

"It seemed reason enough, Khirnari." Not quite a lie.

"I would also prefer to keep their return secret until we arrive in the sacred city," Korathan added.

Riagil noted Seregil's bruised face and nodded. "As you wish. It is enough that they have returned. Come, Korathan í Malteus, you shall be made welcome in my home until the will of the Iia'sidra is known. I'll send word to Sarikali at once."

And so it was, a short time later, that Seregil found himself once more in Riagil's painted courtyard. He and Alec sat apart from the others under the watchful gaze of their guards while Korathan and his people were given wine and food.

"At least he hasn't chained you," Alec remarked hopefully.

Seregil nodded absently, studying Korathan. It had been thirty years or more since they'd roistered through the Lower City stews together. Time had taken a harsh toll on the man, leaving him grim to the point of melancholy most of the time. Seated under the gnarled shade tree, he seemed uneasy with the peaceful setting— unmoved by the warm sunshine or the smiling, generous Gedre attending him.

A man made only for war, Seregil thought. Yet a man of reason as well, or they wouldn't be sitting here now.

Within the hour Riagil rejoined them bearing good news. "The Iia'sidra has granted you entrance to the sacred city, Korathan í Malteus," he announced happily. "There are restrictions, however."

"I expected as much," Korathan replied. "And they are?"

"You may bring your wizards, but no more than twenty soldiers, and you must order your vessels to anchor outside my harbor."

"Very well."

"You must also invoke your blood tie to the Bôkthersan clan in order to declare teth'sag. Adzriel will act as your sponsor before the council."

"So I've been told," the prince replied. "Though I do not understand why my sister Klia was allowed to speak for herself, but I am not."

"This is different," Riagil explained. "Klia came to negotiate. You are bringing a matter of atui before them and, I'm sorry to say, some of the clans could challenge your right to do so. The Tírfaie— any Tírfaie—do not have the same rights under Aurënen law. Rest assured, Adzriel will be a great help to you."

Korathan glowered at Riagil. "You consider us a lesser race, then?"

The khirnari pressed a hand to his heart and made him a slight bow. "Some do, my friend; not I. Please believe that I will do all in my power to see that your sister and Torsin í Xandus are accorded justice."

The column set off that afternoon with Riagil and twenty Gedre swordsmen as escort. There were no pack animals or musicians to slow them down this time. Not one for unnecessary ceremony, Korathan and his riders traveled as if they were on campaign, carrying only what they needed.

Seregil and Alec rode with the Skalans, wearing the tabard and wide steel hats of Korathan's personal guard.

"In uniform at last, eh?" Seregil said, grinning as Alec fidgeted at his helmet strap. "Between that and your dark hair, I doubt even Thero will recognize you."

"Let's just hope the Akhendi don't," Alec replied, warily scanning the cliffs that hemmed in this section of the road for trouble. "Do you think anyone will notice we're the only members of the prince's guard not carrying weapons?"

"If anyone asks, we're Korathan's personal cooks."

They bypassed the Dravnian way station to make camp farther up the pass. At the first stretch of guarded trail, Korathan accepted the blindfold with good grace, commenting only that he wished Skala had such safeguards.

They reached the steaming Vhadä'nakori pool late the following morning and halted to rest the horses. Seregil and Alec remained with the soldiers while Riagil guided Korathan and his wizards up to the stone dragon.

Seregil's mare liked to suck air when being saddled, and he'd felt the saddle begin to slip during the last blind ride. After watering her, he tightened the girth strap, giving her a smart slap on the side to make her exhale.

As he worked, he listened with half an ear to the various conversations going on around him. Korathan's riders had struck him as a dour lot at the outset, but their Gedre counterparts were beginning to win some of them over. Some of them were stumbling along now in a jumbled argot of Skalan and 'faie, trying to make themselves understood. But he also caught a troubling undercurrent from some of the Skalans muttered complaints about blindfolds and "strange, unnatural magicks." It seemed that Phoria was not alone in her distrust of the 'faie, and in wizards in general. This was a new attitude for Skalans, and it troubled him profoundly.

He was just finishing with the strap when suddenly everything went very still.

"Son of Korit," a voice said, speaking close to his ear.

The hair on his neck prickled. Turning sharply, he expected to find a rhui'auros or khtir'bai behind him. Instead, he saw only Alec and the soldiers still going about their business, though he still couldn't hear any sound.

Wondering if he'd suddenly gone deaf, he turned to steady himself against his horse and found a dragon the size of a hound perched on the saddle. Its wings were folded tight to its sides, and its neck was arched back like a serpent's. Before he could do more than register its existence, it struck, clamping its jaws around his left hand just above the thumb.

Seregil froze. He felt its heat first, hot as an oven against his skin, then the pain of teeth and venom slammed up his arm.

He grasped his horse's mane with his free hand, willing himself not to jerk away or cry out. The dragon's claws scraped pale lines in the saddle leather as it tightened its grip and gave his hand a sharp shake. Then it went still again, watching him with one hard yellow eye as blood welled from its scaly mouth and ran down his wrist.

O Aura, it's a big one! Dangerously big. Its jaws reached to the other side of his hand.

"That will leave a lucky mark."

The pain quickly swelled to something approaching rapture. The creature seemed to fill his vision, and he stared at it with an agonized reverence as hazy golden light coalesced around them. Its scales reflected the sunlight with an iridescent sheen. The stiff spines on its face twitched slightly as it held him, and wisps of vapor rose from its delicate golden nostrils.

"Son of Korit," the voice said again.

"Aura Elustri," he whispered, trembling.

The dragon released him and flapped away across the steaming tarn.

Sounds rushed in on him, and suddenly Alec was there, easing him down to the ground as his legs gave out under him. Seregil stared dazedly down at the double line of bloody punctures that crossed his hand, back and palm.

"Larger than Thero's," he murmured, shaking his head in amazement.

"Seregil!" Alec said, shaking him by the shoulder. "Where did it come from? Are you all right? Where's that vial?"

"Vial? Pouch." It was hard to concentrate with his entire arm on fire from the inside. People crowded in to see, overwhelming him with noise.

Alec tugged the pouch free from Seregil's belt and shook out the glass vial of lissik the rhui'auros had given him—the one he'd very nearly left behind.

He let out a strangled laugh. *They knew I'd need it. They knew all along.*

Alec gently worked the dark, oily liquid into the wound, easing the worst of the burning.

The crowd parted for Korathan and Riagil. The khirnari knelt and took Seregil's hand, then called out for herbs.

"By the Light, Seregil!" he murmured, quickly assembling a poultice and wrapping it around his hand with wet rags. "To be so marked, it's—"

"A gift," Seregil croaked, feeling the dragon's venom spreading through his body, turning his veins to wires of hot steel.

"A gift indeed. But can you ride?"

"Tie me on, if you have to." He tried to get up and failed. Someone held a flask to his lips, and he gulped down a bitter infusion.

"You're trembling," Alec muttered, helping him up. "How are you going to manage?"

"Not much choice, talí," Seregil replied. "The worst of it should pass in a day or two. It didn't bite too deeply, just enough to mark me and make me remember."

"Remember what?"

Seregil grinned weakly. "Who I am."

The ride back to Sarikali seemed endless. Beka and Nyal kept off the main road and steered wide of the little villages they passed. Nyal stopped at one to buy a second horse, leaving her in the trees without comment or warning.

She was grateful to have her own mount again; the closeness of riding double with Nyal had been more than she could bear. They spoke little during the day and rolled into their blankets on opposite sides of the fire as soon as they'd eaten.

The entire situation felt ridiculous when she let herself think too much about it. She was, in essence, his prisoner, yet she held all the weapons. Either of them could have stolen away in the night, yet each was there in the morning.

I need to get back to the city and he's been ordered to bring me there. That's all there is to it, she told herself, ignoring the sad, furtive glances he cast her way.

They reached the river the following afternoon and reined in at the head of the bridge.

"Well, here we are," said Beka. "What now?"

Nyal stared thoughtfully at the distant city. "I must take you to the Iia'sidra, I suppose.

Don't worry, though. You're Tír. I imagine they'll just pass you along to Klia. She's the one who must answer for you."

"Will you tell them about letting Seregil go?" she asked mockingly.

Nyal sighed. "Sooner or later I'll have to."

Something in his face brought on another twinge of doubt. If he was telling the truth—

"We'd better put on a good show," she said, handing him back his weapons. This brought on another wave of empty regret; he could have taken them from her if he'd really wanted to.

There was less fuss about her return than she'd expected. They attracted little notice until they reached Silmai tupa. Nyal exchanged a few words with the servant at the khirnari's door, then stepped back and let Beka enter alone. She could feel him watching her but refused to look back. Squaring her shoulders, she allowed herself to be escorted into the main hall, where Brythir sat waiting.

The khirnari's reaction was impossible to read. He simply stared at her for a long moment, then sighed. "I have summoned the Iia'sidra and your own people, Captain. You must answer before them."

She made him a deep bow. "As you wish, Khirnari. But please tell me, is Klia alive?"

"Yes, and I understand she is improving, though she is still unable to speak."

Beka bowed again, too overcome with relief to speak.

"Come." He motioned her to a chair and put a mug of ale into her shaking hands. "And now you must answer a question for me. Have you returned of your own will?"

"Yes, my lord."

This seemed to content him, for he asked her nothing more. As soon as she'd finished her ale, they proceeded under escort to the Iia'sidra chamber.

Here, she found herself facing a far more hostile assembly, although she received nods of encouragement from the Bôkthersans and Akhendi. Sitting in Klia's place, Thero gave her a slight smile. She hadn't had a chance to clean up or change out of the bedraggled clothes she'd stolen. She looked every inch a spy, if not a very successful one.

The Iia'sidra questioned her closely, but she stubbornly refused to say why Seregil left the city or what direction he and Alec had taken. In Skala, such an interrogation might have ended in the torture rooms of Red Tower prison or under the hands of a truth knower. Instead, she was turned over to her own people.

The only part of her story that had raised eyebrows at all was her assertion that the Akhendi she'd met on the road had meant to kill her. If not for Nyal's corroboration, she suspected they wouldn't have believed her at all.

Rhaish í Arlisandin was understandably upset by this news. "I gave orders for their safe return," he protested, making his apologies to Thero.

When it was all over, she was led away under guard by her own riders. Rhylin was in charge and gave her an encouraging grin as they left the chamber.

"They're all right, then?" he whispered.

She shrugged, thinking of the bloodstain on Nyal's tunic.

At the guest house, Thero took her directly to Klia's chamber, where the sick woman lay asleep under Corporal Nikides's watchful guard. Her hands rested on the comforter at her sides, one whole, the other still swathed in bulky dressings. The window was open, and incense burned on a stand across the room, but a sickly odor still underlay it, one she had smelled on battlefields and in hospital tents—illness, poultices, and damaged flesh. Klia was so pale, so still, that for a moment Beka feared she'd taken a sudden turn for the worse.

When Thero touched her shoulder and Klia opened her eyes, however, Beka saw that whether her commander could speak or not, her mind had cleared.

Thank the Flame, she thought, going down on one knee beside the bed.

"She wishes to know all that has happened," Thero said, drawing a chair up for her. "You'd best keep it brief, though. These periods of lucidity don't usually last long."

"There's not much to tell," Beka admitted. "Seregil found his trail and I went on; Nyal caught up with me and sent me back with his men while he went on after Seregil."

Thero made a low, angry noise in his throat. "What happened then?"

"We were attacked by bandits and I escaped in the confusion. Nyal tracked me down again the next day, just in time to get me away from those Akhendi riders. He claimed he'd found Seregil and Alec, helped them out of an ambush, too, and then sent them on their way. But—" She paused, fighting back the sudden tightness in her chest.

"You doubt his word?"

"I don't know what to think," she whispered. Looking down, she found Klia watching her intently. "He had blood on his tunic, my lady. He says Alec was hurt and he bound the wound. I—I don't know."

Thero squeezed her shoulder. "We'll find out," he promised. "What happened then?"

"I was headed back here anyway, so I let him bring me in. The rest you know."

Klia tried to speak but managed only a breathy rasp. Frustrated, she looked up at Thero.

"You did well, Captain. You should clean up and get some rest," he told Beka, then followed her from the room.

"What about her?" she demanded, keeping her voice low. "Have you been able to get any more out of her about who attacked her?"

"No, the poisoning affected her memory. She seems to recall little after the morning of the hunt."

"That's too bad. I don't like the idea of leaving Aurënen before we see justice done."

"That's not Klia's main concern," Thero told her. "Don't let it blind you, either. There's still the vote to come. Your duty lies there."

Returning to the barracks at last, Beka was met with a round of cheers from the riders waiting for her there.

"You look like you had a hard go of it, Captain," Braknil exclaimed, handing her a mug of rassos.

She downed it gratefully, welcoming the warmth it spread through her aching muscles. "No worse than usual," she replied, managing a grin to match those around her. "I just didn't have you all there to help me."

After checking the order of the watches, she left Braknil in charge and retreated to her room to clean up. Smoothing a clean tabard over her shirt, she rested a hand on the regimental device stitched on its front: crossed sabers supporting a crown.

Duty.

She recalled Nyal sitting across the fire from her, watching her with hazel eyes that spoke only of patience.

I wanted to make certain you were safe—

A soft knock interrupted her thoughts.

"Come," she mumbled, wiping quickly at her eyes.

It was Mercalle. Giving Beka a stiff salute, she closed the door quietly behind her.

Here was another situation designed to twist knots in her belly. The two of them had spoken less than ten words to each other since the sergeant had confessed to spying for Phoria. If they hadn't all been trapped together in a foreign land, Beka would have packed her off to another regiment at once.

"I was wondering if there was anything you needed, Captain," she said, clearly as uncomfortable as Beka.

"No." Beka turned away to the glass on the wall, fidgeting with her gorget.

But still Mercalle lingered. "I also thought you might want to know that there's a rumor going around that Nyal is in some sort of trouble with his khirnari."

Beka glanced at her in the mirror's reflection. "How do you know that?"

"I was on sentry duty until a few minutes ago. Kheeta í Branín came by with the news. It's something to do with him not telling folks soon enough that you'd gone."

"What do you mean? He set them on us and led them right to me."

"Well, as I understand it, you three left the night before. He didn't say anything to anyone until the next day, like he wanted to give you a head start. It was the Khatme who broke the news."

Beka fought back a surge of hope. "And you took it upon yourself to come tell me?"

Mercalle straightened to attention. "I'm sorry if I overstepped, Captain. I know how you feel about what I did. But Nyal's been a good help and—"

"And what?" Beka snapped.

"Nothing, Captain." Mercalle saluted quickly and turned to go.

"Wait. Tell me something. Why did you keep quiet about what Phoria told you to do?"

"Those were my orders, Captain. I've lived my life by orders, and for a good part of it those orders came from Phoria herself. That's what you do if you're a soldier." She broke off and Beka couldn't blind herself to the grief in the older woman's eyes, much as she wanted to. "A sergeant can't afford to pick and choose which ones she obeys, Captain," Mercalle went on. "We can't be like you and Lord Seregil, defying the Iia'sidra, or the commander."

Beka opened her mouth to protest, but Mercalle cut her off. "Klia was too sick to have given you any orders. Braknil knows it. So does Rhylin, though we've all tried to keep it from the riders. You did what you thought was best and I hope it turns out the way you want.

But even if it does, don't ever forget that you were lucky; choice is a luxury, one your average soldier can't afford."

She looked away, and when she spoke again her voice was softer. "All the same, if I could change the way things turned out, I would. I never thought it would bring harm to you or Commander Klia. Since Sir Alec caught me out, I've been doing a lot of thinking. Phoria's changed since I served with her, or maybe I've gotten to an age where I look at things a little differently. . . ." She trailed off. "When we get home, Captain, I'll be leaving the regiment. That's what I came in to say, and to ask you to give Nyal a chance to prove himself before you cast him off." She gave Beka the hint of a smile. "It's not my place to say, Captain, but I will anyway. Men like that don't come along every day for women like us."

"And what if I told you he came to me with Alec's blood on his hands?" Beka snapped. "Or Seregil's? There's someone's blood on him, and until I find out whose, I'll thank you to keep your opinions to yourself."

"Your pardon. I didn't know." Mercalle saluted stiffly and went out, leaving Beka alone with a quandary she saw no way of resolving.

Anyone who traveled these mountains carried the necessary medicines for dragon bite. Riagil kept Seregil's hand bound with poultices of wet clay and herbs and had his men brew healing draughts of willow and serpentwood bark. All the same, Seregil's left arm quickly swelled to the elbow like a blue-mottled sausage. Dark spots danced in front of his eyes and he ached in every joint. Clinging grimly to the saddlebow with his good hand, he let Alec lead his horse.

By nightfall they reached the forested foothills of Akhendi and made camp in a clearing there. The grass was soft and the air sweet, but he spent the night tossing through feverish dreams and woke too stiff to rise without help.

"You should eat something," Alec advised, bringing him another dose of Riagil's infusion.

Seregil shook his head but accepted a mug of tea laced with some strong spirit Alec had scrounged up among the soldiers. With help, he clambered back into the saddle and waited miserably for the order to move on.

"Do you feel any better today?" Korathan inquired, walking his horse past.

Seregil managed a grin. "No, my lord, but I don't feel any worse either."

Korathan gave him an approving nod. "Good. It wouldn't do to leave you behind."

Alec grew increasingly watchful as they entered the more populated part of Akhendi. Whenever they stopped for water or news, he made certain that they were safely surrounded by uniformed Skalans. He also kept his ears open and learned that Amali had gone home after he and Seregil had escaped. Rhaish was still in Sarikali.

"What else can he do?" Seregil mumbled, hunched miserably in the saddle. "Either he's innocent and has no reason to run, or doesn't want to look guilty."

They reached the valley late in the day and found a cadre of Silmai lookouts waiting for them at the bridge. Iäanil í Khormai greeted Korathan in the Iia'sidra's name, then sent runners ahead to announce their arrival.

"A better welcome than Klia got," Seregil remarked, sounding more alert as he took his reins back from Alec. The swelling in his arm was already subsiding, though the skin was still discolored.

At the outskirts of the city they found a large crowd waiting to greet them. Foremost among them were nine white-clad members of the Iia'sidra. The khirnari of Virésse and Haman were not with them.

"Rhaish?" Seregil asked softly, craning his neck to see past a tall Skalan riding just in front of him.

"There," Alec said, spotting the Akhendi standing next to Adzriel and old Brythir.

"Good. Maybe he hasn't tumbled yet."

"Ulan and Nazien aren't here."

"That would hardly be tactful, now would it?"

The Silmai khirnari greeted Korathan, presenting him with a heavy golden torque. "I regret that such a circumstance brings you here."

"Or that we should meet for such a reason, my kinsman," said Adzriel, introducing herself.

"When you have rested and refreshed yourself, the Iia'sidra will hear your petition," Brythir went on. "Perhaps tomorrow morning?"

"I'd prefer to settle the matter tonight," Korathan replied brusquely. "I will visit my sister first to learn her condition."

Alec peered out from beneath the edge of his hood, watching

the faces of the various Iia'sidra members. Many were clearly offended at such haste, but no one was in a position to argue. Korathan was the aggrieved party and was within his rights to demand an assembly.

"Come, I'll take you to her," Adzriel said, stepping in graciously. "My sister Mydri is with her now, or she would have been here to greet you."

Säaban brought her a horse, and together they proceeded through the familiar streets.

Alec had never expected to enter this strange place again, or to feel the silvery play of its ancient magic across his skin. In spite of his underlying anxiety, he savored the moment. As if in response, he caught the rich, unmistakable scent of the Bash'wai and whispered his thanks.

"Look there," Seregil whispered.

Several rhui'auros stood beside the street, watching the newcomers pass. As they came abreast of them, one of the rhui'auros raised a hand at him in salute.

"They know!" Alec hissed.

"It's all right," Seregil replied quietly.

At the outskirts of Bôkthersa tupa they were met by a crowd of well-wishers waiting to greet the prince. He acknowledged them with thinly masked impatience and pressed on.

Braknil's decuria were ranked at attention on the front stairs of the guest house. At the bottom Beka stood next to Thero, looking none the worse for her journey.

"Thank the Maker!" Alec exclaimed softly, feeling a weight lifted from his heart.

"Looks like she got back in one piece after all," whispered Seregil. "But where's Nyal? I hope she didn't kill him on sight."

Beka went down on one knee in front of Korathan as he dismounted. "Captain Beka Cavish, my lord."

"My sister mentions you often in her field reports, Captain," Korathan replied, less curt with her than he had been with the Iia'sidra. "It seems her regard for you is well founded."

Beka rose and saluted.

"And in you as well, young wizard," he added, turning to Thero. "You were apprenticed to old Nysander before Magyana, weren't you?"

"Yes, Vicegerent."

Alec thought he caught a gleam of alarm in Thero's eyes; an association with Magyana was unlikely to win anyone favor at court just now. He was also struck, however, by how Korathan seemed to know a bit about anyone he was introduced to.

"A most talented young man," the wizard Wydonis remarked, coming forward with Elutheus to clasp hands with Thero. "Your master and I had our differences, but I see he managed not to ruin you."

Thero returned the greeting stiffly, then clasped hands more warmly with the younger wizard.

Did Thero know who all the Watchers were? wondered Alec.

He and Seregil followed unremarked as Beka led Korathan to his sister's chamber. The nobles and wizards crowded in, leaving the soldiers on guard in the corridor. As soon as Klia's door was safely shut, Alec drew Beka into Thero's room across the corridor and latched the door shut behind them.

"What is this?" she demanded sharply, pulling away from Seregil.

"Don't you know us, Captain?" he asked as he and Seregil pushed back their hoods.

"By the Flame!" She pulled back to stare at them both. "What are you doing back here?"

"I'll explain later," said Seregil. "Did Nyal find you again?"

"Again?" Her smile died, and Alec knew at once that something was amiss. "Then you did see him?"

"See him? He saved our lives!" said Alec.

"He told me—oh, hell." She sank down on the edge of Thero's bed and pressed a hand over her eyes. "He claimed he was trying to help us, that he let you go. But he had blood on his clothes."

"Didn't you notice me limping?" Alec asked. "I took an arrow through the leg. Where is he? You didn't hurt him, did you?"

"No." It was almost a groan. "He brought me back yesterday. But—I still thought he'd betrayed us. Even after he got me away from the Akhendi—"

Seregil's eyes narrowed. "You had a run-in with the Akhendi, too?"

Beka nodded. "Among others. The men Nyal left me with got jumped that same day by a bunch of freebooters. I got away from them and took off into the woods. Later, I met some Akhendi swordsmen on the road and they attacked me. Nyal helped me get away."

"Akhendi riders attacked you openly?" Seregil asked again.

Beka nodded. "Rhaish í Arlisandin is furious."

"Is he?" said Seregil. "Where's Nyal now? I need to speak with him."

"With the Ra'basi, I suppose. I told him to keep his distance. He knows something, Seregil. I saw it in his eyes when I asked about the Akhendi who attacked me."

Seregil gathered her into an awkward, one-armed hug and held her tight for a moment. "We'll sort it out soon," he promised. "I'm just glad to see you safe!"

Beka shrugged. "What did you expect?"

"Has Klia said anything about who attacked her?" asked Alec.

"She can't speak yet, but she's more herself today. She still refuses to demand vengeance against the Haman, though, or anyone else."

Seregil sighed. "That's just as well. I think we've discovered our poisoner. Come, I want to speak to Klia before the others wear her out."

Korathan sat next to his sister's bed. On the far side, Mydri bent over Klia's damaged hand, changing dressings.

"You're back sooner than I expected, Haba!" Mydri exclaimed, glancing up as he came in. "Should I be glad?"

"It was my own choosing," Seregil replied, approaching the bed.

Klia greeted him with a rueful little smile. She lay propped up against a pile of cushions, dressed in a loose blue gown. Her face was still deathly pale, the skin too slack, but her eyes were bright and alert.

When Mydri removed the last of the bandages, however, Seregil's stomach did a slow lurch.

"Maker's Mercy!" Alec whispered, echoing his own dismay.

Klia's first and middle fingers were gone. Mydri had cut away flesh and bone at an angle, from the knuckle of the ring finger to the base of the thumb. The raw edges were sewn together with heavy black silk, and although the flesh was still swollen and red, it appeared to be healing clean. The hand itself, once strong and slender, now looked like a splayed bird's claw.

"Those white patches spread and turned to dry gangrene, just as Nyal said they would," Mydri explained, applying a pungent unguent to the incision. "It would have killed her in time. We were lucky, only having to do it once. I'm afraid she won't draw a bow again, though."

Seregil looked up to find Klia watching him with mute resignation.

"You only need one hand to wield a sword," Seregil told her. She gave him a wink.

"I've explained something of what you two did for her and for Skala," said Korathan. "I'll leave the rest of it to you."

He exchanged a look with Mydri and she withdrew.

"Thank you, my lord." With Alec's help, Seregil explained what had happened once they'd parted from Beka, showing Klia the Akhendi sen'gai and the sealed bottle. Tears glittered in her eyes as they outlined their suspicions against the khirnari and his wife.

Betrayed again, Seregil thought sadly.

"I can't open the bottle just yet, as I don't want to give Rhaish any warning. Before I go to the Iia'sidra, I need you to think, Klia. Did the charm Amali gave you have any marks or cracks in the wood?"

Klia slowly shook her head.

"All right. Now then, did the Haman, Emiel, attack you during the hunt?"

She looked at him blankly.

"She remembers little of that day," Thero told him. "She was quite sick by then."

"That night at the Virésse banquet, do you recall feeling anything prick your hand?" Seregil asked her. "No? Any other time? Do you know when you might have been poisoned?"

Again no.

"Nyal said the snake's bite is painless," Alec reminded him. "The poison must deaden feeling. And the barb on the ring is tiny."

"The ring! Thero, were you able to learn anything more from it?"

"No. Whoever used it masked it well," the wizard replied.

"Just like the charm," Seregil mused, "And yet they were able to preserve the memory of Emiel in it, and turn it white again somehow without disturbing that memory."

"We were just discussing that," said Thero, who'd evidently warmed a bit toward the older wizard. "According to Wydonis, who is much more adept than I at this sort of thing, it's possible to mask the essence of a person, as has evidently been done with the ring. But it's virtually impossible, short of necromancy, to falsely imbue that essence."

Wydonis nodded. "Whoever had Alec's charm, they were careful only to mask its appearance, leaving Emiel's essence to be found when it changed again," Wydonis explained. "I grant you, it's difficult."

"But what made it turn black again, if Emiel didn't attack her?" asked Alec.

"Perhaps merely his proximity," the older wizard said. "As Thero has speculated, these are the doings of someone with greater than normal ability."

Thero passed the ring to the elder wizard. "Perhaps you could divine more than I have from this. We can't afford to miss anything."

Wydonis took the steel ring on his palm, breathed on it, then closed his fist around it. After a moment's concentration, he nodded slowly. "As you say, it reveals nothing of the murderer. However, I can tell you something—it was made in Plenimar, as you rightly suspected. At Riga, I think, by a one-legged smith who slakes his work in goat's urine. The ring was used for a time by a woman named—" He paused, brow furrowed. "She is of the house of Ashnazai, I believe. She used it to murder six people: four men, a woman, and an infant girl—all of them kin to the current Overlord—and then herself. More recently, it was used to kill several calves. It has something of Princess Klia's essence in it, too—blood perhaps—and Torsin's." He tried one last time, then raised an eyebrow at Seregil. "I also sense a fish of some sort, but whoever used the ring to poison the princess has left no trace."

"Could a Virésse or Haman do that?" Thero asked Seregil.

"The Virésse, perhaps, but probably not a Haman. Their gifts don't usually run in that vein. I think it's time we had a chat with Nyal. I'll ask Adzriel to have someone bring him to her house discreetly. We don't want to attract attention."

Korathan shot him a questioning look. "Who is this Nyal?"

"A confidant of Lady Amali's, my lord. These are delicate matters. It would be best if he thinks himself among friends," Seregil explained. "I'll have Adzriel, Alec, and Thero as witnesses. I think Klia will agree that this is best. My lady?"

Klia nodded slightly.

"Very well," Korathan said grudgingly.

"This shouldn't take long," Seregil promised. "Send word to the Iia'sidra that you'll meet with them in two hours." He paused. "Beka, do you want to be there for this?"

She hesitated, flushing a bit behind her freckles. "With my lord's permission?"

"Be my eyes and ears, Captain," said Korathan. "I'll expect a full report."

With that settled, Seregil left the others and found Adzriel waiting just down the corridor.

"I'll send Kheeta to fetch Nyal," she said. "I hope for Beka's sake that he hasn't betrayed you."

"So do I. But I suspect she's right about him knowing more than he's let on."

Adzriel went down the back stairs and he followed, motioning for Alec and the others to remain behind.

At the lower landing, just off the kitchen, he laid a hand on her arm. A ray of late-afternoon sun slanted in through the open door beyond, striking golden glints in her dark hair even as it highlighted the circles beneath her eyes. She looked older suddenly, and careworn.

"I have something for you," he told her, pressing Corruth's ring into her hand. "It belongs here. Who knows what the Iia'sidra will decide. . . ." He faltered, unable for once to find the right words to shape his meaning.

The light struck the ring's large red stone, scattering bright spangles across her palm like tears of blood.

She looked down at it, then leaned forward and kissed him, first on the brow, then on the back of his bandaged hand. "I'm proud of you, my brother. Whatever judgment the Iia'sidra passes, you returned and I'm very proud of you." She touched his wounded hand again. "May I see?"

The teeth marks had scabbed over cleanly, each darkly ringed with blue lissik.

"Make certain the Iia'sidra see this," she advised. "Let them see that the dragons have claimed you. Whatever the khirnari may say, you will carry this mark of favor forever, here"—she touched a hand to his heart—"and here. Come over when you're ready. I'll see that Nyal is there."

Seregil kissed her cheek, then returned upstairs to find the others crowded around Klia's bed.

"She spoke!" Alec told him, making room. "She wants to go with us to the Iia'sidra."

"Is she strong enough?" Korathan asked, looking to Mydri.

"If we wrap her well and keep her from any jolts," his sister said. Looking down at Klia, she shook her head. "Is it important enough to justify the risk, my dear? You're not strong enough to speak at any length."

"Must see me," Klia whispered, her brow furrowed with effort.

"She's right," Seregil said, giving the sick woman a smile. "Let them see just how badly the laws of hospitality have been breached." Leaning down, he clasped her sound hand and added softly, "If you weren't a princess, I'd have had you working with me long ago."

Her fingers tightened around his as she gave him a fleeting grin.

Adzriel opened her own sitting room for the interrogation. Seregil, Alec, Beka, and Thero were already in place when Kheeta ushered the Ra'basi in. Beka acknowledged him with a terse nod, remaining where she was in the embrasure of the window.

Nyal gaped in amazement at the two returned fugitives. "So you were captured after all?"

"No, we brought ourselves back," Alec told him.

"After all the trouble of getting away? Why?"

"We found out a few more things along the way," Seregil told him. "We need your help again. I'm hoping you'll give it as freely as you have in the past."

"Whatever I can do, my friends."

"Good. There are a few things we need to understand first. Tell us why Akhendi would attack not only me but Alec and Beka as well."

Nyal shifted uneasily in his chair. "Akhendi attacked you? When?"

Seregil took out the sen'gai. "We found these among the belongings of those so-called bandits after you left us."

"By the Light! But Rhaish said—"

"We know what he said," Seregil cut in. "I

also know about Alec's run-in with Emiel í Moranthi. You remember that, don't you? Alec says you took his warding charm to be restored? Did you give it to anyone?"

Nyal stared at him. "I gave it to Amali. What has that to do with anything?"

Seregil exchanged a glance with Alec. "Can you explain how that same charm—Alec's—ended up on the bracelet Amali wove for Klia? The very bracelet that she used to accuse Emiel? You see, Nyal, as much as I wanted to, I never believed the bastard laid a hand on her."

Nyal had gone ashen. "No, she would not—"

Alec placed a hand on Nyal's shoulder. "I know that you care for her. I've seen the two of you together several times, and that she shared some fear with you regarding her husband."

"You spied on me?"

"You're not the only one with long ears," Alec said evasively, but a betraying hint of color rose in his fair cheeks.

Nyal slumped back in his chair. "She did come to me, now and then. And you're right in thinking I would protect her. But we're not lovers. I swear it."

Still silent, Beka stared down at her hands.

"But you are her confidant?" said Seregil.

Nyal shrugged. "Before we met again in Gedre, I hadn't seen her for several years. Glad as I was for a chance to be near her without her husband glowering, I could tell that something was wrong. She told me of the child she carries, but also hinted at something amiss. We spoke several times on the journey, and again after we reached Sarikali. She was unhappy, that I could see, but she would only speak vaguely of her husband's fears for his clan, and for the outcome of the negotiations.

"She hinted that his behavior was sometimes alarming, that he was not himself. He grew more troubled after Queen Idrilain's death, but worse was to come. He'd become convinced that Lord Torsin was plotting secretly with Ulan, offering a different bargain, one in which Gedre would be closed again after Skala's war ended, leaving Akhendi as badly off as ever."

"Did you tell him this?" Seregil demanded, ignoring his sister's startled look.

Nyal lurched to his feet, angry now. "How could I, when I knew nothing of it? You have distrusted me from the beginning, but I am no spy! I worked among you in good faith, and resisted Amali's entreaties and even those of my own khirnari to pass on what I heard among you. You know my gift, Seregil; it's one that can strain or destroy the possessor's atui if he doesn't learn restraint. I know when not to listen."

"But Amali did question you?" Seregil pressed.

"Of course she did! How could she not? I gave her what comfort I could and assured her that Klia was acting in good faith, even if Torsin was not."

"Why didn't you come to me about this?" Beka demanded.

"Because I didn't want you to think I was asking you to betray a confidence!" Nyal shot back. "Besides, I didn't believe it. Why would Torsin betray the woman he was sent to serve?"

"Did Amali ever mention Alec's charm after you gave it to her? Did you try to retrieve it?"

"I asked her about it once, not long after I'd given it to her, but she said she wanted to return it to Alec herself. I didn't think anything more of it."

"Would you swear that in front of a truth knower?" asked Thero.

"I will speak anything you like without fear of any wizard."

"And will you swear to these things before the Iia'sidra?" asked Seregil. "The life of the Haman may depend on it."

"Yes, of course!"

"What exactly did Amali say of her husband's behavior?" Seregil pressed.

"At first, only that he was concerned about how the vote would go. As time went on, though, she seemed to grow more frightened, saying he acted strangely, falling into black moods and weeping in the night. Just recently, though, she told me that being here in Sarikali had had a healing influence, for his spirits improved suddenly."

"Just before the Virésse banquet, perhaps?"

Nyal thought a moment, then shrugged. "Possibly."

"And that's as much as you know?"

"Yes."

Seregil rose to stand over the man. "Then tell me this. Why did you go after us? According to Thero, you weren't asked to; you volunteered. You've told Beka that you did it to protect us, yet you claim to know nothing of Rhaish's motives. You must have suspected something; otherwise, why assume we needed protection in Akhendi territory?"

Nyal shifted uncomfortably. "On the day of your disappearance, after the Haman had declared teth'sag, I saw Rhaish approach Nazien í Harí. I—I overheard him say something about a certain pass. I suspected you'd go that way, not knowing it had been destroyed by avalanches. Perhaps Rhaish guessed the same, I told myself, yet why would he tell the Haman? It was then that I began to fear that there was something more behind his melancholy. There was no time to confront him—he wouldn't speak to me anyway, and Amali was gone. I reasoned that if I were the one to find you, I could keep you safe, perhaps even let you escape. I still don't understand what this has to do with the poisonings, though."

"You said it yourself," Alec replied. "Rhaish thought Torsin had betrayed him and took matters into his own hands, discrediting the Haman and Virésse so that they would be kept from the vote."

"And you believe Amali aided him?" Nyal said softly.

"I plan to find that out tonight, once and for all," said Seregil.

"Will you tell the Iia'sidra what you've told us here?" asked Adzriel.

"What choice do I have, Khirnari?" Nyal replied sadly. "I swear to you, Seregil, by Aura's Light, that I thought only to protect you. I trusted that you would not have left without good reason. I hope what I did helps you trust me." He touched a hand to his sen'gai."My rash action may cost me dearly."

"You haven't told any of this to Moriel ä Moriel?" Adzriel asked.

"No, Khirnari. I had hoped I wouldn't need to, but I will not lie to her, either."

Seregil looked over at Thero, who'd chanced a forbidden spell as Nyal spoke. The wizard nodded slightly; the Ra'basi was telling the truth.

"I'll have to take back some of the things I've said about you, my friend," said Seregil, clapping him on the shoulder and giving Beka a surreptitious wink. "Captain, I'm putting him under your escort until this is over."

"I'll see to it, my lord," Beka assured him.

Alone again with Nyal, Beka found herself at a loss for words. An uncomfortable silence ensued, leaving her stranded by the window.

Duty or not, she'd been wrong. He'd risked so much to be her friend, her lover—more than she had begun to guess. In return, she'd been blind, suspicious, ready to believe the worst of him. She wanted to say something, but still no words would come. Forcing herself to look up, she found him staring pensively at his clasped hands.

"Seregil's right about Amali, I think," he said at last. "She's always used me, and I've let myself be used." He glanced up, coloring. "I shouldn't talk of her to you, perhaps—"

"No, it's all right. Go on."

He sighed. "We were to be married, but she changed her mind. For the good of her clan, she said. The khirnari needed her." He let out a bitter laugh. "Her family was delighted, of course. They liked that match far better than the prospect of a wanderer like me coming into the family. That's what's most important here: duty, family, honor."

The last words were spoken with a mix of regret and bitterness that surprised her. "You don't sound like you agree."

He shrugged. "I've traveled more than most 'faie, and it seems to me that sometimes you must step outside the laws in order to maintain what is right."

She had to suppress a smile at this. "That doesn't say much for you, then, does it?" she asked.

He gave a her a hurt look. "What do you mean?"

"I've been talking with my riders and some of the Bôkthersans today. It seems no one knew we were gone until late the next morning, yet you told us just now that you knew where we were going all along. So you kept your mouth shut long enough to give us a head start, then let Seregil go when you found him."

She strode over to face Nyal, fists on her hips. He leaned back in his chair, staring up at her uncertainly.

"On top of everything else," she growled, "I find out that you've stayed loyal for years to a woman who broke your heart, letting her reel you in by the balls anytime she likes, instead of telling her to take a long stroll off the nearest short quay. Extraordinary behavior, all around! I know what I'd do if you were under my command."

"What?" he demanded with another flash of anger.

Straddling his knees, she pushed him back, grabbed him by the ears, and covered his mouth with her own.

For a moment she thought she'd misjudged; he flinched back, lips tight. Then strong arms came up to crush her close. Releasing her hold on his ears, she smoothed her hands back through his dark hair, letting herself be held.

When the kiss ended he leaned his head back and raised a skeptical eyebrow. "This is how you discipline your riders?"

She grinned down at him. "Well, no. In fact, if any of them lied to me that way, I'd tie them to the nearest tree and give 'em twenty lashes. The same goes for lovers, by the way. But I wouldn't mind having someone with your varied talents on my side."

"Are you asking me to go back with you?"

"I already asked you, that night at the Virésse banquet," she reminded him. "You never gave me an answer."

"It would mean leaving Aurënen and following you back to your war."

"Yes."

He reached for her hands, clasping them in his. "When I came back and saw that you'd been ambushed—you know I'm a good tracker. The signs I read as I followed you told me I was going to find you dead somewhere up that road. I had a few minutes to get used to the idea before I saw where you'd outflanked them. You're an astonishing woman, Beka Cavish, and a very lucky one. I think you may just survive this war of yours."

"I plan to."

"Thinking that you were dead, I knew that I loved you," he said, as if that explained something.

"I usually take what compliments I can get, but I'm not so sure about that one."

He squeezed his eyes shut for a moment, tightening his grip on her hands. "Ah, talía! How do I say this? If only you were like Alec—"

"A man?"

Those hazel eyes snapped open. "No, a ya'shel. We call you Skalans 'Tírfaie.' Do you know what the word means?"

"Of course. 'People with short . . .' " A stab of dread killed the words in her throat.

"I love you, talía," he said, reaching to cup her cheek. "You're the only other woman I've truly loved in my life. The first time I saw you, that morning in Gedre, with your wonderful hair blazing in the sunlight—" He sighed. "But pairings between our two races are difficult. Could you bear it, growing old while I stay young?"

"Can you, you mean?" Beka climbed off his lap and walked back toward the window, marveling at the black, aching chasm that lay where her heart had been a moment before. "I see your point. You wouldn't want to be obligated to some wrinkled old hag."

"Stop it!"

Once again, he'd managed to sneak up on her unheard. She spun around, startled. He caught her by the shoulders, his face mere inches from hers, close enough to see the tears in his eyes.

"I am willing to risk it," he rasped. "I just don't ever again want to see hatred and distrust in your face when you look at me. These past few days have been hard enough, between that and thinking you were dead. I will lose you, but while we're together, I need your trust. I need you to have faith that I love the woman I saw in your eyes that first moment we met, now and forever, no matter what your age. Aurënfaie and Tír have loved before; it can be done, but only with trust and patience."

Beka looked into those clear, green-flecked eyes and felt the same rush of heat she had that day in Gedre. "I'm willing to work for that, talí," she replied. "But if you come with me, you could be dead before next spring, too, or I could. Are you willing to risk that?"

"I am, my beautiful warrior," he replied earnestly, lifting a strand of her hair to his lips and kissing it.

Beautiful? she thought, smiling to herself as she pulled him close again. When had she started believing that? "Will your khirnari let you go?"

"She may be glad to get rid of me after what she learns tonight. Otherwise—" The grin he gave her could have beaten one of Seregil's best. "I think I'm a bit past asking permission, don't you?"

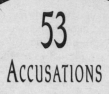

53
ACCUSATIONS

"We never counted on coming back. Now they're going to ask why we left," Alec fretted as he and Seregil changed clothes for the evening's work. "I don't like the idea of lying to the Iia'sidra."

"Don't lie," Seregil replied, stirring through the clothes chest for a coat. "Just stand by me and look convincing. That was one of the first things I decided about you, that day we met."

"What? That I'm a poor liar?" Grinning, Alec reached around him and fished out a favorite blue coat.

"That, and that you have an honest face. Those have their uses." Seregil paused over the somber black coat, then rejected it—too sinister given the current circumstances. A dark green one followed it into the discard pile—close enough in shade to Bôkthersa's color to seem like a clumsy plea for acceptance.

He settled at last on one of Alec's, a russet brown, for no better reason than he couldn't come up with any negative association with the color.

No one's going to care what you're wearing.

Yes, but it's better than thinking about where I'm headed.

Pulling the coat on, he did up the carved

buttons and buckled on a wide belt. At the mirror, he examined the bruises on his face. Those Emiel had given him were going yellow around the edges, and the place where the Akhendi ambusher had kicked him was still dark and swollen. He was quite a sight.

"They'll show better if you tie your hair back," Alec suggested, guessing his thoughts.

"Good point."

A knock sounded at the door and Thero came in. "Korathan is waiting. Are you ready?"

Seregil shrugged. "What do you think?"

Thero looked them over with a critical eye, then went to Alec and tugged at a strand of brown-dyed hair. "You don't want to have to explain this, do you? Hold still."

He closed his eyes for a moment, then slowly combed his fingers through the younger man's hair from forehead to nape, returning the dark hair to its natural color.

"Thank you, Thero. I've always preferred blond men," said Seregil.

"I've taken a great deal of comfort in that over the years," the wizard shot back, tossing them their cloaks. "Now, hoods up until you make your grand entrance. I'll be with Klia."

"I'm beginning to feel like one of those actors back at the Tirari theater," said Alec.

"So am I," Seregil said. "Let's just hope tonight's play doesn't turn out to be a tragedy."

The rest of the household had already assembled in the main hall. Adzriel and her entourage stood with Korathan next to Klia's velvet-draped litter. All Seregil could make out of the princess through the crowd were booted feet below the hem of a silk gown. Beka and her riders stood close by, holding themselves a bit aloof from Korathan's guard. Nyal was there, too, talking quietly with one of Mercalle's riders.

Mydri caught Seregil's eye and came over. Clasping his hands between her own, she held them tightly a moment.

"What do you suppose the Iia'sidra will do with me, once they know I'm here?" he asked.

"I don't know. They're very angry. The Haman have asked for the death sentence this time."

Seregil gave her a crooked grin. "We'll see how they feel after I'm done with them tonight."

Korathan and Adzriel took the lead as they set off. Braknil's men carried Klia's litter, flanked by the Orëska wizards and the remaining members of Urgazhi Turma. Pale but alert, Klia lay propped up on cushions, her ruined hand hanging unbandaged across her chest in a black sling.

Seregil and Alec hid again among Korathan's guard, savoring their last few moments of anonymity.

"Look, the moon's at the half already," Alec murmured.

We could have been back in Skala by now. Seregil silently completed the thought for him.

The Vhadäsoori circle was dark and empty as they passed, but lights blazed at the Iia'sidra.

A crowd had gathered outside, their faces masks of light and shadow in the mingled glow of torches and mage lights.

The Skalans were the last to arrive. Inside, the round chamber and the galleries above were filled to capacity. Seregil and Alec remained with a contingent of guards in an antechamber just outside.

From here, they watched as the others took their seats. Adzriel and Thero accompanied Korathan to the Bôkthersans' place in the circle. Judging by the young wizard's look of concentration, he was channeling what strength he could into Klia.

Seregil watched Rhaish í Arlisandin when Klia's litter was set down less than twenty feet from where he sat. The man's face betrayed nothing but concern.

"What if we're wrong?" Alec whispered.

"We're not." He closed his fingers around the sealed bottle, thinking, *If not him, then her.*

The ritual chime was struck, and the invocation given. The Silmai khirnari stepped into the circle and raised his hands toward Klia. "Korathan í Malteus Romeran Baltus of Rhíminee, brother of Queen Phoria and of Princess Klia í Idrilain, kinsman of Adzriel ä Illia of Bôkthersa, seeks redress for the wrongs committed against his sister, and against their envoy, Torsin í Xandus. Because these crimes have occurred on this, our most sacred ground, the Iia'sidra itself also proclaims teth'sag against the guilty. Adzriel ä Illia, do you speak for your kinsmen?"

"I do, Honored One. The children of Idrilain share with me the blood of Corruth í Glamien."

Satisfied, Brythir raised his hand again. "Present the accused."

Seregil couldn't see the two men but knew by the shifting of the crowd that Emiel and Ulan had come forward.

"Emiel í Moranthi, you stand before this body accused of committing violence against Klia ä Idrilain while she was a guest of your clan," Brythir intoned. "An act which, being proven, brings shame upon the whole clan of Haman. How do you answer?"

"For myself and for the honor of my clan, I refute the charge," Emiel proclaimed loudly.

Brythir nodded, then turned to the right. "Ulan í Sathil, Khirnari of Virésse, you stand before this body for Virésse, beneath whose roof and on sacred ground sacrilege and guest murder were done. How do you answer?"

The Virésse khirnari's smooth voice carried easily through the large chamber. "Should it be proven that these acts occurred within Virésse tupa, then I will accept responsibility for myself and my clan and take the dishonor upon my name. Until that time, however, for myself and for the honor of my clan, I refute the charge."

"He's going to regret those words," growled Alec.

"Don't lay any bets on that," Seregil warned.

Korathan and Adzriel bent over Klia for a moment conferring, then faced the council. Adzriel took a step forward.

"The Skalans seek justice and redress, but not against these men.

Commotion broke out briefly around the chamber, but Seregil still watched Rhaish. The Akhendi sat motionless, hands folded in his lap.

"Surely Korathan í Malteus has been told of the proofs against them?" Brythir asked.

"I have proofs of my own to present," Korathan answered. "With your permission, Elder?"

The Silmai resumed his seat and motioned for the Skalan to proceed.

"Here we go, talí," Seregil whispered, his mouth suddenly dry. Dropping their cloaks, they strode forward together to the center of the Iia'sidra circle.

A spate of excited whispering swelled around them as word of their identity was passed to the back seats and around the galleries overhead.

Stealing another look at Rhaish, Seregil found the Akhendi seemingly no more surprised than anyone else.

"Seregil of Rhíminee?" Brythir said at last, as if he couldn't credit what he was seeing.

Seregil bowed, spreading his hands wide in the ritual gesture of surrender. "Yes, Khirnari. I have returned to ask your forgiveness, knowing I am not worthy of any mercy."

"This man broke teth'sag, my brothers and sisters," Adzriel

announced. "By that act he must be reclaimed by his clan, Bôk-thersa, for justice to be carried out against him. Yet he committed this offense in the service of the people to whom he was exiled, in order to remain loyal to Klia and her kin, as did his companions, Beka ä Kari and Alec í Amasa. I pray you, let them give evidence this day for the sake of justice."

"This is an affront to all Aurënen!" Lhaär ä Iriel objected, rising angrily. "Who is this Tírfaie Korathan, to come uninvited to our land and demand that our laws be put aside for his convenience? The Exile has proven himself a traitor and an oath breaker. How dare he come here for anything other than punishment?"

"Look at the mark the Exile now bears," Riagil called out from his place among the lesser clans. "You Khatme pride yourselves on knowing the ways and meanings of dragons. Examine the mark and interpret it for us."

"What mark?" she demanded.

Seregil stripped the bandage from his hand and held it up.

The Khatme's eyes narrowed suspiciously as she walked out to scrutinize the bite mark. "I know what you are, Exile," she hissed, too low for the others to hear. "This is some Skalan trickery."

"Look closer, Khirnari. No matter how much you may hate me, you're too honorable not to speak the truth."

She gave him a withering glare, then seized the offered hand, handling it as if it were smeared with filth. She made no effort to be gentle, but he endured the discomfort willingly as she prodded and pressed. He'd happily have endured a good deal more to watch the expression of grudging awe that came over the old virago's face.

"He bears the dragon's true mark," she announced at last. "A great mark; a sign of the Lightbearer's favor, though why this should be so I cannot say."

"Thank you," said Brythir. "The Exile will answer for his actions, but for now, I vote that he shall speak, and his companions with him. How say the rest of you, my brothers and sisters?"

One by one, the other khirnari assented.

"I will speak first for Emiel í Moranthi," Seregil began, turning to face the Haman.

Emiel stood next to Nazien's chair, watching Seregil warily, as if expecting some cruel joke at his expense. The khirnari's face was more guarded.

"Honored khirnari of the Iia'sidra," Seregil went on, "as you know, proofs have been given that Emiel í Moranthi attacked Princess Klia, either through violence or poison. From the beginning, however, I had my doubts. I will now lay before you new proofs, ones that show his innocence.

"Klia was brought home from the hunt dying, with the marks of an attack on her throat. Alec í Amasa and others had seen Emiel struggling with her and assumed that he was doing her harm."

He held a hand out toward Klia. "You know Klia ä Idrilain as a wise diplomat. But she is also a warrior, and would not suffer such an attack without fighting back. She had struggled; there was blood under her nails, but it was her own. Emiel bore no marks, no blood. She was choking, poisoned with the venom of the apaki'nhag hours earlier, and had clawed at her own throat in panic. Many of you have seen the effects of this poison; look at Klia as she is now. Speak with Mydri ä Illia and Nyal í Nhekai, who healed her. I believe the Haman speaks the truth when he claims that he was merely trying to help her when she fell ill."

"But what of the Akhendi warding charm Klia wore?" asked the Ra'basi khirnari. "Surely you cannot refute that?"

"The charm proves that Emiel acted with violence, but not against Klia, and not that day." Seregil unsealed the bottle and handed Alec the bracelet, glancing at Rhaish í Arlisandin as he did so. The man still betrayed nothing.

Alec held up the bracelet. "The woven band is Klia's, made by Amali ä Yassara of Akhendi. But the warding charm on it has been replaced. I know this, because this charm was mine. Emiel's violence was directed at me, soon after our arrival in Sarikali. The men who were with him that day can vouch for me. So can Nyal í Nhekai, Kheeta í Branín, and Beka Cavish."

"This is absurd!" Elos í Orian objected. "How could Amali not know her own work had been tempered with?"

"Nyal gave my charm to Amali ä Yassara of Akhendi to restore it. I never saw it again, until I looked more closely at Klia's bracelet after we'd left Sarikali."

"Amali would surely have known the difference," Seregil pointed out. "We believe that she said nothing of it because it was she who switched the charms in the first place, seeking to dishonor the Haman in order to remove them from the vote."

All eyes turned to the Akhendi khirnari and Amali's empty chair.

"I refute the charge," Rhaish said evenly. "She is unwell. Perhaps she made a mistake. She had offered to read it more deeply, but the Exile had already carried it away with him. Perhaps he exchanged the charms, and for the same reason. To dishonor the Haman."

"Oh, Illior," Alec murmured. Before either of them could draw breath to answer, however, the Khatme khirnari spoke again.

"If that were the case, then why would he be refuting the accusation against Emiel now?" she snapped. "And why accuse the Akhendi, who have supported the Skalan cause? Besides, who but an Akhendi could have made such an exchange without destroying the magic?" She turned back to Alec. "Do you know more of this?"

"I—I think so, Khirnari," he stammered. "I believe I saw Amali make the switch the morning of the hunt. Later, when I found the bracelet and brought it back, Rhaish í Arlisandin insisted that she read the charm, though he or another Akhendi could just as easily have done so. At the time, I thought nothing of it, since she was the maker."

"And you maintain that you knew nothing of this?" Brythir asked Rhaish.

"Nothing at all," he replied.

"That may have been true at the time," Seregil said. "She wouldn't have told you that she had the charm because she might have guessed how she came by it and disapproved."

Rhaish colored angrily. "What are you saying?"

"That you are known to be jealous of her former lover, Nyal í Nhekai, and disapproved of their continued friendship. So you didn't know what she'd done until it was too late, any more than she knew what you'd done, or she wouldn't have meddled, would she? You certainly seem to have been at cross purposes."

"Explain yourself," Brythir ordered sternly.

"I can only conjecture, Honored One," Seregil said. "After Torsin died and Klia fell ill, I was at a loss to discover their attackers. Such acts are rare here but I have, as you know, spent most of my life in Skala where it is common practice. I've had years to observe the ways of dishonor. I have even made my way there using that knowledge, though not in the manner some of you assume. I am not a murderer, but I know the minds of murderers, traitors, and assassins.

"I didn't expect to encounter them here, not in Aurënen or in Sarikali. My childish memories blinded me for too long, and kept me from asking the right questions. I kept thinking in terms of who stood to gain by Klia's failure, instead of who would lose the most by it."

"And you claim that someone among the Akhendi is the murderer?"

"Yes, Khirnari. When Alec and I left Sarikali with Beka Cavish, we were careful to cover our tracks. Yet all three of us were attacked by Akhendi intent on killing us rather than capturing us. Alec and I were ambushed by a party of men waiting for us in the very pass I'd chosen to cross the mountains. Someone told them where to find us, someone with the power to track us, since I'd told no one which route I meant to take. After the attack we found these among the ambusher's gear."

He pulled out the Akhendi sen'gai and held it up for all to see.

"We have only your word for that, Exile," noted Ruen í Uri of Datsia.

"You have mine as well," Nyal said, stepping forward. "I was tracking the Exile and his talímenios and came upon them just as they were attacked. With Alec's help, I managed to rescue Seregil as he was about to be murdered, and together we drove off the others. The bodies of those we killed are still there, as far as I know. Later, when I went back to find Beka Cavish, I discovered that she and my men had been set upon, too. I followed her and watched as she was attacked again, this time by men openly wearing the sen'gai of Akhendi."

"You helped the Exile escape?" asked Brythir, arching an eyebrow at the Ra'basi.

Nyal met his accusing gaze calmly. "I did, Khirnari."

The Silmai shook his head, then looked back at Seregil. "I still see no proof that your poisoner was an Akhendi."

"With the guidance of the rhui'auros, Khirnari, I realized that Alec and I had witnessed the poisonings with our own eyes, the night of the Virésse banquet. Rhaish í Arlisandin himself wore the poisoner's ring and killed Lord Torsin with the clasp of friendship. Later, someone placed a tassel from a Virésse sen'gai in Torsin's hand to further place the blame on the Virésse. It was a signal employed by Ulan í Sathil and Torsin to summon one another to secret meetings. Only the tassel found in Torsin's hand was not from the khirnari's sen'gai, nor was any such signal sent by a Virésse that night."

"Why should Rhaish í Arlisandin kill Torsin í Xandus?" the Bry'khan khirnari asked, clearly bewildered.

"Because the Skalan envoy was secretly parlaying with Virésse for a limited opening of Gedre."

Brythir turned to Klia. "Is this true?"

Klia whispered to Adzriel at some length, and the Bôkthersan passed on her words. "Klia learned of this only a few weeks before the envoy's death. He was acting on Queen Idrilain's behest, as a safeguard in case the Iia'sidra would not grant the demands Klia brought. In the meantime, she proceeded with her original orders, hoping to open Gedre permanently."

Rhaish regarded them all stonily, saying nothing.

Brythir summoned the other khirnari, all but Adzriel and Rhaish, to his chair. After several minutes of excited whispering, they resumed their places.

"We would hear more of this supposed poisoning," the Silmai told Seregil.

"As I said, I didn't understand what it was that I was seeing at the time, not until after the attack in the mountains. I believe only Rhaish and Amali knew that we had the bracelet, and its significance if the altered charm was discovered. One of them used it to track us and set the ambushers on us.

"But it wasn't only Klia's bracelet that incriminated them. It was the absence of Torsin's, and for this reason, I believe that Klia's poisoning was an accident, rather than a deliberate attempt at murder.

"When Torsin's body was brought back to the guest house the morning after the Virésse banquet, Alec noted that his warding charm was missing. If the person who poisoned him recognized the charm for what it was, they would have removed it to cover their guilt."

He turned to face Rhaish. "You removed it as soon as you'd poisoned him, Khirnari, knowing that it would give you away. You pretended to stumble and used a common spell to undo the knot holding it on his wrist. The ruse covered this little theft, but Klia surprised you, kindly taking you by the hand to help you up."

"But wait!" Elos í Orian objected. "If that is so, then why didn't Klia's charm give him away in the same manner?"

"Because there was no ill intent, Khirnari. That was the charm's magic, to warn. Because Klia's poisoning was an accident, there was nothing to spring the magic. Perhaps Rhaish could justify killing Torsin—he was old, dying already. He was only a Tírfaie. He was plotting with Ulan to steal away the only hope he had of saving his clan. But Klia?"

He gave the old man a pitying look. "I saw your face as she helped you. If you'd meant to harm her, the charm she wore would have given you away then and there. You knew that, and left it where it was. You told no one what you'd done, not even Amali. Another mistake, Khirnari, given your wife's concern for you.

"It was no secret that Klia was hunting with the Haman the following day. Amali saw a chance to wound those she thought opposed Akhendi's interests and took it. You didn't even know she'd done it until after the bracelet was found, did you? You wanted the blame on the Virésse, and this muddied the waters. The minute I put it in your hands you guessed what had happened and began to stall and try to get it back from me."

Seregil paused, shaking his head. "From the start, the evidence didn't fit the supposed events. There was too much of it, and too readily found. You gave yourself away at last, hunting us down." He held up the sen'gai again. "You couldn't chance the possibility that we had discovered your secret, which brings me back to Nyal."

Nyal came forward again, not looking at the Akhendi as he outlined what he had said earlier in Adzriel's sitting room. "Amali could tell me no reason for his strange moods, and I inferred nothing of what you have just heard until the day I left in search of the three fugitives," he explained. "Like Seregil, I'd seen without understanding. I just wanted to protect Beka, whom I love. I did help Seregil and Alec escape from the men who waylaid them. These men meant to kill them and would have succeeded if I hadn't happened along. I left them afterward still in ignorance. I wanted to protect Amali, too, until I was shown her duplicity with the charm. Even love has its limits."

A hush fell over the chamber.

"You must answer these charges, Rhaish í Arlisandin," Brythir said at last.

The Akhendi rose and drew himself up proudly. "No teth'sag has been declared. I refute the accusations."

"What say you, Korathan í Malteus?" the Silmai asked.

"I stand by what has been said here, and demand justice," the prince said gruffly.

"Have you any other evidence to offer, Seregil?"

This sounded dangerously like a dismissal. "No, Honored One."

Brythir shook his head, looking older than ever. "These are heavy matters, my brothers and sisters. The Iia'sidra must deliberate deeply upon them. Rhaish, you will summon your wife to answer the charges made against her. Until then, this matter is with Aura—"

"What?" Korathan objected, but Adzriel laid a hand on his arm, whispering earnestly.

Alec shot Seregil a dismayed look, but he shook his head and led the way to seats among the Skalans.

The old Silmai raised his voice again. "There remains the matter of Haman's claim of teth'sag against Seregil the Exile. He has broken teth'sag with both the Haman and with the Iia'sidra in defying the conditions of his return."

"Was it oath breaking to follow the orders of those he now serves?" asked Iriel ä Kasrai.

"He is Aurënfaie, and subject to the laws," Galmyn í Nemius maintained.

"But he is exiled, and serves the Skalans," said Ulan í Sathil. "Is he therefore not cut off from the law as well as the comfort of his own kind? If he is not allowed to act as one of the people, is he subject to the same law?"

Seregil gave the Virésse an appraising look, knowing that self-interest lurked somewhere close to the surface of this unexpected support.

"Do the restrictions he and the Skalans agreed to mean nothing, then?" retorted Lhaär ä Iriel. "If so, then may the Tírfaie simply not take what they want from us, regardless of what we say? You offer a dangerous precedent, Ulan. Conditions were laid down and agreed to. The Skalans and the Exile must abide by them."

"The Skalans have been wronged!" Adzriel objected.

Brythir raised his hands for order. "This, too, must be debated with care. We must have time for reflections. Nazien í Hari, do you maintain the claim of teth'sag against this man, Seregil of Rhíminee?"

"I must, for honor's sake, Khirnari," Nazien replied solemnly. "He broke teth'sag. His khirnari must again accept responsibility for him."

Alec's knuckles went white as he clenched his fists. "That ungrateful son of—"

"No, Alec," Seregil whispered quickly. "He has no choice."

Adzriel rose and bowed deeply. "With great sorrow, Khirnari, I accept the justice of your claim. By my honor and that of my clan, I pledge to keep guard over him until judgment has been passed."

"Very well," said Brythir. "We will meet tomorrow morning and resume the debate. Rhaish í Arlisandin, you will summon Amali ä Yassara. Korathan í Malteus, you have until the next half-moon to prove your charges."

Klia stirred, raising her good hand toward Korathan.

He listened, then asked, "What of the vote?"

"That must wait until these other matters have been settled," Brythir replied.

"Damnation!" Alec hissed softly.

The closing invocation was given, and the crowd slowly dispersed. Seregil leaned over to Alec, as if to comfort him, and whispered quickly in his ear. "Ask to stay with me. Make a scene."

Alec gave him a startled look. "What? I can't—"

"Just do it!"

"Come, Seregil," Adzriel said.

"Let me come, too!" Alec blurted out, grabbing Seregil's arm. He blushed as Beka and Thero turned to stare but clung doggedly to him.

Adzriel patted his arm consolingly. "I'm sorry, my dear, but that's quite impossible."

"It's my own fault, talí," Seregil said, looking mortified as he forcefully disentangled himself from Alec's grasp. "Come on now, don't act this way. You're bringing shame on both of us."

"I can't bear it," Alec groaned, burying his burning face in his hands. "After all we went through to get back here!"

"Control yourself, boy. You're making a spectacle of yourself," Korathan growled in disgust.

It took all of Seregil's frayed will to look his sister in the eye and dissemble. "I'm sorry, Adzriel, he's so young—Perhaps I could have my old room for the night? Then at least we could see each other's windows."

"It's as good a place as any," she agreed, clearly shocked by Alec's behavior.

"There now," Seregil murmured, bending to hug Alec. His friend stole a questioning look at him, and Seregil slipped him the signs for "nightrunning tonight."

"Old secrets," Seregil murmured, kissing him good-bye.

"Luck in the shadows," Alec whispered back, and Seregil breathed a sigh of relief.

As he turned to follow Adzriel, Thero grabbed him in an awkward and totally uncharacteristic embrace. "Good luck to you, my friend," he whispered, slipping him something in a little wad of cloth. "Remember your nature and depend on it."

"I will," Seregil assured him, palming the mysterious gift.

54
Teth'sag

Seregil lay on the musty bed, staring up into the darkness and trying not to dwell on all the lies he'd had to tell to end up here alone in his ruined childhood room. Blinding himself to the pain and worry in the faces of the others, he'd shut himself off from them more thoroughly than he had when he'd left the city a week earlier.

And could you sit with them, your sisters and friends, knowing that tomorrow you face judgment, and that Adzriel will be the one forced to carry out the sentence?

Better to lie here alone, conjuring Rhaish í Arlisandin's face out of the darkness as he mulled the events of the day. Seregil had dealt with liars for most of his life and practiced deceit as an art himself. No honest man was ever that calm.

The Iia'sidra might see through the Akhendi eventually, but how many more Skalans would die for want of what could so easily be given? He'd sacrificed his birthright for this mission, Klia her hand, Torsin his life. What else would be lost while the Iia'sidra paced itself in the cold cycles of the moon?

He absently fingered the little wax figure Thero had slipped him, recalling the wizard's parting words. *Remember your nature and depend on it.* Was Thero speaking in double riddles now, like a rhui'auros, or had Seregil merely imagined the challenge, wanted to hear it?

He'd understood, of course. The wax figure was filled with Thero's spell, needing only a key word spoken over it to release it— Nysander had done the same for him many times, since he couldn't manage magic himself. The "nature" Thero had hinted at referred to the spell of intrinsic nature. A favorite of Seregil's from his apprentice days, it transformed one into an animal form said to give the seeker insight into his own heart.

Nysander had cast it on Alec soon after they met, and the boy had, to no one's real surprise, turned into a magnificent young stag.

Seregil hadn't been much older than Alec the first time Nysander had tried it on him. Finding himself in the sleek brown body of an otter, he'd almost wept with disappointment. He'd hoped for something a bit more impressive, a wolf, perhaps, or a great bird of prey like his master, who transformed into an eagle. Looking down at his chinless, whiskered reflection in a glass Nysander had set on the floor, he'd thought himself ridiculous beyond words.

"An otter?" he'd grunted, appalled at his raspy little voice. "What are they good for, except trimming coats?"

"Intelligent, playful creatures, otters. Users of tools, I believe," Nysander had remarked, running a hand down Seregil's supple back. "Sharp teeth, too, and fierce for their size when cornered."

"It's not what I'd have chosen," Seregil sniffed, still skeptical.

"And just what makes you think you get to choose, dear boy?" Nysander had laughed, then made him hump and waddle his way down all those long flights of stairs to one of the Orëska's garden pools, where he'd rediscovered the sheer joy of water.

Seregil shook free of the half-doze that had claimed him and sat up. Stealing silently to the door, he listened to the low voices of his guards. The three men outside were distant kinsmen. Kheeta and his sisters had offered to sit with him, but he'd pleaded weariness.

It hurt a bit, that they believed him and left him to himself.

He pulled a stool over to the balcony door and settled down to wait, knowing it was still too early.

Sitting there, he clocked the moon an hour's span, watching the house next door.

Alec sat awhile with Beka in the colos, then went alone to his room. Seregil saw him framed against the bright rectangle of his own doorway and resisted the urge to wave. After a while the light went out there, though he thought he could make out a dark form still on watch, sharing his vigil.

There was more to being a good burglar than watching the moon. Some inner sense told Seregil when the moment was right, like picking up a scent on the night air, or a certain type of stillness.

He lifted the bed aside and reached beneath the loose stone tile for the grapple, brushing the doll as he felt about. A tendril of ancient hair tangled around his finger, and he caught a strain of strange, sweet music.

"Saying good-bye, my friends?" he whispered gratefully.

Tossing the grapple on the bed, he replaced the tile, then stripped to breeches and a dark tunic for the night's work.

Next, he placed Thero's bit of molded wax under the covers and whispered, "Otter."

A familiar form took shape under the blankets, and he found himself staring down at his own death mask. He lacked the magic to give the simulacrum the semblance of life, so he made do by turning it onto its side and arranging the limbs in a more natural pose. The feel of the cold, unnatural flesh made his skin crawl. It was like playing with his own corpse.

Just pray no one comes in to check on me, he thought as he headed out to the balcony.

The clink of metal on tile sounded dangerously loud as he set the hook on the edge of the roof. His bitten hand ached as he climbed, but the pain was nothing compared to the mix of fear and exhilaration that claimed him as he gained the roof. He felt like a child again, sneaking out to ride beneath the stars; or the Cat, nightrunning across the best roofs of Rhíminee. Either way, he was himself in a way he hadn't been for months—years maybe—and it felt damn good.

His feet remembered the secret way down the disused staircase at the back of the house to a certain landing that overhung the garden wall.

Alec stepped out of the deep shadows to his right as soon as he dropped to the ground. Without a word they set off together, a double shadow against the darkness.

"That was quite a performance you gave at the Iia'sidra," Seregil said when they were outside Bôkthersa tupa. "Well done!"

Alec let out a derisive snort. "Oh, so you like me sounding like a clinging little rentboy, do you?"

"Is that the effect you were aiming for?"

"Bilairy's Balls, Seregil, you caught me off guard and I just blurted out the first thing that came to mind." Alec hunched his shoulders miserably. "I can hardly look Korathan in the eye."

Seregil chuckled. "I doubt it lowered his opinion of you much."

Akhendi tupa was quiet tonight. Keeping to side streets, they skirted the few taverns that were still open and reached the khirnari's house unseen.

With the aid of Seregil's grapple, they scaled the back wall and crept to the edge of the roof overlooking the gardens below. Judging by the darkened windows, the household had gone to bed.

They climbed down and followed a path between banks of flowers. Passing the bower where they'd last seen Amali, they saw that the door leading into the khirnari's bedchamber stood open.

Alec started toward it, but Seregil reached to stop him. There was no mistaking the soft rustle of a silk robe close by.

"I thought you might come, Exile."

They both crouched as a soft mage light winked into being in a nearby corner of the garden. It glowed in the hollow of Rhaish í Arlisandin's palm, just bright enough to illuminate the khirnari's lined face and the arms of the chair where he sat. Raising his other hand to view, he sipped from a clay wine cup, then set it down on a little table at his elbow.

"Please join me," he said, waving them closer. "You have nothing to fear from me now."

"I hope we didn't keep you waiting too long, Khirnari," Seregil countered, searching the shadows suspiciously. Having a light in his face made it harder to see.

"I spend most of my nights here. Sleep is not the friend it once was," Rhaish replied. "I watched you both the day you searched Ulan's house, and again today, as you cobbled together what you think I have done. You may have your mother's face, Seregil, but you possess your father's will, stubborn as iron."

Something in the man's manner sent a chill through Seregil, making his right palm itch for the grip of a sword. Yet Rhaish made no move, gave no signal, just reached again for his wine cup and drank deeply.

"I know you did those things," Alec said. "But I don't understand how you could. Torsin trusted you; we all did."

"You are a good man, young Alec, but you are not Aurënfaie. You don't know what it is to wear the sen'gai of your ancestors, or to stand by and watch the land they walked die. No sacrifice is too great."

"Except Amali?" Seregil asked.

The old man grimaced, then said hoarsely, "She bears my only son, the carrier of my name. What she did, she did in ignorance. The fault is mine and I bear the blame. You might convince the Iia'sidra of her guilt in time, but you would be convincing them of a lie."

He reached into his robe and took out a simple woven bracelet with a blackened charm. His hands were trembling now, making the shadows jitter. "This belonged to Torsin í Xandus. It will prove your claim against me. Let it end there and justice is served."

A spasm of some sort gripped him then, and he clenched the fist holding the bracelet. The mage light still cradled in his other palm flared and flickered.

"Oh, no," Seregil gasped.

The shadows slewed again as Rhaish placed the bracelet on the table and shifted the light to his other hand. Its glow fell across the second cup that had been hidden before, and the small nosegay that lay next to it.

He heard Alec's sharp intake of breath as the younger man recognized the clusters of bell-shaped blossoms. "Wolfbane," he whispered, giving them their Tír name.

"Not cups. Bowls. It's dwai sholo," said Seregil. "This amounts to an admission of guilt."

"Yes," Rhaish gasped. "I considered using the apaki'nhag venom, but feared it might confuse the issue. I want no confusion." Another spasm shook him. Gritting his teeth, he pulled off his sengai and let it fall beside his chair. "The guilt is mine, and I bear it alone."

"Do you swear that by Aura's Light?' asked Seregil.

"I do. How could I ask anyone else to partake of such dishonor, no matter how necessary?" He stretched out a hand to Seregil and he took it, kneeling before the dying man.

"You'll make them believe?' Rhaish whispered. "Let my death absolve the name of Akhendi, and take all dishonor."

"I will, Khirnari," Seregil replied softly. The man's fingers were already icy. Leaning closer, Seregil spoke quickly. "I was right, wasn't I, about Klia's poisoning being an accident?"

Rhaish nodded. "Nor did I intend harm to the Haman. Silly girl—talía. Though I should—" He gagged, then drew a labored breath. The mage light still cupped in his palm was failing. "I should like to

have bested Ulan, the old schemer, and beaten him at his own game
for once. Aura forgive——"

A spate of sour bile burst from the old man's mouth, staining the
front of his robe black in the moonlight. He shuddered violently and
fell back in his chair. The mage light went out.

Seregil felt the fleeting tingle of the departing khi as the cold
hand went limp. "Poor old fool." The silence of the garden seemed
to thicken into something more ominous, and he lowered his voice
to a cautious whisper. "He had too much atui to be good at murder."

"Atui?" muttered Alec. "After what he did?"

"I don't excuse it, but I understand."

Alec shrugged and reached for the bracelet. "At least he gave us
what we need.

"No, don't touch it. All this?" He gestured at the bracelet, the clay
bowls, the cast-off sen'gai. "It's as good as any confession. They
don't need us for that. Come on, let's go back before we're missed."

But Alec remained where he was, staring down at the dead man's
slumped form. Seregil couldn't see his face, but heard a tremor in
his voice when he said at last, "That could be you, if Nazien has his
way."

"I'm not going to run away, Alec." A fatalistic smile tugged at the
corner of Seregil's mouth. "At least not until I'm certain I have to."

Alec said nothing more as they hurried back to Bôkthersa tupa,
but Seregil could feel his fear like a chilled blade against his skin.
He wanted to reach out, offer some comfort, but had none to give,
still driven by the stubborn resolve that had come to him in the
mountains.

He wouldn't run away.

Back in Bôkthersa tupa, they paused outside the guest house.
Seregil searched for something to say, but Alec cut him off, grasping him fiercely by the neck and pressing his forehead to Seregil's.
Seregil hugged him close, fighting rigid limbs to drink in his lover's
warmth and comforting scent. "They're not going to kill me, Alec,"
he whispered into the soft hair pressed beneath his lips.

"They can." No tears, but such misery.

"They won't." Seregil pressed his wounded hand to his friend's
cheek, letting him feel the pebbled rows of scabs. "They won't
kill me."

Alec rocked his head hard against Seregil's shoulder, then pulled
away and scaled the stable-yard wall without a backward glance.

Returning to his too empty room, Alec lit all the lamps, wanting to drive off the shadow of his own dark thoughts.

Anything to block out the memory of that slumped figure, and the two bowls.

Caught between fear and anger, he threw together two small traveling packs, preparing for a quick escape if that's what it took to keep Seregil from a headlong plunge into self-destruction. Time and again he went out to the balcony, but his friend's dark window revealed nothing.

What is he thinking? he raged silently, pacing again.

His own hopes and illusions mocked him now. He'd come to Aurënen to discover some part of his past, and Seregil's. Yet what had it come to? The revelation of his mother's sacrifice, the maiming of Klia, shame heaped on his friend, and now Seregil's inexplicable resolve to face the Iia'sidra.

Thero slipped in just then, looking as if he hadn't been to bed yet, either. "I saw your light. Were you successful?"

"After a fashion." Alec told him what they'd found, and how Seregil had chosen to leave things.

The wizard seemed satisfied with this turn

of events. "It's not over yet, my friend," he said, resting a hand on Alec's shoulder. "Sleep now."

Alec just had time to realize that this was a spell rather than a friendly suggestion before oblivion claimed him.

Alec awoke with the first hint of dawn creeping in through the balcony door. Pushing off the blanket Thero had spread over him, he changed clothes and hurried downstairs.

Noticing that Klia's door stood open, he stopped to check on her. Ariani was with her, talking softly to Klia as she brushed her dark hair. Both women looked up as he entered. He hadn't bothered with a mirror that morning, but the expression on the rider's face served well enough. Klia murmured something and Ariani withdrew, leaving them alone.

"How are you, my lady?" he asked, taking the chair next to the bed.

Her eyes were still deeply sunken, but her cheeks showed more color today. "A little better, I think," she whispered. "Thero told me—the others don't know yet. Rhaish—" Tears welled in her eyes and trickled down toward her ears. Alec blotted them with the end of his sleeve, then covered her good hand with his own. A healthy warmth radiated from her skin.

"Will it help us?" she whispered thickly, forcing the words out.

"Seregil thinks so."

"Good," she closed her eyes. "Don't give up. Nothing else matters now. Too far—"

"You have my word," Alec assured her, wondering if she understood what Seregil faced.

Better if she doesn't, he decided. He pressed his lips to her hand. "Rest now, my lady. We need you back."

She didn't open her eyes, but he felt the slight, answering pressure of her fingers against his. The feel of it lingered against his skin as he continued on to the hall.

The others were there ahead of him. The room was crowded with Korathan's guard and Urgazhi Turma. Craning his neck, Alec spotted Korathan and Wydonis talking with Thero by the hearth.

"There you are," Beka said, emerging from the press. She looked nervous. "Are you ready?"

"What's going on?" he asked.

"Word just came from Adzriel. Rhaish is dead. It looks like you and Seregil were right."

"What are they're saying?" Alec asked, holding relief at bay.

Before she could answer, Thero waved him over. Leaving Beka to her preparations, he pushed past the soldiers and joined the prince and wizards in the small side chamber.

Korathan was sipping tea, the delicate Aurënfaie cup all but hidden in his large, callused hand. Regarding Alec over the rim, he said quietly, "You should have reported to me last night. I had to hear it from Klia's wizard today."

Alec met the man's pale gaze without flinching. "I'm sorry, my lord. I thought—"

"I'm not interested in what you thought. You didn't help the old bastard along, did you?"

"No, my lord," Alec reported. "We—I—" It was too late to wonder just what Thero had told him. "Seregil and I just went to spy. Rhaish í Arlisandin had already poisoned himself when we arrived. We just happened to be there."

Korathan gave him another long, unreadable look. "Is there anything else you've kept back that I should know about?"

"No, my lord."

"There'd better not be."

Setting his cup aside, Korathan turned to the others. "Since you all seem to know what my original orders were, let me make clear to you where we stand now. If Alec and Seregil hadn't brought the news they did, I'd have carried those orders out. I make no apologies for that. I'm the queen's brother, and the queen's man. However, I will confess relief at the way things have turned out. I only hope I can be as convincing as Seregil was that this is a wiser course of action. The best way to do that is to carry out the mission my mother gave you: secure that northern port, and establish a reliable source of horses, steel, and provisions. As Vicegerent of Skala, I will parlay for those as soon as we get this business with Seregil out of the way. I don't pretend to understand this Iia'sidra of theirs, or how they function without a ruler. I know only that Skala has no time to waste in idle palaver."

Rhaish í Arlisandin's unexpected death delayed Seregil's trial until late morning. Alec paced the corridors and stable yard, unable to settle to anything. At last, however, he and the others set off for the

Iia'sidra again. Klia had again insisted on attending, and Thero stayed close beside her litter as she was carried through the streets.

No crowd greeted them today. Their footfalls echoed loudly as they filed into the chamber and took their place with the Bôkthersans. The galleries were empty except for a few robed rhui'auros and scattered spectators. The Eleven were not yet in their seats.

One sight held his attention above all others, however, and set his heart hammering against his ribs.

A lone figure lay facedown in the center of the dark stone floor, arms stretched out to either side. It was Seregil. Alec knew him without needing to see the face hidden by the dark hair.

He was clad in a plain white tunic and trousers and lay utterly still, hardly seeming to breathe. Kheeta and Säaban flanked him like grim specters.

"Courage, Alec," whispered Beka, guiding him to his seat.

Atui, Alec thought, steeling himself. No one would say today that the talímenios of the Exile dishonored him with unseemly behavior.

Seregil had lost track of how long he'd lain there. Adzriel brought him to the Iia'sidra a few hours after sunrise. The stone floor was still cold from the night then, and the chill seeped up through his thin clothes, sapping the warmth from his muscles.

He'd lain on wet grass last time, in his father's own fai'thast. Insects had come and gone across his skin, and the turf had tickled his face as it drank his tears.

His face and chest hurt from pressing against the cold stone, and his muscles were soon twitching from the strain of keeping still. But he did not move, just listened to the distant sounds from outside.

In Bôkthersa, he'd listened to the mocking whispers of children and young 'faie. It hurt worst when he recognized the voices of friends.

Here, it was so quiet that he could hear people passing by in the street. From the bits and pieces of conversation he caught, he knew that Rhaish's death had been discovered, and smiled with aching cheeks and dry lips as news of the man's guilt filtered in to him.

Bilairy's Balls, his back ached. His knees and shoulders throbbed, and the points of his hipbones felt like they were cutting through the skin. His neck and forehead throbbed with the effort of not crushing his nose against the floor, and at last he chanced rocking his head just enough to transfer the agony to a cheekbone. To move any more than that would force his guardians to deal with him, and he couldn't bear to bring that down on Kheeta and Säaban, who stood unmoving somewhere nearby. The scabs on the back of his left hand began to itch, and he flexed his fingers in a vain effort to quell the irritation.

Sometime later something skittered across the back of that hand. *A dragonling,* his overtaxed imagination suggested hopefully. He squeezed his eyelids shut tighter as whatever it was investigated the side of his nose, then allowed himself a quick peek. A green beetle scuttled busily away, its back gleaming like fine enamel work as it entered a nearby patch of sunlight.

No dragons for him today.

He'd thought it would be a relief when the Iia'sidra finally began, but it wasn't. Without opening his eyes, he knew that people were walking close to him as they entered, some pausing to stare down at his exposed back. It was awful, the weight of those eyes upon him, worse than it had been all those years ago in Bôkthersa.

I hadn't spent a lifetime avoiding notice then, he thought dully. His heart was pounding now, shaking him a little with every driving beat. Could they see? He pressed his palms to the floor and silently prayed for the trial to begin.

The shuffling of feet continued for some minutes, and he could hear people settling in, conversing among themselves. Someone was talking about the fresh caneberries they'd had for breakfast. Further away, Ulan í Sathil was talking of trade routes and weather. No one spoke his name. He lay like a forgotten pile of clothing in the center of it all, quivering under the weight of all those accusing stares. The beetle's patch of sunlight touched his fingertips, reminding him of how cold the rest of his body was. His pulse sounded like a bellows in his ears.

Please, Aura, let them begin!

At last, he heard the solemn chime of the Iia'sidra bell. Still facedown, he pictured a face for each successive voice as the Iia'sidra commenced his trial.

"Adzriel ä Iriel," said Brythir. "A man of your clan has broken the laws of teth'sag laid against him."

"Seregil, once Seregil í Korit of Bôkthersa, lies before you. Let the charges be heard." It was good to hear his sister's voice, fix the direction in his mind's eye. Alec and the Skalans would be there, too, seeing this. The thought made his cheeks burn.

"I speak for the Iia'sidra," Brythir continued. "Seregil í Korit has defied the conditions of his return. He has left the sacred city under cover

of night. He has taken weapons and used them against fellow Aurënfaie. He has put on Aurënfaie garb and passed as a spy among us."

He heard the sound of chair legs creaking, then Nazien took up
the litany. "Seregil í Korit has broken the ban of exile laid against
him for the murder of my kinsman, Dhymir í Tilmani Nazien."

His father's long-forgotten voice snarled at the back of his mind.
He has a name, the man you killed!

Yes, my father, I've never forgotten it.

Footsteps approached, and strong hands hauled Seregil up to his
knees.

"Courage," Kheeta whispered.

Seregil kept his hands on his thighs, head bowed. He was facing
the Silmai elder, but could see Adzriel and the others from the corner of his eye. Korathan was there, and Klia on her litter. For the moment, he was thankful not to see Alec.

*He hadn't let himself weep then, facing his kin with grass clinging
to his face and clothes under that clear Bôkthersan sky. He'd wanted
to, but he fought the tears down until they were so far gone he didn't
see them again for years.*

"Seregil í Korit, you have heard the charges against you, acts
which being proven bring shame upon the whole clan of Bôkthersa.
How do you answer?"

His throat was dry, his voice rusty as a crow's, but he faced his ac-
cusers unflinchingly. "I was cut off from my clan. You know me now
as Seregil of Rhíminee, the Exile, and as the Exile, a servant of Klia
of Rhíminee, I acted. Nothing I have done can bring shame upon
Bôkthersa.

"As Exile, I have done all you said and take all shame upon myself. I returned here of my own will to face you and make myself accountable for my deeds. I broke teth'sag, Honored One, but not out
of evil intent."

Brythir stared at him a moment as others whispered. Was his admission of guilt what threw them, he wondered, or the fact that it
was a complete breech of ritual?

"Does anyone speak for this man?" Brythir inquired of the chamber.

"The Exile surrendered himself willingly to me at Gedre," Riagil
í Molan announced.

A pause raveled out, and Seregil caught movement among the
Skalans. Adzriel bent over Klia's litter, then passed on her words.
"Klia ä Idrilain says that Seregil and his two companions broke
teth'sag on her behalf. They risked their lives to meet Korathan and
bring him news of her condition and of the confusion surrounding

the circumstances of Torsin's death. Queen Phoria did not know Klia has thus far forsworn teth'sag."

Thus far? Seregil felt his own eyes widen and knew that others around the room must be, as well. He happened to look Ulan's way and found the man smiling knowingly at him, as if they shared some secret. Perhaps they did, Seregil thought uneasily. The cagey old fox might not have needed the aid of Plenimaran spies to guess what Korathan's real orders had been.

Adzriel continued, still speaking for Klia. "Seregil and Alec's decision to risk their lives a second time in order to clear the names of Virésse and Haman was their own. Klia knew nothing of the matter until they returned yesterday.

"Let the death of Rhaish í Arlisandin speak also for the accused. Though he broke teth'sag, Seregil has brought the truth to light. Will you take his life for that?"

Korathan rose. "Seregil of Rhíminee has served Skala well and honorably for many years. For the sake of that service, I ask in Queen Phoria's name that you spare this man's life."

I wonder what your sister will think of that, if she ever hears of it? Seregil thought.

"We speak for him, as well," another voice rang out, and all eyes turned to the rhui'auros who'd stepped forward into the circle.

"Elesarit, honored as you and your kind are, you know that the rhui'auros do not speak before the Iia'sidra," Brythir remonstrated.

"We spoke for Seregil í Korit the first time he was tried, and do the same now," Elesarit retorted. "He's been marked. The will of Aura is plain on his flesh now, clear for all to see."

"Does anyone else speak for this man?" Brythir asked.

"I do," a deep, persuasive voice behind Seregil said, and he nearly toppled over twisting to look at Ulan í Sathil.

"Whether it was his intention or not, Seregil has proven that my clan does not bear the shame of guest slaying, and did the same for the Haman, whom he has no cause to love. A man lacking atui might just as easily have kept this knowledge to himself."

There would be time later to discover what price this support might carry; for now, Seregil was grateful.

Ulan was the last to speak in his behalf. Now Alec and Beka were called forward and questioned.

Alec wore Skalan blue and Seregil noted with an inward smile that he'd pushed the long hair behind his left ear back so that the dragon mark on his earlobe showed. All the same, he looked drawn and worried. Beka, on the other hand, faced the Iia'sidra with squared shoulders, head held high.

Their interrogation was brief. Having reiterated the story that they'd acted in the interest of both countries, they were sent back among the Skalans.

Finally Nyal was called out. Striding out beside Seregil, he dropped to his knees and spread his arms. He was not wearing his sen'gai.

"Are we to understand from your statement yesterday that you did willfully aid the Exile in leaving Sarikali?" asked Brythir.

"Yes, Honored One." Nyal replied. "When I caught up with him and Alec and saw that they were being attacked, I thought it better to let them go on, in the hope that they would reach safety. I have accepted the consequences of my actions and been declared teth'brimash by my clan."

It was a serious matter to be cut off from one's clan, worse in some ways than outright exile, yet Nyal seemed oddly complacent about the matter.

"You served the Skalans at the behest of the Iia'sidra, Nyal í Nhekai. We may have more to say of this matter," Brythir informed him sternly. "Let the prisoners remain where they are."

The Iia'sidra withdrew to debate and Alec sat watching Seregil. His friend had scarcely stirred a muscle since they'd finished with him, just knelt there, head bowed, face half hidden by his hair. He'd spoken with such confidence in his own defense, prevaricating about nothing except the true nature of Korathan's orders, excusing himself nothing, either, yet making it sound like a challenge.

Alec's gaze shifted to the small side door, willing the Iia'sidra to hurry.

The shadows on the floor had moved less than an hour's span when they filed back into their places. Seregil raised his head a little but otherwise remained still. Beka reached for Alec's hand and held on tight.

Brythir remained standing as he extended a hand toward Nyal. "Nyal í Nhekai, your punishment is deemed sufficient. You shall be teth'brimash for no less than twenty years, cut off from your clan and your name. You will enter no temples, and Sarikali is closed to you. Leave this place."

Nyal bowed deeply and strode from the room in silence. Beka let out a sigh of relief and relaxed her grip on Alec's aching fingers.

Nazien í Hari was the next to speak. Rising, he pointed at Seregil. "For the atui this man has shown toward our kinsman, Emiel í Moranthi, Haman revokes our demand for his life. Let the ban of exile be reinstated against him."

"Thank the Light!" Alec groaned softly. Thero gripped his arm and gave it a victorious shake. There was more to come, however.

Brythir took Nazien's place. "Seregil of Rhíminee, you were granted entrance to Aurënen to serve as an adviser to Klia ä Idrilain. This honor was given to you as one who knows the ways of our people and our codes of honor. Since your arrival, you have acted ably, with great atui, even in the face of insult. In time, you might have won back your name. Instead, you chose to break faith with this body by the breaking of teth'sag. You have become a stranger to us, choosing the ways of the Tír over those of the people who were your own. You have made your choice and must now abide by it. Seregil of Rhíminee, you are declared teth'brimash for life, not by your clan, but by the Iia'sidra itself."

Alec was dimly aware of a muffled sob from somewhere nearby—Adzriel perhaps, or Mydri. Seregil remained very still. Too still.

"You are no Aurënfaie, but a ya'shel khi," Brythir continued. "You are to us as the Tírfaie, an outlander, subject to the same restrictions and the same rights, but you have no claim of blood or kin among the people of Aura. Go with the Skalans and abide among them."

56
Teth'brimash

I expected something like this, Seregil told himself, trying not to sway as Brythir spoke the sentence.

Why then did that one phrase—ya'shel khi—hurt so? The rhui'auros had called him that already, and he'd accepted it as a revelation. Spoken here, in front of his kin, the words cut like a hot knife. He thought he'd understood, but now the world seemed to be slipping out from under him. Exile he knew, but this severing went deeper.

"Go with the Skalans and abide among them," the ancient khirnari ordered.

Seregil's knees ached, but he managed to get to his feet without staggering. Pulling the Aurënfaie tunic over his head, he dropped it on the floor at his feet. "I accept the decision of the Iia'sidra, Honored One." His voice seemed to be coming from somewhere far outside himself. He was dimly aware of someone weeping—several people, in fact. He hoped he wasn't one of them.

He could barely feel his feet against the floor as he went to join the Skalans. Hands guided him to a chair and then Alec was beside him, wrapping a cloak around his shoulders.

The session ended quickly and the room emptied. Seregil pulled the cloak around him and kept his eyes down as he followed Korathan out, not wishing to see the faces of other 'faie just yet. As they neared the door, however, the rhui'auros named Lhial stepped out and clasped him by the left hand. Stroking the dragon mark, he smiled warmly at Seregil. "Well done, little brother. Dance the dance and trust the Light."

It took Seregil a moment to recall that Lhial was dead, and by then the fellow was gone. A group of rhui'auros stood near the entrance, but the apparition was not among them. As he searched their faces, each one raised a hand in silent salute.

Dance the dance? He closed his eyes a moment, summoning a fragment of something Lhial had tried to tell him the first time he'd visited the Nha'mahat. *Looking at you, I see all your births, all your deaths, all the works the Lightbearer has prepared for you. But time is a dance of many steps and missteps. Those of us who see must sometimes act.*

I'm a blind man, dancing in the dark. He thought of the last dream he'd had: the orbs melded into a pattern, and blood coursing down from a succession of weapons. The memory brought with it the same powerful sense of conviction that had overtaken him that night. The power of it straightened his spine and tugged the corner of his mouth up into a little half-smile.

Passing him, Lhaär ä Iriel saw and gave him a scathing glare.

"Do not mock the mark you bear," she warned.

"You have my word, Khirnari," he promised, pressing his left hand to his heart. "I take what the Lightbearer sends."

Adzriel and Mydri clung to Seregil as they followed Klia's litter back to the guest house. Alec willingly gave place to them but stayed close, watching Seregil with growing concern.

Seemingly dazed, the man huddled in his borrowed cloak as if it were winter. What little Alec could feel of his friend's emotions was a whirl of confusion.

At least it was better than pure despair.

As soon as they were in the hall, safe from prying eyes, Klia summoned Seregil to her side and whispered to him. She was weeping now, too. Seregil knelt by the litter, bending to hear her. "It's all right," he told her.

"How can you say that?" Mydri demanded. "You heard what Brythir said; there was hope that the exile would have been lifted eventually."

Seregil swayed to his feet and headed for the stairs. "Later, Mydri. I'm tired."

"Stay with him," Thero murmured, but Alec was already on his way.

They climbed slowly to their room, Alec following a few steps behind. He wanted to reach out and steady Seregil, but something held him back. Reaching their chamber, Seregil shed the last of his clothing and burrowed under the covers. He was asleep almost instantly.

Alec stood beside the bed for a moment, listening to the soft, even breathing and wondering if it was exhaustion or despair he was witnessing. Whichever it was, sleep was probably as good a cure as any. Kicking off his boots, he stretched out beside Seregil, pulling him close through the blankets. Seregil muttered something and slept on.

Alec opened his eyes, surprised to find the room nearly dark and the other half of the bed empty. He sat up in alarm, then heard a familiar chuckle from the shadows near the hearth. A long form uncurled itself from one of the armchairs there and lit a candle from the coals.

"I didn't have the heart to wake you," Seregil said, coming to sit on the bed. He was dressed in the russet coat and breeches, and to Alec's relief, he was smiling. It was a real smile, fond and reassuring. "You've taken this harder than I have, talí," he said, ruffling Alec's hair.

"Is this what you had in mind when you decided to come back?" Alec asked, sitting up to search his friend's face for some sign of madness. How could he be so calm?

"Actually, I think things may have turned out better than I'd hoped, now that I've had a chance to consider. You heard what they said. I'm an outlander now."

"And that doesn't upset you?"

Seregil shrugged. "I haven't really been Aurënfaie for a long time. The Iia'sidra and the rhui'auros—they made me ya'shel khi when they sent me away so young. It was just something I clung to all those years. Remember when I finally got around to telling you that you were half 'faie and you said you didn't know who you were? Do you remember what I told you then?"

"No."

"I told you that you were the same person you'd always been."

"And you've always been ya'shel khi?"

"Maybe. I never quite fit here."

"Then you don't mind not being able to come back?"

"Ah, but don't you see? I'm not exiled anymore. Brythir changed all that. I'm one of you now, and can go wherever you go."

"Then if they do open Gedre—?"

"Exactly. And whenever they get around to lifting the Edict, which I have no doubt they will, I can go anywhere. I'm free, Alec. My name is my own to make and no one can call me Exile anymore."

Alec regarded him skeptically. "And you knew all this would happen, back there in the mountains?"

Seregil's smile tilted into a crooked grin. "Not a bit of it."

Seregil had a harder time swaying the others. Klia and Adzriel wept. Mydri retreated into sullen silence. Deep in his own heart, he still harbored doubts, but the words of the rhui'auros stayed with him: *Dance the dance.*

Fortunately, he had little time to dwell on it. There was still the matter of the vote, this time with Korathan heading the negotiations. Seregil was barred from the Iia'sidra chamber, but Alec and Thero kept him apprised of the progress over the next two days, or rather the lack of it.

"It's as if nothing changed," Alec groused as they sat down to a late supper. "The same arguments go round and round. You're not missing a thing."

Sitting home with Klia through the rest of that week, Seregil grew increasingly unsettled. The initial hope the rhui'auros had given him was wearing thin. For all his trouble, his part in the workings of power was over for now.

Or so he thought.

On the fifth day of negotiations, a young boy arrived at the door asking for Seregil. The lad wore no sen'gai and gave no name, simply handed him a folded square of parchment and walked away.

There was no one else around just then except the two Urgazhi standing guard on the steps below. As soon as he'd unfolded the packet, Seregil was glad of it. Inside he found the words "Cup of Aura tonight, alone, at moon's zenith" written in an elegant, familiar hand. There was also a token: a small tassel of red-and-blue silk.

Seregil examined it more closely, and smiled to himself when he found a few telltale darker threads among the red.

Alec was less pleased when Seregil showed it to him that evening. "What does Ulan want with you?" he wondered suspiciously.

"I don't know, but I'm betting it's in Klia's best interests if I find out."

"I don't like this 'alone' business."

Seregil chuckled. "I cleared the man's name. He's not going to murder me now. And not after putting this in my hands."

"Are you going to tell Klia?"

"You can tell her after I've gone. Tell everyone."

It was a still night. The full moon's reflection lay flat as pearl inlaid in jet on the face of the Vhadäsoori pool.

Seregil entered the stone circle and walked slowly toward the Cup. He thought for a moment that he was the first to arrive; it gave one power to make another wait for you. Then he saw the moon's reflection bob and wink out of sight for an instant as a dark figure glided across the water's surface. Old fears stirred to life, but this was no necromancer's demon.

Ulan slid gracefully to shore and stepped up to meet him. His dark robes blended with the surrounding darkness, while his long, pale face and silver hair caught the moonlight like a floating temple mask.

Seregil distrusted this man, but he had to admire his style. "I had a feeling we might speak again, Khirnari."

"As did I, Seregil of Rhíminee," Ulan replied, linking arms with him. "Come, walk with me."

They strolled slowly along the water's edge as if they were companions. It wasn't hard for Seregil to imagine Torsin in his place. Had the old envoy been able to sense the power that rolled off this man like heat off a forge? Uncomfortable with such proximity, he freed his arm and halted. "I don't mean to be rude, but it's late and I know you didn't ask me here for the pleasure of my company."

"I might have," Ulan countered. "You are a most interesting young man. I'm sure you have many fascinating stories to tell."

"Only with a harp in hand and gold before me. What do you want?"

Ulan laughed. "Truly, you have taken on Tírfaie ways. That's all right, though. I like the Tír and their impatience. It's most

invigorating. I shall adopt the fashion and be direct. Your people still
wish to see Gedre open, do they not?"

Ah, here it was at last. "Yes, and my guess is that you're finding
Korathan a less subtle negotiator than his sister."

"I expected as much as soon as I heard he was on his way to
Gedre with ships of war," the khirnari remarked blandly, gazing up
at the moon.

Seregil refused to rise to such obvious bait. Either Ulan knew of
Korathan's original orders or he was bluffing for information. With
such an opponent, it was best to offer nothing in return.

Ulan tilted his head toward Seregil again, seeming not to have noticed his reticence. "You are clever, and wise beyond your years.
Wise enough to know that I have the power and the will to fight
against the Skalan's treaty until the Plenimaran fleet rides at anchor
in Rhíminee harbor and your beautiful city is in flames. I've been
watching this prince of yours. I don't think he has the wit to grasp
this, but you do, and you have his ear."

"I can't tell him to give up. Gedre is essential."

"I have no doubt of that. That is why I am willing to abide by the
agreement Torsin and I discussed before his unfortunate demise.
Rhaish may be dead, and teth'sag satisfied, but I assure you, there
are few among the Iia'sidra now who will spare Akhendi much pity.
Her new khirnari, Sulat í Eral, is green wood yet, with little backing
among the powerful. Your own clan is under a bit of a cloud as well,
though I'm certain Adzriel ä Illia will do her best. Yet there are so
many who use the actions of her onetime brother as a two-edged
sword. Is not yours a cautionary tale for those who wish no contact
with the Tír? Will not Lhaär ä Iriel point her tattooed nose in your
direction and cry, 'See what comes of mixing with outlanders?'
Then, of course, there is the matter of the new queen's honor. That is
of great concern to us all."

"I've been wondering, Khirnari—what did you pay the Plenimarans for that information?"

Ulan raised an eyebrow. "That information came to *me* as payment.
The Plenimarans are most anxious for the Strait of Bal to remain
open to their ships and to their traders. The Skalans are not the only
ones in need of supplies to wage this foolish war of yours."

Seregil's heart sank, though this came as no real surprise. "Are
you telling me that you've supported them all along? That the
Skalans have no hope?"

"No, my friend, I'm offering you a compromise and my support.
Argue for a limited opening of Gedre—say, the duration of your

war? I tell you as one grateful for what you did to clear my name that this is the best you can hope for. Or has your unfortunate alliance with the Akhendi blinded you to your original purpose? Klia did not come to challenge the Edict but to secure aid."

"Can we even hope for that?" Seregil asked.

"You know what to do, my clever friend. You're the master harpist who knows what strings to pluck. If you agree to my tune, you will have my support."

"Are there verses to your tune? Certain strings you want plucked?"

Ulan's ghostly face loomed closer, the eyes lost in shadow. "There is only one thing I want: Virésse remains an open port. Respect that, and whatever else you need I shall endeavor to provide."

"I don't suppose you can do anything about Plenimaran warships blocking the Strait of Bal?" Seregil asked with a wry grin. The khirnari's smile drove his own from his lips. "You *can*, can't you?"

"There's a great deal the Virésse are capable of, if we choose. Skalan trade has never been adverse to us, and they tend to be more trustworthy. What do you say?"

"I can't speak for Klia or Korathan," Seregil hedged.

"No, but you can speak with them."

"And what should I say to the people of Akhendi and Gedre? That their days of prosperity are numbered?"

"I have already spoken with Riagil and Sulat. They agree that half an apple is better than no apple at all. After all, even in Aurënen, things change with time and death. Who knows what may come of this little crack in the Edict, eh? Slow change is best for our people. It always has been."

"And if things stay the same long enough for you to keep your power?"

"Then I shall die a contented man."

Seregil smiled. "I'm sure there are a great many people who wish for that, Khirnari. I'll speak with the Skalans. There's one last thing I'd like to know, though. Was it you who told the Plenimarans where to ambush us on the voyage over?"

Ulan clucked his tongue. "Now you disappoint me. What use would a princess martyred by Plenimar be to me? Her death would only have united my opposition and created the most inconvenient sympathy for Skala's cause. Besides, I'd have missed out on the delights of the game we've all shared here. That would've been a great loss, don't you think?"

"A game," Seregil murmured. "Or a complicated dance."

"If you like. That's what existence is all about for people like us, Seregil. What would we do if life were ever simple and easy?"

"I wouldn't know," Seregil replied, thinking again of Ilar and the complexities of that long-ago summer. "I was never given the chance to find out."

"You're wondering if I was involved with the Chyptaulos traitors," Ulan said, and Seregil would not have put it past the man to be able to read thoughts and to have the audacity to do it.

"Yes," he replied softly, wondering what he would do if Ulan confessed.

The khirnari turned to look out over the pool. "That game needed no assistance from me, I assure you."

"But you knew about it, didn't you? You could have prevented it."

Ulan arched an eyebrow at him. "In my place, would you?"

Seregil could feel the man's scrutiny, as if Ulan had the power to look directly into his soul and perceive the truth there. In that moment came the humbling realization that Ulan's power was based on nothing so paltry as the reading of thoughts.

"No," he admitted, and the khirnari's approving smile sent a shard of ice through his heart. "I'll speak with Korathan."

As Seregil walked away he had the uncomfortable sensation that Ulan was watching him go, perhaps gloating, and the thought made his skin crawl. Stealing a glance back over his shoulder, however, he saw the old man gliding in slow, graceful circles across the smooth face of the pool.

57

AFTERMATH

It took just two days for the Iia'sidra and Korathan to come to terms. That night, under a waning moon, the Eleven met at the Cup of Aura to cast their vote.

The stone circle was ringed with onlookers. Standing among them, Seregil watched with mixed feelings as, one by one, each khirnari dropped their lot into the Cup. When it was finished Brythir sorted the black stones from the white and held them up in his fists. His cracked old voice did not carry well, but word passed from mouth to mouth through the crowd: "Eight white. Eight white! Gedre is open."

A cheer went up from the Skalans.

But only for forty auspicious turnings of the moon, thought Seregil, watching as Ulan í Sathil congratulated Riagil. Virésse would remain open, as well.

Slow change is best, Ulan had said. Three years for the 'faie was not slow, but within that small space of time, Skala's war would be lost or won. If Skala won, then a precedent would be set, and they could try again for permanent trade.

As it stood now, the Skalans were to be allowed a small trade colony at Gedre but no access yet to the interior. No Aurënfaie troops would be levied, but anyone foolish enough to want to join with the Skalans was free to do so.

"It's a beginning, at least," Alec yelled to him over the rising tide of voices. "We can finally go home!"

Seregil gave him a wry smile. "Don't pack up just yet."

In typical Aurënfaie fashion, it took nearly a month to finalize the details of the agreement. Spring gave way to blazing summer, and many of the 'faie who'd come to witness the negotiations went home, leaving the city more empty and haunted than ever.

For days on end the sun burned down from a cloudless sky, turning the turf in the streets sere and brown, though hardy wild roses and summer flowers bloomed in profusion everywhere. Alec finally learned to appreciate the city's forbidding architecture. No matter how hot the day was, the dark stone rooms remained cool. Everyone adopted the Aurënfaie fashion of loose, flowing tunics and trousers of Aurënen gauze.

Alec once again had time on his hands and a great deal less to do. Beka and her riders however, found themselves in greater demand than ever. A steady stream of dispatches went up to Gedre, and Alec and Seregil sometimes went along with them. Nyal was there, helping Riagil oversee preparations for Klia's departure.

Since the vote, the Urgazhi were suddenly also popular with would-be adventurers, who talked excitedly of joining the Skalan cause.

"If they're as brave as they make out, we'll be Urgazhi Troop before we leave here," Sergeant Braknil observed one evening as they returned from a Silmai tavern.

"We'll need them, too," Alec heard Beka mutter.

"You're anxious to get back, aren't you?" he asked, dreading the prospect. It had been easy, all these months, to forget what awaited her when they went back.

"I'm a soldier, and an officer. I've been gone too long," she said softly, watching Braknil's riders laughing together as they walked along ahead of them.

A few nights before they were to leave, Alec and Seregil were summoned to Klia's chamber. Korathan, Thero, and Beka were there already but none of the prince's people.

Klia sat up in a chair by the window. As they came in, she smiled and held out her hands. On the left she wore a fine leather glove; the empty fingers had been artfully stuffed to hide her deformity. "See, I'll be whole yet!" she said.

"She's gaining quickly, isn't she?" Beka whispered to Alec as he took his place beside her. "She'll be walking again before we know it."

Alec had spoken with Mydri earlier and was less optimistic. Despite all the healer's efforts, Klia still had no strength in her legs and could barely hold a cup for herself. The poison had also left her with a slight tremor. Her mind, however, was as sharp as ever.

"That's all of you," said Korathan, abrupt as ever. "Thero, seal this room."

Standing next to Klia's chair, hands clasped behind his back, the prince looked as if he were about to address a regiment. "As vicegerent of Skala, it falls to me to put Gedre in order. Since Klia is still too weak for hard traveling or battle, I'm placing her in command of the supply station at Gedre. She knows these people better than anyone, now that Torsin is gone, and has the status to get us what we need. Riagil í Molan is preparing lodgings and warehouses at the waterfront."

"I'll need a sizable staff," said Klia. "Captain, you and Urgazhi Turma will remain in Aurënen with me."

Beka saluted woodenly, saying nothing, but Alec had seen her hastily masked shock.

"I've asked Thero to remain with me, as well," Klia added.

Korathan glanced down at his sister in surprise. "I thought Elutheus might do better. He's older, and more experienced."

"I'll take any wizards you can spare, Brother, but I'd prefer to retain Thero as my field wizard. He and I are used to one another, aren't we?"

"My lady." Thero bowed deeply, and Alec saw that he, at least, was pleased with this turn of events.

"What about us?" asked Alec.

"Yes, what about us?" said Seregil.

"I'm sorry. Not you."

"But I thought he wasn't exiled anymore. Can't he go wherever you do?" said Alec.

"Under the law, yes," Klia told him. "But it's not politic for him to overstay his welcome, especially as part of my staff. Many of those who opposed his return haven't changed their minds, and some of them have powerful voices among the clans who voted against the treaty."

"Not to mention the fact that the iron Skala needs is mined in the mountains of Akhendi fai'thast," Seregil added. "I'm not very popular among them. It could raise unnecessary difficulties."

Klia gave him a grateful smile. "I knew you'd understand."

"It's all right," he assured her. "There are matters in Rhíminee I need to attend to. I've been gone too long as it is."

Alec and the others took their leave. As soon as they were in the corridor, Beka turned and walked quickly toward the back stairs, fists clenched at her sides.

Alec moved to follow, but Seregil drew him in the opposite direction.

"Let her be, Alec."

Alec followed grudgingly, but looked back in time to see Beka wipe angrily at her cheek as she hurried down the stairs.

Seregil waited until the rest of the house had settled for the night, then stole down to Korathan's chamber. Light still showed beneath the prince's door, so he knocked softly.

Korathan answered, looking less than pleased to see him. "Seregil? What is it?"

"I'd hoped for a word alone with you before I leave for Skala, my lord."

For a moment he thought Korathan was going to send him away; instead he waved Seregil to a seat at a small table and poured wine for his unwelcome guest. "Well?" he prompted.

Seregil raised his cup to the prince, then took a polite sip. "Through all this, my lord, I haven't heard much of what the queen thinks of your departure from her orders."

"Why do you suppose all those dispatch riders have been wearing out horses since I got here?" Korathan pulled off his boots and scratched his foot, favoring Seregil with a sour look. "Count us all lucky that the Iia'sidra voted in our favor, and that Phoria's too busy with the Plenimarans just now to care about anything but the iron and horses Klia will be sending. Pray to that moon god of yours that the queen remains so occupied for some time. She's in no mood for—distractions. Is that all?"

"No. I also wanted to speak with you about Klia."

Korathan's expression softened slightly. "You've served her well. You all did. Klia and I will both make that clear to the queen. You've nothing to fear in Rhíminee."

Seregil took a longer sip, trying to quell the nagging sense that he was about to do something very unwise. "I'm not so certain one fact leads to the other, my lord."

"How do you mean?"

"Klia served Skala well. What's happened here, the progress we won, that was her doing. If she hadn't won them over the way she did, nothing you or I could have done would have made the difference."

"Are you here to make sure I don't steal my little sister's glory?"

"No, my lord. I didn't mean to belittle what you've accomplished."

"Ah, I'll sleep better, knowing that," Korathan muttered, refilling his cup.

Undeterred, Seregil plunged on. "I'd like to know whether the decision to keep Klia in Aurënen came from you or Phoria."

"What business is that of yours?"

"I'm Klia's friend. Phoria doesn't want her back, does she? She's succeeded where Phoria wanted her to fail, and turned you to her side in the bargain."

"It would be better if no one else ever heard you say these things," Korathan replied quietly, his pale eyes icy.

"They won't," Seregil assured him. "But Phoria must have known what she was doing when she sent you. It takes time to outfit that many warships, and time to get them here. This was no spur-of-the-moment venture. She didn't mean for Klia to come home."

"You're not a stupid man, Seregil. I've always known that, no matter how you played the wastrel with the other young bloods. So I know that you understand the risk you're taking, saying this to me, the queen's brother."

"Klia's loyal, Korathan. She has no designs on her sister's throne. I think you believe that, too, or you wouldn't have come here to help her," Seregil nodded.

Korathan tapped the side of his cup, considering. "It was Klia's idea to stay, as it happens, though I was happy enough to grant her request."

"Thank you, my lord." Seregil rose to go, then held his cup up again. "To the continued good health of all Idrilain's daughters, and their daughters after them."

The prince touched his cup to Seregil's, not smiling. "I'm the queen's man, Lord Seregil. Don't ever forget that."

"Not for a moment, my lord."

The Skalans spent their last evening in the city as they had their first, feasting with the Bôkthersans under a rising moon.

Sitting there in his sister's garden, Seregil searched his heart for some regret, but for once sadness eluded him. He could come back, at least as far as Gedre, and for now that was enough. His thoughts were already turning to Rhíminee.

As they rose to take their leave at last, Mydri drew him and Alec aside. "Wait, my dears. Let the others go. We must make our own farewells."

When she and Adzriel returned from seeing the others off, the older woman was carrying a long, familiar bundle.

"I hope you manage to hang on to it this time," Adzriel said, giving him back his sword. "Riagil left it with me when he brought you back."

Mydri placed a smaller package in Alec's hands, and he unwrapped it to find a long hunting knife. The grip was made of some dark, reddish wood and inlaid with bands of horn and silver. "Only members of our clan own such knives," she told him, kissing him on both cheeks. "You are our new brother, no matter what your name may be. Take care of Seregil until he comes back to us."

"You have my word," Alec told her.

Seregil and Alec were crossing the short distance to the guest house when a slender, robed figure stepped from the shadows across the street. The woman wore the hat and robes of a rhui'auros, but Seregil couldn't make out her face.

"Lhial sends you a gift, Seregil of Rhíminee," she said, and tossed something that glittered softly in the moonlight.

He caught it and recognized the slightly rough feeling of glass against his fingers.

"Such clever hands," the woman said, laughing as she vanished.

"What is it?" Alec asked, fishing a lightstone from his belt pouch.

Seregil opened his hand. It was another of the strange orbs, but this one was as clear as river ice, allowing him to see the tiny carving it held—a dragon with the feathered wings of an owl.

"What's that?" Alec asked again.

Yours to keep. Yours to discard, little brother.

"A reminder, I think," Seregil said, pocketing it with care.

✦

58

RUINS

Seregil stood alone at the ship's prow, watching as the distant outline of Rhíminee's citadel slowly resolved against the dawn-tinted sky. Fog lingered over the harbor, set aglow here and there by a few early lamps in the Lower City.

The sound of feet on the deck above had woken him. Leaving Alec still asleep, he'd gone up alone, thankful for a few moments to himself for this homecoming.

The harbor was as flat as a mirror inside the moles and crowded with warships and merchant carracks riding at anchor. It was so still at this hour that Seregil could hear the rumble of wagons on their way up the walled road to the Sea Market, and the crowing of cocks on the citadel. Closer at hand, a cook on a nearby man-of-war beat on a kettle to summon his shipmates to a hot breakfast. The scents of porridge and fried herring hung on the air.

Seregil closed his eyes, picturing familiar streets and alleyways, wondering what changes the war had brought.

Caught up in his thoughts, he let out a startled grunt when a warm hand closed over his on the rail.

"It looks peaceful enough, doesn't it?" Alec said, stifling a yawn. "Suppose there's any work left for us to do?"

Seregil recalled his last conversation with Korathan. "I imagine we'll find something."

They'd sent no word ahead of their arrival, so no one was at the docks to meet them. As soon as their horses were led off the ship, they set out for Wheel Street.

What remained of the Lower City looked just the same, a maze of customs houses, crooked streets, and filthy tenements. But as they rode on, they saw that whole sections along the waterfront had been razed to make room for supply markets and corrals. Soldiers were everywhere.

In the Upper City, the Sea Market was already busy, but there were fewer goods in the stalls than Seregil remembered.

The wealthy Noble Quarter was the least changed. Servants were abroad on their morning business, laden with market baskets. Trees laden with summer fruit arched their branches invitingly above the colorful tiled walls that shielded the villa gardens. A few trespassing dogs and pigs chased one another across the street. Children's laughter echoed from an open window as they rode by.

Wheel Street lay on the fringe of this quarter and was lined with more modest houses and shops. Seregil paused across the street from the house he'd called home for more than two decades. The grapevine mosaic over the door was as bright as ever, the stone stairway below neatly scrubbed and swept. Here he could only be Lord Seregil. The Rhíminee Cat lodged elsewhere.

"We could just send word that Lord Seregil and Sir Alec were lost at sea," he muttered.

Alec chuckled, then walked across the street and climbed the stairs. With a sigh, Seregil followed.

It had never mattered how long he was gone—three weeks or three years. Runcer kept the place unchanged, ready for his return.

The door was still locked for the night, so they knocked. After a few moments a young man with a long, vaguely familiar face answered.

"What's your business here?" he demanded, taking in their stained traveling clothes with obvious suspicion.

Seregil sized him up, then said, "I must see Sir Alec at once."

"He's not here."

"Well, where is he?" Alec demanded, falling in with the game.

"He and Lord Seregil are away on queen's business. You may leave a message for them, if you wish."

"I do," Seregil told him. "The message is that Lord Seregil and

Sir Alec have returned. Get out of the way, whoever you are. Where's Runcer?"

"I'm Runcer."

"Runcer the Younger, maybe. Where's old Runcer?"

"My grandfather died two months ago," the man replied, not moving. "As for who you might be, I'll need more than just your word for that!"

Just then a huge white hound pushed past the man and reared up to lick Seregil's face, wagging its shaggy tail frantically.

"Mârag will vouch for me," Seregil laughed, pushing the dog off and scratching her ears.

In the end, however, they had to summon the cook to identify them. Young Runcer apologized profusely, and Seregil gave him a gold sester for his caution.

Giving Alec first turn in the small bath chamber upstairs, Seregil wandered the house, feeling like his own ghost. The lavish woodland murals of the salon seemed garish after Sarikali's austerity. His bedchamber upstairs, furnished in Aurënfaie style, felt more welcoming. Opening a door at the opposite end of the corridor, he smiled to himself. This had been Alec's room. They hadn't been lovers when they'd left.

He'd had his own cot at the Cockerel, too.

Turning, he found Alec leaning in the bath chamber doorway, water dripping from his hair onto his bare shoulders.

"We can't just avoid that part of the city forever," he said, guessing Seregil's thoughts easily enough. "I won't feel like we've really come home until I see it."

Seregil closed his eyes and rubbed at the lids, wishing for once that he couldn't feel the pull of Alec's longing. "After dark," he said, giving in.

They dressed in old clothes and dark cloaks, shedding their public personas as easily as the garments themselves.

Going on foot, they followed the Street of the Sheaf west toward the Harvest Market. On the way they passed the Astellus Circle and the Street of Lights. The colored lanterns of the brothels and gaming houses still glowed invitingly there, in spite of the war.

Reaching the poorer quarter behind the Harvest Market, they hesitated at the final turning onto Blue Fish Street. Each had his own memories of the horrors they'd witnessed here.

The ruin of the Cockerel was still there. The land belonged to

Seregil, by way of various false names. Not even Runcer had known of this place or his connection to it.

Chunks of rubble and most of the courtyard wall had been carried off by other builders, but one kitchen wall and the chimney still stood against the night sky, their broken edges softened by a thick growth of creeper. Somewhere among the tangled branches, an owl hooted mournfully. The night wind rustled the leaves and moaned faintly through broken brickwork.

Alec whispered something under his breath, a Dalnan prayer to lay ghosts to rest.

They had their pyre, Seregil thought, fighting down images of blood and dead lips speaking. He'd set the place ablaze himself, just to be certain.

In the back court, they found no sign of the stable, but the well had been cleared and appeared to be still in use. Thryis's kitchen garden had run wild nearby. Masses of mint, basil, and borage had spread to claim earth formerly the purview of the old woman's tidy rows of lentils and leeks.

"All the time we lived here, I don't think I ever used the front door," Alec murmured, picking his way over charred beams to the broken mouth of the hearth. The mantelpiece was still there above it. Mice had taken up residence in the warming oven.

Seregil leaned against the empty doorframe and closed his eyes, remembering the room as it had been: Thryis leaning on her stick as she fussed over her kettles and pots; Cilla peeling apples at a table nearby while her father, Diomis, tended the baby. He could almost smell the aromas: lamb and leek stew, new bread, crushed garlic, ripe summer strawberries, the sour reek of the cheese presses in the pantry. The Cavishs had taken breakfast in this kitchen when they visited the city for festivals. Nysander had had a particular fondness for Cilla's mince tarts and her father's beer.

The memories still hurt, but the edges were blunted.

Dance the dance.

"Damn, what's that?" Alec hissed.

Startled, Seregil opened his eyes in time to see a small, dark form dart out of the hearth. It dodged past Alec but tripped over something and went sprawling. Overhead, the owl and its mate took flight in a flurry of wings.

Seregil pounced on the struggling shadow, which turned out to be a ragged boy. He couldn't have been more than ten, but he rolled to his knees quick as a snake and pulled a dagger on Seregil, cursing him ripely in a high, shaky voice.

"Here's a proper Rhíminee nightrunner, if the stink and vocabulary are anything to go by," Seregil said in Aurënfaie.

"Bilairy take you, spirits!" the boy snarled, trapped between Seregil and a fallen beam.

"We're not ghosts," Alec assured him.

Taking advantage of the momentary distraction, Seregil caught the boy by his dagger hand and pulled him forward. The lad couldn't be making much of a living for himself. His skinny wrist felt like a bundle of cords in Seregil's grip.

"What do you call yourself?" he asked, twisting the knife free.

"Like I'd tell you!" the boy spat out. With another burst of initiative, he kicked Seregil in the shin and yanked loose, escaping with the agility of a rat.

Alec's laughter echoed weirdly off the ruined stonework, but it was full-hearted all the same.

"If the neighbors do think this place is haunted, this ought to put the seal on it." Seregil grimaced as he sat down and rubbed his leg. "Quite a welcome, eh?"

"The best we could ask for," Alec gasped, sitting down beside him. "Owls, footpads—I think it's a sign."

"Take what the Lightbearer sends and be thankful," Seregil murmured, looking around again.

"It was a good place, the first one I ever really thought of as home," Alec said, sobering a little. "If someone were to build a new place here, do you suppose they'd haunt it?"

Seregil knew who "they" were. "If they did, it would be a sorry thing for them to find no one but strangers, don't you think?"

Alec was quiet a moment, then said, "We could do with a bit more room than we had, the way you clutter things up. It might be hard to find someone trustworthy to run it, though. And to do the magicking, too, with Magyana and Thero gone."

"It could be managed." Seregil smiled to himself in the darkness. "You know, I never could stand playing the noble for long, and I've had my fill of it these past few months."

"It'd be bad luck to use the same name. We'd need a new one." Alec leaned down and pulled something from beneath the beam—a long barred wing feather. "How about the Owl?"

"The Dragon and Owl." *Ya'shel khi,* a voice whispered in Seregil's heart. "After all, we'd want to attract the right sort of trade."

ABOUT THE AUTHOR

Lynn Flewelling's first novel, *Luck in the Shadows,* was named a Best First Novel by *Locus* Magazine, and was a finalist for the Compton Crook award in 1996. Both *Luck* and its sequel, *Stalking Darkness,* have received international acclaim. Flewelling teaches writing workshops and has been a guest instructor at the Stonecoast Writers' Conference, the World Science Fiction Convention, and Maine Writers' and Publishers' Alliance. She currently lives in western New York.